SHE'S LEAVING HOME

By the same author:

Fiction
A PARLIAMENTARY AFFAIR
A WOMAN'S PLACE

Non-fiction
LIFE LINES: POLITICS AND HEALTH 1986–88
WHAT WOMEN WANT
THREE LINE QUIPS

EDWINA CURRIE

SHE'S LEAVING HOME

LITTLE, BROWN AND COMPANY

A *Little, Brown* Book

First published in Great Britain in 1997 by Little, Brown and Company

The author gratefully acknowledges permission to quote from the following:
A Thousand Days by Arthur M. Schlesinger, Jr.
Copyright © 1965, Arthur M. Schlesinger, Jr.
Reprinted by permission of Houghton Mifflin Co. and André Deutsch Ltd.
All rights reserved.
Will We Have Jewish Grandchildren? by the Chief Rabbi, Dr Jonathan Sacks.
Copyright © Dr Jonathan Sacks.
Reprinted by permission of Vallentine Mitchell and Co. Ltd.
'Death Knell for Britain's Sense of Civic Duty: Institutions in Decline, says
Report' by Philip Johnston, published 30 October 1996, in the *Daily Telegraph*.
Copyright © Telegraph Group Ltd, London, 1996.
I have a Dream by Martin Luther King, Jr. Copyright © 1963, Martin Luther
King, Jr, copyright renewed 1991 by Coretta Scott King.
Reprinted by arrangement with The Heirs to the Estate of Martin Luther
King, Jr, c/o Writers House Inc. as agent for the proprietor.
Konin: A Quest by Theo Richmond.
Reprinted by permission of Jonathan Cape, London.
Duineser Elegien by Rainer Maria Rilke, translated by J. B. Leishman and
Stephen Spender.
Copyright © 1948, J. B. Leishman and Stephen Spender.
Reprinted by permission of Ed Victor Ltd, London
Every effort has been made to trace the copyright holders in all copyright
material in this book, and the author would like to acknowledge
Vanishing Diaspora by Bernard Wasserstein, Hamish Hamilton, 1996.

A CIP catalogue record for this book is available from the British Library.

ISBN 0 316 64017 4

Typeset in Sabon by M Rules
Printed and bound in Great Britain by
Clays Ltd, St Ives plc

Little, Brown and Company (UK)
Brettenham House
Lancaster Place
London WC2E 7EN

Contents

Part Five

'Before the Second World War the number of Anglo-Jewish marriages was around three thousand a year . . . between the mid-50s and the 1970s it fell precipitously to around fifteen hundred per annum. By the 1980s it had fallen further to some one thousand per annum. Community marriage rates have been consistently less than half the national rates since the mid-50s. They have now reached the critical position where they represent less than one half of Jews of marriageable age, suggesting that *more than half of young Jews are not marrying, are marrying out, or are leaving the community in some other way* . . . This suggests that resistance to intermarriage has collapsed in Anglo-Jewry just as it has in America . . .

These are the facts, and they are very bad news. In the century of the Shoa, they are nothing short of tragic . . . Judaism and Jewish identity are dying. . . A people once known for its loyalty to a unique destiny is vanishing into oblivion. A nation whose seemingly infinite capacity for survival excited the astonishment of historians is losing its will to survive.'

– Dr Jonathan Sacks,
Chief Rabbi of the United Hebrew Congregations of the
Commonwealth,
Will We Have Jewish Grandchildren?
(Vallentine Mitchell, 1994)

'The Jews are vanishing from Europe – and not only because of Hitler. In 1939 there were nearly 10 million Jews in Europe; during the war more than half were murdered. By 1994, emigration and a surplus of deaths over births had reduced Europe's Jewish population again by more than half, to under 2 million...a realistic forecast now is that within a few generations they will disappear as a significant element in the life of the continent . . . And in spite of everything it is not, taken as a whole, the story of Jews as victims of the hatred of their neighbours but rather as victims of their kindness . . .'

Bernard Wasserstein,
Vanishing Diaspora (Hamish Hamilton, 1996)

'Membership of the Church of England has fallen to an estimated 1,468,000 in 1995, 40% of its level in the 1930s. The Methodist church has lost half its members and the Roman Catholic church a quarter over the past 25 years . . .

Neighbourliness has also undergone a collapse. Although 90 per cent of people questioned for a survey in 1995 agreed that their neighbours were "pleasant and friendly", little more than half said they trusted them or felt any sense of duty to be good neighbours.'

Daily Telegraph, October 30 1996,
quoting from *The Deficit in Civil Society*.

PART ONE

Chapter One

Thursday

'Well shake it up, baby, now!'
　'Shake it up, baby!!'
　'Twist and shout!'
　'Twissannshout!!'
　'C'mon c'mon c'mon come on, baby, now!'
　'Come on, baby!'
　'Come on and work it on out!'
　'Workitonnaaht!'
In excited unison Helen and Colette dutifully screamed the responses.
Two heads, one dark and curly, the other black Irish glossy, bobbed and
weaved in time to the thundering beat. On the tiny cluttered stage thin
leather-clad youths shook their guitars with mock menace. A gaggle of
the most daring girls, their faces white in matt panstick, eyes stark with
eyeliner and mascara, mouths open and moist, reached up to touch their
heroes who wriggled away. To each side rose banks of amplifiers, bar-
ricades between the musicians and their fans; chords powered up to the
low curved ceiling, bounced back from the sweaty walls and drove into
the audience like missiles.

'Wanna dance?' a voice yelled in Helen's ear. The music was so loud
her eardrums had gone numb and her brain rattled, but she could lip-
read the offer. At her side Colette was approached by his companion
and with a shrug accepted.

It was too dark to identify what the lanky boy wore but that was
probably a school tie – the Institute, at a guess. A sixth-former if she
were lucky, nipping down like herself to spend his midday break at the
Cavern's cheaper sessions. One hand held a half-full bottle of Coke
while the other gestured away towards another aisle, where couples
were frenziedly jiggling in time to the overwhelming beat.

'Yeah, why not?' She would have preferred a Coke but he was probably as poverty-stricken as herself. A dance, provided she didn't get too

hot, would be marginally less tiring than that steamy crush so close to the stage. To be honest, she couldn't see what was so marvellous about John Lennon. Everybody knew he was as blind as a bat without his spectacles and his reputation was unreliable. Paul with his angelic face and sweet voice was more to her taste, but he'd been in a foul mood since the first note and wouldn't smile or fool around. George had bad teeth and seemed forever preoccupied with intricate riffs on his instrument as if the paying punters were entirely incidental.

'Wassyername?' The boy yelled again in her ear in a pause between phrases of 'Long Tall Sally'. He was a determined and vigorous dancer, his tie flapping against his white shirt. That was definitely a school blazer.

Yet his youth was a reassurance. Dockers came in sometimes when bad weather had stopped work. To beat the no-drinks rule they would get tanked up beforehand in The Grapes pub nearby or a Yates Wine Lodge, then leer at the girls. The alcohol emboldened their hands, too, though often they were barely older than the schoolboys. Occasionally there would be fights. They didn't understand or appreciate the music either.

'Helen!' she shouted back. She had left her navy duffel coat rolled up tight under a chair in one of the darkest corners – what wasn't visible was less likely to be stolen. Her blazer, like Colette's, was still on its peg at school. The black polo neck sweater which concealed the rest was stifling; she tugged ineffectively at it.

'Hello, Lynne, then. My name's Jack.' Or it could have been Mack. Or something quite different: it didn't matter.

'Yeah!!'

The final notes twanged. Without bows or further ceremony the foursome jumped down from the stage and headed towards the food hatch which passed for a bar. Colette was already there, Coke in hand, talking to John's girlfriend Cynthia. Rumour had it they had had to get married the previous summer – she was clearly pregnant. Given the way some fans ogled John and their hostility to their favourites' girlfriends, Cynthia was brave to come at all.

A tubby man climbed up in their place and picked a microphone off its stand. His greasy leather jacket gaped over a red tee shirt; in the red spotlight perspiration stood out on his forehead and his eyes bulged.

'We're very grateful to Liverpool's fab four – the Beatles! A big hand for them, ladies and gentlemen, *pur-lease!*'

The applause was acknowledged with a wry wave of a hotdog by John. George turned his back on the crowd and lit a cigarette.

'And I hope, ladies and gentlemen, that all you good people who have seen the boys live at the CAVERN' – wild cheers on cue from the audience – 'have put your names down for their next disc "Please Please Me" which is due out in February. With your support their first, "Love

Me Do", sold the massive total of *one hundred thousand* copies and made it to the charts to number fourteen in November. It even beat – wait for it – Pat Boone!'

Yells of derision greeted the name of the sanitised American crooner. Although the Beatles' music derived directly from American soul and country music a huge gap existed between what was cool and what wasn't for aficionados – which every Cavern Club member would claim to be. Their preferred singers were mainly black and had been poor: the blues were genuine enough. An exception would be made for a superior white like Jerry Lee Lewis. But Boone stood with Doris Day and Guy Mitchell in the hierarchy of the despised, as far as Helen and Colette were concerned.

The DJ, sweating freely, rubbed a podgy hand over his brow. The fans were becoming restless. Behind him another band had started to erect their equipment. As plugs were tested intermittent squeaks and yowls punctured the remainder of his speech.

'And don't forget your copy this week of the *New Musical Express* and our local music mag *Mersey Beat* – on sale round the corner at NEMS as usual!' Another cheer. The North End Music Store in Whitechapel was the city's largest music shop, owned by the Epsteins; it had been opened in a great flourish four years before by Anthony Newley. In the window gleaming Fender guitars and Hoffner basses tempted schoolboys to abandon their studies. A grand piano filled the foreground, with sheet music ('Hits of Russ Conway') draped artisti-cally over the keyboard. At the back were the precious racks of records where light-fingered truants hovered. The record department had been the brainchild of young Brian Epstein, an idea dreamed up in despair and boredom while running their other shop, a furniture store in Woolton. In a modest upstairs office above NEMS Brian had agreed to represent the Beatles and several other bands.

'And now – the Big Three!'

The lead singer, who was also the drummer, looked and performed as if he had been a docker quite recently: big, rough, loud, tuneless. But he laid down a beat that could be heard across the Mersey and was much imitated.

'Yeah – some other guy now . . .' he chanted aggressively into the mike. He was singing in a different key to his lead guitarist. Neither seemed to notice.

Colette was gesticulating towards the exit. Helen peered at her watch. 'I have to go. Sorry.'

'Me too.' Jack finished his drink, put the empty bottle at the base of the wall alongside a dozen others and moved with her towards the stairs. At the entrance she stepped aside to the dark corner, found a couple snogging on the chair under which her coat was hidden, ignored them as she bent down in retrieval and was rewarded with an oath and a poorly aimed kick. Upright once more she rejoined her escort. He glanced at the 'Ladies' sign in polite inquiry, but the toilets here stank of carbolic and effluent and were best avoided. As they pushed their way across the dance floor he put an arm around her.

As they emerged into Mathew Street the sudden cold made them gasp. A path had been cleared in the snow: it was said by the news-papers that this could be the worst winter for years. Breaths hung in the frosty air. The queue had lessened somewhat compared with an hour earlier. The boys were of all sizes but their haircuts were similarly slicked back, Elvis-style, with a flick up at the front wherever Nature permitted. The more daring sported check jackets with blue velvet collars and shiny winkle-picker shoes with a tendency to curl at the toes. The women stood in clumps chattering like sparrows, bodies encased in long fluffy sweaters and tight skirts just above the knee, feet cramped and frozen in pointed white stilettos. Again their hairstyles conformed rigidly – either straight as a die, a silky frame for the face or else back-combed, piled high on top in imitation of Dusty Springfield and fixed with stiff lacquer with its unmistakable cheap scent. Helen could do neither with her naturally curly hair, which caused her grief every night. Before any big event she would sleep in rollers to straighten it. Lucky Colette, when she bothered, could achieve that sleek look which enhanced her green eyes. Every girl wore the same shade of pale pink lipstick, the colour which Helen now quickly removed from her own mouth with a handkerchief.

'Can I see you again?' The boy shivered on the pavement. Helen fastened the toggles of her coat. Behind them the music rose, diminished and distorted, from the dank warmth of the staircase.

Helen looked him once up and down. 'Which school are you at? I may see you around.'

'Merchant Taylor's. Crosby. You won't, I don't think. We don't go to the same dances as you because we're not in Liverpool. I only came into town today because I'm supposed to be going to the hospital. Bunked off,' he grinned sheepishly. 'Like you, I suppose.'

Helen half smiled. 'Then there's not much point, is there? Thanks for the dance.' She exaggerated the accent, as if she were an ordinary scrubber casting off an unwanted beau. All he could see was the black sweater and the duffel coat: surely it wasn't so obvious that she herself was still at school. It might have been different had he bought that drink – made an effort. She walked away.

The two girls strolled arm-in-arm down John Street to Lord Street, past the big shops towards Lime Street Station. The 79 bus stop was by the Adelphi Hotel. Helen's father told lurid tales of the Adelphi, the city's sole smart hotel, whose management were among his better clients. Its heyday had been in the years before the war when the huge Cunarders were the only way to cross the Atlantic. On embarkation eve, limousines would draw up to its broad steps and disgorge stylish women in furs with mountains of leather luggage. Men in topcoats with white silk scarves would follow, cigars clamped between their teeth. Its sumptuous lounge was a copy of the first-class ballroom of the *Queen Mary* and had been decorated by many of the same craftsmen. For the three-day Grand National event at Aintree the entire place would be taken over by racehorse owners and trainers; on the Saturday, the last night of the meet, the top floor penthouses were the scene of wild parties, including (it was said) cockfights with hooded birds smuggled in via the service lift. Her father would get tips on the day of the big race, but never seemed to win anything.

When the green double decker bus arrived the two climbed upstairs and headed to the front. For the moment, the songs still jangling in their heads, the girls were quiet. It was chilly and the floor was littered with cigarette butts, but from there Helen could drift away, could gaze into back yards and upstairs windows, could fantasise on the lives so briefly observed. Why did people in tower blocks keep lace curtains at their windows, even on the tenth floor – who was there to look in? Why did others, close to railway lines or cheek-by-jowl with nearby properties, have no curtains at all? Helen glimpsed unmade beds; in one a man was still asleep, his face turned away from the light. A shift worker, perhaps – but he would have ensured his rest in a darkened room. A layabout, more likely. She frowned.

The vehicle halted by the bombed-out church at the bottom of Leece Street. Five people had been killed there the night it had been destroyed in 1940. Its blackened spire had been made safe and a memorial garden laid out where once had risen nave and choir. There was no money to replace it, and no call for its services as a place of worship. The neighbourhood had long since been taken over by Chinese.

'They were in a bad mood, today,' Colette mused as the bus began to grind uphill.

'Weren't they just? Must be a bit tense for them – that new record could be really big. Scary.' Helen crossed her legs. 'Pity they lost Stu Sutcliffe. He was the best-looking one: they shouldn't have left him in Germany. Golly, it's only a few months since he collapsed and died. And I still can't figure out why Pete Best was ditched last year. Ringo is so ugly and he has no personality.'

'That was Brian Epstein,' Colette answered authoritatively. The nuances of the group's lives were followed assiduously by their fans. 'D'you know he went to see the boys' parents when he signed them up? In a suit, with his posh accent and tidy hair. Even John's Aunt Mimi was impressed. He was the one who ditched Pete.'

'D'you remember the punch-up at the Cavern after that? Pete's mates were livid. George got a black eye.' The bus lurched and Helen clutched the seat for support. 'Something odd about Brian, don't you think?' she added. 'What's the word – effete? Though he's supposed to be courting. But I've seen him look at John in an odd way, sometimes. Almost yearning.'

Colette did not respond for a moment then returned to the earlier subject. 'They'll cope with fame, if it comes. I was talking to Cynthia. She says the boys learned a lot in Hamburg. John reckons they were innocent little kids when they arrived, but a few sessions in strip clubs down the Reeperbahn left them with no illusions.'

Details from the gossip were repeated. The girls giggled at the image of boys virtually their own age struggling to find the notes as red lace panties were flung over the guitars.

'But you can see why they're so good,' Helen persisted. 'I mean, you can sing everything they play – the tunes stick in your head. They've started to write their own music and it isn't like the stuff anybody else does. I think they're fantastic. What's amazing is that hardly anybody's heard of them outside Liverpool.'

'If they're a big success, they'll pack up and leave.' Colette spoke softly. Her friend gave her a sharp glance but the Irish girl was staring out of the glass.

'Typical. Everybody does.' A pause.

Colette restarted the conversation. 'What was your bloke like? I gave up on mine pretty quickly. He smelled sweaty.'

Helen tried to answer honestly but could barely remember. 'Ordinary, I guess. Merchant Taylor's. Wanted to see me again.'

'And you said no.'

A grimace. Colette flashed that sweet smile showing her small white teeth which Helen so envied. 'Oh, Helen, you'll never find a boyfriend like that. Your standards are too high – you're never satisfied.'

'So what?' Helen did not feel particularly defensive. She was very fond of Colette, whose prettiness, intelligence and willingness to defy authority made her the ideal companion on their occasional forays to the Cavern. 'If I fancied a schoolkid, we can have our pick at the Institute – over a thousand of 'em. No, thank you. I want something better.'

Their destination was the first stop past the brow of the hill. Quickly Helen took off the black poloneck jumper which had concealed her school blouse and tie and folded it into an inconspicuous bundle. Colette dug in her pocket and found a tie – with more devilry in her, she had not bothered with concealment. Both knew school regulations did not permit the partial wearing of the uniform. Either it was the whole works of striped masculine necktie, blazer or belted navy mac, yellow and green scarf and hated green beret, or none of the school's identity could be revealed. Every Blackburne House pupil dreamed of the final day at school when in a ritual ceremony on the Mersey ferry that reviled headgear would be cast onto the waters and would float away like so many shelled pea husks. Both girls flapped arms and ran fingers through their hair to get rid of the tell-tale odour of the Cavern.

Helen walked back into school demure, in her first year of the sixth form, likely to be a prefect next year. With a bit of luck nobody would have missed her.

Thursday afternoon. Not the best moment of the week: double period from two pm till three forty, to be utilised by science students on experiments in the laboratory. Monday and Tuesday afternoons were stolid drudgery, lightened only by her being still fresh after the weekend. Wednesday was survivable – the afternoon was wholly allocated to games for which Helen had little talent but which gave some enjoyment. Energetic exercise on a muddy pitch, hockey stick in hand, had its moments as long as she was not required to take the game too seriously. Friday was a short afternoon, especially in winter; she could leave early in order to be home before dusk. Thursday had none of these advantages.

She sniffed as she climbed the stairs to the chemistry lab. The pong of hydrogen sulphide indicated that the juniors of the Marie Curie Club had been in there between lessons, probably trying to make primitive stink bombs. Miss Clive, the assistant teacher, thought it was fun to impart to the younger children a love of practical chemistry. Helen saw, however, as the teacher did not, that the little horrors simply adored spending their spare time on a cold day making a mess – and making life nastier for the older students who must follow.

The long room was strangely quiet. A dozen girls in stained white lab coats loafed around uncertainly. Some, more daring, sat on the work benches. Near the fume cupboard where retorts and Petrie dishes should have been set out, Brenda Jones was perched. Chubby and bouncy, she was chattering to Meg Findlay, the tall intense girl who would compete with Colette for the top A grades in the year. The latter's slight figure was seated nearby, her black hair hiding her face as she flicked through pages of her file. She had slipped in a moment or two earlier.

Colette raised her head and winked as Helen entered. As ever, the greenness of her eyes was startling. Nothing could conceal Colette's origins, any more than Helen's own brown eyes and strong features could hide hers.

'What's up? No class?' Helen asked. Brenda twisted around.

'We have to wait. Miss Clive got an acid burn at lunchtime – one of the juniors was chucking the hydrochloric around, the idiot. She's had to go down to the Royal Infirmary to have it dressed. And Mrs Egerton came in snuffly and has gone home with flu. We're to stay and revise till we can make a decent escape.'

Helen placed her satchel on the bench. She felt deflated after the released energy at the Cavern; the pulsing noise still vibrated faintly in her brain. Without the discipline of an adult's supervision it would be hard to concentrate. 'I haven't anything much to revise, have you? My folder's up-to-date.'

Brenda considered. Light brown hair framed her rosy face. She would never attain the heights of fashion but her confidence and ebullience made her the self-appointed leader of the coterie, though Meg, bespectacled and angular, kept her in check with sardonic asides laced with veiled sarcasm.

'You've been downtown, haven't you?' Brenda's tone was not accusatory. 'Who was on – any good?'

'It was them – the best. The Beatles, of course.' Helen sighed as theatrically as she could manage.

'They ponce about. I prefer Gerry Marsden – he's a better singer. Or Billy Kramer – now there's handsome for you.' Brenda made the remarks to tease. In response Colette clutched her stomach and made retching noises. By now the two truants were the centre of an admiring circle.

'You'll get caught,' Meg interspersed sourly. The discussion of their favourites' relative merits and talents continued for several moments. A small group over by the far window, who had asserted that the locals were not a patch on the real thing from America, began softly to croon the Roy Orbison hit 'Only the Lonely'.

Brenda spoke sharply. 'Shut it. We'll have Miss Plumb in here if you're not careful.' She turned to Helen. 'You doing anything tomorrow? We have a day off, remember.'

Helen was puzzled. 'It's a Friday. What's up?'

'It's for Founder's Day. Oh, I forgot, you weren't in assembly last week when the date was announced. You know we're entitled to an extra day's holiday to commemorate Emma Holt, daughter of our illustrious founder, whose demise in 1844 at the early age of seven led to his recognition of the importance of education for girls. Have I got that right?' Brenda appealed to her listeners.

'Nearly. Except the child died before that,' Meg could not help correcting. Her fingernails were bitten to the quick; when anyone looked at her hands she would slide them behind her back. 'Still, nice of her Papa. Not many people believed in educating girls in those days.'

'They still don't.' This was said with feeling from Colette.

'Your Dad still being a pest?' Brenda was sympathetic.

Colette put down her file and pushed hair from her forehead. 'He can't see the point in my staying on,' she said quietly. 'I could have left in July and he says I ought to be out earning my keep. Nobody in my family has ever stayed at school longer than the law required, ever, and most skipped off long before that.'

'Can't he see that you'll end up maintaining the entire household if you go to college and get a good job?' Meg spoke with a hint of superiority. 'Anyway, what does he want you to do? You can't exactly end up working in the docks like him or your brothers.'

'There's nothing wrong with dock work.' Colette's response had a touch of irritation.

Meg could not restrain herself. 'Except there's less and less of it. If your brothers want to be sure of wage packets in ten years' time, they'd have been better off staying at school themselves.'

'Fat chance. They weren't learning much at Paddington Comprehensive, were they? But our Billy's applied to the new factory at Ford's. The first cars roll off in March – if they're on time. He says he'll hate being indoors the whole day and the moving track will drive him crackers but the money's great, and steady.'

Helen moved to the large sash window whose design revealed the Regency origins of the grand house which Mr Holt had purchased for his pioneering school. The Anglican Cathedral towered nearby, its red sandstone creeping inch by inch to the sky, still unfinished after half a century. A solitary crane stood gaunt, its small load being raised with infinite slowness up to a solitary workman who sat on the scaffolding, his feet dangled over the edge. Nothing would happen till he had finished his cigarette. When the foundation stone was laid this area had been wealthy and snobbish, the perfect location. Now it had become run-down; the handsome old properties had slid into multi-occupation as the more affluent headed for suburbs and to smart mini-towns over the water. It was not safe to wander around Canning Street and Blackburne Terrace after dark.

Beyond the cathedral the land dipped away steeply down past the old cemetery towards the river. On a fine day Birkenhead and Cammell Lairds were clearly visible. But this afternoon the damp chill made the light soft and misty so that the mythical Liver birds on top of the Cunard building seemed to float, unsupported and ethereal.

The river. You can always leave, murmured the river, as it had to generations of young Merseysiders who had watched its grey-green waters surge and lap on the boards of the landing stage. Each sluggish wave would leave a dirty scum on the rotting wood. You don't have to stay. You can go for a short while or for a lifetime; sail round the world or merely to New Brighton or Hoylake. See New York, or Cape Town, or Zanzibar. You can taste the delights of another life, more exotic, more exhilarating while others, the timid, linger and console themselves with their fear of the unknown. Let them languish, you need not. Nor need you have any fear that you will have burned your boats for ever, for I am the river and I do not change: I will always be here, should you need me, to bring you home.

'Helen! You're miles away. *Your* parents aren't being difficult, are they?'

Helen turned back to the room. 'Yes and no. I wouldn't be the first to have an education but I'd be the first girl. They're so conventional and strict. My worry, Bren, is how to convince my Mum in particular – I know she'd be proud of me, but still she warns me off with comments like "Remember, boys don't like clever girls". It sends me spare.'

Brenda grunted. 'Stuff. Tell her you'll find a clever boy. You will, too. Provided your father doesn't interfere too much. Honestly, Helen Majinsky, I don't know how you put up with it – all those restrictions. Can't go into assembly in case the word "Christ" is spoken or the Lord's Prayer is recited. Can't eat proper food. Can't go out Friday nights ever – I ask you! And your beady-eyed parents vet your friends for their race purity. It must be horrid, being a Jew.'

'We have a day off tomorrow. Founder's Day.'

Helen rose from the table, collected the used dishes and helped her mother clear the table. The *tzimmes* – a sweet carroty stew – had been substantial and filling. Her father picked up the *Liverpool Echo* and began silently to read; Barry had speedily disappeared up to his bedroom from which warbles of Del Shannon (*'Run run run runawayyy!!'*) soon emanated. He insisted on doing his homework to musical accompaniment, which in Helen's view explained his poor marks. Nor did she share his taste. When it came to exams however, he sailed through. That didn't seem quite fair: another minor example of how males were favoured in life, especially younger brothers.

'Oh? D'you have any plans?' In the back kitchen her mother swished soapy dishes in the bowl, rinsed them under the tap and laid them out in an order known only to herself on the plastic rack. This year Annie Majinsky would be forty-five. Her daughter was already an inch or two taller, for Annie was a tiny woman who ate sparingly. Her hair, formerly thick and black, had become straggly and pepper and salt in colour. The face showed fine lines and – at home at least – she wore only a little lipstick.

'Well: I thought I'd spend a couple of hours in the Central Library then maybe go to Dad's at lunchtime if he'll let me. Later I can cadge a lift home with him. I like it when he calls at Mrs Quilter's and the other ladies with the outwork.'

Annie Majinsky sniffed. 'They keep him talking.'

'I won't delay him, Mum.'

It occurred to Helen that her mother was a little jealous. She had solely her husband Daniel's word for it that he stopped merely to collect the bundles made ready with buttonholes or hand-turned collars, to pay for jobs done and to drop off the following week's batch. A quick cup of tea might be shared and pleasantries exchanged as the more intricate tasks were discussed. That he was inside the shabby hallway of a divorced woman's home, or – worse – close to a lonely widow, was enough to worry her. They were *shikses*, known to have fewer moral scruples.

'You could come instead with me to get the chicken for *shabbos* dinner, if you like,' Annie offered. 'You haven't been for ages. They're going to close the Great Newton Street market soon – they say it's not hygienic, though I think it's better to choose your bird yourself, then you know what you're buying. It'll mean we'll have to buy our chickens from Patsky's at twice the price. A real *gonif*, him.'

Helen resented the implied rivalry between mother and father vying for her limited free time. She tried to love them both equally. So why did her mother think up objections to anything her daughter suggested – why couldn't she for once say, 'Great idea, darling, go ahead'? What was there to be afraid of? She finished drying the dishes, but as she lifted a pile of plates Annie stopped her with a yelp.

'Not there! Those are *milchich* plates. That pile is *fleischich*. Don't you know the difference yet? Put them in the cupboard by the sink.'

'I do know the difference.' Helen was cross with herself for her slip. 'I keep forgetting because I can't see the point. Christians cope perfectly well without separating milk and meat crockery and cutlery, and I don't see them coming down with weird diseases. Lots of Jewish people don't bother these days, either.'

'Helen! That's enough. You know perfectly well why we do it. It says in the Bible that you should not boil a kid in the milk of its mother. As for the *goyyim*, I wouldn't want to eat anything that comes out of their kitchens, thank you very much.'

'It says in the Bible, "An eye for an eye and a tooth for a tooth", but we don't do that these days either,' Helen retorted, but she was not in the mood for a fight. To placate her parents she kept the rules of a kosher home and would not have indulged in secret violations or upset them more than she dared. The concepts of duty and filial respect she accepted, at least for the moment.

The altercation had brought her father to the kitchen doorway, newspaper in hand. 'You may not like it, Helen, but as long as you live in this house you will keep the rules. When you have your own home you can do what you like.'

No, thought the girl savagely. I'll never be able to do what I like: all my life, what I fear and shrink away from will have been determined by the taboos I was forced to accept here. It'll start with food – I will always wrinkle my nose in distaste at the smell of bacon. I will never be able to touch an oyster or lobster. I will wince whenever I hear the word 'Christian', as my mother did a moment ago. But it'll continue in my reaction to Christmas and my horror of the Pope, a foolish old man in a gold-trimmed robe who has never known sex but tells half the world what not to do. I've been brought up in a certain way and most of it'll stick. And even as I love you, I resent and hate you for it, you and every mad old rabbi in the last twenty centuries who dreamed up the entire crazy edifice of laws out of *nothing*. And the rabbis' wives with their shorn heads and their wigs so no other man should gaze carnally at them. Dirty-minded lot. Most of all I loathe everybody's insistence that *I have to observe whether I believe in it or not*. But what can I do?

For the present she had no choice, but acquiescence did not improve her temper. Barry's reaction was different, but then he was only twelve to her sixteen. He would shrug: whatever he was asked to do, he performed, with just enough enthusiasm and plays to the gallery to win plaudits. When he was with his pals, she suspected, it was a different matter. As they grew older they would egg each other on to increasing acts of sniggering defiance. It would start with minor peccadilloes – an illegal hot dog from a stand in town, or bars of Cadbury's when they were supposed to be fasting on Yom Kippur – and could finish when they were big enough by getting some *shikse* pregnant. They'd try things with a non-Jewish girl they wouldn't dare with one of their own. Self-preservation, of course; a Jewish girl would have a brother to complain to, or, if the worst threatened, she could tell her mother. The wrath of such a parent, the curse of the community, were not to be hazarded.

Her father retreated to the cleared table, his paper and the inevitable packet of Player's to hand. The dishes finished, and trying to avoid any further errors, Helen followed meekly. She watched his broad shoulders, her face controlled. He was nearly bald now, though the moustache was as luxuriant as ever. It gave him an old-fashioned air, and was worn in imitation of his father whom the photos on the sideboard showed he closely resembled.

Daniel held the pages away from him as if he needed glasses. He was a good man, and more intellectual than most of his contemporaries. Like them he had opened at the sports pages first. Unlike them, he then turned to the national news. He pointed at a photograph.

'Government's in trouble. General de Gaulle's said "No", and the polls are terrible. They seem to be dogged by scandal which doesn't help. Will you have to know about this for your A levels, Helen?'

'Might, for General Studies. I don't have to know what John Vassall got up to, but I may get a question on the economic implications of our not being able to join the Common Market.'

'Macmillan is one of your heroes, isn't he?' Daniel laid down the paper and gazed at his wayward daughter. Was he aware that with that moustache and the quizzical eyebrows and big forehead, he quite resembled the beleaguered Prime Minister?

'Sort of. I like the way he tries to look to the future. New bodies like Neddy and Nicky – the National Economic Development Council, and the National Incomes Commission – I have to be able to write essays on those. And his attempt to get us into Europe. Not all his ideas will work, of course, but at least he *tries*. And he's friends with President Kennedy. Now there really is a man to inspire people – especially young ones like me.'

'All piss and wind, seems to me, Kennedy. And his father was a great anti-Semite when he was ambassador here before the war.'

It was a signal between them; if father and daughter could not easily communicate about personal matters, they could nevertheless dispute energetically and amicably about current events. With her mother such elevated conversations were not possible; her brother was too young but showed every sign of shallowness. Her father made a point of using colourful language in these discussions, a watered-down version of what she could hear on any street corner in town, as if preparing her for the outside world – though he would not let his daughter do the same. It was like his smoking: he had started young and couldn't help it, he declared, but as long as possible he would ban his children from the habit. Helen folded her arms in mock belligerence.

'Well, President Kennedy saw Khrushchev off and nobody else's done that, ever,' the girl countered. It was important to use adult phrases and references with her father, to repay his compliment to her. 'I've never been so petrified as that weekend of the Cuban missile crisis – I thought we'd had it. But the President showed huge courage and leadership.'

Daniel Majinsky considered. 'Easy to do it when you've got half a million soldiers at your disposal. He wouldn't hesitate to put those boys' lives at risk.'

'But you're no pacifist, Dad. And you wouldn't have wanted him to back down.'

Daniel chuckled. 'Right. And if we had to choose between the Russians and the Americans, we know which side we'd be on.'

Helen changed tack. 'D'you ever regret not going to America, Dad?' The family photographs showed his elder sister Gertie, his sole sibling, who had emigrated in the hard years before the war to New York. Cousins Miriam and Eva had fled there at war's end, married to Jewish GIs. Only Daniel had hesitated.

'I was a bit too old.' He looked at his hands. 'That sounds daft – I was thirty-two. I could have gone: Gertie and her husband Joe would have stood surety for me. But I'd decided to marry your mother and set up my own business. My plans were made. Ten years earlier, maybe, it'd have been different. But it wasn't.'

But a decade before he would have faced the same choice. He had never explained why he had opted to stay then, either. Whenever the question arose he referred to the time of decision as the end of the war. So did her mother.

'You'd been ill, though, hadn't you?' Helen ventured.

'That bout of TB didn't help, that's for sure. No penicillin in those days. A man with damaged lungs is hardly prime material,' Daniel admitted. 'But I didn't bother. I wasn't in the army – passed unfit. My war was spent cutting out khaki battledress and on fire-watch on the factory roof. Mostly falling asleep on duty, to tell the truth.'

She waited. Her father seemed momentarily lost in a faraway world. Suddenly he looked up and grinned. 'Right! Haven't you got an essay to write? And I heard you say you're coming to the workshop tomorrow. Tell your mother to do tinned salmon sandwiches. They're your favourite, and mine.'

Helen left the room as her father resumed his perusal of the *Echo*. His jocular dismissal had been as close as he would get to an expression of affection. He had made time for her, talked to her as an adult and had accepted a point she had put, the greatest compliment he could pay.

In this family nobody hugged; there were few spoken words of regard. No one had ever said, 'I love you, Helen,' directly to her. Nor could she recall an occasion on which she had heard her parents exchange words of endearment. Once in a cinema an explosion of passion had erupted on the screen; she had sensed both Annie and Daniel squirm with embarrassment.

Nor could she hope for verbal encouragement. The most she could expect might be an overheard remark: 'She's not a bad kid, on the whole.' If any member of the clan were lauded by an outsider the listener would become deprecatory. It wasn't mere modesty. It was as if praise were dangerous, would expose its recipients to undue attention, make them swell-headed, put the whole fellowship at risk. Complacency might set in, effort might slacken too soon. Jews had learned to keep their heads down.

Her father took his reserve to extremes. He didn't believe in cards and presents at birthdays and anniversaries, and naturally Christmas was forbidden. The result was a fearsome kind of puritanism against which the rest of the Majinsky family would cautiously rebel. Annie in particular looked forward to Mother's Day in March and expected a bunch of daffodils from her children over which she would exclaim with pleasure, though in the same breath she would chide them for the unnecessary expense. She had absorbed from her husband a harsh inability simply to appreciate a gift, or to express thanks without criticism, as if either she or the donor were unworthy.

The street lamps cast a bluish glow as the crowd spilled out on to Hope Street and, taking care on icy pavements, headed for cars and bus stops. It took a long time for two thousand people to find hats, coats, gloves and exits, and to disperse into the inhospitable gloom. Their breaths hung on the frozen air like a misty curtain. Behind them shone the bright lights of the Philharmonic Hall and the hubbub still within.

Rita Nixon linked arms with her sister Sylvia Bloom, as much for the warmth of the latter's fur coat as with any sisterly affection. On a winter's night she was exceedingly thankful for Sylvia's money which had brought in addition the Hillman Minx parked around the corner.

The two women were much the same shape, or would be when Rita, the younger by several years, had caught up. Both had married men they did not love, since marriage was what was expected of them, and was all that was on offer. Both had endured hurried and joyless sex sufficiently long to produce a single child, both girls: first Sarah for Sylvia, then, much later on, Roseanne for Rita. At that point their paths diverged, for once he had carelessly provided cause Sylvia had divorced her husband with relief. Rita merely ignored hers. Scathingly she dubbed him 'Nix' even to his face. Sylvia dreamed of affairs which never materialised but earned her keep encouraging others as informal proprietor of a Jewish introduction agency: a *shadchan*, or matchmaker.

Both doted on their daughters but suspected that the sentiment was not returned, though Roseanne, everyone declared, was the spitting image of her mother both in looks and personality. Rita was not sure this was a compliment and Sylvia was certain it wasn't. Her job meant she understood such nuances.

The sisters had many tastes in common and would frequently meet for a day out, or to keep company at the type of event where a husband was useful if he could be persuaded to appear (or were available), but where a lone woman might find herself out of place. Such an occasion had just finished. The Liverpool Conservatives had welcomed their Leader and Prime Minister. In the heart of the city he had spoken to them, to a rapturous and uncritical welcome. Rita and Sylvia felt quite inspired.

'I didn't think he seemed well, I must say. I don't think that Lady Dorothy looks after him properly,' Rita remarked.

'Not her role, is it? They have servants. She was a Cavendish, you know. Devonshires. Chatsworth. Lovely place,' Sylvia added airily.

'No, he seemed – unhappy, somehow.' They had reached the car. Rita ruminated further as her sister fumbled in the chill air for the keys. 'I suppose it's understandable. President de Gaulle's given him a real brush-off.'

'What did he say to us? Oh, yes, I remember. "If the objections to our entry to the Common Market were so strong in principle, why weren't we told right from the start?" He's got a point.' Sylvia opened her side, slid into her seat and reached over to unlock the passenger door.

'Nothing he can do about it, though.' Rita regarded herself as the more practical of the two. She climbed in, held her coat clear of the door and slammed it hard. 'We're not going to gain entry, and that's that.'

'Would you want to?' Sylvia pulled out the choke and pumped the pedals. She hoped that she could get the engine to start from cold without too much trouble. Although plenty of fit-looking men were milling around who could be asked for a push, their jokes about women drivers would be a pain. With a grunt of satisfaction she heard the motor cough into life on the third try and revved it for a few moments. Her next car would have a heater.

The question took Rita into realms where she preferred to be told what to think.

'After everything the Germans did to us, any links with them leave me uneasy. On the other hand we know what'll happen if they're left to their own devices.' Her face brightened. 'I suppose that's why it's a good idea if the British join. Keep our eyes on the Krauts, and on the Frenchies. Maybe that's what Mr Macmillan has in mind, though he couldn't come out and say it.'

The car moved jerkily away from the kerb. Rita had never learned to drive but had watched her husband Nix many times. She debated silently whether to point out that the handbrake, if that was what it was called, was still on, but fortunately her sister noticed in time and let it down with an unladylike expletive. The Hillman skidded briefly then settled into a slow chug over the slushy snow towards Canning Street.

'You're right, though,' Sylvia concurred. The sisters prided themselves on not quarrelling. 'He was peaky. Drained. Not been a good start to the year for us Tories. Let's hope there's no more bad news to come.'

Helen picked up her bag from the hallway and climbed the stairs to her bedroom at the back of the house. It was too small for a desk as well as two narrow beds, a wardrobe and a chest of drawers. She sat cross-legged on the bed by the window and arranged textbooks and files around her.

The bed swayed and creaked. It had been her father's in bachelor days. He had told her how he had been pulled out of the Hayworth Street house in the autumn of 1944 when for the fourth time his home suffered from bombing. That last occasion it was a direct hit; Helen had seen the gap in the row of terraced houses, like a pulled tooth. Daniel had survived because he had been asleep on the sofa near the fire. The chimney breast had fallen intact across him. He had emerged black as the ace of spades, coughing and wiping the soot from his eyes, but his father – her grandfather – had suffered shrapnel wounds which turned to gangrene. Three weeks later, delirious with pain, the old man had died in the Royal Infirmary surrounded by dozens of similar cases. So when did the bed appear? This narrow bed with its ancient noisy springs? Probably from a second-hand shop soon after, when Daniel must have been taken in by an accommodating friend. It felt older than he was.

This family, Helen sensed, had been affected more by the war in Britain than by the genocide. True, Annie's cousin's family had been wiped out in Auschwitz; a survivor had made his way to Israel after terrible privations. But both Annie and her daughter, like Rita and her sister, were far more aware in their daily lives of acres of bomb-blasted devastation which had not yet been cleared and of the huge effort to restart the economy and to catch up both with overseas competitors and the expectations of ordinary people. All had a sense that the country was falling behind. They were probably culturally closer to their Christian neighbours than to distant relatives in Tel Aviv or Tiberias, though the older generation would have denied it. For them, assimilation was to be fought not welcomed.

Yet despite the tribulations, her father had refused to quit the shattered city. Helen admired him for that. The promised lands – Canada, America, Australia – beckoned. Others couldn't get away quick enough. That was her mother's verdict on the speedy captures by Daniel's cousins of clean-cut young men from the nearby USAF airbase at Burtonwood. The double wedding photos showed both girls smiling triumphantly, their soldier bridegrooms clean-cut in their uniforms. One bride had a baby in arms by the date the ship sailed. At this point in the narrative Annie would sniff audibly. If Gertie her sister-in-law was mentioned Annie would raise her eyes to heaven and mutter. As these women were close relations she could not express outright disapproval, not in her own daughter's hearing. Helen would speculate to herself whether any of her female relatives had behaved scandalously, but suspected it was simply that their choices were far more adventurous than her mother's.

Had Daniel emigrated she, Helen, would have been born in America. Probably in Brooklyn. Gertie boasted an address in Queens, on Little Rock Parkway which sounded like a proper road. An open invitation was extended but the fare to New York was prohibitive. Nor had these newly naturalised Americans, who boasted of having done so well stateside, raised the funds to visit in the eighteen years since: not one of them.

It was dark. The curtains should be drawn, but as with the bus she relished her vantage point. Down in the lighted kitchen of the house across the garden plump Mrs Williams was lifting a large dish out of the oven. At her side a pile of plates, indifferent to meat or milk, awaited the casserole and potatoes, the cabbage and gravy, the suet pudding and custard. Mrs Williams, who was Welsh, was a better cook than her mother; or at least, a more generous one.

A footstep came on the landing; her mother opened the door, her arms full of clean laundry. 'Excuse me. I have to put this lot in the airing cupboard.'

As sheets and towels were folded away Annie chattered inconsequentially about Friday's activities while for a moment Helen continued to gaze out of the window. Her mother paused, hands on hips. 'You've not heard a word I've been saying.'

Helen relaxed. It was the second time that day she had been caught daydreaming. 'I was watching Mrs Williams, Mum,' she explained. 'She seems so settled, like she's been in her kitchen a century and will always be here. Yet she was born in a Welsh village.'

'Here's not a bad place to be,' Annie countered. 'You could do far worse. Liverpool people – Scousers – have some fine qualities. Even the *goyyim*.'

'Oh, I know. Nowhere else are people as warm, as friendly, as kind-hearted. Nowhere else do citizens have the same sense of humour, the same cheeky way with words, the same wisdom. Isn't that right?' Her mother looked puzzled: Helen was teasing. The girl continued, waving her arms as if on a television show, 'Scousers have a keen sense of balance; in particular they know when to work and when to play. It is held to be *wrong* to work a moment beyond absolute necessity. Oh, quite.'

'That's true,' Annie said, a little uncertainly.

'The trouble is,' Helen continued, her brow furrowed in best Cliff Michelmore style, 'outside, these sensible attitudes are misrepresented. Scousers are regarded as a bit of a joke. Their rich accent, thick as soup in a ladle, is a source of mockery. Their attitudes and drinking habits are held up to scrutiny. Their preference for football over hard graft is inexplicably seen as a fault, not as a mark in their favour.'

Annie shrugged and folded the teatowels. 'So stay put. Everything is familiar, everybody talks the same. Nobody'll laugh at you here.'

It dawned on Helen that two kinds of restrictions faced her: being Jewish and coming from a working-class background in Liverpool. Two systems, each elaborate, complete and consistent, separable yet interlinked; two thickly woven blankets intended to protect her. Yet the overall effect was of suffocation.

If Brenda and Meg were correct a third limitation existed. Should she want her own life it'd be much harder *as a girl*. She hadn't given the question much attention; these were obstacles she had tended to take for granted. Girls were not barred entirely: they could try for Oxford, with its thirty colleges for men and only five for women. Cambridge was worse – only three took women. Even Liverpool University would accept far more men than women entrants and set secret quotas to ensure that outcome. But that was a big improvement on times when women couldn't be admitted as undergraduates at all.

So far Helen had regarded it as a matter of ensuring she at any rate was good enough to surmount the barriers. That the existence of the barriers was wrong in principle she knew, but ignored. Hence her preference for science. However tough it might be for a northern grammar-school girl to gain entry to a top university to read chemistry, it'd be ten times harder in English and nigh impossible in politics or history: unless one's education to date had been paid for, and Daddy was a baronet.

She laughed softly. Annie stopped and looked at her, the wayward one. Helen knew her mother found her a mystery: the element of distance between them was increasing.

'So?' her mother demanded defensively. 'What did I say that was so funny?'

'No, it wasn't you, Mum. I was thinking how much easier it'd be to take the next steps if my father were a lord or a baronet. *Sir* Daniel.'

'Well, he's not. Nor am I Lady Majinsky, or Lady Muck. You shouldn't go round wanting what you can't have, my girl.'

Yet Helen continued to smile, if ruefully. As her mother left, arms emptied, the girl picked up a file, then rose and closed the curtains.

Chapter Two

Friday

Annie gazed dubiously at her daughter. 'I'm not sure you should wear jeans, Helen. And that angora sweater. We might meet people we know.'

'So? They'll think you have an utterly modern daughter, Mum, and congratulate you. Anyway it's cold and that's a miserable damp place. I'll put my duffel coat on top. Are you ready – shall I carry the bag?'

One outcome of Helen's musings of the night before had been a resolution to be as well mannered as possible. Unlike both Meg and Colette she had a stable home. It was not her place to attack its foundations.

Annie continued to issue a stream of somewhat disorganised instructions. It was, Helen reflected, as if nobody could close a window nor lock a door without having been told. Or maybe this was a ritual affirmation of her mother's role as mainstay of the household. Not that Helen wished to rearrange that, either.

The girl waited on the pavement as her mother locked the front door. It was a semi-detached, pebble-dashed house like its siamese twin to the left, one of millions of suburban properties built in a wave of 1930s speculation. In the small front garden a few rose bushes straggled behind a dank privet hedge. How Helen hated that hedge. Nothing much would flourish near or beneath it, not daffodils nor lily of the valley; yet privet, as high as it could decently be grown, was a mark of respectability. Too high or straggly or uncut, it would indicate wildness or undue suspicion of neighbours. A hedge too low or viciously pruned revealed a mean streak. Breast-height bushes conferred privacy and confirmed moderation. Her mother joined her at the gate, closed it and glanced back with a nod of satisfaction.

'This is all I ever wanted, you know, Helen,' her mother commented, then turned away with her towards the bus stop. Compared with many at her school the Majinskys were comfortable, though life could be uncertain. They owned their home, albeit on a mortgage. Her father had his own business in the city's heart with a diverse and largely wealthy clientele. Most precious and unusual of all, they possessed a small car, a second-hand black Vauxhall. Daniel drove it, as was normal. Few women learned to drive; the prevailing opinion which Annie shared was that females did not have the right temperament. The fact that Sylvia Bloom drove, a divorcee, served to confirm her prejudice.

A short bus ride would bring Annie and her daughter to their objective behind London Road. On the brow of the hill overlooking the river, the city had once ended at this point. Main arterial trunk roads then wound out into open country before linking up with the villages of Childwall and Gateacre, Aigburth and Prescot, which had been incorporated about the time Annie was born. Just as an ancient tanyard would be banished to the edge of a village because of the smell, so the old slaughteryard stood at the city's original limits, not far from the railhead.

They sat downstairs. Annie paid the fares – 'One and a half to London Road' – and handed over the exact change.

'You going to Harold House on Sunday, Helen?'

'Yes, probably.' That was the youth club to which Helen and most of the city's Jewish youth belonged. Its home was a scruffy Victorian house scheduled for demolition near the town centre.

'It's nice for you there.' Again that nod of satisfaction. As if she might have added, Helen thought, 'God's in his heaven and all's right with the world.' But, faithful to her new-found ordinance, she said nothing. Her mother persisted.

'Does Jerry Feinstein still go? And what about Roseanne?'

'Yes, but we're not close friends, Mum. We happen to go to the same school. We don't even do the same subjects.' She ignored the reference to Jerry. Her mother was endlessly inquisitive about boyfriends.

'Your brother is happy at the King David.'

Helen tried not to scowl. It was not difficult to follow her mother's train of thought. As an eleven-year-old sitting the city's selective tests she had prayed her name would emerge near the top of the Liverpool-wide lists. That guaranteed her entry to the top girls' grammar school instead of allocation to the new comprehensive. As far as she could see the King David's sole advantage – its location close to her house – was more than outweighed by its oppressive religious bent.

'I have to start thinking soon about which university,' she ventured. Annie folded her hands firmly in her lap.

'Plenty of time yet. They tell me Liverpool's very good, if you must go to university. Then you can stay with us.'

'Would you say that if Barry wanted to go away?' Helen was genuinely curious.

Annie sniffed. 'It's different for boys. Now don't start arguing with me, Helen, you know it is.'

'I don't see why. Come on, Mum. You're not thick. If you'd had the chance, wouldn't you have wanted to go to college, and start a new life?'

'I didn't have the chance. Nobody did in those days before the war, not from our street.'

Helen wondered briefly whether she herself might talk similarly some day, with her ideas stuck in the groove established in her youth.

'But if you had?' the girl persisted. Then she remembered. 'You said "nobody" and that's not true. Didn't one of the family qualify as a chemist?'

'Right,' said Annie, but there was a steeliness in her voice. 'Our David. Fat lot of use that was. We had to make such sacrifices so he could go, and then he ups and marries a non-Jewish girl. Not the best example you could have chosen.'

'He lives in London, doesn't he?' Helen was conscious of treading on thin ice. She had never met this uncle whose behaviour had marked him as a black sheep. Her mother was twisting her gloves in her lap. 'Why don't we see him – is that his choice, or ours?'

'We see everybody else,' Annie responded shortly. 'Your uncle Sammy and uncle Abbie in Manchester. Both have nice homes. They're the nearest. My sisters are all over the place. We'd see more of our Becky if her husband wasn't Reform.'

'But we're not close,' Helen mused. 'Not physically or – as friends. You and Dad are the only members of your families still here where you were born. The rest have scattered. It's as if you two are still in the life raft after a storm when everyone else's been rescued.'

'What's that supposed to mean?' Annie shot her a suspicious glance. 'I don't see it like that. I don't hanker after what I can't have and I count my blessings. That's why I'm content. I said it last night. Be content with what you've got, is my maxim. Don't turn your nose up, Helen. You could do a lot worse.' She peered out. 'It's our stop soon. Fasten your coat.'

The bus left them a short distance from their destination. A chill wind whipped through the street. Helen pulled the duffel coat closer. Even a hundred yards away, cattle could be heard lowing in fear, and behind them the screech of chickens.

Underfoot it was wet and slimy. Annie steered her daughter and began to pick her way fastidiously round dollops of manure. 'I'm not sure it won't be a good thing when this place shuts,' she remarked defensively. 'I'll have to wipe my shoes with a bit of newspaper before I get back on the bus.'

Soon rows of steel pens came into sight. Within their confines were pressed dozens of cattle, black and white or reddish brown, their broad cream noses wet and slobbery, eyes wide and rolling. Men in dungarees and donkey jackets, cigarettes on lower lips, prodded the

beasts, indifferent to the steaming odours of faeces and fear. The animals were being herded steadily towards a vast corrugated-iron shed. Its
doors gaped open; a sickly yellow light from inside shone fitfully over
the yards. From its depths clanging metallic noises came with a thumping regularity.

'They don't kill them our way,' Annie asserted. 'This lot'll be stunned
first. We don't allow it.'

The girl shivered but it was as if her mother wanted to press home an
advantage. 'See, the rabbis say our animals have to be free of blemish.
So we wouldn't take that one there.' She pointed at a gaunt specimen
with a gash on its flank. The dried blood attracted flies even in the cold
weather.

'Then for us they have to be put in a sort of cage and turned upside
down so that the throat can be cut in a single stroke. That's also so that
the blood can drain out; we're not allowed to eat any blood, remember.'

'I think it would be less cruel to stun them,' Helen commented.

'Nonsense,' said Annie firmly. 'The animal dies the moment its
throat's cut. It's the best way. In biblical days they'd cut flesh from the
living animal.'

Again that reference to ways of life thousands of years ago, still with
contemporary force. Helen had scarcely thought about it but the need
to be relevant to her own time was beginning insistently to assert itself.
'Something like that still happens,' she said. 'With lobsters and crabs.
They're cooked live.' Both women shuddered.

'I couldn't touch them. And people who eat them claim to be
civilised!' Annie continued. 'Anything which crawls along the sea bed is
dirty. Fish are permitted if they have gills and scales but no shellfish.
Winkles and cockles: ugh. No thanks.'

They had left the cattle sheds behind and entered the area reserved for
fowl. The noise was as loud, more urgent, more of a shriek than a
bellow. On one side fat farm-raised chickens with glossy brown plumage
sat eight or ten to a wicker basket; their vendors resembled the birds,
plump men or women in tweeds from the dunes of Lancashire. Nearby,
lorries unloaded their wares, banks of metal cages crammed with
scrawny ex-layers with white feathers and raw patches around their
necks. The air was more sour than near the cattle, less earthy, acrid.

Women worked around here, some in black aprons, their heads
swathed in scarves, hands cold in fingerless gloves. An auctioneer in a
white coat moved down a wall of cages prodding chickens and uttering
a steady stream of prices. He was followed by three attentive men.
One, young and thin, the auctioneer's clerk, took notes; the others, evidently more prosperous, were buyers for local shops. Whatever was
purchased would shortly grace marble slabs decorated with plastic
parsley in emporia throughout the region, and appear on dinner tables
with roast potatoes and mushy peas on Sunday.

'This way.' The buyers ignored Annie as she threaded her way past. Just one more housewife with an old leather carrier-bag, off to fetch her dinner cheaper than she could get it from them. Wanting to see the live bird for herself: as if that were any guarantee of its quality. How could she know more than they did?

In a moment the two arrived at a roped-off area arranged as a small yard. On one post hung a white plastic notice with lettering in blue, English and Hebrew, plus the six-pointed star of David, the same as was exhibited in every Jewish food shop. It indicated the jurisdiction of the Beth Din, the guardians of *kashrut*.

A corrugated awning provided shelter from rain or snow but not from the wind. Underneath sat several ancient hags dressed in black each with a leather apron covering the lower body. Behind, acting as an inadequate wind-break, was a double row of black iron pots, like chimney funnels. Helen suspected they were exactly that – liberated in a job lot from a builder's yard, exactly the right shape and size. The bottom of each pot was open; each was nailed to a metal bar and suspended over a small open drain filled with black blood which oozed in sluggish rivulets. Some of the pots held chickens, upside down, their legs sticking up helplessly, red or yellow, the long claws packed with grime. The smell was overpowering and made her want to retch.

'Good morning, Mrs Ginsberg.' Annie greeted the nearest old woman with deference. The sticky eyes peered back at her glumly.

Mrs Ginsberg was completely bundled up in black from top to toe. Under her apron and stained skirt thick stockinged legs could be glimpsed which disappeared into heavy boots laced up past the ankle. Like the other women who glanced up in momentary curiosity then returned to their tasks she wore black fingerless gloves stiff with blood, mucus and feathers. The fleshy face was wizened and red with cold; a headscarf was tied tightly around her head but wisps of grey hair had escaped unnoticed. A couple of small white feathers had lodged in the tendrils. On her lap lay a headless chicken which she plucked with speedy ferocity, the feathers dumped in handfuls in a sack at her side. The other women were similarly engaged but worked more slowly.

'Mrs Majinsky. Not a good morning. Bloody freezing.' Mrs Ginsberg sniffed and wiped her nose on her sleeve. 'Go choose your chicken. Brigstone's got some nice ones. Watch out for the old man.'

That meant the wily old Rabbi from the Beth Din was in the vicinity. Like a malevolent vulture he would scrutinise as animals and chickens were dispatched. If he did not like what he saw he might declare the carcase not kosher. Then a noisy row could ensue as the purchaser demanded her money back and the vendor, the sale completed as far as he was concerned, refused. Customers had been known to come to blows. On one occasion a butcher, driven to distraction by the Rebbe's pernickety ways on a singularly bad day had grabbed his beard and threatened him with his *shochet*'s knife. He had been heavily fined by the Beth Din for that.

Mr Brigstone stood nearby, a wicker basket at his feet. He came in from Formby. Annie preferred his birds as they were mature and healthy, as was evident from the red wattle and clear eye; often several eggs would be found in the oviduct, semi-formed and delicious. Once the abattoir was closed, these opportunities would vanish too. Whatever was inside the live bird at the moment of purchase was hers to use – giblets, liver, heart: all except the gizzard, solid with stones and half-digested corn, which must be discarded, along with the guts. That was a skilled task. A careless hand would yank out the intestines and break the bile sac or duct; then the flesh would be tainted and useless. But the remaining innards made excellent soup, and by family tradition were Annie's own to nibble with the meal.

For a moment, for the sheer pleasure of it, Annie debated with Mr Brigstone the virtues of each of the six hens remaining in the basket, then chose the middle-sized one as she usually did. A ten-shilling note was handed over, change counted and put away. Chickens were not cheap, but they were essential for a proper Friday night dinner.

Respectful of her delicacy the farmer reached into the basket and hauled the squawking bird out by the legs. With it held firmly in front of him as it struggled he marched straight over to the butcher and put the hen into his hands.

It was now the turn of the butcher to nod amiably to his customer. He was a fat but muscular man, in shirtsleeves despite the cold, his blue striped apron tied twice round his middle and streaked with gore. On his head was pinned a *yarmulkah*. Annie knew him to be a robustly religious man who would take no chances. He had to be so, to hold down the key job at the heart of the Jewish community.

'Mrs Majinsky! A fine one here.' So saying he quickly examined the hen thoroughly. Then in a swift movement he tucked the flapping bird under one beefy arm, bent back the neck and with his knife cut the head clean off in a single stroke.

Blood spurted from the wound. The thing continued to jerk about. As Helen watched in horror it suddenly leaped out of the butcher's hands and jumped awkwardly around in the mess at his feet. Other faces turned around at the commotion. The butcher, hands on hips, began to laugh heartily, then spotted the alarmed faces of the Majinsky women. Quickly he scooped the creature out of the mire, holding it firmly in both hands till suddenly it flopped. 'Poor thing – I know just how it feels,' he murmured, and stroked the quivering plumage.

Then the corpse, its golden feathers muddied, was turned upside down and unceremoniously dumped into one of the metal chimney pots to drain alongside half a dozen others.

Helen felt exhausted: by the stink, by the racket, by the savagery of the headless bird as it clung unknowingly to life. The butcher was already joking with a fresh lady customer who clutched another wriggling chicken by the legs as he deftly stropped his knife. But his hand shook slightly.

In the distance she could see the skinny black-coated figure of the Rebbe. Head bowed, eyes restless he swung this way and that and muttered into his beard. His presence chilled her. His piety seemed to encompass not love but inhibition, ritual observance and denial, without room for compromise or compassion.

Two more tasks remained. Old Mrs Ginsberg rose, tugged the bird out of the pot with an audible *plop* and shook it so that a last few drops of blood spattered the floor. Then she settled it lovingly on her knees as if it were a baby about to be fed and plucked it thoroughly. Small under-feathers floated up in the air and made Helen sneeze. As the naked flesh emerged the hen was transformed into its oven-ready state. The pinkish yellow skin stretched over the rib cage and the fat curved thighs reminded her of the torsos of half-nude women she could sometimes glimpse on hidden magazines in the station bookshop. Such material was banned, of course, but merchant seamen brought it in from abroad; it was easy to find if you knew where to look.

The old woman finished her plucking with a last determined tug at a broken feather stub on a wing. 'Clean it out for you?' she offered. Annie assented gratefully. That was a task she did not care to do herself. Mrs Ginsberg carried the bird to a wooden block and eviscerated it with firm neat strokes. The slithery discards, still steaming, were dropped into an overflowing bucket at her feet. A smell of hot chicken faeces filled the air. Helen shut her eyes.

There was no point in being squeamish, she chided herself. As long as she ate meat and enjoyed it, the brutality of its preparation was unavoidable. Butchers! Horrible word. The men who ran the concentration camps were called butchers. Their victims were dispatched with similar attention to orderliness and rather more to record-keeping. Yet she knew she would eat the food, suitably cooked and trimmed, without a second thought, and wondered what hardness lay within her that made it possible.

The chicken, gutted and wholesome, was wrapped first in white paper then several layers of newspaper in case it leaked, and deposited in the carrier bag. Annie patted it in triumph and relief. It would make an excellent dinner.

Daniel Majinsky tweaked the worsted cloth across the broad shoulders. 'That shoulder wound made you slightly lop-sided, did you realise?' he commented, and pinched a fingerful of excess fabric by the right armhole. Instantly the overcoat sat better.

'I never noticed, but you're right.' Captain Armitage turned sideways and breathed in his abdomen. He smoothed the material appreciatively. Only one sleeve had been pinned in for the session. The vacant armhole revealed layers of brown bindings and stiffener; on the front, white tacking stitches ran like tram lines down the chest. 'Hand-stitched lapels, Danny, as usual. If I'm going to pay good money for a tailor-made Abercrombie I might as well let everybody know it.'

The tailor was as tall as the sea-captain. He inserted a pin, then deftly marked the neckline with white chalk. 'You wouldn't get a good coat cheaper in Owen Owen's. Not one that would last.'

'True.' His client preened himself in the full-length mirror. 'And it'll have to. This next voyage is the end of the line for me. Could be the last new coat I can afford.'

Daniel straightened up, measuring tape in hand. Although the garment was designed to last a decade or more, the loss of a good customer would be a blow. 'But you're not yet sixty!'

'Yes, but the shipping company is beginning to reduce its British flagged fleet. Cheaper to get crews from Panama or Hong Kong. And even where captains are British I don't fancy the life – sailing around the tropics with a crew you can't talk to isn't an old man's game. They made me a fair offer and I'll take it.'

'But you don't want to leave the sea, do you? It's in your blood. Four buttons or five?'

'Four. That's true, but it also makes sense to get out while the going is good. There's change in the air. Look, Danny, the Red Book lists seventy-four shipping companies registered in Liverpool this year. Within twenty years there'll be hardly a dozen. Men like me with maximum seniority are too expensive these days. Our seamen on union rates are ten times dearer than the Chinks who work harder and do what they're told. The company has no option.'

'Bloody unions.'

'Couldn't disagree with that, but our blokes couldn't live on those wages, union or no. Can't blame 'em: neither could I.'

The two men talked on. Daniel remembered the first time Armitage had climbed the stairs into the first-floor showroom. He was not likely to forget: the Captain had been one of the early patrons of the new business in the days when the tiniest piece of cloth had required reams of clothing coupons. Like many seafarers Armitage picked up his requirements overseas and had carried a mysterious bolt of Harris tweed into the workshop with him.

The master mariner had spent the war years in convoys from the States dodging U-boats. Miraculously he had avoided trouble until the last few months of 1944 when a maverick destroyer, far from its wrecked Bremen home, had fired a few desperate salvos. The bridge of his vessel suffered serious damage and so did its master. But Daniel suspected that had the Captain emerged unscathed when so many brave Liverpool men had been lost in the merchant navy he would have felt guilty at his own good fortune.

Daniel stood back, brushed an imaginary hair from the sleeve and admired his own handiwork. 'Buttons on the cuffs as usual?'

'As usual. You know me, I don't like change.'

It was only the third coat he had made for Armitage, who was also regular in his order of two suits every other year. Change nevertheless revealed itself in the slowly expanding measurements in that small note-book on the workbench. Not that Daniel Majinsky would have been so tactless as to mention it.

Steps could be heard. Daniel helped the Captain off with the precious half-finished coat. The two men turned as Helen hesitated at the door.

'Have you met my daughter? Come here, Helen, and say hello.'

It did not occur to Daniel to name his customer to his daughter. The confidentiality of his clientele was vital, partly for business reasons, for such a list of names and addresses was worth real money, called good-will, if ever he sold the firm; and partly through an innate sense of decency, for he had seen these men in their underclothes at moments of great vulnerability.

The girl approached, murmured 'Good afternoon', shook hands and withdrew quickly to the back workshop. She heard the two men laugh. Probably they referred to her, or young people in general, whose tastes in mass-produced garments were Daniel's bane.

At last solid footsteps retreated down the stairs. The street door clicked. In a moment her father came in, a pack of sandwiches in hand. He indicated the gas ring in the corner. 'Put the kettle on.' He lit a cig-arette and inhaled deeply. 'So: how was the abattoir?'

Helen grimaced.

'I can't stand the place either. Something else that's about to disap-pear. Have a sandwich.'

She accepted and began to eat hungrily: the cold air and an early breakfast had left their gap. 'I'm sorry I wasn't properly dressed, Dad. I didn't know you'd have a customer.' A tailor's daughter should proudly wear his handiwork.

'Oh, you youngsters! I shouldn't complain, though. Look what walked in this morning.'

He pointed at the far corner. A large roll of green velvet rested upright, its edges wrapped in tissue paper. In the soft light through a grimy window its surface shimmered.

'Ever heard of the Remo Four? They're one of the groups Brian Epstein's signed. He told 'em to smarten themselves up, so one of them went down the market and bought that. It's lovely stuff, fine silk velour, and they want four suits out of it.'

Their eyes met and both giggled. 'They'll look like a bunch of frogs.'

Helen helped herself to another sandwich then started to make the tea.

'Won't they just. Exotic, but that's the effect they want. One of them's portly so I'll put a couple of hidden elastic panels in his trousers. Sewing it is a bugger. Every needle mark shows in weave that fine – no room for mistakes. I'll probably make a *toile* first to get it right. That's an old dress-making technique – haven't done it in years.'

As she poured tea from the chipped teapot and stirred in milk and sugar Helen saw that the musicians' need of his highest talents delighted her father. He continued, 'They'd have done better with curtain mater-ial – damask or whatever, which would have taken some wear. Those outfits won't last five minutes, but they're for a TV programme. I told 'em it'd cost. They just hooted and said Brian'd pay.'

'Customer is always right.'

'Absolutely.' Daniel reached for the notebook and scribbled a reminder to himself. He would ring NEMS before he laid a finger on the fabric.

Helen bit into a small apple. The discussion at school came back to her. Brenda's careless remark that it must be 'horrid' to be Jewish, rein-forced by her mother's demand for conformity to rules – rules that produced that disgusting slaughterhouse – plus an increasing necessity to establish herself and her family in some sort of context, led her on. 'Did you always want to be a tailor, Dad?'

'God, no. I dreamed of being a draughtsman. At Cammell Laird's. But that apprenticeship cost money – you had to buy your own tools if you didn't have your father's – and tailoring didn't. So here I am. But I'm not a *tailor*, child. The tailor is Mr Mannheim upstairs. A tailor sews. I'm a tailor's cutter – much more skilled. And more important: if the tailor makes a wrong stitch he can unpick it. If the cutter makes a mistake he ruins a whole bolt of cloth.'

He accepted the mug of tea. On its side was a faded coat of arms flanked by the two Liver birds and the legend '1207–1957' underneath, a relic of a civic celebration. 'In the factories it's done by machine now. The jeans your pals wear: they're cut fifty at a time by automatic knives, each pair identical. Don't need an apprenticeship to learn that.' He paused moodily. 'But there'll always be customers who like a jacket that fits, a pair of trousers which sit well, and who'll pay the extra. I hope.'

With a hint of weariness he rose and went out on to the landing. Helen could hear him use the tiny smelly toilet and wash his hands. Quickly she gathered up the remains of their lunch. The greaseproof paper was folded and could be used again.

She settled herself in a corner. 'Can I watch?'

'Sure.' Daniel lit another cigarette and balanced it carefully next to the previous stub which had gone out. On principle he would not relight a cold butt; he declared that they tasted awful and that he was not yet reduced to such penury. The hot raw smoke caught his chest and he coughed. In the morning he would rise and torture the family with much clearing of mucus. Since that happened in most homes it excited no concern.

He whistled softly under his breath as he switched on the worklight, a large oblong contraption below head height. At once the bench was bathed in a golden glow, like a billiard table, while Daniel's face remained in shadow.

The workbench was covered in linoleum and was some twenty feet long, roughly the length of a piece of fine wool fabric, sufficient to make a man's suit, trousers, jacket, waistcoat. Daniel selected a roll of suiting to which was pinned a scrap of paper with his back-slanted scrawl. With a flourish he spread it out and matched the edges double, for each piece had to be cut with its mirror image, left to right, trouser to trouser, cuff to cuff. He ran his hand lovingly over the cloth, relishing its softness and fine weave. A flaw was checked and marked with chalk, to be avoided during the process of cutting out.

'Pure wool, this, Helen. Here, let me show you.'

He pulled a single thread from the cut end, held it up and put the flame from his lighter to it. The thread twisted and sparkled but did not catch fire.

'Pure wool smoulders. Cotton will burn. Terylene, now, and artificial fibres are another matter.' He dropped the burned thread on the floor and stubbed it out with his toe, then rummaged under the bench and pulled out a scrap of blue. Again he lifted a thread high between finger and thumb and put the flame to it; this time it melted and he dropped it quickly.

He kicked the rubbish back under the bench. 'These mixtures are the devil. I can get a fair payment for trimmings from wool – they're shredded and used for cheaper cloth. But the offcuts from Terylene blends are practically worthless.'

At the end of the room hung a horizontal pole laden with stiff pieces of cardboard turned yellow with age. The templates were as essential to the business as were his shears: had the premises been destroyed Daniel would have tried to replace these before anything else. He checked the details of the order, looked up the name in his notebook, chose several boards and began to arrange them on the cloth, ensuring that stripes matched exactly. The task took several minutes. When satisfied he began with swift sure strokes to draw a line around each in pink tailor's chalk.

'You draw with your left hand, but you use the shears with your right,' she commented. She had not considered it before. 'Are you left-handed, or ambidextrous?'

Her father rubbed his left shoulder. 'Wish I were. No, I was taught to cut with my right hand. When I was younger than you.' He did not elaborate.

Helen watched quietly. Her father was a craftsman, the finest level of achievement a working man could reach. Other men might be better paid, but they could not function with such grace and *pride*. His knowledge was such that men, and the handful of women customers he worked for, felt comfortable and looked smart in what he created. To watch him was a wondrous thing. Whatever she might attempt in the unclear future would never have this flowing elegance, this artless match of hand and eye. Daniel, a well-read man, had once remarked that the poet William Blake had been a craftsman and had never let his trade be derided. There was poetry here, too, and beauty, and manliness.

Yet he enjoyed discussing politics with her. That, too, was a tradition: the working man who took a close and learned interest in the world beyond his workshop. He might have made a politician himself, had the means been available. Helen blinked. Once more, she realised, her parents' lives had been stymied years ago by their exclusion from mainstream society – by lack of money. Yet the options facing Helen were much wider. The problem might be to get her parents – Daniel and Annie both – to see that what had stopped them would no longer stop their daughter. As long as their imaginations had not been destroyed as well.

Daniel straightened. 'This one's a bit tricky, Helen. He's a disabled man, not a standard fit. I'm going to have to concentrate. Sorry.'

A dismissal, again. It was as if a master surgeon had barred students or Michelangelo had told a novice to leave him in peace. She could not help, only get in the way. The girl rose without demur, picked up her coat, and went out into the cold square, where shoppers laden with carrier-bags silently trudged past her.

Later, Helen returned to the workshop for the promised lift home. She was tired, more so than had the day been spent in class. Visits were paid to the out-workers, but mostly she stayed put in the car, declining invitations to cups of tea. Her father took a long time in some houses.

At last she snuggled down in the front passenger seat of the elderly Vauxhall as it pulled away from the kerb, turned left into congested Wavertree Road and headed for home. On the back seat was a tumbled heap of finished out-work: it comforted her, this reminder that the system functioned and brought honest cash into several households, and that the hand-made buttonholes with their small neat stitches, the exquisitely turned collars without a ruck or wrinkle, her father's trademarks, would continue.

Ahead a green Crosville bus stopped to disgorge buttoned-up figures who scurried away with children. Street lights were coming on; it was nearly dark.

'Mrs Quilter looked upset when she came out on to the step,' Helen remarked, to start a conversation. 'She usually asks me about school and whatnot and tells me about her Sandra, but not tonight.'

'Her daughter's the same age as you.' Daniel had been regaled indoors with the story. 'Bit of a minx, from what I hear. Left school last summer, then threw up her job at Littlewood's Pools. Now she's running around in town at all hours. Mrs Quilter's worried sick.'

The quiet cosiness of the old car, the background chunter of its engine, her father's concentration on overtaking the bus, made intimacy easier. During this brief journey undertaken about once a month Helen could broach subjects with her father which might have been awkward at the dining room table.

'You glad I didn't leave school like Sandra Quilter, Dad?'

Daniel looked in his mirror and adjusted his speed. His legs were aching; a calf muscle cramped. The quack called it atherosclerosis or some such and said he should cut down his smoking.

Helen was waiting.

'Well: if it benefits you or your brother, we'll find the necessary to keep you, if that's what you mean.'

The girl tried again. 'I have to start deciding what to do next. Miss Plumb wants me to try for university.'

Daniel grunted and changed gear so clumsily that the car protested. He worked the pedals with a muttered oath.

'Sorry. Your mother and I are in two minds about your plans. You'll need to persuade me. Why don't you go to the College of Commerce and do shorthand and typing? You could earn a fair wage as a secretary. Or teacher training.'

'I'm not sure I'm cut out to be a teacher, Dad. And I know I can do better than a shorthand typist.'

'Now, don't you go being snobby about typists. Mrs Quilter'd be delighted if her Sandra had a well-paid office job at the Royal Liver Insurance instead of – you know.'

'I'm not being snobby, Dad. It isn't snobbish to want to do the best you can, is it?'

She is as stubborn as I am, Daniel realised. Without reply he steered the car around the Clock Tower roundabout and turned into suburban Childwall Road. Not far now.

'In some circumstances, it is,' he answered quietly. 'We're born into a certain strata of society. We can dream, of course, of bettering ourselves. But often it's wiser to stay close to what you know. Wiser and safer.'

'Stratum,' she corrected without thinking.

'What?'

'Stratum. One stratum of society, two strata. It's Latin.'

'Oh, it is, is it? You see what I mean. I never did Latin. Now you correct the way I talk. That's snobbishness. And I don't want a daughter of mine looking down on her parents.' He was annoyed.

She took a deep breath. 'Maybe an education would make me

appreciate you more, not less. Oh, Dad, don't hold me back. I asked Mum this morning whether if she'd had the chance of university she wouldn't have wanted to seize it, but I don't think she had a clue what I was talking about. She said we should be content with what we've got.'

'It's not a bad recipe for life, you know.'

Helen suddenly felt self-conscious. 'It can become a recipe for – for ossification. And it's hopeless if the world about us is changing. We have to adapt.'

'Not if it means losing your grasp of what truly matters in life. A home, family. Roots. That's especially important for you as a woman, and for us as Jews.'

She was silent for a moment. Then she stirred herself once more. 'But you would sign the papers, wouldn't you? For the entrance exams?'

How could he refuse her? He stole a quick glance at her then as quickly regretted it for he saw that she caught all the mixed emotions of affection, anxiety and distaste in his face. He was not a man to express his feelings, nor to analyse them, nor face them. But Helen could. She'd drive him hard as Annie did not, as Barry never would. She was a chip off the old block. Daniel shivered.

They stopped before the house. 'Open the garage doors, there's a good girl.'

Helen did not budge. 'Will you sign? Please, Dad.'

Both hands on the wheel, Daniel stared sightlessly ahead. The residential street was quiet in the dusk. He bowed his head and listened as the engine idled.

'We'll see,' was all he could offer, but she grinned and squeezed his arm.

'Thanks.' The implication was that a deal had been done. As the girl opened the wooden doors and stood helpfully by, Daniel had the sense of being outpaced.

In the house the lights were on. A fire had been lit in the grate and carefully banked. Once the evening drew on and *shabbos* had commenced the humping of coals was not allowed. Strictly speaking, to carry anything was forbidden, especially if it smacked of work or labour. In the morning, should the family want a fire, they would have to ask their young neighbours John or Marie from next door to clear the grate, lay and light it: a dirty task nobody undertook willingly, a servant's job. That required knocking while the young couple were still abed and enduring their vaguely hostile mutter. It was impossible to explain to such people why to break the sabbath was a sin. Only on a very cold day could Annie bring herself to put the request.

Helen took off her coat and hung it up with her father's. The sudden rush of warmth after the chill air made her cheeks tingle. From the kitchen came a tantalising smell of roast chicken. As she entered the living room she bit her lip.

On the table was outspread a white linen tablecloth which had belonged to Annie's mother. In the exact centre, on a mat to save the wax, stood two tall brass candlesticks, a wedding present, which Annie had polished as usual that afternoon. She was in the act of fixing securely the plain white candles while Barry watched idly from the sofa. Next to the candlesticks was a small silver tray with a bottle of 'Palwin' Israeli wine and four crystal glasses. A bowl of hyacinths on the window ledge gave off a heady perfume. The light of the fire flickered lovingly over brass and silver and cast a glow on a nearby dish of oranges and bananas, the weekend treat.

Daniel reached in the top drawer of the sideboard and took out two *yarmulkahs*, one black for himself, one silver, white and blue, embroidered, for his son. Lazily Barry came to his father's side and slouched, lop-sided. 'Go on, Mother.'

Annie picked up a patterned headscarf and covered her head, tying it peasant style at the nape of her neck. Women too had to cover their heads. She, who had lived in a city since her birth, could not explain why she tied it this way; only that her mother had when she was a little girl, and her aunts, and every woman of her acquaintance. Helen knew she ought to do the same but retreated behind her father and deflected her mother's glance.

Inside Helen something sighed. It was as if the room had been transformed into a place of worship, the ordinary table into an altar. Jews did not have churches or altars or incense. Nor priestesses. Yet the impression of a holy place, presided over by her mother, inviolable, matronly, was very powerful.

'Ready?'

Husband and children gathered around.

Annie took a deep breath. *Erev shabbos*, the eve of the sabbath, was so precious. The sanctification of the candles, the Friday night meal when the whole family was present without fail was the high spot of each week, but more, of her very life. No guests tonight; ancient law said that any stranger of whom they were aware must be invited and made welcome. Jewish strangers only, of course, which meant they were probably not entirely unknown but distant relatives or contacts. To do so was a *mitzvah*, and thus a step forward on the path to heaven. It was a splendid custom. No Jew was ever without shelter or friends. A Jew always had family, somewhere.

And here, for a few moments, the woman stood supreme. This was her realm – hers and nobody else's. Though men governed in all the great decisions, although in an orthodox synagogue men took charge and relegated females and children to the gallery upstairs, in a Jewish home the *mother* was the head. Especially on Friday night. Deference and respect were expected and freely given. For in the end the mother, not the father, held the key. Who was a Jew – how was that precious

Jewish identity secured? Through the mother, not the father. As the rabbis pointed out, you could tell absolutely who a child's mother was. You could not be certain of its paternity.

Daniel shifted impatiently. Annie picked up the match box, struck a light and put the flame to the candle wicks. It seemed to presage good luck that they caught immediately. The bright flames rose, swelled and settled.

She reached out her hands and passed them in a circular motion over the candles, three times, then covered her eyes. She paused as was traditional for a few seconds of private prayer. Then together the family spoke the blessing of the lights.

'*Boruch atoh, Adenoi elohanu . . .*'

Blessed art thou, oh Lord our God, King of the Universe . . .

Chapter Three

Sunday

Nellie McCauley opened one eye and peered out resentfully at the alarm clock. She reached an arm from under the covers to bang its top button and stop the noise, then groaned. It would be easy as pie to drift back to sleep, but she needed the job. Who didn't?

Five o'clock in the morning! What kind of time was this to be woken up? And on a Sunday too. Not that there was anybody to keep her, no one to whisper insistence that she stay buried in the warm nest of blankets and pillows. With a grunt of resolution she swung her feet over the edge of the bed and felt for her slippers. The room was dark and freezing cold; her teeth chattered as she pulled on a robe and padded to the bathroom.

Sunday: the busiest day at Feinstein's Famous Delicatessen. Between opening time at seven and lock-up soon after two in the afternoon takings would nearly equal those of the rest of the week put together. Mad busy, they'd be. And were she to be late Mr Feinstein would yell at her, and customers would be banging on the door and cursing her as a lazy *shikse*.

Damn Jews. Why couldn't they treat Sunday as a day of rest like everybody else? They took Saturday off instead, they claimed. Nellie sniffed: many were the familiar faces she had seen in town laden with packages on a Saturday morning when they were supposed to be at prayer in their synagogue. If she were recognised she would be greeted with a curt nod; the guilty party would scurry away faster, usually in the direction of a car park. Not supposed to use their cars on the holy sabbath, either. She knew the laws. She'd worked for them long enough.

It had to be admitted that many of the locals patronised the shop. The big convent down the road was a prime source of business as people stopped on their way to or from Mass to collect fresh bread, smoked salmon, bagels, soft cheese or roll-mop herring. It was amazing how readily these savage tastes had been assimilated by wealthy Catholics who drove such a distance to hear the Sisters' fine choir. The deputy Chief Constable and his lady, last year's Lord Mayor, the city's Medical Officer of Health: Nellie knew them all, and their preferences in dill pickles or kosher garlic sausage. Their cars blocked the drives of neighbouring property and regularly caused complaints. Nothing could be done: word had gone round at the city's most exclusive Masonic lodge that Feinstein's was the place to go.

Nellie checked the clock and began to speed up. On went lipstick, bright red, her trademark. Then dangly earrings, like a pub landlady's. Not much point in gay clothes when a white overall covered everything, so a woolly sweater and trousers would suffice and gumboots with men's socks down below – it was cold out in the yard. A quick tug of a hairbrush through jaded yellow hair: the dark roots were showing. Back to the peroxide bottle tomorrow night. If she were paid what she was truly worth she could've afforded to have it done properly at a salon in Bold Street.

The boss wasn't mean by nature – far from it. But did he realise how much he depended on her? If the shop were clean – and as a food shop it had to be, spotless – it was because she harried the dull sloth of a cleaning woman, chased her to reach into every corner, to shift boxes and wipe lino and walls behind, to rub counter glass with vinegar and old newspaper until it sparkled. The big fridge in the back room she defrosted herself every Monday morning – a grotty job but it must be done. And if the shop's reputation for high-quality fresh specialities were renowned that was to her credit too – she it was who dealt with the reps, insisted on the best, tried the samples, checked the deliveries, threw the rubbish back at them, and – if Mr Feinstein but knew it – haggled hard to get better prices than rivals in Manchester and Leeds. Yet he still saw her as a common shop assistant, only a cut above the dim-witted cleaner and the student who came in to help. It set her teeth on edge.

The customers, though. They knew her value. They would ask for her to serve them, would stand patiently until she was free then ask for their 'usual', confident that Nellie had everybody's habitual order secure in her head. She had, too: she could reel off the names and purchases of a hundred regulars and price their totals almost to the last penny. And she retained in the depths of her sharp memory who was to be trusted to pop in with a pound note later in the week and who wasn't. Feinstein, the big soft dope, would have given everyone credit, then wondered why the shop was packed but making no money.

Feinstein wasn't a bad boss. In his bumbling way he was kind and often put upon. He would accept her suggestions and allow her to do with the shop much as she saw fit. When he disagreed with her it was with a hesitant and apologetic manner. Her exasperation towards him was at its worst in the ghastly grey light of dawn but would dissipate later as they worked side by side. In truth she felt a little sorry for him, and treated his slapdash errors with affectionate respect. He was easier to cope with than most bosses she might have had. In all probability, that was why she stayed.

So much to do. The bread man would arrive at six with his first fragrant loaves and buns. It was a moment she adored. She would check and count, every time: the baker was an honest man but his delivery boys could be light-fingered. Sometimes she would pick out a damaged *cuchon* or slightly burned loaf, deduct it from the total and make the man sign for the number accepted – but the offending article tasted just as good for elevenses with salty Welsh butter, if she could grab a few minutes. Some customers, Sunday papers under their arms, would time their arrival to coincide with the second bread delivery about ten. Then would appear Danish pastries stuffed with almond paste and stewed apple or half an apricot, and cinnamon rolls and marbled cakes with their swirl of coffee and cream sponge, and best of all warm *chalahs*, the sweet milk loaves perfect for Sunday afternoon visitors, shaped like a plait of burnished brown hair, queenly and womanly; so much more tempting, in her view, than the masculine hardness of the pale bagels which had to be dunked in a cup of tea to make them chewable.

Five-forty. Not too bad. Time to pull the moped out of the shed and kick it into life – no buses at this hour. Still dark out, and would be for hours yet. But a bird could be heard somewhere down the park, singing sweetly if slightly desperately, totally alone. Bit like her own position in life: doing her best according to her lights, even if nobody took a scrap of notice.

Helen rose at seven. She could earn more if she arrived as the shop opened, but in truth her presence was not needed until the first rush. And Nellie was so irritable early on that it was wiser to keep out of her way. By eight-thirty the manageress, as Helen thought of her, was metamorphosing into a more human creature and could be expected to greet her cheerily, and slip her a knob of Cheddar for her breakfast.

She would see Mr Feinstein twice that day, for he would come to her house at night to play bridge with her father and other friends. Not that she would be around, of course: Sunday evenings were reserved for Harold House, the youth club.

The shop was close enough for her to walk to, though had it been wet she would have begged a lift from her father. As she arrived it seemed the cold bright weather had drawn more custom than usual, until she remembered that today was a Catholic feast of some kind and the convent would have laid on extra masses. From a hundred yards away she could hear the chatter inside.

Feinstein's Famous Deli stood in the middle of a row of suburban

shops, its double frontage proud and disordered all at once. To one side
was a newsagents run by a recently arrived Pakistani, to the other a
barber's: all three were busy in these few hours. Painted in white on Mr
Feinstein's window were that week's special offers – Canary Island
bananas at 10d a pound, Norwegian salted fish at two shillings a quarter. Outside rickety trestles covered in green plastic carried boxes of fruit
and vegetables, onions in three sizes and colours, potatoes and carrots
and pale cabbage for sauerkraut. Labels on oranges and tangerines
proudly proclaimed their Israeli origin. Mr Feinstein would not buy
from South Africa. His cousin in Jo'burg had recently seen a sign on a
golf clubhouse door: 'No coloureds, dogs or Jews.'

Helen pushed her way inside and hurried into the tiny back room
where she hung up her coat and collected her overall. With a twinge of
disgust she noticed it had not been washed since the previous week,
though Mr Feinstein had promised. No sooner was she installed behind
the counter than the calls started.

'Oi! Young lady! I've been waiting ten minutes. You gonna serve me
or not?'

He was a fat elderly man, red in the face, a large string bag in his outstretched hand. Nellie was absorbed with another customer with a long
hand-written list. A brassy woman next to the shouting man poked him
indignantly and announced that she was first. Some half-hearted pushing ensued. Helen ignored the fat man who was often at the centre of a
fuss, as if it were a necessary adjunct to his shopping. Instead she
addressed the woman: Sylvia Bloom, another regular, in a red coat, as
stout and florid as a jar of jam. The racket in the shop was deafening as
bodies shoved and shouted.

'What can I get you, Mrs Bloom?'

'A carton of smetana, a dozen bagels, and a quarter of smoked
salmon.'

'Bagels over there on the rack – help yourself. Big carton or small?'
The soured cream was a favourite over fruit, or eaten greedily by itself,
sweetened with brown sugar.

'My doctor says I shouldn't – make it a small one. Full up, mind. And
take the salmon from the centre, not the end – I don't want any skin or
brown bits.'

Mr Feinstein loomed close, stropping the thin blade of the salmon
knife. 'I'll do this, Helen. Morning, Sylvia. How much did you say you
wanted – half a pound?'

Sylvia, hands full of bagels, dimpled immediately. 'Morry, you're a
card. You know I live by myself. For what would I be wanting half a
pound of salmon?'

Feinstein grinned, half roguish, half shy. In the shop as proprietor he
felt confident with women, could tease them and bask briefly in their
admiration. It was a totally different matter away from his beloved

almond biscuits and Rakusen's Matzos. With any female he met outside he would become tongue-tied, would not know what to say, would shuffle his feet and stare at the ground, then flee back to the sanctuary of his solitary bed and sigh with relief at his deliverance.

There had been another time, of course. There had been Rosetta, as timid as himself; he had been a gawky youth, pushed into early marriage by his parents who wanted the joy, they said, of grandchildren, to see their seed sown. Rosetta and he had obliged though the whole exercise had been deeply embarrassing to both. The result was Jerry, who was supposed to come and help when the shop was busy but who frequently had better things to do. The degree to which the pregnancy and birth had weakened Rosetta's already frail constitution had been apparent to nobody; when she had fainted one day after taking the boy to school it had been a shock for which neither was prepared. Heart disease, the doctor said. Must have had rheumatic fever as a child, though her mother stoutly denied it: for a girl with such a condition, had it been known, would not have been marriageable.

And so one cold winter day his wife had collapsed and been rushed to hospital, and with a husky whisper had slipped away from him a few days later.

Her death had come when the boy was about eight. The child's grandparents had rallied round and the boy had been dragged up, one way or another, in the homes of various relatives nearby. In his teens Jerry had elected to live permanently with his father, more for the freedom that promised than through any excess of affection. Nevertheless Mr Feinstein was grateful. The boy's presence gave him an excuse to love something, and the occasional glimpses in his son's face of Rosetta, her wistful smile, her large dark eyes, bound him to his wilful offspring as nothing else could.

That Jerry lived at home in the flat over the shop gave his father another useful shield, this time against the army of unattached women who wanted to improve on his widower state. Sylvia was one, a divorcée, and not at all to his taste. She claimed to be his age – fortyish – but had a daughter much older than Jerry, so that seemed unlikely. She simpered, she wriggled, she batted her eyelashes, but Mr Feinstein kept his eyes on the razor-sharp knife as it slid beneath his fingers over the pink oiliness of the salmon. He wished she would stop. Yet his shopkeeper mentality would keep pushing itself to the fore. Sylvia was a wealthy woman and would not miss a few shillings. If by a little harmless flirtation he could persuade her to spend more, particularly on the most expensive perishable items in the shop, then he would not hesitate. And it was part of her trade as a matchmaker, to get him into the mood. It was a game played out every occasion they met. In truth both enjoyed it, along with the flicker of hope it brought.

He weighed out six ounces until she began to protest. With a heavy sigh of regret he wrapped the delicacy carefully in greaseproof paper and wrote the price on a corner. He should count the bagels she had dropped into her bag, but she was a good customer. If she intended to eat the lot herself, nevertheless, it was no wonder she was so tubby. His Rosetta had been tiny. He should have guessed she was not robust, but her slimness had established his predilections from there on.

'How's Jerry – how's your boy?' Sylvia had not finished yet, though the protests behind her rose to an indignant crescendo.

'Fine – still in bed, I think.' Feinstein jerked his head in the direction of upstairs.

'So idle, the younger generation,' Sylvia commiserated loudly, ignoring Helen who counted her change into a beringed hand. 'He should have a mother, poor boy –' But her words were lost as the fat man succeeded in elbowing his way to the counter.

Helen worked hard and steadily until about eleven when there was a lull. As she stood brushing hair from her eyes the door opened. Her face broke into a smile: her favourite 'uncle', Simon Rotblatt, had entered the shop.

He was not a relative but her father's oldest friend. The squat, solidly built figure in the camel-hair overcoat came towards her, a rolled-up newspaper in one hand, car keys in the other. Despite living barely a quarter of a mile away he would usually drive, though he handled the big car with difficulty and could not park straight. He did it, as everyone knew, to show off: but so good-natured and beguiling a character was he that none but the most spiteful would criticise.

'And how's my gorgeous girl this morning?' He came to the corner of the counter and gave her a hug, then held her back to examine her. 'So tall. And beautiful, like your mother.'

Only Simon Rotblatt had ever called Annie 'beautiful' and it had more than once made Helen ponder; she took it that there was no adverse intention in the remark, only an oblique compliment to herself.

'I'm fine, Uncle Simon. You look well. What would you like?'

Simon considered. 'You got a new delivery of schmaltz herring? Yes? I'll have two small ones, there's a good girl.'

He turned to a neighbour and began to swap comments on the previous day's football game. Although nobody in the shop would admit it had a rabbi challenged them, several had witnessed Everton's defeat of Manchester City at Goodison Park and revelled in the fact.

Helen retreated into the chilly yard. Fetching herring from the barrel was the one task she loathed, for the fish were pickled deep in brine with oil which in this cold weather became a horrible caustic mush. Yet intelligent people like Simon Rotblatt adored the result. She pulled on rubber gloves turned brown and brittle by contact with the liquid and manfully wielded the wooden tongues, but still it was an effort to entrap the slippery silver bodies and remove them into the plastic bowl at her side.

'Need a hand, Helen?'

She ignored him. Jerry had not arrived to assist her; he must have seen her struggles through their kitchen window. In an ideal world it would be he balancing a dead fish between barrel and bucket and not herself. Instead he stood in the way with an amused smirk on his pimply face, hands on his hips.

The youth had other ideas, as his flushed cheeks indicated. Casually he sloped closer as Helen was forced to bend over the barrel for the second herring. Standing behind her, he moved to put his hands around her waist. She glanced over her shoulder in annoyance and with her free elbow gave him a dig in the ribs but he was only momentarily dislodged. He was dressed warmly in jeans and sweater but had moccasins on bare feet. Without meaning to she slopped a little brine on his foot.

'Damn!' Jerry rubbed ineffectually at the stain, then yelped as the salt found microscopic cuts in the skin of his fingers.

Helen had completed her task and was heading back inside.

'Sorry, Jerry. If you really want to help, come and put an apron on and cut up some cheese.'

'You've got to be bloody joking,' the youth muttered, sucking angrily at a cut in his palm. He slouched in after her but slipped back upstairs. He had no intention of becoming a grocer: nor did he like being humiliated by a girl, even if nobody had witnessed it.

In the tiny bathroom Jerry ran his hand under the cold tap and winced with pain. He'd bide his time. What a stuck-up minx that Helen Majinsky was. Every Sunday he tried, and each time she slipped from his clutches. Her resistance didn't make her more sexually attractive but did increase his determination to have it off with her, sooner or later. Then he could boast about it, and that alone would pay her back. If the opportunity came to show Miss H a thing or two, he'd grab it. And hang the consequences.

Sunday. January. If I don't talk to somebody I'll go mad.

That's no way to start. Do it properly. My name is Colette O'Brien, I am sixteen years old and this is my diary. Not a proper diary with dates and space for addresses and phone numbers – just a spare exercise book with a blue cover nicked from school. I shall write in it when the thoughts in my head start to scream at me. I'll pretend the pages are a special friend, somebody in whom I can confide but who'll never tell my secrets.

Of course it'd be better if I wrote nothing down at all but there are limits to human endurance. I'll hide the book carefully at the back of the cupboard. Nobody'd find it. It isn't meant to be found.

But I promise myself I'll be honest in this book. Daft, you
could say, but it's the only place I could be honest. I won't
describe exactly what happens – even I would find that
difficult – but I will set out how I feel about it. It might help me
come to terms. Help me work out if there's any solution.

So all I'll say for now is that it started when I was about
twelve, after my mother left. She had been pretty when my
brothers and I were younger. I'm supposed to look like her a bit.
They say I get my brains from her too. Certainly not from him.
She got fed up with his drinking, and being skint and kidding
the National Assistance. He's not bad when he's sober – calmer,
more rational. But he needs the drink to give him courage. Then
he's a big man.

One day there was a big row and she put on her coat and left.
She didn't kiss us goodbye. And that was it; we've not seen her
since. She might be dead for all we know. She doesn't write, but
then we're not a writing family. I'm the first O'Brien who likes
putting pen to paper. Then I'm in a different world.

A better world than this one.

Throughout Liverpool the day of rest slid by with the afternoon spent
reading the newspapers and sleeping off the week. The weather was predicted to worsen. By four it was dark and snow flurries drove people
home. Teatime – a high tea of tinned Canadian salmon with a garnish
of lettuce leaves, a sliced tomato and half a boiled egg was eaten
throughout the city, followed by jelly and fruit cocktail if there were visitors, or a sliced banana with custard otherwise. None but the most
intrepid would venture out after seven o'clock.

Or the young and foolish, who recognise no risk. Jerry parked his
father's Ford under a street light, climbed out, forgot to lock it, walked
half a block across brown slush, remembered, and with an oath
returned to ensure its security. His father may be an easy touch but the
use of the car was a privilege not to be abused.

The streets around the neglected square were gloomy and deserted.
Dirty snow still lay underfoot, uncleared and neglected. Nobody much
lived in the neighbourhood, though once these great Georgian houses
with their porticoes and pillars had rung to the sound of balls and
splendid dinners. Some had been bomb damaged; others were shored up
and awaiting demolition. Jerry skirted the wooden stanchions which
kept one frontage upright and kicked litter out of the way. A cat yowled
in the distance.

The expanding university had purchased the land and as many leases
as it could lay hands on. All it required was the wherewithal to rebuild.
A veterinary laboratory and graduate school were planned for the site,
it was rumoured. That left Harold House on the corner as an oasis of

former grandeur, and perfect to be wrecked in its turn, albeit more slowly, by the coterie of Jewish teenagers whose parents had clubbed together to buy it. Lost in the mists of time was the 'Harold' whose name was thus commemorated.

The main door at the top of the imposing steps was shut fast; nobody knew when it had been opened. Probably for the funeral of the last occupant, Jerry supposed. The steps were covered in rain-pitted snow disfigured by the footprints of a couple of dogs. Nobody had bothered to sweep or salt the pavement. He went around the side and clattered down a metal staircase to the former tradesman's entrance and pushed open the door.

To his irritation Helen was already there, at her post. He had to hand it to her: she was reliable. Since she was smart at figures she had been appointed as assistant honorary treasurer – the real 'hon treas' was somebody's father who did not like coming out on a cold Sunday night. Her job was to check membership cards and collect the evening's half-crown entrance fee from each arrival. At the night's end she totted up the whole takings, plus receipts for crisps and soft drinks, signed for the total, and sent the small sums off to the nearest night safe with one or two of the biggest lads. No one minded that she was the brains of the operation, but carrying money was a man's job.

For two years Jerry Feinstein had been secretary of the club. That was because nobody else was willing to volunteer, and Jerry liked to feel important. The duties were unclear but hardly onerous. They included, when he felt like it, imposing his choice of music. He headed for the main room where the record player was as yet silent, rifled through a pile of singles, chose six and put them on the automatic turntable. In a moment the pure country sound of Connie Francis warbled through the building.

A hand touched his sleeve. 'Hi, Jerry. Howya doin'?'

The mock Atlantic accent heralded his girlfriend, Roseanne Nixon. Sweet sixteen. She was short and pretty, her nose turned up, a smaller version of her formidable mother Rita. Her brown hair was sleek and firmly controlled by lacquer. Had Jerry touched it, it would have felt like spun sugar, hard and brittle.

'It'll be quiet tonight, I reckon,' he offered by way of reply.

'Yeah, we could do with some life here, y'know?' she grumbled as she traced the title on a record cover with a pink varnished fingernail. The record ended, clicked; the next one fell neatly on top and began to play Eddie Cochran, King of rock'n'roll with 'C'mon Ev'rybody'. The beat rhythm set his pulse a-tingle.

'Wanna dance?' he asked, and without answer took her hand and whirled her into the middle of the floor. Another two couples followed their lead. Jerry and Roseanne were the best jivers and enjoyed showing off their skills. That didn't stop him talking at the same time.

'The problem is,' he pointed out between twirls, 'we don't have a drinks licence. Not likely to get one either as there's no adult here, mostly. And that's how we like it. So anybody who wants booze has to go elsewhere.'

'We've debated that in committee a dozen times,' puffed Roseanne. She was neither as lean nor as fit as her partner. 'Alcohol'd bring in the wrong sort. Rough area, this. We're lucky we've had no trouble.'

Jerry concentrated for a moment as he grasped both her hands and conducted a complicated movement which required both dancers with split-second timing to pass under the arch of their arms.

'And we only want Jewish kids, remember that.' As she spoke Jerry recalled his promise to himself that he would go out with her officially for only six months. Otherwise Mrs Nixon would have him a marked man, and would be planning the ceremony.

'My Dad had some American customers the other day,' he answered. The tune ended and was replaced by Chubby Checker singing 'The Twist'. Jerry had picked it though he regarded the silly dance as suitable only for simpletons: but the younger members loved it. The floor filled as he moved a disappointed Roseanne over to the bar and opened a Coke for her.

'So? Where were they from?'

'Dunno exactly. New York, I think. From that air force base on the East Lancs Road. But they were chuffed to find what they called a real deli in Liverpool. Dad hopes they'll come again.'

'Were they young? Did you see them?'

Jerry noted sourly that Roseanne's eyes were shining at the faint possibility of James Dean lookalikes in his father's shop. He affected indifference.

'Haven't the foggiest. American national servicemen are usually a bit older than us, though not much.' He had reached the limit of his knowledge. He recognised the first chords of his favourite, 'Peggy Sue', and held out his hand. 'C'mon – we're wasting good music. Tell you what. If they come in again we'll invite them here. If they're Jewish, that is. That'll make the place jump.'

The Majinskys' bell rang, once, then again. Outside could be heard stamped feet then a muffled shout: 'Danny! Hurry up. It's effing freezing.'

Annie untied her pinafore, hastened to the door and opened it wide. Two figures stood on the doorstep, shuffling their feet and breathing gusts of white breath into the night air. A vast silver car, parked askew, blocked the drive; beyond it another vehicle drew up, headlights ablaze. Annie peered into the gloom.

'Hello, Simon, Mr Mannheim. Come in, come in.'

Old Mr Mannheim entered first, shown respect by the others, a bowed, slight man with a gaunt face. He worked upstairs from Daniel and was, strictly speaking, his tenant. He smiled and shook Annie's hand as he spoke: 'Good evening.' *Gut efening*.

'Annie, my dear.' Simon Rotblatt was the same age as her husband. As genial as ever, it was a puzzle that he had never married, though his courtesy with women was legendary. He placed big hands firmly on her shoulders, looked her full in the face and kissed her on the cheek. 'You look adorable as usual.'

Embarrassed but flattered she moved deftly away and helped Mr Mannheim with his coat. Daniel came into the hallway and ushered his guests inside the living room. The dining table flaps had been folded down and it had then been pushed aside. On it cups and saucers waited, and a bottle of whisky, glasses and a plastic ice bucket on a tray. Pride of place was reserved for the square baize-covered card table. In its centre stood the big cut-glass ashtray and two packs of new cards with a sharpened pencil and bridge notepad at each place. With so many occupants the modest room soon became overcrowded and stuffy.

The last to arrive, in a flurry as ever, was Maurice Feinstein. He too kissed his hostess but with a noisy smack, a brotherly greeting which made Annie dimple. 'Go on in, they're waiting.'

It would not have occurred to the players to ask the lady of the house to join them. Women did play bridge just as they played golf, but Annie was reckoned not one of those fearsome viragos with nothing better to do than muscle in on men's pleasures. Instead she would sit in the adjoining room in front of the television and would regard herself as clever if she guessed most of the occupations on 'What's my Line?'. At about nine-thirty she would intervene with tea and home-made madeira cake. Soon after she would go to bed; the boys would tidy up, after a fashion, and kindly leave the dishes for her in the sink.

'Cut for partners.'

Danny liked to do everything properly. The four men bent over the spread pack. Each withdrew a card and turned it up.

'Two of hearts.' Maurice Feinstein.

'Jack of hearts.' Mr Mannheim, with a wintry grin.

'Four of diamonds.' A shrug from Simon.

'Queen of spades.' Daniel. Highest card, highest suit.

'Fix!' laughed Simon, and the men arranged themselves around the small table, Simon at west opposite Maurice, Mannheim at north with his back to the window, facing Daniel. Their host poured whisky for the two drinkers, Maurice and Simon. He and the old man would wait for refreshments. That the cards had deemed them partners meant they would probably win.

Daniel dealt. He noted pleasurably that he held a moderately strong hand with an ace, a king, two queens and three jacks spread around the suits. Mannheim opposite also looked pleased – that meant at least a second ace, possibly more. When movement ceased Daniel started the bidding.

'One no trump.' Safe: and 'no trump' would beat any suit.

'Two of spades,' Simon followed. He had noticed the quick glance between his opponents, their comfortable demeanour.

'Two no trump.' Mannheim was curt, cool. The raise was the lowest possible: so his hand was not brilliant.

'No bid.' It might not be that Morrie Feinstein had such poor cards, Daniel reflected. It was more likely that he could not work out what to bid.

How Daniel adored his bridge. It was the one moment in his life when his mental agility made him supreme. All week his livelihood came through his fingers; though he had to concentrate on the line of a jacket, the jib of a lapel, yet half his brain was not engaged and would niggle in its inactivity. In his youth he had been an avid reader, mostly of works with a strongly political theme. Before he was twenty he could quote passages of Robert Tressell's *The Ragged Trousered Philanthropists*, much of it learned during a long illness. Tressell was buried in a pauper's grave in Walton. Blake was another favourite. Had it not been for the war he might have aspired to a political life, but fate had not dealt him the best hand. Nor could he have easily campaigned for a pacifist Labour Party with that idiot Lansbury in charge, a man who forswore resistance despite those terrible stories which filtered from Germany. As for Churchill—

Under the table Mannheim kicked him gently. Daniel jerked upright. He was in danger of forgetting his task. He bent his head to the cards. In a moment South (himself) had won the contract at Three no trump – a bit risky, for it meant a promise to take nine out of the thirteen tricks – and was declarer. Mannheim as partner laid down his hand, face up: the dummy. Splendid – that added two aces and a king to the arsenal.

Simon led with a low spade and his partner, delighted, threw down the ace of spades. Aha, thought Daniel, that's where it was. Nice to get it out of the way so soon. Feinstein took the trick with a flourish, laid it face down and tossed in the nine of spades. Daniel offered his Jack, and took the trick. One each.

Then Daniel took a chance and switched to diamonds, playing the Queen. But Feinstein gurgled happily and threw down the King. Daniel had been right – the chap held a hand whose value he could only grasp once in play. Fool: far more spectacular results could be obtained by thinking ahead. A grocer didn't need to, a craftsman did. Yet Feinstein's impulsiveness was part of his rather feckless charm.

Simon took the next trick with a King: they must've had one each. Then Simon threw down his ten of spades and took the trick with competent satisfaction. Four tricks to one. 110 points-worth to only 30.

They'd have to play every single card to the bitter end. The air was vibrant with effort.

The balance shifted back. The next three tricks were Daniel's with more high diamonds. Four each. But to match his bid he had to take all five which remained. He could call on the two aces, two Kings and Jack in his combined hand – that made another four. In a moment they'd be down to one card each, with eight tricks to four on the table. The question was, should he take a chance by leaving himself the Jack of clubs? The last trick would depend on clubs. Who had the Queen?

Simon was staring at the ceiling, forehead furrowed. No clue there. But Feinstein was shifting about, mouth a-twitch. Daniel looked at Mannheim who flicked his eyes in Feinstein's direction: so he too reckoned the grocer must hold it. That meant Daniel should hang on to his best card. He could feel himself sweat as he played steadily, competitively. Then, to his delight, suddenly he had it: one card remained in his hand, the King of clubs.

He paused, then threw it down with a flourish. Feinstein tossed in the Queen with an oath.

'You bloody did it! Amazing,' the shopkeeper congratulated.

'Close run thing.' Daniel grinned in relief.

'I wanted to keep a good card to the end.'

The winner chuckled. 'Yes, we could see that. Written all over your face. Good job you don't play poker, Morrie.'

The evening continued. The air became pungent with blue smoke as Simon lit a cigar. The heavy ashtray began to fill with curls of ash. It was an absorbed four that eventually greeted Annie as she cautiously brought in the tea. Feinstein went to the bathroom, Simon drew out a large handkerchief and blew his nose. Under its cover he watched Annie's movements wistfully but did not speak as she put down the tray, poured tea and handed it out, left the room and closed the door behind her.

'She's a wonderful woman, your Annie,' Simon remarked at last. 'She puts up with all this' – he indicated the littered table, the fuggy air – 'with not a murmur of complaint. I live alone, like Morrie, so I can do what I want in my own house, but my daily cleaner moans at me like a fishwife. And when I go to my sister's – oy! It's "Don't put your feet there", and "Pick your newspaper up". She makes my life a misery.'

Maurice grunted. 'Most important, she puts up with him.' He jerked a thumb in Daniel's direction. 'You're such a stubborn bugger there must be moments. Don't you ever fight, eh? Doesn't she ever chuck a plate at you? Or is it all domestic harmony?'

Simon continued the teasing as Mr Mannheim added sub-totals. 'Got her under control, Danny, is that it? But beware of hidden depths. Mind she doesn't end up like my sister. When my brother-in-law was alive, *olvershalom*, his wife once got so mad at him she tipped a whole pan of hot chicken soup over him. He had a lot of explaining to do down the Royal Infirmary.'

'He deserved it,' Maurice defended stoutly. 'He'd been playing around with a *shikse* at work and she found out. She should have finished him off.'

'Yeah, but he wasn't insured. She'd found that out too,' the devoted brother revealed. The men laughed contentedly. 'Funnily enough, she did make him take out insurance after that, so when he died of his heart attack a year later he left her *very* comfortable.'

'Got a good business head, your sister. Ever thought of taking her into the firm?' This from Daniel as he stubbed out a cigarette. Rotblatt's made jeans and men's trousers for Marks and Spencer. The company was a substantial commercial success, which explained the gleaming three-litre car strewn across the path.

In answer Simon placed a palm on each side of his head as if in pain and rocked to and fro. 'My life! The very idea. It's bad enough eating *shabbos* dinner there. I wouldn't wish her on my worst enemy.'

The play continued for a further hour with the more able pair, Daniel and Mr Mannheim, steadily amassing a huge lead in points. That much of the exercise was a mystery to Maurice Feinstein was repeatedly evident. When within a few minutes of the start of one rubber Mannheim calmly claimed ten tricks before he had played anything Feinstein threw down his hand in disgust.

'I don't get it. How do you *know*? You haven't played 'em yet. How can you be so sure?'

Mannheim said nothing but looked up quizzically at Daniel. It was understood that the old German, who could converse with rapidity and elegance in Yiddish and his native language and several others, and who, it was believed, had once been a physicist with Werner von Braun, did not feel at ease in English.

Daniel started the cut for the next deal.

'Look: it's all logical. In this hand, Mr Mannheim won the contract, so I as his partner had to lay down my hand face up as the dummy. Then he plays with both, see? That means he also knows which cards you two hold. He can make an intelligent guess at the split. Your bids earlier demonstrated where you're strong – say, a run of five cards in a suit – and where you're weak. It doesn't take a genius to work it out.'

Feinstein grumbled cheerfully but Daniel allowed a tinge of impatience to enter his voice. 'The trouble with you, Morrie, is you won't concentrate. You'd prefer to have a conversation –'

Feinstein leaned forward and pointed his lighted cigarette at his host. Three whiskies had loosened his tongue. It had been a long day. 'And the trouble with you, Danny, is you like winning. You're really aggressive at the table, you know that?'

The atmosphere turned cool. Mannheim began to deal, clucking softly between his teeth. The intrusive sound obliged the others to return to the cards.

Daniel did not want Feinstein to have the last word. 'No, I'm not aggressive. I'm an ordinary bloke. Why, if that were true – if I'd been a hard man in business – I'd be rich as Croesus like Simon here, and could afford a Bentley and have my name inscribed in the book of donors at the *schul*.' But he laughed as he said it, and Simon took the remark as a compliment.

Soon it was nearly midnight and long past the point at which the children had been heard to return home and Annie had trudged upstairs. To restore harmony Daniel had allowed Feinstein to win a rubber; the man had bragged happily as a child as he had loudly reckoned his total. Humiliation had been avoided. Simon Rotblatt, who did not think deeply about his play but had a natural aptitude and a good memory, had instantly spotted the courtesy and liked it. Only Mannheim had frowned but his host's quickly shaken head had deflected any rebuke.

At last they rose and stretched. Glasses and cups were drained and the last slice of cake nibbled as the friends prepared to depart. Mr Mannheim collected tea plates and tried ineffectually to stack them. His hands were not strong and the pile suddenly tottered. Before anyone could reach it the large dish with its floral pattern slipped and broke. Crumbs scattered on the rug.

The old man mumbled disjointed pleas as Daniel bent to retrieve the pieces. He had seen a fleeting look of terror in the watery eyes, as if some nightmare had returned. He laid a reassuring hand on the thin arm.

'Your wife is so good and she will be upset,' Mannheim persisted. *She vil pee oopset.*

Daniel murmured, 'No, don't worry. Not the best china,' though Annie would rant a little. Their stock of crockery was not so extensive that such a loss could be ignored.

'You don't understand women, Mannheim,' Feinstein joked gruffly. 'When you're not a married man—'

'I was a married man.'

The sibilant *vass* startled his listeners. It had long been assumed that Mannheim who had fled from Berlin in his twenties had been single. Whenever the wedded state of Daniel as the only one of the four was aired, Mannheim had never demurred.

Daniel straightened, the broken dish in his hands. He spoke slowly. 'What happened to her?'

'Ach! She went up in smoke, like the rest of them. Buchenwald. After she broke a dish. She worked in the kitchens—' Mannheim stopped.

All eyes swivelled as one to his right arm as if to pierce through the fabric to the parched skin, to the tattoo which now each of his friends was certain was there. His other hand moved protectively as if to hide the mark, but in so doing answered their unasked question. He grimaced and turned away.

We will never get away from it, thought Daniel moodily, as he let his companions out into the night and shut the door. The *shoa*, which others call the Holocaust. The Final Solution. Genocide: the determined attempt to rid the world of the Jews, to cleanse it of my blood.

His eyes caught a photograph on the wall, of himself and Annie dressed in their finery at somebody's wedding, a showy orchid corsage on her tailored suit, the children at her feet.

Yet my flesh and blood do not know any of this. Ah, yes, they are taught at *schul* and *cheder*, but they do not *know*. How can they know? They are not touched by the horror. It is not they that cannot shake off the memory, that pay the price: it is my generation, who will never be free of it.

By the waters of Babylon Rachel sat down and wept: yeah, Rachel wept for her children.

Across the city another front door opened and then banged closed. Booted steps could be heard along the uncarpeted passage, dragging and irregular: two sets, her father and a brother, or perhaps one of them with a drinking mate. The rancid waft of fish and chips entered with them. In the kitchen a plate was banged on a table. Somebody clouted a shoulder hard on a door jamb and muttered a curse. So thin were the partitions which passed for walls that the jarring could be felt throughout the flat. On her dressing table a dish rattled.

The bedroom was in blackness. Street noises came up to it fitfully – a youth shouted and was answered by a raucous female, a lone bus ground its way up the hill. The little room was, for once, not cold. Heat came from a single-bar electric fire plugged into the wall. That cost money, but for the moment the meter had been successfully by-passed so the power was freely squandered.

At the window the curtains were thin and ragged. Through their open weave and holes a neon street lamp flickered. At midnight it would be extinguished. Then he would come.

Colette shrank under the bed covers and drew her knees up to her chin. Her thin arms pulled the nightie down over her legs, then wrapped themselves around her limbs like a parcel. Despite the warmth her teeth began to chatter.

She made herself think of school in the morning. Double physics followed by maths: God, what a grind. She would have to force her mind to it with the utmost dedication. Those subjects did not permit guesswork, however tired she might be. She had to know the procedures and get them right. Accuracy was all. How she envied the girls in the arts classes. It didn't matter if they couldn't produce quotations absolutely spot on – what counted was to present a convincing argument. Not that she was confident she could do that, either. What if there were several opinions about an extract, apparently of equal value? Some of the better students could judge for themselves which was right. Teachers declared those girls had natural taste and judgement. Faced with competing passages of English, however, Colette was frequently stumped. She could grasp their sense: she could join in a discussion about their quality. But left to her own devices, without guidance or hints, she could make little headway in picking out which was 'best'. In that sense, therefore, the rigid certainties of science were much easier for her. Its rules created a known territory which she could memorise in detail. The way it was taught for A level meant no debates. Only one line was correct, and it was a straightforward matter to learn—

'Ah, Colette darlin'.'

The whiff of vinegar had entered with him, and the smoky smell of the pub. And the unspeakable sourness of undigested beer on his breath. Once he had been so drunk he had needed to vomit first; he had leaned over the bed to try to reach the floor, but his aim had been so bad that some had landed on her shoulder. Its acrid stink had barely made things worse. He had been clumsily apologetic. He had not meant to do that.

He did not mean to do anything: he could not help it. That was the most he ever said by way of excuse.

She shrank away and curled up as tightly as she could into a ball. Her breathing became shallow and rapid and she strove to make it silent. If he thought she was sound asleep, mightn't he stop and think again –?

'Ah, no, Colette, don't be like that. Be a good girl for me.'

A hand on her shoulder pulled her roughly on to her back. She could not see his face in the shadows above her. She would not look at him and kept her teeth and lips clamped shut. She would not give him the satisfaction of acknowledging him. That would recognise him as a human being. He wanted that.

He fumbled in the dark with his clothing. She heard the clank of a belt buckle as it hit the floor.

Then he climbed roughly on to the bed and thrust his hand under the bedclothes. Rigidly she resisted him, but tonight it was no use. If she fought back, as she used to, he would hit her hard across the face until she subsided, sobbing. Or he would reach for the belt and strop it across her body, creating weals she'd have to conceal for days. Then he would carry on, so there was no point.

No point in resistance. No escape. Nowhere to go. What idiots those kids at school were. How little they knew.

Yet school was the only way out. If she could take those exams next year – if she could hold on – she could get away—

He had it in his hand. He seemed to be testing it for size and strength, and little grunts came from him. She suppressed a scream and turned her face away, but tonight he didn't want that. He tugged the bed-clothes back and knelt up over her.

'Now then, little girl. Open up.'

She was trembling violently, all over, as he pushed his other hand roughly between her knees to make room for himself. The skin on his fingers was rough from his work and the endless exposure to cold and wet. Big fingers. Rummaging around inside her. If she were too dry he complained she made him sore. He seemed to think that was her prob-lem, not his. He'd have been pleased if she had done something about it, like Vaseline. Mostly, like tonight, he was in too much of a drunken hurry to care.

Then he was inside her, and his heavy body flopped down on hers as he grasped her bony shoulders and heaved himself in and out. His breath came in rasping spurts, interspersed with a loud belch which interrupted his rhythm. For a moment she was terrified that he might be sick right there on her face, but he wriggled deeper inside and carried on. She tried her hardest not to move with him, but the momentum of his body made the bed rock and creak for them both.

Then suddenly he shuddered, and shook himself like a dog. In a moment he had raised himself up. A sliver of light from under the door glinted on his teeth. He must be smiling.

'God, Colette, but I needed that.'

She was shivering, lying there exposed. With a shamed movement he shoved the blanket roughly over her. She clutched the edge and pulled it up to her chin. She had made not a sound.

At the bedside he pulled his trousers on again and fastened buttons and belt. Then he bent and kissed her wetly on the cheek.

'It's good for you too, little girl, don't forget that. In fact I've a treat for you tonight.'

He had never spoken that way before. Usually he was shamefaced, almost despairing. He would slouch off mouthing phrases about mortal sin and his doomed soul. This bravado was new, and no change for the better. She wondered dully who had been talking to him at the pub. Who had he come home with?

He went to the door, opened it and went out. The lightbulb in the hallway illuminated his sweaty unshaven face. A bubble of spittle hung on his chin like foaming pus. He was not looking in her direction. Then she heard him call out, and froze in horror.

'So, Jimmy, my man, are you ready? She's here and waiting for you. Got the hots tonight, has my little darling. Come on now.'

Chapter Four

Green Shoots

One supposed advantage of Liverpool, Helen reflected, was that it seldom suffered prolonged cold weather. When reports on the radio described blizzards elsewhere, when Derbyshire or Scotland were snowed in, Liverpudlians faced chill winds but not much worse. The Gulf Stream on the west side of the country kept the climate mild. The price was more wet days. Whatever else it did not do in Liverpool, it rained a lot, and often.

Every morning that week, in fact. While the rest of the country was still gripped by the worst winter in recent memory, they had rain instead, though weather reports gleefully predicted more snow. Becalmed in the sixth-form cloakroom with sodden raincoats swinging wetly around her shoulders, she groaned at the prospect of either.

It would have helped had chairs been available for that handful of pupils whose parents withheld permission for attendance at the morning religious service. The excuse paraded was that there were too few to make such a fuss worthwhile. Instead they had to sit on the narrow benches under the coathooks where children would perch to remove their outdoor shoes, surrounded by the rubbery smell of mackintoshes.

Helen and Roseanne Nixon were the two oldest Jewish girls, with a handful of others from younger forms. One abstainer came from a strict Unitarian home where her father was a Minister; she was forbidden to take part in prayers which referred to the Trinity. In a corner apart sat two shy Muslims, the dark-skinned daughters of that Pakistani whose shop adjoined Mr Feinstein's. Their father had tried to obtain agreement for them to wear trousers and had been rebuffed by the chairman of governors with a snort. They were lucky to be at Blackburne House at all, he was informed. Lastly came three girls, two sisters and a cousin, from teacher Mrs Egerton's family who proudly proclaimed themselves humanists. The teacher herself remained discreetly in the staffroom. To the others, each a believer in her way, humanism meant denial of the existence of God. At times that provoked heated arguments in the cloakroom, as distorted snatches of Church of England hymns floated in from the assembly hall nearby.

'*He-e who would valiant be*
'*Gainst all disaster,*
Let him in constancy
Follow the Master –'

' 'Gainst all disaster. Appropriate, this morning,' Roseanne commented. She had forgotten her beret and her limp hair dripped.

Helen looked up from the back page of the *Daily Telegraph* on which she was attempting, unsuccessfully as usual, to complete the crossword. It would help to find fourteen letters ending in 'ent' meaning circular bravery. The hymn had moved on:

'*There's no discouragement*
Shall make him once relent –'

Ah, yes. 'Discouragement' would do.

'*His first avowed intent*
To be a pilgrim.'

Roseanne prodded her crossly. 'Wish we weren't in this stupid school.' Helen shrugged. The two were much the same age, but Roseanne's laziness condemned her to the lowest class in her year while Helen was in the top stream of the next year upwards. Since Helen had chosen sciences for her A levels the gap between them had widened; for Helen had become a member of a small elite open to girls with qualities and aspirations which Roseanne lacked, and rather resented.

'My mother is thinking of moving me to the King David.'

It was intended to be a provocative remark, and succeeded. Helen folded the newspaper and laid it in her lap.

'What would you gain?' she asked. 'This is a grammar school and that's a comprehensive. However brilliantly you got on there it'd never have the cachet of this place.' And why, was the unspoken query, might you think you'd do better there?

'I'd meet boys: it's co-educational,' Roseanne smirked. The two Pakistanis covered their mouths with their hands and whispered to each other.

'Better not let Jerry hear you talk like that. Jealous lover, that one.' Helen meant to tease but Roseanne reddened and gestured towards the younger children who were pretending to do homework in the dim light.

'Hush. Not in front of the babies.'

Helen turned. 'Are you and Jerry serious? I thought it was a bit of fun. He's a flirt, you know.'

'Certainly we're serious.' Roseanne tossed her head. 'We plan to get engaged on my eighteenth birthday.'

The idea seemed so incredible that Helen could not stop herself smiling. It was evident that Roseanne knew little about her putative fiancé. Girlish solidarity required her to warn Roseanne even though they were not close friends. Yet she hesitated. It was safer for Roseanne, who was headstrong and tended deliberately to misheed advice, to discover for herself. If she, Helen, were to recount Jerry's Sunday morning lurches she would promptly be accused of making the play. The broad rule frequently annunciated by Miss Plumb, that if you can say nothing pleasant about a person you should say nothing, would serve. She preferred her name not to be linked with Jerry's anyway.

Roseanne was clearly put out that her announcement had failed to impress. Although she had blurted it out on the spur of the moment, on cursory reflection it seemed like an excellent notion. A schoolgirl who was engaged was one step ahead of a schoolgirl taking exams, any day. She began to repeat it, then thought better of it. She pointed. 'Anything in the paper?'

Helen turned to the front page and scanned it quickly. 'Mr Wilson is expected to be chosen as the new Labour leader. He says he's proud to represent Huyton.'

Roseanne sniffed. 'Pity he doesn't sound as if he represents a Merseyside seat, then. He talks odd. Yorkshire, isn't it? I don't like it.'

'He's called for a general election.'

'Won't affect us.' Roseanne was not interested.

From the hall came the low murmur of voices. The rhythms of the Lord's Prayer indicated that the devotions would soon be finished. Helen felt a need to mend fences with Roseanne, whom she did not actively dislike. These morning sessions of exclusion in the cloakroom conferred an element of comradeship: at least between themselves they should not fall out.

'Beatles' new single is out next week. It's called "Please Please Me". They played it in the Cavern yesterday for the first time. Have you heard it yet?' This might be a better subject.

It was. Roseanne's eyes widened. 'Ooh! You are lucky. I put an order in to NEMS but they won't sell it till the day. Said they want it to go straight to the top and not dribble out. D'you think it will?'

Helen nodded vigorously. 'Yes. Number one. And the next one, and the one after that – they'll be so big, you watch.'

'Then they'll be off – Royal Command Performance and that. And we'll never see them again.' Roseanne was wistful.

'Stuff. They're Liverpool boys. They won't leave.' Even as she spoke

Helen could not recall where recently she had heard a similar assertion. It sent a frisson down her spine.

The doors of the hall were thrown open and the small band of dissenters trooped in under the gaze of the entire school.

Helen went first, her head held high. Though she hated this moment of humiliation it also gave her legitimate communion with the long line of those who had suffered for their faith through the centuries: Rabbi Akiva, Galileo, Joan of Arc. That made her proud, and secretly pleased. The decision which led to this moment was significant. Her parents cared enough to insist on her removal from the pernicious influence of alien incantations and had had to answer questions and sign papers. Yet her ears burned each time. Whenever possible she would avoid it. That was how she had missed the announcement of Founder's Day: instead she had hidden in the Library and buried her nose in a book. This morning however she had been warned that Miss Plumb required her presence. She could not escape.

Each class stood in lines, youngest at the front, with staff ranged like guardsmen down the sides of the hall. The girls were told to sit, and did so, row upon navy-skirted row, cross-legged, knees red and protruding. Teachers posed primly, backs stiff, on canvas-seated tubular chairs, their hands folded in their laps. Most were dressed in simple tweed skirts and plain blouses fastened to the chin with cardigans for those who felt the cold, and no make-up other than a hint of lip colour. Miss Pennington who taught history wore a man's tie and shirt. But the head of languages Miss Hodgson sported a red sweater and a tight black skirt and crossed her splendid legs in defiance of school injunctions while at her side her *assistante* daringly sported a vivid chiffon scarf at the throat. At the piano Miss Tyrone, a wizened relict from the first war, fussed over her sheet music. Mrs Egerton was absent as usual but her fellow chemistry teacher Miss Clive still nursed a bandaged hand. The acid injury was taking ages to heal.

Messages were given out. The results of sports fixtures at the weekend were announced and success rewarded with polite applause. The term's charity, to which the pupils' efforts both with the collection plate and regular sales of work would be devoted, was to be a mission in central Africa run by an old girl of the school.

Helen sat at the end of a row at the front, her back to the piano. Miss Plumb's well-shod feet were a bare few inches away. Miss Plumb was not tall but had a trim, full-bosomed figure which showed to advantage in her narrow-waisted suits. She had been born soon after the Armistice: that put her in her forties. Her eagle stare was legendary. Helen kept her own eyes down. Miss Plumb had neat legs and ankles, not normally visible from an upright position. Under the pale seamed stockings faint brown hairs showed on the headmistress's shins.

Miss Plumb's plangent tones carried her words throughout the large hall with ease. Miss Plumb did not sound as if she came from Liverpool, nor from Yorkshire. Indeed Miss Plumb made no effort to hide the fact that she came from the south, from Kent, which to most of her listeners was impossibly remote on the other side of the country, further even than London. In Kent, had they known, she was not regarded as speaking with a Kentish burr either. In Tunbridge Wells polite circles that was not done. To the children at her feet, their parents and most of their teachers her speech was distinctly upper class, and very distant.

'And so we offer our congratulations to the under fifteen netball team and send our good wishes for their further success in the semi-final.' She turned over a piece of paper. 'And would those first year sixth-formers who wish to be considered for Oxbridge entrance please come to my room after lunch.' She glanced at Helen but mentioned no names. 'We will discuss the matter together first, then I will talk to each of you in turn. And now, Miss Tyrone, *if* you please.'

A lively if inaccurate march was struck up on the piano. In meek obedience pupils rose and marched out, the little ones swinging their arms at their sides while older girls did their best to slouch. Helen stood and waited. She caught Miss Plumb's eye, and nodded. She would be there, and both knew it.

Sylvia Bloom was hard at work. In front of her on the dining table were propped a notepad, a small black address book, a card index in a lockable box, a folder stuffed with press cuttings mainly from the *Liverpool Jewish Gazette* and the *Jewish Chronicle*, plus telephone directories for Liverpool, Manchester and Leeds.

She nibbled the sugary edge of a Danish pastry then licked her fingers. Her best time was in the morning, after a cup of strong Viennese coffee, the kind her mother used to make. Her mother had embroidered the linen tablecloth on which Sylvia worked: she touched its curlicues and roses with reverence. *Olvershalom*: may God rest her soul. Morrie Feinstein stocked the same coffee. He'd charge her the earth, then his conscience would prick and he would slip in a wedge of fresh Wensleydale or a couple of roll-mop herrings for free, to keep her sweet.

Morrie Feinstein. Sylvia selected a press item of a recent wedding which showed guests and close relations lined up in their finery. Morrie was in the middle of the back row, slightly indistinct. She began to scribble on her notepad. A young man – well, youngish: well set up with his own thriving business, not ugly, and unmarried. It wasn't right.

It wasn't right, for a start, that he lived alone. His son Jerry didn't count, for the boy would be off his hands soon and would have his own place as soon as he could afford it. Bit of a *schlemiel*, that one. Jerry wouldn't need a matchmaker – more likely a divorce lawyer to extricate himself from some mess he would be certain to get himself in. Probably more than once. She should warn her sister and niece Roseanne, who was sweet on him.

Morrie's lifestyle was totally wrong. Weren't Jewish people naturally gregarious? They eschewed solitude. Hermits were not honoured. Above all, celibacy was frowned upon. Hadn't the sages urged the people to 'Go forth and multiply'? The rabbis, the priests, were enjoined to set a fine example, to marry and have lots of children, at least four, though more might be regarded as overdoing the enthusiasm. That had been the pattern for centuries. In modern days the Holocaust had given more urgency, an obligation to replace those millions, *olvershalom*, who had been lost. In the community a single man was anathema. Didn't that mean that her own calling was a sacred duty?

So, perhaps she herself was a bit old to 'go multiply' – and with Sarah, her daughter, she had done her bit. Grandmotherhood should beckon, though the daughter showed not the least desire to get hitched. With regret Sylvia finished the last crumbs of the Danish, wiped her hands on a paper napkin and wished she had bought two.

Not that Sylvia was keen to tell the truth about her own age nor that of most of her clients. That would not do at all. Exaggeration of wealth and minimalisation of personal faults were her stock in trade. The truth got in the way. Heavens, if she had a pound note for the number of times she'd glossed over imperfections or dodgy back histories: the times without number when her black book and index had held unsavoury information about a member of a family, imprisoned in Jersey, say, or facing bankruptcy proceedings in Glasgow, or with a tendency to drink, and she had kept quiet, or pooh-poohed the very suggestion: if she had a pound, she repeated, she would be a rich woman.

Thank God, she was not exactly destitute. The divorce settlement all those years ago when her ex had been so desperate to go off with his floozy had been shrewdly invested and the house was hers, unencumbered. Better than Morrie's home, in fact. Nor was she such an undesirable catch, though she said so herself. Solid and healthy: well rounded, it had to be admitted, but some men preferred their women cuddly. On the other hand, she liked to earn a living. There was no money to be made from the grateful parents of a suitably placed old maid if she were to land the reluctant Mr Feinstein herself.

Sylvia poured more coffee and looked around her kitchen in satisfaction. Fitted cupboards from Owen Owen's. The latest double fridge-freezer which her friends envied and schemed to buy in imitation. A Kenwood mixer with attachments, bigger than her sister's. An electric kettle which whistled when the water was boiled, *and* an electric toaster. She congratulated herself on these acquisitions, though often they would remain in their packaging and be exhibited only when visitors or clients appeared. Houseproud was one thing, but slave to the stove was quite something else, and not Sylvia's style.

So why did Morrie Feinstein interest her so much? It wasn't his money. It wasn't status, though to be a wife again, the head of a household, would be far preferable to queening it alone. Sylvia returned to the table, picked up the press cutting with Feinstein's photograph and allowed herself to stare at his face for fully five minutes.

He was a man: and having been married once, he might be a captive again. Others, equally eligible like Simon Rotblatt, had so long resisted her blandishments that (though she would never admit it) Sylvia had virtually given up on them. Morrie, however, with his flirtatious wielding of the smoked salmon knife gave hints that with finesse he might be caught, someday. That was it.

Sylvia propped his picture on her cup and slowly began to circle the table, humming to herself. Then she ran her hands over her thighs and let them rest, there, at the groin, pressed together, where she could feel them on her pubic bone: the spot a man might slide his hands to if he were standing behind her, his arms around her, touching and pleading . . . She bent slightly and exhaled, her upper arms pushing in her fleshy breasts from the sides so they swelled up before her, and thrilled at the sensation. And if it was a man – Morrie or – *anybody* – she would feel something else, too, pressed into the small of her back, into the cleavage of her buttocks: and he would not need to use words, other than endearments, to tell her what he wanted, what he could give. That half-remembered hardness would be its own supplication. And she would turn and put her arms around his neck and raise her face to his to be kissed—

Sylvia Bloom caught sight of herself in a mirror, a stout middle-aged woman in a skirt that was too tight, belly bulging, blouse ridden out at the front, her fat arms upraised and a flush on her cheeks, solitary in her empty house. She dropped her hands lifelessly and stood still.

It had been fun trying to get Morrie into the mood. If he were attracted to her – really attracted, instead of playing the pliant shopkeeper – he had shown no signs of it. To be honest he was much too young for her. It was probably wiser to abandon any dreams of entrapping the grocer for herself and instead to persuade him to consider remarriage as a genuine proposition. For that she had no end of suitable clients who would pay nicely.

With a deep sigh she tucked the blouse back into its waistband, returned the press cuttings to their folder, and began to scribble notes in her private little book.

'You planning to come, Colette?'

First lesson was a prep. The four friends were huddled around a table in the library, textbooks propped open before them. The room was two doors away from Miss Plumb's office and, like hers, had been one of the main entertaining salons of the old house. It was high-ceilinged and airy, with an oak parquet floor in curious patterns, much eroded at the edges. The elaborate ceiling rose no longer bore a magnificent chandelier but a neon strip light which dangled and swung slowly in the draught. An electric bar fire provided limited heat. The walls were hidden by dusty shelves filled with several thousand old books in cloth and leatherette bindings, arranged in some idiosyncratic order clearly understood only by Miss Tyrone who had set it up four decades before. A display cabinet by the door bravely showed a selection of 'New Books', their garish covers protected by opaque plastic. The cabinet was locked.

Helen did not need to elaborate her question. The discussion with Miss Plumb would dominate their thoughts the whole morning.

'I'm not sure there's much point. My Dad wants me to leave now, never mind after the exams next summer.' The girl spoke quietly; her green eyes were veiled.

'Simplest way to fight your horrible kin is through education,' Brenda hissed, and prodded Colette's arm with a pencil. The warmth behind the urging made the Irish girl smile.

'Let her be, Brenda,' intervened Helen. 'It's possible to have a marvellous family and still find that persuading them to let you go to university is an uphill task.'

'Yours still being difficult too, then?'

'A bit. They're like Colette's dad in some ways; can't quite see why I should want to spend another five years studying – two here at school and three at university – with no guarantee of a better job. They calculate, I suppose, that the cash I lose won't be made up, specially if I get married not long after leaving college. Though when I talk to them they say money's not the problem. Seems to be something deeper – an anxiety that I'll change and grow away from them.'

Brenda tossed her curly head. 'Well – I'm not giving up my job when *I* get married. I don't see why I should, and you don't have to these days. My grandmother told me she had to leave the civil service when she got wed – that used to be the rule. She ticked off my Mum when *she* suggested that was still best. My lot are keen I should go to college. And have a career too.'

'I'm not sure it's that easy,' Helen mused. 'The best jobs go to men – always have. And what happens if you want kids? Lots of places aren't keen to employ women with children. Most husbands won't allow it – my Dad won't let Mum get a job, even a part-time one. Her place is at home, they both say, and I can see their point. I wouldn't want to come back to an empty house and have to make my own tea.'

All eyes turned to Colette. For some years since her mother had abandoned the children it had been the girl's role to make tea for her brothers and her father. The men were sometimes home the whole day but it was known they did not lift a finger. She bent her head and did not respond.

'There's one easy answer.' Meg sat up and pushed her spectacles more firmly up her nose. A didactic tone entered her voice. 'Don't get married. Don't let them dictate to you! Have your own bank account and your own home, make your own friends. Maybe have a car some-day. Do your own thing. Why not?'

The others were dubious. That sounded like sedition. Helen lowered her voice: 'One reason you've forgotten. You can't open a bank account without a man's signature. So you'd have to keep well in with some-body you can trust, such as your father.'

'Or campaign for a new law,' Meg muttered. She began to chew her nails savagely.

Helen shrugged. 'Meanwhile we have to live with the law as it is. Hush now, or we'll have the librarian on the warpath. Has anybody fig-ured out the answer to test question three?'

The object of Sylvia's cogitations was in the back room of his shop. He was bent over nearly double, one hand on a battered box of grapefruit, the other pressed to the small of his back. His face was scarlet and he was panting hard, with little gasps escaping between clenched teeth.

'Nellie! Where are you? Will you come?'

It was difficult to make oneself heard when facing the wrong way and addressing the wet floor. It was the rain which had caused the problem: on the slippery concrete he had lost his foothold just as he had managed to lift the heavy box. As it slipped from his hands he had felt something crunch in his back. And now he could not move.

'Nellie!' he yelled as loud as he could, and yelped as the effort sent stabs of agony across his lumbar region.

The shop was busy. Nellie McCauley noticed at last that her employer had been absent for some time and bustled out to rebuke him. His elevated backside which greeted her was a source of amusement and she debated with herself whether to tap it playfully. When she did so the howl which emanated from the other end stopped her in her tracks.

'Oh, God, Nellie! I've done my back. Can you get an ambulance?'

Poor Mr Feinstein, the customers commiserated. Such a dreadful shame. They watched agog as the figure of their grocer, doubled up and seated on an old chair, was carried out gingerly to the ambulance.

Nellie scurried about and assisted as well she could with the blanket. Her reward came quickly.

As the white doors were about to close, Mr Feinstein grasped her hand and held it tight. 'Nellie, mind the shop for me, won't you? The fruit delivery I've checked, those apples need to go back – and the bagels were burned –'

Nellie squeezed the hand in response. Her heart, which had started to thump the moment she had realised the trouble her employer faced, was still beating oddly. His cracked voice, his evident pain, touched a nerve

in her. She was needed, as never before in the years she had worked for
him. She made herself smile reassuringly into the twisted face. 'Don't
you worry. It'll be in safe hands.'

He relaxed briefly and grunted. 'It will. I know that. You're a grand
girl, Nellie. I don't know how I'd manage without you.'

It had to be admitted that Miss Plumb terrified them. It was not only
that reverberant accent which made her so alien, nor the self-confidence
expressed in that basilisk stare, nor the clothes, almost tight-fitting, of
a cut which would have been frowned upon had any of the pupils
worn similar. Helen's father, remarking the fine quality grey tweed,
had once commented in his daughter's hearing that for a schoolteacher
Miss Plumb was an attractive woman. The cling of the skirt, the curve
of the bosom hinted at an undertow of sexual energy which the adolescents recognised, though they had not the least doubt that her
sexuality was totally sublimated to her profession. The notion of Miss
Plumb with a man, doing his bidding and sighing with distracted passion, was too droll to contemplate seriously. Whatever else she was,
Miss Plumb was *formidable*, and as such certain to put men in their
place.

Brenda, the self-appointed leader of the quartet, knocked on the
door.

'Come!'

Miss Plumb had followed precedent and used the main room of the
Georgian house as her study. The oak parquet here was polished to a
shine and she had imported scarlet rugs found on holiday in Isfahan. To
one side was a carved stone fireplace with baked blue Liverpool tiles
alongside the grate. No one had ever seen it lit; heat came instead from
a cream-painted radiator behind Miss Plumb's back, which left the rest
of the room cool. The ceiling edges and corners still sported elaborate
if flaky mouldings, though here also the chandelier had disappeared to
be replaced by a standard issue Bakelite shade. Over the mantelpiece a
heavy mirror, its gilded edge faded, was screwed to the wall; before it
were ranged a handful of invitation cards, the print too small to be read
by nosy eyes from a distance. A vase of daffodils stood at the mantelpiece's centre and a carriage clock, locked away every night. On all
sides solid wooden bookcases rose, some to the ceiling, others to waist
height laden with the fruits of a lifetime's erudition in several languages – Miss Plumb rightly judged that no burglar would be interested
in those.

The headmistress was seated at her large desk, head down, her back
to the bow window, facing the door. Papers were ranged in neat piles
before her and she was annotating a folder. Behind her the city stretched
out, the truncated red cathedral to the left, the Cunard building straight
ahead, the river a silvery ribbon in the distance. The test thus set was to

hold her eye and not let attention wander to the forbidden temptations of the port or its shops, cellars and clubs. The world inside this room should be sufficient.

The girls trooped in and stood uncertainly in a semi-circle. Miss Plumb let them wait a pregnant few moments when she finished her writing, then looked up briskly. 'Good afternoon. Bring those chairs over and sit.' They obeyed meekly.

'Helen, Brenda, Colette, Margaret.'

Meg squirmed. The girl hated her given name.

'You are intelligent young women with an excellent future ahead of you. Your teachers are well pleased with your application and progress. We take it for *granted* –' she paused and swept her gaze from one solemn young face to the next '– that you will apply to university to read for an honours degree. So will others in this school. But you are judged capable of entry to the highest establishments. I mean of course Oxford and my own university Cambridge.'

She was met by four studiously blank faces.

'We'll come back to the details in a moment. I should warn you at once that if you are willing to try, that will mean extra classes to prepare you for the General Studies paper. Especially as you –' she consulted her notes '– as you are all scientists.'

Miss Plumb was not a scientist. She allowed her head to turn towards one of the bookshelves. 'It will be hard. I will myself tutor you in preparation for examinations and the necessary interviews. Remember Longfellow's wise words – if you would hit the mark, you must aim a little above it. You will need to read a great deal which may be unfamiliar – ancient history, literature of several countries, philosophy. Has any of you, for example, heard of Kant?'

Blinks. Helen swallowed. She had an inkling of what might be coming next and had prepared herself.

'Aha! Well, you will by the time I've finished with you. Now, tell me. What are you reading for pleasure right now?'

Meg, too, was ready. 'Thomas Hardy's *Far from the Madding Crowd*, Miss Plumb. It was a school prize.'

Miss Plumb's eyes flickered at the unnecessary boast. 'Good. I want you to try *Tess*, then. And you can write me an essay on Hardy's treatment of women in both novels when you have finished. Brenda?'

'Baroness Orczy,' Brenda confessed. '*The Scarlet Pimpernel*. I only read it for relaxation –'

'*A Tale of Two Cities* for you. And if you don't see why when you have reached the last page, I have made a mistake with you. Colette?'

'I have been trying *War and Peace*, but I keep forgetting which character is which.'

Miss Plumb suppressed a smile. 'A common problem. Keep it for the holidays. Here –' she went to a bookshelf, ran her finger over the volumes, then selected one and handed it over, '– try Tolstoy's short stories instead. *Master and Man*. Superb. Helen?'

'Grahame Greene. *Brighton Rock*.' It was a slightly mischievous answer, and Helen knew it. The headmistress pretended to be shocked.

'A modern novel? Good gracious. And such seedy characters. Did you buy it?'

That was impossible. 'No – I have a reader's ticket for the Central Library in town. They have a new fiction section –'

With a dismissive gesture Miss Plumb moved on, but she did not suggest any alternative, and it occurred to Helen later as she rolled the conversation back through her mind's eye that the teacher must have read the novel to have made the remark she did.

For the next ten minutes Miss Plumb outlined the Oxbridge system, the college and tutorial peculiarities, the byzantine entrance requirements and the additional studies necessary were the girls to have any hope. The discussion was littered with the names of Miss Plumb's roommates and fellow-students who had risen to positions of academic importance. It was name-dropping and intended to impress, and largely succeeded.

Normally the colleges, each of which conducted their own examination papers and interviews, would not consider candidates until the seventh term of sixth form, that was until the autumn *after* A levels when results were known. For the private sector that arrangement was understood and built into timetables and curricula. For state schools whose families had little to spare it presented a serious barrier, for staying on required an additional year which could have been spent on a degree course elsewhere, hastening the arrival of a proper pay-packet.

'However, I have had a long conversation with my friend Dr Swanson who is the Dean of Admissions for my former college, St Margaret's,' continued Miss Plumb. 'She tells me that the Cambridge authorities have expressed alarm at the exclusive nature of the undergraduate intake. Far too high a proportion comes from privileged homes, especially from the Home Counties. Far too many boys, it is alleged, are made offers because their fathers were there, or because of sporting prowess. The worry is that future academic achievement might be at risk.'

'Or that a future Labour government might change the rules,' murmured Meg.

Miss Plumb pursed her lips. 'Be that as it may, these worries may be to our advantage at Blackburne House. St Margaret's is keen to attract more applicants from the state sector and from the north of England. Particularly in science. You, in other words.'

The girls sat quietly. Then Brenda spoke.

'It's natural you should want us to go to your old college, Miss Plumb, or one similar. But is that best for us? We don't come from down south like you and our families haven't got money to burn.' She hesitated.

The headmistress's eyebrows shot up. 'Aha! This happens every year. I smell foolishness and ignorance. Just because you hail from the north and speak with Liverpool accents – scouse, isn't it? – you think you're not suited to our most ancient seats of learning. You think you'd be unhappy there, discriminated against, is that it?'

'They're a long way from home,' Brenda explained half-heartedly. 'Not many people like us.'

'All the more reason for you to choose them,' Miss Plumb concluded briskly. 'Goodness, Brenda, I wouldn't suggest it if I didn't think you were all quite capable. And you are. Handpicked, each of you. Is that clear?'

Her gaze swept from one pale face to another. 'Good, then we'll have no more argument about it. I want four entrants next year – a record for this school – and I'd like four successes.'

She paused to let the message sink in. Before her Brenda relaxed and grinned broadly. Meg snorted. Colette kept her eyes down but ran her fingers through her hair, almost furtively. Only Helen, eyes fixed firmly on the teacher's face, did not move.

'It means that they will entertain applications from grammar schools *before* A levels – that is, this autumn, on the basis of our assessment of your likely grades. You can apply for the greatest centres of academia in Europe at the same time as you try for, say, Leicester.' A note of triumph.

'Does that mean we are more likely to get in?' Brenda could not conceal her curiosity. She is like a big daft Labrador puppy, Miss Plumb thought, with all that breed's energy, loyalty and generous nature. Meg is a snappy inbred terrier, Helen a long-established workmanlike sort with a touch of class – a spaniel, perhaps, or an old kind of hound which ran with kings. And Colette? Poor Colette, such a brilliant mixture, with no pedigree whatever, and no predictability about either stamina or temperament. But were I obliged to choose, it would be Colette.

'On the contrary,' Miss Plumb answered sternly. 'You will be attempting papers when you have completed barely half the A level syllabus. And you will be competing with girls a year older – or in Helen and Colette's cases, two years older and that much more mature. You won't be the only ones, of course,' she added hastily at the look of alarm on the two faces, 'and these considerations will be taken into account. The college is seeking potential, not mere paper qualifications.'

The prospect of being pioneers intrigued them. Miss Plumb waited. Helen broke the silence.

'So: are we guinea pigs, or are they genuinely keen to break the mould?'

'Mixed metaphors, Helen. You will have to learn to avoid them. But I take your point. My own view is that we have a unique opportunity and must endeavour to make the most of it.'

She reached for a pile of folders. 'Now will you please go and work in the Library and come back in one at a time. Helen, you will be first, so stay where you are.'

As the others filed out and shut the door Miss Plumb flicked through Helen's dossier. The girl sat patiently. Yet it was all she could do to keep her hands from trembling.

'So: Helen Majinsky. You are supremely capable of going on to university; your previous examination history is exemplary and your current teachers think highly of you.'

Helen nodded. 'I like the courses. Mrs Egerton in particular teaches very clearly.'

The headteacher smiled inwardly at the tact and grace of the remark. 'Have you persuaded your parents to let you go?'

'So far. My father has said he will sign. At least he said "We'll see" when he could have refused point blank. But nobody mentioned Oxford or Cambridge. That's different.'

'Why?'

Helen shifted restlessly. 'It'd mean being away from home – so would, say, Manchester or Leeds, but they're not so far and I could get home for weekends.' She did not add, they have big Jewish communities and synagogues which I would be expected to join so they could keep an eye on me. And relatives, so I would be denied the freedom of hall. Denied freedom of any kind.

'Thoroughly bad proposal. The greatest benefit of undergraduate life is the friendships you make which you'll keep for ever. The student who endlessly dashes home misses a great deal. Anyway Oxford and Cambridge are hardly the end of the world. Your parents could come to visit you.'

'I don't think they will – or that they would see it like that. It's not mere physical distance – it's so hard to explain and I don't quite understand it myself, since I don't *feel* the same way they do. It's broader than that. Something to do with a fear that if I do go, I'd be pulled away from them for ever.'

Miss Plumb's eyes narrowed. 'That does not have to happen unless you want it to.'

Helen could feel a lump form in her throat. It came to her suddenly that if she were not very controlled she might cry. From her sleeve she pulled out a handkerchief and began to twist it in her hands.

'But if I do get into Oxford or wherever, it's much more likely that I – wouldn't ever properly come back. I'm aware of that, and my parents are too. Yet I don't want –'

She stopped. In an effort to keep her eyes from filling with tell-tale tears she lifted her chin and stared out beyond the teacher's head to the rooftops and skyline beyond. Miss Plumb checked herself and swivelled around so that her back was almost to the girl.

'You don't want to stay, yet you don't want to leave, is that it?'

Miss Plumb turned back and leaned across the desk, fixing her most potent glare on Helen.

'Now listen to me. You owe it to yourself, Helen Majinsky. What have you been taught daily in this school? That you should do your best under all circumstances. You are very bright – not quite up to Colette, who I know beats you in exams. But you are more certain to complete a degree course and put it to good use. If you develop that potential, you are doing with your brains what God intended when He gave them to you. You have a commendable sense of duty to your family, Helen, but you also have a duty to yourself. In so doing, you're far more likely to benefit the rest of mankind, and your own race, if I might venture an opinion. Far more so, than if you stayed in this city and became a – became a secretary, say.'

Helen looked both startled and downcast. The teacher pressed home her case.

'I believe in you, Helen. You have a spark in you which can best be nurtured by the finest education you can lay hands on. Then, my dear, you will be the better equipped in future to cope with the conflicting choices which are being forced on you now.'

The handkerchief was screwed into a tiny ball. The girl herself probably needed no convincing. What she did require were the arguments and vocabulary with which to convince her opposition. Miss Plumb tried one last time. She rose and moved to the other side of the desk and laid a hand on Helen's shoulder. Her voice softened.

'Your parents are proud of you, are they not? Of course they are. And you would do your utmost to make them even prouder. Helen, my dear, I can guarantee you this. Should you win a place at St Margaret's younger than nearly everyone else, your name and photograph will be on the front page of the *Liverpool Echo* the day after your success. Writ large. Your parents' friends would stop them in the street, wave copies under their noses and congratulate them. That'd work, wouldn't it?'

Annie rolled over and opened one eye. 'What's the matter?'

It was pitch dark and quiet. Not a chink of light came through the curtains. The street lamp outside the house had long since switched itself off.

Daniel had thrown back the blankets and eiderdown and was seated on the edge of the bed, thin legs planted wide on the rug, bent over, his head between his knees. The white woollen vest and underpants, his usual night attire, were the same garments he wore in daytime. That was normal, but his silent distress was not.

He raised his head for a moment. She guessed that his face would be screwed up in misery. He ran his hands up and down his calves and the inside of his thighs, pressed hard and kneaded his knuckles in at the tight places.

'Cramp,' he muttered.

She peered drowsily at him. She ought to offer to get up and make him a drink. 'That's the third time this week. What did the doctor call it? Something sclerosis.'

'Atherosclerosis. Fancy name for hardening of the arteries.' He rubbed his thumb down the inside of one calf and pressed back his toes. The action made his feet tingle; the blood supply was returning. 'Full of smart-alec information, the quacks, but they don't give you anything to help.'

'You been to see him again?'

Daniel ignored the question and Annie knew better than to repeat it. Her husband's hatred and distrust of doctors was impelled by his fear of hospitals. He had seen sufficient of them when he was a kid and smelled enough carbolic, he declared, to last a lifetime. Had surgery been suggested he would have refused.

'Says I got to stop smoking.' Daniel stood up gingerly and moved around the room, slowly and quietly to avoid disturbing the children. The two spoke in low tones. 'And not to drink. I don't touch a drop, I told him. Shows how little they know.'

He had walked round to her side but did not sit. Instead he paced back to his own side, then repeated the manoeuvre, stretching the calves at each step. As her eyes adjusted she could see that his mouth had a grim twist.

It must have been eight or ten minutes before he stopped pacing. 'Bit better,' he murmured and sat down on the bed. He did not apologise for waking her, but tiredly patted her arm. 'Getting old, lass.'

Then he lifted the covers and slipped his chilly legs inside.

Annie lay still. 'You're only fifty. Too young to be an invalid yet, surely?' Daniel did not answer, though she could tell from the flicker of his eyelashes that he was awake.

She tried again. 'Did the doctor offer to prescribe you a painkiller at least, or sleeping tablets?'

'Oh, yes. Dope addict stuff,' Daniel grunted in reply. 'Barbiturates. If I'd have taken them I couldn't drive. And you know, Annie, that without the car I can't run the business.'

What did it mean, this hardening of the arteries? It obviously gave her husband a lot of pain. Combined with the interrupted sleep it made him peevish. His daytime behaviour was less tolerant and more erratic than it used to be. The pattern worried her. He could dismiss the repeated incidents and pretend they hadn't happened but she could not. She had anticipated, naturally, that the time would come when age and decrepitude would overtake them, but not so soon. She was still capable of having children – it was out of the question, of course, but in her mother's generation babies had arrived to women in their forties. Her own periods came with brutal regularity, so she must still be fertile.

Not that there was any danger of pregnancy. Sexual intercourse was apparently off the agenda these days. That was a relief in its way, though it brought an obscure sense of failure to do her wifely duty. Daniel seemed to have lost interest in *that* some time ago.

Perhaps it was part of the same process. Did men suffer a menopause? One of the women's magazines at the hairdresser's, *Woman and Home*, had coyly raised the issue. This decline must worry thousands of other wives. Annie had always assumed that the signs of ageing would be external and easily identifiable and could be treated as life's unkind joke. Grey or white hair, for example: both had it, though Daniel's had thinned over the years to make him bald. His chest hair had become like wisps of cotton wool. Lines and wrinkles she could cope with – a man's appearance in fact improved, though Annie had long despaired of her own looks.

What was troubling was the hidden, internal damage. Her husband seemed to have deteriorated – quite sharply, if truth be told, in the last year or so. If the arteries were seizing up in his legs, maybe the circulation was failing a bit throughout his whole system. He was no longer a red-blooded man. She glanced sideways at him.

'What happened to us – when did we stop, Danny?' Her voice was a whisper and he did not reply nor give any sign he heard her. 'The night of my birthday a couple of years ago you certainly came trotting up to bed with a gleam in your eye.' He had patted her bottom happily and hummed as he undressed while she waited, resigned and a little rigid as usual. But then he had puffed and panted and taken a long time over it, and had seemed a bit depressed afterwards. There'd been another couple of occasions, at weekends when he could lie in the following morning, after he'd had a whisky or two with his friends. Come to think of it, years ago she had been his regular after-bridge chaser. Now the game went on later and he was fatigued when he came upstairs. The liquor made him snore.

Not that he'd ever been a great lover with her. He'd known what to do – the bridegroom had not been as shy as his bride and went to with a will. She was not the one who had taught him. But intimate relations had never played a powerful role in his character, nor did he go in for protestations of adoration. Not the most romantic personality, her Daniel. Annie guessed that given the choice he'd rather talk than make love, but on the whole in recent years the two of them hadn't done much of either.

She chided herself silently. Daniel was a fine man. In his youth he'd had ideas and ambitions, but absolutely way beyond his station. The responsibilities of married life and parenthood had necessarily put paid to that sort of silliness.

He had excellent qualities. He liked a tidy kosher house as did she. He preferred a set routine which could be dull and resisted proposals for modest change: maybe that was part of growing older too. He'd never be rich – he'd never exhibited much commercial acumen, which meant to his credit that he didn't take foolish risks with the family's security. But he worked hard, had few debts since he didn't believe in hire purchase, handed over generous housekeeping every week without fail, paid the mortgage and major expenses, didn't waste cash in the pub or on horses, or carouse or embarrass her. And was respected in the community, though he chose not to play much part in it. That was an irritation for it diminished her own status. The wife of a prominent donor, or of a *frummer mensche*, was treated with deference. But the Mrs Majinsky whose husband saw customers on Saturdays and was low down the list of contributors was an also-ran and was sometimes made to feel it.

She wished she knew what impelled him these days. Sometimes she wondered if some part of Daniel hadn't given up – he seemed willing to pass his days year in, year out as before, until old age and infirmity overtook them both. But infirmity had crept up without warning and threatened to turn a vigorous middle-aged man into a curmudgeonly old one in the wink of an eye. That boded ill, for herself and for the children.

'Drift,' she murmured unhappily. 'We are drifting.' Daniel's breathing had settled into a regular rhythm but it was unclear whether he was asleep or merely ignoring her. She could visualise it: they were floating together idly downstream on a sort of river of life towards a wide open sea of eternity, making no attempt to influence their direction any more. Choices had been made when they had married. No alteration had been contemplated since, let alone discussed.

Annie lay still. If the marriage were not quite as warm and loving as she might have hoped – if she felt a bit lonely at times, and a mite hard done by – these were minor considerations compared with what many women had to put up with, poor souls. The children were their future. Daniel had matured into as reliable a husband as she could have asked. Her role was to be as supportive a spouse as he had the right to demand, and not to complain.

'I made my bed, husband. So did you, all those years ago. Now we must both lie on it.'

Ten days later both of Helen's predictions had come spectacularly true. On the night of St Valentine's Day Harold Wilson beat the Labour Party's deputy leader George Brown by 144 votes to 103 for the position of leader and chairman of the Party. The love affair between the

British electorate and the broad-vowelled Yorkshireman was about to begin.

And the Beatles' 'Please Please Me' which had entered the charts immediately on its release made it to Number One on 16 February.

The pupils of Blackburne House were ecstatic on both counts, though naturally Meg was more taken with the enhanced possibilities of a future Labour government while Helen and Colette sat in dazed excitement, and read and re-read the front pages of *Mersey Beat*.

'My God, it's started. The revolution. Here in Liverpool.' In the Library Helen giggled as if drunk. She was perfectly aware that this was an over-reaction, but nevertheless the atmosphere of regeneration, of redemption almost, of fresh hope was irresistible. Heads nodded about her in agreement. She took gulps of air to steady herself.

'I can't believe it. But it's ours, kids – ours, and John and Paul's, and funny little Mr Wilson's: the future is ours.'

Chapter Five

Lost Youth

'C'mon, lad, rise and shine.'

Daniel Shmuel Majinsky kept his eyes tight shut. A fourteen-year-old boy has the right to behave childishly if only for a few minutes in the grey dawn of his first day of adulthood.

Beside him his elder brother Izzy stirred. A hard heel kicked him painfully in the shin. Whichever was first to the kitchen would get hot water straight from the kettle. But the will to shift was not there. The bed beside him went cold.

His father sat down beside him.

'You're making heavy weather of it, lad. It's easier to jump to it.'

His father, the old man. Harry Majinsky couldn't have been more than forty, but to his children the slight, stooped figure with its spider's web of lines around the eyes and the droopy moustache might have been a thousand years old. Before he had left for the front in 1916, those who were big enough recalled that the eyes had often crinkled with laughter; the wiry body had stood upright. As a married man with several young children Harry had not been in the first wave of volunteers or conscripts. But after a million men had fallen in a war which showed no signs of a conclusion the recruiting officers were not so considerate. He had been away two years. When eventually he came home with a mention in dispatches, a shiny service medal and a scar on his neck he bore with him a melancholy which cloaked and separated him from all those who had not served. Yet he avoided the company of former soldiers. Questioned about his experiences, he would shake his head and stare moodily at the floor.

Daniel's eyes were still closed but the flutter of the eyelashes told his father he was not asleep. It was all Harry could do to stop himself touching his youngest son's tousled head with its hint of copper in the dark hair.

The father rose with a shrug. 'Well, lad, if you don't budge soon you'll be late. And that would not be a good idea on your first day at work. Tough taskmasters, Berman's. Set high standards. That's why you're lucky to be going there.'

As soon as his father had left the tiny room Daniel jumped quickly out of bed and began to pull on his trousers and second-best shirt. He was taller than his father but had the same narrow frame and bony shoulders. Pa was right, of course. He was fortunate to have a job of any kind, let alone a proper apprenticeship, when throughout England grown men stood meekly in dole queues. Soup kitchens had appeared down Scotland Road and on the dockside. The Mersey Mission to Seamen stayed open all day and most of the night. From its small red door down in Water Street wafted a sour smell of cabbage soup and scouse, the thin stew made with barley and old mutton bones which gave the city its sobriquet. And many were glad to have it.

Yet a week from now he would enter the house with shillings a-jingle in his pocket: money from gainful employment. He would proudly hand over the coins to his mother who would reach up and drop them into the brown pot on the mantelpiece behind the clock. She would say very little, as was their wont. The act of placement told everything, that now he could help the family to pay its way. He would be earning, as a man. Or nearly.

The clothing factory was a familiar sight and within a short walk of his home. That made him doubly blessed, for nothing would be wasted on fares, nor would he face a long trudge on penniless days. He kept firm hold of his snap, a couple of thick-cut egg sandwiches prepared by his mother, with a penny bar of chocolate. The new cap on his head, a gift from his mother, felt rough and strange. He found himself in a steady stream of people, men and women, most of whom seemed to know each other, who talked and chattered and teased. The swelling crowd spilled out into the road and surged through the gutters with a gusto and confidence he did not feel, but which roused in him a mingled excitement and fear. They headed in the same direction as himself, for several factories were crowded together in a street near the rail depot which brought coal for their boilers.

He gazed in wonder at their faces, unnerved at their deportment. The girls seemed to be as forward as the men; they marched in twos and threes, arms linked, shrieking with laughter and energy, many with wooden bases to their working boots which clattered merrily on the stone pavements. Would he ever be like that – would he conduct himself with such confidence, such swagger? Could he ever feel at ease and draw attention to himself and his pals in that manner? No: he would not behave so. But he hoped he might feel similarly inside at least. Not sick in his stomach, as at present.

It had not been his choice. He was lucky: he clung to that, as to his packet of sandwiches. He had not dreamed of employment on the shop floor in a dusty, noisy factory. He had not wanted to work in tailoring at all, even though it was assumed, as a boy from a Jewish family of limited means, that such would be his fate. You had to stay with your own: and your own would look after you. So it was no use Daniel Majinsky yearning for a life as a draughtsman in a shipyard where great liners were crafted, whose magnificence would bring cries of amazement as they hove into view: there were Protestant bosses and Catholic bosses, but nobody with a grasp of how to put in a rivet would have given a position to a Jewish boy when good Catholics and Protestants were waiting in the outer office.

Berman's, on the other hand, was owned by Jews. Its directors with only a couple of exceptions could be seen on holy days in various synagogues, their prosperity like a sheen on their smooth jowls and barrel-shaped chests. The mention of his name and pedigree in the right ear had guaranteed an interview. His obvious quickness and good health were all that were required. Indentures were signed. He would start Monday. Now.

Inside the door he hesitated and was buffeted as workers shoved past. Older men gazed sadly at the tall thin figure; one directed him to the manager's office. He waited nervously at the door, cap in hand.

Around him swelled the power-driven clatter of the factory as it got cracking again after the weekend break. A steady whine of machinery filled the air – not the crash and rattle of weaving machines, which he had seen once in a cloth factory in Manchester where an aunt was a supervisor, but the hiss of a big steam engine somewhere nearby in a boiler house matched by the fizz of steam presses where trousers were laid and the irregular whirr of industrial sewing machines row upon row into the distance, their treadles pumped by five hundred pairs of feet.

The air was thick with decades of dust given off by the fabric. It hung in grey globules from the rafters, it lay in a thick fur on top of door lintels and window ledges, it smothered light shades and filled corners, it lay like a carpet under worktables. It too had rested on the sabbath but now stirred. At the least movement particles lifted lazily and hovered, only to settle once more. As girls found their seats their skirts disturbed the accretions; fibres floated aloft in shafts of light then fell softly, visibly, on to the nearest surface. Nobody took the slightest notice.

The place smelled dirty, and smoky, for ventilation was not regarded as paramount. Of course the place would be a death trap in the event of fire, but nobody bothered much about such things either: risk was a fact of life and unavoidable. All the men smoked anyway though they were expected to be careful. So did a few of the girls as they bent in concentration over their black Singers, but had any cinders damaged their work they would have been charged for it. It was true that one prized older female employee, a foul-mouthed virago whose piece-rate wages were nearly a man's, had a cigarette permanently stuck to a lower lip as her hands guided collars under the whizzing needle, but she was regarded as generally odd and not for imitation.

Daniel was directed to a small ill-lit room with two workbenches, one on either side. Several apprentices were at work under the supervision of a thick-set man in a brown overall. Daniel knew him slightly.

'Mornin'. I'm Solly Goldsmith. You must be young Majinsky? Know your father. Bit tall for this job, aren'tcha?'

To tailor meant bending over: tall men were prone to bad backs. But then, so were coal miners. Daniel shook his head. At least he would see daylight. 'I'll make sure I don't grow any more, Mr Goldsmith.'

He was shown where to stow his tuck, cap and jacket and handed a blue overall. Its cost would be deducted from his first week's wages. It was not new and smelled strongly of the last man to wear it.

'Sign here for the locker. Then there's no argument if you go into somebody else's.'

Daniel took the pencil and bent to sign his name. As he did so the manager chortled.

'Cack-handed, are we? Ho, we'll have some fun with you, my lad.'

Goldsmith called to one of the other boys, who had been eyeing Daniel with curiosity while still bent studiously to their work. 'Benson! Bring your shears.'

The powerful steel shears were black on the outside but white and silvery on the cutting edges and must have weighed several pounds. The handle was deeply curved and shaped. Goldsmith took the closed blades in his fingers and pointed the fingerholds to Daniel. 'Go on, take them.'

A small crowd gathered. The manager's tone had promised amusement and he expected an audience. Automatically Daniel reached out his hand – his left hand. The finger holds would not fit though he twisted his wrist and tried different poses. The shears were made for a right-handed person. The apprentices suppressed giggles and nudged each other. Awkwardly, with a growing sense of panic, he tried the other hand. The holds fitted, but when he tried to make the blades open and close he could not do it. His brain began to scream, as always when people tried to make him do things right-handedly.

'Now then! You'll have to learn, lad. And there's only one way. Come here.'

The manager had a length of thick string in his hands and a gleeful smile on his face. He twisted the cord around Daniel's left wrist and bent his arm behind him. The string was then tied around the thin body several times until the left hand was immobilised behind his back. Then Mr Goldsmith stood back, checked the tightness, and held out the shears once more.

'We use the right hand. Only the right hand. You'll have the other tied back till you've learned. If it takes days or months. It's for your own good, if you want to be a cutter.'

It was all Daniel could do to stop himself crying out. The bonds bit into his wrist and he could feel his hand going numb. Gingerly he eased then clenched his fist tight. Part of the pain transferred itself to his chest and he found himself breathing hard through his open mouth like a frightened horse. The other boys pointed and whispered. With a huge effort he bit his lip, squared his shoulders and looked the manager in the eye. He held out his right hand awkwardly for the shears.

'I'm ready, Mr Goldsmith.'

It took three months before the restraint could be removed. His left wrist hurt the whole time where the string had cut even after its release, as if the limb feared amputation entirely. Three months in which he felt his world turn upside down: in which his very nature was derided and he himself became an object of ridicule. The cruelty of forcing him into an unnatural mould was not lost on Daniel. Once he asked why, when steel could be fashioned in Sheffield into any shape, nobody made left-handed shears; but the question was regarded as hilarious, and as evidence that he was still a child underneath the gangling exterior. He heard many times the statement 'Because that's how things are' usually accompanied with a shrug, and came to associate it with the dumb acceptance of beasts of burden. Rules were arbitrary but had to be obeyed. Life was hard and grinding but with luck could be endured, even enjoyed. The petty irritations of the factory should be reduced to just that and not allowed to intrude into the real world of family, friend-ships and leisure time, not least because such time was so limited. Had Daniel taken his troubles home he would have cast a pall on the whole Majinsky household which nobody deserved: sympathy would have been in short supply. It was hard luck that he was different, but that was that.

The pain did not recede. The ache in his chest, which had begun as he had breathed in too fast the instant the ties were tightened, stayed with him. It resurfaced at night when he relived in dreams the horror of that moment, and later as he began to walk out with friends in the evenings. He would come home a little early and tired more easily than his companions, though he never complained. It was accepted that he did not have quite the stamina of his older brother but the slight weak-ness was put down to growing pains. His mother gave him anxious looks from time to time as he grew but did not fill out. He kept to him-self the nagging pain and told no one.

One day at the factory, not long after his apprenticeship was com-pleted, he began to cough. It had happened before and was nothing new; in that thick atmosphere, everybody coughed. He placed the shears on the workbench and pulled out a large handkerchief.

In a moment the handkerchief was covered in bright red blood. At the sight, and with a weary sense of exhaustion, Daniel closed his eyes and collapsed. When he had revived somewhat it was found he could no longer walk. He was carried home on an old door to his mother.

Thomas Leadenthall jammed his Homburg firmly on his head, heaved his flannelled bulk from the upper level of the tram, clutched the black Gladstone bag in one hand and puffed his way clumsily down the steep curve of the stairs. His demeanour was grim and resentful at the indignity of public transport. Were his talents properly recognised, were he more appropriately remunerated, he could come and go by hansom cab.

On the pavement as the tram clanked away he took his bearings. Although this quarter of the city was familiar, its rabbit warren of streets was a confusion. An urchin plucked his sleeve, its grubby face upturned hopefully.

'Got a penny, mister?'

Leadenthall looked down magisterially. 'I might have, young man. But in return you must tell me where I might find Grenville Street.'

The boy screwed up one eye. 'Why d'ya want to know? Somebody important live there?'

'Of course someone lives there. And that's why I want to know.' He glanced with distaste at the child who was wiping a greenly snotted nose on a sleeve. He tried to guess its age. From the diminutive size, barely four foot four, it could be six or seven years old. But that wizened pinched face and sharp manner suggested otherwise. More like twelve or thirteen. The product of dreadful diet and poor parental habits, no doubt. Far too many like that around here.

Thomas Leadenthall pulled out a handful of change and selected a shiny copper penny. 'Tell me straight, young man, and it's yours.'

For answer the child pointed towards a jumble of houses, their blackened walls overshadowed by the gritty outpourings of a thousand chimneys. In the still air the smoke hung acrid and immovable. 'By the baths in Cornwallis Street,' it mumbled, then grabbed the penny and ran.

The streets were full of such urchins. They crouched in the gutter and played marbles, the brilliant blues and fiery reds aglow in the hazy sunlight. They sat on broken walls and swung their bare legs and scarred knees at him. Little girls in torn dresses and overlarge hand-me-down shoes pushed rackety toy prams and crooned to dolls. As Leadenthall passed they stopped their play to observe him, at once curious, indifferent and hostile. Some called to mothers who came to doorways, their hands sudsy from washing, and watched with suspicious eyes. One or two recognised him and turned away. A Catholic mother crossed herself and hurried her children inside.

He found the address he wanted, knocked on the door and waited.

On the door jamb was nailed the tiny metal capsule the Jewish people called the *mezzuzah*, which one of his patients had informed him contained religious scriptures and was supposed to protect the household from harm. Nothing else distinguished this terraced house from its neighbours, except that the curtains of the front bay window were tightly drawn. The doorstep had been scrubbed recently and an effort made to remove grime from the window ledges, but in this area that was a thankless job. From inside came voices and a door slammed. He knocked again.

The front door creaked open. On the threshold stood a small, thick-set woman.

'You're not taking him to no sanatorium.'

Thomas Leadenthall was accustomed to such a greeting on doorsteps but still it made him sigh.

'If I let you take him away, he won't ever come back.' The woman folded her arms obstinately over a substantial bosom. She filled the narrow doorway as if she would physically prevent his entry. He had the right, since the disease was notifiable, but co-operation was sought wherever possible. He took a deep breath and removed his hat. A red weal from its brim and beads of sweat marked his brow.

'Madam, my name is Tom Leadenthall. *Doctor* Leadenthall. I am employed by the Corporation of this city under its distinguished Medical Officer of Health. Now do you want us to conduct the rest of this discourse on the pavement, or may I enter and examine the patient?'

The woman grunted and hesitated. On the opposite side of the street a small crowd of children had gathered. Under their unbending gaze, still unwilling, she gave way and stepped back. As the two trudged into the gloom towards the back of the house, she wiped her hands on her apron as if absolving herself of responsibility.

He was not shown into the parlour. That, he guessed, was where the invalid might be. Instead it was the kitchen with its black-leaded range emitting excessive heat, the kettle pushed to one side. A wooden rack near the ceiling held damp under-garments and sheets. Through the open back door he could glimpse a tiny yard strewn with old wheels, a mangle and tub, a couple of empty tea chests, a broken hutch. He put the Homburg and his black doctor's bag down on the kitchen table with a slight thump, as if to grant himself greater authority.

It was his task to try to overcome her fears. Consumptives had little chance in conditions like these. Those great open air hospitals in their own parkland, developed in the years before and after the war, had done untold good. Based on Swiss and German ideas they practised the virtues of healthy outdoor living, a strictly disciplined regime, plain food, abstinence from strong drink and the rigour of hard work, at least for those patients well enough to undertake it. Beds were strung out on verandas in all weathers. It was reasoned that if the lungs were diseased the more fresh air that could be forced into them the better. And since it was widely known that foetid overheated rooms and smoky atmospheres, not to speak of the ale-house and staying up late at dances – in other words, ignorance – were among the causes of the higher incidence of the disease among the labouring classes than the gentility, the doctors were clearly right. To persuade the indigent to accept their superiors' knowledge and advice had however proved an insurmountable problem, especially in the slums of Liverpool.

'It is my duty to urge you to reconsider this question of Fazakerley—' he began again, but she cut him short with a snort.

'You tell me then, doctor. How many patients leave there alive? If you've got nothing infectious when you arrive, you have for certain within a week. And more's the point, how many last five minutes after they've come home? Many's the one I've seen sent back here a wraith, supposedly discharged "cured" because it improves your damn-fool statistics. Well: they ain't cured. Helps you get more money from charity women, them rich ladies as likes to do good for the rest of us.'

She made as if to spit, then caught the look of alarm in his face and stopped herself. The two glared at each other with equal belligerence. Leadenthall could have answered that three-quarters of all sanatorium patients died within five years of discharge, and that her criticisms were increasingly being voiced by public health specialists including his own boss. Those who were claimed as cures, particularly the younger ones, were more likely to have been the victims of malnutrition. To have given her that satisfaction, however, was neither in his brief nor his character. Nor did he have much else to offer.

'I will not dispute with you, madam. I can see your mind is set. The young patient can be cared for under the auspices of the Netherfield Road clinic, which I believe is the nearest. Not as good as the sanatorium, but . . .' The mother turned from him and he shrugged.

He was ushered at last into the front parlour. Its drawn curtains made the room dark, while the spluttering coal fire rendered it airless and stiflingly hot. A narrow bed filled most of the space; the normal furniture of the room, a large sofa and an armchair, had been pushed to one corner and covered in an old rug. A small table by the bed held a bottle of lemonade and a glass, a packet of Woodbines and an ashtray in which a cigarette burned. A fusty smell came from the bed, in which lay the fragile shape of Daniel.

Dr Leadenthall motioned at the curtain. 'Mother, I cannot see to examine him. Would you please allow us a chink of light?' His voice was suddenly gentle as he removed his jacket and placed it over an armchair.

For several minutes the doctor concentrated and made notes. Deftly he wielded his stethoscope like a talisman, listened to the noises in the thin chest, examined the tongue, palpated, checked the shallow pulse. For a quiet moment he placed his cool hand on the sweaty brow and held the boy steady, as if his own goodwill might enter and purge the contagion, or at least sustain the youth. Then from his bag he pulled out a small glass bottle and from a selection found a wide cork that fitted. 'For the sputum,' he said, and handed the bottle to the woman. He rose.

'If it isn't TB, Mother, I shall be surprised,' he murmured. 'The tests on what he brings up will tell us for sure.'

The mother clutched the bottle and bridled again. 'There's no bad blood in our family,' she protested. 'It could be something else.'

'There is nothing whatever wrong with your family, madam. We have known for nearly half a century that the disease is caused by the tubercle bacillus. That idea of inheritance, of bad blood, is nought but foolish superstition. No stigma should be attached to this infection, for that is what it is, and you should permit none to attach to your son. Nor to any member of this household.'

She pursed her lips. 'Well, then, tell me what I have to do.'

'First, he must have light and air. As much fresh air as you can get into him. Simple hot food, eggs and butter, Ovaltine before he sleeps. Make sure you only buy TT tested milk – none of your cheap milk-cart rubbish. Plenty of fluids – your Jewish chicken soup is as fine a remedy as can be devised. There is disagreement as to whether consumptives should be kept warm or not, but I prefer it – stone hot water bottles rather than stuffy rooms, if you please. And clean, simple surroundings: all this stuff harbours dust and dirt –' at her glare he added hastily, '– though I can tell you are very house-proud. Look, I'll show you.'

He always enjoyed this part of the consultation, the expression of surprise and horror on the faces of relatives who preferred to hide what they believed was their familial shame. He rose, his bulk filling the crowded room, approached the window, flung the curtains open wide and wrenched open the upper frame, pushing it out as far as it would go on its hinges. A blast of cool air entered and the patient began to expectorate.

'Good! Excellent! That's what we want. Get it up, but don't share it with anybody – that's how the contagion is spread.'

The doctor began to whirl round the room like a dervish, thumping furniture as he went. Clouds of dust danced after him in the sunbeams. 'Get rid of this dreadful stuff – take it out at once. And take up the car-pets. Bare floors, Mother, scrubbed every day. The bacillus likes to lurk and will reinfect whenever it can. Ah, that's better!'

In demonstration he stood in the bay window and sucked in lungfuls of murky air. He found himself observed by a dozen astonished children who had crossed the road and had their noses pressed to the lower pane. Impatiently he waved them away; they did not budge, but murmured to one other.

'Can he smoke or not? He likes his cigarettes.'

'Oh, yes, no problem there. Helps clear the lungs. Good for him. And cod liver oil, every morning. But no alcohol. Drink is one of the root causes.'

He rummaged in his bag, took out a notepad and began to write busily. 'You will present yourself with this and the sputum sample this afternoon to the clinic, where you will be issued with medicine. A tea-spoon three times a day to begin. If it does not agree with the patient, continue but reduce the dose. It can cause a rash and sickness, but it is efficacious, I assure you.'

'What'll it cost? And what do we owe you?' The woman stood upright and proud. A gust of wind slammed the kitchen door shut. The boy in the bed gagged at the noise and began to moan softly.

'Madam, my services come free. The government says we should charge, but opinion in this city as in Manchester and Birmingham is that to attempt to recover charges from such as yourself would deter . . .' The bitterness on her face at such condescension halted him. He was at heart a kindly man, or he would not have sacrificed a promising med-ical career, in which he might have had rooms in Rodney Street and tended women in furs for substantial fees, for this dreary employment.

Hurriedly he continued, 'We are obliged to make a charge for the medicine as it contains gold. That seems to be the best treatment at pre-sent. It will cost twelve shillings a bottle.'

The woman gasped and staggered. 'His insurance benefit comes to fifteen shillings a week and we've lost his wages,' she muttered. 'And after three months off sick it'll go down to half that.'

'At least he was an insured worker when he contracted the condition, or he'd get nothing – or have to go to the Poor Law Guardians. There is that consolation. And if you take care of him as I've instructed he has every chance. Now: any more questions?'

She shook her head, and with an effort at politeness showed him first to the kitchen where he washed his hands then to the front door. 'Thank you, doctor.' It was the first time she had called him that. 'I don't know how we'll manage, but we will. My son will recover. I swear to God Almighty.' She touched the *mezzuzah* on the door jamb lightly with her fingertips then raised her fingers to her lips, as if to seal a bond.

The doctor was halfway down the street and surrounded by a chirruping crowd of awed children before he realised he had forgotten his hat. He turned back and found the woman on the doorstep, the Homburg in her hand. With her forearm she brushed the battered felt respectfully, and without a word she handed it to him. Her face, he noted, was wet with tears.

Mrs Majinsky was as good as her word. By dusk the sickroom had been emptied of unnecessary furnishings including the carpets. The floor was scrubbed with vicious energy. A smell of carbolic pervaded the room briefly until dissipated by the breeze wafted in from the window, by now propped open with a stick. Security was not a consideration: nobody would be leaving this house for months and anyway there was nothing whatever to steal.

The father came and went silently. In the synagogue he lingered and brokenly mouthed prayers. As the weeks passed with little apparent change but no worsening, the old man became more bowed and silent. It was as if he had offered his own life and vitality for his son's as Abraham once did for Isaac, and the offer had been accepted.

The smell of cooking pervaded the house as marrow bones were scrounged for soups and stews, as nourishing as could be afforded. Whereas in normal times such tantalising odours would have attracted those even poorer than themselves, particularly from other nearby Jewish families who would then be invited in to share, now nobody appeared except those overcome by morbid curiosity who stayed but briefly and would not enter the parlour. This TB thing was infectious. That was why patients were taken away and isolated. Hadn't it once been compared to leprosy, and didn't it carry the same terrible fears?

Izzy his brother considered staying with friends for the duration but nobody would have him. Who was to say that he wasn't infected too, or a carrier? So he trudged off to work and at night read his brother the paper borrowed from a workmate. Money became a matter of silent desperation. Every penny was needed to sustain the cost of the illness. Nothing could be spared.

It was three months later, and high summer, before Daniel was well enough to sit up in bed and gaze out of the window. His breathing was still stertorous and painful but his lungs seemed somehow more elastic and easy. The doctor had said the lesions might heal with the right attention. The medicine had made him repeatedly nauseous and his sisters had muttered about the folly of swallowing metals, but he had persevered and was convinced that it had helped. In his estimation the taste of cod liver oil was worse, especially a whole tablespoon of it forced down his throat every morning by his mother. If he recovered he would never touch the stuff again as long as he lived.

One bright day he sat out on the pavement on a chair, bundled up in blankets, his face turned gratefully to the sun. The effort of having tottered even a few steps from his bed had exhausted him, but he slept soundly during the night and did not cough. From then onwards he sat out every day unless it rained, and spoke haltingly to passers-by. As neighbours could see he was on the mend, more came shyly forward to help. The spectre of death began to recede. The burdens on his mother eased.

It was early autumn when the after-care ladies came. This time it was a hansom cab which drew up at the end of the street. The cabby pointed to the house and to the figure seated on the step, a blanket around its knees, reading a book. Two ladies emerged: a middle-aged woman in old-fashioned black moiré silk who descended, adjusted her large feathered hat, and brought the veil down over her prominent nose. Black gloves, a beaded bag and a parasol completed her ensemble. She was accompanied by a younger girl in a shorter and more modern dress with a cloche hat pulled well down over her ears and a bored expression. The senior lady told the cabby to wait and began to walk the short distance, picking up her skirts against the dusty street.

The women stopped in front of Daniel. Clearly he was expected to stand up, but though he was by now perfectly capable of the walk to the corner shop he decided to stay put. He turned his book over on his lap, his finger inside the page.

'Good morning!' the older woman boomed. 'And would you be –' she consulted a note '– Mr Daniel Majinsky?'

He nodded curtly. He had a notion he knew what was coming.

'Splendid. My name is Ivy Titchfield – the Marchioness of Titchfield. I am from the National Association for the Prevention of Tuberculosis.'

The patient appeared uninterested and certainly not impressed. Lady Titchfield sniffed and glanced at her companion who pulled a face. She ploughed on: 'The NAPT is considering making a grant – a substantial grant – to the after-care committee of the city of Liverpool, as you have here one of the highest incidences of tuberculosis in the country. Quite dreadful.'

At 'quite', which she pronounced 'kwait', she shook her head solemnly. Daniel remained immobile.

'So I resolved that I must come and see for myself. I have brought my assistant, Miss Arabella Simpson.'

Daniel allowed his eyes to roam briefly over the young woman's fashionable fringed dress, her silk hose, the white kid shoes. She had thick knees; not far above them as the fabric of her frock moved he could detect the nubs of her suspenders. Her strong sweet perfume hovered about her like an expensive aura. The grander lady smelled of violets and wore too much jewellery.

Street children had gathered at the corner and peeped round. A mangy dog trotted cautiously over from the far side of the street and sniffed from a few steps away. At home Miss Arabella probably had a pet dog, a pampered mite fed from her own plate. She looked like a dog's dinner herself. The mongrel came closer.

Lady Titchfield pulled out a notebook. 'So tell me: what after-care do you get, and what do you need?'

From within the house came the crash of pans. His mother must have seen the visitors and chosen to ignore them. Daniel, however, decided to explore a little: it could do no harm and for his mother's sake, might do some good. 'My mother looks after me. The main problem is that money is short. When I was in work I earned two pounds fifty in a good week, and—'

Lady Titchfield tittered. 'Oh, we do not permit hand-outs of money, you know. It is important that the patient should be taught that, although the disease has left him with a perhaps permanently damaged life requiring constant care, self-denial and watchfulness on his part, it is still his duty to seize every opportunity of becoming a useful and self-supporting member of society. It follows that a Care Committee should restrict actual giving of financial assistance as much as possible.'

She smiled benignly. Daniel choked and raised a handkerchief to his lips, but the sputum was clear as it had been for weeks. He shaded his eyes awkwardly and avoided looking the woman directly in the eye. 'I'm well cared for, thank you. If you can't give money, what can you give?'

'All life's little necessities,' the lady answered gaily. She waved her arms expressively and gazed around for inspiration. 'The aim is to avoid as far as possible anything which will undermine your self-reliance. The intention is to help you help yourself, rather than to continue your dependence on others. Now: do you have a job to return to?'

'I hope so.' One visitor had come from Berman's. When fully fit Daniel could expect to go back, unless trade turned bad.

'And will you need anything in particular – tools for example?'

Daniel shook his head. His own new right-handed shears with his initials stamped on the handle were wrapped in an oilcloth in the kitchen cupboard. He observed from the corner of his eye the mongrel which, unnoticed, had sidled close behind Arabella and was taking an interest in her shoes.

A sly thought occurred to him. In his enforced idleness he had found himself devouring whatever free reading matter he could lay hands on. *The Ragged Trousered Philanthropists* had greatly appealed and he could now quote much of it by heart. He was up to 'P' in the cherished second-hand copies of the *Home University Library* purchased in happier times. Daniel had also heard and read a great deal about the charitable ladies of the NAPT led by their renowned Scottish chairman Sir Robert Philip. Their lunches and dinners were famed, including one grand event in the Mansion House in London which had raised the staggering sum of £17,000 in a single night. He would not want them to leave disappointed.

'One suggestion – I don't know whether it would be possible.'

The two women smiled contentedly. The Marchioness paused, pencil in hand and nodded encouragement.

'When I get back to work, I'm not supposed to travel on buses and that. But it's a bit far to walk, to begin with. Also I should get exercise, the doctor says. So a new bicycle –?'

The ladies crowed and danced with delight. A bicycle! The very thing. Lady Titchfield composed herself and spoke sternly.

'I can promise nothing, Mr Majinsky, but I will put it to the Committee. It seems like a very good idea to me. Not a new one, of course, but—'

Then a yowl of rage came from Arabella, who to that point had said not a word. She squealed and raised her left leg and shook it, then stared in horror at the dark wet stain now soiling her stocking and shoe. The smell of urine mingled with her scent. A poorly aimed kick missed the dog, which ran off barking joyously.

Down the street children whooped and screamed as they scampered after the dog. Miss Arabella uttered a word Daniel had never heard on the lips of a woman before, which brought a sharp reprimand from the Marchioness. Daniel covered his mouth with his hand and endeavoured to keep a straight face. Arabella pulled out a handkerchief from her reticule and scrubbed ineffectually at her ankle, then burst into tears and stalked off in the direction of the cab.

He should have offered help: he should have shouted inside to find a towel and a bowl of water. But the towel would have to be thrown away afterwards and the bowl no longer used for food, all of which would incur expense which could not be afforded. Had the women been genuinely kind, it might have been worthwhile. He did not budge, and did not call his mother.

'I am sorry, ma'am,' was all he could manage. Then: 'Thank you for coming. I know you mean well. You'd better get after the young lady.'

'A bicycle . . .' the Marchioness muttered. She dropped her pencil, recovered it, hesitated, looked around anxiously for the dog, then pulled herself together. Soldier on!

With a curt farewell off she swept, head held high, ostrich feathers bouncing regally, and climbed into the cab which disappeared rapidly.

That night Daniel slept uneasily and dreamed of his return to the workbench, which after a spell of convalescence by the seaside could not long be postponed. When he awoke, the pain in his chest had vanished for good.

Instead his right shoulder felt cramped and uncomfortable, though there was nothing obviously wrong. His wrist, his left wrist, the source of all his trouble, flexed with ease. No rubbing would make the phantom ache disappear. He knew then it would always be with him.

PART TWO

Chapter Six

Dance Time

It was freezing. Goddamn England.

Sergeant Andy J. Newman trudged along, his bullet-shaped head bowed against the sleet, high-laced leather boots slipping on drifts of wet snow. He could feel his uniform grow heavier as flakes on it melted and wished he had remembered his waterproof. Out in the field white hillocks had formed, their surface ruffled by the wind. Aircraft in forlorn clumps dotted the desolate turf. He peered into the gloom but their outlines were increasingly sketchy. There would be no flying today.

He reached the shelter of the mail hut and stood for a moment in its doorway. Drips fell from the snow on his cap.

No place for a Texas boy. He'd love it, he had been told; he'd find England eye-poppingly green. The moist climate'd be a relief after the aridity to which he was accustomed. But they didn't know the desert. At home the air was dry, so high temperatures were not oppressive. Wherever he cast his eyes the horizon shimmered and beckoned. In the badlands you could ride a horse and camp for days without coming across any other sign of life except a few coneys or a sly fox but at night the air was alive. A man could find himself, there, and know what he was. A man could speak to his God without having to reach for a mackintosh.

Wet was worst. Hell on earth had been a teenage vacation to an aunt's in Florida where the humidity had made his lungs seize up, the stifling heat had given him hives, bugs had made a meal of every square inch of exposed flesh. Excursions had brought further horrors. The beach was evacuated in short order when sharks appeared in the surf. A boat ride in the Everglades had been abandoned after he fell in. His aunt's screams about crocodiles had been as nothing compared to the agony of the doctor's efforts to remove a leech which had lodged itself in his crotch. Even today he shuddered at the memory.

Maybe he simply didn't like leaving home. So? As one of Uncle Sam's conscripts he had little choice. It'd have been different were he likely to see some action. The British military had an advertising slogan: 'Join the army and see the world.' Americans joked that the Limeys should add an imperial polish: 'See lots of interesting and exciting people, and shoot 'em.' Instead he was stuck with five square miles and two million square feet of storage at Burtonwood USAF base on the wind-swept treeless plain of south Lancashire, one of the most god-forsaken holes on earth. And one of the chilliest.

The bad weather would mean that indoor entertainment would be required to keep the men happy. That was his job. The camp was not big enough to qualify for a full ranking officer to organise events, but Andy had seen his chance. Whoever it was that tried the latest movies first and checked out nearby clubs and strip joints gained both status and opportunity. He had grabbed at both with alacrity and volunteered his help. The downside was the work involved. Tonight it'd have to be a film – possibly the new one, *Hud*, with Paul Newman, or *South Pacific* yet again so they could wolf-whistle Mitzi Gaynor washing her hair – *There is nuttin' like a DA-AAAME* – and maybe five-a-side basketball. Inactive days like these were bad news.

He wished he'd been drafted some years earlier. Camp legend told that during the Berlin airlift crisis, Burtonwood had been a hive of activity with planes screaming overhead, landing and being refuelled; every man jack worked round the clock in a fuzz of exhaustion. Nobody needed artificial fun laid on then. As for the real alert, when Kennedy was nose to nose with the Soviets over Cuba: that stomach-churning terror was brought home whenever a red-lined memo turned up at the bottom of a forgotten tray, its capitals spelling out laconic instructions in case of nuclear war. He was glad to have missed that.

He pushed open the door and entered. As he shook feathery flakes from his arms and shoulders and stamped his feet the mail orderly handed him several items and packages. Two airmails, one from that auntie in Florida, no doubt pestering him to return, one from his mother. Nothing from his girl in Galveston. It'd serve her right if he found a replacement. Rumour had it the Lancashire mill girls were keen, especially if plied with American nylons and tales of mythical acquaintances in Hollywood.

A radio played loudly in the background. Andy Newman prided himself on his knowledge of popular music; the base had its own station where he took his turn as disc-jockey. This was new. The harmonies were harsh but effective. He stopped.

'*Please please me, oh yeah,*
Like I please you –'

Guitar chords swept down the scale with an excited confidence. Andy whistled through his teeth.

'What the hell's that? What are you listening to?'

The mail man grinned. Shorty was a thirty-year-old regular from New Jersey. A tidy, squat man with his shiny scalp visible through the crew-cut, his close friendship with the landlady of a nearby pub was said to have influenced his decision to remain on this base.

'Radio Luxembourg. Pirate station. The Limeys ain't caught up with commercial radio yet.'

'No – I mean that music. Wow! Not heard anything like that before. It sounds like country and western from home but all mixed up with your nigra tunes, and then some.'

Shorty shrugged. 'Dunno. They're Brits. It's the new Number One here – the kids are going crazy about them. Stick around, they'll play it again in a couple of minutes. I'm getting sick of it.'

'You, me, oh yeah, like I please you –!'

'Christ,' Andy muttered. 'Powerful stuff. They don't believe in holding back, do they? Stiff upper lip, my arse.'

The orderly pointed. 'You got a local lady, now?'

Andy shook his head glumly. 'No. Though I'm considering the matter if Gloria don' write me soon. Next thing I know I'll get a Dear John letter from her. Why do you ask?'

'You've got one with a Liverpool postmark.'

Andy turned the letters over with surprise. He had been distracted by the blizzard and his worries about Gloria, then his attention had been diverted by that song. The envelope was small and blue and addressed in a neat hand to 'The officer in charge of Entertainments'. He reached for a paper-knife and slit it open.

'Hey! Listen to this. Could be my big chance. "Dear Sir, we are a Jewish youth club in the heart of Liverpool. We play great music and have discos on Saturday nights. We would like to extend a welcome to any young American airmen who would like to join us." "Young" is underlined, so that's you out, Shorty. And an address. It's signed "Jerry Feinstein aged nineteen".'

'Well now: ain't that nice. We could send a couple of guys this weekend.'

Andy considered. 'Plenty of nineteen-year-olds here. Place is lousy with 'em. Wouldn't do any harm to include a couple of older guys too, to keep them in order. I s'pose they'd have to be Jewish.'

Shorty never missed an occasion to pull the rank of experience. 'I remember a story told me by my Pa who served in Lincolnshire during the war. The Brits couldn't get their heads round the notion that we had mixed troops. One day an invite was delivered by a butler – real old broken specimen, my Pa said, every fit man had been called up. Lady Bountiful would like to welcome six servicemen to traditional Sunday lunch. And she'd scribbled on the bottom, "No Jews."'

Andy parked his backside on the table. 'What happened?'

'It was her bad luck that the troop leader was a Brooklyn boy with a sense of humour. Come the appointed day the lady heard the butler fall down with a thump: he had fainted on the doorstep. Outside stood six of the biggest Negroes you have ever seen, all in freshly pressed US uniform, very solemn. When she said that there must have been some mistake, the sergeant answered, "No Ma'am. Cap'n Cohen, he don't make no mistakes."'

Andy Newman snickered. The two men swapped further stories of muddled contacts with neighbours whose culture was a mystery. Andy concentrated and re-read the letter. 'Better get it right this time.' He groaned. 'Oh, mercy, does that mean I have to go through all the camp personnel records? How many men we got here – couple of thousand or more?'

For answer Shorty picked up another pile of mail and began to allocate it to the named cubby-holes behind him. 'They won't want more than half a dozen, at least to start. There's the two Cohen brothers, a Kahan who I know is Jewish because he gets letters from Tel Aviv, three Levys and a Levison. That'd do for starters, wouldn't it? I should try them.'

Helen found herself walking slowly against a sleety wind and huddled into the duffel coat. The sweater and skirt she had chosen for the evening gave little warmth. She was early for the session at Harold House, but since visitors were due the committee had to arrive an hour ahead. The cleaner had been requested to put in extra effort, but as a rule the woman spent more time chatting and smoking than at work. It would not do if the toilets were dirty or if the bar and dance area looked scruffy. If nobody else had swept the steps clear of snow she would do it herself. The new blood might make their club a regular venue. That'd be great. Or would it?

The youth club members, Helen realised, had precious little idea what to expect from their invitees and even less of what was desired in return. A bit of noise and colour, naturally. More money: it'd be terrific if the servicemen, who were not only paid but paid handsomely, started to splash out. Not that there was much to buy – crisps, peanuts, egg sandwiches and kosher hotdogs were the limits of the members' virtuosity in the kitchen. The maintenance of *kashrut*, particularly keeping milk for the coffee separate from the savaloys, drove everybody mental.

After hours, however? There was an unspoken hope that following the disco the GIs might invite club members to join them downtown in an exploration of more adult pursuits. Were she asked she would be tempted though it'd be wiser to refuse. It took no imagination though to picture Jerry Feinstein enthusiastically on the razzle. He'd lead the guys on (or try to) and boast loudly about it for days.

That was jumping ahead a bit and might not happen. How might the Americans behave in the club? Perhaps they'd come laden with bottles of unfamiliar yellow beer with German brand names, or even whisky. Given the rickety fridge it might be awkward if they demanded ice. They'd been warned Harold House had no licence but it was not against the law to bring your own alcohol though that was frowned on when younger children were present. The Saturday night dance however was not an event for thirteen-year-olds. Most present would be her own age or older. They certainly did not think of themselves as children and were used to sliding into bars and lying, wide-eyed and red-faced, about their ages as a sweet cider or lager and lime was ordered. The very choice of drinks betrayed the deceit. Not that anybody would challenge them, not the publican nor the police: provided no trouble ensued, no fist fights or glassings, everyone colluded contentedly.

The boys were bound to be an improvement on what was available. Boywise, that is. Helen sighed and her walk slowed. Not that there had been so many boys in her life to date. She wrinkled her nose and tried to remember the schoolboy in the Cavern. His tie flapped against his white shirt as he danced energetically with her. She could have her pick of blokes of that sort had she wanted. What was he called? Jack. Or Mack. Something like that – quite unmemorable. Just like him.

A point in his favour was that he came from Merchant Taylor's, a fine school out in Crosby to the north of the city where comfortable families had begun to drift. The fact that they were no longer Liverpool citizens was seen by them as an advantage: that also avoided payment of high Liverpool rates. The subject had come up in school when Meg's grandparents had moved there. They did not want to hand over their hard-earned money to be spent on riff-raff, Meg had explained with a toss of her head. When asked about loyalty to their home town such emigrés shrugged. The drain of brains and financial power which weakened what was left behind was not their concern.

The shift of population was not yet a flood but it made Helen instinctively uneasy. When she was a small girl the city's official population had been over 800,000. Now it was expected to fall to barely 600,000. So: 200,000 in twenty years or so was only 10,000 a year. There was probably nothing much to worry about.

Her father had told her that fears expressed post war had been exactly the opposite, of cities overflowing with people in the wake of the baby boom. With the enthusiastic concurrence of the local council, government policy encouraged removal to overspill towns in the countryside. To places like Kirkby with its ultra-modern high-rise flats, or Skelmersdale, the garden city of the future; the latest, Runcorn, had just been announced. Few voices were raised in opposition.

Helen enjoyed life in a big, vibrant city: she was an urban animal, she knew quite well. Yet if Liverpool's population continued to slide, might it cease to be like that? Was it possible that some day it'd stop being a great sea-port and turn instead into a clutch of decayed slums bedevilled by high unemployment and social problems, too far gone for the decline to be reversed? Surely that was unthinkable.

Her father had expressed his alarm. Cities die, he argued, and nobody notices soon enough to cry halt. His attitude was in part a reflection of his distrust of the municipal grandees whom he regarded as a bunch of idiots.

He had brandished the front page of the *Liverpool Echo* whose photographs showed aldermen, councillors and the Lord Mayor in velvet robe, feathered hat and chain of office at a foundation stone ceremony in Skelmersdale.

'What they don't realise, Helen, is that it's the best people who leave. Those who stay behind often are the worst. The dregs of humanity.'

She was shocked at his tone. 'Surely not. It's going to be hard to get one of those new houses, Dad. There'll be long waiting lists.'

'It'll be a question of who you know, then. The old pals act, as usual.'

'That's not fair, either. The point is, Dad, that you can't generalise about who will settle out of town. They'll all be council tenants for a start. That might increase the proportion still here of owner occupiers like ourselves. We might be seeing the back of the weaker families, not the stronger.'

He had chewed his moustache for a minute. Then he turned towards the end of the paper and with a triumphant shake found what he wanted. 'Look at the property ads. What's on sale for the likes of us? Crosby, Southport, even over the water in the Wirral. Beautiful new houses, all mod cons. Fitted kitchens included, for heaven's sake. Semis ideal for newlyweds, it says here, or detached houses for the family seeking a pleasant environment for their children. Excellent schools – big play made of that. I tell you, Helen, that if you and your brother were still little your mother and I would be on our way, Liverpool born and bred though we are.'

He waved a finger in the air. 'As for your council tenants: yes, the gullible ones will scramble off to the new towns. Then they'll find it's an hour's bus ride back to the bright lights on a Saturday night, and no decent alehouses or shops, and those that do open'll have to charge a fortune to make ends meet: no competition, see, and not enough customers. Soon people'll be clamouring to get back, mark my words. Those won't be happy communities. But families which choose to leave and lay out their *own* money will dig their new gardens and plant roses. Their kids'll blossom in those smart schools. Top results, no discipline problems. They won't return and neither will the next generation. Lost to us for good. Once that kind of change starts it's permanent.'

As she remembered her father's heated remarks Helen found she was debating with herself. This was exactly the sort of material which might appear on the General Studies paper with which Miss Plumb had threatened them. 'Are cities a thing of the past? Discuss.' But she was not in an examination room, not yet.

Harold House was time off. She could think about herself. She could think about boys, even if the drip from Merchant Taylor's who had started off this set of reflections was not to her taste.

Colette had accused her, though lightly, of setting her standards too high. Was that true? Up to a point. For choice she would have preferred a boy who could join in proper conversation of the kind she had just conducted with herself. That only occurred at school with her closest friends, or with her father. No boy on earth had she ever met with whom such a discussion was possible.

Maybe being at a single sex school had something to do with it. A few eccentric establishments had opted to be co-educational, but mostly it was feared that the constant presence of the opposite gender would be a distraction. Boys and girls behaved differently in scholastic terms. In mixed schools a powerful natural differentiation asserted itself. Girls leaned towards the arts, and boys more to maths and science: nobody knew quite why. As a girl scientist Helen didn't feel herself that she would have been put off had boys been around – indeed she'd have bridled at any suggestion that only boys could manage chemistry and would have worked the harder to prove them wrong. But it undeniably affected girls *en masse*, while the boys seemed to feel that a passion for Jane Austen or poetry was cissy. So separate was better: both sides could make clearer choices.

Boys and girls in the same classroom at the same age didn't gell. That was a well-known and an uncomfortable truth. The girls were more mature – physically, intellectually. A fourteen-year-old female was nearly a woman, with a woman's secrets and hopes and fears. Give her *Romeo and Juliet* and she would weep; give it to a fourteen-year-old boy and he would giggle, if he understood the emotions at all.

It had to be admitted, nevertheless, that this separation turned *all* boys into sex objects. Their daily absence paradoxically made the girls much more excited about them, and probably had an identical effect on the boys. Maybe that explained why it was impossible to discuss anything intellectual such as politics with a member of the opposite sex: the whole time she was sizing him up as a possible partner, and he was almost certainly doing the same to her. It made simple friendship unattainable.

It'd have been better had she had brothers. Barry didn't count, partly because he was so young. But he didn't seem to care about anything important. You could grab his interest with a remark about football but he could never in a million years have held his own on, say, the prospects of a General Election. Had the topic come up he'd have slunk out of the room and regarded it as a signal to vanish upstairs and turn on his record player. The really depressing fact, Helen reflected glumly, was that most of the young males she knew were similar, with the addition, which doubtless Barry would acquire before long, of a unwholesome if furtive obsession with sex.

Sex. She would have argued with Colette that she wanted a boy to be serious, and a friend, and had found nobody who came within a mile of either. But Colette might have countered that she was ignoring the sex angle – no, Colette wouldn't. She didn't talk like that and kept her head down, literally, whenever the subject arose. Meg just looked angry as if the question of sex was an intrusion. Brenda was more forthright, maybe because she had older brothers who, though protective, would try to explain how boys *felt*. That they felt the same way as girls, often – anxious, eager, exposed – had come as a revelation to Brenda's circle though her accuracy and authority were undoubted. Both her mother and grandmother were sources of information as well. Helen envied her. No wonder Brenda faced the future with equanimity and cheerful optimism.

None of them had had sex, Helen was fairly certain. In that sense none of them knew what they were talking about. No one respectable did. No one.

It was wrong, for a start. Every religion said so: sex was for marriage and procreation. Catholics especially were taught to believe that these were its only purposes: the activity undertaken with any other aim – just for fun, perhaps, or out of passion or lust – could be mortal sin. Oh, people did it outside marriage, but most of them *were married* or had been, if to somebody else. You could read about what went on every Sunday in the *News of the World*. Dad had caught Barry engrossed in a copy and had hidden it thereafter but her father still bought it, for the sport, he claimed. Divorce cases involving adultery littered the pages, sometimes with spectacular and hilarious results, but always with the killer phrase, 'intercourse took place'. Intercourse: sex. But 'sex' was a word never used, not in the context of the act itself. It was too simple, too direct. Too stark.

The inhibition against sex was also a practical matter. To do it – to 'have intercourse' – needed several prerequisites not readily on tap for people her age. Somewhere private, for a start. Somewhere quiet, and warm. A bedroom at home, perhaps. But parents were everywhere, and horrible little brothers. And neighbours, who would spy and report.

And – precautions. My God, to get pregnant would ruin everything. It'd probably mean a speedy wedding to somebody you might quickly discover you couldn't stand – and then you'd be stuck: husband, baby and all.

Precautions were supposed to be a man's responsibility but Helen suspected that the boys she knew were as ignorant about sources and systems as she was. It was hard to see how a sixteen-year-old youth could lay hands on – whatever. A chemist would laugh at him and threaten to phone his mother. Gentlemen might ask their barbers for something for the weekend – at least, they did in *Carry on Doctor* and Ealing comedies. Everybody in the cinema fell about with laughter at such innuendoes but the adolescents in the audience were left frustrated and cross. Why wouldn't anybody help? Why wouldn't any adult tell them what to do, and how to avoid trouble? Why was the evident pleasure only obtainable by those in the know, and how on earth did you get to *be* in the know?

Once when rummaging in a wardrobe for an old cardigan of her mother's Helen had come across a cardboard box. Inside was a mass of red rubber tubes and a booklet in small print with diagrams. Perplexed, she had sat on the floor and started to read. Her mother had found her and bundled the box and its contents back into the cupboard with a sharp remonstrance, but Helen had grasped only scraps of what she had seen. It remained an enigma. The message was clear: pregnancy was an ever-present danger, not to be risked by those like herself who had other plans for their lives.

Her mother wouldn't talk about it. Whenever the subject came up she would purse her lips and look skyward. She gave the impression that those who indulged deliberately in sex had somehow abandoned their better selves. But some in the family knew – those American women relatives, for example. They could have been an invaluable source of information. But they were 3,000 miles away.

In reality nobody she had met so far had awoken in Helen any sensations other than boredom. And distaste. Pimples, mostly. So much acne on pale, thin cheeks. Dirty fingernails which scratched at the pustules and made them bleed. Brown stains on teeth and the stink of cigarettes on the breath. The thought of kissing that! Bloody marks on shirt collars from inefficient attempts at shaving. Dark patches of sweat under armpits. Broken cracked voices with no timbre or resonance. Greasy hair – why on earth did anyone wear that Brylcreem with its pungent perfume which she found so disgusting? Look at what made the Beatles so fantastic: they were clean, their hair shone. When they shook their heads the well-cut manes tossed like lissome rivers then settled back into shape across their brows. George Harrison had pimples, that was true. But Paul didn't. If any of the American visitors looked like Paul, she might be interested.

That had not occurred to her. The GIs might be more than well-off and intriguing strangers whom it was her job to entertain. They might be terrific to look at. If any of them resembled James Dean – she checked herself. That was unlikely. The invitation had made it quite clear that it was a Jewish club and only Jews would be welcome. Sal Mineo, then. He would do.

She quickened her pace, turned the corner to the clubhouse, opened the door and entered.

'Right. Are we ready? Nurse Wilkins, tidy that curtain, *if* you please.'

Sister folded her arms over her well-corseted bosom and frowned. The reputation of the male orthopaedic ward of Sefton General Hospital was at stake. Outside it was snowing yet again. Behind her the clock ticked loudly towards seven fifteen pm.

The long row of beds was neat, each bed precisely parallel to its neighbour. Sheets and blankets were turned down at right angles, corners folded at exactly forty-five degrees. Temperature charts and notes on metal clipboards hung vertical. Over-bed tables were carefully aligned. On them vases were placed ready for flowers – left in their wrappers they'd droop petals in a frightful mess. Sister was sure Florence Nightingale had never permitted flowers in *her* wards but she had been unable to ban them except at night.

Patients who were well enough sat up, watchful in pyjamas or dressing-gowns. Two insisted on reading their newspapers and ignoring her. She swept her gaze over each body. Every button was fastened: nothing lay loose or unattached. And *nothing* was exposed. What a pity about those three beds at the far end. Patients in traction with elevated limbs in plaster made the ward appear so untidy. Bother orthopaedics. If a transfer came up to a general medical ward, she swore she would apply for it.

Now to the nurses. Their tasks complete, they lined up, led by the qualified SRNs in crisp navy blue cotton dresses clinched at the waist by a broad belt with an elaborate silver clasp, the lower grade Enrolled Nurses in pale blue. At the end the two girls in training wore blue and white gingham. Firmly muscled legs were encased in seamed stockings and black laced shoes. No jewellery but wedding and engagement rings was allowed: each had a fob watch pinned upside down to her chest. On each head perched an alarming starched cap secured by several hairpins which owed more to the attire of medieval nuns than to the demands of modern medicine. Every face was supposed to be scrubbed clean but some had suspicious traces of lipstick. Sister sniffed.

'Nurse Thomas! What has happened to your cap? It looks as if it has been through the mangle.'

Nurse Thomas stayed rigid but her eyes glazed. Her accent was ripely scouse. 'Sorry, Sister. It has been through the mangle. It got mixed up with my uniform and my mother—'

'Enough. If it happens again you'll be fined. I cannot have Ward Six letting the profession down. And Staff Nurse, I know you are exceptionally busy but we are privileged, we *trained* nurses –' she glared at the probationers, who cringed on cue '– to wear the silver buckle at our belts. It behoves us to keep it polished. Gleaming, do you understand?'

'Yes, Sister.' It was all the staff nurse could do not to curtsy. Her glance wandered uncontrollably to the clock.

Sister turned on her heel. Outside the ward doors a murmur could be heard, but at her step it fell silent. The small crowd in snow-sodden coats and scarves fell back, bunches of flowers and brown paper bags of fruit secreted like contraband.

'Visiting time!' Sister announced as she opened the doors. 'Forty-five minutes only! All visitors will be asked to leave—'

But the determined jumble had swept past her. Soon most beds had acquired one or two huddled figures. The junior nurses gratefully slipped away for a cup of tea while Sister kept watch.

Nellie had decided to wear her fake fur. The journey on the moped had made her wetter than she had expected. In the warmth of the ward the soggy coat gave off an odd faint smell which added to her unease. She did not like hospitals and had never before visited anyone other than her mother and sister. It was even odder to see Mr Feinstein flat on his back in a bed. Despite the plaster cast up to his chin it did not seem quite respectable. For the first time she noticed the hairs on his forearms – long, fine and silky. She wanted to stroke them.

'Oh, Nellie. It is good to see you. A human face, for a change.'

Nellie grinned with more reassurance than she felt and was glad she had worn her boldest earrings. She kept hold of the bag of grapefruit she had brought. They seemed suddenly to have been a tactless gift and she wondered whether it would be too obvious if she took them back. She tugged off her gloves.

'You must have loads of visitors, Mr Feinstein. Lots of people in the shop asking after you. Mr Rotblatt, and . . .' She reeled off several names.

'Yes, but nobody likes coming to see an invalid. They're scared they'll catch something. My Jerry's only been once; the moment he saw a nurse carrying a full bedpan he turned green and skedaddled.' His voice was mournful. 'I'm stuck here another three weeks in concrete from my chin to my hips. Can't move. If I read I give myself a crick in the neck. If I listen to the radio that bloody pop music drives me mad – why can't we have *Rose Marie*? Nothing to think about but the shop. Nothing to do but worry.'

A strange ache overcame her which she could not resist; Nellie patted his hand then quickly withdrew her fingers.

'Shop's fine. No need to worry. I am managing, honestly.'

She was, too. Once she had realised that the proprietor would be out of action for at least a month then was unlikely to be able to lift heavy weights, Nellie had set about a clearance operation. With huge energy she had checked every box upstairs and down, inside and out and thrown out or sold off cheaply all the slowest lines. Those tinned kippers Mr Jacobs liked – but he'd died two years ago. The *matzos* from Poland which smelled musty. Jars of olives from before the war. A part case of oily Moscow vodka which had given rise to jokes about spies – disgusting stuff. And the peach brandy. From here onwards deliveries of perishables would be more frequent. As word got about over the bargains to be had, business had been very brisk. Feinstein's Famous Deli had had its best couple of weeks in years, and the fresher goods and brighter packages now making their way on to the shop shelves bode well to continue the trend.

'We're making money, Mr Feinstein,' she added and quoted him the totals.

Morrie Feinstein twisted his head as far as he could and gazed at her in surprise. She had a solid grasp of the business: he had always known that, but here she was, turning over far more than he had imagined the shop could produce. He questioned her gruffly and was delighted at her answers. She found herself reading his expression with pleasure, then saw his anxiety return.

'You're a great asset to the business, Nellie,' he began. 'You know I appreciate it. You are important to me too – it helps to know I have someone there I can trust.' She blushed and did not reply. Emboldened, Mr Feinstein warmed to his theme. 'If my Jerry was in charge I'd have reason to worry myself sick. As for our Jewish people, if I'd asked any of them to help out: to be honest I can think of one or two who'd have had their fingers in the till and I couldn't complain, could I? Have to be loyal to them, couldn't make a fuss.' He paused. 'So how many years have you worked for me, Nellie?'

'Too many,' she joked, then spotted an anxious flicker. He might infer from that a threat to leave or a demand for more money. 'I mean, ten years since you took over, and I was there before that. I've grown up in that shop, you might say.'

'We've grown old together, you mean.' He sighed deeply.

'Nonsense.' Nellie was brusque. 'Don't talk like that. You're not old. You're quite young – about my age, in fact.'

Feinstein turned his head and looked at her again, full in the face as far as he was able. Nellie felt herself colour and kept chatting. His eyes seemed to rest on her earrings. She touched them gaily. 'I bought these down the market. Thought they might cheer you up. D'you like them?'

Her boss appeared to be weighing her up. 'Yes,' he answered slowly. 'I hadn't noticed before, but you always brighten the place, Nellie. And I like that lipstick too—'

'*Well*! What have we here?'

Nellie sat up rigid. Her grip slackened and the concealed grapefruit escaped from the bag on her lap. The two yellow globes rolled away, one under the bed and the other towards Sister's desk. With a little cry

Nellie jumped up to retrieve them. By the time she returned, panting and confused, the chair had been taken by the beaver lamb-coated figure of Sylvia Bloom.

Sylvia smiled coldly at the shop assistant.

'You've just about finished, haven't you, Nellie? I should throw those away. The floor in here may be spotless, but . . .' The suggestion was left to float in the air that in the shop the fruit in Nellie's hands might have been returned to its display.

Mr Feinstein opened his mouth once then closed it. If a slight sigh came from his direction perhaps it was merely a movement of the sheet. Nellie dumped the unwanted grapefruit in the bin by the side of the bed, bade a curt good-bye and stalked off to the exit. Both sets of eyes followed her.

'Well!' Sylvia said again. The syllable conveyed an infinity of affront at the cheek of the woman and at Morrie Feinstein's foolish tolerance of it. Her meaning was not lost on the patient.

'Hello, Sylvia.'

He did not add, 'Nice of you to come.' Sylvia unfastened her coat and arranged its folds to show the moiré silk lining. She crossed her legs at the ankle. There was no time to lose.

'She has designs on you, that woman. I saw the way she was leaning over you. It's not right, Morrie.'

'Don't be silly,' he protested weakly. 'Nellie? She has a boyfriend – I think.' He realised he had no idea what Nellie did with her spare time. She had been married, of that he was fairly sure, but no name of a lover or spouse was ever bandied around. He had put that down to natural discretion, but now began to wonder.

'It's not right,' Sylvia repeated. 'And I'll say this, Morrie Feinstein. You'll be the gossip of the community if you let it continue. So I tell you what I'll do. Once you're out of here, I'll fix up a couple of dates for you – nice women of the faith. I'd have you myself but I don't think I'm your type.'

Her target winced at the thought. 'I've told you before already, I am not interested. Why don't you fix somebody up for –' he hunted for a name '– Simon Rotblatt? Wealthy man, on his own, lovely catch . . .'

'Too old. But I'll keep him in mind.' Sylvia itched to take out her little book and read out a few choice details. She glared down balefully, a mother quelling a difficult child. 'I will find the perfect match for you. That's my job. On the way you'll enjoy yourself. It's you I'm after, Maurice Feinstein: you'll be perfect for one of my selected lady clients. You're not going to escape.'

'*Comma liddle baby let's jump the broomstick*
Comma let's have a baa-a-all –'

With a proprietorial air Jerry gazed around the noisy room. It had to be admitted that the addition of the Americans was a great success. He wondered whether their style was exportable and if by observation he could learn anything. Nevertheless he felt slightly apprehensive, almost naked, before their magnificence. He wished he had a cigar to wave. That might impress Roseanne even if it had no effect on the USAF.

Was it their appearance, these clean-cut young men in their tailored pale blue, the flashes on their shoulders neatly sewn, their identical black boots hard and shiny, their crewcuts blunt and close like the stiff pile on a clothesbrush? And those accents, straight from the silver screen, enough to blow your mind, however courteously they spoke. It fair took your breath away.

'*Mamma don' like it – Papa don' like it –*'

Several airmen were on the dance floor gyrating happily with the bolder girls. Determined competition came from the better jivers amongst the club members. The floor had been crowded with whirling bodies for over half an hour. It was hot and the windows had steamed up. The joint, he had to say it, was jumping. Next to him the group leader, his sleeves adorned with three upside-down stripes, drank Coke politely and tapped his feet.

'You didn't have to wear uniform,' Jerry gestured, Coke in hand. It was like a conversation with John Wayne, he realised, or with Robert Mitchum in one of those war movies. A dream come true, almost. His heart beat faster than usual and not just to the rhythm of the music.

Senior Airman Caspar Cohen, known as 'CC', shrugged easily. 'First time, see. Regulations. If we come again we can wear what we like.' He was a mid-height, swarthy man from a Chassidic family. A black *yarmulkah* was carefully pinned to his stubby hair. For his taste the club was not nearly observant enough: two kitchens were necessary, not one.

Airman Buzz Cohen was his younger brother, a smaller more wiry version with a ready grin. There were ten children in all: their parents felt this was the surest way to increase the number of adherents of the Lubavicher Rebbe, Rabbi Menachem Mendel Schneurson of New York. Buzz's attitudes were a mite slacker than his brother's – for example he did not grieve for the loss of his *payers*, his side-locks, when he was drafted. Nor did the intensity of his religion stop him seeking out the most important item in short supply in the camp: female company.

Buzz had approached Roseanne, who was delighted to show off her laboriously acquired skills. Jerry wished he had the nerve to break in, but his role was to act as host. As he watched they joined hands and twirled expertly. He tried not to frown: he was too tall to do that movement with her.

'*Comma let's have a ball!*'

The record ended. Couples stood around, chests heaving, ready for
the next one. Jerry bit his lip. In Liverpool it was considered forward to
hold hands between dances unless you were going out together but
Buzz didn't seem to know and Roseanne apparently had forgotten. He
could feel his pride become tainted with jealousy but there was nothing
he could do. At last came a click. The clear voice of The Springfields
and the 'Island of Dreams' filled the ether.

'*Far, far away from the mad rushing crowd*
Please carry me with you –'

For several minutes CC had had his eye on one young woman in a
group as he and Jerry had chatted. Now he headed towards her. In an
instance the two were energetically prancing as if they had been an item
all their lives. Jerry, alone, puzzled furiously. Not every one of the newcomers was handsome. In fact only one or two were taller than himself:
in most surrounds the Cohen brothers would have made an unprepossessing pair. The fact that there were another half dozen Cohen siblings
at home, each one born a year or two after the other, all 'very alike'
according to CC, made Jerry think of a collection of Russian dolls in
descending sizes. The other GIs, not related though several shared sur-
names, were equally ordinary once their attributes were closely
analysed. Yet there was not a shred of doubt that the whole club was
bowled over, and not only the girls.

Jerry groaned in frustration. The sheer dominance of American culture
overwhelmed him. It gave no room to the home-grown kind. There was
Dusty Springfield, a stunner if ever he saw one, with her candy-floss
hairdo and black-rimmed eyes and that terrific voice: but to get anywhere solo she'd have to make cover versions of US songs and was
reported to be considering a move to California. Petula Clark was under
pressure to do the same. In the States the Limeys were adored – how else
could you explain the appeal of David Niven and Richard Burton, for
God's sake, the one a quintessential Brit, the other a smouldering
Welshman? Even Elizabeth Taylor was proud of her birth. Everyone
admired the British. They had won the war. So why didn't the British
admire themselves – why did they allow the Americans to take over?

'You do look solemn, Jerry.'

It was Helen Majinsky. Her pink sweater and full skirt drew attention to her slim figure. For a moment Jerry recalled that he was not
supposed to like Helen and had vowed to get even with her for her
rejection of him, but with Roseanne almost out of sight with Buzz on
the far side of the room, her company was welcome.

'They've taken over. I was trying to see how they do it.'

Helen laughed. 'Money. Glamour. Strangers. This is a sea-port. We aren't suspicious of strangers – we adore them. Open arms, you might say.'

Jerry's heart sank. The next record he had chosen was a slow number, ideal for a gentle smooch: Pat Boone's 'Love Letters in the Sand'. He felt certain Buzz and Roseanne would stay together for it. 'Let's dance,' he said, and before she could resist he put his left arm firmly round Helen's waist and swung her away.

'*On a day like today*
We'll pass the time away
Writing love letters in the sand –'

She was trim, a neater shape than Roseanne. The gentle resistance she put up when he tried to get closer excited him. He was glad he had splashed on some 'Old Spice' before he left home. He nuzzled into her neck and hoped Roseanne was paying attention. Helen kept her face turned away so he could not kiss her.

'*How my broken heart aches –*'

'Can't stand him,' Helen confessed.

'Who?' Jerry pulled back to stare at her.

'Pat Boone. Haven't we got the Beatles' record?'

'Oh, that. Yes, but we've played it twice already. The Americans will think we're barmy.'

'They'll think like us before long. The record's been issued in the States. Maybe if they enthuse about the Beatles when they go home it'll help make them famous.'

'What do you think of them? The Americans, I mean?'

Helen pondered. 'I've not talked to them really. They got whisked away by – the others.' She meant Roseanne, but did not say so to spare Jerry's sensitivities.

The ruse worked. As soon as was decent Roseanne marched across the room with an annoyed expression on her pert face. She stepped smartly between Jerry and Helen.

'Thanks for taking care of him for me. Jerry, my dance.'

Jerry gestured helplessly but left Helen alone. CC was at her elbow and shrugged politely. 'Lover's tiff, I'd say. I'd ask you myself but I gotta find the john. Why don't you try Mike over there? He's a bit shy, only posted last week. Go look after him for me.'

As she walked in the direction indicated Helen was buffeted by a triumphant Roseanne in a particularly flashy move. Cautiously she edged out of the way. Thus she did not examine the partner to whom she had in effect been allocated until she was right next to him.

'Hi, Mick, is it? I'm Helen.'

The flash on his uniform pocket announced *Michael R. Levison.*

'Hi, Helen. My name's Michael. I'm glad to meet you.'

She had to look up, startled. His voice was deep and came from far above her head. He must have been about twenty or so and was broad shouldered and regular featured, with a square jaw and well-defined almost aquiline nose which indicated that, unlike most of the boys she had met to date, he had almost finished growing. His skin was smooth, acne-free and he was smooth-shaven, with a slight uplift about the corners of his mouth. He smelled faintly of soap. CC had said he was shy, but he did not twitch or fidget, just stood there, quietly.

She took a small step back and scrutinised him more thoroughly. His neck was wide. He seemed to fill his shirt as if he carried muscle there, biceps and such, instead of the weedy teenage tendons and ribcage of a Jerry or Jack. His wristwatch was large with an expansible gold bracelet. The belt of his trousers was on a level with her ribcage; his shoulders were on a par with the top of her head. Yet he gave the impression not so much of being tall – though he was that, certainly – but of being *big.*

Not a schoolboy, not a pimply youth. No deadbeat, this one. Not like anything she had ever been as close to before.

Not a boy at all. A man.

She should answer lightly but the devil seemed to have grabbed her tongue. With an amused lop-sided smile he held out his hand to shake hers formally. She felt almost faint. This could not be real. Was it her fancy, or did he really take her hand in his own and look into her eyes? And was it for a little longer than was absolutely necessary? She swallowed hard. If so, she was not about to object.

'I think,' Michael said gravely, though his own eyes were lively, 'that we are supposed to dance. Will you do me the honour?'

Helen tried to get a grip, to shake herself out of her stupor. She could not speak, only nodded. She, so ready with easy talk as a rule, knew that if she opened her mouth she would make a complete fool of herself. The right approach was a light disdain but she dared not try anything of the sort. Playing hard to get would be *impossible.* But after the dance she would get him to sit down in the side room and talk. Where did he come from? What were his family like? Did he have a girl-friend? Suppose he was intelligent and – nice? It did not bear thinking about. If for a mere half an hour, provided she hung on to him, she might well be in the company of somebody quite extraordinary.

Together they took hands and swept out on to the dance floor to the next record.

'Sweet little sixteen –
She's just gotta have –'

Chapter Seven

Making Plans

Another Sunday afternoon. Still frozen outside: the snowy winter seemed set to last for ever. The garden looked forlorn under a grubby white blanket though the apple tree was struggling into bud. A coal fire burned smokily in the grate. Lunch had been cleared and her mother had waved Helen out of the kitchen. Barry had disappeared to a pal's.

She needed to talk. She still felt dazed after the encounter of the night before.

At the end of the evening to Jerry's chagrin the GIs had elected to return straight to Burtonwood. Those *en route* had been offered a lift and dropped off at their doors. The sheer luxury of personal transport had left the British youngsters thrilled and breathless. The GIs would return to the club provided they were not on duty. Michael had said he would make a point of it.

They had not kissed. Not on the first night – that would have been unseemly and excessive. As she climbed out of the back doors of the van he had squeezed her hand and said, 'See you soon.' That was all; he had not followed her nor insisted on a doorstep tryst, an omission for which she was grateful. As it was, she had had to explain repeatedly to her mother about the boys, the unheralded vehicle and the lift. She was glad it had vanished before Annie could start the ritual of inviting its occupants inside to check them and their credentials. It was enough that the boys were Jewish, she told her mother firmly. For herself she felt relieved that the first boy who had made a positive impact on her might meet with her family's approval.

Not a boy: Michael R. Levison. She had forgotten to ask what the 'R' stood for. He would have told her. He practised an easy old-fashioned courtesy which captivated her. In bed alone past midnight she had tried to repeat his style of speech, not only the slurred 'r' and the longer vowels but his manner, and was still murmuring as she drifted off to sleep. How lucky that she had been pushed in his direction – friendly as the other GIs were they didn't hold a candle to Michael. No doubt about it, he was the best of a fabulous bunch. In fact, so far, with as yet no evidence to the contrary, she had to admit it: he was *wonderful*.

After a couple of dances they had retired into a quieter room and sipped Coke. He told her briefly that he came from a military background. His older brother was a pilot stationed in West Germany. His father worked in Washington as an adviser of some kind – on that Michael had been vague. Helen had not known what further questions to ask or whether to do so would have been rude. Perhaps he did not know much about his father's job. Or perhaps it was secret. Then she rebuked herself: it was enough that he was terrific without inventing an enigmatic history.

Helen let her imagination wander downwards from his face. The smooth curves of his chest and shoulder muscles had been visible under the well-pressed shirt. Underneath he probably wore a tee shirt, regulation issue, again more close-fitting than most locals would dare: men and boys were not supposed to show off their figures in tight clothes but to hide undistinguished torsos under shapelessness. She wanted to touch that flesh, and flushed hotly as she thought about it.

But such a man would expect to be taken seriously, whether they saw each other regularly or not. Helen swallowed hard. She wanted to dally with visions of him taking her in those strong arms, but felt apprehensive. He would not mess about, such a man. He would expect her to keep up with him. He might rapidly get to the stage where he would not take 'no' for an answer.

She frowned. He was big enough to be a bit frightening, if she crossed him. With the gawky boys of her acquaintance Helen was sure she could take care of herself and felt reasonably street-wise – you had to be, in Liverpool. This stranger was an unknown quantity even with those impeccable antecedents. If she meant to go further with him she must keep her wits about her.

Meanwhile she had had to endure an extended Sunday mealtime during which her brother and parents began to plan the celebration of his thirteenth birthday in May. The whole subject irked her, wicked though she felt her reaction to be. She played no part in the discussion, just as she would have virtually no role in the event itself. It was assumed she'd attend alongside her mother in proud support of Barry and Daniel Majinsky, the chief participants. Money for a new outfit was the likely limit to her involvement. The exclusion rankled obscurely, but it troubled nobody but herself.

The barmitzvah festivities would stretch through an entire weekend. On the Saturday morning the Majinskys in their glad rags would attend synagogue. Barry would swagger about in his first adult suit, made by his father. He'd demanded in addition a waistcoat faced in a bright fabric.

In the synagogue males and females would be separated. The women would climb upstairs into the gallery; they could join in the prayers but most ladies did not read Hebrew. Her brother would be called up to read his portion of the law in a sing-song voice, an initiation for which he was being prepared with other candidates by Reverend Siegel the Minister. After the boys were done and congratulated their fathers would be called up too. For that privilege a substantial donation to the coffers was expected. Daniel's grunt indicated his resentment at this form of compulsory levy.

Wealthy parents were expected to share their joy with the rest of the congregation and invite the lot into the hall immediately afterwards for a *kiddush*, a glass of sherry and a piece of sponge cake before everyone went home for dinner. Annie fretted that the Majinsky budget did not run to such generosity but another boy, Stuart Freeman, was to be processed in the synagogue the same sabbath morning. His family had a mail-order company and boasted of their wealth, so they'd do it. That solved the problem nicely.

Then on the Sunday – Helen sighed and felt almost murderous. You couldn't have the main party on the sabbath. Too much cooking, carting, washing-up. It had to be the Sunday. At three o'clock the Majinskys would take over the synagogue hall (the Freemans had already booked the Adelphi for their Sunday splash, so poor Reverend Siegel would have to scuttle between the two). A sit-down meal would be served. Speeches would be made, wine poured and blessings uttered. Telegrams read, the works. The barmitzvah boy would be permitted to get mildly drunk.

Then the four-piece band would strike up. It could play both standards and pop, its leader had assured Annie. Two hundred people including all Barry's pals were to be invited. Helen could name five of her own, including a couple of school-friends. Non-Jewish friends, that was. Quite a concession.

It dawned on her that the American servicemen might be suitable guests. Their presence would liven up the occasion tremendously, bring her some attention and provide someone to dance with other than Jerry Feinstein. But the dinner dance was a couple of months away yet. The GIs might have been posted home or elsewhere by then. Better to wait.

For the moment her frustration expressed itself in half-hearted efforts to badger her father. She suspected he wanted merely to settle down in an armchair and fall asleep till tea-time. If she had to behave impeccably on the great day, she could still make herself felt *now*.

'Dad. Why does Barry have a barmitzvah when girls don't?'

It was not Helen's intention to sound peevish. She genuinely wanted an answer which would satisfy her and which she could quote to others who posed the same query.

Daniel shrugged. 'That's the law. It's always been the law. If we were members of a Reform *schul* you could have a *batmitzvah*. That's common in Israel too, I'm told. But we're Orthodox and we don't. It wouldn't feel right to me to challenge that. To be honest I'm more worried about being called up to read from the *Sefer Torah*. My Hebrew's rusty. Could you give me a quick lesson? Reverend Siegel will tell you which chapter. If I ask him myself he'll nag me about attending every week.'

'Why don't you?'

He shot her a look. Helen sensed that he wanted to avoid the interrogation but she persisted out of an obscure sense of injustice. She was attention-seeking and knew it.

'Don't believe in it.'

Helen was surprised. Her father could have countered that as a businessman he had too much to do on Saturdays. That would have been both true and fair. Yet he had as a rule treated her to the truth, if not the whole truth. Something warned her to be cautious, but her response came out fiercer than she intended.

'What don't you believe in, Dad? You believe in spending pots of money on this great event.'

He reached for his newspaper with an aggressive movement. 'I'm not sure I believe in any of it. But that won't stop me doing what's right for my son. And for you too. For a girl it's her wedding, so find yourself a suitable boy and it'll be your turn. Now I'm going to have my rest. A working man's entitled.'

The answer baffled her. Maybe her father had been irritated by her mother's enthusiasm and desire to splash out, or by Barry's excitement. The purpose and meaning of the ceremony seemed to have got lost in the scramble. She had half hoped her father might recover it for her. Yet his response hinted at a frustration as profound as her own, though from what cause she could not fathom.

Helen backed away and headed upstairs. With a heavy schedule of school work and, out of the blue, Michael, she had enough on her plate. That tricky essay on the nature of aldehydes and ketones had to be written tonight and submitted in the morning. Miss Plumb had also insisted that the potential Oxbridge candidates commence a programme of reading: Plato's *Republic* lay unopened in her satchel alongside *Emma*.

For the moment she wanted to do no more than think quietly. Her father's brusqueness disturbed her. If she could not figure out what he meant, then she would switch off and luxuriate in daydreams about Michael. Maybe he could be the 'suitable boy' her father had idly referred to. If so, he might bring her closer to her family. She lay back on her bed, arranged the pillows under her head, and stared at the ceiling.

'Time for the six o'clock news. Nix'll be home soon. Bring your cup in with you.'

Monday. Rita Nixon and her sister Sylvia had spent the entire afternoon at Rita's Menlove Gardens house in a most satisfying gossip. The
reputations of many acquaintances had been taken out, dusted off and
restored to the cupboard of memory gloriously dismembered. Various
friends' ailments had been analysed and their chances of survival
clucked over; a medical dictionary was consulted twice. A former pillar
of society had died, permitting delicious speculation over the subsequent
appearance of unknown children. The cemetery had as a result been the
scene of a disgraceful row. A memorial stone was due to be erected on
the first anniversary of a death as was customary but the deceased's
legitimate offspring, disappointed in their inheritance, had started a
fight; brothers-in-law had come to blows and the Rebbe, whom everyone blamed, had ended up in Casualty. No less trivial, the allegation
that the Jewish retirement home's new cook had used lard by mistake in
her pastry had fortunately proved groundless. Then of course there
was the question of the new boys – the GIs. For both sisters their arrival
at Harold House brought intermingled concern and hope but club
members had been reticent. The *coup de grâce* was saved for the end –
Sylvia confided that society nuptials would soon take place at which she
would be a discreet but welcome guest: another success. Business was
good. After a moment's hesitation she decided not to mention her visit
to the hospital to see Morrie Feinstein, or the peroxide blonde in the
damp fake fur and vulgar earrings whom she had found already present.

Sylvia picked up her cup and plate, selected one more *small* piece of
ginger cake and followed her sister into the front lounge. There, as
Rita had hoped, she halted, mouth agape.

'You have a new set! Oh, very nice. Will it get the new BBC channel
when it starts?'

'Yes, though personally I think two are quite enough.' Rita had
resisted the temptation to bring a duster in with her but ran her fingers
proudly over the fine walnut veneer before opening the two neatly
fitted doors at the front. 'Twenty-two inches,' she added proudly, as if
boasting about a new-born child. Which, in a sense, she was.

The television took a moment to warm up then BBC News flashed
on to the screen. Rita could not quite work out what the newscaster was
talking about and glanced at her sister in puzzlement. She started to ask
but Sylvia, listening intently and munching cake, hushed her.

At last the item was finished. Sylvia sat back, a smirk of unalloyed
malice on her face.

'I don't believe it. Do you?'

'I'm not sure,' Rita answered cautiously. The newsreader had moved
on to bloody events in Mississippi which seemed even more abstruse.

'He's lying. I am sure of it. My job, you know.' Her sister looked
blank so she took a final sip of tea, put down the cup and expounded.
'Mr Profumo says he had nothing to do with this girl Christine Keeler.

Yet George Wigg keeps on. Horrible man, but he doesn't usually get things wrong. No smoke without fire. She's a tart, I tell you.'

Rita sat down slowly. Though both were paid-up Tories in a city where nine of the twelve parliamentary seats were held by the government she considered that she was more unswervingly loyal than her sister whose profession made her a bit cynical.

'But that can't be. It'd mean Mr Profumo lied to the House of Commons. And to the Prime Minister. To everybody, in fact.'

'He's probably started with his wife, if you think about it. Couldn't ever figure out what she saw in him. Looks like an emaciated beetle in my opinion. And those tiny frightened eyes. Don't trust him.'

'I liked Valerie Hobson when she was on the stage,' Rita mused. 'D'you remember her at the Liverpool Playhouse? Lovely, she was.'

'Well, it appears our esteemed Secretary of State for War has a taste for actresses. Some as are, and some as aren't.' Sylvia glanced at the green marble clock on the mantelpiece. 'Heavens – is that the time? I must go.'

At the front door her sister helped her into the black wool coat with the astrakhan collar. Sylvia laughed suddenly. 'I doubt if we'll ever hear the truth of this Profumo business, and I'm not sure I want to. It won't do poor Mr Macmillan any good.'

Rita concurred. 'It'll help Harold Wilson, true or no. Ugh! I hate that 'orrible Yorkshire accent. The notion of him actually becoming Prime Minister! Really puts me off.'

On that the sisters were as one. Sylvia kissed Rita on the cheek, promised to phone, pulled on her gloves and was gone.

The post landed with a plop on the hall rug. Barry was first to reach it, though seldom did any arrive addressed to him. The pile appeared to be larger than usual. He brought the envelopes into the dining room and tossed them one by one on the table, deftly avoiding his father's breakfast cigarette.

'A bill – another bill – a brochure of some kind for you, Dad – ooh!'

He stopped. The envelope was pale blue with stripes of red and darker blue around the edge. 'Air mail,' he announced portentously. 'From the United States of America.'

'Give it to me, Barry. Go get ready for school.' Annie snatched it away before her son could read out the addressee's name. It would have felt like sacrilege had anybody else opened an air mail letter first: that was her duty, and pleasure.

In the doorway Helen pulled on her blazer, a half-eaten piece of toast held in her teeth. Mouth full she mumbled, 'Who's it from, Mum?'

Annie turned the missive this way and that, examining its exterior as if its contents might be revealed by telepathy, but in reality enjoying the postponement of knowledge in case of disappointment. '"Mrs G. Ahrens",' she read. 'Who's that? Oh, it must be Gertie. Haven't heard from her in ages.'

'Who's Gertie?' Barry did not want to know about his far-flung relatives, but contrariwise hated being left in the dark.

'Gertie? What's she up to now?' Daniel's curiosity was equally aroused. 'Born lucky, that one – always landed on her feet, whatever she got up to.'

'Hush, Daniel. Gertie may have been wilder than us, but . . .' Annie cast a veiled glance at the two youngsters. 'Of course she's a lot older.' She reached for a clean knife. The envelope produced two rustling sheets of thin blue paper. Annie read in silence, her lips moving slightly, and ignored the chunter of impatience from her children. Then she yelped.

'Oh, heavens. Dramatic's not in it. She's coming – here.'

Daniel stood up. The chair fell over behind him with a clatter on the lino. 'She's what?'

Slowly but with a tremor in her voice Annie began to read out loud. '"It is much too long since I have seen any of you and it doesn't look likely that you'll have the chance to come across here to visit for the time being. So the family on this side of the Atlantic had a confab and we decided one of us should represent the rest at the forthcoming bar-mitzvah in May of your son Barry, *kinnenhorror*, which you wrote us about. As I have fewest commitments it'll be me. I propose to make a long stay of it if you'll have me." Oh, no!'

'What is it?' the others chorused in unison. Annie had gone white and now held the pages by her fingertips as if they had grown hot. Her voice dropped to a whisper. She looked up at Daniel with mournful eyes.

'Your sister is proposing to come for two *months* and wants to stay – here. The whole time. Except for a few days in London to see the sights. She's taking the Cunarder *Sylvania* next week and will arrive in time for *Pesach*. Oh, my God.' With trembling hand she reached for the fallen chair, set it upright, sat down heavily and used the letter to fan herself. 'Gertie! But how will we cope – on top of everything else?'

A startled silence had descended as the momentous news sank in. A relative from the States, instead of remaining incorporeal if glamorous, had decided to materialise in the flesh.

To Barry, excluded by his age from contact with the GIs at Harold House, the news felt like heaven-borne revenge on his sister. A pukka American, not the celluloid version he and his friends envied at the cinema and aped outside. A rich person, of that one had no doubt. *Very* rich: all Americans were. The boy was the first to recover.

'Will she bring us presents? Will she take us out? What'll I get for my barmitzvah? Can we ask her to bring us some records?'

But it was Helen who had spotted the dilemma posed by the arrival. From her mother's face she was not alone.

'Mum,' she said slowly, 'this is only a three-bedroom house. Where is she going to sleep?'

Her mother looked helplessly from one to another. Then she squared her shoulders, glanced upwards as if she could see through the ceiling to the cramped bedroom beyond, and back to the girl.

'Well, she can't stay in a hotel for weeks, I'd never hear the last of it. I'm sorry, Helen. You'll have to move your books and papers off the spare bed. She's hardly the companion I'd choose for you but your Auntie Gertie'll be sharing your room.'

The author of the air mail letter smiled to herself as she emerged from the mirrored walk-in wardrobe of the master bedroom in Little Neck Parkway, Queens, New York, her arms full of folded garments. It would have arrived by now. A transatlantic phone call could have been booked, but in the flurry details might have been misheard or forgotten. It had been better to write and set out dates, times, dock number.

Methodically she began to compile a list for her packing. Senior citizenship was not a problem except when it came to her immediate memory. Toothpaste, cleanser, two flannels. Ten pairs of stockings – no, double that at least, they'd be great for gifts. Two months' stay would justify the expense, especially if her sister-in-law Annie agreed to let her stay with them. Funds simply did not run to a hotel for the whole trip, though no doubt the Brits were convinced she was loaded.

Lucky that Joe trusted her to come alone. Sweet Joe, husband and distant kin. Same stock, same history, nothing to explain. Not that he had much choice: he didn't travel well and would bid her *bon voyage* quite happily. On the quay he'd wave her off with a fluttering white handkerchief and a tear in his eye. Their next-door neighbours Marty and Lil would look after him. In her absence he'd have a fine old time. He and Marty would go to the game and play golf to their hearts' content. They'd sit around the American Legion Club, swap a few tales, drink a few Budweisers and roll home late, to Lil's pursed lips and curlers, but no harm would result. She hoped the two oldies would not overdo it. Nursing duties on her return would not be to her taste.

It was funny when you thought about it, that Joe was so keen on the Legion. He'd avoided the first war, as she knew, and spent the second entirely as a storesman on a base in New Jersey, from which he escaped frequently back to New York. Such a contrast to the family's experiences in Britain which were described in terse censored letters, but which could be pictured with chilling clarity against the background of Ed Morrow's London broadcasts. It remained to be seen to what extent the damage, psychological and physical, which the bombing must have wrought in her old home town had been eradicated.

Life stateside had been good to her and Joe, what with their sons set up in their own homes, and money in the bank, and their own detached property in one of the smarter suburbs of New York City. Her only regret was not having had a daughter. But leaving Liverpool had been the best thing they'd ever done. So many shackles had been thrown off, so many restrictions abandoned. In middle age she'd enrolled at City College of New York and taken a Bachelor of Arts degree in social history: ah, the satisfaction of that graduation day, as she held in her hand the proof of her endeavour and ability! None of that had been possible, or would have been, had they stayed in Europe. She had no regrets, and was certain Joe hadn't either.

The two of them had willingly acted as sponsors for so many friends and for her cousins. They'd have done the same for Daniel, but his abrupt refusal to leave had been a puzzle. Gertie as the elder harboured a sense of responsibility, though that had not extended to staying at home to help her mother any longer than necessary. That episode when she was sixteen – but that was before Joe, and such a long time ago. It made her blush still to remember, and to sigh quietly whenever she heard a Scots accent.

For those days it was a modestly sized family. Gertie was the eldest, born at the turn of the century. A brother born in 1906 had died in adulthood – Izzy, short for Israel, so Daniel was her only sibling now. The girls – the two cousins, Miriam and Eva – had been in and out of their home so frequently they were almost like sisters. There must have been more, for mothers became pregnant every couple of years as the last child was weaned, but babies were miscarried or didn't survive. That was how women had to live. Their mother had had a terribly hard time. God rest her soul.

Gertie hesitated before the dressing table. Was all the jewellery to come? She felt torn – in American terms they were far from wealthy and had had to withdraw savings for her trip. On the other hand, it would be grand to show off a bit to the folks back home and watch their eyes widen. All the jewellery it was, then, and maybe Miriam and Eva could also lend her a brooch or bracelet.

Daniel had been the brainiest. If he'd had the chances, he could have gone to college. It was out of the question then for a working man, especially one in poor health. As she mused Gertie felt slightly anxious. She had emigrated while Danny was a boy. The two had not been close, and now he was all of fifty.

He had once dreamed of change, or so she'd heard second-hand. That Annie had not been his great love nor his first was a whispered tale – hardly surprising as he'd been in his mid-thirties before he married. The cousins had nothing positive to say of Annie, who was too reserved for their taste and who had disapproved of their capture of American airmen as husbands. The conflict between old world and new world values had made sparks fly then but had softened with time and distance. It meant however that Gertie was unsure what she would encounter, while Daniel and Annie could have precious little notion of her. It was to be hoped that no new sources of conflict would emerge.

What might she find? Gertie pulled out a photograph album and scrolled through the pages. Her brother didn't send many pictures; perhaps he didn't have a camera, for everything here was taken by somebody else, mostly at *simchas*. One showed Daniel and Annie at somebody's wedding a few years ago with the children. The adults probably wouldn't have altered much but these small ones would have grown a bit. Barry would be nearly as tall as his mother, though that cheeky manner would still be present. Miniature charmer, in all probability, and soon with an eye for the girls. He did not attract her.

The daughter, though. Helen. Where did that name come from? Greek, wasn't it? Their mother, her grandmother had been Edith or *Itah* in Hebrew; the plan must have been to name the child for her as was customary but in a more up-to-date version. Edith, Elaine, Eleanor, Helen. That was it. So in their search for modernity they'd chosen a name far older than Edith, which was itself an assimilation to the Victorian taste of their contemporaries. Jewish people liked camouflage. So the baby girl was named, probably by mistake, after the whore of ancient times whose beauty launched a thousand ships and destroyed a nation.

Helen might have inherited her father's wits. From Annie's letters it sounded so, and the pictures suggested she was not a plain girl. Maybe she had a measure of the Majinsky spirit of adventure, at least as it had manifested itself in its women. As Gertie put away the photographs she found herself looking forward to meeting her niece for the first time.

Gertie chuckled. Getting to know Helen could be the best part of the whole trip.

'So! How did the night out go? Make progress?'

Sergeant Andy Newman carried his tray into the canteen, found the man he had been seeking and sat himself down at Mike Levison's side. 'I was asking for professional reasons. Helps to know if the invite was worth while.'

'Sure.' Levison pushed his plate away. Was it his fancy or was the food getting worse? 'We were made real welcome. Funny old place, bit like a fraternity house, but respectable. No booze.' He grinned.

'Wouldn't suit everybody then?'

'No–o. Not the wildest joint in Liverpool, but I liked it. Couple of us have promised to go again. Members are a bit young, I think. The oldest can't be more than nineteen or so.'

The sergeant blinked. Michael tried to explain. 'It's a youth club. Mostly they run it themselves – real fine kids, don't get me wrong, and not dull. More like a church group, but the music's great. The girls are cute and smart. But if any of our guys wanted "cigareets and whiskey and wild, wild women", they'd be best advised to go elsewhere.'

Camp rules were strict. Nobody wanted trouble. Andy was satisfied. As he rose, Michael Levison laid a hand on his arm.

'Say: it's a Jewish club. How did you decide to send me?'

The sergeant shrugged and pointed. 'Your name.'

'Just that? Not that I mind. I was brought up not to have any prejudice, and I don't expect folks to have any against me. I wondered, that's all.'

The square brick building was tacked on to the side of the synagogue, a cheap fifties design with a flat roof which in due course would cost the congregation far more than they expected to refurbish. The big hall with its expensive parquet floor where barmitzvahs and wedding parties took place was at the back, furthest from nearby residents who had objected strenuously to its construction. Next to it were four classrooms. Each, like the Marcus Liversham Hall, was named after its donor.

Helen pushed open the door of the *cheder* and went in. A shimmer of warm air enfolded her from the big radiator inside the entrance. At five o'clock on a quiet Tuesday only two of the classrooms, the Bertha Morris and the Lionel Blumsky, were in use. Through the glass window of one she could see Mrs Siegel, a tubby solemn woman with scraped-back black hair, in front of a class of seven- and eight-year-olds. On the blackboard Hebrew letters were written out neatly from right to left. The class appeared to have reached about halfway through the alphabet, to *mem* and *nun*, the precursors of modern M and N. In the other room Yehudah Siegel, the Reverend's intense older son, had pinned up a map of Israel. He was gesticulating and pointing to it, his mouth moving, as barmitzvah candidates and a few girls learned about their putative homeland. Helen craned her neck but could not see whether Barry was present. His attendance at best was unreliable.

She headed for the office. As she paused at the half-open door she could hear a voice within. Its cadences and central European accent were unmistakable, and made her smile.

'I don't care what Princes Road *schul* say. Here we bring our old people together for second night *seder*. They like it, and it brings in a bit of money.'

A pause. Reverend Siegel appeared to be arguing testily with the voice on the other end of the phone. Although he was invisible to his interlocutor, he danced around and waved his free hand expressively. He spotted Helen and motioned her inside.

'I agree it's a *mitzvah* that their families should do it. That's for first night *seder*. But some of the families don't bother with the second night, and some want to go away. Not every home will make welcome Auntie Sadie and Cousin Millie. And heaven knows whether they're eating *kosher* when they get to Bournemouth or wherever. Selfish lot, the next generation.'

The altercation continued a few moments longer. At last it seemed that the Reverend may not have convinced his opponent but had mollified him. He bid goodbye and replaced the phone.

'Ach! I could swear at times, Helen. Sit, sit. Some minion in the Chief Rabbi's office has raised an objection to our communal *seder*. Can you believe it? It'll detract from family life, they say. Much they know.'

'I think the old people enjoy it,' Helen concurred. 'They're conscious of being a burden, some of them. And you do it right, the way they were brought up. I'd offer to assist but I think my mother would expect me at home.'

'Naturally.'

It was warm in the office. He was still in his black silk vestment; perhaps he had been conducting an afternoon service for a few keen adherents. He removed the garment and hung it up behind the door, and ran a finger inside the white dog-collar which seemed a tad tighter than a few months earlier. The Reverend, so well cared for by his efficient and loving wife, was putting on weight.

Reverend Siegel, Minister and cantor of the relatively new Childwall congregation, was in his early forties. He had arrived in Britain as a small child and could speak perfect English when he chose; but in his world it cut more of a dash to emphasise his impeccable cultural origins. His short figure was both comfortable and muscular and he had a tendency to bustle. He was smooth-shaven but struggled unsuccessfully against a dark shadow of persistent beard over almost his whole face except for a small patch round the eyes, which would begin to appear about an hour after his ablutions each morning. The effect was to make him resemble a benevolent panda, an impression enhanced by his short-sightedness.

He was not a full rabbi. The congregation could not afford one – or at least, that was their excuse. In reality those learned and pious scholars who had presented themselves for interview had intimidated or alarmed the committee. There had been the consideration, unspoken but widely recognised, that a full rabbi would be a law unto himself and could make life very difficult, whether on a ruling of *Torah* or interpretation of *Talmud*. A real rabbi, in short, however pliant his manner at the start, could turn out to be a fanatic. A lesser qualified man might be more beholden to those who had chosen to ignore his lack of key certificates. The word 'malleable' was never used. But it was clearly given to the new appointee to understand that he'd be expected to conform to the easy-going standards and style of his principal employers and not to any higher authority.

'Now then! *Purim*. You will help with the babies, won't you?' That was his term for the under-sevens. 'Bit special this year as it's twenty-five years since this *schul* was founded, and fifteen since the establishment of *Eretz Yisroel*.' He half bowed towards another map of the State of Israel which adorned the wall, surrounded by framed photographs of events held in the hall and synagogue. A flicker of doubt must have shown on Helen's face for he added hastily, 'I know the tale of Queen Esther hasn't a lot to do with the spread of your parents' generation from the slums to the suburbs nor with the War of Independence in 1948, but I want everything to be splendid this year. First *Purim*, then *Pesach* after. Call it pride, if you like.'

Helen nodded. 'What exactly do you want me to do?'

'Well, there'll be the reading of the *Megilla*, and the singing. The children need to know when to boo and when to cheer, and that means drumming into them everything about King Ahasuerus and Queen Vashti, and Mordechai and his beautiful ward Esther and how she became Queen in Vashti's place and saved her people.' This last phrase was uttered with a note of triumph. 'And then the fancy dress competition. Some of their parents will have bright ideas but one or two always get left out. Or get it horribly wrong. Last year little Francine Lewis came as Queen Vashti because her mother didn't know the difference. Poor kid was in floods of tears when everybody laughed. Of course if Francine's mother had ever brought *her* as a child to *cheder* – but never mind. No mistakes this time if we can avoid it.'

'I think there are some old costumes in the cupboard. Shall I get them out and tidy them up? Then we can be sure everyone has something suitable to wear, even if we end up with six Esthers.'

'We always end up with six Esthers. Conventional lot, our *yiddishe* people.'

He rose and scrutinised the framed photographs, then gently lifted one down and placed it in her hands. 'Remember when you won the competition? You must have been about eleven.'

Helen tilted the picture to capture the light. It showed the raised catwalk installed in front of the Ark, the better to permit the parade of hopefuls. Underneath were only a couple of planks on barrels covered in an old blue carpet, but the effect was quite grand.

Ten young faces stared back at her. The photographer had stood in the well of the synagogue and looked up, so the perspective was of a row of towering statues. Several girls as Reverend Siegel had intimated were swathed in the regulation sheet or curtain complete with yashmak, which symbolised the modest purity of the young virgin queen. Others were draped in gaily striped bathtowels as wicked Haman or benign Mordechai; local imagination was restricted to the fashion of the Old Testament prophets rather than the glamour of the Persian court.

On the end Jerry Feinstein, then a fat boy, was dressed incongruously as an insect. The costume had been left over from a primary school play and was all that came to hand in that motherless household. His face was painted in yellow and black stripes and antennae wobbled from his forehead. But his grin was broad: he had won a consolation prize for the placard he carried, inspired at the last minute by Nellie, which claimed he was a bee from Ahasuerus's garden.

The winner had been Helen herself. That year she had been determined, conscious that it might be her last entry. Puberty was already interfering and she would soon become too embarrassed, as would her friends, to pose in public. She stood proudly, her costume nothing to do with the *Purim* legend. Instead she had recalled the tale of another woman who had ignored the instructions of her husband not to look back at the destruction of Sodom and Gomorrah, the great revenge of a wrathful God, and had shared their fate.

Helen's arms, legs and head protruded from a large cardboard box painted white. Every scrap of visible skin had been dusted with talcum powder and her hair stood out in white tendrils. Painted on the front of the box was the legend: 'Lot's Wife.'

'Turned into a block of salt. Inspired,' sighed Reverend Siegel. 'Got you into the *Liverpool Echo* that year.' The possibilities of press coverage were never far from his mind.

'What do I answer if the children ask me if the Purim story is true?' Helen queried, as he replaced the picture.

'Oh, but it is. Ahasuerus was King Xerxes. He was King of the Persians in – let me see – the fifth century BCE. The modern version is a bit coy at times – for example, Queen Vashti is alleged to have been put away for having refused to dance for the king, but in reality she angered him by mutilating the mother of one of his mistresses.' He stopped, confused. 'Shouldn't tell you that – you're a bit young for the juicier details of Herodotus.'

Helen blushed. 'Go on. I'm old enough.'

The teacher needed no encouragement. 'Anyway, there's no doubt from internal evidence that it's authentic, and written by somebody who knew the court well. Maybe Mordechai himself who's raised to the highest office at the end. And there's something very curious about the whole Book of Esther, you know. It never mentions God, or prayer, and has no religious teaching nor direct moralising. That suggests it was written for the Jews of the Persian empire as an account which could be circulated without offence to other religions. It's authentic, all right, Helen, as most of our holy books are.'

She had gone quiet. Reverend Siegel, who loved each of his charges but retained a particular affection for the dark-haired girl seated opposite on whom the marks of womanhood were clearly apparent, felt a sudden unease.

'You do believe, don't you? The latest discoveries, the Dead Sea Scrolls, the cuneiform tablets, show the Old Testament's not merely a collection of myths. We were the first to work out that God is one and indivisible, and to stick to that throughout centuries of persecution. Through divine intervention, nothing less, we were given the finest set of ethics ever known, and charged never to forget or abandon them. That is our law; that is why we are the chosen people.'

She raised her head, her expression anxious. 'Do you think so? Do you think Abraham, Isaac and Jacob were factual? Do you believe our father Jacob wrestled with an angel? Honestly?'

He responded in a sober, slow tone. 'I believe those three men existed and that they are our blood ancestors. And yes, I do hold from the bottom of my heart that the knowledge imparted on that terrible night, of which we are the custodians – however symbolic Jacob's ladder might be – has set us apart for ever.'

'I wonder sometimes.' Helen spoke as slowly. She could not get out of her mind her father's remarks. Perhaps he was speaking through her; maybe it was simply that the two of them, father and daughter, were so alike that their thoughts might run uncannily along the same grooves. 'We deride the Christians who set so much store on a man who may never have lived. He's not mentioned in any records of the Roman Empire, anywhere. We even avoid using his name – that's why you said "BCE" – Before the Christian Era – instead of, well, you know. Yet we base the whole of *our* philosophy on a collection of ancient fables which probably didn't happen. Or else are a folk memory. And however useful those endless rules of *kashrut* were for survival in a hot desert, they're a bit shaky and pointless for today's world.'

She stopped. Silence hung heavy in the room. Reverend Siegel rose and folded his arms, slowly. 'I hope you don't start saying that to the babies, Helen. Otherwise I'll have to get somebody else to help, and I'd much rather have you.'

He came to her side of the desk and placed a hand on her shoulder. 'It's good, I suppose, that you should ask. Seek knowledge and ye shall find. Better than blind acceptance any day. Zangwill wrote that we are not merely a chosen people, we are a *choosing* people. So, think hard, ask your questions, then choose. In time you will pass on your love of our traditions to your own children. You're one of the best, Helen. You're intelligent, principled, and kind. A modern *balaboster*. You'll be the type of Jewish woman everyone will be proud to know.'

From a nearby room came the clatter of a class being dismissed. He moved to go, but could not stop himself from quickly wagging an affectionate finger.

'You may well have a point about our forefathers, though you'd be foolish to dismiss our way of life. There is nothing better, should you seek from hell to high water. Only make sure you don't search too hard in the wrong direction.'

He pointed to the photograph he had replaced on the wall.

'Or you too could end up like Lot's Wife: turned by God from a human being into a pillar of salt – cold, dead, and lost for ever.'

Chapter Eight

Headlong

'Six-thirty! Docking in half an hour!'

Gertie Ahrens had not slept. The steward's call was a relief: she could rise, shower and dress with no further guilt or debates over whether it was wise or dangerous to take another sleeping pill. She slipped her feet over the edge of the bunk and cautiously hunted around with her toes for her slippers. Across the cramped cabin her cabin mate snored rhythmically, a sound remarkably close to the throaty rumble of the ship's engines. The two noises, combined with the swell and heave of the Atlantic, had nearly driven Gertie crazy in the previous four days and nights. Had she ever considered the joys of a cruise, the lesson had been learned.

She pondered. If she were quick she could use the facilities before Mrs Hattenscheiner woke up. In fact it would be possible to be out of the cabin and away before the unwanted companion had surfaced, which would avoid phoney farewells, an exchange of useless addresses, and insincere promises to look each other up. It'd been hard enough having to share a cabin at all, but the boat was full; and sharing was cheaper.

Mrs Hattenscheiner stirred, threw out a fleshy arm with its two *diamanté* bracelets and blinked enquiringly.

'Not yet – plenty of time,' Gertie assured her. 'I'm just going on deck for some air.'

When vigorous rumbles again filled the cabin she slid a packed suitcase out from under the bunk, quickly stuffed her toilet bag inside, pulled on her new coat and with handbag under one arm and a second suitcase under the other, tiptoed out.

Halfway down the corridor the steward stepped neatly from his cupboard and greeted her. She had hoped to avoid him, too. The level of service grudgingly offered to lower-deck passengers did not deserve thanks, let alone a tip. But here he was, barring her way. She put down the bags and fished in her pocketbook for a five-dollar bill. He would have to be satisfied with that.

In the cold air her spirits, battered by lack of sleep and the miseries of the voyage, began to sink yet lower. The ship had crept close to the jetty; its engines throttled back to a low hum. For the first time in days their vibrations no longer jarred her teeth. She leaned over the rail and gazed at her native city, and understood once more why she had left it.

The morning was not dark but gloomy and dank, with no hint of sun or light. Grey clouds threatened rain. On the breeze came the smell of burning coal and rotting vegetation. Warehouses bordered the quay of assorted shapes and sizes, but uniformly blackened and grubby with broken windows and redundant winches. Dockers in overalls lounged in clumps and smoked. There was none of the excitement and joy supposed to be associated with arrival. All sea-ports have their depressing corners but Gertie decided that Dock 42, the home of the Cunard liners, must be amongst the most dismal in the world, and wondered how long it would take before the company, which sold glamour along with its tickets, would abandon Liverpool for ever.

A faint voice called up from far below. A man was waving. She waved back cheerily: the figure in an overcoat could be anybody. Without her glasses she could not see clearly. Suddenly she caught her own name. The man was jumping about and motioning frantically at her. She peered down uncertainly then straightened. Her own features stared back at her, albeit with a man's moustache. It must be her brother Daniel.

She was home. A rush of emotion choked her. She found a handkerchief and fluttered it at him, then began to cry, and gesticulated and laughed, all at the same time.

By the time brother and sister came together on the dockside as the big ship loomed over them like a protective wall, and hugged and shouted all at once, surrounded by other noisy family groups doing exactly the same, Gertie's anxieties had vanished. The horrible Mrs Hattenscheiner, the supercilious steward, the miserable tub of a boat, were behind her.

An unforeseen problem emerged. As heavier luggage was unloaded Gertie identified her trunk. Daniel blanched at its size and weight. 'It's full of presents,' she apologised proudly, and, 'It won't go into the car,' he explained. She did not believe him; it had arrived easily enough at the New York dockside in Joe's Chrysler. Not until the Vauxhall was brought from the car park to sit alongside the offending object and had been measured by eye was it obvious that Daniel was right.

'Pity your car is so small,' she commented as they debated what to do.

'It's the biggest I can afford, Gertie.' Daniel was hurt. 'Look, before we start. I hope you're not going to spend the whole holiday complaining that everything in Britain is smaller or less grand than you've got at home. You may not intend to give offence, but I have to live with Annie afterwards. We'll do our best for you and make you very welcome.'

Thus Gertie's luggage had a taxi to itself, an expense neither could easily justify. The bemused cabbie followed the elderly black car to Childwall and helped unload the trunk with much puffing and groans inside. In the hallway came more hugs, though Gertie and Annie had not met before.

Annie fussed, fluttered, patted her apron. Her sister-in-law removed her coat and looked around for somewhere to hang it, but Annie seized the garment from her and folded it over her arm. As they spoke Gertie noticed that the fine fabric was caressed lovingly, as if Annie had never held anything quite so good before. In American terms it was a perfectly ordinary coat.

Annie pushed back a lock of hair. 'Good journey?'

'Yeah, terrific. Nothing like an ocean liner. You live in the lap of luxury for days.' As Annie's eyes rounded in envy Gertie could not resist elaboration, though her examples came mostly from glimpses along the gangways of first-class passengers on their way to dinner.

At last politeness intervened. 'Where are the children?'

'Gone to school.' Both had begged to be allowed to stay, or to go to the dockside with their father, but Annie had insisted on routine. In truth she wanted a few minutes to herself to assess the visitor. Would Gertie be an intruder? A revealer of secrets? While any challenge to the orderliness of their lives was dangerous, this live invader posed particular risks: though Annie would have been hard put to articulate exactly how. Gertie was new, untried, unbridled. Gertie would not know the rules, and would scoff and deride. Both physically and in age and seniority Gertie was bigger than her hostess. Not to speak of vastly more prosperous, as the watch, brooch and gold chains at her neck with the diamond-crusted Star of David bore witness. The presence of this tall angular woman in her home, whose outer clothing was obviously of cashmere and who wore rich perfume at nine o'clock in the morning, made her apprehensive.

Practicality asserted itself. 'I'll show you your room,' Annie said and started up the stairs. 'Mind your head as you go up. You're sharing, I'm afraid. Bit cramped. Hope you won't mind.'

Gertie pursed her lips. More of the same, it seemed, but for weeks this time, not days. She picked up the smallest of her bags and grimly followed.

Miss Plumb settled her charges at the large table in the corner of her study. In its centre stood a vase of red tulips; window-boxes on houses nearby were showy with yellow and purple pansies. The air outside was balmy and a gentle breeze nudged the window frame. Late spring, long overdue.

This was the part of teaching which she most enjoyed: four clever girls, expressions eager, their futures ahead of them, their characters as yet part-formed and open to influence. *Her* influence.

For, as Miss Plumb knew, every teacher is a secret Svengali. There might lurk within one such child the seed of genius just begging to be nurtured. Some of humanity's greatest ideas (as refined by herself, of course) might thereby be instilled. If the result were a series of Plumb copies – what was that term from botany, a clone? – that was as good, if not better, than breeding children of one's own, whose outcome was far more unpredictable. That the nation might gain from her cultivation of such ability was naturally a powerful justification. The botanical allusion was, however, too flaccid altogether for what Miss Plumb felt. Pedagogy was a hunt with live quarry, with all the thrill of pursuit: success needed that combination of passion, persistence and cunning that any Master of Foxhounds would instantly recognise. Her task was not to kill her quarry but to capture it, to feed both mind and spirit, then release it, hugely improved, to go out into the world with *her* stamp on its brow. As Aristotle had for Alexander, as Socrates for Plato: the teacher had a sacred, God-given task.

By contrast the grind of administration bored and frustrated her. The daily cajoling of academic staff, the threats needed to keep cleaners and domestics in line, detracted from those hours she could spend teaching face to face. Yet it was reported that some heads no longer saw pupils at all. To Miss Plumb's mind that was a disgrace, and a negation of everything she had come into the profession to do.

'So how did you get on with *Emma*?' she asked.

Three of the girls grimaced or stared down at their notebooks. Only Meg sat ready. 'I liked it very much. The character of Emma's done awfully well. She feels almost real.'

Brenda tossed her head. 'She's such a sourpuss. And she's so mean to poor Harriet.'

'But Harriet's a goose too. She's only interested in fine clothes and a rich husband.' This from Helen. 'I agree, though. I hated the book and had a struggle to finish it. I'd much rather read Charlotte Brontë – her characters are warmer and more sympathetic. Jane Austen's seem so – brittle, like china dolls.'

'I can see why Meg likes Emma. She's a mischief maker, and doesn't care who she hurts.' Brenda spoke in a solemn murmur but her eyes danced: she meant no malice, though Meg flushed.

'Now, girls.' Miss Plumb encouraged her charges to argue but not to try each other's patience. 'Tell me how you saw Miss Austen's portrayal of the relationship between men and women.'

Brenda frowned. 'She doesn't seem to like women much, does she?

Her treatment is almost catty – whether it's Emma or Harriet or the older women. Jane Fairfax is so drippy I could shake her. I mean, it's funny and you can picture them exactly – the picnic on Box Hill, for example, when everybody jockeys for position and Emma is so cruel to poor Miss Bates. By contrast the men are the fount of wisdom, like Mr Knightley. I think he was stuck-up, but it's clear you're supposed to admire him.'

'Not all the men. She clearly doesn't have much time for Mr Elton the vicar.' Meg warmed to her theme. 'And Emma's father is horrendous – can you imagine having a whinging old slob like that as a papa? Heavens!'

Miss Plumb suppressed a chuckle. 'You're talking about one of the greatest novels of English literature, continuously in print since it was published nearly one hundred and fifty years ago, as if it were a penny dreadful from a cheap bookstall.'

The girls were not impressed. Helen spoke. 'We aren't paying it homage, we are studying it. And we're entitled to say if we aren't wildly enthusiastic. If I had to read this sort of stuff all the time I'd loathe it. Emma Woodhouse is a pain, Miss Plumb, you have to admit. She's vain, silly, rude and a crashing snob. She doesn't know what goes on outside her tiny world, either –'

'Perhaps. Though Jane Austen herself wrote that pictures of perfection made *her* sick. But if I were you, I wouldn't criticise too strongly should a question on Miss Austen feature on your general paper. You may be scientists but you don't want to appear fools. Grit your teeth, my dears, say how remarkable the author is, and *then* give your analysis. Which, incidentally, carries considerable merit.'

The discussion continued for several moments. Miss Plumb had planned to set the group another of her favourite author's works but the prospect of rebellion made her reconsider. Instead she would check before the next session whether Mrs Gaskell's *North and South* was available in school in sufficient quantity. If the quartet preferred a gritty tale of smokestacks and romance from the previous century, that might do the trick. Then maybe in the autumn a put-upon heroine like Maggie Tulliver might excite their sympathy rather than further derision.

In her neat hand she made a note for herself. Modern girls: so hostile to the notion that a marriage proposal was (or should be) the prime objective of a lady. In that respect they had more in common with Miss Austen than they realised. And with George Eliot. And with herself, come to that.

'Now for next week, girls. Let me ask you about your current cultural intake. Do any of you waste your time with the magazine *Private Eye*?'

Glances were exchanged. Colette had been in the middle of a yawn, but collected herself and grinned. The girl seemed overtired. 'Since we subscribe to it in the sixth-form Library you can't condemn us for swallowing every line as gospel, Miss Plumb.'

'I'm pleased to hear that the council's expenditure is not in vain.' Miss Plumb tried the glare, but its effect was to seal a bond with the quartet, not enforce a distance. 'What about television? Are you familiar with *That was the Week that Was*?'

All four nodded. The programme was essential viewing at ten thirty pm on Saturdays even if that did mean getting home early.

'How good to know that you keep up with current affairs,' Miss Plumb teased dryly. 'My attention was caught by a piece in the *Daily Telegraph* about such trivia in our society, which as you know come under the collective heading of satire.' The article lay on the table before her. 'The great satirists of the past, the writer says – and I imagine he has in mind classical writers, or Jonathan Swift – were moved by indignation to mock at stupidity, hypocrisy and vice in the name of intelligence and virtue. Swift regarded it as a mirror held up to nature, but pointed out that in it you can see everyone but yourself. Dryden believed that the true end of satire is the amendment of vices by correction. And Robespierre was brought down, there is no doubt, the instant the citizens began to laugh at him.'

The girls were scribbling furiously. The change in their teacher's tone indicated that she had become didactic.

'But what we have today is a kind of mass satire in which the whole population has joined. Everyone pokes fun with no respect. Nor are any institutions held sacred. That dratted television programme thrashes away at the props of our lives, including the Church and the Royal Family. Conventional morality is become a source of mirth. Now is that safe, or destructive? Is it a necessary cleansing of Augean stables, or a nihilism which will demolish the pillars which hold up the house, and so make matters infinitely worse? That is the theme for next week.'

Her students looked puzzled and began to ask questions, but Miss Plumb held up her hand for silence. 'What you make of it is up to you. I will prepare a reading list based on what's in the Library. Don't be so alarmed – you're quite familiar with *Gulliver's Travels* and *Animal Farm*, so it's not as tough as it sounds. We'll use one of the *Telegraph*'s more portentous quotes as our title. Yes, here it is. "Is mass satire desirable in a liberal society, or is it a 'cannibal dance around the idea of Authority'? Discuss." Consider the use of the word "cannibal". Not more than ten pages of foolscap by next Tuesday.'

The girls' groans were sufficient acclaim. With a wave she dismissed them. 'Good morning.'

Miss Austen's acerbity and the levities of such TV stars as David Frost and Bernard Levin were not in Helen's mind as she jumped from the bus and ran, satchel in hand, up the road to her house.

What would she be like, the new auntie? Would she look like Dad? Or terrifyingly alien? She was much older – an old woman. Would she be decrepit – would sharing a room be an ordeal? What happened when somebody spent the whole of her adult life abroad, in a country as powerfully self-confident as America? Would she sneer at them, call them old-fashioned and try to change their ways? But then, Helen reasoned as she arrived panting at the gate and waited a moment to catch her breath, that was understandable in those who'd left and returned on a triumphant visit. They'd be bound to show off a bit. Otherwise it might be inferred that they'd made a mistake by leaving in the first place.

Don't be petty, she chided herself. How can you believe boasting must be part of their style? Michael isn't like that. He's dignified and polite, and somehow finds a pleasant or complimentary remark to make about everything. That's quite a talent. All too rare in Liverpool.

The reflection on Michael made her pause a moment more. He and the boys were coming to the club tonight, but it might be fun instead to introduce him to the Cavern. The dilemma was that she'd be expected to stay in for her aunt. It'd be the height of bad manners to disappear on her first night. Helen leaned on the gatepost and bit her lip in despair. She had to see Michael; there was no argument about it.

Michael R. Levison. Airman first class, but hoping to be promoted before long. He could have tried for an officer but preferred to stay with the enlisted men. Tall and wide. A strong neck, angled jaw. Ruby-stoned fraternity ring on his finger: she had never seen one like that before, nor did most males of her acquaintance wear rings or anything fancy other than a watch – they'd have condemned the idea as cissy. But Michael could not be called that, not in a million years.

Tonight he had said he would be in mufti, as he called it. She wondered what a young American might wear, and how obviously his nationality would be advertised: she'd be torn between pride and embarrassment if he stood out or looked silly.

She murmured anxiously to herself and glanced at the door. Tonight was for Michael and no one could dissuade her or badger her into giving him up. Perhaps she could get away with it. It might be best simply to lie.

What was it about him? Why should she want to conceal this friendship? Why had she already misled her mother, and deliberately refrained from sharing the delight she felt at meeting Michael? It was new, this urge to have secrets. She shivered, as if a cold finger had touched the nape of her neck. There was absolutely nothing wrong or wicked about this slight connection with a young GI who might disappear back to the US at any time. Yet her natural honesty and desire to please her parents was under threat. She would not tell her parents the truth about her intentions that evening. She would not allow

Michael to enter the conversation nor the realm of family discussion. Knowing him was a private matter.

Thus it was with a jagged sense of shock, and of a decision inadvertently taken, that Helen put her key in the front door lock and walked in.

Noisy chatter came from the living room. Shyly Helen hid in the hallway. The new relative stood in the middle of the room as if she owned it, with the parents hovering like lackeys.

Helen took a long steady look. This lady wasn't ancient – far from it. A rangy elegant woman above average height in a fine knitted suit, the aunt had a handsome mane of reddish hair folded at the back of her head in a French pleat, the like of which Helen had never seen before. The eyes were hazel and the face carefully made-up, with mascara and eyeshadow discreetly applied as if by a professional. Her fingernails were shiny scarlet. It was odd to see a woman with crinkly skin around the eyes and deep smile-lines etched each side of the mouth who refused to admit the depredations of age – Helen knew the aunt was much older than her father. Before, the notion of a respectable elderly woman wearing make-up would have seemed disgusting but on Gertie it was cleverly done and acceptable. The suit was strange, too – it was made of a sleek silvery thread which swished as the wearer moved. Perhaps that indicated that it was very expensive, a conclusion supported by the numerous items of jewellery which winked and gleamed. The overall effect was magnificent.

Barry was excitedly unwrapping a large present, his eyes alight with greed.

'Oh, wow,' he breathed. From the tissue paper emerged a briefcase in tan leather with a brass clasp. On the flap were stamped his initials in gold.

'A gift to see you through from childhood to manhood. See, it has a combination lock,' Gertie drawled. 'Put in some numbers you won't forget – your birthday, perhaps.'

'That'll look great at school,' he murmured. 'Nobody else's got one like this. Golly, Auntie Gertie. Thanks a million.'

The woman held out her arms for a hug but Barry hung back. 'Boys don't kiss, sorry,' he muttered and withdrew. Gertie laughed and dropped her arms.

'Gawd, I'd forgotten how uptight the English can be. My own kin! OK, but would you please call me Gertie? I hate that auntie bit.'

'No,' intervened his mother stiffly. 'We can't have them using your first name. It's Auntie Gertie and don't forget it.'

Barry sauntered off down the hall and rehearsed carrying his briefcase. Gertie turned.

'Well, hi! You must be Helen. Do I get a hug from you, if not from your brother?'

Helen came forward awkwardly. In a family which did not hug she was not sure how to do it and sensed that she failed to respond as required. Her aunt smelled flowery – that must be scent. The skin was fair and papery.

Her gift was prettily wrapped. 'Aren't you going to open it?' her mother asked, disappointed. The girl glanced at the aunt who winked conspiratorially: it was her niece's right to choose when to put the item on public display.

'I'll open it later. I'm sure it's something very special.' It felt like a leather vanity case. Her mother pouted but the girl continued to resist. Helen realised she was mentally pushing Annie aside to make room for the aunt. And to clear space for herself.

'Sure, kid. I gather we're in the same room? We'll have lots of chats. You can try my perfume.'

Her mother turned away, obviously put out, and busied herself with setting the table. Helen suddenly grasped that the two women did not know each other and would find it awkward to become friends, so different were their fields of reference. But something extra was at play. Her mother found the visitor overwhelming and a source of fear. Maybe it was already obvious that Gertie would dazzle them, but her mother feared most the effect on the vulnerable young girl.

That suggested the American aunt had something to teach her. And though her mother was afraid of it, she, Helen, was not: and wanted to learn all the more.

Daniel was as hesitant as his children, once the tensions released on the dockside had subsided. Had the rest of the family been on hand that morning he would have restrained himself. Now, however, he had a suggestion. He clapped his hands.

'When you've unpacked we'll go out to dinner. Somewhere nice, to celebrate your arrival.'

Faces fell all round.

'But I've put a pot-roast in the oven –' began Annie.

'Does that mean I have to dress up?' lamented Barry.

Helen said nothing but caught her aunt's eye in a flash of panic. With easy grace Gertie took her brother's arm and chuckled at his crestfallen expression.

'Great idea, Danny, but not tonight. I'm bushed. How about tomorrow – or better still, Saturday? Then we could step out in our finery, like Barry says. Where did you think we might go?'

Daniel lifted his chin defiantly. 'The finest restaurant in Liverpool. The manager's a client –' he added hastily at Annie's squeak of alarm. 'The Rembrandt.'

Helen had heard of it. The Rembrandt was a private club. It was the location of the smartest twenty-first birthday parties and dinners – the ideal of many of her schoolmates but quite beyond their parents' pockets. Her father must have decided to hang the expense.

Annie was tugging at his sleeve and spoke in an urgent whisper. 'But it's not kosher.'

Daniel looked at Gertie who shrugged slightly. 'So what?' he countered shamelessly. 'I'll book the table tomorrow. It's not often we have my big sis with us and I intend to make her stay here a truly memorable event.'

As Helen moved quickly away upstairs to change, she caught a glimpse of the expression on her mother's face. Annie was suffering. Her mother was no longer in charge in her own home. That meant she was in charge nowhere, and counted for nothing.

'You feeling a bit better, love?'

Sylvia Bloom put down the cup of tea on the bedside table and paused, hands on hips. As much concern as she could muster was in her voice, but she kept her face averted. Playing nurse for an hour was one thing. Catching flu in sympathy was quite another even if the invalid were her own sister.

'Dough, dot really.' The bunged-up nose of Rita Nixon was red and swollen. 'Pass me the Kleenex.'

'I'll sit with you for a bit,' offered Sylvia. The patient groaned and blew her nose, which both took as consent.

Sylvia had brought the newspaper with her and began to read as her sister dozed, but at the first flicker of awareness sought a suitable topic of conversation. However extraordinary the goings-on in Parliament might be, the daily details of their own lives were vastly more important.

'You going away on holiday this year?'

Rita sneezed. 'Yeah, if I ever leave this bed. Nix says we'll need some sunshine after that terrible winter.'

'There's an ad here. "*Make Madeira your island paradise this summer. Bananas and tropical fruits ripen all year round. Breathtaking scenery –*" they all say that, don't they "*– wines are cheap and plentiful.*" That's more like it. I enjoy a drop of Madeira. Stay in an exclusive hotel from twenty-five bob a day, or two weeks' holiday all in from sixty-nine guineas.'

'That's still a lot. Anywhere cheaper?'

'Um, let me see. How about Belgrade? Fly with Pan Am on big jets. One month return flight for fifty-five pounds and sixteen shillings. Full Rainbow Economy Service.'

'You'd have to get a hotel on top. And who'd want to stay in Belgrade for a month? Where the hell is it, anyway?'

Sylvia pondered. 'Yugoslavia, I think. It's past Italy. You know, Tito's place. Not sure I'd want to go to a country ruled by a dictator. I'd probably say the wrong thing and get arrested.'

'But Madeira's not much different. Doesn't it belong to Portugal?'

'Bloody dictators everywhere. Blackpool'd be safer. At least if I get into a row the policeman speaks the same language.'

'Doesn't have the weather, though. Or cheap wines.'

'True.'

Rita's stertorous breathing filled the room. Her sister looked around. The Nixons had installed fitted bedroom furniture in a pseudo-French style. Doors from floor to ceiling hid cupboards, wardrobes and drawers. Mirrors with gilded surrounds and hidden lights conveyed hints of a royal boudoir. White woodwork with gold filigree was handsome, Sylvia conceded, but collected dust and would soon look tatty. Had she herself been attracted by something similar, her sister's choice made it out of the question. Pine was altogether more modern.

'Fancy a trip to London one weekend?'

Rita stirred. 'What's on?'

'We could try and get tickets for *My Fair Lady*. It's been at Drury Lane five years and I still haven't caught up with it.'

'It'll be coming to Manchester soon, I read in the *Echo*.'

'Much better to say you saw it in London. We can catch it up north as well. Costs less here so you can take the family.'

'The kids'd rather see the Beatles. D'you know Roseanne paid three pounds for a ticket for them with Tommy Roe and Chris – I can't remember – Montez, yes, at the Liverpool Odeon? She says it was "fab". I don't understand the way they talk these days.'

Sylvia flicked through the paper for the cinema listings. She brightened.

'So: d'you fancy this new film with Elizabeth Taylor and Richard Burton? *Cleopatra*. Four hours long. Steamy antics on set, apparently. In and out of each other's bunks. I adore Burton but he's a dope to fall for her. Married man, too.'

'She's gorgeous, though.' Rita's voice became dreamy. 'Big bust and tiny waist and those eyes – d'you think she puts drops in to make them violet, or was she born like that?'

'Remember her in *National Velvet*? She was such a pretty little thing. Not had a happy life since she left England.'

'Fame and money. Doesn't buy happiness.'

Since Sylvia's assessment of her customers turned more often on their financial strengths than their beauty she felt bound to disagree. 'Don't be silly. Money can buy you anything.'

'Talking of the kids,' Rita moved on, 'have you heard any more about those American boys at Harold House?'

'What about them?'

'Well –' Rita glanced around furtively as if expecting eavesdroppers '– one or two have got quite keen. Roseanne says they take girls out to clubs and the like. I think she's a bit miffed that nobody's asked her.'

'She's got her Jerry, hasn't she?'

'Sure, but she wouldn't mind playing hard to get with him, if you know what I mean. And those GIs have plenty to splash around.'

'Your Roseanne's probably just jealous.'

Rita sniffed loudly. The sisters were not as one in their judgements on the remarkable qualities of her daughter.

'That Helen Majinsky,' Rita persisted. 'Roseanne says she's stuck up – home's not good enough for her, she wants to leave and go away. Bit of a smarty-pants. Anyhow, she's been seeing one of the GIs. Keeps missing Harold House with no explanation. That means my Roseanne has to do the till all night and she gets fed up with it.'

'Won't do her any harm to learn a bit of business,' Sylvia commented. 'Anyway, it doesn't matter, as long as they're Jewish. Drink your tea, it's going cold.' She turned a page. 'Oh, good. Lord Beveridge has died. Remember him? Welfare state and stuff. Cost us a fortune.' She read out a few lines of the obituary.

'I heard him speak once at Liverpool Town Hall. He said if we could afford fifteen million a day to fight the war, we could afford the peace and his grandiose schemes.'

Sylvia snorted. 'We can't afford them. The Americans paid for the war. We were skint.'

'But it's nice to know the Health Service's there if you need it.' The tablets on the bedside table were not paid for in full; the doctor who had prescribed them had come free. Only Sylvia's richest clients could afford private health care and they made sure everyone knew it. The two sisters briefly contemplated a life without socialised medicine and were silent.

Sylvia rose. 'I'll make a fresh pot before I go. Tea's the best remedy. Anything else? Right, then I'll pop by tomorrow.'

'My God.'

Michael paused in the darkened street and sniffed. From the gaping yellow hole of the Cavern stairs rose a powerful draught of sweat, urine, disinfectant and setting lotion, mingled with rotting fruit from the nearby market. Up too came voices and the twang of guitar chords and drums. 'You want us to go down there, Helen? It's like the gates of Hades.'

'Sure. It's the only way in – or out. But don't be surprised if people stare. I did warn you that most boys wear jackets and ties. But you knew better. In that lumberjack shirt and jeans you have *American* written on every inch.'

'Maybe they'll think I'm some kinda talent scout.'

'Not a bad idea, though in that case you'd be in an Italian suit. In this place that'd count more than money.'

The burly figure of the bouncer loomed. 'You two members?'

Helen produced her card. 'I am. And this – gentleman – is my guest.'

Doorman Paddy Delaney, huge and curly-haired, was guardian of the club's reputation. He checked Michael over suspiciously. 'No jeans,' he grunted. 'We don't have no teddy boys here.'

Michael spoke easily. His nose was on a par with the doorman's eyes. 'I'm in the Armed Forces, sir. Would you like to see my ID?'

Around them girls twittered and nudged. A US accent would lend tremendous authenticity to their activities. Michael calmly reached inside his tee shirt and showed his dog-tags, displayed on the palm of his hand: his manners and charm were not in question. One girl pulled Delaney's sleeve. 'Go on, Paddy. Let 'em in.' The doorman shifted reluctantly and motioned them inside.

Helen was excited. A session in the evening was rare for her. At lunchtime she could conceal her visits in the guise of shopping or going to her father's. But to attend at night with a boyfriend required an elaborate tissue of lies about Harold House with an enhanced risk of discovery. That gave added bite. She reached for Michael's hand and led him firmly down the packed staircase into the noisy cellar beneath.

Under spotlights the band on the tiny podium were belting out a rhythm and blues number. The atmosphere was smoky and acrid. Sweat dripped from brows, guitars thrummed frenetically. The drummer, a cigarette stuck to his lower lip, had a glazed wide-eyed expression as if hypnotised. The effect was overpowering.

'Long distance information
Give me Memphis Tennessee
Help me find the party
Tryin' a get in touch with me –'

'We're a long way from Memphis.' Michael had to bend and shout into Helen's ear.

She shook her head. 'We're not. This is Liverpool.'

The packed mass of youngsters were not jiving – there was no room for that. Instead they bounced vigorously up and down, heads bobbing, mostly without physical contact with their partners.

'What kind of dance is that?' Michael pointed.

'We call it the Cavern stomp. Come on, it's dead easy.' And Helen pulled him into a small space and proceeded to bop along with the rest.

'She would not leave her number
But I know who placed the call
The bootboy took the message
And he wrote it on the wall –'

The guitar riff pulsed around the low curved roof and set his teeth a-tingle. He had to bend to avoid bumping his head. The flip-joints of Chuck Berry's poor southern towns were beyond Helen's imagination,

Michael realised, though similar filthy dives existed not half a mile away near the docks. Not that he wished to explore any, though some GIs, drawn to the low life, had done so and invariably returned with more than they bargained for.

> '*Long distance information – more than that I cannot add*
> *Only that I miss her, and all the fun we've had*
> *Marie is only six years old, Information please –*
> *Try to put me through to her in Memphis Tennessee.*'

'That's a cop-out, that song,' commented Helen breathlessly as the last drum roll crashed. 'He's talking about his daughter, for heaven's sake. Should be his girlfriend.'

'Don't you think it's sadder, though? His kid's trying to contact him and he's frantic to return the call – and doesn't have her number? It's quite sophisticated stuff.'

'They play it because it was always the Beatles' opener,' Helen explained. 'The Cavern was a jazz club originally, then skiffle. That's sort of rock and roll, but amateurish. The Beatles are different – ambitious. "Besame Mucho" and "Till there was you", which none of the others would tackle. Most groups aped Cliff Richard and the Shadows or Shane Fenton, sanitised *yuk*. But the Beatles are explosive: they go straight for raw stuff, then mix it with romance but in black leather and Cuban boots. Or at least, that's what they wore till Brian Epstein got at them. Paul sings like a choir-boy – he *was* a choir-boy once – and John like a demented chain-saw. Mesmeric, I tell you.'

'I'd love to hear them live. When are they on next?'

'Dunno. Bob Wooller the DJ would know. Been around the joint for years. He's over there.'

Wooller was short and dapper, with a white shirt, dark suit and tie, the exact opposite of the more flamboyant versions of Michael's experience. It was as if the focus were so strongly on the music, with its evocative accompaniment of that distinctive Cavern odour, that everything else could be exactly as in the offices and streets above them. Or perhaps Wooller's respectable dress was a peculiar form of camouflage: the unobjectionable face of a revolution.

'Him?' Michael chuckled. 'He looks like a bank clerk.'

'Part of his talent,' Helen riposted. 'He used to be a clerical worker, but for the railways, not a bank. Perfect for keeping everything running smoothly in here, if you think about it.'

Wooller took the microphone as the band scrambled to remove their kit. Beside them fidgeted the next bunch of gawky youths, new Fender instruments in hand, fifteen-watt amplifiers stacked behind them, anxious to set up.

'Hang on,' he told Helen and Michael. 'They've got exactly the time of two records to change over. Move outa the way.' He raised the mike and consulted a scrap of paper. 'And this record's been requested for Val, Sue and Rosie. Brenda Lee, "All Alone am I". Where are you, girls? Wave. There you are, fellahs. Three luverly Liverpool lasses, all alone and waitin' for you.'

Good-natured whoops greeted this sally as the vocalist's high warble rose. The entire audience joined in and swayed.

'*All alone am I*
Ever since your goodbye
All alone, with just the beat of my heart –'

'Now then. What can I do for you?'

'When are the Beatles on again?' Helen asked quickly. Wooller's attention could be held only for a split second.

'Oh, you've missed 'em. They were here 12 April, Good Friday, big event, from four in the afternoon till well after midnight. With the Foremost, Faron's Flamingos, the Panthers. Nine groups in all. Fantastic night. But we had to lay it on specially. They're off to London.' His expression became dreamy. 'God, I can remember when the Beatles got a fiver a session and a quid for the driver. Even last autumn it were only fifty nicker. This time it was three hundred quid, and the fire service only let us sell five hundred tickets at ten bob each and we still had to fork out for the other groups. Bloody nerve – we got nine hundred in 'ere last August when they came back from Hamburg. Outa pocket, the Club was. They've got beyond us.'

'But you'll get them at the Cavern again, surely?'

Wooller shrugged but looked distressed. 'We'll try. Maybe August Bank Holiday. Look, kid, they can fill the Liverpool Empire. By them-selves. Two number ones so far and even their LP's in the charts. They're going to be big, we both know it. Plans for a film. And America next spring if the records go well – Brian's talking about a baseball sta-dium in New York.'

'Shea Stadium? But that's huge.' Michael's eyes widened. 'And they don't have concerts. I'm sure that's wrong.'

Wooller checked over the quartet of youths in close-cut suits, shirts and ties who had succeeded in plugging their equipment into the ampli-fiers as the second disc spun to silence. 'Cilla's gonna sing. Stick around.' He moved away.

'Who's Cilla?' Michael was mystified.

Helen pointed. 'Priscilla White. Calls herself Cilla Black now. She works here – she helps with the bands, takes your coat in the cloak-room. If you've left anything in your pockets, you have to take it out, get what you need then pay a second time. She's a bit fierce, is Cilla. *Her* voice is like a foghorn. Here we go.'

The skinny red-headed girl with buck teeth and a tiny mini-dress took the microphone and with total aplomb began to belt out the Peggy Lee torch song she had made her own.

> *'Fever! When you kiss me*
> *Fever when you hold me tight –*
> *You give me fever –'*

'I've never heard of any of these names,' Michael confessed as he examined the poster of future attractions in the dim red light. 'The Swinging Blue Genes – Rory Storm and the Hurricanes – the Four Just Men – Wayne Gibson and the Dynamic Souls – Freddie Starr and the Midnighters . . .'

'We've about three hundred and fifty bands in the 'Pool at the moment,' Helen preened. 'The Blue Genes are about to be Swinging Blue Jeans with a J: they have a deal with Lybro, our local overalls factory. Freddie Starr is fun. Mad, rather. Ringo was with the Hurricanes till last summer when he joined the Beatles. Jimmy Powell and the Fifth Dimension, who are on next month, have a crazy harmonica player called Rod Stewart with the tightest bum you've ever seen.' She swaggered away from him. 'Don't you realise that right now, here in the Cavern, you're at the very epicentre of the known world? There is no better place. Come on.'

The new band had started up an old Emile Ford number, familiar to the customers who again joined in the riff.

> *'What do ya wanna make those eyes at me for,*
> *When you don' mean what they say?*
> *You make me cry, you make me sad,*
> *You make me want a lotta things that I never had –'*

'He was the first black British pop star.' Helen seemed determined to give him a guided tour of both the club's geography and recent history. They found themselves at the hatch and bought two Cokes. 'And the first big pop name to appear here. Three years ago. Before Kennedy was President. Seems like another century, doesn't it? Soon they'll all be famous.'

The ill-lit corner was hardly quiet and, since the gents' toilet was nearby, suffered even more grossly from its assorted odours. Helen slipped her arm through Michael's.

'Look at them,' she motioned at the stompers, at the band. 'They believe to the letter what I've just said. *You make me wanna lotta things that I never had* – and they think they're about to have it all. This is no mere music. This is claimed as our renaissance – the revival of this great city. Yet in the end it's utterly insubstantial. We have no Tin Pan

Alley. That's in Soho. The moment the guys sign a contract they're off to London, and beyond.'

She squeezed Michael's arm. 'You're much more real, I think. You and what you represent. What we see here are the last throes – the city is dying. Real life is elsewhere. But let's enjoy it while we can, shall we?'

April 20th. I can't stand it. He's so bloody rough it hurts every time. He doesn't realise – or if he does, he doesn't care. Women are supposed to get hurt, in his canon. That's what they're there for.

He swears it's good for me and mutters about my not being a child any more. What he forgets is that I'm his child, and always will be. That doesn't give him the right to do what he wants with me. He may think so, but I don't.

I still go to church but I'm beginning to wonder what for. I pray every night that he won't come, that he'll be too tired or drunk. Sometimes when he has his wages he goes down Berry Street and finds a prostitute, then he doesn't want me. They're better than I am, he says, they know what a man needs. Know how to give a man a good time.

His mate Jimmy came again. If his wife knew she'd kill him, but she's expecting their third, he told me, so she won't let him have any. He wasn't as rough as my Dad. When he'd finished a clouded look came into his eyes and he whispered that if ever I needed help I should let him know, but down the docks, not at home. After he'd gone I found two pound notes under my pillow. I didn't know whether to laugh or cry, but I kept them.

Where's it all leading? What is this doing to me? I feel cut off from reality, in a horrible little cage I cannot escape. My poor soul cries out in anguish and terror. But can anybody hear?

Chapter Nine

A Good Dinner

It was after ten in the morning when Gertie sauntered into the kitchen. Her white satin dressing gown, tied at the waist, was trimmed with rabbit fur as were the matching mules on her feet. She found her sister-in-law working busily, surrounded by piles of dishes, with two opened boxes at her feet full of crockery half-wrapped in torn newspaper. Annie seemed out of sorts; plates and soup bowls banged and clattered alarmingly.

In turn Annie noted with some satisfaction that despite the painted toenails and tinted hair, once deprived of panstick and rouge the person before her was without doubt an old lady.

'Would you like a cooked breakfast? I can manage eggs –'

Gertie yawned. 'Oh, Gawd, no. Thanks. I'd kill for a cup of coffee, though.'

Annie looked dubious. 'I've got a small jar of instant coffee and chicory somewhere. We drink tea.'

Gertie blinked awake. 'You got a percolator? No? OK, then I'll go downtown later and buy you one. Glass of hot water and lemon'd do for now.'

Annie gulped. Lemon?

Gertie knew she was not at her best first thing in the morning. It was the only time of day when she felt her age. A superhuman effort was required, therefore, not to respond rudely. She settled for a glass of warm water from the kettle sweetened with honey, a piece of toast and a cigarette.

Annie returned to her task. She appeared to be removing one set of plates from boxes and putting the current sets, carefully wrapped in the same scraps of paper, into other cartons. The activity seemed to require the two sets to be kept completely separate and, since little surface space was available in the small kitchen, much of it annulled by Gertie's spreading herself and yesterday's newspaper over the table, it was a complicated manoeuvre.

A decorated tureen fell to the floor and broke with a crash. Annie wailed, flapped her hands helplessly, then bent to pick up the pieces.

Gertie raised her eyes from the paper and peered over half-moon spectacles. 'What are you doing? You don't need to go to any trouble on my behalf.'

'I'm not,' Annie responded crossly. 'This is for *Pesach* next weekend.'

'You change the dishes?' Gertie was incredulous. 'What – all of them? Cutlery too?'

Annie nodded and stood, two large shards in hand, trying to fit them back together. 'Of course we do. You can't mix Passover dishes with everyday stuff. Don't you?'

'Doesn't bother me one bit. I keep separate for *milchich* and *fleishich*. Mostly. And I won't have *treife* in my kitchen, though with processed food you never know for certain what's been used. But changing over the lot for Passover – that'd mean four sets of dishes! No way.'

Annie coloured. It was clear she was deeply offended. 'This is how we do it here. It's how I was brought up and it's how my friends operate. I don't know any other way. I won't have any other way; it'd feel like – like contamination. So I'd be grateful if you'd observe with us during your stay. I've enough problems persuading the children that these rules are for their benefit, without you . . .' She left the rest unsaid.

Gertie removed her spectacles, drew on the cigarette and blew a pensive stream of blue fumes out through her nostrils. Annie's nose wrinkled. Gertie had not taken the hint from the lack of an ashtray. Instead the cigarette was stubbed out on the toast plate.

'I must get dressed. Can I use the bathroom now? Pity you don't have a shower. Is the water hot?'

'Yes,' Annie answered stiffly. 'I put the immersion heater on specially for you. A couple of hours ago. I didn't know what time you wanted to get up.'

'It'll be earlier tomorrow. Say, you gotta let me pay for a few things. That extra heating must be costing you. Can I give you some money?'

How dare you, Annie wanted to scream. I will not be humiliated by you. You march in here and you casually assume you can simply take over. My husband decides to go to a restaurant for the first time in years, for you, not for our anniversary or something for *me*. You give my son a briefcase that costs as much as my weekly housekeeping: next he'll demand more pocket money and think we're mean when we refuse. And my daughter, who ought to be growing up in my own image, who should be planning to settle in a semi-detached house just down the road so I can see my grandchildren daily: silly Helen gawps at this newcomer like she's the pantomime fairy come to grant every wish. But no good can come of it. After this interloper's gone there'll be a price to pay, in discontent and restlessness. And who knows what else.

Annie forced herself to stare calmly into her tormentor's face. She

shook her head. 'No, of course not. You are our guest. Daniel would be
furious if I accepted a penny.'

'Then I'll pay for dinner tomorrow night. You can't refuse me that.'
And without waiting for a rejoinder Gertie swept out.

As Nellie crossed the shop towards the door she could tell that her boss
Maurice Feinstein was more than usually preoccupied. She wondered
what might be on his mind.

As usual Passover was an exceptionally busy period for a grocery
store, since (if anything was to be sold at all) the premises had to be
closed and scrubbed in their entirety before a single piece of *matzoh*
could be allowed to enter, let alone the myriad varieties and huge quan-
tities of food necessitated by the eight-day feast. The idea was to remove
any trace of leavened bread or flour – whether biscuits, cakes, instant
potato, pancake mix or anything which might have been tainted – tea,
jams – to be safe, the lot. That meant a complete spring clean with
attention devoted to the remotest corners where suspect crumbs might
lurk.

The clear-out had required the closure of the shop after Sunday trad-
ing. All hands had then worked late into the night, ready to reopen on
Monday morning, albeit an hour late. The shelves and glass gleamed.
Paintwork had been completely washed down and shone. The lino had
been swabbed by hand, with a toothbrush at the awkward edges. A
faint smell of disinfectant hung in the air, fresh and flower-scented.
Behind the counter a big Rakusen's sign in English and Hebrew wished
all customers a very happy *Pesach*.

It was fortunate, Nellie reflected, that the edicts only worked one
way – that *chometz* (leaven) could render *matzoh* unsaleable and useless
but not *vice versa*. So once the holiday was over, sealed boxes could be
retrieved from the locked back room and the erstwhile banned packets
of biscuits returned to the shelves. Had the exercise been required twice
in a month she would have protested and probably left. Instead, as she
crossed the floor to unlock the door, her breast swelled with pride at her
handiwork. She could justify that sort of annual effort. Other shops
she'd worked in never got the sniff of a damp rag from one year's end
to another.

The next few hours were busier than normal for a weekday morning.
It was not till after eleven and a quick coffee break (with a new jar of
Nescafé covered in *kashrut* stickers stating 'Kosher for Passover' and a
set of mugs kept solely for Passover) that the two had a quiet moment
together by the cheese display.

'You did a magnificent job, Nellie.' Mr Feinstein never lost an opportunity to be appreciative.

'Looks nice, doesn't it?' his assistant agreed. There was a moment's
silence.

'Nellie –'

'Mr Feinstein –' Both spoke at once, and laughed in embarrassment. He started again by patting her hand.

'You mustn't call me Mr Feinstein. After the years we've known each other. Call me Morrie. Anyway I wanted to ask your advice.'

'I'm not sure I'm the person to ask, Mr Fein— er, Maurice.' It felt strange to call him that, but 'Morrie' was absolutely too familiar.

He looked at her directly. 'I'm thinking of getting married again. Do you think I should?'

Nellie nearly dropped her cup. Her mouth fell open and she gaped at him with round eyes. Was this – did he mean –? He had dropped no hints. It would be madness to jump to conclusions. She coloured furiously, and to hide her confusion bent her face and took a large swallow of coffee. It was too hot and she spluttered.

He waited patiently with an anxious expression.

'Well,' she gulped at last, 'it depends on the person, doesn't it? Do you have anyone – particular – in mind?'

'Oh, Nellie, I wish I had,' he responded gloomily. 'She would have to be as capable as you and as pretty as my dead wife, God rest her soul. She'd have to help me with Jerry – stepmothers always have problems.'

'Jerry's nearly grown up. You could concentrate on your own needs now. You deserve it.' Nellie heard her voice tremble.

Mr Feinstein did not seem aware of her turmoil. 'Yes, that's what my dear Rosetta said. My wife. She came to me in a dream the other night and told me it was time to remarry, and that she would give me her blessing.'

The thought of a dead wife reappearing like some latter day Mrs de Winter to interfere with a new relationship gave Nellie pause. Her chance, however, might slip away. She took a deep breath.

'I think you should be extremely cautious. You don't need to get married again, Maurice, if all you're after is help in the business. I'll stay here and take care of – everything.'

How she longed to tell him that she would take care of him too if he wanted. He swirled the remainder of the coffee in his mug and stood brooding, but did not argue with her.

Outside the door two lady customers were about to enter, their identity hidden by signs and notices Sellotaped to the glass. The bell tinkled as the handle was pushed.

Hurriedly Nellie asked, 'I suppose she has to be Jewish – your new wife, that is?'

'Yes,' Mr Feinstein affirmed, but he sighed sadly. He turned back to her with anguish on his face. 'Oh, Nellie, if only—' he began.

There was no more time. The two women approached in a jangle of bracelets, shopping bags and noisy greetings. One was Mrs Cohen, the sprightly little octogenarian from Dudlow Court who had come for butter and half a pound of cheese. The other was Sylvia Bloom.

Nellie collected the two empty mugs, nodded at the old lady and shot the stout newcomer a glance which she hoped was full of recognisable malevolence. The *shadchan*, such people were called – matchmaker. Nemesis had just walked in.

'I've brought my order to be delivered Wednesday,' Sylvia announced. 'And guess what? I've found the ideal girl for you, Morrie.'

From the back room came a wail, then the sound of breaking china followed by a blunt curse. Customers and shopkeeper half twisted uncertainly towards the noise then returned to their transactions.

'Having one of her bad days, is she?' Sylvia exuded false sympathy.

Feinstein shrugged. Some instinct told him not to run Nellie down in front of Sylvia, even if she was a *shikse*. Ultimately he needed Nellie's services far more than Sylvia's, as the sparkling shop bore witness. 'She's cross with me, I don't know why,' he confessed, then realised he had no evidence for his statement apart from the muffled growls behind the partition.

'As to this girl – such an excellent match for you,' Sylvia continued. 'You're going to the Majinsky barmitzvah?' Feinstein nodded. 'Fine, so is she. You can get to know each other then.'

A few more details were exchanged which Feinstein received with a morose air. The news should have filled him with excited anticipation. His days of loneliness would soon be over. Yet as Nellie failed to reappear until the front door shut and the bell tinkled once more, he realised he did not view his course of action with the pleasure it deserved.

'Hi, it's great to see you. Twice in one week.'

'They'll be talking about us.' Helen grinned up at him, and allowed him to kiss her lightly on the cheek. Behind him the cathedral loomed into the sky, its red walls warm in the midday sun. Michael had left a message at the Post Office on the corner of Hope Street where the school pupils bought their sweets that he would be nearby during her lunch-hour, if she could get away. It had not been difficult.

'Well, I so enjoyed our time at the Cavern. What an incredible experience!' He was wearing the same check shirt and a pair of slacks, with his airman's leather jacket, almost too warm for the spring weather. In his hand were two paper bags of snacks purchased at the shop. She did not bother to hide her uniform: he was going out with a schoolgirl and ought to realise it.

'So's this.' Helen pointed round the back of the cathedral, where a stone grotto ran down and out of sight. The two began to stroll. 'This is where the kids from the Institute – boys' and girls' schools – come to learn to smoke. It'll be quiet and safe now. Gets a bit dangerous at night sometimes.'

The descent was steep, through a natural stone arch which formed a dank tunnel. Michael reached out to steady himself on the slippery path then recoiled at what he had touched. 'Jeez! That's a gravestone.'

'Sure.' Helen had a touch of mischief in her voice. 'It's the old grave-yard. St James's. Much older than the cathedral itself. An abandoned quarry, I think. Very gothic. Come on.'

He took her hand as they reached the level. The unfinished cathedral towered overhead, with no sign of movement up above. Any workmen would doubtless have disappeared for a long meal-break. Together they began to pick their way through weed-strewn paths, peering at the monuments and statues, some at angles or broken, many dotted with green and yellow lichen. Brambles trailed over catafalques, trees creaked mournfully in the wind. A scruffy tramp turned away at their approach and shuffled off into the undergrowth. In the distance a tall circular mausoleum stood forlornly, its marble columns cracked, isolated and forgotten. Yet the atmosphere was silent and dignified, despite the dis-order and insidious neglect.

'Loads of Americans here.' He pointed and read out loud. 'Captain William Wildes, born at Arney Town, state of New Jersey, USA, 3 July 1793, died Liverpool 4 March 1835. Captain Charles H. Webb of the barque St Lawrence of New York, US, died 25 January 1856 aged forty-five. There's another one, from Miami.'

'Sea-port,' Helen explained briskly. 'Look, this headstone's full of Finnish sailors – Carl Alexander Ingmar of Kristinestad, died 30 September 1869 aged twenty-eight. Another from Uledborg aged thirty, two years later. A dozen of them – there must have been a little com-munity. So much for the assertion that Liverpool couldn't cope with our entry into the Common Market because our trade is with the Americas. We've had a Baltic Exchange here for generations.'

'A sea-port with a lot of dead children.' Michael had half knelt at a series of graves in one corner and began to trace out the inscriptions with his finger. 'Liverpool Female Orphan Asylum. Ann Davis aged eleven, 1844. Maria Hughes aged thirteen, 1849. Lots of them. Why so many deaths in 1849? Was that because of the Irish famine?'

'No, that'd be earlier – 1846 or '47. Anyway, the Irish wouldn't have been in an Anglican cemetery. Cholera epidemic, perhaps. Kitty Wilkinson's buried somewhere near. She campaigned for public baths and washhouses for the poor in the last century. A blessed woman, my Dad once called her.'

Michael turned and gazed around. 'I haven't got long. Let's find somewhere to sit, shall we? I'll spread out my jacket.'

In the shelter of a cliff overhang they found two substantial family graves, handsomely cut in granite with flat tops and low wrought-iron surrounds. 'Not the Rathbones,' said Helen firmly. 'They are great benefactors of this city. We'll sit on the other one.'

For a while they chatted amicably. Michael wanted to take up the conversation where it had been left off in the Cavern.

'Why did you say that dive wasn't real?' he asked. 'I've never been anywhere so – magic, so vibrant in my life.'

'Oh, the council will catch up with it sooner or later. It's a fire-trap. The warehouses overhead are collapsing. So its success is temporary in every way: in a couple of years or so it'll have closed. Anyone with any talent will have been spirited off to London.' Helen reached inside the paper bag and selected a chocolate bar. 'I mean also that its appeal is false. Those lads on stage – some give up good jobs to play and are thrilled when they sign a contract. They're everybody's heroes. But they'll find they've been fleeced or lost every penny and will end up on the dole, permanently. It's not the way forward. It's not real.'

In the Cavern itself or with adherents it was not possible to utter such doubts. Helen continued, 'Down there if I said such things I'd be lynched. Oh, I love being a member and I have my favourites. But I don't want to be like them. I want something far more substantial in my life.' Artlessly, she grinned at Michael. 'Like you.'

Michael smiled down at her, then opened two bottles of sarsaparilla and handed her one. He looked around. 'You sure chose the right spot to debate the permanent and the ephemeral. Everybody who sleeps here once thought their experience was absolute truth, and now it's vanished and so have they. Their attitudes were held with total certainty. But in our days change is the watchword. And I think that is wonderful.'

He expanded with references to Franklin Roosevelt, that passionate exponent of the necessity of change in whose footprints his own heroes the Kennedy brothers wished to follow – no mean feat, and no mean ambition. Since her admiration for Macmillan was in part based on his links with the youthful John Kennedy, Helen willingly concurred. The discussion flowed easily, but on a higher plane than Helen expected. Michael was a sensitive and thoughtful man, utterly to her taste.

'I wish you liked our pop groups as much,' she teased. 'For all my hesitations, I am certain that the Beatles and some of the other groups will be world-wide successes.'

'I do,' he protested, mouth full. 'But mostly what I've heard so far has been loud. I like intelligence and wit in a lyric.'

'Oh, you do? But so much of what comes out of Nashville is such rubbish.' She began to warble, imitating the American long vowels and tapping her foot in rhythm: '*Laallipaap, laallipap, ooh lally lally lally* or how about *Who put the bomp in the bomp-a-bomp-a-bomp, who put the bam in the bama-a-lalla ding-dong*?'

'Mercy,' he chuckled. 'I can do better than that.' He sat up, an empty lemonade bottle in one hand like a microphone. 'This is the ideal spot.

Remember the Eddie Cochrane number? *Oh, there are three steps to heaven, Just listen and you will plainly see –'*

Above Helen his broad shoulders blocked the light. Something about his appearance, his bulk, made her catch her breath, but he seemed oblivious to their closeness. He gazed merrily down at her.

'Step one – you find a girl to love –
Step two – she falls in love with you –
Step three – you kiss and hold her tightly –'

Helen joined in the familiar last line.

'Well, that sure seems like heaven to me –'

The two laughed, but Helen suddenly averted her eyes. Who was he, this man whose physical presence had such power to excite her? The fine hairs on her forearms and at the back of her neck rose as he bent over her and every nerve tingled. Surely, she did not know him well enough to love him. She did not need to know him well to fall in love with him, of that she was fully aware. But the sheer intensity of the sensations he aroused, and the fact that she had no control whatever over them: this was new and thrilling, but scary.

Michael seemed to catch her tension. He put down the bottle and took her hand, but continued to sing in a fair baritone.

'How about this one, Helen? *Please help me, I'm falling, In love with you –'*

He finished the song, then looked quietly at her. 'I dedicate it to you. Don't be frightened of me, Helen. I mean you no harm. I'd break the leg of any guy who tried to do you harm.'

She could not answer. He put a finger under her chin and lifted her face, then kissed her full on the lips.

'You're a very special girl: I've never met anyone quite like you before. I don't know how much time I'll have in the UK, but as long as I'm around I'd like to go on seeing you. Is that OK? Do say yes, dear, sweet Helen.'

Her head was spinning. For answer she looked him in the face and touched his cheek with her fingers. He leaned across her and she lay back, nestling in the warmth of his jacket, and she let him kiss her, long and lovingly. For the first time she felt his warm weight press upon her body, though he was considerate and gentle. Yet the messages were paradoxical and confusing. Above his head the empty branches of dead trees, devoid of bud, bent and sighed at her in the salt breeze. Beneath the sheepskin under her shoulders the tombstone was hard and chilly.

'I must go.' She jumped up. 'We shouldn't fool around in this weird place. Angry ghosts might pursue us.' His question was unanswered.

'Yes, I'd love to see you. But it might be best not to broadcast it, not just yet.' She could not have explained why not, but some instinct had intervened. She laughed shortly to cover her embarrassment.

'You don't believe all that superstition, do you?' As they climbed back towards the cathedral entrance Michael was clearly making an effort to return them both to normality. He avoided using the carved headstones as a support this time.

'About ghosts, and that? No. I live in the present, and I sometimes resent the hold the past wants to exert upon us. They should let us go. The future is ours.' The two had reached the top once more. Helen added cheerfully, 'I'd much rather be cremated than buried, wouldn't you? But it's not allowed for us.'

He looked oddly at her but said no more. Across the street by the Post Office a group of younger schoolchildren were watching them with unconcealed curiosity. Quickly she bid him goodbye and walked, outwardly calm, towards the school entrance.

Michael would let her know when it might be possible to meet. She did not need to press him: he was determined to see her again, and as often as possible. Already, she realised with a jolt, she was beginning to read his mind, and to like what she found there.

When Helen returned home that evening it was to a smell unfamiliar in the Majinsky home – a warm, rich aroma which, after some puzzlement, she identified as ground roast coffee.

'What I should also have got', she could hear her aunt intone, 'was an electric coffee grinder. But d'you know I went everywhere in town and couldn't buy one? "Try a catering supplier" was the best advice. In the end, joy: I found Kardomah, and tins of ground coffee. You have to keep it in the fridge.'

'In the fridge? Tins?' Her mother's voice wavered.

Helen stuck her head quickly around the door to announce her arrival and slipped upstairs. It might be safer to stay out of the way for a while. In a trice the hated uniform was on its hanger and had been replaced by cotton trews and a baggy sweater. The satchel was emptied on to her bed and papers rearranged.

For a few moments she sat and ranged through the file. Damn Miss Plumb. The essay on satire was in confusion; the ideas wouldn't come clearly, though in a group discussion Helen knew she would have no hesitancy.

Naturally it was wonderful to poke fun at established institutions and defy the conventions. That was the role of the young in every age. Hadn't her parents' generation done the same? Helen was a bit vague about social history, but she could well imagine her mother dancing the Charleston with gay abandon, or her father voting Labour in an earnest desire for radical, compassionate government. He gave the impression he had had faith – in the political system perhaps, though maybe not in God. There must have been a time when he sincerely believed in something, before the apathy and middle-aged inertia which lately had infected him had taken grip. Was there a particular event which disillusioned him, or did it happen so gradually he didn't notice? On the other hand, her mother had probably always been quite a conventional person. Annie had the capacity to close her mind, to shut it tight. Helen could not picture her engaged in energetic rebellion, ever. Maybe Gertie would offer her some clues, if the chance arose and it wasn't impertinent to ask.

This was no help. She badgered her brain to think further back. In her grandparents' day people had been critical of old ways. Victorian *mores* had vanished once their war was over – votes for women came in, skirts went up, wholesale illegality was condoned at least in Prohibition-ridden America. At home a decade later in 1936 even the monarchy was briefly under threat as love for a divorcée had brought about the Abdication. So her parents' resistance to change, bolstered, as far as she could tell, by their friends' conformity, was not merely an irritation but an anachronism.

Michael's references to Roosevelt and Kennedy came back to her. It was unusual to hear anyone talk with such enthusiasm of a nation's leaders; that was not the British style at all, where (at least in her own circle) those in authority were regarded with derision. He approved of them precisely because they espoused change and were determined to make it work for their citizens. That, too, seemed far more transatlantic than European.

She had found the discussion remarkable and thoroughly enjoyable; in his company she had begun to feel more assured. Was this the 'serious boy' she had been seeking? Was that the reason, without understanding exactly why, she had a need to keep his friendship a secret? It came to her, though, with a faint melancholy, that conversations of this ilk with her own generation had all but displaced those she used to have with her father.

In her own time examples abounded of attacks on once-settled regimes. Censorship had vanished – officially, anyway – both from the printed word and on the stage. A much-thumbed copy of *Lady Chatterley's Lover* had found its way into the prefects' satchels if not yet visibly on to Library shelves. Established notions of God were being brutally demolished: Miss Plumb had sought their views on Dr John Robinson's *Honest to God* which derided the commonly held picture of the deity as a hirsute old man 'up there somewhere' as painted on the Sistine Chapel ceiling. Then the notion of marriage as the sole destination of normal women was uproariously sent up in Helen Gurley Brown's *Sex and the Single Girl*. Ms Brown propounded the scandalous theory that women might enjoy sex, and seek it, and have boyfriends – sexual mates – without ties or contracts, or regrets.

Pregnancy was not an unavoidable outcome, nor unhappiness. Meg bought the book and wrote her name boldly inside the cover but Colette, to her friends' bafflement, was scathing about its casual immorality and the likely risks.

So everybody was at it – the pillars of society, as Miss Plumb and the *Daily Telegraph* described them, had been seized and shaken vigorously. Would they stand, or were they so weakened that collapse was inevitable? Nor was this satire, in the sense of poking fun – it was a deliberate attempt to alter the way people lived. The air sang with brilliantly fresh ideas; her time at university could be filled with joyous experimentation. If only she could get there.

'Penny for 'em,' came the aunt's soft drawl.

'Sorry?' Helen was nonplussed. She folded the file on her lap.

'Penny for your thoughts. You were a million miles away.'

'No, not really. I have an essay to write and I can't get my head around it. All about challenges to an accepted way of life.' Helen grinned sheepishly.

'Oh, my. I'm beginning to feel I know chapter and verse about that.' The aunt sat heavily down on her bed. Her knees were close enough to touch her niece's. 'Say, Helen, what have I done wrong? Your Ma seems mad at me. I don't want to get in the way. But every time I offer to do something for her or the family, she looks daggers. I don't mean to upset her, not a bit.'

'She's a bit edgy. The barmitzvah's a big headache. And she's often a bit tense. Worries about us, I guess.'

'I guess: you're picking up a bit of American. That makes me feel more at home. Did you like your present?'

In answer Helen reached in the top drawer and brought out the red leather vanity case with its stainless steel clippers, its tweezers and emery boards and tiny scissors. As with her brother's gift, her initials had been embossed on the corner.

'You must have gone to a lot of trouble – and yes, it's splendid. I'm very grateful.' With that, she leaned over artlessly and kissed the aunt on the cheek.

'I gave your Ma a bottle of Chanel Number 5 – I know she used to like perfume – but she didn't react at all.'

'She thinks it's a waste of money.'

Gertie raised her eyebrows. Maybe money – her money and its obvious abundance – was at the root of the matter. But for that she refused to apologise. There was no virtue in poverty, of which she had had her share, long ago.

'Do you agree? Here, I offered to let you try my perfumes. Would you like to?'

Helen relaxed and laughed. 'Sure. Though they might be too sophisticated for me.'

For the next ten minutes the two bent their heads and rubbed aromatic drops on the back of hands, on the inside of wrists. Lipsticks were also brought out, and nail varnish, and tips about mascara discussed. Soon the small room was filled with delicious fragrance with a headiness that lightened Helen's spirits. The shared cosmetics were like a conspiracy.

'I think I prefer *Miss Dior*, though I'd only wear it to go out. Not for the Cavern,' Helen mused. 'It'd be wasted there.'

Gertie indicated the books and files. 'I'm glad you're interested in girly things as well, kid. Your Dad gives the impression you're a bluestocking. Got a boyfriend?'

A month ago Helen might have confided. But she hardly knew the lady seated on the opposite bed. It would be foolish to assume so quickly that Gertie could be completely trusted. If Helen were desperate to discuss Michael with anyone – which she wasn't – she'd start with her closest pals at school. Her own age, her own philosophy. Not Roseanne. Not Jewish.

So she dimpled in a show of shyness, conscious that she was deceiving her aunt who presumably merely meant well.

'Not at the moment.' She closed one of the files. 'Dad's right. I do want to concentrate on my studies for a while. Plenty of time for boys later.' She hesitated, then: 'I'm glad you're here and I hope we'll talk some more. Lots I want to ask you. And thank you for the lipsticks and things – that's so kind of you.'

Gertie rose. 'Kid, you're welcome. I forgot: I came up to tell you your Ma says tea's on the table in half an hour, and be sure to wash your hands before coming down.'

'She thinks I'm still nine years old,' Helen murmured.

'Of course. No mother can see that her children are no longer infants. What's worse, let me warn you, is that no father ever accepts that his daughter has stopped being his little girl and become a grown woman. That'll bring you most misery of all.'

Father Aidan O'Connor walked stiffly down the main aisle of St Mary's and St Joseph's, turned, genuflected as deeply as his arthritic knees would permit and with a beatific smile acknowledged the row of penitents waiting for confession.

Fourteen this time. At least an hour, even if they were quick. They came to him, he knew, because he had been there so long he had heard it all before. As they unburdened themselves of their minor peccadilloes they had no desire to sin further by shocking the priest as well.

He had noticed nevertheless, and with some relief, that several of the middle-aged female penitents, after a decent pause of several weeks to assess the new man's demeanour, had begun to drift towards Father Gheoghan's stall. So earnest he was, so anxious to do right. Yet the young man's handsome looks could prove a mixed blessing. In these days of turmoil for the Church, with so many ancient certainties upside down, the demands of the flesh could too easily undermine a man's commitment. Should the new incumbent decide eventually to abandon his vows, as many priests and nuns were now doing, Father O'Connor would not be in the least surprised. Nor would he condemn.

Father O'Connor regarded himself as fortunate. The temptations of females and the desire for family life, or indeed any kind of life outside his vocation, had never taunted him. Perhaps because there'd been no chance: into the seminary from the age of eight, destined for the priest-hood by a devout mother who'd handed him over without fear from her own care to Mother Church's. How he had been overawed at the high ceilings, the tiled walls, the running water in the ablutions area. The soaring wonder of the Mass had filled him with a joy which had never receded. The old Abbot, a revered and saintly man, had been fierce but kind; in his fellow novitiates, amongst the teacher monks he had found both brothers and parents – thus his needs both spiritual and physical had been tolerably well met. Given, moreover, the dirt floors in his mother's cottage in County Donegal, the lack of anything recognisable as modern amenities and the absence of any possibility of employment other than through labouring or emigration, a sound choice had been made which the beneficiary had never regretted.

He upbraided himself as he opened the door and settled his bones. He was committing the sin of hubris and would have to atone for it to Father Gheoghan in due course. He would also ask permission for a cushion.

Over an hour later it was a weary confessor who barely noticed that his next supplicant was a young girl. Hardly had she started the ritual incantation when he said, 'Say two Hail Marys,' in the hope that she would be satisfied and scuttle out.

The girl did not move. Father O'Connor glanced up in momentary annoyance. He could not see her face; her hair was hidden under an old scarf too big for her small frame. His voice softened. 'What is it, my child?'

It was a long time before she spoke. 'I wanted to know, Father, whether if you're involved in a sin, it's still as much a sin if you don't want to – do it?'

He peered through the grille, but her head was bent. He had to strain to catch the whispered words.

'Well now, that depends,' he began. 'God gave us free will, so we can say no. If you let something happen which you are sure is wrong, you can't simply shrug it off by saying you don't want to. We take respon-sibility for our own actions, you know.'

She was silent, but he could hear movement at the level of his knees, as if she were twisting a handkerchief in her hands. A process of elimi-nation might help.

'So tell me, my child. What sort of sin might we be talking about? Might it be that somebody you know is stealing – shoplifting maybe? Or perhaps you've been involved in some bullying at school?'

'No, nothing like that.'

He dropped his own voice. He knew his flock. 'Is somebody in the family being hurt – is that it? Does your Pa come home some nights and belt your Ma and you're too scared to interfere?'

She shook her head but did not speak. Father O'Connor was tiring of the game but tried once more.

'So it's something you're more directly involved in?'

That worked. 'Yes. And I truly don't want to be, Father, I hate it, but I can't stop him.'

Sex. It had to be. A snuffly noise came from beyond the grille.

'But you have to stop, my girl. Until you're married it is mortal sin. And if he's using some artificial means of contraception, that compounds it – much worse. You have to find a way to avoid him.'

A moan came from her as if she were in pain. 'It's not that easy, Father.'

'It's a man, isn't it? My daughter, you must understand. Men can't help themselves. That is their nature. But if you let him have his way you share the sin, no doubt about it.'

'I can't – stop him. He's – he's stronger than me.' She was sobbing, her breath coming in ragged gasps, each word forced out.

'Compose yourself, my dear.' Father O'Connor sighed deeply and shifted his buttocks on the wooden seat. If God had any mercy on him this one would be the last for the day. He waited till the desperate sobs subsided, then said quietly, 'I will pray for you, that the Blessed Virgin grant you the strength to resist. I suggest you go into the Lady Chapel for a few moments and do the same. Three Hail Marys and four Our Fathers. If you get completely stuck, go talk to the sisters at the convent. In the Name of the Father, the Son –' and without further ado he made the sign of the cross.

With leaden movements the girl rose to leave. Father O'Connor wondered if he had been too brusque. 'Wait a moment,' he urged. 'I meant what I said about offering a wee prayer of intercession for you. What shall I call you?'

The girl struggled to regain control and blew her nose. For a moment the priest thought she would not reply, then as she pushed open the door she turned her face to him.

'Yes, Father, pray for me. Take pity on my soul. It's the only thing which might help. My name's Colette.'

Though Annie made it plain she would have preferred the visit to the Rembrandt to be postponed or forgotten entirely, neither Daniel nor Gertie would hear of it. Given the imminence of Passover it was best to go without further delay.

'Can I wear my barmitzvah suit?' Barry demanded.

'You shouldn't – it'll be bad luck,' Annie quickly interposed.

'Where d'you get that nonsense?' Daniel had come home early and bounced around giving instructions. 'That's fine. Then if it's tight anywhere or needs a quick alteration there's still time.' He summoned his daughter. 'Your best frock. No trousers or other foolishness or they won't let us in.'

Up in the bedroom Gertie surveyed her niece's lavender gingham dress with its close-fitting bodice, narrow waist and full skirt.

'That shows off your figure beautifully. You're a very pretty girl, Helen. Make sure you smell good too.' Helen dabbed as instructed from the big bottle of *Miss Dior*.

The club was on the first and second floors above ground level of a fine old sandstone building in the centre of town, not far from Daniel's workshop. The car parked, the Majinskys gathered on the pavement a little overawed before an impressive carved door. The bell push, a shiny disc of brass almost a foot across, waxed and waned as car headlights passed. Through bay windows above their heads could be glimpsed chandeliers in a rosy glow. The main decor appeared to be red – crimson flock walls and ceilings, almost as if the place were a high-class brothel. Maybe it had been, once: in Liverpool such a history was not unlikely. Its current usage was betrayed by the discreet tinkle of wine bottle against crystal, of silver cutlery on porcelain. A fine smell of roast beef floated down from an open shutter.

Helen saw her mother sniff in disgust and bury her nose in the lapel of her coat. The girl was unsettled by the animosity between mother and aunt but was determined not to let anything spoil her enjoyment. This was the way her father desired to celebrate the arrival of his sister, the first visitor ever from his far-flung tribe in America. He'd have pondered deeply how to impress. His contacts included the most refined names in the city: Helen did not doubt that in such respects his taste was impeccable. If she were to risk a future beyond the confines of home such knowledge might come in handy. Not least, it'd be easier if her first experience of a smart restaurant could be in the comparative security of her own family.

Maitre d' Mario Belloni smoothed the lapels of his tuxedo as the group approached. His face creased into a practised smile.

'Ah, my dear Mr Majinsky! How wonderful to see you in our establishment.' He ticked them off his list and deftly removed coats, complimented Helen on her dress and scent, then whispered confidentially to Daniel: 'This suit you made me is superb. I must come and see you for another.'

It did not escape the women in the party that Daniel had claimed the manager, not the head waiter, as his client.

The property consisted of interconnected salons in each of which three or four tables were set. That gave privacy and cosiness though it limited the opportunity for covert examination of other diners. Mario bustled smoothly, collected menus and ushered them into the far room.

The table for five was circular, with a blush pink tablecloth which nearly reached the floor. It was laid with bone china in white with raised gold edging: the club symbol, the self-portrait of Rembrandt the painter, was on every piece. Each place had three forks and knives parallel, silver-plated with heavily chased handles in decreasing sizes, and another fork, small knife and spoon horizontally at the top, plus three differently shaped cut glasses. With a shiver of pleasure Helen fingered the elaborately folded linen napkin and the centrepiece with half-opened rosebuds and a red candle. Mario winked at her and hovered expectantly.

Gertie promptly ordered a Martini, though the rest could not be budged to more than orange juice. When the juice came Barry pulled a face.

'Ugh! It's got bits in it.'

Helen sipped hers. 'It's real juice, you dope, not bottled squash.' She drank carefully to imprint the sweetly acidic tang. Never again would she accept orange-coloured cordial.

'Wine with the meal?' Gertie asked with a hopeful air.

Annie began to demur but Daniel laid a hand on her arm. 'Why not? What do you recommend?'

Mario looked from one to another to assess their probable spending power. 'Depends what you are eating of course, but we have a delicious fruity Fleurie, or if you prefer a white a Meursault –'

Daniel's brow furrowed. To her own astonishment it was Helen who came to the rescue. More than once the girls at school had daydreamed what might be served at their weddings, just supposing they and not their mothers had the right to choose.

'How about Mateus Rosé? Everybody likes that.'

'And it goes with everything,' Mario agreed hastily. He lit the candle in the centre of the table. 'Now have you decided on your main course?'

Helen picked up the huge menu in both hands. In the dim light it was difficult to decipher. Many of the terms meant nothing to her. What were Lyonnaise potatoes? or *crème brulée*? or tagliatelli? *Was any of this kosher?*

Her father ordered poached salmon, with tomato and herb soup as a starter. Gertie asked for Dover sole preceded by an avocado vinaigrette. Annie began to order the same, then sighed and with an apology for her small appetite asked whether a mushroom omelette might be possible. Mario bowed. 'Certainly, signora. Whatever you want.' And Barry after much prevarication asked for the same as his father.

All eyes were on Helen. She picked up the wineglass and tilted it to examine the candle flame. Through its facets her parents' faces were distorted as if in a peculiar dream. She looked up. 'Are there any rules about what I can have?'

'What do you mean?' Daniel was impatient.

'I mean, can I have *anything*? If I choose what I'd like, you won't say I can't?'

Two of the three adults shrugged. Mario grinned at her. 'The kitchen is at your disposal, signorina.'

Helen hesitated, but only briefly. She took a deep breath and spoke quickly. 'Right! Then I'll have avocado with Dublin Bay prawns, and a steak. A big one.'

In the background she could hear her mother's sharp intake of breath and Barry's disbelieving 'Wow – prawns! And meat! That's *treife*. Disgusting.'

'How would you like your steak, signorina?'

Helen was stumped. She glanced in supplication at her aunt.

'First time you've had a steak, is it?' Gertie asked softly. Helen nodded. 'Then I should try it well done to medium. Later you might develop a taste for rare, but I guess it'd be too bloody for you right now.' Mario collected menus with a flourish and vanished.

'Helen! How could you? Everything you've picked is forbidden!'

Helen stared coolly at her mother. 'You said I could have anything, and I'd like to try steak. It's not as if we'd ever eat it at home, is it?'

'Absolutely not. It'd have to be soaked in cold water for half an hour then salted for an hour to get the blood out. We don't have blood, Helen. And we're permitted only forequarter meat. You know that. And you top of the class at the *cheder*.'

The wine came and the girl drank half a glass quickly, her nose wrinkled against the fizz.

'You don't care, you little madam,' Annie muttered furiously. Helen bowed her head and studied the sketch of Rembrandt on the plate. He gazed back inscrutably.

Afterwards Helen would admit that prawns would never be a favourite, not with that fiddly de-shelling. It was a struggle not to mark her dress and she had to be shown how to use the fingerbowl; then, after all the effort, their fishy blandness was a disappointment. But as the entrées were served with scrupulous ceremony she knew her temerity was worthwhile.

The steak was magnificent. Surrounded by onion rings, mushrooms and fried potatoes the sirloin sat richly inviting in the centre of the warmed dish in chargrilled glory. When cut, a slight purple ooze came from the soft flesh.

Under veiled lashes and with not a whisker of contrition she watched her mother avert her eyes. Her brother stared in horrified fascination as Helen raised morsel after morsel to her mouth, chewed happily and swallowed, as if he expected her to be struck dead on the spot. The waiter brought various mustards to try; as Helen savoured the milder French version mixed with the ravishing taste of the moist beef, it would, she decided, forever remind her of this magic moment: freedom.

The meat took a while to eat. To shield herself from her mother's grimness Helen did not protest when the waiter refilled her glass. By the time her plate was empty the girl was feeling distinctly tiddly. Her companions' attention had been diverted from her inexplicable wildness to their own meals, though Annie had merely toyed with the delicate omelette and declared it underdone. At that point the girl knew for certain what she had but dimly suspected in the past – that her mother, trammelled by both *kashrut* and stunted ambition, was a terrible cook.

'What would you like for dessert?' Mario hovered once more, but Gertie was alert.

'Sweet trolley please. I may try a bit of everything.'

Barry gurgled in delight at the gateaux and charlottes, the trifles and fruits marinated in brandy, the syllabubs, zabagliones and smooth mousses in stemmed glasses with angelica leaves on top. He chose an enormous slice of chocolate cake laced with black cherries and liqueur. Annie and Daniel refused any more; Gertie settled for mixed fruit salad and custardy trifle. Again Helen was left to last.

'No cream, Helen, you've had flesh.' Annie's voice was curt. 'You can't mix milk and meat.'

'Oh, yes, I can,' the girl muttered. She felt as if she could take on the world and beat it. The wine made her head expand, made her feel enlarged and more powerful: and gave her courage. If this were the effect of alcohol, she would not resist it in future.

She pointed. 'I'll have – what did you call it? Strawberry charlotte. And *loads* of extra cream, please.'

Her aunt had to show her how to use the fork and spoon, a combination unheard of at home. Her mother looked away with a groan. Even as she lifted delicious forkfuls, Helen wondered hazily what streak in herself could make her so cruel to her mother. Annie's anguished face was not far from tears; a bitter tinge had crept on to her mother's features. Yet the other adults were not so affected. Both her father and aunt, after clucking a little at her cheek, ignored her amiably and were engrossed in their own conversation. Surely what she ate did not matter *that* much?

What was going on, Helen wondered, between herself and her mother? She had long chafed at the proscriptions. More than once she had begged Reverend Siegel to justify the dietary laws in themselves, but his explanations had run lamely to the wisdom of avoiding rotten meat and the lack of refrigeration in hot countries. That would not do. Nor was it the whole truth. The deeper purpose of such arbitrary codes, she realised, was the differentiation of a culture. Identity, in other words – hers, her mother's, everyone with Jewish blood. But surely there must be

more to being an orthodox Jew than that? A culture which depended so
heavily on silly food taboos must offer more, or be exposed as hollow
at heart. A religion which clung so tenaciously to such unsustainable
maxims – to such trivia – raised issues about its most basic credibility
and values.

Far more significant ought to be the guidance for life which the faith
could offer. That must include the way people should relate to other
people. And here, Helen feared, once she started to investigate she
might uncover the biggest vacuum. That code of ethics which Reverend
Siegel had so lauded ought to have tolerance and compassion as its very
soul, but apparently – self-evidently – it did not. The tendency of Jews
to practise against others the racial discrimination they had themselves
suffered through the centuries was too often present. It was there in
Israel, it existed in her own home. It disturbed her and was profoundly
wrong. It was not her way – she, Helen Majinsky, could not behave like
that. She could *not* see other races as different, as inferior. It was not a
question of trying to believe: she refused point-blank to try.

Yet that was how she had been brought up. And the conundrum was
that her parents, these decent souls seated opposite whom she loved,
respected and had longed to please, held such views and expected Helen
to hold them also. Against non-Jews they would freely express (even,
sometimes, in the subject's hearing) such prejudices as would have made
liberal critics scream 'anti-Semitism' had they been uttered against Jews.
Intermarriage was absolutely forbidden – by Jewish law. Racial intermixing was not allowed – every subterfuge would be employed to
prevent it and to deter anyone tempted. Because it was Jews who said
and did such things, a deaf ear was turned. But she, Helen, could not do
it.

She wondered what Michael might think. Michael R. Levison: the
name suggested an Ashkenazi background not dissimilar to her own.
He did not behave much like Jerry or her brother, a fact which in itself
made him more, not less attractive. But then his *Americanness* – that
exotic combination of accent, dress, courtesy, dignity, as well as his age
and uniform – these were the dominant factors about him. His attitudes, however unfamiliar, might form the tentative basis of a fresh
philosophy for herself. And her reading – and Miss Plumb: with a rush
of relief Helen knew she was not alone. If a journey of discovery, however painful, stretched ahead of her there would be no lack of guides to
help.

As to this food. Helen tugged her reflections back to more mundane
levels. Was this cuisine better? Her reactions could have gone either
way. Did she prefer the taste, the mixture of flavours, the liberty of
action accorded to the chef? She ran her tongue slowly over her lips as
her aunt, who had been observing her, chuckled indulgently. The answer
was yes, this food was superb; and with it came the realisation with an

undercurrent of sadness that never again would she be able to enjoy kosher cooking and Jewish living as she had done before.

The strange battlefield had claimed its victims. Barry was defeated halfway through his cake, which was solemnly wrapped in a paper napkin to take home. Daniel and Gertie lit cigarettes and gossiped quietly over coffee. Annie sat rigid, pale and upset. And Helen finished the last crumbs with a dazed smile and her eyes bright. With regret she folded her napkin the way her aunt had. 'Gosh, that was fabulous,' she announced to the room in general. 'Thank you. Marvellous meal, great evening.'

'Why, hello.'

The family twisted around. Before them stood four new arrivals, young men with shorn crew-cuts and multi-coloured jackets. Both style and accents were unmistakable: American airmen from the Burtonwood base. Gertie sat up smartly and stubbed out her cigarette. She glanced quickly at her niece with new-found interest.

A little wobbly, Helen arose. 'Oh, hi.' She tried to focus, her heart hammering. 'Mum, Dad, I'd better introduce you. These are the boys who come to Harold House. This is CC Cohen, and his brother Buzz. And this is –' She could not continue.

He stood there in the candle-light, so tall, grave and polite, and her spirit churned inside her. She had hurt her parents enough that evening. She was brutally aware that, at least as far as her mother was concerned, the defiance had gone much too far. Some devil had got into her. But now – to bring Michael into it, and thus to advertise her growing independence and youth – that might be to rub salt into an open wound. This was not the time, surely.

As she hesitated CC stepped forward and shook hands. 'Hi! Pleased to meet you, sir, ma'am. This here's our friend Sergeant Newman, and Michael Levison. Is the fish OK? There's no Jewish restaurant in this town so we've been recommended to eat here.'

Gertie checked over the newcomers with undisguised approval. Pity they hadn't shown up earlier – it'd have been a much merrier evening. At her side Daniel motioned for the bill. 'It's grand. Great food. Say, how d'you know Helen here? My name's Gertie Ahrens. I'm her aunt. From New York.'

'They come to the youth club. We wrote to the base to invite them and they came,' Helen began hastily to explain. She waved a hand. 'Oh, tell you another time, Auntie. But we like to make *all* Americans welcome.'

Michael was at the back of the group. He made as if to speak, but Helen shook her head slightly, a warning that all the boys caught in an instant. Michael shifted his gaze elsewhere as if seeking an empty table.

'Time to move, I think,' Annie remarked crisply. Her expression suggested that one American companion at dinner had been too much for her, let alone a whole troupe. 'Where's my coat?'

'Yeah, that's right. We must go,' Gertie concurred. 'School in the morning for the babies.'

Barry's howl of protest made everyone laugh and gave the opportunity to slide past the GIs and away. As they paused at the door Helen glanced back. Michael was watching her; he winked and put a forefinger to his lips, then fluttered his fingers, just once, in a tiny wave.

In the car Helen sat as still as possible and ignored her mother's reproachful sighs. In the mirror she caught Gertie's eye: the aunt had been intrigued and would interrogate her further, of that she was sure. Her father had noticed, or chosen to notice, nothing. Her mother had been terribly hurt and would not forget it. And Barry would be confirmed in his view that his sister was a raving lunatic.

As the Vauxhall drew up to the darkened house Helen shivered. A profound metamorphosis had begun as if she were shedding a skin which had grown too small. It had started in the cemetery, as the cold stone pressed her shoulder blades through Michael's sheepskin jacket. It had continued with the meat, the cream, the wine, while Rembrandt smiled enigmatically from the food-smeared plate. She turned her face towards the stars. Their pinpricks of light had not altered in millions of years. But something had changed in her that day, for ever.

Chapter Ten

May 1963

The barmitzvah dominated everything. Before the day dawned Helen was heartily sick of the entire business. It seemed that nothing in the faith could be commemorated in a simple fashion – the more elaborate and showy, the better. As with her father, the excessive display went against the grain.

Her irritation was best suppressed. She tried to be as helpful as possible, which included collecting her brother's new suit from the workshop. At the Rembrandt it had been stained and had proven a bit big in the sleeves. Before Daniel arrived home her mother would have ensured it was tried on, twitched and adjusted, then pressed and put on a hanger.

There was no sign of her father. The entrance to Williamson Square was unlatched at usual, but a note was pinned to the door of his office: 'Back soon. Upstairs (Mannheim's) for inquiries.'

Helen trudged up the next four flights. However unprepossessing her father's premises might be, higher up in the gloomy murk from a dirt-encrusted skylight she was transported to another world. This terrace was old – it had been constructed in the late eighteenth century by a speculative builder for the lesser merchants and captains of the burgeoning port. Their wealth had soon led them further up the hill with its clear air, cleaner water and views over the river. The salons were too pokey, the bedrooms too few for their broods of children and servants. By the Great War the houses were mainly workshops and storage. The far end had been destroyed in the Blitz.

Helen gingerly held on to the banister. Fragments of grubby rococo plasterwork and rickety iron balustrades recalled former grace. Above the first storey the floors were bare planks; no paint had been applied for decades. It smelled musty. A patch of slimy mould revealed a leaking pipe. If the roof were intact it would be a miracle.

At the top she hesitated. Only one door was open. A light was on inside. From within filtered the soaring notes of a violin concerto on an old gramophone.

She peeped in. The place was a replica of her father's with its elongated workbench and shaded lamp above, but was much smaller and very untidy. It was dominated, as Daniel's was not, by a heavy deal table in the centre with heaps of cuttings in disorderly piles. A crescendo signalled the end of a movement. Helen knocked and entered.

'Hello, Mr Mannheim. You have good taste in music.'

'Ah yes, but then Yehudi Menuhin could make a cat's wail sound wonderful, my dear. Come in, come in.' *Fonderful*.

Mannheim bustled about. 'You have come for your brother's suit? I have it here. He will look a *mensch*.'

Three pieces were laid out on the bench – full-length navy trousers, Barry's first; the tailored single-breasted jacket; and a waistcoat, its front in figured blue velvet, the back in navy silk, with four bright brass buttons.

'I made the waistcoat by hand myself. Will he like it, do you think?' Mannheim showed her.

Helen fingered the silk wistfully. 'He'd be mad not to.'

The old man watched her shrewdly. 'So, pretty Helen, a cup of tea, yes? Your father will be back in forty minutes or so.'

The bent figure scurried into an enclave, evidently a tiny kitchen. Through another opening Helen could see an unmade bed. There came a clatter and the noise of water as a kettle was filled and placed on a stove, a whoosh as the gas caught, more clatter as crockery was located. Soon Mannheim reappeared looking quite pleased with himself, with two cups of hot sweet tea.

'Sit, sit.' He indicated a battered chair. 'You will not mind if I take my usual spot?' With that he perched his bottom on the table and in a surprisingly spry action lifted his thin shanks and tucked them under.

Helen giggled. 'You're exactly like the Tailor of Gloucester – I mean, a traditional tailor, sitting there cross-legged. Isn't it uncomfortable?'

'Not at all. You get used to it. You can get used to anything.' But it was obvious her remark had pleased him.

She sipped the tea willingly. The old man was quite clean despite frayed shirt-cuffs and a day's growth of beard. When he came to play bridge his dress, though shabby, was immaculate. She itched to ask how he managed in such limited surrounds. But he might be offended – or anxious, since to sleep here was probably against the law or fire regulations. Instead she remembered a comment made by her mother.

'Were you always in this trade, Mr Mannheim? I heard that you were an educated man.'

Mannheim screwed up his eyes. 'Ach – a long time ago, in another world. I was a scientist. I believe your father said you want to study sciences at university?'

Helen was startled; the tone implied that her father had spoken with pride of her ambition. 'Yes, if I can – chemistry.'

'You should think twice. The sciences can be a force for good – or evil.'

She had heard that canard before. 'So can any knowledge, Mr Mannheim. It's what we do with it that counts. I'd like to do something useful – research in medicines or whatever.'

Mannheim drank his tea, head bowed. Then he put down the cup and picked up a semi-finished jacket in which a buttonhole was half done. 'I felt the same as you, once, though in my day it was sulphonamides and internal combustion,' he murmured. 'I was a physicist, of a sort. I studied at the great institutions of pre-war Germany. My doctorate was on the early development of the turbine engine. They said I had a brilliant future.'

She waited. He sewed, in, out, until he had a steady rhythm. His voice took on a sing-song quality.

'But then Hitler was elected to power – you did not know he was elected? Of course – the people admired the National Socialists whatever they may claim today. So much poverty and unemployment. The Germans were starving. Inflation was so high we had to take a wheelbarrow of paper money to buy a loaf.'

He shrugged defensively and appeared about to break off his narrative. Helen gazed at him gravely. 'Please go on. This is my history too. Nobody talks about it much and I want to know.'

'It is in the reference books. I was no different to thousands – millions of others.' He sewed a little faster, then stopped and spoke as if to himself. 'No, you are right, *schöne mädchen*. I have a duty to tell. But you are not to feel sorry for me – only angry that such things can happen.'

The sewing resumed. 'I got out. I saw what was coming. I heard it in the lecture halls – you had to be blind and deaf not to realise what was going on. In Berlin the books were burned. When my professor was sacked from his job and deprived of his ration card I knew there was no choice. I tried to get my fiancée Sonia to come too – she was my assistant – but she wouldn't listen.'

He looked up with a wintry smile. 'It was not difficult to emigrate then – the authorities were glad to see the back of us. But she argued, like many others, that she was German, that her grandfather had been a Lutheran minister, she would not be affected. She told me the days of the wandering Jew were over. I could not persuade her that even to live in a land which could make such distinctions was no longer acceptable.'

'You left without her?'

'Yes, may God forgive me.' He finished his buttonhole, bit off the end of the black thread and for a moment stared unseeingly at his work. 'But I went back for her.' He selected another length of twist and started the next.

'You see, she pushed me away. She gave me a poem to make her point about the wandering Jew. It was by Rainer Maria Rilke – well, he never settled anywhere. Born in Budapest, lived in Paris and Munich, died in Switzerland, wrote his finest work in Italy. I carried it with me many years. Later I lost it, but I remember every word.'

Eyes half-closed he began to recite, beating time with one hand:
'*Wer hat uns also umgedreht, dass wir,*
was wir auch tun, in jener Haltung sind
von einem, welcher, fortgeht?. . .'

He opened his eyes at the mystified Helen. Then, like a teacher, he translated.

'*Who's turned us around like this, so that we always, do what we may, retain the attitude of someone who's departing? Just as he, on the last hill, that shows him all his valley for the last time, will turn and stop and linger, we live our lives, for ever taking leave.* It's from the Duino Elegies. You get Sonia's argument? She wished to remain in the place called home, to which she felt great loyalty. She virtually accused me of cowardice by running away, did she not? We quarrelled furiously but she took no notice. I – I could not stay in such a country.'

Helen wanted to ask a dozen questions but feared the narrative would stop. Mannheim sighed.

'I am ahead of myself. I was here in England, that is right. I went to Derby for Sir Henry Royce. They were happy to have me, with my background. Not so many qualified engineers and physicists in Britain then. I helped design the engine which went later into the Merlin and Spitfire. So in the worst times, when I looked up and saw a British plane, I felt proud.'

He paused. 'Have you heard of *Kristallnacht*? You have heard of it but you don't know what it is.'

'It was mentioned by my father once in a family discussion over the fate of distant relatives. All in hushed whispers. When I asked they refused to continue. It's as if everyone wants to forget, but I need to know. Please go on.'

'It was November 1938. In one night Jewish businesses throughout Germany and the occupied territories were destroyed – set on fire, looted. Respectable families were dragged from cellars and beaten up, women violated, little ones held by the feet and their heads dashed against the wall. The name is from the broken glass which littered the streets. It was the signal. I went to get her out – my papers gave me the right to return to Britain. We got married: I thought that might give her some protection. The *chuppah* had to be in a field as the *schul* was a heap of rubble. But I was wrong. We were arrested a week later.'

She listened, barely taking it in. The old man faltered. 'You will understand if I do not describe the camps. We were sent to Buchenwald because we were intellectuals and so of value. You should read *The Scourge of the Swastika* by your own Lord Russell of Liverpool – he was at the Nuremberg trials. It is all there.'

'And afterwards?' Helen prompted gently.

'When we were liberated? She was ashes and I was alone.' *She voss ashess unt I voss alone.* 'We stayed in the camps under military guard. It took weeks to sort out the dead from the survivors. In some ways it was worse, not knowing what was to happen. Short of food, clothes, still sleeping in the same lice-ridden huts. I wore my striped prisoner's pyjamas – you know? – I had nothing else.' His voice rose in bitterness. 'The alternative was the uniforms abandoned by the SS when they fled. Some wore those – not me. Three months later we were visited by a lawyer, a Mr Earl Harrison from Pennsylvania sent by the American President Truman. He was appalled. He wrote that the sole change from before was that we were not being exterminated. Then things began to move. And I came back to England.'

'To Liverpool?' She was puzzled.

He chuckled softly. 'No, my dear. Back to Derby. Most DPs – displaced persons – were refused entry by the UK but again I was "useful", as you put it. I threw myself into my research at Rolls-Royce and forced myself not to think or remember. My brain was a blank except for my calculations; my best friend was my slide rule. Then—'

The needle slipped from his fingers and was still.

'Then one day it hit me. In 1950. I was transferred to the new company set up to receive the latest atomic science from the Pentagon. Top secret. We were to make nuclear submarines – not the warhead, that was never my job, but the power generator. Such was my assignment: to ensure that the new nuclear turbines would function properly. If my team succeeded, submarines would be able to travel for months, perhaps years, under the sea with no need to surface.' His face became animated; his hands described arcs as if to bring alive the miles of tubing and mysterious control boxes before her eyes. 'Every drop of water would be redistilled, the air refreshed with liquid oxygen. Enough fuel for a year you could hold in your hand. We had the technology: it was merely a practical matter. Then such carriers of terror could become invulnerable – if attacked they could dive to the bottom of the oceans to hide. *Mein Gott*, what a weapon!'

He leaned forward. A savage edge had come into his tone.

'I saw I was creating the most lethal armaments which man could devise. They can start the next war and wipe out humankind altogether. My system could not take it. I had what you would call a nervous breakdown. I was found on the dockside here in Liverpool – I don't know what I was doing there.'

He shrugged and returned to his sewing. 'So: I was in Clatterbridge hospital a year. Completely mad, raving. On discharge I did not want anything to do with my former life. Your father took me in and now I earn my keep as you observe.'

The mottled hand shook. Helen gazed pensively at him. He must be – what? Maybe sixty, though he looked much more. Those terrible experiences would have aged him. Perhaps he was not much older than her father, yet he seemed left over from another age.

One question nagged at her. She took a deep breath and blurted it out. 'The Israelis were recruiting in the camps. Did you never think of going there?'

'It was called Palestine then. And yes, the offer was put to make *aliyah* – to go up to the Holy Land. In fact only the Zionists wanted us. Everyone else preferred to forget about the DPs. We were an uncomfortable remnant, and nothing special in the fleeing masses of refugees.'

'Britain took in lots of people,' she defended stoutly, content to allow him to digress for a moment.

He snorted. 'The British? The British were hostile because of their links with the Arabs and their need for Middle East oil – even then. One MP, a Mr Austin Hopkinson, demanded in Parliament that Jews who had found sanctuary pre-war in the UK should be repatriated. To *Germany*. Churchill gave him a raspberry. The Attlee government was no wiser. The British gave passports and entry papers to an entire company of SS – Ukrainians who presented themselves in civilian rags as stateless persons. Gullible lot, British immigration officers. Or fools. Or maybe not so gullible.'

She was silent. He took the hint.

'But Israel? Well, no. Several reasons. Firstly it didn't exist in 1945. It was a romantic dream, touted since 1897 but with no result we could hold on to. America existed, Rolls-Royce existed. My Derby workmates pressed for my release once they heard I was alive. And there were – other problems.'

The old man looked sideways at her, but her earnest face willed him to continue. He spoke gravely as if examining afresh issues long shelved in his own mind.

'When David ben Gurion came to Landsberg KZ – that is the concentration camp – he was heard to wonder how some of us had survived. He said we must have been hard and selfish. It's true that certain inmates helped run the camps and had virtually become collaborators to save their own skins, though not myself. I feared that in Israel I would be a burden, or reviled. I didn't have much affection for the place or the idea. And you might say I was sick of being a Jew. I had had enough.'

'But you might have felt at ease in a country where our people were in the majority.'

The old man sensed that Helen was testing points put to her by others. 'Not me. I was never religious. I felt comfortable on a test-site with other combustion physicists. To me the theory of relativity was more important than the Pentateuch. I needed nothing else, and no reminders of why I had been put in the KZ.'

'Mr Mannheim,' she asked slowly, 'do you think, then, it's possible to be a Jew and not accept most of what Jewish people believe in – or at least are supposed to believe in?'

He tilted his head like a scrawny bird. 'Such as?'

'Oh, the laws of *kashrut*. All the festivals like *Purim* and *Pesach* – changing the plates. Only going round with other Jewish kids. That sort of thing.'

'These are superficial matters. You are a Jew if you feel a Jew. If your heart leaps when you hear of Jewish achievement, if you are in pain when a Jew is attacked. If you will run to their aid before anybody. If your door is always open to a fellow Jew. If that's how you feel, then you are part of the tribe.'

That was no help at all. 'But what if you don't? What if you feel British, and part of a new world, and keen not to be dragged back by these superstitions and by the dead weight of centuries? And if you've those warm feelings towards everybody, not just a single section of humankind? What if – like you said – *Eretz Yisroel* really doesn't feature in your plans? That try as you might, you don't – can't – care about it one jot?'

'Aha. They want you to go to Israel, is that it?'

She bit her lip. 'It comes up. Any time I suggest I might leave home. I don't have to and nobody will make me. Only I don't fancy it a bit. And *that* makes me feel –' She paused, searching for the word, yet knowing it all the time.

'Guilty?'

Helen nodded unhappily. Mannheim patted her on the shoulder with a sad smile.

'So now, dear Helen, you have matriculated. You are truly a Jew. For centuries Jews have oozed guilt from every pore – about the burden of being God's chosen people, mostly. It is the Almighty's way to keep us in line. And do you know what?'

She shook her head, eyes brimming. He had not been much help yet she was glad she had tried.

'The day you cease feeling guilty, you will have grown up. And that day you will also begin to cease feeling Jewish too.'

The words lingered in the dusty air. A sob rose in her throat: Helen could not reply.

Old Mr Mannheim put down his handiwork, slowly unfolded his legs and came down from the table. Then he picked up the new suit and began to wrap it, first in white tissue then in brown sheets of paper, which he tied with string in an elaborate parcel. He stood, bundle in both hands, as once he must have stood with his entire belongings clutched before him when he quit his homeland for ever. She took the parcel and fled.

Blindly she left the workshop and stumbled out into the street. At the bus stop she leaned against the shelter and prayed for the bus to come quickly. The parcel was held tightly to her bosom but she nearly forgot her satchel – another passenger had to nudge her to remember. Kindly faces murmured at her. They probably thought her misery was something simple like boyfriend trouble.

On the top deck in her usual spot it was some while before she could raise her eyes. The conductor had noted the uniform, muttered 'Pass?' at her and left her alone.

Nobody spoke much about the death camps, nor about what befell the survivors. Their stories were so horrible the human mind could not enfold what had taken place; the numbers so huge – millions dead, efficiently and systematically killed – that no sane person could comprehend their scale. It was as if there arose from the blood-stained earth a piercing unholy scream, a shriek which split the air in two and left it shivering, which never ceased, and from which normal people must cover their ears or go mad themselves. It was impossible to absorb, detail after detail: no wonder denial surfaced. To turn one's back was a form of self-protection.

'Yet if we forget, it could happen again,' Helen whispered to herself. The moments in the graveyard with Michael returned to her with conscious irony. 'But if we dwell on it, what does that do to us? That crushing weight: such grief is itself destructive. Not least it can turn to hatred.'

She felt lost. And, at the same time, overwhelmingly grateful to have been born after the war, in England. Faced with such persecution she doubted she could have performed bravely, and was glad her courage had never been put to the test.

The thought came to her that a Christian wouldn't find it so hard to start afresh. To forgive, to turn the other cheek: a Christian would find pardon obligatory, however ghastly the events. But in Judaism the sole person who could exonerate a crime was the one against whom it had been committed. So a thief could gain forgiveness, or a slanderer or mugger; but murder lay forever unabsolved, whether the killers showed remorse or not.

Thank God it was a long journey. The bus was embroiled in a traffic jam at the corner of Smithdown Road, but rather than become fidgety Helen was relieved. At home all would be noise and chaos. Later that evening there would be time to herself, when she and Michael would slip away to the Cavern again. She patted the parcel on her lap and tried to smooth out the creases where it had been held too tight.

As the driver swung out once more past Nicander Road a new emotion was borne in on Helen – to her disgust, one of resentment. The Nazis had left a terrible legacy. Not just the smoking camps and the mountains of skeletal corpses, but the awareness that so few were left from a civilisation which had graced and enriched the whole of Europe. The survivors included herself as well as Mr Mannheim. And that conferred obligations to preserve the way of life which those monsters had sought to destroy. The duty lay not merely with her parents' generation, those lucky enough to have escaped – it included her own as well.

Helen shifted miserably. Here was a role for which she felt utterly unready. No, more than that, quite unsuited. Like Christ in Gethsemane she did not feel strong enough to confront such a dilemma. To devote herself to preserving the traditions would be – what? emptiness: negation. An abandonment of herself. It would mean an end to choice, an end to her dreams and hopes of a different life. Mentally at least, and probably physically as well, it would mean *staying put*.

Mr Mannheim had bid her: be angry. With that instruction, uncomfortable as it made her, she could concur. She left the bus, head reeling. The ache in her heart was close to fury, but suffused with fear.

The school was quiet. The caretaker had slipped away early, twittering glibly about investiture night at the Lodge. He was an Ulster-born Protestant of around fifty with sandy hair and erratic ways. Miss Plumb wondered to what invented office his cronies might elevate him, and how he would look in a black bowler hat and orange sash.

His absence meant she had to go round and lock up herself, a task she quite enjoyed. Conscientiously she checked radiators were off, windows shut tight and locked, doors closed. By the time her tour had brought her back towards her office her arms were laden with lost rulers, pencils, a blazer and two berets, and a forbidden glossy magazine with the Beatles on the cover.

It had been a fine school, Miss Plumb reflected as she paused in the hallway by the grand staircase. Under her guidance it would remain so, though the maintenance of quality was a battle royal. Above her hung half a dozen honours boards, the names of dozens of successful pupils since 1844 emblazoned in golden letters on varnished wood. One listed the headmistresses: only twelve in over a century. Such stability and commitment were rare these days. Her own was last: Miss E.M. Plumb, MA (Cantab), Cert Ed. 1955 –

Elizabeth Mary Plumb had gazed upwards at similar boards as a child in Kent and picked out numerous Plumbs, aunts, great-aunt, a cousin. Both mother and grandmother had attended the same ancient establishment but had never quite made it into the top two or three spots. Their relative failure had spurred Miss Plumb upwards and outwards, away from their complaints and self-pity.

A Victorian copy of Canova's Three Graces adorned the hall. Their elegance and sweet faces drew the eyes to their nakedness: that took some explanations occasionally. When a Bishop made an official visit, pots of flowers would conceal bare toes, and strands of ivy would be draped artistically across breasts and buttocks. Miss Plumb was amused at the delicacy, and traced the curvaceous line of a thigh with her finger.

A noise behind made her jump. She turned and found herself face to face with Colette O'Brien.

'Goodness! What are you doing here? It's after five.'

'Miss Plumb – sorry. I was finishing my homework in the Library. Didn't realise the time.'

The girl seemed weary. Miss Plumb observed her thoughtfully.

'Nowhere suitable at home, is that it? You have been looking a bit peaky lately. Come into my office a moment, Colette.'

Miss Plumb observed the girl taking a chair. Dark circles were unmistakable under the eyes and the skin had an unattractive pallor. The body was thin and gawky. The teacher could recall the bright youngster who had skipped into school as an eleven-year-old; her mother had been around then. Although the child was small for her age, which hinted at a degree of undernourishment, her manner had been energetic and cheerful. A sea-change had happened since, mainly in the last year or so.

Miss Plumb reached in a cupboard and took out a jar of boiled sweets. She offered them apologetically.

'I give these to the little ones, Colette. But I haven't any other refreshment, I'm afraid, so help yourself.'

Colette half smiled and took a blackcurrant flavour. Miss Plumb switched her gaze to the window.

'Colette, I do not interfere in the lives of my girls, but you do realise that you can speak to me? You are a very able young woman. For you – more than most, perhaps – education is a route to a far better world.'

The girl's eyes flickered. Sucking the sweet gave her the excuse to weigh her words with care. 'I know. You are good to all of us, Miss Plumb.'

'Thank you, but I wasn't searching for compliments.'

The girl bent her head. 'I don't know if you can help. I don't think anybody can.' She crunched the candy. Miss Plumb began to feel a flutter of impatience. Colette's next remark startled her.

'Were you ever married, Miss Plumb?'

'No, indeed. I put my career first and never regretted it. It wasn't allowed when I was young and – I am no longer so young. Why?'

Colette shook her head. 'If you were married I might be able to ask. But not otherwise. It's nothing to do with schoolwork.'

'Ah,' said Miss Plumb. She sat back. 'It's to do with – all that.

Boyfriends and so on, is it? Then you're probably right: I may not be the person to speak to. Your mother – no, that won't do.'

Miss Plumb was uneasy. The girl had a distant air, as if she wasn't concentrating on the conversation: as if she were not entirely connected. Miss Plumb knew that expression all too well. It manifested itself sooner or later on the faces of the majority of the pupils these days, usually at the juncture when they had decided that school wasn't worth it any more. Without vigorous parental support the changed attitude was impossible to budge. If that was true in Colette's case, it would be a very great pity.

Miss Plumb cast about worriedly. The discussion was drifting. If sex were the problem, she had certain duties. 'Have you tried your doctor, Colette?'

'Him? He's Catholic.' The tone was scornful.

Miss Plumb felt distinctly out of her depth. Colette raised her head and looked straight at her.

'You ever had a lover, Miss Plumb? There are – things I'd like to talk about, but only if you've done it. I wouldn't want to embarrass you.'

Miss Plumb sensed herself blush to the roots of her hair. What was she to reply – were the two of them about to exchange sexual confidences? Her mind raced. The French count in Anjou – that ten-year liaison which flourished solely during the vacations when Madame could be packed off to the mountains – before him, the Deputy Principal at the teachers' training college, also married, who had taught more than didactic skills?

Oh, dear. Spinsters in her position were supposed to be virgins – or virginal, at least. Any suggestion of impropriety could lose her her post. And she had not been trained, as a doctor or nurse would have been. Her usual approach to such topics was to call in the suitably qualified. And, naturally, to utter such injunctions as were proper to the time. She frowned at the young girl, but spoke quietly.

'I'm not sure my personal life is an appropriate subject, Colette. Nor am I allowed to give you any kind of – medical information. All I can do is to remind you that at your age sexual intercourse is barely legal. It is moreover unwise, and it is terribly risky. If you need advice you must go to the people who can help.'

The young face hardened. Miss Plumb tried another tack.

'I have to write reports for university entrance next term. It might be kinder if there were some aspects of your personal life I didn't know about. I want to say the best about you.'

The glance which flashed in return was laced with animosity, yet behind lurked something unfathomable, heart-rending.

'Thanks, anyway,' the girl said off-handedly and rose. Miss Plumb allowed herself to feel a little put out. Obscurely she sensed that a chance had been missed.

'Goodnight, Colette. Take care going home. And don't forget, if I can help –'

But the student had gone, and the door had closed behind her.

Nellie McCauley did not often appear down in the dumps, but it was clear to her closest friends that something was eating her. That same Friday night two of them decided to take action.

A knock came. The tiny television in the corner of the room had its sound up but she could not pretend that she did not hear. The knock came again, more insistently. 'Bugger,' said Nellie, and lurched to the door.

The chain went on automatically as she peered through the peephole. 'Who is it?'

'Doreen. And Trixie. C'mon, Nellie. We haven't seen you for yonks down the Ancient Mariner. Whoever he is he's not worth it. There's a country-and-western singer on tonight. Get your glad rags on and join us.'

Nellie unlocked the door and let them in but with scant interest. 'I'm tired,' she announced, and slumped back in the chair.

Doreen was a blousily battered forty-year-old with an optimistic outlook on life no matter how it treated her. She left her husband regularly when the couple came to blows but was as often reconciled. As a Catholic, divorce was out of the question. A former schoolmate of Nellie, they had known each other back in the days when the latter's surname wasn't McCauley. Her younger sister Trixie was a C&W fan and tolerably happily wed: but then her husband, deck-hand on an oil tanker, was seldom at home. Provided neither heard of misdemeanour by the other the liaison was secure.

An opened bottle of beer in one hand, cigarette in the other, Nellie looked dully at them. She had done the housework the previous week-end but not bothered much since; dirty clothes had been thrown on sofa and chairs, dishes remained stacked in the sink, the ashtray was piled high. Curtains and windows were closed. Nellie did not encourage invasions of her privacy so no one would see. In a perverse way it satisfied her. The state of the flat represented fairly accurately the condition of her soul.

'So what's eatin' you, kid?' Doreen loosened her coat and sat on the sofa arm with a sympathetic air. Her hostess sighed.

'That damn cow Sylvia Bloom. No, cow isn't right – vulture. Eater of flesh.' The two newcomers exchanged glances. 'She's a Jewish matchmaker, would you believe,' Nellie explained brusquely. 'Got her claws into my boss Mr Feinstein – well, got him lined up with one of her choice cuts. Won't let go till he's in some synagogue under the silk canopy, a wineglass crushed under his foot for luck.' Nellie could not clearly picture what he would marry, only that it would be a female shape in shimmery white, curvy, dark-haired – and younger than herself.

She took a doleful swig of the beer. Her second bottle. In truth she did not care for the taste, but her sorrows needed to be drowned, or at least dowsed.

'But what's it to do with you? Here, give us one of those beers,' came from Trixie. Nellie indicated the kitchen and her visitors helped themselves.

'You're right,' Nellie swallowed, and wiped her mouth. 'I dunno why I care, but I do. It'd never be me. Not in a million years. The orthodox Jews wouldn't have somebody like me unless I converted – and that takes ages and could be refused. You have to take lessons, like somebody marrying a Catholic.' Doreen nodded and Nellie continued. 'I'd have to learn Hebrew, God help me. D'you know it's written the wrong way round and hasn't any vowels?' Mr Feinstein had helped her read the three consonants which made up the word 'kosher'.

'It's a mystery, designed to keep intruders out. Like me. In our place. Underneath. When Feinstein gets married I won't even be invited to the *chuppah*. And I've worked for him over ten years.'

'My grandmother said they bring a lot of it on themselves,' Doreen commented. 'Racial hatred and that. The old pawnbrokers pre-war were so mean, and bullied their poor customers.'

'Glad I'm not a Jew,' Trixie laughed shortly. 'Wouldn't want to work for them, neither. British through and through, me.'

Nellie had no difficulty understanding such dislike. The exclusive nature of the Jewish faith reinforced such intolerance. That did not mean she had to practise it herself, nor allow it in her presence.

'Oh, yeah? You sure?' Nellie pointed the bottle at her friend. 'This is a sea-port. Nobody in these streets can claim purer blood than anybody else. You never know which sailor your granny went with forty years ago.' Trixie and Doreen giggled but did not remonstrate. 'Anyway,' Nellie continued stoutly, 'two wrongs don't make a right. However mean the old Shylocks were, that doesn't give a reason for exterminating them. Live and let live, is my motto.'

She did not want to be one of them. She did not care much whether they wanted her or otherwise. But she did hate how her boss, a good and decent man, was about to be entrapped, and how he would be quite content without her.

Doreen picked up Nellie's handbag with a threatening gesture. 'You're coming out tonight, girl. For God's sake, stop brooding. You can wear ordinary clothes – not everybody will be dressed up.'

At this juncture Nellie looked at them crossly. Their coats had been removed in the warmth of the flat and slung over the sofa. With a start she absorbed what her friends meant by 'dressing up'.

Doreen wore a cowgirl's outfit in tan imitation leather, with a low-cut

white blouse to show off her substantial cleavage. The buckled belt cut
her nearly in half and must surely be abandoned after a couple more
pints. Fringes everywhere jigged and flipped. In one hand but not yet on
the hennaed curls was a white Stetson, matched by the white high-
heeled ankle boots on the feet. Trixie was younger and slimmer; her
outfit of dark blue denim jeans and jerkin, red kerchief tied at her neck
suited her. The boots were black knee-length and she had left out the
hat.

Nellie's mouth twitched. 'Merciful God,' she muttered. 'The pair of
you look like a dog's breakfast.'

Doreen and Trixie sensed they were winning. Nellie was half pushed,
half pulled towards the bathroom. 'You've got ten minutes, girl. It's
Johnny Cash tonight.'

'Johnny Cash? What, the real one?'

'Well, nearly,' Trixie demurred. 'He does Johnny Cash. And Jim
Reeves and Slim Whitman and Tex Ritter. Lots of others. Ask him nice
and he'll sing one for you. Now gedda move on!'

It was a good half-hour later that the three women clattered along
the main highway towards the pub, from which came raucous chatter
and snatches of amplified music. Nellie had found a pair of tight
leopard-skin trousers and a black scoop-neck sleeveless top to go with
her fake fur coat. The effect was tackily glamorous.

By the time the three women entered the Ancient Mariner the entertainment was in full swing. The bar was crammed, mainly with men.
The three new entrants were greeted rapturously. In a trice the women
were seated at a prominent table and pint glasses of beer appeared as by
magic.

Nellie threw off her coat and wriggled happily at the wolf whistles.
It was a pleasure to have left behind the shapeless sweater, those scuffed
shop boots and thick socks, and show off her buxom figure. She
reached for her glass, aware that her bare arms were tidily muscled from
humping that grocery. Her earrings dangled merrily. She pressed her lips
together to smooth out the lipstick and laughed loudly at someone's
joke.

Doreen and Trixie were spot-on. He was definitely not worth it. Not
worth moping over, anyway. And she was mad to let herself ever contemplate life with – but no. She pushed the name away. It was a
complete waste of effort. He'd never have her. He was too set in his
ways. For him Nellie McCauley was not in the frame.

'I keep a close hand on this heart of mine –
I keep my eyes wide open all the time.'

The crooner wasn't bad though he had trouble with the key
changes – but so did Johnny Cash himself, Nellie recalled. Two pints of

bitter later life was much more mellow. Merry, indeed. On all sides came whoops of cheery ribaldry, great gales of it, as Doreen and Trixie brought more pals to join them.

A rum and peppermint appeared from nowhere and she sipped appreciatively: how grand to be treated like a lady. She leaned her elbows on the wet table and gazed hazily around. This was her sort of place: not that stupid shop. These were the types she had grown up with. Rough they might be but kind-hearted. Cracked a joke, liked a cuddle. Didn't mind who you were.

'*Because you're mine – I walk the line*'

'Nellie. I thought it was you.'

The broad-chested man in a dark blue jersey eased himself into a seat left temporarily empty by Trixie's new beau. Nellie began to say 'That's Bob's', when she stopped dead.

'It's me, Nellie. Aren't you glad to see me?'

The haze refused to clear. She prodded Doreen in the ribs but received only a chortle in return; her pals were too engrossed in their own conquests to come to her rescue. She grabbed the glass to steady her shaky hands, then drained it.

'Cheers,' said the man with a grin. He was clean-shaven, though jowly and with less hair than she remembered. Around his blue eyes, white crows'-feet stood out in his sunburned face. 'Thought you'd like that. Your favourite – or used to be.'

'Oh, my God,' Nellie gulped as she put down the glass. 'Pete McCauley. I thought you were dead – or in the French Foreign Legion, or whatever.'

'Not quite. But the Costa Brava seemed like a good idea for a while, then I got a berth on a Spanish tanker on the Barcelona–Caracas run. Been sweet-talking the senoritas ever since.' He winked.

'The Costa Brava? Then you *were* on that bank job. You told me you weren't, you stinker.'

'Heh! heh! I wasn't about to spill my beans on my mates, was I? Anyway it's eleven years ago. Trail's gone cold. Detective Inspector Slipper's busy elsewhere. So I thought I'd chance it. Hitched a ride on a tramp steamer loaded with oranges. Great to be home.'

Some reserve in Nellie sagged just as Pete's face registered that boasts and bombast were no longer as effective as before. He would have to work harder than that, she told herself.

'You could have written—' she began to protest.

'Oh, Nellie.' He took her hand; she did not pull it away. 'I couldn't, see. If the police were tracing your mail it'd have given us away. Same if I'd sent money. Most of it went in living expenses – you can call it Costa Packet as far as I'm concerned. Plenty disappears into the pockets of them Franco police to keep 'em quiet. Bribery and corruption isn't in it.'

Nellie hesitated and bit her lip.

'I thought a lot about you, Nellie.' His deep voice sounded earnest. 'Them foreign women – they aren't the same. Do you know they said I didn't talk proper English? I'm Scouse, I told 'em. I talk English like she was meant to be spoke. It's the other buggers who don't.'

Nellie blinked at him slowly. It'd be best to get up and move away. He was a rogue, this husband of hers, and always had been. Yet what else was on offer? Not Mr Feinstein, that was for sure. Perhaps Pete's return was both a punishment for her dreaming of a different world, and a reminder of the only world in which she was at home. A timely reminder – and one she should not lose hold of, not this time.

She smiled and raised her eyes to him.

'I'm not here long, Nellie,' he pleaded. 'I could still be put away for five years. Got to see my Mam, she's not been well.' He saw his chance suddenly. 'So I can't stay there, know what I mean? I thought . . .' His toe nudged a long blue kitbag on the floor.

Of course you could bed down at your Mam's, Nellie thought. The lazy old duck never did look after you – and as a seaman you're more capable of cooking your own breakfast than most in this pub. That's not what you're after.

She rose and swayed slightly, still smiling. 'Can sleep in tomorrow – shop's shut,' she mumbled.

Pete held out her coat in an exaggerated display of chivalry. 'Still work for the yids? Why don't you get a proper job?'

'Long story.' She could not control it: her speech was emerging slurred. A gurgle broke from her, half-belch, half-laughter. 'You'll have to hold me up, love. Gimme your arm.'

Paddy, the doorman at the Cavern, greeted Helen and Michael this time with easy familiarity, and joked about the attractions of the best club in Liverpool for US servicemen. Michael promised to spread the news back at base. Yet in truth the noise, smell and heaving bodies were more to Helen's taste than his own. After an hour or so Michael could take no more. Hypnotic as the music was, it prevented conversation. By ten o'clock he had persuaded Helen to leave. The two of them started to walk in the mild night air till they came to the El Cabalah, a half-empty coffee bar.

Michael carried two cups from the counter and placed them on the tiny table. Outside pink neon flashed on and off. It was quiet at this time of night, while bars and cinemas were still full. He fed the juke box with coins, pressed buttons. Then he seated himself. From a glass dispenser he poured two large teaspoons of brown sugar into his cup, took a sip and grimaced.

'You have joshed me, Helen, about how I'm complimentary about everything here. So let me tell you that you Brits haven't the faintest notion how to make half-decent coffee.'

The soft vibrato of Elvis filled the café. '*Wise men say, only fools rush in.*' They had passed a cinema showing the film, *Blue Hawaii*, which featured the song.

Helen grinned and drank a little. The froth clung to her upper lips and she licked it.

'My American aunt says much the same and it really annoys my mother. We can complain to Steve over there. He's very proud of his espressos and cappuccinos.'

'That's what you call it, huh? We're a long way from Little Italy, that's all I can say.'

'I've never been to Italy,' Helen spoke dreamily. 'In fact I haven't been anywhere much.'

'Little Italy's in New York. They have a marvellous parade every September for the feast of San Gennaro. Everyone has a whale of a time. I'd take you to Paolucci's or the Café Roma on Mulberry Street. Great ice cream sodas and pizzas with olives and mozzarella – oh, I forgot, you don't have pizza here.'

'We have spaghetti. In tins with tomato sauce. Heinz.'

'*But I can't help –*'

Michael pulled a face but laughed. 'Well, I'm not Italian so I won't take offence. But I'd love to show you my native city; take you riding on the subway, sit out with you at the Verrazano Narrows bridge, swim at Fire Island: Helen, you'd adore it.'

'*– falling in love with you –*'

He told her more about himself. That he was twenty-one and had graduated, but was keen to complete his compulsory military service without delay. That he was unsure what to do afterwards but might stay in the Air Force for a while. That his father held a senior post in the Justice Department which required frequent attendance in Washington. That he also had a younger brother about Helen's age, the apple of his parents' eye. He spoke with energy and enthusiasm, emphasising points by tracing circles on the table with his index finger. The family he described had a warmth and closeness which made her wistful.

'*Like the river flows surely to the sea –*
Darling, so it goes: some things are meant to be –'

Still she had not placed him in context. It was time to try.

'In New York, when you're home, do you go to a big *schul*?'

'A big what?'

'A *schul*. You know, a synagogue.'

He frowned. 'I don't go to a *schul*. Helen, I'm not Jewish.'

The air froze, and sang, and whirled away from her. Not Jewish? Her heart stopped beating and she could feel the blood drain from her face. She held her breath then slowly let it out, as if frightened ever to breathe again.

Not Jewish. Not allowed.

Forbidden.

Somehow it had been there from the start. He had not swaggered, he had not made a speedy play for her. He was obviously used to money but didn't chuck it around. His manners came from another culture, one less frenetic, less troubled, less persecuted, less desperate to impress. She might have guessed, had she allowed herself to consider. What instinct had suppressed a casual inquiry? Was it the same instinct which had led her to keep his existence a secret, though there was no obvious reason to do so? Had she subconsciously realised, and feared knowing? Until now.

'Take my hand – take my whole life through –'

Quietly she put down her coffee cup. He gazed at her gravely, only dimly aware of the importance of his announcement. Then he placed his hand on hers and squeezed it. She did not pull away but looked steadily into his face. Her voice was faint: it was an effort to speak.

'You do realise that the Harold House invitation – and your sur-name—'

'Sure. But not at the time. My name often throws people; my grand-father was a Jew from Poland. But we're Episcopalian. And what's more –' he leaned forward anxiously and held her hand tighter '– I was brought up in a liberal-minded household. My parents are New York Democrats. They would tolerate no kind of prejudice, not against Negroes, or Jews, or "Polaks", or "Ities" or anybody. My Pa won't allow derogatory talk in our home.'

He could see she was confused. Without pause he continued, his voice low and urgent. 'Hey, Helen, I sure hope you feel the same way. It's a new world for our generation. Remember what Kennedy said at his inaugural, about the new generation taking over? He meant we should look outward, put away old divisions which separated us. My Pa has campaigned for his brother Robert, our Attorney General. He's an even finer man, my Pa says. We *are* tackling prejudice and those inequalities which have made a mockery of our constitutional free-doms. That means we too must live our lives without hatred, respecting every man as our equal. And every woman.'

He laughed lightly to soften the solemnity out of consideration for her. Helen saw that he expected no less a declaration in return. But though at the highest level – in her reading for example – she would empathise with exactly the same sentiments, to hear them uttered as a recipe for real life was new and quite bewildering.

How he reacted in the next few moments would determine whether they could continue their friendship, deepen it to an alliance, or whether she would walk out and go home alone.

'For I can't help falling in love with you . . .'

The record clicked and ended. Behind them the shiny coffee machine hissed and gurgled, coins tinkled on the counter. The neon sign winked, pink and lilac.

Helen turned her hand palm up on the table, so that Michael could grasp it more firmly. It was an invitation from her to share her dilemma, but not to belittle or ignore it. He responded at once without a word. He had not lifted his gaze from her pale face, but stared solemnly and unblinkingly at her as if he wanted to transfer to her the depth and strength of his own convictions. The power and confidence of his grip, his hand warm without being clammy, gave her overwhelming reassurance. She had her answer.

'No Jew can be prejudiced,' she responded at last. 'Look at what's happened to us over the centuries. Don't worry, Michael. I'm not going to give you up because of that.'

A strange sound came from him, as if he were suppressing a cry. He rose, grabbed his jacket and pulled her up. 'Come on.'

His back as he marched ahead of her out of the café and up Leece Street had a firmness of purpose about it. They came to Hope Street where he had parked the Austin car borrowed from a civilian on the base. Away from the main road it was darker; street lamps cast ineffectual pools of light into the night. In the distance she could hear a bus grinding its way up the hill, a snatch of music.

Within a few yards he stopped and pushed her gently with her back to a brick wall. They were in an alcove, protected from the street. She looked up at him, not afraid. He had kissed her before, but briefly: enough to create a nagging hunger for more. However clumsy she might be with relatives whom she barely knew, with Michael it would be easy. His jacket collar was of sheepskin, comforting, inviting. Beneath it in the hollow of his throat his skin glowed and a pulse beat, far faster than normal.

Without hurrying he took her in his arms and held her close.

'Oh, Helen, you are so lovely, and so young. I don't want to cause you any grief.'

'Hush.' She laid her cheek on his shoulder. 'You won't. But I've never met anyone like you. It takes a while to get used to.'

He smoothed her head under his hand and buried his face in her hair. 'Your hair smells of apples. Why aren't you like other girls – all hard-faced and made up? Everything about you is genuine and sweet. Yet you're smart as a button. Whatever I say to you, you're way ahead of me.'

She lifted her face to him. 'You're talking tosh, Michael. Now stop messing about and kiss me.'

'Stop messing abaht . . .' He imitated her accent, teasing, making her wait. Then he bent and kissed her, gently at first, then harder, and let the tip of his tongue explore, not too aggressively in case this was new to her; and she clung to him inside his unfastened jacket so he could feel her breasts against his ribcage, and she arched her back and was standing on tiptoe, and her hands were kneading the small of his back . . .

He broke off. 'If I touch you, will you scream?' he whispered. In response she lifted his hand and placed it where he most wanted, under her sweater on her left breast. He slid eager fingers under the bra and found the nipple. She sighed and half closed her eyes. He pressed her harder against the wall, aware that she would feel his erection—

'I say. What have we 'ere?'

The policeman was right behind Michael who jumped as if shot. The law officer struggled to keep a straight face and prodded them gruffly with his truncheon.

'It may be true love, but not in the street, if you don't mind.'

'Sorry, officer.' Michael grabbed her hand as she pulled down her sweater. Both were red with embarrassment and warm with the sensations of the other's body. In a moment they were in the car and driving furiously towards Helen's home, giggling at the ludicrous interruption, sure that neither would tell on the other to anybody else.

Michael parked round the corner on Woolton Road where anonymity was more assured. He switched off the engine and kissed Helen again, but the little car cramped his long legs and banged his elbows.

'It's horribly late. I have to go in,' she said suddenly and wriggled out of his embrace.

He leaned back, one arm still around her shoulders. She reached behind to hook up her bra once more and tugged down her top. Her skirt had remained demurely over her knees.

'You've never done it, have you?' he asked. She shook her head and turned from him. As she pulled away her hand knocked against the gear lever; she let her fingers rest lightly for a moment on the knob, as if to indicate she knew what was to come.

'Would you like to do it with me? I'd make sure it was safe.'

A great shout came from her soul, but all she could utter was a sigh and a slight shake of the head.

He ran the back of his hand slowly down the side of her face and across the lips he had moistened only a second before, then picked up a dark curl and twirled it between finger and thumb as if committing every detail of her to memory.

'I won't press you. But think about it.'

She nodded, reached up and kissed him lightly one more time, then opened the door and climbed out.

Every inch of her was on fire: she could feel arteries pound in unaccustomed new places, in her neck where he had sucked a tiny love bite, across her breasts where he had squeezed her, deep in her belly, between her legs, though he had not ventured there or further. Yet his words had set her whole being to smoulder: as if she were a barrel-load of gelignite, packed, primed, and about to explode.

As she walked rapidly towards the house she listened for the car driving away. For a long time there was only the click of her own heels on the pavement. It was several minutes before the engine revved then roared off.

Nellie and Pete left the pub entwined; his swagger told his fellow drinkers all they needed to know. Catcalls and ribald suggestions followed them into the street.

Nellie, for all her intoxication, kept her wits about her. Her Pete was tall, and had worn relatively well. The money he'd stolen must have helped, but he'd been a handsome bloke in his twenties – that's why she'd fallen for him. What a stupid berk he'd been, getting involved with that gang. Too greedy to live on a labourer's pay, he'd sworn he'd never go to sea. Now that he'd been forced to, it seemed to suit him. Smelled of Senior Service cigarettes and Red Barrel – strong, masculine. Still handsome. And available.

At the door of the flat Pete McCauley wrinkled his nose. Nellie said nothing. Good housekeeping was not what he was after.

'*Mia carina*,' he whispered, and held her tightly.

'Oh, God, Pete. It's been such an age.'

'You're still a peach, Nellie. *Bella, bellisima*.'

He slid the jacket slowly off her shoulders so he could grasp the bare flesh of her upper arms. Then he bent to kiss her, but was unprepared for the ferocity of her reaction: hungrily she reached up for him, her two hands on his cheeks, and pressed her mouth and tongue wetly on to his. For a moment they clung till he broke for air. He enfolded her in his arms and rubbed her back with his thumbs, so that her breasts pressed into his own body.

Somewhere below she sniffled. He lifted her chin.

'You won't get any daft ideas, will you? I have to go back.' An idea of his own appeared out of the blue. 'But if we hit it off again you could come with me. Not a bad place, España. No extradition treaty. Lovely sunshine.' Another sniff. He didn't fancy her maudlin: better get on with it.

So Nellie found herself in her own rucked-up bed with the man to whom she had once been married, and, she remembered with a shock, from whom she had never formally separated. They undressed in a blur and crashed heavily down in a tangle of limbs. Fuzzily she gauged that Pete'd not learned much in his years away and was still as rough and speedy as before. He weighed a lot more, too. But he did the business with more than a little passion and it felt far better than nothing; with practice who knew what heights they might attain?

Later they smoked and talked, meanderingly, until he failed to answer and began to snore softly instead. Nellie lay back and studied the ceiling for a moment, then responsibility reasserted itself. She leaned over the supine torso, found the dying cigarette, stubbed it out and then her own. She yawned. Her mouth tasted furry but would wait till daylight. They could attend to their hangovers together. Gently, like a caress, she pulled the blankets over them both and snuggled close to her warm sweaty husband.

'Goo'night,' she mumbled, and turned out the bedside light.

Chapter Eleven

Barmitzvah

It meant 'son of the law', Helen knew. The Law was *Torah* – not just the five books of Moses around which everything else was built, but Kings and Judges, Daniel and Ruth, Ezra and the Maccabees, told and retold as if their adventures happened yesterday, and Ecclesiastes and Isaiah whose texts had to be treated with such caution since the Christians had pinched so much. But never the New Testament.

As the singing below swelled into a chorus she opened her own prayer book. The Law included, in addition, the *Talmud* and the *Shulchan Aruch* from which as a girl she was excluded. To study the medieval and later texts required years at a *yeshiva*; the main one in Britain in Gateshead would have been shocked to the marrow at the notion of taking females. That seemed odd, since the Law was a comprehensive system of ethics which women were supposed to observe as well as men. How could you be expected to obey if you couldn't investigate the sources?

Helen did not doubt that the Law was wholesome and worthy. The word *mitzvah* had various translations, all positive in implication. For example a *mitzvah* was a good deed. The road to heaven was paved with them – though in the strictest interpretation, a good deed counted only if nobody else knew about it: except God. The altruism and modesty pleased her.

But the Law was a protection and an identity, so there was little point in doubting it, or the way it was administered. At least not today.

She leaned over the balcony to gaze at the participants below. The *schul* was full, partly as a mark of respect to the two families whose boys were on the *bimah*. Only men were permitted in the body of the hall. The front row included her mother's two younger brothers, Uncle Sammy and Uncle Abbie, both businessmen from Manchester, and Aunt Becky's husband Leonard, who was a member of a Reform synagogue and clearly lost in the complex liturgy. The rest of her mother's extended family was either dead, ill or dispersed. Jack Feldman and his wife had emigrated to Australia, Ruth was working in Glasgow, Rosie had a sick husband and had declined. David the pharmacist and his non-Jewish wife in London had not been invited, a matter which nobody sought to query: their presence would have been both controversial and an irrelevance.

As in every Orthodox congregation women and small children were banished upstairs. The balcony end nearest the Ark was reserved for Mrs Siegel and her brood who sat bolt upright and followed every word. Aunty Becky and the other sisters-in-law and their children sat in a well-dressed gaggle around her mother. Gertie's transatlantic style, her choice of silvery grey for an outfit, the sweep and charm of her hat, made her the object of intense whispered curiosity. Downstairs, beside his father, Barry looked unnerved in the new suit, his head covered with a white *yarmulkah*, his shoulders with the silk prayer shawl Gertie had brought from the States as a special gift.

At the eastern end facing the worshippers, at the top of three balustraded steps, supported on carved and embellished pillars and surmounted by mottoes and exhortations in Hebrew, was the Ark of the Covenant, the *Aron Kodesh*. The doors were hidden behind a blue velvet curtain thickly embroidered in gold filigree with representations of the tablets of stone brought down the mountain by Moses. A tiny eternal flame flickered above.

The most holy moment was about to arrive.

Reverend Siegel raised his voice in a paean of praise; the congregation came to its feet and sang with full-throated enthusiasm. The elders, faces full of piety, stepped forward. The curtain was drawn aside and the Ark opened.

It was simply a cupboard set in the wall, but the sight never failed to make Helen pause in awe. Inside, it was lined in white ruched silk. Like grand eminences the holy scrolls were revealed in their splendour, rolled up and laid vertically in coats of purple, with silver bells on the handles and engraved breastplates which twinkled in the light. Each elder touched the edge of his prayer shawl to a scroll then pressed the tassels to his lips with a murmured blessing. Both parchment script and decorations might be of great antiquity; when a *sefer Torah* was too old to use, it would be buried in consecrated ground with a complete funeral service. The chorale swelled as the appropriate scroll was selected and carried on Daniel's shoulders to the *bimah*. There, with further incantations, it was denuded of its velvet and rolled out on the lectern ready for use.

Barry began to intone his portion of the Law, following the hieroglyphics with the silver pointer held by Reverend Siegel. His voice cracked a little with strain. Every note and inflection was sighed over by relatives both upstairs and down.

Barry made a tiny mistake and Helen winced. She could have done it perfectly. Yet in the Orthodox *schul* it could not happen. The Reform and Liberal synagogues permitted barmitzvah for girls – it was called *bat-mitzvah*, daughter of the Law – as they allowed many other depredations, but their approach was regarded as back-sliding rather than modern. What was the point in having a religion that was too easy?

But what was taking place below was not about religion. The barmitzvah was an initiation ceremony – an induction into manhood, an admission to the ranks of adult males who controlled the community as they had in the village or pale or ghetto from which their forefathers had come. So women took no part, and she suspected that the men might have preferred to get on with it without female chatter from upstairs. For the behaviour of the gallery during the two hours or more was to a degree disrespectful and certainly a distraction.

It was not their fault. Helen could translate the service, but since most women had not been taught Hebrew they could only chant the best-known lines with virtuous expressions. In between they caught up with family events in a buzz of gossip and showed off their best clothes and hats. Yet few had ever protested or considered their exclusion strange.

In the Roman Catholic Church the Vatican Council had denounced such parrot-fashion devotions. The Holy Mass should be in the language of the country its adherents could understand. The comprehension of the common people had also been at the heart of the Reformation: that such arguments stretched across centuries surprised Helen not a bit, accustomed as she was to quotations from second-century Rabbi Akivah in the same breath as Herzl or Chaim Weizmann. Nor was she surprised that clergy like Archbishop Lefebvre from France had denounced the proposed changes as heresy. The Church would be weakened, the Archbishop claimed, if it opened eyes and ears. Piety needed no compromises. Should the pious begin to think for themselves, there was no limit. It would end with men making their own pact with God, needing neither priests nor intervention nor churches, nor heaven and hell either.

It intrigued Helen that she could glean more from newspapers about the agonies of the monolithic Catholic church than ever was possible about her own. The *Jewish Chronicle* was not taken in her house; only one Jewish paper could be afforded and the *Liverpool Jewish Gazette* with a single reporter-cum-editor was mostly tittle-tattle and wedding photos. Since photography was not permitted on the sabbath, snaps from tomorrow's party would appear in next Friday's edition, with every invitee listed.

Time for the *Kadesh*, the holiest part of the service. Girls weren't supposed to join in the responses, but she couldn't see why not. Around her the women rose to their feet and were cowed by shushing from downstairs into comparative silence.

'*Kadesh, kadesh, kadesh – adoshem yevoretz –*
Veloe kol ho-oretz ke'vodo –'
'*Holy, holy, holy, is the Lord God of Hosts -*
The whole earth resounds to his glory –'

Below the men fell to *davening*, their prayer books held close to their noses. Their bodies swayed, heads in *yarmulkahs* or trilbies bobbed up and down with the rhythm of the language. A hum as of bees rose from the assembly. Near her, Mrs Siegel was doing the same. The interlude would take several minutes. Pages flicked over quickly as if there might be a prize for whoever could finish first.

The formalities were nearly over. Reverend Siegel, sweaty in his black robes and black velvet *couronne* hat, crooned a final verse and bowed to the now closed Ark. Men removed their prayer shawls, folded and kissed them and put them away in braided velvet bags. A man's prayer shawl would go to his grave with him. The bags would stay in the space built under their seats till next needed along with the prayer books; it was a sin to carry anything, even religious items, on the sabbath.

Now the women could descend though they could not enter the main body of the synagogue. Everyone gathered outside in the spring sunshine. Barry was kissed many times by effusive ladies till his cheek was multi-coloured with lipstick. Daniel's hand was seized and shaken. Annie was the target of attention also and basked in compliments.

Helen stood to one side, and did her best to feel proud.

All afternoon visitors came to the house until Helen and Annie, had they dared admit it, were exhausted. Gertie rode to the rescue – her friendliness and continued interest in the minutiae of Liverpool society were inexhaustible. Nobody protested when, once it was dark and the last visitor had gone, Daniel wearily suggested turning on the television for the news. And as the family sagged in front of the set, it seemed reasonable to watch the film afterwards, and slowly to doze.

Helen had debated going to Harold House but tonight was for familial duties and the GIs were away on a weekend exercise. More excitement was afoot. Michael had invited her to the base, an excursion planned for the following Sunday. He had spoken a great deal about his work; in fact, as she realised, he wanted to introduce her to more of his pals. The trip felt rather as, she imagined, the first contact with a lover's family might be. Would she pass muster? Would they like her? Whether she liked them or not was immaterial – it was Michael who counted. But a fair impression made on his companions could strengthen his regard for her. That mattered.

Michael was in her mind every moment. Apart from a few casual remarks at school (not in Roseanne's vicinity) she had instinctively kept quiet about him. Some inner sense had warned her early that Michael was not in the ordinary run of boyfriends.

For a start he was older than most of her crowd. He had completed the stage none of them had yet entered – he was a university graduate and treated her anxieties about gaining entrance with what amounted to a gentle contempt. Of course she should try, of course she would get in. This approach she found encouraging rather than the opposite: he took her abilities absolutely for granted.

And he was a foreigner. That gave their exchanges greater piquancy and verve. For whatever she disliked about her city or its inhabitants, whenever Barry or Jerry Feinstein made her despair, she could fall back on the certainty that Michael was not like that at all. He was not part of this decaying port, did not share its lackadaisical and cynical attitudes. He was honourable, educated and kind. His manners were a delight. That he was an outsider was a huge attraction for her, whereas for almost everyone else she knew – including her parents – such foreignness would rule him out at once.

It wasn't merely that he wasn't Jewish – as yet she dared not let herself think too deeply about that. But Michael presented a dramatic challenge which most of her family would deplore. Anything fresh or new would produce flickers of worry from her mother, hoots of derision from her brother, illogical reasons not to proceed from her father. Proposals which might lead to an altered state would be ridiculed until dropped. The presupposition was that everything should stay much as it was.

Yet the times were changing, or at least that's what Michael declared, and what the television news showed. The Beatles' sudden success was an example. Down in Mather Avenue, Paul's father and brother had had to hide behind their curtains as hordes of teenage girls descended to catch a glimpse of their hero. They would not be told that the group was in London and periodically had to be removed by the police. On the screen their faces were contorted and tearful as they were lifted bodily away. A new word, 'Beatlemania', had been coined.

And with politics too, an election could not long be delayed. After so many years a new government might take office. The Prime Minister and Cabinet seemed to have lost their grip. The new Leader of the Labour Party sounded confident, his supporters determined and united. The old guard would be swept away. What was it Michael had referred to – Kennedy's comment at his inaugural? '*Let the word go forth that the torch has been passed to a new generation*': that was it. By contrast with that superb rhetoric British Ministers' speeches were dull and old-fashioned, but at last it felt as if some ancient blockage was being shifted. How she longed to be part of the movement. She would have to contain her impatience until she was a proper student and away from home.

The television was switched off. Helen climbed the stairs, her mind still engaged. At her bedroom door she remembered that not every one of her relatives was so hide-bound. One, indeed, was a foreigner. She undressed thoughtfully and slid into bed. Gertie entered.

'Wow! What a day.' Gertie began to unbutton her exquisite silvery suit and found a hanger.

'Big event for us. Not often our routine is disturbed so.'

Gertie smiled. 'I guess the next time will be your wedding.'

'Shouldn't think so,' Helen murmured. She half sat up, her arms round her knees.

'Why not? It would please your mother. You surely can't think of a register office ceremony – it'd break her heart.' Gertie pulled a lace-trimmed nightdress over her head. She cast a curious glance in Helen's direction. 'Or do you plan not to get married, is that it?'

Helen took the plunge but tried to sound off-hand. 'Not exactly. I don't know. I see my mother, and I know I don't fancy her life. She's nothing but a housewife – a drudge, of sorts. I wouldn't be so different from most of my friends if I preferred a career, and not merely as some boss's secretary. Or as a nurse. I don't want to spend my time cleaning up after other people.'

'That's quite a rejection of motherhood, my dear,' mused her aunt. 'You don't have to do it your ma's way, you know. Don't have to martyr yourself. And motherhood can be a joy, especially if you've a happy partnership.'

So many questions came rushing into Helen's head. Was her mother a martyr? Or perhaps she acted one? And if so, was the marriage perhaps – not happy? Was that Gertie's view – and on what evidence? Helen had tended to assume that her own home was a normal model. Certainly it had been held up to her as such by both parents. What she had just heard disturbed her. For the moment however she held her peace: caution was essential. From Gertie right now she needed something else. She spoke again, choosing her words with great care.

'I wanted to ask you. D'you think it's possible to love somebody quite different from yourself – successfully, I mean? Everyone says it's safer in the long run to stay with what you know. But I get so bored with that. Is it bound to be a failure?'

Gertie sat on the edge of her bed and began to cream off her make-up. The circular motions gave her time to consider.

'That depends. I fell in love with somebody from my own street, but at the same time we struck out into the wide blue yonder. My Joe and me. Never regretted it for a second.'

Helen took a deep breath. 'My mother said you were quite wild when you were young. Especially around my age.'

'Did she now! I was a lot wilder than she was, that's for sure.' Helen bent her head: she was not about to get involved in any personal battles. Gertie wiped her hands on a Kleenex and reached for the hairbrush.

'Oh, Gawd. It's a million years ago. The family scandal – or one of them. D'you really wanna know?'

Helen nodded. 'All they ever do in this house is nudge and talk in half-sentences. Nobody ever tells me anything, Aunt Gertie. My mother seems to believe ignorance is good for the soul. It gets so that I want to keep secrets myself: it begins to feel like the natural thing to do. But I want to know about my family history, not just riddles. You seem the most – honest and open person about. So I am listening.'

'And you understand that you don't go spraying it around, yes? Fine. So listen.'

The elderly lady composed herself. She did not look directly at her niece.

'I was a kid. Your age, I guess. One day I couldn't stand it at home any longer. I was suffocating – I had to scram. So I ran off with a sailor – not hard to do in Liverpool! We got as far as Cherbourg. I'd hoped to board a steamer to New York from there though I hadn't a bean. Thought I'd sign on as a kitchen hand or whatever. Got hauled back pronto. My mother was hysterical.'

'Was he Jewish?' She hardly dared ask.

'No. Matthew Campbell, his name was – hardly kosher. No Jewish boy would've run away. He'd have got engaged and married me.'

'What was he like?'

A nostalgic note came into Gertie's voice. 'Matt? Drop-dead gorgeous, if truth be told. Ten years older than me. Tall and skinny with grey-blue eyes. Stomach flat as a board. He was Scottish, from the lowlands, from a dirt-poor background – ten of them in a two-room hovel, he said. Off to make his fortune, and more than willing to have me tag along.'

'Were you in love with him?'

'I thought so at the time. Ah, to be young and in love.'

'I mean,' Helen continued slowly, 'were you – lovers?'

Gertie stopped brushing. 'I suppose I should be flattered that you want to talk to me like that. But if I tell you, I don't expect to hear it repeated in the parlour downstairs.'

'Course not. I promise.'

'Sure we made love. He was terrific at it. I dunno who tutored him – not me. But I was a fast learner. You know, Helen, when you're young, fit, got enough to eat, when those limbs start to entwine and the ol' heart starts pumping – Jees, there's nothing on earth to match it. Ecstasy – you wait. Human beings were built to enjoy it, you know. Little buttons in the right places – press them and – *pow!* That's how Mother Nature guarantees the survival of the species.'

Helen stared at her fascinated. Gertie laughed.

'Hell, kid, if it wasn't fun, nobody'd bother. Take your parents, for example.'

'What do you mean?' The girl was suddenly defensive.

'Well – maybe I shouldn't say this. But those cousins of ours who were closer to her age got the impression your mother thought sex was a bit – well, dirty. Beneath her. Plenty of women thought like that in those days. Your Mom'd put up with it to have children, and to satisfy her husband but she didn't believe it was possible to have fun in bed. Miriam told me Annie was quite shocked at the idea that women could get completely carried away. But our side of the family – the females anyway – have healthy lusts. It's good for you, is my view. Always has been.'

'Do you still do it?' Helen could not hide her curiosity.

Gertie sighed. 'Joe and me? Not as much as we did – you get decrepit, the joints creak and you need your rest more. Once I'm recumbent I'm in the land o' nod. But if it's once a month, so what? It's still wonderful. I'd say I have a lively sex life for my age.'

'I don't think my parents do it much,' said the girl softly. 'I'm right next door and I think I'd hear. Mostly it's Dad's snores, or I hear him pace around when his legs are bad.'

Her voice dropped to a whisper as if her mother might be hovering nearby.

'D'you see what I mean? I don't want to get trapped like that. Stuck. Dependent on a husband for my money, and on my children and relatives for my hopes of the future. Living through other people, with my head filled solely with who's getting married, who's having a baby, have I enough to pay the milkman. Mum's horizons are so foreshortened it drives me nuts. I'm interested in what goes on *beyond* these four walls. It's not her fault, it's me – I don't think I'm cut out to be a conventional Jewish momma.'

Gertie climbed into bed. 'That's quite a confession for the weekend of your brother's barmitzvah. You don't have to be the same as your own mother.'

'That's easier said than done, Aunt Gertie. Your approach is much more open. You seem so much more alive.'

'Hm. Well, I try. Life's great – but it's what you make of it. Say, though. I meant to ask you when we had a moment alone. Those American boys we met at the restaurant. They were real cute. They come to your club?'

'Well – that'd be an exaggeration. They've been a couple of times. They're a lot more sophisticated than us and can go to pubs and that.'

Gertie cast a veiled glance in Helen's direction. 'You might make a play for one of them. Did I catch the name Cohen?'

'Them? Buzz and CC's family are Lubavicher Chassids. I don't think they'd be interested that way.'

'But the others?' Gertie persisted, her eyes bright.

Helen paused a long time. She could confide, now. She could take a chance and trust this elegant, unconventional aunt. She could seek advice, as she had with Mr Mannheim. Yet something held her back – perhaps that natural reticence inherited from her mother, or a more British reserve picked up at school. Most likely it was a deeper instinct that Michael was too precious to be a suitable subject for idle chatter.

'I think that's a matter of ask no questions and you'll get told no lies, Aunt Gertie. But I don't want that to surface in the parlour either.' The assumption that the other GIs may well be suitable was allowed to lie uncorrected.

'Poor Helen. You don't fit into any of this, do you?' Gertie leaned across and patted the girl's knee. 'I need my beauty sleep, so goodnight. And you can escape, you know. If you planned to emigrate to the States I'd sponsor you and so would your other family. You don't have to stay put and be miserable. In fact you can do whatever you want, honey. The world's at your feet, don't you realise that?'

By Sunday afternoon the Marcus Liversham Hall had been transformed. A huge red and gold banner was pinned to the wall: HAPPY BARMITZVAH – MAZELTOV. Between the lights and the windows hung streamers and bunches of white and blue balloons with ribbons. Trestle tables had been decked out with blue linen, flower arrangements and pretty white crockery. Everything had been hired from the synagogue as both accessible and cheap; most items had been bought by a committee in a fit of patriotic zeal for an Independence Day supper, so were in the colours of the Israeli flag. That too was present, tacked up on the far side.

Helen had decided against an invitation either for Brenda, Meg or Colette, or for the GIs. Her schoolfriends would have been treated with distant condescension by other guests and would have required endless explanations and shepherding. As for Michael: once his origins had been established his appearance would have been courting disaster. It was unthinkable to invite the other boys without him. Though she felt lonely and missed him, she concentrated instead on the active role as dutiful daughter. The alternative was to hover at her mother's elbow and be greeted as an afterthought, mostly with a comment about how big she had grown.

Conscientiously she slipped into the kitchen to meet the hired staff, then walked round to check. On the stage the four-piece band were setting up their instruments: drums, saxophone, bass, and an innovation – an electric organ. Her mother's own candlesticks were on the top table for the blessing. The microphone was in place and appeared to work. As the caterer bustled about, the girl fingered the serviettes, specially printed for the event in silver on white, with the date, Barry's full name, and 'Mazeltov Daniel and Annie'. The five Hebraic characters for 'mazeltov' were beneath.

Quite suddenly two hundred people turned up at once, it seemed. Not for Jewish people any exaggerated delay or dramatic late entrances at a *simchah*. Where there was food and wine going, Helen reflected wryly, her kith and kin were bang on time.

Most she knew: her father's friends, every in-law that could be traced, the usual pillars of local society. Gertie swanned about, magnificent in a gold sheath dress which showed off her still lithe shape and red hair; Annie by contrast looked bland and a little tired. Others were less familiar, such as a young second cousin over from Israel whose family had escaped the Holocaust, and a 'dear lady friend' wheedled in at the last minute by Sylvia Bloom. Yet as guests filed in and found their seats, as the band began to play songs from the shows, with a glass of wine inside her and compliments received about her dress (pink shantung with a tiny waist from Blackler's) and hair (in a French pleat like her aunt's and very grown-up), Helen began to relax.

For the photos, the meal and the speeches she stayed demurely on the top table. As the musicians struck up waltzes and foxtrots she moved away. She did not want to dance if it could be avoided.

Maurice Feinstein was not noted for his dancing skills either but Vera Wolfson, the lady to whom he had been introduced, obviously expected it of him. It'd been no accident that the two were on the same table and facing – a phone call from Sylvia to Annie had seen to that, in return for a marginally fatter cheque as a barmitzvah present. Sylvia herself, a vision in navy satin (a bit excessive for a mere barmitzvah, Maurice thought), was located at the table end to keep a motherly eye on her charges. His son Jerry was mercifully out of earshot in the young people's corner near the drummer.

Maurice Feinstein felt extraordinarily shy. Stupid, really, a grown man. Vera was thirtyish, though Sylvia had insisted she was twenty-seven. Not married – had been working abroad. That sounded fishy: but he would explore the matter further when they had time to themselves. Not pretty, exactly – the nose was a mite too long and pointed – but presentable. Quite smart: a cream dress and jacket, genuine pearls, make-up. Hands clean, nails varnished in pink. Gold bracelet watch on slim wrist. No rings.

Maurice sighed inwardly. That was the trouble. His soul did not leap. Nothing about her called to him. She seemed determined to play down anything dramatic about herself, yet her manner had an eager hopefulness that made his heart sink. He risked a look at Sylvia who nodded vigorously. Better get on with it.

'Dance?' he asked heavily and in a trice Vera was in his arms. Not till they were well out on to the floor did Maurice realise he hadn't the faintest notion how to do the cha-cha. He shuffled and jiggled in approximate time to the music. His partner however was on her toes, bending neatly at the knee, twisting and turning. Her face bore a bright smile. He noticed her fine calves and trim ankles. She seemed to know what to do.

'You're a lovely dancer,' he puffed as the music came to its closing bars, and added 'Cha cha cha!' without much enthusiasm. He turned back towards their seats but she held his fingers tightly and did not budge.

'Yeah, I love it. Got prizes for it. Let's do the next one.'

Thus it was a heavily perspiring Maurice Feinstein who, half an hour later, announced firmly that he was not going to attempt the Black Bottom and plodded to their table without her. Vera took the hint and headed demurely for the ladies'. Maurice sat and poured a beer from the jug, drank it in one greedy gulp and poured another.

'So? You like?' Sylvia was instantly at his side. Her eyes darted from his reddened face to the door of the toilet.

'Up to a point, Sylvia,' was the guarded answer. 'We've not had much chance of a conversation.'

'She's perfect for you. Such a delightful couple you make. Everybody's talking.' After a couple of drinks Sylvia began to speak like her mother, whose language had been Yiddish. She prodded Maurice's belly. 'She'd be superb for you, a younger wife. Get some of this off.'

Put me back in hospital, was the desperate if unspoken reply. The ladies' toilet door swung open and the cream dress began to emerge. Maurice rose and headed doggedly to the top table.

Daniel saw him coming. He raised his own drink in salute. 'Do we say Mazeltov to you yet?'

Maurice drew up a spare chair and plonked down in it. 'Get me outa this, Danny. Can't we start a game of cards or something? Plenty of card tables in the back room where the old people play canasta and I'm sure we'll find a couple of packs. Not everyone wants to dance – or to get plastered, either.'

Daniel chuckled. 'Annie'd have a fit.'

Maurice fixed him with a glare. 'You're the host. You're paying the bill, for heaven's sake. If I don't sit quietly for the next hour I swear I'll have a heart attack. She may be Sylvia's idea of perfection but all night with a champion ballroom dancer isn't mine.'

Daniel was still laughing inwardly but considered how to tackle Annie. It was best done as a *fait accompli*. Mr Mannheim was eager. So were Annie's brothers and several others, delighted to be relieved of the obligation to cavort with wives and cousins. It was the women who adored the dance floor: the men found the whole business uncomfortable. There was no tradition of it, not of couples twirling around. In the old country men would dance in a line, arms linked across each other's shoulders, with bottles balanced on tall stovepipe hats, but nobody

present knew how or was sufficient of an exhibitionist to try. Only
Simon Rotblatt demurred: he was reminiscing happily with Gertie. He
could play cards any time he said, and concentrate better without the
noise.

Two foursomes were hastily arranged. As the cardsharps slipped discreetly away to the back room, Danny squared his shoulders and
marched to Annie.

'I'm going to play cards for a bit,' he announced.

'You're what? But you can't. It's your son's barmitzvah.'

'The men want a game.' He gestured helplessly.

'You mean *you* want a game.' She prodded him, furious but impotent.

Daniel spread his hands self-deprecatingly. 'Look, Annie, I can't
prance around like these youngsters. I've never been keen and my legs
bother me. You don't want me keeling over, now do you?'

She pursed her lips. 'What are you going to play?'

'Oh, nothing serious.' Not all the volunteers could manage bridge.
He failed to meet her gaze.

'Poker. You're going to play poker, aren't you? Men!'

There was no response since it was true. He wouldn't gamble, not
properly. No question of him losing his shirt. A few quid at most.
Shamefaced, with Annie's eyes like gimlets in his back, he disappeared
to the card room.

Sylvia and Vera reached for the wine bottle. 'So?' Sylvia asked.

Vera considered. 'He'll have to learn to dance,' she said firmly.

Helen took her glass and sat down near the young Israeli. His prove-
nance was a bit obscure. A relative of her mother's had emigrated: he
was the second generation offspring and lived in Tiberias. But since he
was visiting Europe, he had been included. His name was Shlomo.

Shlomo was short and solid. His eyebrows met in the middle over
black eyes. On his thick black hair a knitted *yarmulkah* was perched
which he would lift and replace in agitation. He seemed to point a lot
too. He would be about nineteen, Helen guessed, dark-skinned, lightly
stubbled (it was many hours since the morning) and fierce of manner
not softened by a guttural accent. Next to him Jerry Feinstein appeared
languid by comparison.

'But of course you should come to Israel,' Shlomo was saying loudly.
He punched the air. 'Look at me. I'm a *sabra* – native born. A soldier in
the Israeli Army soon. I fight for my homeland. I have something to be
proud of. What do you have to be proud of, here?'

Jerry leaned back and contemplated the ceiling. 'I'm not the type to
be proud,' he confessed. 'And I can't say I fancy being in the Army.
Getting shot at? Not me.'

His lazy resistance produced an agitated reaction. The index finger
jabbed the air, the *yarmulkah* was lifted and replaced twice.

'But you're a Jew. You have no life here. And you have a duty to *Eretz Yisroel*, the new state. It is surrounded by enemies. Young men like you, and women –' he turned to Helen, who was quietly attentive '– we have equality, you can serve too in the Israeli Army, the finest in the world. You are needed to defend your homeland. The Arabs have sworn to sweep us into the sea. It will be a second Holocaust. How can you live with that on your conscience?' He paused, panting.

Helen leaned forward on her elbows in what she hoped was a mild posture.

'I'm not sure about this homeland business. You say it's our homeland. I can see it's yours – you were born there. But Jerry and I were born here. If he wished to he could join the British Army – if they'd have him.'

Jerry giggled but Shlomo was not amused. 'It is yours too,' he insisted. 'Blood was spilled so that every Jew could live in freedom without discrimination. Where else is that possible?'

Jerry pulled a face, but mischief crept into Helen. Elaborately she gazed around – at the noisy dance floor where couples were clumsily jiving and her brother was swinging a pre-teen girlfriend, at tables littered with remains of a delicious salmon meal, at gaggles of relatives engaged in chatter, glasses of wine, beer, whisky and lemonade to hand.

'How about here?' she asked.

'Rubbish. You are not free in this place. Only in your own land where Jews are a majority, where Jews decide the laws. There you can be a Jew without asking anybody's permission.'

'I don't ask anyone's permission here.' Helen kept her voice calm. 'But real freedom comes from being neither majority nor minority. It means being able to decide your own fate without interference. From anyone. I'm not sure I fancy Israel. I read that ultra-orthodox Jews prevent shops opening on *shabbos*, and attack women who walk around old Jerusalem with their arms uncovered. It's supposed to be a secular state. Doesn't sound like freedom to me. Or equality.'

The *sabra* mumbled about having respect. Helen could feel her heart pound. Here was an easy target, this man who wore arrogance like a badge of honour: but he was also a guest. Yet the opportunity to interrogate him and learn in the process was not to be forgone. He was far more of a stranger, she suddenly realised, than Michael. She pressed on.

'And what about those Arabs who live within Israel's borders? They don't have the right to vote. Where's the freedom for them?'

'Israel is a country in a permanent state of war.' The *yarmulkah* bobbed up and down. 'We cannot give rights to our enemies.'

'Perhaps if you gave them rights they wouldn't be enemies.' Helen was aware that this was naive. It was also heresy. 'It looks to me a terrible shame that, coming as they did from such mayhem, the founding fathers couldn't have set *Eretz Yisroel* up as a truly multi-racial state.'

Shlomo looked horrified. 'But it's a Jewish state,' he insisted.

Helen and Jerry exchanged glances. The same argument had been repeated many times at Harold House. Jerry yawned and poured himself another drink.

'All I know, Shlomo, is that I'm British and quite content with that. For the time being, anyway. I'll go to Israel on holiday, and no doubt when I can afford to I'll contribute to its upkeep as my Dad does. But I live here, thank you very much, and I intend to stay put.'

'As long as they'll have you,' the *sabra* muttered darkly. He reached into the bread-basket, found a last roll and bit savagely into it.

The exchange came to an inconclusive end. Helen felt curiously elated. The *sabra*'s arrogance and bellicosity had been distinctly unappealing, but he had found no converts. As the band tried a Chris Montez number, Jerry took Helen out on to the floor.

'Well let's dance – let's dance –
We'll do the twist and shout and mashed potato too
Any old dance that you wanna do
Let's dance –'

The card room was fuzzy with blue smoke, mainly from cigars. The Majinsky barmitzvah was, after all, a big social event, though thankfully not so grand that penguin suits had to be worn. Ties were loosened, jackets removed and hung over the backs of chairs. Several male guests stood about, waiting a turn. A hum of concentration pervaded the air, with the slap of cards, the occasional jingle of coins, and brief snatches of conversation.

It was, most definitely, not a place for the ladies, which was precisely why the gentlemen had gravitated to it. So when Gertie appeared at the door and lounged, Marlene Dietrich-like in her gown, her presence dismayed several of the key players.

One portly man threw down his cards. 'Lady Luck not in it for me tonight,' he said. He addressed Gertie. 'Hey, no female spectators. This ain't a casino. Either take my place and play, or leave the big boys to get on with it.'

Eyebrows were raised as Gertie slid into the proffered chair. Before anyone could put the obvious query of whether she knew how to play, she motioned to the man on her left. 'Cut for dealer,' she instructed. With a gulp he complied. She grinned cheerfully, laid her gilt handbag on the table and perched half-spectacles on her nose. 'Ready?'

The bandsmen took their break and sat about sipping pints thirstily. They were regulars at such functions, and as usual related to several of the guests. One was a brother-in-law of Simon Rotblatt who took the opportunity to exchange a few words.

'Bernie! Good to see you. Don't you go deaf playing that kids' stuff – what was it?'

The band's last effort had been a version of the Four Seasons' 'Walk Like a Man'. Even Bernie the bandleader had to admit that their falsetto had been inadequate. He mopped his brow with a crumpled handkerchief. 'So what'd you prefer, Simon? Always glad to oblige.'

Simon put his head on one side. 'I like my music romantic. Haven't had a dance yet. How about a Strauss waltz? I can manage that.'

'Dunno 'bout Strauss. What about "Tales of Hoffman"? The Barcarolle. I got that music.' The bandleader hummed the tune and Simon smiled.

And as the bitter-sweet strains of the lush waltz floated out to cries of acclaim, Simon Rotblatt approached Annie, bowed formally before her and asked her to take the floor with him.

'*Oh, my love, my dearest love*
No other love have I –'

They started slowly, a little awkwardly, the dapper man, the small faded woman, his arm firmly round her waist to guide, her hand lightly on his shoulder, their other hands linked and outstretched to balance. The gap between their bodies closed, cheek brushed cheek. As their timing and confidence in each other improved they whirled faster, almost as one entity, toes and legs in step to the lilting melody. For a few moments the pair were the centre of admiring attention, until new couples swept in and they were lost from sight.

Daniel had been on his way to the gents, cigarette in hand. His calves ached and he stopped briefly to observe the dancers. At first he was pleased to see his wife enjoying herself: she had put so much into ensuring the success of the *simchah* that her own pleasure had taken a back seat. But it was Daniel and only he who saw that the expression on Annie's face was one of utter yearning, while Simon Rotblatt, his arm about her, had his eyes half closed in a look of inextinguishable devotion.

Daniel turned abruptly into the toilet. He entered a cubicle and locked himself in. It was ten minutes before he emerged, driven by the realisation that his absence might be noticed. The card game had lost its savour; he collected his small winnings and returned slowly to the top table. His wife, flushed and bright-eyed, was engaged in animated conversation with her sister and two women friends, her daughter at her side. Simon was nowhere to be seen.

Daniel touched Helen's elbow to draw her away. 'Had a good time?' he asked. 'Bit hard being big sister today, I know.'

In response she squeezed her father's arm. 'It's been fabulous, Dad. You and Mum should be delighted.'

Side by side they surveyed the boisterous, happy scene.

Daniel spoke. 'So: you think you can give all this up, Helen? Wouldn't you miss us if you went away?'

'That's a bit extreme, Dad. I'd come back. Especially for *simchas* – of course I would.'

'Once you go you lose contact, you know,' her father warned.

'I don't see why necessarily,' she defended. 'Unless we meant to. If a family wants, they'll stay in touch from anywhere in the world.'

'It's not that easy. Air travel costs a fortune. Globetrotting isn't for the likes of us.'

Once again that attempt, so depressing, so insidious, to keep her in her place. In *their* place, the one they had chosen for themselves.

'Well, Dad, you send the invites and I'll turn up. Especially for functions like this.'

That was tactless: her father needed no reminder that their ordinary life was much more mundane, and that it was its very emptiness which pushed her elsewhere.

She turned to him, abashed. His face had a bleak air. What she should immediately have said was that she loved her parents, loved her home. There would have been no obligation to follow that up with a declaration that she would never leave – Daniel would not have believed her. Their relationship had never been based on deliberate falsehood, even if absolute truth had sometimes gone astray.

Her parents' style had defeated them all. 'I love you' was not in their vocabulary. And at times, in her darkest moments, she wondered whether she did love them. Or whether they loved her, if loving meant understanding at any level at all. Naturally they 'loved' her in the sense that they worried about her, and wanted her to be a success – in their terms. Nothing would make her mother more deliriously happy than another *simcha* just like this one in five years' time, for her own nuptials. But surely there had to be more to it than that?

She stayed near her father a while longer. His remarks had been spontaneous: he had not been attempting blackmail – nothing so crude, merely an emphasis on what was at stake. But Helen had no illusions. Her family would adhere to the rules. Ostracism would come into play. Should she choose to marry a *goy*, there'd be no celebrations in the Marcus Liversham hall, no clutches of aunts and uncles, no table littered with gifts and congratulatory telegrams. At least not from her side. Her family would not attend her wedding at all, and could well refuse to see her again. The unremarked absence of her mother's pharmacist brother Davy and his *shikse* wife was mute testimony to that fact.

Soon the waitresses entered and began to clear up. Like the band they were paid till ten; their darting presence hinted strongly that the evening must draw to its close. In one corner small children ran round with ragged energy. Barry was smoochily doing a slow dance with his leggy partner. Jerry and Shlomo had drunk most of another bottle and made friends once more; football had proved a more amenable topic of discussion. Sylvia and Vera had bopped with each other, their handbags on the floor between them, as had numbers of the keener women. On one young mother's lap a fat baby lay contentedly asleep. In an armchair an elderly man, head back, was in the same peaceful state, his aggrieved wife seated next to him, wide awake and lips pursed.

Maurice Feinstein staggered out of the card room followed by the other players. Several had astonishment writ large on their faces and the remains of much-chewed cigars clamped between their teeth. Behind them, last, came Gertie with a triumphant gleam in her eye, her handbag firmly folded under her arm.

Annie was surrounded by guests saying their farewells. Her cheeks were still flushed and she radiated a pleasure which made her sweetly pretty. As Maurice passed he muttered hoarsely to her and jerked a thumb over his shoulder.

'Your Gertie. Amazing woman.'

'What's she done?'

'Only cleaned us all out, that's what. Cleared the tables and broke the bank. Took fifty quid off me.'

Annie's mouth dropped in horror. Gertie approached looking immensely pleased with herself, picked up a half-empty glass and downed it.

'Great party. Great! Nearly paid for my passage. An' they think they can play poker. We goin' home now?'

Then the American pulled her sister-in-law's face towards her own and roughly planted a wet kiss on the cheek. 'I adore ya. Adore ya all.'

Annie could not reply; she seemed overcome. She fished out a linen handkerchief and blew her nose. 'You're right. It's been wonderful. What a pity that it has to end.'

Chapter Twelve

Into the Abyss

March 1938. The wind blew fitfully off the Pier Head. Below the parapet near the floating landing-stage, rubbish welled and disappeared – empty bottles, bits of wood, half a child's pram. The air was a smoky blur from the newly equipped diesel engines of the motor vessels *Royal Daffodil* and the *Royal Iris* as they wallowed at the dockside, waiting for passengers. Yet the wintry sun glinted on the windows of the Cunard building in a hint of spring while the Sunday afternoon crowd, though warmly wrapped in overcoats and scarves, milled around cheerfully.

At spaces of four or five feet apart, sufficient to avoid physical conflict between the occupants, several soapboxes had been erected. On these makeshift platforms with their backs to the river were ranged half a dozen men speakers and one woman. Leaflets in hand (the woman had a bible), lungs expanded, they punched the air, pounded the shaky lecterns and harangued onlookers. Bolder characters yelled rudely back. A couple of the orators kept up a running dialogue with their audience while others were ignored. This was Liverpool's version of Speakers' Corner in Hyde Park, and every bit as popular.

The Bible-toting lady came from the Catholic Light League. A fat woman squeezed into a tightly buttoned brown coat, with a pair of steel-rimmed spectacles jammed on her nose and a small black hat perched on grey curls, she shouted hoarsely in a County Cork accent with barely a pause for breath. On her lapels were tin badges from many pilgrimages, at her throat a prominent crucifix, in her free hand a rosary which was waved vigorously at her critics.

Next to her the Anglican clergyman was also a regular, his tall lanky figure with its grubby dog collar and black fedora hat a familiar sight. His adam's apple bobbed up and down like the ball-cock in a cistern, to the fascination of small boys looking on. He affected a public school manner to which, as his hearers well knew, he was not entitled. His objective (seldom achieved) was to fill the nearby church for Evensong and so replenish the coffers left bare by his Depression-hit flock. The Bishop, as he was dubbed, was noted for his tendency to quote scripture which did not quite fit his point. The throng before him was good-natured and noisy.

'How can you prove the existence of God?' demanded a man in the front row.

The clergyman sighed theatrically. 'When I see people like you, my good fellow, I am convinced of the existence of Lucifer. And somebody must have created *him*. Ergo, God exists. Romans ten, eleven: for the scripture says, "Whosoever believeth on Him shall not be ashamed." Next question.'

'It is blasphemous to suggest that God Almighty does not exist!' yelled the stout woman. She jabbed a finger at the questioner. 'May St Michael and all his angels strike ye dead on the spot for saying such a thing!'

'I didn't!' the heckler riposted. 'But it's not a sin to—'

'On yer knees!' The woman had a voice like a foghorn and a commanding presence which would have done justice to Joan of Arc.

The Bishop raised a pseudo-aristocratic eyebrow as if too fastidious to interfere. The woman leaned forward, hands gripping the edge of the lectern, eyes boring into the hapless sinner. 'You'll rot in hell, that's what.' She bared her teeth in anticipation then swept her finger round the audience which recoiled in mock awe. 'All of you. Return to God! Be washed in the blood of Christ Jesus! Oh Holy Mother –' She crossed herself, clasped her hands together, rolled her eyes to the clouds which scudded overhead and began a Hail Mary.

Annie Feldman sucked a boiled sweet and watched, mesmerised. The dramatic exaggeration of the woman, her fierce faith, were strange and exotic. The disdain induced in her listeners was, Annie felt, unfair. It was a brave act to speak up like that – she, Annie, five foot nothing in her stockinged feet and not yet twenty, could never do it in a million years.

It was only recently that Annie had made a habit of joining the anonymous strollers on the Pier Head. Not that there was much else to do on Sundays, and it was free. Something drove her, engrossed but repelled, towards the religious speakers. She would never be tempted to convert, of course; her own religion was quite sufficient without the complications of any other.

After the rants of the pious her attention was drawn to the politicians. Their competing cries and the derisive catcalls of their audiences made the place chaotic, almost like a funfair. It was an education to listen to them for an hour or more in the hazy sunshine. What she heard and but dimly grasped helped her understand remarks in the canteen at work or over the counter. It stopped her feeling a complete nincompoop. It did not, however, compel her to believe, nor to join in.

She stopped before the first, a supporter of the eclipsed George Lansbury faction of the Labour Party. He was in his thirties, probably unemployed, an off-white muffler at his throat, no hat, no overcoat. He had been moved a few yards downwind of the Blackshirt, a Mosleyite, for on previous occasions they had come to blows: but free speech meant just that, so both were permitted to continue. A police officer, baton in hand, patrolled warily nearby.

The Mosleyites had something to celebrate. Armfuls of party newspapers were being handed around by acolytes. On the front page were pictures of Hitler's victorious entry into Vienna the week before when his birthplace was incorporated into Germany, the day after a plebiscite had been due on Austrian independence. As he drove through the cheering masses, Hitler looked extremely pleased with life. A new word, *Anschluss*, had entered the English language. In front of the podium three scowling bodyguards in black uniforms with Sam Browne belts and very short haircuts stood with legs planted wide apart, fists clasped behind their backs when not giving the Hitler salute. Their eyes flitted over the crowd. Above them their man did his best to emulate his hero Sir Oswald Mosley but succeeded merely in looking faintly risible. The bodyguards were a different matter: their menace made Annie shiver. It was rumoured they'd follow anyone who disagreed and teach him a lesson. Two already had criminal records.

'The bomber will always get through,' Lansbury's supporter mourned dolefully. 'The League of Nations is our only defence. Collective security – sanctions. Britain should not waste money on armaments. Beware the war machine. Churchill is a war-monger, a killer. He would put the working man back in the trenches –'

'The Jews are traitors! All war is the result of conflict caused by Jews and moneylenders. What Herr Hitler wants is peace! If our government wasn't so infiltrated by Jews and Americans they'd see that. A treaty with Germany would give England peace for a generation!'

The two shouted virtually simultaneously, but each had an ear open for the other. Both orators used the slogan 'No more war!' repeatedly, as if its incantation like a magic spell would alone bring harmony. The promise, or hope, was batted back and forth between pacifist and Blackshirt. In the throng, men of conscriptable age shifted uneasily from one foot to the other.

Annie knew she ought to be sympathetic to the Labour speaker. It stood to reason, given her background. Even Mosley had called himself a socialist not long before. He'd been tipped as a future Labour Prime Minister, but ambition and haste had driven him first to found his own party – 'New Labour', it was called – then rapidly to shift towards the more intolerant and aggressive movements in Europe. A general sense that the adulation of jack-booted foreign leaders was distinctly un-British, plus a degree of refined revulsion among his erstwhile apologists, had caused his star to wane.

The third political speaker was relatively new. Annie had seen him once before. He was younger than the others, about twenty-five. He did not seem to have much control of his tall gawky body which jerked as he spoke as if it operated independently from his brain. His lectern carried no identification stickers so perhaps he did not represent an official party. Nor did he have any leaflets to hand out.

'You should listen to Churchill,' he was urging a woman as Annie approached. 'What he writes in the *Daily Express* is right. There will be war. Hitler and Mussolini are busy carving up Africa and Europe between them. Today Abyssinia and Austria, next it'll be Czechoslovakia, then us. They've already forced Eden out of office. Watch.'

The bare-headed young man was thin and earnest. His lack of any official link was not unusual. Aspiring politicians of every sort came here, for the spot was famous throughout the north west. Perhaps he had designs on office in his trade union. It'd do him no harm to be known as a forthright debater who had honed his skills at the Pier Head.

Annie was spotted on the edge of the sparse group and beckoned forward. 'Good afternoon, young lady. Come and listen. This concerns you.' The courtesy sat oddly with his local accent and awkward manner. She took a couple of steps, shyly. Close to, he was quite pleasant to look at, with a respectable suit, a shock of brown hair and a moustache, but thin-faced as if he had been ill.

Annie tossed her head and laughed. 'How can it concern me?'

The youth frowned impatiently. 'If there's war it'll affect everyone. Our friend there –' he gestured at the pacifist '– may be correct about the bombers. Liverpool will be a target. You will be a target.'

She laughed prettily and dimpled. 'Me? Why should anybody want to make a target of me?'

'Don't be complacent. If Hitler invades, no one will escape. We should demand that our government arms itself before it's too late. Mr Churchill should join the Cabinet – he should be Minister for War—'

'Preposterous idea!' roared the fascist. 'Nothing is more likely to lead to disaster! With Churchill in Whitehall instead of on the backbenches where he belongs there would never be peace! A million men will die! Two million! It has happened before and will happen again –'

Annie covered her ears against the tirade and turned back to the young man. 'So: what on earth can I do about it?'

'Write to your MP – tell him what you know. And when the time comes, vote for candidates who hate war as much as anyone but are realistic –'

'I'm too young to vote,' Annie countered with a flourish. Several of those nearby hooted and clapped her as the boy flushed and closed his mouth wordlessly, as if she had won a game. With as good a flounce as she could muster she walked off. Yet she felt obscurely ashamed of herself.

As the afternoon grew more chill the audience drifted away. Speakers collected bags and papers, folded away their lecterns and moved them flush against the railings ready for the following week. Nobody would steal them, for what good were the ramshackle contraptions other than to provide repeat entertainment? Cloth-capped boys made snowballs of abandoned posters and pelted each other and passers-by. A stall selling tea and buns had done a lively trade during daylight and now its owner lit a paraffin lamp which swayed in the breeze. Customers gathered and rolled sparse cigarettes whose red nubs glowed dimly. Litter blew around, tracts from the testaments, leaflets advertising lectures and rallies, pages from the *News of the World* and the *News Chronicle*.

Annie was reluctant to leave and bought herself a cup of tea. Once she was home, that was the end of her free day, with Monday morning and an early start for work that much closer.

'You'll be able to vote soon. You can't be that young.'

He was suddenly at her side, his hands around a chipped mug, a Woodbine between his fingers. He was more than a head taller. He looked cold.

Annie Feldman sipped her tea and shrugged. 'I'm twenty. Nearly. And I'm not stupid. What would I vote for? I probably won't bother.'

The young man groaned. 'You should. People died to give you the vote. People are dying now, in Germany and other places, because they didn't use the vote when they had it.'

'Just Jews?' she inquired mischievously up at him. He looked Jewish. Her own origins were unmistakable.

'Mostly, but not just us. People who object to the regime – Communists, trade unionists, churchmen. Democratic politicians. Anybody.' He nodded in the direction of the clergyman's receding back. 'I may not agree with what they say but like Voltaire I'd defend to the death their right to say it and be heard. And not get beaten up by bully boys or spirited away and shot.'

'You've no evidence that happens,' Annie countered. She had heard such sentiments both forcibly expressed and countered in the canteen. 'You talk like a Communist.'

'Now you are being stupid,' the youth answered brusquely.

She should go. The young man's intensity disturbed her. His narrow shoulders writhed as he spoke and his eyes burned, but with sadness and passion, not hatred.

A moment's silence. 'Sorry,' Annie offered. The boy was looking unhappy. Then, 'You're a bit young to be on a soapbox on the Pier Head, aren't you? What's your name?'

He warmed his hands around the mug and bent his head to drink. The steam curled up around his nose and wetted the straggly ends of his moustache. Annie suppressed an urge to take out her handkerchief and wipe it for him.

'I'm Daniel Majinsky.'

The name rang a bell. 'Have you got a cousin Eva?'

'Yes. Do you know her?'

'Not very well. She worked in Blackler's hair salon for a while, didn't she? She's a bit older than me. I think she did my hair once.'

The boy did not reply but lifted up his jacket collar against the salty wind. It was apparent that, still wrapped up in his hour-long performance, he did not seek a social chat. He finished his tea and handed back the mug, then took a long drag on his cigarette, sucking the smoke into his lungs and expelling it in a blue stream through his nostrils. He turned as she did towards Water Street and kept pace with her. Annie tried again.

'Were you speaking for a political party? You didn't tell us how to vote, only that we should.'

He sighed. 'Well, there won't be an opportunity for a while. The government has a majority of almost three hundred with the National Liberals. Not likely to put that at risk for ages with a General Election.'

'You haven't answered my question.'

He stopped and rubbed an invisible mark in the dust with his toe, hands thrust deep into his pockets, head down.

'That's because I can't. I don't know which party to support any more. The ILP broke with the Labour party six years ago. It'd been mostly skilled men like myself. Keir Hardie was a wonderful leader – a man you could believe in. Ramsay Macdonald too, for a while, till he went wrong. Then they changed the name to the Socialist League and now it's all bloody intellectuals.'

He peered at her and hesitated. 'Look at the leaders of the left – all over the place. Ernie Bevin wanted to be chairman of the League but they wouldn't have him. Lansbury is loved by everyone but he's an impractical idealist and he's old now. I was glad when he finished as party leader. He's the sort who'd plead with the fascists and be the first they'd kick over the cliff. Attlee's not much better – he'll criticise every request for arms by Mr Chamberlain till after war starts, if it does. As for the hunger marchers, what good did they do? The National Unemployed Workers movement is in the hands of the Communists and I've no truck with those. They say capitalism has broken down but I don't believe that. And Stalin's as bad as the rest – worse, perhaps.'

'So if you don't know what or who to believe, why do you come down here and make –' she was about to say 'a spectacle of yourself' but that would have been cruel. And his honesty was admirable. '– A fuss about politics?'

'Somebody must. Silence – not shouting about it – would destroy us all. If anybody'd have me I'd stand for Parliament. Not much chance of that – no money, no connections. But first I have to clear my head. So many lies are told. When I get up on that soapbox it's myself I'm trying to convince. I work my way through the issues to find the truth. Those blokes in the crowd who argue with me – or girls like yourself – are helping me, though they don't realise it. I'm in marginally less of a muddle by Monday morning.'

They had arrived at the terminus shed. A tram stood ready. Annie stepped up; on its platform her face was suddenly on a level with his. She held out her hand. 'This is mine – I must go. I am pleased to meet you.' She hoped her expression was slightly mocking though without malice. This young man took himself and his agonies far too seriously.

He took her hand absent-mindedly and for the first time she looked directly into his eyes. They were brown, and deeply set, with long lashes which added to his melancholy demeanour. As they touched he seemed to shake himself back to the present.

'I don't know your name. Could we meet again? Will you be here next week?'

'Probably, I can't promise.' Suddenly it did not seem a wise idea to make any kind of liaison with him. She twisted away and climbed on to the first step of the tram's staircase, then relented. As flirtatiously as she could – it'd be good for him – she smiled.

'I'm Annie,' she said.

She would be home in time for the babies' bath. Time for a long read before bed, perhaps – the latest Agatha Christie from Boots' lending library lay under her pillow, if only her sister Becky would let her have some peace.

Annie's preference was for romances. Margaret Kennedy's *The Constant Nymph* had passed through her hands three times. She'd dropped strong hints about a copy of *Rebecca* by Daphne du Maurier for her birthday: both *Jamaica Inn* and *Frenchman's Creek* had been terrific. Everyone at work was talking about the new book. The forbidden word 'sexy' had been whispered in the ladies' toilet. A hardback novel read but once was an outrageous extravagance. She'd have to wait until Boots stocked it and put her name down in the queue.

The babies, now. Four little ones, ranging in age from Sammy aged eight through Rose, six, Ruth, nearly four and the toddler Abbie. They'd go into the tub one after the other, biggest first, with the girls together. They'd be flannelled all over and their faces scrubbed, and the backs of their necks, knees and behind their ears. Pear's soap for them: amber clear and soft. She loved handling it and sniffing its clean fragrance.

Annie should by rights have been home already, but the task of supervision fell to Becky her older sister. It was the eldest girl's job to be mother's helper. Mother's drudge, more like. The boys wouldn't be involved other than by humping the big zinc tub and bringing in an extra scuttle of coal. Their bath-time was Friday, *erev shabbos*. Had the family been *frum* the boys would have gone to the *mikvah*, the ritual bath, but that would have meant time off work and money lost. The Feldmans tended in the modern way to put practicality before fervour. There was no need to apologise since most of their neighbours did the same.

A family of eight children, in total. Hardly unusual; a gap divided the older and younger groups when her father had gone down south searching for work and her mother had quietly miscarried through worry. Four of them with jobs – which was out of the ordinary. The Feldmans were grafters. They'd take whatever was offered, not turn up their noses and were blessed as strong and healthy. They came, it was said, from sturdy stock.

Dad was a cabinet maker, the mainstay of a furniture workshop of some renown in the city. He had been shrewd. Jacob, her elder brother, he had decreed should become a kosher butcher. 'People have to eat; a butcher never starves,' he had stated. That had turned out sound common sense as the young man, made strapping by his trade, would march home in his bloody apron even in the hardest times, with a bagful of chicken legs and a fine piece of topside. Jack was secretly courting, however, and would soon be seeking his own home.

The next boy down, David, was a year Annie's junior. He had been clever at school and had won a Central Class place at the age of eleven. Hours of agonised discussion and consultation had been expended: the parents, solid and earnest, had sat at the table over pot after pot of tea, scraps of paper in front of them on which they scribbled hierarchies of figures. Davy's future was settled eventually on much the same principle as Jack's, though the family would be deprived of a wage for far longer. He was sent to college for two years to qualify as a chemist. 'You'll never be out of a job. People will always need medicine – and they'll come to you before they'll trouble the quack,' had been the father's judgement. So now the young man was an assistant manager at Boots and wore his pharmacist badge with pride. It meant, however, that Davy worked Saturdays without fail, and was drifting unobserved away from his family.

Davy's extended education had had implications for Annie. She had also won a Central Class place and had attended St Margaret's in Anfield, not the Hebrew School. She could have continued after the age of fourteen like her brother – but the family could not afford both. With a fresh baby on the way her mother dared not take on a skivvy job, though it had been considered. Instead Annie left school the moment it was legal. She had not felt resentful: pleased, rather, to be independent and to help feed the growing number of mouths at home.

Seldom did she lament her lack of education, though she was conscious of it at moments like those on the Pier Head when her ignorance pushed her out of her depth. She could not help but feel awed by genuine seekers after enlightenment. Yet what would have been the point in carrying on? In any occupation where more certificates would have been useful, such as a private secretary or the civil service, she'd have had to finish on marriage or soon after. That was the rule and unchallenged. And most men would regard it as an insult if, after their own careers had been established, their wives continued at work. It would imply they didn't earn enough and might be inadequate husbands. Anyway, girls weren't supposed to be brainy – that was left for the male side of creation. Ladies should not usurp men's role in life and should not hanker to be gentlemen. To do so was unnatural.

The year Annie left school aged fourteen was 1932, about as bad a time as could be remembered. The soup kitchens were full and dole queues drifted endless and without hope around corners, especially in a Liverpool desperate for a revival in world trade. To balance national budgets, jobs paid for out of taxes had been cut. Thus it had been a godsend when Auntie Ida Bernstein, owner of clothes shops in the poorer parts of the city, offered her a position as shop assistant at twelve shillings a week.

The memory of her first day made Annie giggle now, but then she had burned with shame and fear. Auntie Ida, it had to be said, was a ferocious personality who enjoyed instilling terror in her staff. That was why they didn't stay; hence the vacancy.

The chosen establishment was in Tunnel Road. It had been new in 1926; its paint had soon peeled and turned grimy under the onslaught of city-bound traffic. The frontage grandly announced 'Gents' Outfitters', but as was evident to the most cursory glance it was a hat and cap shop. Still, every man and boy had to wear one; it was not respectable to go out with the head uncovered, so a fair trade was possible though with little to spare for staff.

Ida Bernstein stood on the doorstep as Annie arrived at eight o'clock. She was of medium height but enormously heavy, her expanses engirthed in brocades and a fox fur stole. The furry snout was tucked greedily into the folds of her chins and the ruby button eyes glittered in the light. Ida wore make-up, with lipstick which detached itself and played on her teeth. Her thick legs were encased in lisle stockings, for she suffered from the family ailment of varicose veins; her feet disappeared into small black shiny shoes which looked as if they pinched.

'Twelve shillings a week and you're not worth that,' was her greeting. Annie did not know how to reply. Ida turned with a sniff, unlocked the street door then led her inside.

The interior smelled musty and chill. The tiny back room where Annie was told to hang her coat had green stains on the walls. Stock would have to be turned over quickly in such a place or it would go mouldy.

But the shop itself was a wonder. The girl fought down her delight as she began to familiarise herself with its contents under Ida's suspicious gaze. Hats and flat caps everywhere, mostly the latter: brown and blue and beige, tweed and corduroy and cheap cotton for summer, workmen's navy blue, old men's in smaller sizes, tam o'shanters in dark green and red tartan with pompoms on top, boys' caps for local schools, striped larger versions for young swells: drawers floor to ceiling were crammed with them, the more expensive models wrapped in tissue paper. More were kept in sliding trays under the glass-topped counter, folded to keep their shape, alongside handkerchiefs in spotted red or plain white cotton or (for best) Irish linen. Ties and cravats in tasteful styles and colours were folded lengthwise to show off their designs. Scarves and mufflers did good business. And gloves! Not that a man must have gloves, but a lady should not be seen out of doors without. Big leather driving gloves had made their appearance, and knitted versions and some without fingers or with leather palms. Leather patches for elbows could also be obtained, and invisible tape for frayed cuffs, and a multitude of collars in stiff white with collar studs – boxes of them, mostly in cheap metal which snapped if handled carelessly.

The window display was reserved for proper hats: a handsome bowler, the type which might be worn to work by a railway stationmaster or the gaffer of a small factory. A Homburg, which might appear at *shabbos* service when a man was called up. Two brown trilbies in slightly different styles, their brims turned rakishly, for the man who refused to wear a cloth cap, whatever his social calling. A deerstalker with a pheasant's feather stitched to the ribbon. And, magnificently, a top hat, which was in fact Ida's father's second best and not for sale, but which splendidly announced the shop's nature and pretensions.

The topper sat elegantly on a pedestal with a white silk scarf arranged cunningly around its brim, as if its wearer had deposited it briefly before going in to dine at the Adelphi. Ida had toyed with perching an embossed invitation next to it but had reluctantly concluded that such display would incur not respect but guffaws.

The proprietor hauled her small new assistant outside. 'You'll take everything out of the window once a week to dust, then put it back *exactly* where you found it, do you hear?'

Annie nodded, eyes huge. The idea of handling that top hat with its silky sheen and the sweep of its brim thrilled her to the core.

Ida smirked and folded her hands across her bosom. 'Nice, isn't it? Real rabbit fur, that one. Silk lined with the maker's name inside in gold – you'll see. Cost five guineas new. They used to dress 'em with mercury to make 'em shine. That's a poison so the workers would end up going doolally. Mad hatters – that's where the saying comes from.'

As she spoke Ida licked a finger and wiped it over a spot on the window, then examined her dirty fingertip with an exclamation of annoyance. 'Filthy! What a lazy minx that girl was – the one you're replacing. Well, my lass, you have your first task. You'll find a step-ladder in the back and a bucket and rags. I want this whole window cleaned, at once. And I expect it done properly whenever it needs, which is probably once a week. Off with you.'

Thus it was that twenty minutes later Annie, all six stone of her, found herself clinging precariously to the top of the ladder as she tried to reach the upper expanses of the plate glass. To her horror it trembled whenever she touched it and so did she. From her vantage point she could see that the putty was frail and brittle, and absent altogether for inches at a stretch. Were she to lean on the glass, or put one hand out to steady herself, the whole window could cave in.

'I will not let myself be frightened – I will not,' she muttered under her breath. Her hands were becoming sore and chapped and her dress down the front was sodden. She forced into her mind images of the new baby, of her careworn mother, of other members of the family who worked unstintingly without complaint. They would expect her not to give up at the first hint of adversity. She was nearly finished; Auntie Ida in her finery would not risk a climb up the ladder to check. With teeth gritted she rubbed gingerly at the stain left by a seagull.

'Made a bit of a mess of your clothes, haven't you?' was all the thanks she got, but after another hour's scrutiny, when her aunt was sat-isfied that she could be trusted to work the till and give the right change, she was at last left to her own devices.

That job lasted six months. Annie had brooded. She was supposed to feel, and exhibit, gratitude. It was made crystal clear that no pay rise would be possible for years, if ever. Instead she was not far off a skivvy, since Ida refused to employ a cleaner. That was endurable; but it was the terror of that weekly window which drove her at last to action.

She began to hover wistfully outside Priceman's in St Homer Street which, though similar in appearance to Ida's, was larger and specialised in women's and children's garments. It was open Wednesday after-noons when most shops including Ida's were shut.

At first she had bought little things for the children or a modest gift for her mother, a tiny embroidered handkerchief or a wisp of a scarf. Then her attention turned to herself – a pretty blouse with *broderie anglaise* for which she had to save up five weeks, a pair of finer quality wool stockings, a blue silk ribbon for her hair.

One Wednesday she had to wait in line as a flustered assistant tried to total the half-dozen items purchased by the woman in front of her. Annie could not help blurting out the correct sum. 'That's right – that's what I make it too,' said the customer. The slight disturbance brought the manageress. The assistant's incompetence and Annie's quickness were explained; the manageress eyed the diminutive girl up and down and said, 'If ever you want a job, miss, you come to me.'

So Annie boldly asked for a pound a week from Priceman's and got it. The window was dealt with by an elderly man and the general cleaning by his wife, so life improved dramatically. Auntie Ida's shrieks of fury could be ignored; her father had chuckled, her mother looked shocked, and Jack had slapped her on the back and said, 'Well done.'

For years to come Annie would recall with pleasure the moment she had defied her fate and bettered herself. Priceman's was to be her employer for two years until she had grown a couple of inches. Then she marched in neat black gloves and a pert hat into the ladies' dress department of Owen Owen's, the largest department store in town. No vacancies existed at present, she was informed, but her pretty face could be an asset elsewhere. At a remuneration of two pounds, rising by steps to three when she attained the age of twenty-one, would she be interested in the perfumery counter?

Would she? Ah, joy!

Thus Annie Feldman, of below-average size, truncated education and narrow horizons, who once had stood up for herself and who knew her own worth, became adviser to Liverpool ladies on which scent to wear for what, and to their husbands and beaux on the purchase of alluring gifts. She was astonished at how much money people were prepared to waste on smelly water. Not a shred of doubt assailed her, nevertheless, that she had found her métier.

Her own taste was for Bourjois *Evening in Paris* perfume – 'young, romantic, a little sophisticated', the ads said. Mitcham's Lavender Water was her recommendation for any woman over fifty, or Atkinson's Gold Medal Eau de Cologne if the buyer looked slightly threadbare – perfume, soap and talc in a box could be had for four shillings and threepence. Coty had lots, with the most evocative names she struggled to pronounce – *Emeraude* ('rich, sensual, and strangely individual'), *Chypre*, *Le Nouveau Gardenia*, *Le Vertige*, *Paris* – for Christmas a gilt-capped bottle in cut crystal of any one of them had cost a whole guinea. *Mischief* perfume came in three sizes at three shillings, five and six and twelve and six: the largest bottle, she had noticed, was bought with furtive glances by men with thin moustaches.

The mixed events of the day occupied Annie's mind as she bathed the small slippery bodies. That boy, so earnest, so solemn: it was rare to find someone so young deliberately courting ridicule in that way. She resolved not to mention him to her fellow shopgirls who'd jump to the wrong conclusions. Her attachment was entirely driven by curiosity, and by compassion.

A chap like that could not be a suitable lover. He would never put earning a living as a high enough priority, for a start. Nor did he know how to treat a lady. Not compared with, say, Simon Rotblatt, who had bought a lovely present for her last birthday. He'd have been her beau in an instant had she let him. Kind Simon, with his round face and willing heart. He told her whenever he had a pay rise, not boastfully but as if giving himself a character reference. Yet he was not Mr Right: far from it.

Simon knew where she worked. Annie suspected he'd waited out of sight one lunchtime till she had gone for her break then checked with her fellow assistant what she'd most like. His choice must have been made as much to dazzle as to please, for it was three Helena Rubinstein perfumes in a red box with cupids, which she knew cost eighteen and six, a fortune. She was duly impressed and not a little anxious. If the gift presaged a proposal, she was not in the market.

She finished her tasks and excused herself. When her sister Becky came into the bedroom they shared, wiping her arms and hands on a towel, Annie was lying back on the bed, her head hung behind her, staring upside down at the far wall.

'That's done – heavens, what are you up to?'

'Hanging head downwards brightens eyes and reduces wrinkles,' Annie responded dreamily. 'At least, that's what it says in *Woman and Beauty*. We get the old ones from the hair salon. It also suggests a gentle massage of the eyeballs through the lids to stimulate circulation.'

Becky shrugged. 'That nonsense is read by women who have nowt better to do. Don't get the wrong ideas. You're a working girl.'

'But I don't want wrinkles.' Annie sat up and pouted. 'In my job it is important to look one's best at all times. You never know when Mr Right might show up.'

Becky took off her apron and hung it over the end of the bed to dry. 'Simon's keen on you. What's wrong with him?'

'He's a show-off. And he's only interested in money.' That was not fair and she knew it. 'He has no imagination.'

'So what? He's on five pounds a week at Berman's, one of their best cutters.'

'A tailor! I don't want to marry a tailor. I can do better than that. Anyway I'm enjoying myself. I don't want to get tied down into marriage and motherhood for ages. Maybe never.'

Becky slowly sat down on the bed beside her sister. A concerned expression settled itself on her broad features. No man had come forward for her yet; if she could not find a husband for herself, assistance would be sought, but for the moment her usefulness in the house was paramount. She placed a clumsy soap-roughened hand on Annie's shoulder.

'I hope you don't mean that. You don't want to be an old maid. Plenty of those already. A woman's fulfilment lies in her home, her family, her children –'

With a toss of her head Annie rose and went to the chest of drawers.

She wished there was room for a proper dressing table. She felt cross and out of sorts, though usually bathtime with the babies brought lightness to her spirit. 'Yes, but just look at our mother, and all the other mothers we know, Becky. Every other year a new infant, endlessly expecting, backache and – that. And such a struggle to feed and clothe them all. Is she truly happy? Is that what I want? It may be what I have to settle for, but as long as I have a choice –'

'You've met someone,' Becky spoke accusingly. 'Is he Jewish? Some *goyische* bloke's come into Owen Owen's and been chatting you up over the cold cream, I'll bet. Be careful. You won't be the first to hear a packet of lies and live to tell a tale of woe.'

'No, no. It's not like that.' In defiance Annie unscrewed the middle Rubinstein bottle and dabbed the stopper behind her ears. That was a waste of good perfume but would rub in her sophistication as against her sister's simplicity – more, her control of her life as compared with Becky's passivity. She loved her sister and itched to confide in her about Daniel Majinsky; instinctively she saw it as unwise.

'Too independent, that's you.'

Annie shrugged. The perfume filled the air of the little room with dreams and whispered promises. Becky made as if to say more, then left the room and shut the door behind her a mite too sharply.

'I just want – what do I want?' Annie murmured to the closed door. 'Not to be stuck here for ever. To get out, to get away, if I can. To be adored, to be swept off my feet. The question is how, and to that I have no answer.'

The strange young man had forecast correctly. War was to come, though not for another eighteen months. In the meantime Mr Chamberlain flew to Munich with a copy of *Rebecca* in his briefcase. The British government expressed their conviction that German expansion in central and eastern Europe was a 'normal and natural thing'. By March 1939, a year almost to the day that he had entered Vienna, Hitler was in Prague, a move condoned by the British Prime Minister as 'inevitable'. In the House of Commons Conservative members were impatient at Churchill's urgent warnings; but equally they resented Hitler's interference in their affairs.

Annie sensed rather than understood a change of mood. The fascist disappeared from the Pier Head and was rumoured to have been arrested. All the orators now spoke openly about the likelihood of conflict and were joined by Polish and Czech refugees. The throng increasingly included foreign sailors who smoked strong-smelling tobacco and whispered among themselves. No one from the government parties dared to appear to utter words of continued appeasement; any such would have been shouted down.

Daniel Majinsky, increasingly respected, took his place with other speakers who urged realism and effective preparation. Annie openly came to listen to him. The two had also walked out, not every week, but whenever he could spare the time and money, or drag his attention temporarily away from politics.

She found him a total puzzle. He had escorted her at her suggestion to dances at the Tower Ballroom in New Brighton, but after a few polite foxtrots would retire to the bar and engage in heated debate with acquaintances he found there. She was included in the conversation, however, an experience she found unsettling. He preferred the cinema and would sit forward intently for the newsreels then mutter and fidget through the films. He seemed oddly immune to the glamour of Fred Astaire and Ginger Rogers.

To Annie, nurtured on a diet of glamour and recipes from *Women and Beauty* and *Vogue*, Daniel's obsessions were embarrassing but intriguing. Any attempts at coquetry on her part met with an irritated frown on his. He was not a boyfriend in any conventional sense, though frequently she felt the need to defend him; he was a friend, no more, no less. She continued to accept the attentions of Simon Rotblatt who would look at no other, but regarded herself as free of promises or entanglements. The special man of her fantasies had resolutely refused to materialise at the perfumery counter. She wondered in her darkest moments whether he ever would.

Annie waited as Daniel finished his session and packed up. This Sunday he was quite hoarse: he must have been making speeches during the week when she did not see him.

He took her arm without ceremony and headed for the tea stall.

'Annie, what are you going to do when war breaks out?'

She stopped. 'I still don't think that will happen –'

'It will. They're digging trenches in the London parks. The newspapers are full of evacuation plans for the children – your little brothers and sisters will be sent to North Wales. Mr Chamberlain's announced the return of compulsory military service. Your big brothers will be called up.'

She recoiled, shocked. 'Not our Davy. We'll still need chemists here. Or Jack – he's just married and a baby on the way.'

'So? He may not be in the first wave, but after that.'

'Don't, Daniel. You're frightening me.' She looked up, her face puckered. 'Anyway, what about you? You're not married. Will you volunteer, or will you wait till you're sent?'

His shoulders sagged. He seemed to have grown even thinner. 'I wouldn't pass the medical. Not a chance, or I'd go like a shot. The doctors say I'm lucky to be alive.'

They drank their tea, a sombreness in their manner. Around them similar conversations in low tones were under way. He put down the mug and lit a cigarette.

'Look, Annie. It won't only affect men, you know. Selling perfume will hardly be a protected occupation if we're at war with Germany – you'll be sent somewhere, on the farms or to a munitions factory. Unless you do something more useful.'

She began to protest but the firmness of his expression silenced her. He hurried on.

'In Berman's some of the boys in the reserves are already packing their bags. And we have big new contracts for army uniforms and the like. They're trying to take on extra cutters but there's a shortage. So they want to train up a few girls. I could put in a good word for you.'

'A *tailor*? Goodness, that's a man's job.' She did not add that, as a girl who had no intention of ever marrying a tailor, the notion of becoming one herself was preposterous.

'You could come into my workshop. They're a friendly enough bunch, nobody too rough. You already know Simon Rotblatt – he's on the same shift.'

'But I'd be teased – I'm so small, how on earth would I reach over the workbench?'

He laughed at last. He had such a sweet smile, she realised, though it was rarely on display. His gaze swept her up and down, as if it were the first time he had appraised her.

'You'd have to stand on a box. C'mon, Annie, you can't stay where you are. Berman's is well paid. And you know the best thing?'

She shook her head. It was bewildering. The future which she had daydreamed over was about to slap her in the face.

'I'll look after you. I'll train you myself.'

She bent her head and murmured that she was not sure that was such a recommendation, but it felt as if a brother had pledged to care for her – somebody she could trust absolutely, who would immediately think of her welfare in troubled times. Yet he seemed to want so little in return.

At the tram she turned to him anxiously. 'Do you honestly think there will be fighting?'

'Yes. And, Annie, we have to hope there is, we Jews. And that the confidence the government shows in our forces is well founded.'

'What do you mean? Nobody wants war to break out.'

'No, but think. If we continue to make room for Herr Hitler and his stormtroopers there's only one way it'll end for people like you and me.'

She waited, but guessed what was coming.

'Mass executions. Firing squads. The grave.'

'Oh, Danny.' Her hand flew to her mouth, her eyes brimming with fear. She took a step closer to him. Her voice shook. 'I'm glad you're around, Danny. You and – and Simon, and my family. We'll stick together and we'll get through this. Won't we?'

PART THREE

Chapter Thirteen

Whitsuntide

The emergency meeting of the Childwall ward branch of Wavertree Conservative and Unionist Association slowly got under way. The minutes would record in due course that ten members attended, though not that every jacket had been thrown off in the summer heat, or that both Mrs Queenie Bennett and Mrs Sylvia Bloom were hatless and had committed the unforgivable sin of not wearing stockings. Bulges around their midriffs hinted that corsets had been abandoned also. The two ladies, of indeterminate ages, sat at opposite ends of the table like a pair of bulbous book-ends, Queenie in a floral print dress, Sylvia in a cornflower blue suit. Both were obviously hot and unhappy. When their weight shifted a faint squelch could be heard down below from sweaty thighs. The secretary, tidy Mrs Myra Fitzsimmons, who was not bulky enough to need corsetry, shook her head in despair. The two must have colluded by telephone. But perhaps one should be content to get anybody to show up for politics in a heatwave.

The branch met as usual in the room above the greengrocer's at Childwall Fiveways. It was furnished with little more than a trestle table and chairs, a filing cabinet and a battered typewriter. The table's roughness was hidden under a baize cloth pockmarked by cigarette burns. A heap of undelivered party newspapers cluttered one corner, beneath a broken Gestetner. On the dusty floorboards lay an ancient rag rug which Myra had frequently sworn she would throw out. The light was filtered by years of dirt on the outside of the windows – unavoidable, it was asserted, on such a busy roundabout – and further reduced by blue fumes from the smokers present. Above the empty fireplace gazed down a framed print of their Member of Parliament Sir John Tilney, aristocratic and remote, while opposite hung the wartime portrait of Winston Churchill. It had been their intention for years to obtain a picture of the current Prime Minister but somehow they'd never got round to it. A space had been kept; Myra worried privately that, given the forthcoming election and the state of public opinion, perhaps they'd better get a move on while he was still in power.

Charlie Marples the chairman was the proprietor of the shop beneath. A cousin of his, Ernest Marples, had been Minister of Transport and was still MP for Wallasey. That gave Charlie status but not much else. He had removed his green overalls before climbing the stairs, but the whiff of onions and earthy potatoes still clung to him. The smell made the hot air more oppressive; dust floated in the slanted beams of the dying sun.

'Well, ladies and gentlemen. Thank you for coming. It's been a remarkable week.'

'Terrible week, you mean.' Mrs Bennett crossed herself and sniffed dolefully.

'Aye, well, we're not here to discuss the death of the Pope. Very sad, that. The secretary will note –' he decided rapidly against a minute's silence: they were Unionists, after all '– that condolences were expressed to communicants of the Roman Catholic Church present. We have other matters to consider.'

'I can't believe it of Mr Profumo,' was the tearful response. Queenie was capable of rapid changes of tack. 'He lied to the House of Commons. He lied to the Prime Minister. He lied to us all. And solely because of that – that—'

'That prostitute,' said Sylvia firmly. 'That's the word. A common prostitute. With a Russian boyfriend. He's skedaddled off home quick – seen the last of 'im.'

'What were they doing at Lady Astor's country home, I'd like to know?' This from Albert who had been footman to the Earl of Derby till retirement and was the staunchest Tory on the committee. He tamped his pipe with a nostalgic air. 'Dear Nancy. She's still alive. Did she invite them in?'

'She's gone doolally. But her son was there, or at least the papers say so,' advised Sylvia, who made it her business to know such matters. 'It was quite a society crowd. Titled people and the like. Cavorting around the swimming pool starkers. No wonder poor Mr Profumo fell. It'd take a man of stone to resist.'

Albert stirred in indignation. 'This 'ere Stephen Ward. Did you see him on TV last night? Said he was an osteopath, whatever that is. Denies living off immoral earnings.'

'Pimp,' Sylvia translated crisply. 'Hers, and a few others too. Can of worms. She's got a couple of nasty West Indian fellers in the background as well – one was up in court for punching her.'

The comments flowed freely as the loyal members unloaded their grimmer assessments and rolled their eyes heavenwards. It was not long before plausible connections had been established between Miss Keeler, her disappearance when a key witness in an earlier Old Bailey trial, certain allegations in the *Sunday Mirror* and the War Minister's resignation. The whole story seemed too bizarre to be true. When Albert stuck his refilled pipe in the corner of his mouth and began to recount a yet more salacious tale from a former colleague in the Windsor household in Paris, the chairman called them swiftly to order.

'Enough, now,' he chided gently. 'I don't know what things are coming to. There's a debate on the whole affair in the House of Commons after Whit recess. On whether Mr Profumo attempted to pervert the course of justice by spiriting the lady away, though personally I doubt it. Plus an inquiry into the security aspects. The constituency executive has suggested it'd help if we sent a message of support to the Prime Minister. Our secretary has drafted some suitable words. Is that agreed?'

'The polls are horrible,' Sylvia murmured to Mrs Bennett as Mrs Fitzsimmons read out the proposed motion. 'We're down below thirty per cent. That's the worst since the war. And Labour's fourteen points ahead.'

'We ain't gonna be in trouble in Liverpool,' Albert intoned stoutly. 'Don't be daft. There's nine seats in this city and we hold six. Labour's only safe MPs are battlin' Bessie Braddock and ol' Logan in Scotland Road. Irvine holds Edge Hill for 'em by the skin of his teeth. Tories'll be fine here.'

'God help us if that bunch get in – they're not much better than Communists, some of 'em. They'd abolish Church schools, the Royal Family, the lot.' Queenie Bennett crossed herself again.

'We don't mention Labour in this room,' Chairman Marples growled. 'Now come on, ladies, let's concentrate. The quicker we pass this motion the sooner we can go home. All those in favour?'

A hundred yards away Maurice Feinstein in his best suit and tie was seated in José's Spanish Wine Bar, which he had been assured was the finest in town. The fact that it had been opened barely a month explained the strong smell of fresh paint, but that was in its favour since it virtually overcame the odour of garlic from the kitchen. Across the table, her face carefully made up and rosy with wine, sat Vera Wolfson in a shocking pink dress with white polka dots. Her pearls gleamed in the candlelight. Maurice was about to pour a third glass for her. His own was untouched.

Maurice felt slightly sick. Usually he cooked for himself or grabbed whatever was handy in the shop. The seafood paella, or whatever it was called, had been pungent, oily and filling. Despite his injunction he suspected it had contained *treife* – half a shrimp had caught his eye and been pushed in disgust to one side. But Vera had eaten the lot with evident relish and wiped her dish, 'continental-style' as she excused it, with a chunk of bread. Maurice was fascinated.

'You like this sort of stuff – you eaten it before?'

'Oh yes. You get it quite often abroad.'

He had never been further than Blackpool, nor wanted to, though a trip to Jerusalem before he died was a half-hearted ambition which would probably never be fulfilled.

'Sylvia mentioned you'd lived abroad.'

'Not exactly lived there.'

Vera had given no special instructions; the empty dish before her was littered with the blue-black shells of mussels. She was now licking her fingers. More paper napkins were called for and she wiped her hands. Her nails were a delicate shade of pearlised pink, Maurice noticed. He raised his eyes to her face. She was really attractive in the soft light. He was proud to be with her, this sophisticated lady.

Vera sighed in satisfaction. She removed a stray piece of fish from a tooth with the nail of her little finger. Her accent, refined before the aperitifs, had slipped a bit. 'That was terrific. I'll have ice cream for dessert. Thanks a million. My mother makes me stick to the rules at home. Gets frightfully tedious when you're accustomed to variety like me. On board ship we had a choice of five courses, both lunchtime and dinner. Oh yes.'

He must have looked puzzled. 'Didn't Sylvia tell you? I was a hostess for Cunard on the big liners for ten years. Called myself Venetia – a bit smarter than plain old Vera, don't you think? You name it, I've sailed in it, or to it. New York, Caribbean, Mediterranean. Round the world twice. Wonderful life. Mostly thirty days on, ten days off. And as much food as I could eat.'

'Venetia,' Maurice repeated with wonder. 'You don't look like a Venetia. I think I prefer the old-fashioned name. It suits you better.'

She laughed prettily. 'If you like. My Venetia days are over. Please may I have some more bread?' As he passed her the wicker basket he blurted out the query which had sprung into his mind. 'You're lovely and slim. Most people who go on the cruises come back – well, a bit heavier than when they left. How did you manage?'

'That was easy. Burned it up. I was a hostess – ah, you don't get it. I was on the go day and night. And in particular, I was a dancing partner for any single gentleman – or if, say, a passenger's wife was poorly or not keen on the light fantastic. That's where the championship certificates came in handy. I was the sole lady engaged, though there were three gentlemen hosts – some old widows booked a particular cruise purely to lay their paws on their favourite. Imagine!'

Maurice pushed away his plate, his eyes rounded in disbelief. He feared the next reply.

'And you – were there men with their eyes on you? I mean, were you expected to do anything more than dance?'

Vera broke out into a peal of laughter that made the other diners

twist and stare. Maurice had the impression that she was somewhat out
of control. She gave his chest a playful shove.

'What do you think? No, never. Not officially. The whole thing was
ultra respectable. You'd get to know the guys to avoid – the word
would get round. But if a chap was a charmer, and you'd spent hours in
his arms, and he offered a big tip – well!'

And she rolled her eyes suggestively, then pouted.

'But it's behind me now. I mean, you dream some cheesecake'll carry
you off to a mansion in Georgia with dozens of servants and a chauf-
feured Rolls, but they never do. I enjoyed my years on the ships and
wouldn't have changed a thing but it's finished. My Ma's been going on
at me about grandchildren and said I'd better get a move on because of
my age. So here I am.'

'Children? How many do you want?' He might as well have asked
how many sugars in her coffee. (The answer to the latter, he noticed,
was two.) It was a struggle to keep up with the pace of her conversation, its twists and turns.

'Me? None at all preferably. Can't bear 'em. But Ma won't be content with fewer than four. She says she dreams about babies.'

It was the kind of discussion a man should have with a putative
wife, Maurice knew, but still it was a shock. *Babies?* Was he to be a
father all over again? Nappies – teething? Two in the morning, pacing
with a howling infant? That had not occurred to him. On the other
hand, Vera was a peach. His pals would call him a lucky dog. In a
dream himself, Maurice called for the bill, blenched, paid without
demur and accompanied her to the door.

Around the corner they began to walk down Queen's Drive then
slowed near the traffic lights of Woolton Road. They were outside her
home.

'I'd invite you in but my mother's there,' Vera said archly. Her escort
shuffled his feet in embarrassment. She prodded his arm. 'We're not far
from your place, are we? Perhaps we could go there for a – nightcap.'

Maurice gazed down at Miss Wolfson. He needed to ponder much
that she had said. Especially about babies and her former profession,
which left him uneasy though he was unsure quite why.

'My son's home. Can't,' he responded shortly, though he knew that
was not true, at least not till midnight. There would have been plenty of
time had he been tempted.

Her mouth fell. Devoid of its guile it was a pleasant face; were she
slightly less artificial she would be truly comely. He wondered how
Vera might react if he told her so, as tactfully as possible. She didn't
need so much make-up. A good woman would listen. He resolved to try
when an opportunity arose. Who knows, he told himself, she might be
grateful.

*

Sergeant Andy Newman parked his tray at a table near the door next to Michael Levison and poured himself an ice-cold Budweiser.

'Love the weather,' he said. 'If England could be like this the whole time, it'd be not half bad.'

Michael laughed. 'Not hawf! Where did you pick that up – been in the local dives, have you?'

'You bet. My favourite's the Pelican in Warrington. I grant you the beer's an acquired taste – they serve it warm, even in summer. The landlord says it's dead these days compared with a few years ago. But I can make myself understood here. In Germany it was terrible – not that we were supposed to fraternise with the Krauts. No, gimme Blighty any day. Haw haw, what? I say!' and he practised the typical American imitation of a high-class Englishman.

Through the open door stretched almost fifteen hundred acres of the base, flat grey land with warehouses. The biggest building was Header House which covered around three million square feet of space – as with much else at Burtonwood, one of the largest in Europe. Its main post-war task had been to support, repair and overhaul the whole of the 3rd US Air Force in Europe, which involved supervision of some thirty daughter bases scattered across England and North Wales. For thousands it had been home, albeit temporarily: by 1945 almost 18,000 officers and men were stationed there, while at its peacetime peak over 5,000 US troops and their dependents lived on the site on a three-year tour. Some of the results, particularly the sprawled ugly buildings and miles of concrete runway now sprouting grass, were permanent.

'Pity this base's such a dump. It's seen plenty of action in the past but now it's not much more than a glorified storehouse.' Michael had walked around to select sights to show Helen. His spirits had fallen at the seedy emptiness.

'Its great days were in the Berlin airlift, I was told,' said Andy. 'It had the longest runway in the UK and could overhaul nine Skymaster aircraft in every twenty-four-hour turnaround. That's some record. But the whole lot could close next year.'

'Really?' Michael was not entirely surprised. The air of redundancy, less apparent in the busier sections such as the canteen, was pervasive the further he had trudged from the centre.

'Stands to reason, once our key squadron moved to Alconbury and others to Mildenhall in Suffolk. Look, it used to be perfect to land men and *materiel* from the States in Liverpool, but now we can fly the lot in big transports straight to their destinations. Time's moved on.' Andy Newman took a long swallow of his beer. He enjoyed playing the expert with more recently arrived men. 'And far less gets lost in transit, or disappears at the docks. The number of times you hear about things falling off the back of a lorry! It's a national joke. Not that anybody could say so in public, of course.'

'It's not a bad spot, though. I like the locals.'

'Oh, sure.' Andy chuckled. Michael's disappearances into Liverpool and the tiny photo of a pretty dark-haired girl pinned up in his locker were already common knowledge, and hardly unusual. 'Always made us welcome. In the fifties, legend has it, one in every three unaccompanied US airmen here married a girl from Warrington or nearby. And plenty left behind unwanted baggage when they went home – illegitimate children. But that happens near every army base, I guess.'

'What'll happen to it, d'you reckon?'

'I'd say it'd be handed over to the RAF. And we'd be sent forward – Wiesbaden, probably. Or, if the Indo-China theatre doesn't calm down, Saigon, Lord help us. Unless the French government get tricky and carry out their threat to withdraw from NATO. If General de Gaulle serves notice on Uncle Sam, we'd have to clear off our bases on French territory. Then maybe Burtonwood'd be useful.'

They had been joined by 'CC' Cohen who brought over a plate of bread and cheese.

'I bet in the old days they had kosher food,' CC grumbled as he nibbled the cheese.

'I bet they didn't – on active duty who has time for such niceties?' Newman teased. 'Anyway, aren't you allowed to break any dietary law in order to save life?'

'It'd save my life if I had a nice bit of my uncle Babar's *wursht* right now,' CC answered cheerfully. 'I wrote my mother that I was dying for it and she put one in a parcel with books and soap and such for me. But it stank so much by the time it got to the dockside that the Customs threw it out. They didn't realise it's supposed to be a bit strong – garlic and that.'

The two others held their noses in mock horror, then Andy tentatively raised the issue both had in mind. 'How's this date of yours, Mike? You still planning to show her off to us?'

Levison nodded. 'Sunday. But the idea is to show us off to her. Any suggestions? I thought the control tower – you can see for miles – and the workshops and hangars are impressive.'

CC put his head shrewdly on one side. He wondered how devoted Michael, whom he liked, was about the young lady from Harold House. Her family was respectable – that much had been obvious from the glimpse at the Rembrandt. The fact that she had introduced himself but not Michael had told him much. It grieved CC that a girl of his own faith was to be courted by a Christian; he felt some obligation to keep a watching brief.

'You could try serenading her. D'you know the song the Yanks here used to sing in the forties? Listen to this –' And CC broke out in a yodel to a tune derived from *No one can love like an Irishman*:

'When the heavenly dew whips through the breeze
And you walk in mud up to your knees
When the sun don't shine and the rain flows free
And the fog is so thick you can hardly see –

'When you live on Brussels sprouts and spam
And powdered eggs aren't worth a damn,
In town you're eating fish and spuds,
And washing it down with a mug of suds –'

He waved his arms and conducted the chorus:

'Dum diddy diddle diddle dum –'

As his companions urged him on, CC paused for breath and explained, 'There are dozens of verses, much in the same vein – they get worse . . .

'There's no transportation so you'll have to hike
And you get knocked down by a "Gosh Darned" bike,
Where most of the gals are blonde and bold,
And think every Yank's pocket is lined with gold.'

'More, more!' came from Newman. Michael was laughing and keeping time with his palm on the table.
CC obliged: 'It finishes:

'This isle ain't worth saving I don't think,
Cut loose those balloons, let the darned thing sink,
I'm not complaining, I want you to know,
But life sure is tough in the ETO!'

The ETO was the European Theater of Operations. The three linked arms and warbled the last lines barber-shop style:

'You all may say what e'er you can,
But no one can love like a New York *man'*
('Texas!' yelled Newman loudly).
'Dum diddy diddle diddle dum!'

'Oh God, I can't start crooning crap like that to her,' gasped Michael as he wiped his eyes. 'She'll think we're nuts. And idle loafers with one sole thing on our minds.'
'And haven't you?' Newman was inquisitive. 'She's quite a looker. Kinda cute – no, demure. But no English rose with those wicked black

eyes. Wassername – Helen?' He gave Michael a dig with his elbow. 'Anyhow, what else is there – wedding bells?'

'No, of course not. She's much too young.'

'So – how young? Eighteen? Nineteen?'

'Seventeen. Nearly. She hasn't graduated from high school yet.'

'Baby-snatcher,' Newman began to tease, but was warned off by a shake of Michael's head. He might chuckle about the ditty but would brook no remarks about Helen.

'Girls marry at seventeen in the Chassidic community,' said CC plaintively. 'My sister was furious. She wanted to go to college but our grandfather the rebbe said education was wasted on a girl. She should focus on bringing up a family.'

'What did she do?'

'She gave in, naturally. Got three infants under three now. My nephew and nieces! I'm a very proud uncle. You wanna see some pictures?'

Michael cleared his tray and left the two men together. He did not want to risk further joshing from them about Helen. Partly because he had scarcely dared to sort out in his own mind how he felt about her; but mainly because he feared his image of her might be sullied by the casually lewd comments that would invariably follow. He strolled out into the late sunshine, found a quiet corner and sat down, with his back to the warm corrugated-iron of the shed.

When he thought about her, which was often, it was with a surge of affection of a kind normally reserved for his parents and brother or for a special buddy. Most girls were in a different class and at times operated like a separate species: you wouldn't reveal to them any deep emotions. With them, an extra layer of skin intervened to prevent vulnerability. You didn't get close. You didn't want to. You didn't need to.

But Helen was not like that. She didn't go about with a band of twittery girls. She had an air of solitary composure which he found fresh and intriguing. He was fairly sure she did not share views about him with her friends or anyone else, and that she maintained a cool silence if asked. It wasn't merely that her co-religionists would strongly disapprove, which he knew about though found hard to grasp: that imposed secrecy. It was also a natural reserve, as if Helen would automatically keep things hidden. Perhaps she preferred it that way. For all her youth she came over as a private person, a quality that made her appear more mature, more intensely interesting. Yet she was not limp: strong-willed, definitely, or he wouldn't have been in the least attracted. He longed to get to the heart of her, to find what made her pulses race, what inspired her. Such was her intelligence and thoughtfulness that he was certain that in her company would come revelations, simply expressed maybe but none the less significant, which might serve him well in life too. She had something to teach him. How very strange.

His deliberations made him frown in surprise. Normally when he pictured a girl the first element that sprang to mind was physical – her appearance, the sensation of her body, how she moved, how she smelled. How she scored in the sack, if truth were told. Like many boys of his generation (particularly American) he'd never bothered much with a girl's personality unless it got in the way, and seldom considered her brains – though anyone totally moronic would be ruled out. Yet with Helen he was drawn by something magic about her, not physical. Almost spiritual. It made him wonder what he was getting into.

He felt a burden of responsibility, of that he was sure, which he had not experienced with any other female. To her substantially, and to himself. It was easily justified by her age. More than that: from remarks she had made he was fairly certain he was her first real beau, whereas he for sure was no beginner.

It would have been hard to attend a typical American high school in the late fifties and emerge a virgin, he reflected with a grin. At least, for a full-blooded male. Certain girls were known to be extra friendly. Co-operative. Competent, even with the fumbles of virgins like himself.

He had been fourteen and already nearly six feet tall. The guys on the junior football team had decided it was time he became a man. They were sick of telling jokes whose nuances their gangly quarterback didn't grasp, an ignorance evident when he snickered in the wrong places. At the memory Michael smiled. So the captain had made a deal with Kiki, already a major, who was known to boast how many times a night she could do it. How many of the team could she cope with? If she made it to fifteen there'd be a cash bonus and her reputation would soar.

It was arranged that he would go in at number three. Another rookie would go after him. More like baseball than football, he'd kidded at the time, but his knees had been weak from mingled excitement and terror.

So Kiki, blonde hair piled on the top of her head, gingham skirt a-flounce, had met them in the clubhouse two hours after practice ended. Her heady perfume mingled confusingly with the prevailing stink of wintergreen, but her smile was wide and genuine. She wiggled tantalisingly into the treatment room carrying several towels and a jar of Vaseline. After a moment came the call: 'Let's get cracking, one at a time. Biggest first!'

When Michael's turn came, he could hardly walk, so tumescent was his erection. Kiki had been on the bed, long tanned legs crossed at the ankles, skirt demurely to her knees, a cigarette in one hand, her panties in the other. She had waved at him.

'Hi! What's your name?'

And she had lifted her skirt and patted her moist pussy. So it had been damned easy: she'd gone so far as to help his trembling fingers

with the unfamiliar rubber. The fact that it came so quick was not a disappointment but more like respect for her. When he had shuddered and
was done Kiki had caressed the top of his head, drawn on her cigarette
and wiped herself delicately as he shambled back into his trousers. She
made him pirouette to ensure everything was tucked away, then blew
him a kiss. 'You were a darlin'. Send the next one in.'

He had stumbled out and felt, God forgive him, deliriously happy. A
complete man, a finished-off human being. The initiation had been
stupid but had not disgusted him; she had been a volunteer. Indeed by
dawn she had succoured all fifteen with a half-hour rest and shower
after the tenth, or claimed to have done so. Since every boy had entered
the room, none (and especially not the tailenders) would have dreamed
of admitting a lack of capability.

His recall of the event had always been pleasurable: in fact he had
told the tale in a self-deprecatory fashion whenever the question, 'How
did you lose yours?' was broached. He'd been a kid, totally wet behind
the ears and desperate to learn. He would not do anything like that
now. Yet to his own discomfort and shock he felt newly ashamed of the
entire episode.

Should Helen inquire he would imply that he had been Kiki's sole
suitor, that night at any rate. Then it hit him: for Helen, if she could be
persuaded, the situation would be reversed. Not only her first real love,
but her first time. It was up to him to ensure that it'd be memorable,
and precious, so that never in future should she have reason to feel
queasy as he now did.

Dammit. Surely she guessed what she was taking on – an adult US
airman? Wasn't his greater age and experience exactly what attracted
her? If she felt safer with a pimply boy she had her pick at Harold
House. That she had preferred him, a masculine man some years older
who had made no bones of his sexual desire for her, was consent in
itself. Wasn't it?

She was a virgin. Michael began to feel helpless and unsure. He had
never made out with a virgin before. Willing or otherwise. Not that he'd
force her. He doubted he could force anyone – but how to arrange that
she desired it too, as much as he did himself, and right the way through
to the end? Would she need to be coaxed? Would she have the faintest
idea what to do? When he needed her to touch him, would she shrink
away and start to cry?

In which case he would lift his hands from her and roll away. That
much was decided. Never mind Kiki's reputation: it was his that mattered, not as a stud, but as a gentle and loving person. Not only in
Helen's eyes, but in his own.

Michael rose; his back ached and he flexed his shoulders to restore
circulation. So much introspection was unaccustomed, especially about
sex. Correction: especially about one particular girl, whom in truth he

barely knew, from a country he regarded as outlandish and a religious background which would reject him bitterly. And to whom nevertheless he was driven so strongly, like a bee to the sweetest honey, or a white dove to its lofty home, as if it were his soul which he could not deny.

Michael wished he could discuss the matter with somebody. It was unthinkable to toss it around with pals on the base. The name which came to him was his father's: after thirty years of marriage his Pa might have some advice, without being too prescriptive. But that would have to wait till furlough in July.

As he moved away, head still bowed in thought, Sergeant Newman caught him up.

'Say, Mike. I dunno if this will help. I'm out all day Sunday – going to explore the Lake District while the weather holds. You can have the keys to my bungalow. Better than shared barracks, hey? No sweat. Enjoy yourself, and your little lady.'

The younger generation coped better than their elders with the heat. School was out for a few days. So Brenda proposed an evening on the *Royal Daffodil* on its two-hour round-trip cruise to the estuary and back. An added incentive was the bar, and the blind eye of its staff to the age of customers.

Helen had chosen black drainpipe trousers and a plain top, with a sweater thrown over her shoulders. Out on the Mersey the air could be breezy and cool. Brenda and Meg were also in trousers; Colette had on a cotton dress and cardigan, both of which had seen better days.

The wait at George's landing stage while the boat chugged its way across from New Brighton, its previous destination; the surge as the iron gates were opened and people flooded down the long ramp; the rush on board to find the best spots, near the front on the upper deck, where both a seat and a good view from the rail were to be had: all were part of the delights of a ferry trip on the river Mersey, to be enjoyed as much in anticipation as in the event.

'Here'll do!' panted Meg, as the four girls raced up the stairwell and planted themselves firmly in their chosen place, well forward of the smoky funnel. She glared at three boys who had been hard on their heels. Beaten, the youths slunk away.

The boat wallowed, unstabilised. It was soon full with families, courting couples, kids like themselves. Helen mused that in 1940 those soldiers snatched from Dunkirk must have had a thoroughly unpleasant voyage back across the Channel, and worse with German planes strafing them constantly overhead. Still, the alternative was death on the beaches. The city had taken enormous pride in the intervention, among others, of its two little boats (or ships, as it insisted on calling them). Under the funnel a brass plaque commemorated the rescue, with another on the sister 'ship' *Royal Iris*.

The three boys sauntered nearby, pints of beer in their hands. Meg pulled out her purse. 'I'm going to get a lager and lime. Anybody else coming?'

'If you were pally to them they'd probably buy you one.' Helen indicated the boys but she was only semi-serious. She had brought enough money for two Cokes, as much as she could absorb without having to use the boat's toilets, which were always foul.

'Yuk,' was Meg's response. She disappeared into the hatchway.

Below them seamen in oily dungarees slipped the hawsers and the vessel began to chug out into the channel. Brenda and Helen sprawled on the metal benches, arms stretched out along the backs, feet on the stacks of lifebelts and faces raised to the salty breeze. Colette, a little apart, leaned over the rail to watch the murky waters churn. Gradually the Liverpool seafront slipped behind them, first the Docks and Harbour board office with its dome copied from St Paul's Cathedral, then the squat portico of the Cunard building in Portland stone, and third the tall Royal Liver building – an insurance office – an edifice magnificently strident, both symbol and product of a prosperous society, its Liver birds perched on the clock towers, mythical creatures like a cross between an eagle and a turkey, with a leafy branch in their beaks.

'What d'you think the branch is for?' Brenda pointed.

'It's like Noah's dove, isn't it? The idea is that the Liver bird was at the flood too and came back with a proper branch, not a few crappy leaves. So the merchants who sail from Liverpool could expect to return well laden. I think.' Helen giggled.

'I love the place,' Brenda sighed. 'It has such style. Pity we ever have to leave home, isn't it?'

'Yeah – I like coming from a sea-port. If Miss Plumb were here she'd probably be quoting Longfellow,' Helen answered. 'You know the bit:

'I remember the black wharves and the ships,
And the sea-rides tossing free;
And Spanish sailors with bearded lips,
And the beauty and mystery of the ships,
And the magic of the sea.'

'Lead me to the Spanish sailors,' Brenda commented dreamily. 'But this isn't exactly the most romantic river, is it? Black wharves and junk in excess but not much magic or mystery.'

At the barrier Colette bowed her head and fiddled with the hem of her dress, but did not join in. The engine was up to full throttle; she would have had to shout, or move nearer, which she seemed loath to do.

Helen concurred. 'I wish we'd known it in its heyday. A hundred years ago, say, when its great achievements and wealth were still in the future. I feel as if we've been born too late. Wherever you look it's going downhill.'

'My father says it's the Common Market,' Brenda continued. 'Liverpool's now on the wrong side of the country. We've been attuned to the Americas – first the slave trade and cotton, and sugar and rum and tobacco, then manufactures, now oil from places like Venezuela. Over on the Continent they've picked themselves up very quickly and trade is booming. Rotterdam's doing brilliantly. They were smashed to pieces in the war same as we were, but they used their Marshall Plan money to reconstruct industry whereas in Britain it was spent on new housing. At least, that's my father's theory.'

'We certainly didn't splurge much on industry. Or the railways. The opposite, in fact. If Dr Beeching gets his way we won't have any railways.'

Meg reappeared with her own drink and three Coke bottles with straws on a plastic tray. 'If you want something different, go get them yourselves,' she said. 'It's a bit rough in there.'

The other three accepted lazily and paid her. Brenda and Helen made room for her beside them. The boat had neared the opposite shore with its gaunt cranes and blackened shipyards and lifted in the swell. At the bow, eddies and vortices formed and swirled. The tide was turning.

'Not much trade on the river tonight,' Brenda remarked. 'My mother remembers some days when being on the ferry was like trying to cross a busy main road. Ships from everywhere. Not now. And Cammell Lairds isn't doing a lot of overtime either.'

'Their own bloody fault,' Meg interspersed. 'They won't work and they won't modernise. They think it's all right to hand over a ship when *they* want to; the men'll go on strike for more money two weeks before it's due and then it'll be three months late. My uncle's a ship broker and he says the Swedish shipyards deliver on time, always. Their initial contracts look expensive compared with ours but you get what you pay for – no hidden extras. The big yards at Bremen and – where did you say, Bren? – Rotterdam, are the same.'

'But it doesn't have to be like that,' Helen countered. She had donned the angora sweater and snuggled down in its softness. 'We used to have trade with the whole world, not just with America.' She recounted the details of the Finnish gravestone she had seen in St James's cemetery. 'There's no law says this port has to go downhill. The workpeople here are as smart as anywhere else. With better management – if they realised they were up against the competition, that they couldn't take their position for granted –'

'It'd need more than management.' Brenda was paraphrasing remarks she heard at home. She ticked off on her fingers in unconscious imitation of her father. 'You'd need huge investment – the docks are in a dire state. They were old fashioned before the war so can you imagine what they're like now? Meg's right. Every single job in those workshops is done by tradesmen, by hand like before the *first* war, let alone the last one. You'd need modern methods such as the Japanese have pioneered – preconstruction, standardisation. Mechanisation. And guess who'd put a stop to all that?'

'The unions,' Meg and Helen chorused together.

Brenda gazed at the cranes overhead. 'My Dad says the Japanese are already launching more shipping tonnage every year than this country. Bulk containers, each one an exact copy of the next. No need for fancy design – off the shelf, virtually. Cheap, and reliable. Like their cameras. No class whatsoever, but the customer doesn't give a damn. We're still operating in another century.'

Helen persisted. 'Liverpool does *not* have to deteriorate. But it'll have to be quick. I mean, if you asked around at school, how many of our Sixth Form plan to stay put? Not many. It upsets me a bit, but I can't see what we can do.'

'If people like us leave, then the life blood drains away,' Meg commented sombrely. None of her hearers thought comical or conceited the notion that the senior pupils of the Liverpool Institute High School for Girls, and by implication their fellows in the Institute for Boys, were the future life blood of their native city. They were the elite: that had been drummed into them since day one, and was precisely the reason they had been selected from their age cohort throughout Liverpool.

'Makes you worry, though,' Brenda mused. 'If we clear off we may in a small way hasten the decline, 'cause we won't be around to notice or do our bit. On the other hand, if we stay we may get dragged down ourselves, either 'cause we'll be as complacent as the next person, or because it'll be too damn difficult for one small group to do anything about it. So you may be wrong, Helen – it may be inevitable.'

'I'm not going to hang about and find out.' Meg bit her nails. 'You have to think of yourself.'

'So: where do we go, then?' Helen grinned at her friends. 'As far away as – Manchester?'

'London for me,' said Meg suddenly, as if she had just made up her mind. 'I like big cities and a woman's got a better chance there than up north.'

'I'll try for Oxbridge.' This from Brenda to Helen. 'You should too, don't argue. I won't get in, though. But Colette there would. Hey, Colette! We're talking about you. Northern grammar-school girl scientist, and with blazing green eyes and an Irish accent to boot! Perfect.'

A wan smile came from Colette but no answer.

'Maybe it'll get easier for all of us girls before we finish college,' Helen suggested. 'If Labour get in there's talk of legislation to ban discrimination on grounds of sex.'

Brenda hooted. 'Can you just see Bessie Braddock in charge? Our Scouse battlin' grannie as a government Minister. She's thick as a plank nailed together at both ends. Come off it, Helen, the idea's ludicrous.'

'There are others,' Helen defended. 'Barbara Castle from Blackburn. She's smart, and pretty. Oxford – Somerville.'

'Next thing you'll be telling us you'd like to be a lady MP. Storm Westminster in high heels and *Miss Dior*.' An edge of malice crept into Meg's voice.

'No,' said Helen softly. 'I could never do it. But change'll come. And either we'll be part of it, or it'll bear down like a steam-roller and flatten us.'

The boat left the silent shipyards and headed west towards the open sea. The estuary was broad and dangerous, with unpredictable flows. Here the vessel lurched and groaned in the heavy waters. One of the boys staggered out of the bar, his face ashen, reached for the barrier, leaned over and threw up. After retching noisily for several moments he wiped his face with the back of his hand, pushed himself upright then tottered back to the bar.

'Charming,' sniffed Meg.

Brenda settled herself deeper in her seat. The wind was quite strong and smelled sulphurously of the ICI works at Runcorn and the power station. She nudged Helen. 'So: how's the love life? Your parents still threatening fire and brimstone if you dare sigh over anybody adorable?'

'Aren't they just,' Helen muttered. 'I don't want to deceive them but I can't see how to avoid it.'

'You should come round to my house. One of my brothers, Ally, quite fancies you. We could make a foursome. Your parents couldn't object, surely?'

'They could,' said Helen firmly. 'It's not that they worry I'll get in with a bad crowd. I'm sure your Ally's super. It's simply that unless he's circumcised and never eaten pork in his life, he's *verboten*.'

'I think he's circumcised,' Brenda snickered. 'I mean, most baby boys are these days, for health reasons. Not that I've ever taken a dekko, of course,' she added hastily.

'Shows the old Jewish teachers were right. Problem is, it's all or nothing. You're either Jewish or you aren't. My parents would *never* accept somebody like Ally however wonderful he was because he's not a Jew.'

'So what's a Jew, then?' Brenda was genuinely curious. 'Is it somebody who says he is, or that other people thinks is, or do you have to have a big nose and look the part? Is there a test? D'you have to be born one, or can you convert?'

'It's blood only. Conversion is skin deep, my Mum says. And you can't inherit through both parents – it goes through the mother.'

'So that means your kids will be Jews whether they want to be or not?'

Helen struggled. 'Depends what you mean by Jew. My children can decide for themselves – I'm set on that, and I'll love them whatever they are. But to be accepted by the community – the answer's yes. Whether that's an advantage or not . . .'

'Damned complicated.' Meg rose and stood facing them, and leaned on the rail, her back to the wind. 'Any other religion, you're in it if you believe it, and nobody makes you believe. Colette's a Catholic not only because she was brought up that way, but because she goes to church and confession – don't you?'

Colette nodded. She had not uttered a word and seemed lost in her own reverie.

'So most faiths, people choose for themselves. But not yours.'

'Ours isn't solely a faith. It's a people. A race, if you want to use that word, though I don't like it. A culture, is better, that's lasted thousands of years. And what you say's not true. I have free choice.'

'Oh yeah?' Meg, sharp as ever, had worked it out. 'And if you choose not to be a Jew, to marry out or whatever, what'll happen then? But Colette can decide to be RC, and Brenda and I can go to church or not, and nobody'll make a fuss. We matter for ourselves, see, not for what we were born.'

'The RCs can be ferocious too, if you hope to marry in church. Have to promise the kids'll be brought up RC, sign papers, the lot.' Colette's intervention was so quiet her companions had to strain to hear.

'My Mum said she wouldn't mind if I came home with a coal-black Hottentot, as long as I was happy.' Brenda sat up. 'But I reckon I'm bloody lucky with my family. They're great.'

The other three could not counter with claims of their own. It was getting dark. The *Royal Daffodil* had returned to the calmer waters closer to the port. The night had become still and stuffy. Lights twinkled from windows along the harbour front. On the distant hill the half-finished Anglican cathedral was silhouetted blackly against the purple sky. A smell of vinegar wafted up to them from the winkle stall on the dockside.

'I'll take the bottles back and get the deposit,' Helen offered. She picked up the tray and, stepping gingerly on the slippery floor, entered the bar.

It was packed, noisy and aggressive. No different to a thousand pubs in the city, Helen reminded herself, and she was used to those. Men drank in clusters, standing up, hands firmly around pint mugs; women and older couples sat squashed around tiny tables. Every surface was awash with stale liquor whose sour-sweet odour filled the low-ceilinged room.

At the bar she had to wait as a late customer was served. The barman jangled a small ship's bell attached to a pillar. 'Time, ladies and gentlemen, please. We berth in five minutes.'

The customer in front was female, tarty, in a tight red skirt and revealing top. Two cocktails slopped in her hands, a cherry on a stick in each. As the bouffant hairdo turned around Helen found herself gazing straight into the rouged and lipsticked face.

'Hello. It's Sandra Quilter, isn't it?' Helen said politely. Though she had not seen her father's outworker or her daughter recently, she had met Sandra many times over the years.

The woman was drunk and swayed uneasily, but managed a grin that was close to a leer. 'Yeah, thass me. Having a lovely time. Who're you?'

'Helen Majinsky. Your mother does some work for my father.'

'Oh, yeah,' Sandra muttered vaguely. 'Nice to see ya, love. Gotta get these down us. Bye.'

Helen handed over the bottles and collected the penny deposits. She watched Sandra slump next to a much older man who appeared as plastered as she was. The man took no notice of Helen, but with a start the girl realised she knew his identity also. He had come to school once or twice, making a fuss about some triviality. If she were not mistaken, it was Mr O'Brien: Colette's father.

By the time Sandra was seated half the drink had been spilled and she and her escort were laughing hysterically. Helen was ignored.

Sandra was exactly the same age as herself. Helen decided not to mention the contact at home, nor to tell her friends what she had observed. The man's wife had left him and so he had a right to companionship, but the sight had dismayed and disgusted her. Colette had given no hint that she knew her father was on board; Helen concluded that, with hundreds of jostling passengers on the cruise, she simply hadn't seen him, nor he her. Back on deck, a little pensive, she rejoined her friends on the bench. Above their heads the funnel let out a smoky hoot of arrival.

Brenda put her arm around Helen's shoulder and pulled Meg in the other side. 'C'mon, Colette. You've been ever so quiet. 'S been a smashing evening, hasn't it? Let's promise, that whatever we do, wherever we go, married, single, or divorced, even when we're grandmothers, we'll meet up on the ferry again. Every ten years, say – in 1973, and 1983.'

'That's assuming there'll still be ferries across the Mersey,' Meg pointed out irritably. Brenda and Helen looked at her, startled. No ferries? The idea was unthinkable.

'That's assuming we'll all be here, too,' whispered Colette, but nobody heard her.

Chapter Fourteen

End of Term

Two women, had they but known it, came to Liverpool dockside at roughly the same moment early one morning a month later, but with different purposes.

One, Gertie Ahrens, of indeterminate age but lithe and fit, arrived at Prince's landing stage with her baggage in tow to catch the *Sylvania*. She had left behind an entire suitcase of clothes and gifts. Whenever one of her female relatives admired an outfit or an accessory or sweater, Gertie made a mental note. At the end of her stay the items were wrapped in tissue paper and presented in an unrefusable flourish. Thus Annie's wardrobe was to have an American flavour for a decade though the skirts had to be shortened, while Helen became the proud possessor of a real silk blouse, a cashmere sweater, several colourful scarves and a pile of costume jewellery that was much too old for her.

Gertie had shrugged with nonchalance as she was thanked. It was part of her triumph to pretend that these beautiful garments were insignificant since she could afford to buy more. That was not strictly true, but Joe would be as generous as he was able. She'd see to that.

Daniel and Annie came to see her off with Annie wedged in the back next to the trunk, which was now light enough for them to lift. The farewells were stilted and awkward. Gertie understood that Annie regretted her ill will. This had been but a short visit and no rivalry had been intended. The contrast between the two women's lives and convictions had been impossible to hide; in some senses, Gertie guessed, their conflict had been inevitable, since each clung to attitudes which were in direct contradiction of the other's.

It irritated Gertie that her sister-in-law should make such heavy weather of a woman's lot. She herself had found it relatively easy to function both inside and outside the home at the same time: no sacrifice need result from holy matrimony. Sure, it wasn't perpetual wedded bliss. The shine would come off romance with the passage of years. But a wife wasn't a slave, a kitchen wasn't a prison cell. Gertie had used the word 'martyr' in an unguarded moment of frankness with her niece, but did not shrink from it. Maybe Helen would make a better fist of her opportunities than her mother.

Gertie kissed Annie and hugged her brother but felt uncomfortable with him too. She had barely known Daniel, who had been a small boy when she had quit Britain for good, as soon as it was safe to sail after the first war. Most of her acquaintance with him came from letters, and from the remarks of her younger cousins who had grown up alongside him. They had painted a picture of a thoughtful, vigorous man, alive to his surroundings, compassionate and politically aware, though illness had robbed his youth and poverty wrecked his chances. At least, that had been the family theory.

In many respects the visit had saddened her. Daniel was less than she had hoped. Perhaps it was merely that he was older: her personal picture of him had stuck in the groove of his twenties. Nor was he physically well, a fact obvious to a newcomer. Yet few of those unusual qualities which had made him an attractive, even magnetic, figure in his young days seemed to have survived. To be sure, he had taken them to the Rembrandt, a grandiloquent gesture, though Gertie had eventually paid. And he'd been as amused as she was at his daughter's defiance, as if he reasoned that to ignore the rules of *kashruth* was, if one must, the least violent way to break with tradition. The spirit and good humour then exhibited, and the tactful way he had later soothed his wife, had endeared her to him. But as for anything more dramatic: it was as if he had begun to fade long before his time was due.

He did very little more, from what she could judge, than go to his workshop, come home, turn on the TV, and play an occasional game of bridge with the same bunch of pals year in and year out. He didn't bother to watch his favourite football team in person as the crowd had become too rough. His attendance at synagogue was perfunctory – holy days and special celebrations only. He seemed to receive no joy from his Jewishness; instead he appeared to regard his faith as a chore and an imposition. That did not bode well.

He belonged to no boards, contributed to no charities. He was not a Freemason, though Simon Rotblatt had explained that many of Liverpool's Jewish businessmen, denied membership by certain hostile Lodges, had formed one of their own. It had become virtually an obligation to join and take part in the ritual. Daniel had been pressed frequently. But when she had inquired, her brother had been scathing about those who performed their charitable functions in public and with their trouser legs rolled up. Yet nothing else took his fancy. There was nothing he cared about.

They had kept off politics but she had established that he felt no deep-seated loyalty to the state of Israel. The blue and white tin of the

Jewish National Fund stood by his telephone as it did in most house-holds, and he emptied his spare change into it on Friday evenings. But he claimed in all seriousness that that was because coins in a pocket tended to wear out the fabric, and he didn't like being the kind of man who jingled coins when talking. It was as if the new country did not exist for him. It had no part to play in his life whatever.

You have to believe in something, Gertie had chided, but he had deflected her puzzled strictures with a wave of his hand about the room. 'This is what I believe in – this is what I've got, what I've built. It's sufficient.' He meant his home, his family. He was a paterfamilias and had resolved at some point in the past to accept that limited role. But from everything she had heard Daniel had been capable of better things – or rather, of more than mere owner-occupation and fatherhood. Her cousins asserted that Daniel had had the capacity and vision to go much further. She wondered what had happened.

Maybe he had simply absorbed the deadly lassitude of his native city. She was amazed at how difficult it was to get a simple job done as promised and without additional trouble and expense. Look at the hassle of coming here today: no taxi was willing to come out at six am to Childwall, at least nobody reliable. Every discussion was peppered with examples of somebody's failure to perform and the preposterous excuses, often in vivid language, which would follow. They had a terrific sense of humour, these Liverpudlians, and a way with words. What they didn't have was a healthy respect for hard work and a sense of responsibility – a work ethic – the sort her own parents had drummed into their children. Daniel had summed it up neatly and cynically for her: 'You'll get fifty thousand cheering fans on the Kop for the game on the dot of two-thirty Saturday afternoon. But can you get them to clock in at seven-thirty Monday morning? Not a chance.' He clearly took it as read. That depressed her mightily, the more so as he declared this state of affairs as immutable. He seemed to have given up, on this as on so much else.

Gertie found her cabin and was relieved to discover that she would not be required to share for the return voyage. She unpacked her toilet bag, then went back on deck. Daniel and Annie were still on the cobbles below, as if uncertain when it was polite to leave. She waved and yelled, aware that they could hear her only indistinctly. The ship's hooter sounded loudly and made everyone jump.

Annie would be relieved to see her depart. Gertie felt genuinely sorry, but suspected her own emotions on the high seas would be the same as her sister-in-law's. The son, Barry, was a bit of a *schlemiel* – a sly, narrow child who would survive perfectly well whatever befell him. Not her type of boy but no doubt he'd not cross his parents and would keep them happy. Gertie would not miss him.

The daughter, Helen, was a different matter. Gertie half wished the girl was on board with her, on her way to a new life in the States.

There, released from the confines of the Old World and especially of its tattier elements, the girl would flourish. When the pettier restrictions were lifted, in an environment where originality was encouraged and ambition admired, the kid's adherence to the more fundamental tenets of the faith could be resecured. At the moment, Gertie sensed, the child was so frustrated by petty rules that she was in danger of throwing the whole thing over. That wasn't an uncommon reaction amongst the young. She had recognised it in herself all those years ago. Fortunate, therefore, that Joe's wisdom and calmness had been available to rescue her. Perhaps one of those American GIs, with a surname like Cohen, would perform the same trick for her niece.

From the deck Gertie Ahrens took one last look at the dilapidated warehouses and seedy litter of the quay, at the flotsam of unidentifiable rubbish jammed between the ship's side and the brick dockwall, one last gaze at the stolid, blackened buildings on the waterfront. Then she went inside. She was glad to be going home.

The *Sylvania*'s hooter had also made Nellie McCauley start. She was two hundred yards away, where a much smaller cruise ship was bound for the Canary Isles. Pete had signed on as a leading hand, but intended to jump ship in Bilbao.

Nellie stared round the tiny cabin in the bowels of the vessel. 'God, it's not exactly the lap of luxury, is it?' she remarked.

Here no effort was made to hide pipes or bulkheads as on the upper passenger decks. No panelled wood or veneers, no stainless steel or chrome had penetrated this far down. Doors, walls and fittings were of iron plates, the rivets standing proud, each surface covered in many layers of flaky green paint. A dribble of dank fluid seeped from a rusty weld. On one side of the tiny room were two bunks, one above the other. The third was below the porthole. Opposite was a minute sink and splashed mirror with razors and toothbrushes in a slimy mug, while the fourth wall held the door and a narrow floor-to-ceiling cupboard. Lino covered the metal floor, its edges curled up, and in front of the sink it had worn through to its jute back. A large pair of sea boots with thick socks still inside had been slung carelessly under one of the bunks; their ripeness soured the entire cabin.

'It'll do,' said Pete gruffly. He opened the cupboards and stowed away a pair of trousers and a jacket. 'If you'd been on board I'd have got us a double. They're a bit better.'

'When I come to Spain I'll fly,' Nellie replied with as much verve as she could muster. She smiled at him coyly. 'Not made my mind up yet, anyway.'

'Don't take too long about it. I want to know I haven't lost my touch.' He turned and put his hands on her arms, squeezed, then gathered her close and kissed her.

When they relaxed, Nellie rested her head on Pete's shoulder. There had been so much she had wanted to ask during his brief stay, but whenever she was home he had needed her either to cook or make love. She seized the moment. 'What exactly would I do in Spain, anyway? Be a lady of leisure?'

'No. I told you most of the money had gone. Christ, d'you think if I was a millionaire I'd be travelling like this? No, I've got a part share in a bar. You could work there.'

'A barmaid?'

'What's wrong with that? You weren't born with a silver spoon in your mouth, Nellie. It's not a bad way to earn your keep.'

She disengaged, and smoothed her hands over his rough jersey. No doubt about it, nights with Pete had beaten sleeping solo hands down. He didn't trouble her with much introspection and expected no finer cuisine than what she managed for herself, supplemented with fish and chips from the corner chippie. A life in the south, of Sangria and sand, of days off to sunbathe had its appeal, especially compared with the grotty streets of Liverpool. Nothing better loomed on the horizon. Her friends would die with envy. It was worth weighing up, very carefully.

'Better clear off, Nellie, or you'll be on the high seas whether you want to or not. Be good now.' And he gave her one more cuddle, though it was a little peremptory compared with the first. He held open the door. 'Out of here, turn left, up three flights and you're there. Bye.'

It was a disconsolate Nellie who disembarked down the crew gang-plank. She had been left with a choice: that at least was a vast improvement on a month before. What precisely that choice might be, and whether it was a bed she wished to make, let alone lie in, she was unsure. Perhaps events at the shop would help her make up her mind.

Helen turned over the examination paper and checked the clock. Three solid hours, four questions to complete, twenty minutes left. 'Compare and contrast the properties of aldehydes and ketones' had come up as she had hoped. 'Describe the qualities of the benzene ring and discuss their value in modern life' had been twice revised. 'Explain the processes of making nylon' was easy, to be honest: it demanded merely a good memory. She was not required to wax eloquent. The fourth question, her weakest, had been left to last. She did not find ethanol and its derivatives in the least entertaining and was aware she had not done the subject justice.

The mock A levels occurred in the spring as practice for the real thing in June. By then the entire syllabus would have been completed, they would have practised variants on the prescribed experiments, she would have memorised chunks of historical biography, on Semmelweiss and Mendel, on Pasteur and Marie Curie, in case a question popped up on the lines of 'Which chemist or biochemist in recent history would you

Edwina Currie

names inspired her; their struggles were leaven to the stodgy diet of
everyday chemistry and physics. Their successes showed that the public
view of science as brainwaves and sudden revelation was far from the
truth. On the contrary: Helen marvelled how these scientists had
slogged away in the face of hardship and disapproval. For the women
the injustice was pervasive and blatant. When Pierre Curie was awarded
his Nobel Prize his wife was ignored; it took a prolonged outcry for
Marie to receive hers some years later and only after his death was her
own genius recognised.

It was finished. She laid down her pen and read through the script.
The marks would be included in confidential reports to universities.
Helen had worked hard and had no fears. If her score were below sev-
enty per cent she and her teachers would have been astonished.

Fifteen minutes left. She began to doodle on the back of the exam
paper. It would not do to leave, for that would disturb entrants still
scribbling furiously nearby. Brenda never managed to finish since she
would be too engrossed in the first two questions. Meg would answer
as necessary, but a slapdash approach and unreadable calligraphy
would cut her marks. Colette was staring straight to the front, pen
between her teeth, brow furrowed. As Helen watched, the Irish girl
described a six-sided polygon before her eyes, then appeared to grasp
what had eluded her and started to write busily once more. Helen loved
to discuss the answers afterwards with Colette who could always
analyse them more clearly than the others and whose quick brain made
mincemeat of the calculations. In the right circumstances Colette would
make a superb specialist.

What might she herself achieve? It was not arrogant to want her
name up in lights and not vain to assume it was possible. As she had
outlined to Mr Mannheim, her preference was to be associated with the
development of some commodity which might have future science students learning her name – a wonder drug, or a dramatic new fabric.
How wonderful it would be if the 'Majinsky method', a technical break-
through as yet undreamed of, should some day make her famous, like
the Salk vaccine or Fleming and penicillin. Along with Mr Mannheim
she would shy from research into weaponry of any kind, though staff in
such laboratories were well paid. Not that she was a pacifist – but
others would do it, and she would leave it to them. The odds were,
however, that she'd end up in Port Sunlight, buried in the endless search
for a soap powder to wash whiter.

Her doodles had synthesised into two columns. At the top of one she
had squiggled 'Don't', and the other was headed 'Do'. Seven minutes till
the bell. She began to put into each column the first notions that came
into her head in no particular order.

'Do' soon had a long list. *Hard work, politeness, fulfil potential.*

Keep hair nice, nails clean, stockings free of ladders, polish shoes. Save money, followed by (!) *Read more, especially novels. Get more sleep. Give essays in on time. Go to dentist before it hurts. Learn to love Miss Plumb. Love Michael.*

The 'Don't' list was shorter, mainly because her natural turn of mind was positive. *Don't be rotten to Barry even if you hate him. Ditto Jerry Feinstein.* (She then wrote 'Make friends with Roseanne Nixon' under 'Do', pondered, and crossed it out.) *Don't interrupt. Don't snap at your mother.*

What a peculiar collection, she realised. All the 'Don'ts' but one were to do with other people. The only 'Do's' with people were for her headmistress and her American boyfriend and both used the word *love*. And two of the most important individuals in her life, her father and Reverend Siegel, did not feature at all.

'One minute left,' came the supervisor's call. Helen drew a line with 'Don't know' above. Under she wrote two words, then hesitated and wrote two more. After the latter two she put a large question-mark. The list then read, *1. Dad 2. Rev Siegel 3. America? 4. Israel?*

'I have more research to do yet,' she murmured to herself. 'And I think I know who might help.' The bell sounded, short and sharp. Pens were laid down, sighs echoed around the room. Helen collected her answer sheets and held them up for collection. The exam paper, obliterated by doodles intelligible only to herself, she put in her pocket.

Roseanne Nixon returned to the solidly respectable detached house in Menlove Gardens with its pebble-dash exterior and paved drive she shared with her parents, and plonked her satchel on the kitchen table with her beret.

'Don't do that, dear,' responded her mother automatically. Mrs Rita Nixon was talking on the phone which had been newly installed on the kitchen wall. The girl opened the fridge door and took out a bottle of Coca Cola and a slice of blackcurrant cheesecake. She sat at the table and began to eat.

Her mother said goodbye and replaced the phone on the hook.

'Heavens, Roseanne, have you never heard of a plate? Look at the mess. Crumbs everywhere. And couldn't you have made a cup of tea instead of drinking that rubbish?'

Roseanne responded with as much dignity and self-control as she could muster.

'Mum. I've been in the house five minutes and all you've done is moan. Don't you want to know about the exams?'

Mrs Nixon paid attention as bid. 'Of course, dear. How did you get on?'

'Dunno yet.' Roseanne was gloomy about her prospects. 'It would've helped if I'd read *Bleak House*, I suppose. And the history – I get so mixed up between Charles I and Charles II. I swotted up the Restoration so I wrote about that, but the question mentioned the Long Parliament. I think I got it wrong.'

'Never mind, dear. I'm sure you'll pass.'

Roseanne flashed her mother a withering look and went on with her snack.

Mrs Nixon wiped her hands on her apron and sat down sympathetically beside her daughter. 'These don't count, though, do they? It's next summer which matters. Plenty of time between now and then.'

'Yeah, but they won't get any easier. I don't think my grades will be exactly brilliant. Don't expect too much, you and Dad.'

Mrs Nixon gave Roseanne a hug and kissed her on the cheek. 'Whatever you do you'll still be our lovely daughter.'

Roseanne deduced correctly that her mother must have been reading women's magazine articles about bonding with wayward teenagers. At times she felt quite murderous towards her parents.

'No, Mum, listen. If I don't do well, we have to decide what's next. I think university or whatever is out. I'm not sure I want to be a student anyway – especially when I look at the kind of girls who do want to go. The thought of another three years kowtowing to the likes of Helen Majinsky and Brenda Jones makes me want to puke.'

'Roseanne: language.' Her mother swept the crumbs off the table with one hand into the other. The bits were dropped into the sink. 'Fancy the College of Commerce? No? Then we could have a word with Uncle Solly and you can go work in his dress shop on London Road. You won't be without a job, anyway.'

The girl brightened. 'Would I get a discount? He's got some smashing stuff.'

'You'd have to ask.'

'And, Mum –' Roseanne stopped until she was sure she had her mother's full attention. 'What about getting engaged? You said I'd have to wait till I finished my exams. Then I'd have something to show those others. They'd be jealous as cats if I had an engagement ring.'

That was a point in favour of action. 'It'd be my dream to see you married. The best day of my life that'll be, your *chuppah*. Still on with Jerry, is it? What does he think?'

Roseanne had not broached the subject recently. Jerry was weak enough, however, to give in to relentless pressure. The only effective opposition could come from her parents.

'Well,' she began diplomatically, 'he feels he ought to be ready in a year or two. If I'm bringing in some money, that'd be sufficient to get by. You'd help us out with a mortgage, wouldn't you, Mum?'

Rita blenched. 'With the deposit, anyway. I'd have to talk to your father about it.'

Roseanne knew with enormous precision how to blackmail her mother.

She leaned her chin on her hand and gazed airily upwards. 'I'd like four children – two boys and two girls. Boys first. We could have the whole family to the *bris*. Just visualise how Dad would be congratulated.'

Tears pricked at Rita Nixon's eyes. 'You'd make us both very happy, Roseanne. A proper *yiddishe* wedding, and a *bris*, and then barmitz-vahs, and more weddings.'

Roseanne pushed home her advantage. 'And you could come to my house for second *seder* night, and listen to your little grandchildren asking the four questions.' She spoke in a high lisp: '*Mah nishtanoh, ha-layloh hazeh, mikol haleylos?*'

'"Why is this night different to all other nights?"' translated her mother. She gazed proudly at Roseanne. 'Why is this daughter different to all other daughters? Other daughters cause their parents grief. They want to forget their *yiddishkeit* and marry a *goy*. They'll change their names to Johnson and pretend they were never Jews. Oy! They deserve everything they'll get. But not you. A *balaboster* you'll be, a source of joy to everyone. Thank God.'

Roseanne smiled sweetly. 'You won't mind if I fail a few silly exams, then. And I'll choose the right moment to tell Jerry everything's settled.'

They had decided to make a day of it. Helen had agreed with Mr Feinstein to miss one Sunday morning and told her mother she would meet friends in town then go in a crowd across to the Wirral. She was not sure where they'd end up but would be home around eleven. Since it was virtually the end of term with no further pressure of study, Annie was reassured that the girl could afford the time off, deserved it almost.

Helen pretended not to hear her mother's inquisition about her companions' identities. To avoid argument she accepted the offer of a packed lunch and so set off with cheese sandwiches wrapped in grease-proof paper, a banana and a bottle of lemonade. It suited them both to see the excursion as a children's picnic.

Town was quiet. The meeting point was obvious – under the Epstein sculpture of 'Man at the Helm' atop the main doors of Lewis's opposite the Adelphi. Michael was already there, lounging against the wall. In the open they did not embrace, but walked quickly to the Jeep parked behind the hotel.

Ten minutes in the Mersey Tunnel brought them out into daylight amid the grimy bulk of Birkenhead warehouses. 'Dismal spot, this,' was Michael's comment. He consulted a map and written instructions obtained from Andy Newman, then threaded his way straight through the town and out the far side. Within half an hour he had picked up the National Trust sign for Thurstaston and found a spot in the shade to leave the vehicle.

Helen watched in delight as he reached into the back and took out a large tartan blanket and an enormous wicker basket. 'That puts my little packet of sandwiches firmly in its place.'

'Gotta impress. This is what the US Army is for. Here, can you carry this?' He handed her the blanket. 'It's to sit on,' he added quickly when he saw a flicker of anxiety in her face.

She had debated whether to wear jeans, or a skirt. Trousers would be easier to scramble about in on the rocks at Thurstaston, and more modern. A skirt would be cooler, and better if he wanted anything . . . She made herself stop thinking like that. But she had chosen a cotton skirt, in blue with a flower pattern, and had tied her hair back with a ribbon to match.

He wore his Levis as if accustomed to them, as if he never thought twice what to wear when not in uniform. The check shirt had short sleeves. How practical Americans were. When her father could be persuaded to venture on to a beach his sole concession was to remove his shoes and socks. His white bony feet and toes would wriggle about shyly in the sand. A jacket would be worn, however hot the day; short sleeves were unheard of. Like many of his generation he kept his hat on. The contrast made her laugh.

'What's so funny?' Michael had begun to climb ahead of her, to find a vantage point. The broad flat red rocks were already warm in the sun. Between the stones was fine dry sand, with tufts of sea-pinks and rye grass. The wind whistled softly around the point. Above their heads gannets and terns wheeled and cried, endlessly argumentative and busy.

Helen explained. 'Michael, to us you seem to have arrived from another planet. You're an alien creature in my world. And I love it.'

They settled near the top where both shade and shelter could be had. He spread out the blanket and sat, his back against an outcrop. They looked towards the south west.

'Now that's the river Dee, not the Mersey? I need to get my bearings.'

'Yes. That's north Wales over there. Chester is off to our left. Liverpool is directly behind us.'

He shaded his eyes then pointed across the estuary. 'Is that some kinda castle?' He consulted the map. 'Yeah, Flint, it says.'

'There's a whole string of castles down there. Queensferry, and Caergwrie. That's how we used to keep strangers out.'

'Ah, the Welsh! But strangers can be smart. "I can call spirits from the vasty deep", as Owen Glendower put it. *Henry IV Part I*, yes?'

She responded instantly with Hotspur's quip. 'Why, so can I, or so can any man. But will they come?'

'Clever clogs.' For several moments they allowed the sibilant whisper of the reeds to take the place of speech. Michael stretched out his long legs. 'Come close. I want to talk.' She snuggled near him. He put an arm around her and kissed her almost absent-mindedly. 'We don't live in separate worlds, Helen. I don't want to be a stranger to you.'

'You're not,' she murmured. 'I feel as if I have known you my whole life. It's as if I have been waiting for you.'

'The Chinese believe that when a child is born a single soul is split in two. When he or she finds the other half, the result is perfect happiness. If the two halves never find each other then they'll seek for ever and never rest content with what they've got. That's how they explained love, I guess.'

'I know what they mean.' She avoided looking at him directly.

'I'll be off home soon for a month. I wanna tell my parents about you. Would you mind?'

'Of course not. But what on earth will you say?'

'You're fishing. I shall tell them I've met a tricky, awkward young lady, with big dark eyes, an old head on her young shoulders, a very rich American auntie and an ogre for a daddy.'

'He's not an ogre. He's simply stuck in a medieval time-warp. At least, that's how it feels.' She turned her face to Michael. How natural it was to be near him. 'He wants what's best for me, as he sees it.'

'And that wouldn't include little ol' me, would it? D'you see how bewildered that leaves me? As for my folks – well, my mother would be aghast that anyone could reject her perfect son. I gotta figure out exactly how to broach the subject.'

'You don't have to mention me at all,' Helen murmured. She picked up his hand and kissed his fingers, one by one.

'Yes, I want to tell them,' said Michael firmly. He did not elaborate, but Helen's eyes widened. He did not need to spell out that she would be the first romantic attachment he had spoken about to his parents, and that this set her apart.

'If you came to America you'd love it,' Michael said suddenly. 'You'd get on real fine. Away from Liverpool, and your Dad, and the tired old outdated ways which I know you hate. I don't want to tread on any toes, but to me the UK looks shabby and broken. You won the war and have been resting on your laurels ever since, a kinda snooty but ragged bunch on the isolated edge of Europe.' His voice took on an urgent rhythm. 'America's a young country. Most of it's still empty. We have hills and rivers – this place is fine, Helen, but I'd love to drive you coast to coast, go west, stand with you by the Grand Canyon.'

She was listening attentively, so he pressed on.

'Anybody that grafts can make money and live well. Here you're tied in knots, seems to me. Your class system would drive me nuts – all those titles! However much a kid like you will try, you're going to be kept down. In America you could be free. It's a "can-do" world – you don't hear the phrase "Can't be done, old boy, impossible", which pops up every five minutes around here.'

Freedom again. She had heard that before. Her response was deliberately cautious. She did not want Michael to realise the extent to which she had begun to assess the options.

'But in the States,' she said slowly, 'I'd have to pay to go through college. In Britain I'd get it free, plus a grant – assuming I get in, that is. And – I know it's odd to mention this, but it matters – I'd have to pay for health care, wouldn't I? Again we get it free.'

'It's free this and free that which has beggared Britain. In America you'd win scholarships – no question. You're so smart you'd sail through college. And people plan – d'you know my Dad started to save for my education the moment I was born? And I took a night job in a diner to help out. It did me no harm – knocked a bit of sense into me, rather. I rubbed shoulders with these guys with no qualifications whatsoever condemned to a lifetime of fast-order hamburgers, and I stuck to my studies. Graduated Dean's List,' he grinned with pride.

'As for health care, it's much the same. You plan and take out insurance. People earn enough to pay for these things. In Europe where you're accustomed to earning a pittance you can't get your heads around it. We earn a lot, Helen. It is true that Americans have piles of money. We can make any necessary provision for our needs, and have a lot left over. That's what it means to be citizens of the richest country on earth.'

She was solemn in the face of such conviction. 'But what happens if you're not insurable? If you're diabetic, say? Or old? What happens if you have a handicapped baby? Here you'd be looked after. But you can't tell me nobody falls through the net. We have a safety net in the end, you haven't.'

'That is true, and the Kennedy administration would say you're right. There are big city hospitals which do treat people without charge but nobody'd say they were sufficient. Or much good. There are ideas for something on European lines, but more limited – the Medicare Bill, for example. The President is making haste slowly because he couldn't get it through Congress just yet. He quotes Jefferson that great innovations should not be forced on slender majorities. Maybe after the '64 election he'll have bigger popular support and be more secure.'

'You think he'll win?'

'Oh, sure. Especially if the Republicans choose Goldwater. Wipe the floor with *him*. Look, young voters will plump for Jack Kennedy in a solid mass. So will the Negroes, and millions more are registered now than used to be. He may not be flavour of the month with urban intellectuals like James Baldwin, but one endorsement from Martin Luther King and he's away. And he'll get it – nobody wants a right-winger in the White House instead.'

'I find it hard to credit that anybody could be prevented from voting. At least in this country everyone has the vote.'

'Don't kid yourself. I went to a St Patrick's Day meeting last year – out of curiosity, I hasten to add. You have to own your house in Ulster to be able to vote. That rules out most of the Catholics. You didn't know that? It's your country too.'

'But look, when a Sinn Fein candidate is successful they won't take their seats. The first woman MP elected was Countess Constance Markievicz in 1918. She never took the oath or attended. That's how Lady Astor got to be the first to take her seat, in a by-election the year after.'

'Prejudice rules, OK?' Michael lightened the atmosphere. 'Maybe all it shows is nobody has a monopoly on wisdom. But we got a written constitution, Helen. Our rights are explicitly laid down. Better than the bitty common-law arrangements you have here. And Kennedy is terrific: he's so keen for change. His instincts are spot on – after all, as a Catholic himself he knows about discrimination. As long as he's President we will make progress. I truly believe that.'

The sun was high in the sky. Above their heads gulls flapped and called incessantly. A clutch of cheeky sparrows scrapped over crumbs nearby. Below, the sea lapped lazily on undulating sand dunes. The noise of children was carried on the breeze. On a grassy bank nearby an impromptu game of cricket had started, with shouted instructions and yells.

Michael unpacked the basket. Out came a tablecloth, two Thermos flasks, a chicken pie in an earthenware dish, bread rolls, muffins, little pats of butter, brownies, big Florida oranges, a green watermelon, plates, cutlery, cups and glasses. With a flourish he spread a teatowel on her lap and one on his own as napkins. She added her modest contribution with a laugh to the pile of food and they set to with a will, hungry in the sea air. He had to show her how to eat the watermelon and spit out the pips. The sweet juice ran down her chin.

The afternoon passed in a lazy blur. It seemed to both remarkable that they could range so widely over every subject that came into mind: over religion, and the organisation of society, and the relative merits of rhythm 'n' blues versus country music or Elvis compared to the Beatles, and whether the movie of *Gone with the Wind* was as good as the book and exactly what Joseph Heller's *Catch 22* really meant; whether Jackie Kennedy was beautiful, and what had constituted the special appeal of Marilyn Monroe, and whether her recent death was an accident or otherwise. One topic neither raised was the movie of *West Side Story*: its theme of star-cross'd lovers seemed altogether too close to the bone.

It was a tired but contented pair who turned into the main entrance of Burtonwood at around six in the evening. Michael showed his ID. Helen shrank down in her seat, timid at the guard's scrutiny.

The base was virtually empty as many airmen had obtained weekend leave passes. For an hour Michael drove her round the vast acreage until she was giddy with its size. They climbed the stairs to the top of the control tower and gazed out over the flat scrubland towards the Mersey. The controller cheerily showed off dials and screens and explained that few planes had landed at Burtonwood in recent years – mostly they arrived in crates for assembly or repair. Nevertheless, everything was kept operational.

Michael had hardly touched her. A finger on her arm to guide her, a hand on her back to say it was time to leave. Yet she was conscious of his body, warm from the sun, familiar yet strange, at her side yet separate. As she smiled and nodded at his earnest colleagues she compared them. In most cases Michael was physically broader, and surer in his movements, with a decisive manner which suggested that were he to choose the military as his profession, his innate qualities of leadership would be promptly rewarded. He was greeted with warmth everywhere, and she with dignified politeness. It made her feel coolly adult, and ready for anything.

At last he parked the Jeep behind a small bungalow, one of a row which looked deserted. The hamper was at his feet as he found the keys and unlocked the door. 'We might be hungry again,' was his comment as he put the remaining food on the sink unit. 'Come on in.'

The door opened straight into a tidy kitchen with a table and four chairs in the centre. On the table was a neat red check tablecloth, GI issue, and a jamjar with daisies, white and pink. The effect was homely and welcoming. Helen's pulse began to beat faster. To one side was a bathroom with both bath and shower. To the other a bedroom.

A transistor radio stood by the sink. Michael switched on and fiddled with the dial till Radio Luxembourg could be heard. Helen noticed that he fumbled. He was silent.

Then he came to her and put his hands on her shoulders and stared down at her quietly. The disc jockey announced the next tune, a Bruce Channel number which had been a big hit the previous year. Michael's face lifted and he smiled as he heard the first long chord and opening lyrics:

'Hey – hey, baby!
I wanna know-ow-ow –
Will you be my girl?'

'That says it better than I can,' he said softly. 'Will you be my girl?' And he bent his head and pressed his lips to hers, so she had to stand on tiptoe and arch her back to reach him.

She had not answered. He held her face in both hands, his thumbs circling her cheeks, his fingers intermingled in her dark hair. 'God, kid, you have eyes to dive into. You have me bewitched, you know that?

Whatever I'm doing I can't get away from you. My head is so full of you it feels it would burst. Oh, Helen.'

'Only your head? Not your heart?' she teased in a whisper. Her hand rested lightly on his shirt where she could feel the live warmth of his flesh. Between them lay a hair's breadth of empty air. It was still possible to pull back.

From somewhere above her came his voice, steady and grave, as if he had rehearsed the request many times. 'Will you let me? Please? I promise I won't hurt you. I can't tell you how much I've dreamed about being with you, dearest Helen –'

This was a man who had never asked before, never begged. She could picture the girls who had flirted before him, their skirts a-twitch: high school cheerleaders with tanned thighs, the freestyle champion in a high-cut swimsuit, the sassy waitress at the all-night diner. And he had had his pick.

In response she slid her arms around his body, behind his back, and in that single gesture gave him permission to come close, to press himself against her. As their hips came together he groaned slightly and she felt with shock the strength and hardness of him against her belly. Her mouth was half open and she could hardly breathe, but in answer she let her trembling hands slide down from the small of his back to his buttocks, and willed herself to caress the muscular curves.

'Helen, if you do that, you are saying yes, you realise,' he warned. 'I won't force you. We can stop now if you want.'

'I want to know you,' she murmured. 'I love everything I know about you. I want to know more.'

He broke away, went to the front door and locked it. The key he placed on the kitchen table: this was no incarceration, merely the avoidance of interruption. Then he took her hand, led her into the bedroom, drew the thin curtain and shut the door.

The bed, a small double, was made up. Beside it was a wooden chest of drawers with an alarm clock. Quickly Michael pulled off the top sheet and blankets. Outside, house-martins twittered unconcerned in the eaves but in the charged dusk inside nothing moved but the two of them.

Helen waited. It was as if time had elongated, as if everything were in slow motion. She could savour each second as the clock ticked unobtrusively. In the background the song had changed to the Rooftop Singers:

'*Walk right in, set right down,*
Baby let your mind roll on –'

She should ask him to be gentle. She was at a loss to know the words, the terms, the argot. She hadn't the faintest idea what to say or do. All she could imagine was that, as she wanted him to be kind to her, so perhaps that was the best approach in return. As Michael bent to plump up the pillows, she placed her hand on his shoulder. The effect on them both was like an electric shock: each stared at the other, startled.

'I want to see you,' he said, and lifted her sweater up and over her shoulders. The hair-ribbon fell away and her curls framed her face. Then he reached behind and unhooked her bra, and draped both on the bedpost. She undid the button on her skirt and kicked it away, and stood before him in her panties only, shoulders back, her breasts held proudly. He gazed at her for a long moment, arms at his sides.

'Don't be shy. You are so beautiful. And remember, whatever we do, it's not dirty. When two people care about each other, there is no shame, only love.'

Her mouth was dry and she could feel her heart pounding so hard: surely he could see it just below her ribs. Involuntarily she sought the spot as if to invite his attention. He placed his fingers over hers and laughed softly. 'Mine's doing that too,' he said, and pulled his shirt off over his head in one swift movement. 'Here, feel.'

Hesitantly she gazed where he indicated, but ached to run her hands over the muscles of his chest, to feel that wiry hair: suddenly she realised she too could do whatever she wanted, and with a sudden sparkle in her eyes began to move her hands over his upper body, letting her skin begin to know his. Michael caught her and kissed her palm inside, his eyes holding hers. 'My, my. You catch on fast, don't you? Hang on.' And he unzipped his jeans and dropped them to the floor.

'Give me your hand, Helen.'

She did, and he guided her to his penis through the fabric of his shorts. She folded her hand over it and was surprised how firm and hot it felt. 'Don't be frightened,' he whispered. 'Come on, lie down.'

She obeyed and he slipped off her panties. Then he was kneeling over her, naked and erect. She closed her fingers over him once again as if in acceptance and encouragement and he cried out, then bent and kissed her mouth hard, pushing his tongue inside. Then he broke off, reached into the drawer of the bedside table, found the tiny silver packet and as she watched rolled its contents on. Again she held him and both smiled. Then he lay beside her, one hand under her shoulders to raise her mouth to his, the other fluttering and exploring her breasts, her nipples, her belly.

'I have to open you up a little or it will hurt you. Trust me now,' came the words in her ear. She felt his hand slide down to the place between her legs, but he kept her head buried in his neck so she could not see, only feel. His fingers found her and began to rub. She seized him and looked into his eyes in amazement: it was as if pulses had sprung up where none had existed before. Is that what Aunt Gertie meant by the buttons? Oh, my God—

'Oh, Michael – I am on fire for you!'

Suddenly he had two fingers inside and was massaging her. It was a fantastic sensation, terrifying, frantic. She could feel herself moisten, tissues fill and engorge and open. She spread her legs out to make it easier for him. 'Now. Oh, please, now.'

For a second he could not enter, then with a grunt he pushed strongly. A jagged edge of pain shot through her as he shoved himself deep inside and she cried out. He put a hand lightly over her mouth.

'Hush. We don't want anyone coming to investigate.'

'I'm OK, honestly. Don't stop.' Hoarsely.

'I wasn't intending to. Hold on tight, here we go –'

Then came thrust after pounding thrust: he was big and she pulled her knees up and around his trunk to accommodate him, as above her his head blocked the faint light from the window; then he rose above her on his arms, muscles bulging, his brow reddened and sweaty, and she was filled with his strength and power, and let herself go completely to him and called his name in yearning . . . at last with a long sigh he came inside her . . . and then slowly, slowly, subsided over her until their two damp bodies in the rumpled bed seemed about to coalesce into one.

They lay still until with a regretful lunge he slipped himself carefully out. Gingerly he removed the condom which was streaked in blood. 'Couldn't send you home pregnant,' he joked to cover the manoeuvre. 'Your father'd cut my balls off.'

He knelt up. She let her eyes roam over his body, and gazed with undisguised inquisitiveness at his private parts. She ran her index finger over the wizened brown skin.

'Not as pretty as yours, little lady,' he chuckled. 'You never seen a man before?'

She shook her head. 'Is everyone as big as you?'

He laughed out loud. 'Now there's a compliment! We're available in every shape and size. But I'm told that *your* equipment is remarkable and can expand to fit any measurement.'

She shifted uneasily. 'I wasn't planning to try anybody else just yet, Michael.'

'Pleased to hear it. You're my girl now.' And he relaxed beside her contentedly, and kissed her, and nibbled her ear.

Eventually he looked up. 'Jeez, it's nine-thirty. We'd better get a move on. Go take the first shower.' He had to show her how to operate it.

When she came back into the bedroom wrapped in a towel it was to find a rueful Michael stripping the bed. The bedclothes in his hands were widely stained with her blood. She bit her lip, horrified.

'You were a virgin, Helen. This is normal. It's a bit torn and sore down there, yes? In the old days sheets like this would be hung out of a window the morning after a wedding to prove the marriage was consummated. So congratulations. You're a woman now.'

He dropped the bed-linen and took her in his arms. 'I hope it wasn't too awful. Next time will be easier. But you were marvellous.'

She nestled her cheek against his bare chest and smelled the reek of sex on him. To her own surprise she wanted to stroke him again, and watch him rise, and laugh with him over it, the funny, ridiculous thing. A great warm rush suffused her.

'It wasn't awful. It was just – new, that's all. Next time. I shall dream of next time. Oh, Michael, I love you so.'

He had not meant to say it. He had never said it before to any woman, not with any sincerity.

'Dearest Helen, lovely girl. I think I love you too.'

Chapter Fifteen

Summertime

Elizabeth Plumb put away her passport, kicked off her shoes and stretched out her legs. Outside the train window slid the flat green lands to the south of Paris. Within half an hour clumps of forest would appear. She would be struck as usual that the trees were much taller than the tidy red-roofed farmhouses. That was seldom true in England.

Near Tours the sun beat down on the first neat rows of vines. Tiny in the distance, an old man in blue overalls with a cart and a shabby horse ignored the train. He would be on his way home to his *déjeuner du midi*, Miss Plumb calculated, and would not expect to return for at least an hour and a half. And he would drink wine with his meal, as she would, every day for the next three weeks. Bliss.

At Tours she must change to the local service which meant an hour's wait. On the station forecourt she bought a coffee and baguette larded with *rillettes*, the spicy meat paste, and chewed contentedly at a table under an umbrella.

Charles would be at Chinon in his big silver Citroën. The low-slung car, the type which featured in French gangster movies, thrilled her to the core. The chauffeur knew about them, but would have been packed off to the Riviera to take care of Madame, and to phone Monsieur le Comte should his wife take it into her head to return early. Miss Plumb smiled, and spoke his name the French way, *Sharl*, slurred and sexual, under her breath. At times like these she felt like a minor character in a film whose real stars were Louis Jourdan and Leslie Caron, but despite the slight corniness she relished the opportunity thus afforded her.

It was such a delight to escape. The last few days had served as a reminder of everything distasteful at home. It had rained, heavily. That had drowned out the Orange Lodge march on July 12. Miss Plumb had hugged herself over the *Echo* picture of the school caretaker in a bedraggled bowler hat as the wet sluiced off the shoulders of his one and only suit. In the city centre, sodden orange lilies soon lay broken in the gutters. The excursion to Southport for Lodge members' families had also been a wash-out. Their return off the train, the men drunk, the children bawling, had been the signal for Catholic matrons to close the curtains and drag their own belligerent and hardly sober menfolk inside.

Not that the Catholics were any better. St Patrick's Day, March 17, was mainly celebrated indoors – in the pubs. Fighting, even riots, were *de rigueur*. One of her pupils had told her, as a simple and unremarkable fact, that in her street off Scotland Road twenty pubs existed within a hundred yards. Before the war there'd been more: one minor point in the Nazis' favour, Miss Plumb reckoned grimly, though it looked as if the Corporation would in its slum-clearance zeal demolish more than German bombers ever had.

One would mind less if conditions were improving. But they weren't. Since her school drew pupils from the whole metropolis she could observe what passed for progress. As the last of the back-to-back properties with their windowless rooms and dank cellars were bulldozed, some families were transferred nearby into municipal flats – monstrous towers which, once the lifts were vandalised, became hated prisons. But most tenants were moved out and areas rapidly became depopulated. The pubs remained, often isolated on street corners and surrounded by heaps of rubble, but still open. No brewery would willingly give up a licence.

Elizabeth Plumb was no teetotaller, far from it. Yet the demon drink dominated and destroyed the homes of too many of her pupils. The poor children had no chance, despite the fact that their natural aptitude afforded them the chance of elevation via the grammar school system.

Take that dreadful man O'Brien, for instance. He had barged into school just after four o'clock one day and demanded to see her. He must have been imbibing for hours; she could not avoid inhaling the sour winey smell from his skin and his hair, its odour like peardrops as the alcohol metabolised. He stank, and so did his disgusting donkey jacket and leather bib. He had carried with him two unopened bottles of whisky, which he deposited on her desk.

'Now that's for you, for all yer doin' for my lass,' he announced.

Miss Plumb picked up the bottles and examined them. Sixty per cent proof was unusually strong. Nor did she recognise the brand name, though the product was Scottish right enough. Around the neck of each was a narrow gilded label: Export only.

'You didn't purchase these in Yates's Wine Lodge, Mr O'Brien,' she said sternly.

He shuffled and shrugged. 'I'm a docker, Miss. Them's perks.' At her glare he swayed, then remembered why he had come. 'I want to ask you. Our Colette. She will pass her exams, won't she?' He nudged the bottles a little further across the desk.

Miss Plumb was frosty. 'I have not the least doubt, Mr O'Brien, that she will perform well without any extra assistance. What precisely is your question?'

'Well, it'll help when she leaves school. Get a better job. I didn' want her to stay on: we could do with the money. But if we 'ave to wait, it'd be best if she gets her grades.' He spread his hands. 'I mean, if she's gonna fail, then she can leave now. But you can keep the prezzie. Thass for you.'

Mr O'Brien, Miss Plumb wanted to say, you are an utterly horrible creature. Instead she bristled.

'If I have anything to do with it, Mr O'Brien, your daughter will go to university. She has an excellent mind and will gain entry I am sure.'

'University? Don't talk daft. The likes of us don' go to no university.' The man's eyes flickered. 'Don' you go putting stupid ideas like that into her head. Gotta getta job, our Colette. An' if she's that smart, she'll get more dosh. Yeah.'

He peered at her, then marched unsteadily up to the desk and picked up one of the bottles. He wagged a stubby finger.

'You go givin' 'er daft ideas and I'll be back. I'll smash this 'ere bleedin' bottle over yer head, see? University – bloody rubbish. Good girl, our Colette. Does what her Dad tells her.'

And with that he had slouched out, the single bottle cradled in the crook of his arm.

The *locale* chugged to a halt, stood like a patient donkey until its straggle of passengers arranged themselves, then groaned and tugged, and with puffs of black diesel smoke swung to the south-west. Each name whispered magic: Ballan-Miré, Druye, Azay-le-Rideau, where she caught a glimpse of the exquisite château in its tiny lake. As the two-car vehicle emerged on to chalky hillsides between more vineyards Miss Plumb craned her neck out of the window. The white limestone fortress of Chinon dominated its escarpment, its battlements glinting in the sunlight, like all the magic castles of fairy stories. Beyond it was the sheer drop to the river Vienne.

'About as different from Liverpool as could be,' breathed Miss Plumb in satisfaction. 'In fact the only thing the two spots have in common is King John. He tread these slopes as King, and gave Liverpool its first charter in 1207. And he was a miserable good-for-nothing. How appropriate.'

The train slowed and stopped. She pulled down her small suitcase; experience had taught her to travel light. She stepped out on to the platform and shaded her eyes.

Half an hour later Miss Plumb was still on the platform. In her hand was a crumpled note. At the last moment, Monsieur le Comte had written, he had been obliged to accompany his wife. A room had been reserved for her at the Hostellerie Gargantua in rue Voltaire, to which the boy who had brought the note would lead her. *Chère Élizabeth*, he was *désolé, mais . . .*

Miss Plumb allowed the boy to pick up her valise and followed him numbly into the sunshine.

That same evening Maurice Feinstein sat in the back room of the shop, surrounded by boxes and packing cases. On the desk were scattered papers and bills. A bag of flour had burst earlier in the day; the fine white dust hovered and shimmered. In the background he could hear Nellie banging about with bucket and mop. The cleaner had gone to Morecambe for the week with her grandchildren. His routine disturbed, Mr Feinstein felt out of sorts.

'Haven't you finished that yet, Nellie?' he yelled testily. 'I could murder for a cup of Nescafé.'

The response was indistinct, but soon Nellie had washed out the bucket in the yard and stored the implements by the sink. She appeared looking as irritable as her employer and rolling down her sleeves.

'I was off home, to be honest,' she said shortly.

Maurice Feinstein blinked in surprise. There was a time when Nellie would have leaped at the chance to make him a hot drink and waste a few moments in idle chat. In fact she used to spot his needs before he recognised them himself. She would, indeed, have put a mug, sweetened the way he liked it, before him without being asked. He frowned.

'Nellie, come here a mo'.'

With evident reluctance Nellie complied.

'I'm having trouble with these accounts. When I was in hospital the shop did fine and we had money in the bank. Now I've got a five hundred quid overdraft. Where's it gone?'

'I hope you're not suggesting—' Nellie bridled.

'No, no. I just can't make it add up. Here.' Absent-mindedly he patted the old chair by his side. A dust cloud rose and lingered. 'Take a look. I'll make the coffee. Two spoonfuls?'

'I don't take sugar,' came Nellie's answer as she sat down. 'All these years and you've forgotten? That'll be your lady friend, not me.'

Maurice opened his mouth but decided not to argue. Nellie's co-operation was urgently required.

When he returned from the kitchen, mugs in hand, his assistant's blonde head was tilted towards the ceiling and her eyes were half closed in concentration. A pencil was clamped between her teeth and both hands were outstretched to count on her fingers. Her lips moved rapidly despite the pencil. He tiptoed around her and put the mugs on the desk.

'Got it?' he asked hopefully.

She opened one eye, removed the pencil, sucked her teeth, rummaged about among the bank statements and scribbled a couple of numbers.

'Oh, yeah. I know where your money's gone.' She paused to let her superiority sink in.

'Well then?'

'It's here. See? It's not the shop; turnover is down a bit for the summer, but that's normal. But you hardly take any out usually. Then since May – whump! You've withdrawn a hundred quid every other week or so. And other big cheques. What are you up to? Gambling? It's your money and nowt to do with me, but . . .'

'Gimme that here.' Maurice scrutinised the columns where Nellie indicated. 'Christ, you're right.' He gazed at her mournfully. 'No, I haven't been near the bookie's. Lost a bit at the Majinsky barmitzvah but that's a one-off. It's that woman. Vera. Likes to eat out. Never anywhere cheap. Last week it was the Adelphi – can you imagine? She must think I'm made of brass.'

'If she's only after your money, Mr Feinstein, she has a disappointment coming up. At this rate you'll be bankrupt before you can get her to the altar.'

'Call me Morrie,' Feinstein muttered. 'I shouldn't have to keep telling you, Nellie.' He perused the paperwork with the utmost gloom, tried a few calculations then threw down the pencil and chewed his fingernail in silence.

'If she's nice, you can explain to her,' Nellie suggested tentatively. 'After all, if she's going to be your wife –'

Her boss was still engrossed in his thoughts but did not correct her. She rose and stood before him, hands on hips.

'Well: it's none of my business. But this is. I think you should know I'm considering emigrating.'

Feinstein groaned and held his head in his hands. Through his fingers he peered at Nellie who stood uncertainly by. 'I'm not sure I can cope with any more bad news tonight, Nellie. Can't it wait till tomorrow?' Her face was stony and he saw she was upset. He sat up wearily. 'OK, tell me. Emigrating – where?'

Nellie turned and flounced out, earrings oscillating wildly. 'A long way from here!' was all he caught as she banged the door, but there was also a strange noise, as if she might be crying.

Three thousand miles away to the west it was not yet lunchtime. The temperature was in the high eighties and men sat about in shorts cut off just above the knee. Even respectable men, and their sons.

'It has been a long hot summer, and more to come, son.'

Colonel Levison wiped his brow with a white handkerchief. They were seated in the yacht club bar overlooking Fire Island, New York. Before him the daiquiri glass misted over with condensation then dried in the sticky heat.

The Colonel was of medium height, thickset but not flabby, in his early fifties. His steel-grey hair and piercing blue eyes made him attractive to women while his directness and lack of mannerisms endeared him to men. He wore an open-neck shirt and navy-blue Bermudas. After lunch he and his son would take a club boat for a sail.

The Colonel's rank had been earned in the Supreme Commander NATO's HQ in Europe but he was a lawyer rather than a career soldier. Nevertheless it had suited him to remain in uniform. In Washington titles counted. Should Capitol politics get him down he could shift to less fraught pastures. In the office of the Attorney-General, however, neither boredom nor disillusion was a problem.

The Colonel raised his glass and toasted his elder son.

'So, Michael. How is the Air Force? Better than the Army?'

'It's fine, Pa. Though if I were to stay I'd want to train as a pilot.'

'They all do. But I don't suppose you get much flying at Burtonwood?'

Michael chuckled. His father did not miss much and would have checked. 'Not a scrap. If I wanted lessons I'd have to sign on at the civilian weekend glider school.'

The two men were at ease in each other's company. Michael prompted. 'You having a tough time in Washington?'

The Colonel leaned back. 'You could say that. What with violence in Alabama, burning crosses in Mississippi, the clamour for rights and votes – and noises off in Vietnam. Madame Nhu is a bitch of the first order, I swear. One of these days somebody's gonna cut off her nose and ears and make her eat them, if he hasn't chopped off her husband's head first, and Diem's too. Won't be long. I'm afraid we've backed losers there.'

'Being in Britain has given me another perspective.' Michael was cautious as he sipped his cold beer. 'Some of the drinkers in the Pelican pub served in Malaya and Burma. They reckoned you can't beat an insurgency unless you persuade the people you're fighting for them. If the foreign force seems to be propping up an unpopular regime, villagers will go over to the other side in droves.' He let the comments sink in. 'Let me put it their way. The Limeys say we'll get a bloody nose in Vietnam – they think we're going about it totally wrong. There's not a man-jack of them wants to see any British troops involved.'

'Well, the French got more than a bloody nose in '54,' his father mused. 'Trouble is, we have to work with the leadership that's in power. South East Asia is hardly a breeding ground for democracy. So we are stuck. In the end, the army bosses will decide who's in charge in Saigon.'

'Which army – ours, theirs or the Viet Cong?'

'Hush – not so loud.' His father smiled ruefully. 'Don't kid about it. When Ike retired we had under two thousand men in the country. Now we're up to sixteen thousand, though that's not trumpeted about. If the situation deteriorates you could find yourself in pilot school whether you choose or not. They're short of crews for the big 'copters. Guns mounted on the struts – vicious buggers.'

'You don't care for that line, Pa, do you?'

'I do not. I hear the flexing of muscles and the crack of knuckle-joints too often. We are being drawn into something we cannot control and it costs lives – thirty-two US boys dead in the last two years and eighty wounded. Your Limey pals are right. I counted twenty-seven Americans with the rank of General currently in Saigon, and d'you know how many have attended the counter-insurgency course at Fort Bragg? Not a single one.'

The two conversed sombrely for a while then ordered sandwiches and more beers. To eat more formally in the dining room would have required ties and jackets. Michael reached hungrily for the food.

'I do love a BLT,' he munched. 'Nobody in England has heard of them. When I suggested putting a little mayo in what they call a "bacon butty" they thought I was mad.'

'Learned to like the ale yet?'

'No, sir.' Michael grinned and pulled a face. He wiped his fingers. 'So: I'm here till Labor Day. What gives?'

His father considered. 'I should steer clear of southern cities during August if I were you. Go stay with your grandma in the Berkshires – Massachusetts is superb in summer and she'd be pleased to see you.'

Michael honed in on the warning remark at once. 'Why steer clear – what's going on?'

His father sighed. 'Because the Negroes have stopped listening when we say "Wait". Trouble is in the air – tangible, almost. Dr King and non-violence, and his friend Roy Wilkins with his insistence on the rule of law, are under attack, not only from racists this time but from their own brethren. King was pelted with eggs last week.'

'It was going to happen sooner or later, I guess.'

'Maybe. Fact remains that in the south still hardly any Negro children attend school with whites, whatever the Supreme Court might rule. And in the north we got *de facto* segregation – as James Baldwin claims, the Negroes are segregated but nobody did it. Life can be desperately tough in northern cities like Pittsburgh and Chicago or New York – there are no support mechanisms, family or church. Dr King is not a product of a Harlem slum. He and his wife and children come from the Southern Baptist Conference, and it shows.'

'Who's making waves – is it these Black Muslims?'

'Are they bad news! I'm not a literary man as you know, but I like to keep up with what's talked about around Washington dinner tables. Have you read *Negroes with Guns*? Robert F. Williams, came out this spring. He's done a bunk to Cuba but it's being quoted everywhere. Congressman Adam Clayton Powell, who is from Harlem, says the white man is afraid. I'm not, but some are.'

Colonel Levison's brow furrowed. 'The Attorney-General is determined to stay with these shifts of opinion. I was privileged to attend a session with Baldwin at Bobby's apartment here in May. Private, but I know you won't gossip. Lena Horne and Harry Belafonte were there, and several writers, and Professor Clark of City College of New York, Assistant Attorney Burke Marshall plus Jerome Smith, the young freedom rider who got beaten up so badly. It gave me quite a start, I tell you, to see so many intellectuals with black skins – maybe the dearth of educated Negroes in high office is something we can tackle. But the atmosphere was not good.'

Michael waited. His father needed only an audience.

'Smith started by telling Bobby that being in the same room with him made him want to puke. Nice guy. He should not have to plead, he said, for rights to which he was entitled as an American. And as long as Negroes were treated so – dogs set on them, beaten up, denied access to schools – he felt no moral obligation to fight for the USA in war.'

'Christ. They don't believe in asking politely, do they?'

'Exactly. Though in their place I might feel the same.'

The Colonel offered his son a cigar, lit his own and puffed for a moment. 'Most of the guests backed Smith's line. It got increasingly hysterical. They stood and ranted, they cursed, they wept. They were not interested in any practical points or any declarations the President had made. It was absolutely terrible. Bobby Kennedy sat there for three solid hours and took it but he was badly shaken. And d'you know what? Two of those present contacted him later and thanked him for his efforts. When he asked why they'd not spoken up, they said they could not speak in front of the others or they'd have lost credibility.'

'All that is needed for evil to triumph is for good men to do nothing – as the Brit Edmund Burke might have said.'

'And how. So we have a new Civil Rights Bill sent to the Hill with no assurance of an easy passage, even as the potential beneficiaries sneer. I think that's why the President has decided to tour the southern states this fall – partly to prepare for the election, but also to suss out who's where on this issue.'

'It can't improve the President's popularity.'

'God, that's true. The Harris poll suggests four million white voters have turned against us. National approval of the President has fallen from sixty to forty-seven per cent in a few months. We have a new phrase here, "White Backlash". But what's so great about the Kennedys is that they don't give in. They see no alternative to prevent the isolation of moderates like Dr King. Expectations have been aroused and must be met. Somehow.'

'I wish I could help. I feel so out of it in Lancashire.'

The Colonel laughed. 'Oh, you kids.' He thought for a moment. 'If you're in Washington on 28 August, you might stroll over to the

Lincoln Memorial. There's to be a peaceful march organised by Bayard
Rustin and old Philip Randolph – they're hardly revolutionaries. The
leaders are worried that it won't be well attended. You could show your
face, but take care.'

'I might do that,' said Michael thoughtfully. He looked out of the
window. 'And now if we don't get a move on, somebody will pinch our
boat. Shall we go?'

Back in Liverpool there were no yacht rides for Michael's lover, and no
brilliant sunshine either. In a home where money was short her spare
time was spent in paid work. A summer job as shop assistant and official first-aider at Boots The Chemist in Allerton Road filled the bill. It
gave Helen a hefty discount off cosmetics, clean surroundings and polite
companions – all a distinct contrast to Feinstein's Famous Deli, where
the atmosphere had become distinctly frosty since Nellie had announced
her departure. Plus she had time to think in the quieter moments, and
an improvement in her bank balance. Suddenly it had become important to save.

Michael was away: it seemed like a distance of a million miles and
ten light years. She could not phone him and had resorted to pre-paid
air mail letters, her handwriting as tiny as possible to cram in her news
and ideas. One had come in return for her to the Post Office near
school, but he was not as easy a communicant as she. Only in person
could he express himself well.

He was the right one. Of that she was sure. The right one for her at
this time, anyway, and for what they had been doing. She had not lost
her virginity: she had given it away, made a precious gift of it, and carefully chosen the recipient. Their consummation was a benediction
bestowed on them both. The memory filled her with delight, and with
frissons of sheer sexual electricity. It felt as if Michael had been sent to
her for exactly that purpose. *Michael, Michael, Michael.* Adored and
wonderful. A man, who had created her a woman.

With a jolt she came back to the present: the small back room off the
pharmacy, and her task as the shop's first aider.

Before her stood a small child. The little girl's face was wet with tears
but she made not a sound. Her narrow shoulders heaved with mute
sobs. One arm, hand twisted inside, was clutched to her abdomen and
cradled by her other hand. She was trembling violently.

Helen sat the child on the chair and motioned the mother to crouch
at her daughter's side. There was only one other chair and she needed
it herself. Her mouth felt dry but it was important not to let them
know she was almost as scared, when she was supposed to be the epit-
ome of professional efficiency.

It was her own fault. The first-aid certificate framed on the office
wall was no fantasy but had been obtained years earlier. A Red Cross

cadet troop, left over from the war, met in a church hall near Harold House. The commandant, a broad-beamed matron in a blue uniform, had offered to train the Youth Club members. Helen had become adept at triangular bandages and how to place bodies in the foetal position. Mouth-to-mouth resuscitation, a relatively new technique, had caused much embarrassment. What she was trying desperately to remember, however, was the safest way to remove splinters.

'Come on, now, let me see. I won't hurt you,' she lied.

The child opened her mouth and gagged. 'I c-c-c-can't—'

Next to her the mother, her hat askew, gloved hands clutching a leather carry-bag, began to argue. 'I told her not to play with that rub-bish but she took no notice. My back was turned talking to Mrs Jarvis. Oh, you are such a naughty girl.' The woman made as if to cuff the child, who cringed.

'Would it be easier if your Mam was outside?' Helen whispered. The child nodded. The mother, protesting, was firmly shown the door. Helen washed her hands nervously at the pharmacist's sink and col-lected the implements from the cupboard.

'Now then. It has to come out, you know. You can't go round with other people's property in your finger.'

The little girl sniffed but her heaves subsided. Very slowly she uncurled the afflicted joint and showed the angry red finger where the black sliver had entered under her nail.

Helen breathed a sigh of relief. The thought of poking around to find the offending object had terrified her. 'Well now, that's easy.' She lifted the child's chin. 'And do you have a name?'

'Lucy,' muttered the child. 'I hate my name. What's yours?'

'I'm Helen.' As the child gazed fixedly into her face, with a quick tug of the tweezers Helen had the splinter out and held it up triumphantly. 'There you are!'

'Ow!' Lucy yelped.

'Hush! You want your Mam to think you're smart and clever, don't you?'

A deadened look came into the girl's eyes. That their home was a miniature war zone was more than apparent. It occurred fleetingly to Helen that Colette's might have been similar when she was a small child and her mother still lived there, though her friend never talked about it.

'Then I'll check there's nothing else in there, put some antiseptic cream on it and give you a bandage. Big or small?'

'Big,' came the decisive answer. 'Then she'll feel sorry for me and we'll have sausages for tea.'

The conspiracy was concluded. The child, dwarfed by a balloon of white net over the injured digit, emerged into the shop. Helen had debated whether to include a sling but suspected the woman would have difficulty paying for it. As it was she grumbled at the shilling for the bandage.

Helen slid back to her place on the hair products counter. It was the second year she had worked at Boots. The store was light and airy, the toilets and staff areas spotless, their white coats were laundered at no charge, and her boss Mr Clay the pharmacist was a gentle-mannered man at the mercy of his staff.

There was no possibility of going away for the summer. Where would she go? Relatives? Three weeks in the spare bedroom at Aunty Becky's did not appeal. Butlin's was not kosher so she could not get her parents' permission to go there. And who would she go with? Their families would have been scandalised at the idea of a bunch of teenagers sleeping unchaperoned in adjoining chalets. Anyway, nobody had a car. Only Jerry could drive. Maybe next year after the exams were over Harold House should organise a week on a camp site at Pwhelli in North Wales. If Yehudah Siegel were officially in charge, the Minister's son, surely nobody could object.

She sighed at the project's bleakness. It was grim enough to be young and penniless without the additional strictures of Judaism. No wonder youngsters skipped off to Israel on the free ticket: on a typically damp day like this, its sunny beaches and orange groves had enormous appeal to a British youngster. And not come back, either. Life in the kibbutz did not sound particularly onerous. No shopping, no individual cooking. All done collectively. Children were cared for in nurseries so that their mothers could work. She suspected that Lucy for one would regard that as paradise. So might the child's mother.

Mr Clay the pharmacist emerged from his dispensary. 'Well done. You dealt with her beautifully.'

'Thanks. She was a sweet kid.'

He peered over his spectacles. 'You going to train as a nurse, Helen?'

'Heavens, no. I'm not the type. Not good at taking orders or making beds.' The possibility had entered her head briefly in a careers discussion. It was one of the few professions dominated by females and with equal pay. It had been as quickly dismissed.

He gestured at the arrays of aspirin and cough drops, of toilet tissue and deodorants. 'You could go on working here. As permanent staff you'd get more money. Two weeks' paid holiday a year and a pension scheme.'

As amiably as possible Helen shook her head. 'I'm doing my A levels next year.'

'Ah. Then had you thought of qualifying as a pharmacist? You'll always be employable; you can travel with it if you like.'

Helen was nonplussed. 'A chemist? I suspect that's what my mother assumes I'm going to be. My A levels include chemistry. So Mum makes the connection that I'll be a chemist in a shop. Like her brother, years ago, though I don't know if he is still in practice.' Helen laughed. 'She'd be quite proud if I did. But no.'

The pharmacist turned, disappointed. 'It may not be the most challenging occupation, but it's worthwhile,' he said gruffly, and went back behind his counter. Helen gazed after him a little penitently: there was no kindness in kidding Mr Clay along, though she had not intended to hurt his feelings. She returned to tidy up the office.

Elizabeth Plumb was given to understand by *le patron* that her bill would be paid for ten days. Madame *Plon* – the closest the innkeeper could get to her name – was to be treated with the utmost respect. He hoped she would enjoy her stay in this town of Rabelais, Descartes, Joan of Arc and the Plantagenet kings. A table had been reserved for her for dinner each night.

Madame *Plon* had taken a couple of days to recover from the shock. She could well understand that Charles could not warn her in time. Had he tried to contact her in Liverpool he would have failed: since it was too far to travel in one day she had broken her journey both in London and Paris. Or perhaps he had not known himself till the last minute. Madame la Comtesse could be a peremptory creature, he had frequently implied. And quite unreasonable. He was not permitted to come to England for fear he would catch a chill – the French were a nation of hypochondriacs. It suited her too, however: had he ever appeared in Liverpool it might have been embarrassing, to say the least. Their romance had been confined to the holidays, and to his home, in the lady's absence.

The Hostellerie Gargantua was not unfamiliar. It was the real thing, an authentic fifteenth-century magnificence in the midst of the town's cobbled streets. Rabelais' lawyer father had practised in its rooms while the author himself had supped often in the painted caves at the back. She had dined here with Charles in the tiny room in the tower, a rather self-conscious dinner *à deux* by candlelight. The view over the river below was at its finest as the sun set after a hot day, when pink and silver light would steal into the chamber to stroke her bare arms. The French knew how to seduce a woman, that was for sure. She had adored every minute.

Miss Plumb pondered how to use her unexpected solitude. The *patron* suggested excursions to the abbey at Fontevraud, to Saumur with its horses, to the dolmens at Bagneux, to Bourgueil's wine festival on the Feast of the Assumption, August 15. Charles had preferred to stay on his estate with her and regarded such *touristique* activities as rather beneath him. Miss Plumb squared her shoulders. Though her heart was heavy there'd be a next time – half term, or after Christmas when Madame might go to Monaco. For the moment she would occupy herself as best she could.

First there was the château in Chinon itself to explore, its tall ramparts a short walk from her hotel. Equipped with a book on its history she pottered around. The great moat was grassed over now, but it was easy to visualise marauding invaders being beaten off and bloody corpses piled in triumph. With care she passed through the archway where Charles VIII banged his head, fatally – or was it poison? It was creepy to stand on the spot where Joan the Maid was imprisoned after her betrayal to the English. Two floors beneath and a century earlier Jacques de Molay and his Knights Templars had also been incarcerated. On the wall her fingers traced the strange cabbalistic symbols carved by the captives. Perhaps the Church was wise to regard them as dabblers in the black arts. They ended up roasted alive on the Pont Neuf in Paris.

As the afternoon wore on she rested on a bench in the shade. She had expected to feel lonely and a little sorry for herself, but the combined exercise of mind and body had brought an element of release which was itself pleasant. The affair with Charles was a source of hedonistic enjoyment, but it was not love and both knew it. More a fusion of like minds which had acquired the quality of ritual, year by year, as if to refresh and strengthen the two of them to withstand more conventional lives during the winter. In her case that meant Liverpool. Miss Plumb shuddered. After such delight, such exquisite beauty, the journey back would seem like a return to Bedlam and the treadmill.

The site attracted a great many foreign visitors. One family sat down on the grass near her: young parents with three children, two leggy boys aged about fourteen and ten and a chubby little girl of perhaps seven. The entire group wore shorts, tee shirts and open sandals. How sensible, Miss Plumb thought as she twitched her corduroy skirt. They chattered in English and passed a bottle of water. Miss Plumb, apparently engrossed in her guide book, began to eavesdrop. She recognised the accent with a blink of pleasure. This family came from her home county of Kent.

'England was governed from Chinon for hundreds of years,' explained the father. The children formed a semi-circle at his feet, alert and engrossed. 'King John was married here in the year 1200. He stole his wife, Isabel of Angoulême, from her betrothed the Comte de Lusignan.' His voice took on a sing-song quality as if he often spun such tales. 'That gave Philippe, the French king, the excuses he'd sought to seize John's French territory. So he became known as John Lackland. He also lost the crown jewels – not here, though, but in England.'

'Careless sod.' Miss Plumb smiled to herself.

The father pointed at the tower. 'The saddest story is about his father, King Henry. This was his palace. He came here when he was old and sick, still determined to hang on to both kingdoms if he could. Philippe swore he would destroy everything unless poor old Henry gave in. He promised to produce a list of Henry's former vassals who had switched sides. When he did so, John's name headed the list.'

'Gosh,' said the older boy. 'Betrayal of the first order. What did Henry do?'

'He turned his face to the wall.' The father pointed again as if to indicate the exact square of limestone. Miss Plumb involuntarily craned her neck. 'And he died of a broken heart.' The little girl sighed. 'But,' said her father mysteriously, 'his wicked son did not inherit his crown. Not then, anyway. Do you know who did?'

'The eldest, of course,' said the eldest. 'King Richard. The Lionheart.'

'Correct, Rupert, top marks.'

'Go on, Daddy, don't stop,' pleaded the little girl, but her father reached mischievously for the bottle and took a long gulp. He wiped the neck with his palm and handed it around.

'No: enough for today. Tomorrow we will pay homage at the tombs of our Kings and Queens at Fontevraud, and I will tell you about King Richard and his exploits. D'you know he didn't speak a word of English? Only French.'

'Golly.' The younger boy rolled his eyes. Miss Plumb deduced he had recently commenced the struggle with gallic declensions. The family rose to their feet and sauntered towards the exit.

She lingered as shadows lengthened, her book upside down in her lap. How she would love to teach children like that. Bright and attentive, but more: they took for granted that knowledge was not merely useful and necessary but *fun*, that their nation's chronicles and legends were a living, exciting study, neither dry nor irrelevant. They had hung on every word. Men and women long dead had become for them live creatures with blood in their veins and ambition in their souls.

How often had she tried to stir such enthusiasm among the girls of Blackburne House, but with a few exceptions it was a thankless task. Too many were determined to ridicule all scholarship in their restless search for the modern. The prevailing culture valued instant gratification over perception or wisdom. Anyone who threatened to break out, like Helen Majinsky and her coterie, was subjected to not-so-subtle mockery. Under these pressures, unless the city council offered a great deal more encouragement, the school might not survive.

Up till now, Elizabeth Plumb had convinced herself that this danger to education existed throughout the country: she would stumble over the same obstacles wherever she went. That family's behaviour gave the lie to such a generalisation. Wherever they hailed from, in that area were schools which taught well, pupils who listened and relished their studies, adults with much the same views as her own. Parents' evenings would be a joy. They'd attend and ask intelligent questions. They'd applaud the staff and demand their utmost from each. Teachers and parents would share with a sense of solemn responsibility the nurture of the next generation.

One thing was certain, she told herself as she rose stiffly from the bench and brushed down her skirt. Nobody would arrive at her office to bribe her with stolen bottles of whisky.

Pensively she strolled down the steep cobbled hill towards the old town, taking a different route from her entry. At a bend in the path she paused and leaned over the parapet. The cars below on the embankment near the Rabelais statue were tiny, like toys.

One, an elongated silver outline, caught her eye. It was quite like Charles's. In fact, unless he had changed his model, it was identical. Yet he had boasted that they were rare and difficult to obtain. As she watched idly the car slowed in front of a big modern hotel on the edge of town. Not Charles's sort of *auberge*. Or rather not hers – she preferred the biggest contrast possible with home and had often said so.

The car parked and the driver's door opened. A man's figure climbed unhurriedly out and entered the hotel. A few minutes later two shapes emerged, the man with his hand on the elbow of a slim female in a summer dress. They climbed in the car which purred off in the direction of Azay.

Miss Plumb clutched the ancient stone to steady herself. Of course it might have been an hallucination. Or she could accept the evidence of her own eyes. She would recognise that sleek grey hair, that slight bow anywhere. There was no doubt whatsoever.

Charles was in town, not on the coast. In the company of another woman. And he did not care much if anyone saw.

Michael knew at once that he would remember it for ever. By mid-morning it was obvious that the march, billed as 'a great moral protest against racial bias' was turning into a day when the peaceful might of the American Negro was to be on display as never before, when a good-natured mass of ordinary people might decisively alter the course of history.

He stood quietly and gazed around in wonder. Most of the people, to his surprise, wore suits – black suits for the men, as if on their way to church or a wedding, despite the sweltering heat. The coloured women wore gay cotton dresses and hats. Their children were miniatures of the adults, their hair brushed into orderliness, small boys in white shirts, blue suits and bow-ties, tiny girls with tight coils and plaits tamed with fluttering ribbons in every hue of the rainbow, and ready smiles on every face.

A battered bus drew up near him with Mississippi plates, one of hundreds from every state of the Union. It disgorged a score of workmen in well-pressed dungarees with new straw hats. They grinned lop-sidedly and shook hands with everyone they saw. One seized

Michael and slapped him heartily if inarticulately on the back. Above their heads planes homed in towards the airport. One, they heard later, contained the singer Josephine Baker who had entertained the passengers in the hours since Paris. The airport, rail stations, the bus depots, car parks were jammed. Every taxi had been commandeered, every piece of municipal transport, but they were not enough. And so people walked, in their thousands. One man announced to all and sundry that he had roller-skated all the way from Chicago. And still they kept coming.

Clergymen abounded: thick-necked men in clerical collars who moved easily among the crowd, Bible in hand, praising the Lord, sweat on brows, eyes alert for trouble. The numbers swelled. For the first few hours Michael and the new arrivals strolled happily from the Lincoln memorial past the reflecting pool to the Washington Monument and back down the other side, but gradually movement became sluggish. Every inch of possible space was filled. The marchers sat down where they were and swapped food and drink with those around them, and described their adventures on the journey, both physical and spiritual.

Michael found he was one of a substantial sprinkle of whites, mostly young people like himself. The blacks called him 'brother' without affectation and he murmured 'A grand day', over and over again. He did not trust himself to say more. Oh, how Helen would love this. He resolved to remember every detail to recount to her. To tell his children and grandchildren some day: 'I was there.'

On the steps of the Lincoln Memorial, as the solemn golden statue peeped out from behind the huge pillars, microphones had been set up. It seemed wisest to wedge himself near the steps from where he could observe most easily. He noticed uncomfortably how old habits of deference die hard: whenever with thanks and apologies he headed in any particular direction, the way parted and children were pulled from his path.

He shaded his eyes and saw the stocky figure of Marlon Brando, up there mumbling an incomprehensible speech. With mounting excitement Michael recognised other stars who waited their turn – Judy Garland, Burt Lancaster. He was not surprised to see Sidney Poitier and Lena Horne. Small and dapper in his mohair suit, Sammy Davis Jr scuttled forward and began to sing snatches of show favourites. His voice soared over the crowd as his spectacles reflected the sun. The haunting notes of 'Summertime' floated over the water and many joined in –

'So hush little baby, don' you cry-y . . .'

Centre stage passed to black baseball star Jackie Robinson who smiled and waved shyly, and was cheered to the echo. Then the Chicago rollerskater was half pushed, half carried to the front, spoke haltingly of his exploits and admitted his legs were tired.

Suddenly there was a commotion: another white man nearby had unfurled a red flag with an indistinct emblem and began to run towards the steps, yelling as he went. He wore a black shirt with the same emblem on the pocket and black gloves. The crowd separated and tried to scatter but there was no room to get away. For a moment shocked spectators froze in their seats. From what Michael could distinguish the man was a supporter of George Rockwell, the American Nazi leader, and was screaming for the right to speak.

Michael's gorge rose in fury. Bloody Nazis! If they'd had their way there'd be no freedom marches. No free elections. No John Fitzgerald Kennedy. No Sammy Davis Jr. No Helen, come to that: her people had filled gas chambers by the million. No freedom of speech for anybody. The man had to be stopped, and preferably by another white.

As the fascist breasted him Michael lunged with his best football tackle, knocked the man off balance and wrestled him to the ground. By the time state troopers loped up three burly Negro stewards were astride his victim who was still spewing out maddened vituperation. The lone demonstrator was handcuffed and his rights read. As he was frog-marched away the Nazi flag was torn into shreds by those nearest and spat upon.

The solemn business started. Michael melted back into the crowd and listened in respectful silence as Bayard Rustin, credited with the day's organisation but who would have been destroyed had it turned sour, spoke with tears in his eyes. 'Already one of our objectives has been met. We said we would awaken the conscience of the nation, and we have done it.'

'Amen!' 'Yes, man!' 'Tell them, tell them.' The cries and chants surged around the hundreds of thousands in his audience. A camera turned towards Michael who nodded and smiled. A young black slapped him on the back. 'We shall overcome, brother.'

At last a sigh went through the vast throng as Martin Luther King Jr mounted the rostrum. His head was bare in the sun. He raised both arms above his head and they shouted and stamped their feet for him. This was the hero, the leader, the man who walked with princes and Presidents, who articulated what lay deepest in their hearts. They had travelled for days to hear him. They had waited for him through the forenoon and the heat of the day. A collective hush fell.

He declaimed like an Old Testament prophet, measuring the time it took for each phrase to roll up to the Capitol building a mile away and return. Whoops and yelps greeted every pause.

'Let us not satisfy our thirst for freedom by drinking from the cup of hatred and bitterness. The struggle continues, and will continue, until justice flows like water and righteousness like a stream . . .'

'Halleluya! Amen, brother, amen.'

'Even though we still face the difficulties of today and tomorrow, I still have a dream . . .'

'Oh, tell it,' murmured the multitude, entranced.

'I have a dream, that on the red hills of Georgia the sons of former slaves and the sons of former slave-owners will sit together at the table of brotherhood. I have a dream, that the state of Mississippi, a state sweltering with the heat of injustice will be transformed into an oasis of freedom . . . I have a dream!'

The people joined hands and rocked, slowly and ecstatically.

'Dream some more . . .'

'I have a dream, that one day every valley shall be exalted, every hill and mountain shall be made low, the rough places shall be made plain, the crooked places will be made straight . . . and the glory of the *Lord* shall be revealed and all flesh shall see it together . . .'

My God, thought Michael confusedly, this is how it must have been at the Sermon on the Mount. He grabbed the hands of both his neighbours and held on tight. Everyone scrambled to their feet as the old Baptist hymn began to float over their heads. With a quarter of a million others he opened his mouth. Throatily at first, then with increasing courage and conviction, he started to sing:

> '*We shall overcome, we shall overcome,*
> *We shall overcome, some day.*
> *Oh, deep in my heart I do believe*
> *We shall overcome some day.*'

PART FOUR

'Enveloped in a common mist, we seem to walk in clearness ourselves, and behold only the mist that enshrouds others.'

George Eliot, *Leaves from a Notebook*

Chapter Sixteen

Back to School

The girls commented on it with both wonder and fear in their voices. Miss Plumb seemed to have lost some of her fierceness. The basilisk stare was still present but was no longer switched on at the least excuse. Her step down a corridor was perceptibly less dominant. Instead she appeared preoccupied. On more than one occasion pupils became aware that she was observing them, but privately, and she had passed on without remark or command.

'Fallen in love,' was Meg's verdict as they sat in the library. 'Somebody she met on holiday. A widower. A headmaster, I bet. Not a lady of great originality, our Miss Plumb.'

'Don't be daft,' Brenda chided. 'She's too old. A confirmed spinster. She must be nearly fifty. People don't fall in love at that age. They start counting the days till they can retire.'

'Maybe it's not a man but another woman.' Helen wondered at her own mischievous remark; her adventures with Michael had opened up such possibilities for her, broken so many taboos. She had begun to glimpse what a sexual relationship could mean, even for those who concealed their feelings under a stony exterior. 'Like Virginia Woolf and her Violet. Don't you think it'd fit dear Miss Plumb perfectly?'

Brenda was shocked, Meg amused. 'You shouldn't talk like that, Helen, it's not nice,' said Brenda. 'I don't know about Miss Plumb, but you've changed too. Not quite the reserved little Jewess you were a year or two ago, are you?'

Helen smiled. Where once she might have regarded Brenda's words as hurtful now she recognised their truth. She spoke calmly and without offence.

'We are on the cusp, Brenda. Look, our schooldays are nearly over. The law says we're adults, or nearly: we all have National Insurance cards, we can get married without a parental say-so.'

'God! Why should you want to do that? Anyway, you can't vote, and you can't do much else without your father's signature till you're twenty-one.' This, with a sniff, from Meg.

But Brenda had not missed the mention of marriage. She touched Helen's arm. 'Might you run off and get married? Without your parents' permission, I mean? I know you're keen on your Michael – you moon about him often enough – but you're not planning a midnight dash to Gretna Green, are you? Honestly, it's not a great idea.'

'If you do, let us know. We'll be your witnesses.' Meg's narrow face reflected a wistful envy.

Helen had not responded. The question of a quick marriage had never arisen – indeed, marriage had not entered the frame – but she let herself consider it briefly, then slowly shook her head. 'Marry in haste, repent at leisure. I agree – it doesn't seem too smart to me either. And girls like us don't need to. We can clear off far more responsibly, and have the option to return, if we get into university.'

'A shotgun marriage is exactly what Colette's father would fix for her, though.' Brenda began to sort out her books. 'Talking of Colette, where is she? She doesn't seem to be part of our gang since the start of term. I worry about her. This morning she looked like death warmed up and when I went into the cloakroom before break she was standing over the sink like she'd been sick. I asked her but she said she hadn't.'

'I think they knock her about at home,' Meg said shortly. 'But if she won't pipe up, what can you do? Her best bet is to stick at her studies and get out that way.'

The three settled soberly to their tasks. Helen glanced at her friends under her eyelashes. All of them had changed. Their companionship was less jolly, with a sharper edge than before: friends since they had entered the school six years earlier, they were no longer children. Brenda was a handsome, curvaceous young woman. Her bosom strained against the girlish white blouse; the school tie looked provocative against that smooth throat. Brenda would have no trouble with boyfriends, not least because her expectations of men were set by the brothers she adored. Provided Brenda never suffered hardship or bad luck she would be content, and radiate contentment to those around her.

As for Meg, her ambition drove her harder than before. The slight frown between the brows had become permanent. Her caustic tongue created distance as if she were reluctant to allow affection or consideration for other people to hold her back. It was becoming harder to like Meg, though she showed no signs of wishing to quit the small coterie.

And Meg was right, Colette's behaviour had become erratic and more secretive. Not that the girl had ever been forthcoming about the unpleasant circumstances at home, other than to hint that they were best not described. Loyalty must come into play here, of course: none of them willingly, publicly, criticised their families, for that was equivalent to running down oneself. And it could be that the Irish girl felt that once expressed and given substance, her problems could no longer be rationalised away. Perhaps she was afraid that the authorities might try to interfere, which could only make things worse. Her friends were accustomed to the world-weary impression she gave that she knew far more about the outside world than they did, but that this unasked-for maturity brought her no peace.

If she got the chance, Helen would cajole it out of her at lunchtime. Neither was rostered for playground duty; they would be at liberty for a precious ninety minutes. Faron's Flamingoes were on at the Cavern, a good group but not one which would pack the place out. Together they could let down their hair and recapture some of the carefree innocence of a bare few months before.

And as for Helen herself: she needed no reminder that a Rubicon had been crossed. The line between herself and her childhood was receding fast into the distance. In the weeks after their first love-making there had been as many meetings as could be arranged both before and since Michael's furlough home. Her body, her entire system had responded to him, with a flush of hormones which made her eyes sparkle and skin glow. She was quite certain that her breasts had enlarged a little and her hips filled out, though she had not put on any weight. The mirror told her she looked more womanly, with a sweeter aura than before. No one would any longer dismiss her as a mere schoolkid.

Helen pondered what might have happened to Miss Plumb. Could it have been something similar? Love it might well be: the most surprising people fell in love and were transformed as she felt she had been. Michael, she reckoned, had become more confident, more courteous, if that were possible. Her love had made her more outspoken, braver, as well as far more sexually aware, but she could well understand that if love came late it might make a person turn in on herself. Perhaps it was love rediscovered, or love challenged in some way. If Miss Plumb were indeed distracted by an affair of the heart, and if that induced this milder, more considerate manner with her charges, long may it continue. Helen let herself daydream, and hoped the teacher was as happy as she was.

'She's probably going through the change of life,' Meg muttered sourly, as if she could read Helen's thoughts. Brenda threw an exercise book at the cynic, and brought the speculation to an end.

The object of their interest was in her study nearby. On the desk lay the three-page letter in exquisite French which had arrived at the weekend. How elegantly he listed his excuses, how obliquely he hinted that a repeat visit would not be appropriate. His wife had not discovered their liaison, he insisted, but had made it clear that he was expected to dance attendance on her more often. Opportunities were limited. It might be preferable not to risk – and so on, complete with an apposite quotation from Verlaine.

The recipient was distracted, yes, but not distraught. In fact that was the source of the greatest puzzlement as she read the letter for the umpteenth time.

He deserved her hatred. Miss Plumb knew from the evidence of her own eyes that each page was a pack of lies. Though it had been hard to tell from the distance, that woman on Charles's arm had not walked like an elderly lady nor one yet middle-aged, so it could not have been Madame herself. He had no daughter. Had she been a daughter-in-law, surely his son would have been present.

Miss Plumb recalled her favourite fragment of early philosophy – Occam's Razor. Don't invent entities, was the maxim of the fourteenth-century Franciscan friar. If several unconnected scraps of information lead to one rather obvious conclusion, then that conclusion is probably the correct one. If thunder and lightning were in the air, Gods might appear, spirits might dance, but the most likely outcome was – rain. If two men stood over a recently killed corpse and one looked guilty, he was more likely to be the murderer. Miss Plumb chuckled – it didn't always work. But if an ageing Lothario were spotted with a pretty young woman on his arm in circumstances in which he had half-heartedly endeavoured to cover his tracks, she was quite possibly his new mistress. It stood to reason.

'I am getting old,' Miss Plumb whispered to herself. 'It had to happen sooner or later.' Then she realised that the emotion most strongly urging itself to the fore was not self-pity but annoyance. 'But then so's he. He's ten years older than I am. Silly fool.' She swivelled round in her chair and stared grimly out of the window, then back again towards the fire-place, having gauged that Charles, to the south east, was roughly in that direction.

'Well, here's my prayer for you, *cher* Charles. Thank you for our wonderful years. Thank you for saving me from a fate as a loveless dried-up husk: at least I know what it's all about. But may you find no joy in your new conquest. May your manhood shrivel to a flapping bag of useless skin. May it humiliate you from now on, you who were so proud of your prowess. Serve you right, dammit. Grow old gracefully, and be kind to your wife.'

It dawned on her that Madame knew about her husband's escapades and may even have been entertained by assessments of her rivals' attributes. To have been the subject of such tolerant condescension was dreadful. Miss Plumb swallowed hard and raised an invisible toast towards the mantelpiece. 'And thank you for bringing me to my senses. If I'm to enjoy my remaining years it won't be through you, or any man.

Unwittingly you've enabled me to see so clearly that I must rely only on – myself.'

There was a tap on the door. With a guilty start Miss Plumb dropped her hand and bid farewell for ever to her Frenchman. The letter was scooped up; it would not be destroyed, but put away to be mulled over when she was past caring any more, and then only as a source of nostalgic amusement.

'Come!'

Helen Majinsky stood on the threshold with a blue Basildon Bond envelope.

'Yes, Helen? Come in.'

The girl held out the envelope. 'The usual at this time of year, I'm afraid. Request from my parents to let me have time off school for the High Holydays.'

'Oh, you do have a most inconvenient religion.' Miss Plumb took the note, saw Helen's flush and immediately regretted the remark. 'Let me see. Two days for the New Year, then soon after one more for the Day of Atonement. Is that the lot? I seem to recall there are more in the pipeline – Roseanne Nixon has asked for two more days for something else.'

'That'll be *Succos*. I persuaded my parents not to bother about that. The Oxbridge exams are right afterwards and I don't want to lose any more time. It is not me that's asking, Miss Plumb, it's my mother and father.'

The dignified admonishment hung in the air. Miss Plumb sensed anger in the girl's demeanour and felt slightly ashamed.

'It is not *I*, dear,' the teacher corrected automatically. She sighed. 'I know it's not you, Helen.' That was the best she could offer by way of apology.

Miss Plumb swiftly recollected how to make amends. She rummaged in the top drawer of her desk. 'Here, take these since I've seen you. That's the main application form for UCCA, the Universities' Central Clearing House for Admissions. And these – ah, got them.'

Two more printed forms were uncovered and handed over, together with, after a second's hesitation, a new buff folder.

'Yes. Those are for Oxford and Cambridge.' Miss Plumb found herself speaking rather fast. 'Take them home, get your father to sign each one. Do try to keep them clean, please. But don't fill in the rest till I've gone through your answers with you.'

Helen had not sat down. Her face had become a mask, her eyes unnaturally bright. She stood perfectly still, the new folder in her outstretched hand, as if unwilling to break a spell.

'I think that's your route out, Helen, is it not?' The teacher's voice had regained some of its dry humour. 'Go now. Bring them back as quickly as you can. And, Helen –'

The girl had reached the doorway but paused.

'Yes, Miss Plumb?'

'Not that you'll need it, but just in case. Good luck.'

'Golly, look at that. There must be hundreds here.'

Colette and Helen paused, crestfallen. From the steamy staircase of the Cavern came wails of an old Gene Vincent number, *Be Bop a Lula*. The long line of girls in high heels and men with slicked-back hair, hands in pockets, swayed and moaned as they shuffled forward:

'She-e-e's my baby now –'

Helen approached Paddy Delaney, the bouncer. From his greater height he stared around, bored and watchful.

'Who's the crowd for?'

'There was a rumour the Beatles would appear. I keep tellin' 'em, fat chance. An' if they were, we'd've advertised it in *Mersey Beat* and charged a quid a time if we could have got away with it. But they don't believe me.'

As he spoke a girl in the crowd began to groan. 'Oh Paul, I love you so!' Behind her, convinced that McCartney must have appeared as from nowhere, other girls took up the cry and began to surge forward. 'Paul! Paul! He's here! Oh, let me at him – Oh, Paul—' Near the staircase a girl slipped and fell on her knees. The person at her side fell on top of her, and the youth behind, like dominoes. The noise increased; at the far end of the line out of sight it had turned to screams, steady and high pitched, as if a band of feral wolves had scented prey.

'Bloody 'ell,' muttered the doorman, and waded into the mêlée. He hauled the fallen girl off the ground and she stood trembling for a moment, crying and rubbing her grazes. 'He's not bloody coming, do you hear? Now stop that caterwauling or you won't get in today or any other day.'

'The place has gone mad,' Helen commented, but her expression was troubled. She moved closer to Colette who stood pensively beside her.

'Started with the Orbison tour in May,' the doorman informed them as he returned to his post and tugged down his cuffs. 'Ringo told me the screams started in Glasgow. Not much else to do up there, I suppose. Then there were riots. Crazy when you think about it – this time last year nobody'd heard of them.'

'Except us,' Helen swaggered. 'We were yelling for them even then. D'you remember how the keenest girl fans would arrive in hair rollers and jeans and queue for hours to get seats in the front row? When the supporting bands came on they'd go to the ladies and do their hair and make-up and put on a dress. So when John, Paul, George and Ringo took the stage, they'd see a sea of gorgeous women, all panting for them.'

'The queue started at midnight for a lunchtime session,' the bouncer reminisced dreamily, his eyes alert. 'Those were the best when the boys'd fool around on stage and cadge chip butties from the little typists. Before Mr Epstein told 'em to behave. But it's become a lot crazier since then, you know. Ringo's girlfriend Maureen got chased the last time they appeared. Ended up with nasty scratches down her cheeks.'

'Crikey. But who'd do that?'

'Other girls who fancied Ringo, I suppose. They told her to keep away from him or they'd put her eyes out.'

Despite the late summer sunshine Helen shivered. She turned to Colette. 'We're not going to get in – no chance,' she said. 'I'm sorry I dragged you down here. But let's go into Lewis's and wander around a bit before we have to get back to school.'

The big department store was on the corner opposite the Adelphi. Over its main doorway the Jacob Epstein statue 'Man at the Helm' drew their glances. Gaunt, skinny and quite naked, his large-toed foot extruded on the prow of a ship. This was the spot where Helen had met Michael on that fateful day out. It was not polite in Liverpool to stare at the statue, which had caused a furore when first installed.

The two girls looked up, daringly, deliberately. The male figure was blatant and ugly. Helen felt herself blush.

'Funny how when you love someone, it doesn't look so peculiar,' she commented. 'In fact all that equipment is fascinating.' Colette turned away and refused to meet her eye. Helen caught her arm. 'Sorry, Colette. I didn't mean to – to boast. Or embarrass you. But nobody tells you these things. It's hard work finding out for yourself.'

The two took the new escalator and found themselves in the ladies' clothing department. They wandered around, two school pupils despite the black polo-necked sweaters which covered their blouses and ties, and stopped before an angular model sporting a narrow-waisted suit.

'My Dad makes ladies' suits like that but he can't match the price. He says the ladies' side of bespoke tailoring is dying.'

Colette did not respond. Irritated and anxious, Helen drew her into a corner near a tall mirror where two wicker chairs had been placed, presumably for menfolk to sit and admire their spouses' choice before paying for it.

'What's the matter, Colette? I suggested coming out today because you looked really peaky. Aren't you well? You act as if you're carrying the burden of the world on your shoulders. We're best friends. We've always talked. You can tell me.'

Colette shook her head slowly and allowed the black hair to hide her eyes.

'We are still friends, aren't we?' Helen persisted. 'We haven't had a fight – I haven't said anything to upset you?'

Again, that puzzling slow shake of the head and a refusal to meet her gaze.

Helen sat back on the cane chair and swung her legs aimlessly. For a moment she felt once more like a schoolgirl. She spoke into the air, making a more oblique attempt to engage Colette.

'Things have changed since the holidays, haven't they? Before that we could pretend that school would go on for ever, though of course we knew it'd come to an end. Now the end looms. It's like the last few minutes of a voyage – as the ferry boat swings in close to the landing stage. You know that the suspension of belief is over, that real life is about to begin.'

Colette had not moved or responded. Helen continued, almost to herself. 'We will go in different directions, unless we end up at the same university – and even then we could be in different colleges. We'll go our separate ways. Oh, we'll meet, and swap stories. But it'll never be the same again. The closeness we've shared will be gone for ever. Boys and lovers will be more important to us in future than girlfriends. Husbands will get in the way, break the links. Grown-ups are never the bosom mates that young people can be. Never quite the same trust as between kids, is there?'

Colette's silence provoked her irrationally. Helen dug the girl in the ribs, quite hard. 'So what is it, Colette? If something's bothering you it'd help to share it. I may not understand, not being Catholic and that, but at least you'd feel better for having spoken to someone. You don't have a mother to talk to, but I bet you don't confess everything to the priest, do you?'

A strange noise came from behind the curtain of hair. Regretting the sharpness of her tone Helen turned to Colette, gently peered under the fringe and ascertained that the sound had been a swallowed sob. She waited, but still no confidences were forthcoming.

'We've grown apart already, haven't we, Colette?' Helen murmured sadly. 'I can witter on about my hopes and plans for next year but you've heard all that already. I won't describe the intimate details of what Michael and I do, because that's too precious to giggle over. I think you grasp that. But I'm unhappy that you can't share what's eating you. You shouldn't push your old friends away. I care about you a lot, Colette. Whatever it is, even if you say it's private it can't be so horrible that you can't even hint at it. Can it?'

'It can,' said Colette shortly. 'Nothing you can help with, anyway.' She jumped up and began to move towards the staircase.

'Boyfriend trouble?' Helen spoke in an encouraging tone as they descended the stairs together. The store could afford only one escalator and had chosen one going up.

'No. Nothing like that. God, what a joke.'

'Why a joke? I don't get it. Have you got a serious boyfriend you don't want anybody to know about? I wouldn't sneak on you. I wouldn't tell your father or anything like that.'

Under the hair the green eyes blazed. 'I don't have a boyfriend of any sort. And I'd much rather not have an interrogation the whole way back to school, if you don't mind. If you want to be a real pal you'll let me be.'

Helen sighed. 'Suit yourself.' In the open air she stole one more glance at Colette. The girl seemed to have atrophied somehow. Her whole shape seemed smaller, shrunken almost, along with her personality. Had she always been like this Colette would never have made it into the inner circle of Brenda, Meg and Helen, who expected a lively contribution from each member. The foursome of *Little Women* – all bright, keen, yet distinguished from each other, complementary, contrasting – had often appeared to them a fair model. Yet Colette seemed to be withdrawing deliberately from the partnership.

'We'll be late if we don't get a move on,' was all the Irish girl would say.

On the bus back both were occupied with sombre thoughts. As they turned into the school Helen was left with a strong sense of disappointment, and of foreboding.

The train pulled out of Bletchley station with a lurch. In the corner of a 'Ladies Only' compartment, Dr Edith Swanson, Dean of Admissions at St Margaret's College, Cambridge, settled herself with *The Times* crossword, a bag of peppermints and the Liverpool Corporation guidebook to the city.

Her friend Elizabeth Plumb had briefed her over the years in a series of letters filled with insight and wry observations. It was widely acknowledged that the City of Liverpool was run not by any of its women, but by three great men. They were not politicians, for those were a universally despised profession seen as incompetent, irrelevant or on the make. The Lord Mayor in his ermine-trimmed robes was chosen entirely on seniority not ability. Local MPs were by any yardstick a rum lot, with only the formidable Mrs Braddock, built like a small tank, of any national interest. Between her and her husband Alderman John Braddock, both good-hearted and rough souls, the complacency and diminished horizons of the masses they served were well represented.

Yet that complacency was not without foundation. Liverpool had long been a leader: its pre-eminence was widely believed unchallengeable. Blackburne House, Elizabeth's school, had been the nation's first girls' day school, a generation before compulsory education. City fathers had been in the vanguard of the Victorian public health movement in 1847 and had built the first municipal housing anywhere in Britain in 1869. They gave free school milk to their schoolchildren and refused to charge for tuberculosis treatment decades ahead of the

National Health Service. The progressive spirit lived on. Thus Liverpudlians in the mid-twentieth century felt they had cause to be quite pleased with themselves.

The three wise men were universally respected. One was Glaswegian Professor Andrew Semple, Medical Officer of Health, holder of a distinguished role created by the great municipalities. A small, rotund, clean-shaven man with fiercely intelligent eyes, he it was who provided the drive behind the slum clearance schemes whose outcomes so troubled Miss Plumb. He it was, too, who urged immunisation against smallpox, explained the polio vaccine, introduced BCG against tuberculosis, waged war on head-lice. The city's children believed that they chafed under liberty bodices in winter, a kind of cross between padded body armour and stays with ribbons, because Professor Semple said so. Their morning cod-liver oil capsules, swallowed whole (since to bite one was to have the mouth filled with a disgusting oily fishiness for the rest of the day) were certainly his edict. That their generation reached adulthood in better physical condition than any previous one in the port was largely due to his Scottish charm and competence.

The second person was Catholic Archbishop Dr Heenan, smooth-faced and benign. A sea-port had to be tolerant – after all, the Chinese quarter celebrated their New Year with noisy cymbals, the Orange Lodge marched unmolested through the town centre and Congregational chapels with signs in Welsh dotted suburban street corners. Nevertheless it was quietly acknowledged that the city 'had a lot of Catholics', not simply because of numbers boosted by frequent Irish transfusions but because the faithful attended Mass, put their money in the plate, and did what their priests told them. Especially the women. Thus what if anything the RCs lacked in quantity they made up in discipline, a fact reinforced by the status of their spiritual head.

Yet Heenan was no bitter zealot. His determination to construct his own cathedral – situated with emotional symbolism at the far end of Hope Street from the Anglican version – brought widespread approval. The design, reminiscent of a spacecraft on its launch-pad, was regarded as splendid. The Metropolitan Cathedral, as it was to be known, would elevate its adherents to their rightful position in the cosmos. No longer would they be a downtrodden proletariat despised by all and sundry. The pain of emigrations from the Great Hunger of 1846 onwards which brought boatloads of desperate ragamuffins to the sea-port would be expunged. Respectability beckoned.

Heenan was grudgingly admired by the Jewish community who were intrigued by his performances at the Second Vatican Council. His attitudes were long held: in the fifties he had vigorously criticised the Holy See's boycott of the Council of Christians and Jews. Heenan shared their view that as long as the Pope's followers prayed every Good Friday for the veil to be lifted from the hearts of 'the perfidious Jews... so that they too may acknowledge our Lord, Jesus Christ', then anti-Semitism would continue and be condoned, as it was in darker regimes such as rural France and Poland. The hostile wording of the liturgy had to be erased, insisted Dr Heenan: 'The Catholic Church, in the name of all Christians, should make some strong gesture by way of repentance for the unheard-of atrocities committed against Jews in our own time.' Ranged against him were men like Cardinal Ottaviani who had allegedly prayed to 'die before this Ecumenical Council ends, so that I may die a Catholic'.

Had Miss Plumb but known it, the battles in Rome were meat and drink to such as Reverend Siegel. When prayers for the Royal Family were offered in his synagogue each sabbath he would murmur a private request that Heenan's efforts meet with divine success. It was glumly feared, however, that Liverpool's Primate would in due course be rewarded with a Cardinal's hat and be swept away to Westminster.

The third man was Mr Magnay, the Director of Education. H.S. Magnay, to be precise. A Tynesider. Unlike Dr Andrew Semple's his given names were never uttered, yet his surname was known to every Liverpool family, and by many he was deeply admired and loved.

Mr Magnay's dumpy figure in its navy suit and waistcoat, the wavy hair streaked grey above a podgy face, was familiar to a fair proportion of his thousands of charges, for he took his duties seriously and frequently inspected schools himself. His signature in ink – not a rubber stamp – had appeared on the letter advising Helen's parents of her place at Blackburne House. Every head teacher had had to parry his gentle but effective questions to obtain the job, and other staff as well. He set the educational standards of the city and reinforced them by the most positive means. It was taken for granted that he would attend the prizedays of as many of the city's secondary institutions (at any rate, its grammar schools) as he could manage year by year, and that he would be photographed for the *Echo* with certificate winners. As in many other households, the framed picture of him with Helen graced her parents' sideboard with the hope that Barry's would some day accompany it.

Thus the populace felt themselves to be in honourable and reliable hands, at least those who read newspapers, listened to the BBC Home Service, wanted the best for their offspring and bothered to vote. And should aspects of urban life threaten to intrude – should one become too aware of litter or vandalism or crime – one could move, spread out beyond the city's boundaries to Sefton or the Wirral, to reside with like-minded neighbours and pay much lower rates, yet continue to benefit from the proximity of the great port without any sense of obligation towards it.

As she flicked over the pages, Dr Swanson was struck by how often Mr Magnay's name appeared in both the booklet and Elizabeth's correspondence. If he were truly as benign as Elizabeth said, what was he doing with these new schemes to create comprehensive schools and to abolish selective tests at eleven-plus? Very little such pressure emanated from the Macmillan government, though if Harold Wilson won the General Election that was certain to alter. The City Council's desire to be progressive was leading them in *quite* the wrong direction. She would mention it tonight. It would not be rude to highlight these errors to Mr Magnay's face: on the contrary, it would be her duty.

Dr Swanson sucked her third peppermint. Whenever anyone peered into the compartment at the vacant seats she snorted intimidatingly till the person moved away. She was a thin, whippet-like woman with perpetually pursed lips as if she wished to say more than propriety permitted. Her grey hair was cut severely short. She wore neither make-up nor jewellery except a man's watch. Her clothes were shapeless and mainly brown in colour, with trim laced-up shoes. The effect was both academic and arrogant. Yet her role as Dean of Admissions required her to be uncompromising and incorruptible. Personal likes and dislikes must not intrude. If occasionally a twinkle came to her eye; if sudden acts of impulsive kindness suggested a softer interior; if her preferred authors were John Donne and W. B. Yeats, Rupert Brooke and Elizabeth Barrett Browning, these facets would not emerge until her retirement, when she, believing herself largely friendless (and necessarily so) would be moved at how warmly both pupils and colleagues spoke of her.

Dr Swanson counted Elizabeth Plumb as one of those to whom she would give, were it required, unstinted help and advice. Of a professional nature, of course. Since the two worked at opposite ends of the country their relationship could not be much more than a warm acquaintance conducted mainly in writing. True, there had been avid discussions over tea and crumpets in Elizabeth's room at St Margaret's during undergraduate days, but exclusively over the virtues of *Portrait of a Lady* compared with *Middlemarch*. True, at moments she had gazed covertly at Elizabeth, but the right opportunity had never arrived. Neither then had had a taste for men, nor indeed for anything beyond academia.

Now Elizabeth had asked her to join Mr Magnay on stage for her school's annual prizegiving at the Liverpool Philharmonic Hall, and Dr Swanson had graciously deigned to accept. Not least because it would give her the chance to meet, albeit briefly, the school's likely candidates for St Margaret's later in the year.

I should have told Helen. She's a good sort. I should have blurted it out when we sat on the chairs at Lewis's. I'd have twisted it a bit so as not to shock her. I could have said, I have a boyfriend, see, but it's somebody in the family and we shouldn't.

I wouldn't have said it was my Dad. How could I tell anybody that?

But she had a point when she complained we were growing apart. Put her finger on it exactly. We used to share confidences, used to laugh. I never liked talking about sex much because – well, I knew more than them and my knowledge didn't come from magazines. I knew it wasn't fun. I let them put it down to my being an RC, that we were a bit prim. Or else I let them think that without a mother I didn't feel so ready to chatter about – feminine subjects. Helen is lovely, and so smart. She's brave and prepared to challenge the rules. She knows something's wrong and she's hurt that I won't confide.

Brenda's the next best. She's solid and wise. She doesn't have a boyfriend yet, but she'll find somebody eminently suitable at college and they'll get married when she's got a proper job. Bit predictable, Brenda, but that's her strength and attraction.

Meg, on the other hand, is more mixed up than I am but doesn't know it. Real sourpuss sometimes; I don't entirely trust her. The centre of Meg's world is Meg. She'd tread on others if she had to. But she's scared of sex, deep down. Scared of commitment, perhaps. Or maybe as she says she doesn't want to be dominated by men or be obliged to live her life through them. Is it always that way round? If she met the right kind of woman friend she might be happier. What am I saying?

We've got a lot in common – or we had. We're the first generation of girls to take our education for granted, to be determined to make the most of it. It's a ladder up and out for the four of us, though Brenda is contentedly conventional so she'll return or not go far. Meg'll scoot as far from home as she can. I'd have said the same about Helen but this American boy could prove a genuine alternative to college. He could be a spanner in the works – if her parents discover and throw her out. What would she do then? I don't think she'd give everything up to chase after love, but you never know.

I don't want to lose them. I want to cling to them, keep us together as we've always been. They're all I have. Yet I can't confess, so Helen believes I'm being difficult and want out. It's not true, quite the opposite.

There must be a way I could broach the subject. How would Helen react, I wonder, if I started asking her about contraception? The word is taboo in my church. It's a mortal sin – sex is for procreation and that's final. I bet she leaves it to her Michael but the pair of them will be careful, they won't take chances. They have too much to live for and look forward to. I have nothing.

Nothing. Not even my Dad's mate Jimmy who tried to be kind. He got killed, I heard. Unloading a cargo of pineapples which had gone half-rotten and started to ferment. The fumes in the hold must have been a mixture of alcohol vapours and he passed out instead of staying alert. When he didn't come up they found him crushed under a pallet. The men had a whip-round for his wife and kids. These accidents happen down the docks all the time.

It means I have no one. No one who knows and might help. Nobody. I am completely alone.

Prizegiving will be such a farce. Pretending to be normal. Everybody smiling and applauding. It should be branded on my forehead that I sleep with my father. And that I can't stop him. I can't see an end to it. I can't see anything at all.

'Pleased to meet you! We are honoured to have you with us.' Mr Magnay shook Dr Swanson's vigorously. What a bouncy little man he was – as different to the etiolated dons of Cambridge as could be imagined. No wonder everybody warmed to him. Dr Swanson permitted herself the ghost of a smile.

The introduction took place in what must be the green room for concerts. A diminutive glass of sherry had been accepted. Behind in the body of the hall the noise rose steadily to a loud hum. Since attendance was compulsory, all 400 girls were present in uniform, most with several members of their families. The concert hall, one of England's finest and a short walk from the school, would be full.

Academic gowns were to be worn. Mr Magnay didn't bother: his status came from something more significant than a mere degree. Dr Swanson's PhD in red and blue edged with white fur was the most distinguished, rather more so than Elizabeth's more modest version. Nearly half the staff, it appeared, had studied at Liverpool or Manchester – fine in their way, but how dull to stay so close to home. No graduates of the new universities mooted in Dr Robbins's report had yet appeared; Dr Swanson rather approved of such ancient cities as York, Norwich and Exeter as fresh locations. They'd give the frightfully staid Redbricks – the Victorian seats of learning – a run for their money.

Dr Swanson buttonholed Magnay. 'I really must tackle you, Director.'

He was instant solicitude, his voice betraying a slight Geordie accent. 'So pleased you could find the time to come. We want to send you our best—'

'That's the whole point. If you persist with your plans to – ah – *comprehensivise* the schools, isn't that the jargon? – then you'll ruin the best and waste a great deal of effort on the riff-raff.'

Magnay's earnest brow furrowed. 'We are anxious to improve education for all,' he explained. 'The children attending such establishments as the Liverpool Institutes reach levels among the highest this country can achieve. But that applies to less than twenty per cent of each age cohort. I have a responsibility to the rest, whose standards, frankly, are deteriorating.'

'But you can't have it both ways.' Her bold stare to the fore, Miss Plumb joined in. She had told Dr Swanson of those Kentish children in the lee of the ramparts at Chinon: clearly she felt emboldened. Around the three of them conversation paused. 'Either you ensure that the most able children become an elite or you'll strive mightily with the masses and get nowhere. You'll have to level down, not level up. The cult of mediocrity will rule. This country, which we both care about, Mr Magnay, will go down the plughole. Not to speak of this city,' she added gratuitously.

Magnay looked uncomfortable. Dr Swanson divined that he had put much the same points to his councillors, most of whom had left school at fourteen or earlier, and been rebuffed.

Miss Plumb drove on. It might be the sole chance she would have to say her piece to somebody influential, and to satisfy her own conscience. To stay silent on such an important issue was no longer an option. 'A child needs some basic ability to appreciate history. And you can't half teach science, for example. Either pupils can handle calculus or they can't. Either they're smart enough to master Latin – which, may I remind you, is still an entrance requirement for Oxford and Cambridge –' (Dr Swanson nodded vigorously) '– or they are not. If my best staff are obliged to spend most of their time with the bulk of the pupils – let alone with the dimmest – then the most able children are certain to lose out. And, let me add, the brightest graduates will refuse to enter the teaching profession. A wholesale degradation will take place. Then where will you be?'

Mr Magnay opened and closed his mouth like a fish and looked dolefully from one formidable woman to the other. Miss Plumb glared, then pointed to the clock and steered her guests out.

The Philharmonic Hall itself, as they trooped out on to the stage, was to Enid Swanson a revelation and a delightful surprise. Its art deco lines swooped gracefully overhead to create a vast space without pillars or restricted views, airy and light. But it was Edmund Thompson's carvings on the high side walls which caught Dr Swanson's eye, as they did those of every pupil, in whom annually were induced suppressed sniggers. For the good burghers of the city had agreed in all virtue a series of vivid depictions of gods and muses. Naked and prancing came Diana and Pan, Apollo and Bacchus, breasts high, thighs extended, nipples pointed skyward in ecstasy. Dr Swanson caught herself calculating the dimensions of Pan's buttocks and suspected that the pubescent youngsters who blushed and smirked under her gaze had done much the same.

'Remarkable,' she commented to Elizabeth, who coloured slightly as she rose to her feet.

The next hour passed for those on the platform like most similar rituals. The choir sang Purcell without enthusiasm, Britten without skill and Rodgers and Hammerstein without panache, though the latter brought the most spontaneous applause. The first year recorder group, twenty children in a solemn semi-circle, played 'Nymphs and Shepherds' excruciatingly out of tune. A wind quartet of fourteen-year-olds murdered Schubert. Dr Swanson peered at her programme and noted with relief that Blackburne House did not run to a violin tutor.

Elizabeth was reading out her headmistress's report. It had been a good year for hockey and netball. Examination results had been excellent. Why, oh why, Dr Swanson reflected, do these city grammar schools try to ape the great private schools? And not merely the girls' versions such as Cheltenham Ladies' College or Malvern which might have been understandable. Instead with their striped ties and subfusc uniforms they aped *the boys*. How bizarre and foolish. Eton or Harrow Blackburne House was not going to be, nor Winchester or Marlborough.

Yet the municipalities had something fine to offer in their own right. What was this school's motto? *Non nobis solum sed toti mundo nati.* 'Not for ourselves alone, but for the whole world was I born.' In upperclass mouths that would sound pompous and condescending. Here it referred with pride to the tradition of service and of high-quality endeavour inculcated by the city, its forefathers and governors. And by such models as Mr Magnay, at least till now.

Dr Swanson glanced down the waiting lines of winners. First she must concentrate on the prizes themselves; every single certificate and sports shield had to be handed to its recipient. Fortunately Elizabeth was superbly organised and the girls well drilled. Up the steps they marched like martinets, shook hands, collected their awards, marched off. One or two, cheekier than the rest, waved to supporters in the audience and were raggedly cheered. Flashes popped on box cameras, mainly from the balcony.

The group that drew Dr Swanson's main attention were the sixth-formers, applicants to university within the next couple of months. She made a mental note of Jones, B.R., Findlay, M.R.P., O'Brien, C.M. and Majinsky, H. amongst others. The scientists would have a marginally easier time than the rest, especially if they could offer evidence of all-round competence. Newer educationalists declared that Oxbridge interviews were inconsistent and tended to promote and perpetuate prejudice, but the Dean of Admissions knew better. Any of these who could talk her way through the ordeal, who had something to say for herself, who was – ah, interesting – would be much more attractive as a candidate. The 'gift of the gab', it had been dubbed, though Dr Swanson would not have employed the vulgarity. But it made those interviews such tremendous fun. At any rate for the staff.

The girl Majinsky caught her attention. Carried herself calmly; bright eyes, steady gaze. Had taken the chemistry prize and another for the short story competition – that augured well. Dr Swanson gave her hand a quick shake but did not let go.

'You will be applying to university, I hope?'

'Yes, I think so.'

'Cambridge?' The question was an order.

'I don't know if I'd get in.' The eyes were lowered, modestly, but only for a split second.

'Nonsense.' Dr Swanson stopped herself. Hopes must not be raised. She yearned to lift the child's chin with her fingertip but a thousand people were watching. Instead she cleared her throat so that the girl looked at her sharply. 'You must apply. If you're good enough, you'll have the same chance as everyone else.'

Majinsky nodded and seemed reassured. It was so difficult, Dr Swanson reflected, to convince these northern girls that her college sincerely desired to accept more of them, although naturally merit alone would determine that private schools would fill most places for many years yet.

The next pupil was also on her mental list. A slight figure, pale face with black hair tied back in a lacklustre style, head down. As the girl mounted the steps she almost stumbled, and walked the twenty yards across the platform with a diffident air. Dr Swanson pursed her lips. Something about the child was not quite – clean.

'Colette O'Brien – physics and form prize,' came Miss Plumb's voice, as if from far away.

Dr Swanson shook the hand held out awkwardly to her. It was limp and clammy. Alarmed, she tried to peer into the girl's eyes but caught only a glimpse of their unusual hue. 'Congratulations, Colette,' she began formally. 'And are you planning—?'

A deep groan came from Colette, as if her body had been winded by a blow. Her grip slackened, then she began to sag. Dr Swanson put out her other hand. Behind her Elizabeth Plumb took a quick step: 'Colette – are you all right?'

'Help me – oh – o—' came the sigh. There was a sudden terrified plea in her green eyes. Then the eyeballs rolled upwards so the whites showed, and she staggered a step away from the two women. In a second she had collapsed into a crumpled heap at their feet.

Helen had reached the far end of the platform when she heard the thump and ensuing commotion. That Colette was in trouble somehow did not surprise her. Promptly she dropped her books and ran back. The two academics were standing over the insensible girl in mute shock; in the background Mr Magnay danced and yelped for a doctor. Other teachers flapped about in their gowns like old scarecrows. A hubbub arose as the audience craned to see.

As carefully as she could, Helen knelt at Colette's head and cradled it in her lap. The girl's skin was white as a sheet and tinged blue around the nostrils and lips. Gently, unsure what to do, Helen patted her friend's face. 'C'mon, Colette, wake up,' she murmured anxiously. The eyelashes fluttered and a little cry came. Helen looked up at the adults. 'I think she's only fainted. She hasn't been feeling too well in class lately.'

A doctor, all stolid eminence, had emerged from the stalls and climbed the steps to the platform. The prone figure in its crumpled school uniform was lifted by the men and set on tottering feet, then assisted backstage to the green room. Helen went with her, for Colette would not let go her hand. It would not have occurred to Helen to do otherwise.

Elizabeth Plumb and Edith Swanson stared fixedly at each other. In the hall the inquisitive chatter had crested then calmed to a fierce buzz. It was the don who broke the impasse.

'Duty first, my dear. I think we'd better carry on, don't you? The other girls are waiting. Who's next?'

Chapter Seventeen

Rosh Hashanah

'*Tekiah – Tekiah –*'

The ram's horn was lifted reverentially to the young acolyte's lips. A hush fell upon the congregation. This was the instant they would be called to account: when their sins, and *mitzvahs* if they had any, were being weighed in the divine balance. To most of the assembly the shofar-blower looked ridiculously youthful for such a weighty role, indeed barely old enough to be out of school. The thin strands of beard on his cheeks did not reassure. His tongue flickered wetly. Then he took a deep breath and blew.

For a dreadful moment nothing emerged but a puff of air. The entire assembly swayed, open-mouthed. Surely the young ordinand, sent specially from London, would not fail them? A silent ram's horn would be too humiliating, not to speak of a dismal portent for the new year.

Red in the face under his horn-rimmed spectacles and white velvet hat the youth tried again. His elbows flapped as he raised the horn to a sharper angle and his silky robes, white for the New Year, billowed about his thin figure. A raw squeak emerged, then suddenly he got the hang of it and blew hard and true. The unearthly noise rose in the synagogue, piercing and ethereal. No one spoke, but on the front row someone sighed deeply.

'*Tekiah – Shebarim – Teruah –*'

This time it was short blasts, angry and unpredictable, like an alarm bugle, the echo of tribal trumpets as a rallying call to war. Wrapped in their fringed shawls the elders moaned and swayed. The blower gained the instrument's measure and barely paused as each cue was called:

'*Tekiah – Tekiah – Teruah – Tekiah Gedolah—*'

The wail of the ram's horn rose and sobbed and drove into the furthest corners of the synagogue. In the gallery the women leaned back as if to avoid it. One old lady twisted her head this way and that as if she had heard it long ago in some more terrible circumstance. To every listener the cry seemed to go on for ever until the pain was almost too much to bear.

Then as brusquely as it had begun, the utterance came to an end with a single drawn-out note, high and fine. The faithful let out their breath with a slow hiss. Murmured words of gratitude came as they bowed and nodded to each other. For another year their identity had been revealed to them, their godly covenant confirmed. They knew themselves once more.

'Excellent,' commented Reverend Siegel. Shofar-blowing was not the Minister's forte and it did no good to the singing voice; he was happy to see it delegated.

The visitor adjusted his hat on his head and slumped in his seat. He had played no formal part in the devotions up to that point and had appeared morose and self-absorbed, as well he might, for he was required to do no more than to blow for service after service during the ten days of prayer and penitence from the New Year to Yom Kippur.

In the next to back row, partly protected by a pillar, Daniel Majinsky stared down at his feet. That weird sound, so powerful yet so full of grief: unmistakable, and unreproduceable by other means. It chilled the bones as if some genetic memory had been disturbed – he felt himself like a wild animal, drawn to bay aloud in unison. The shofar troubled him in ways he could not easily analyse.

For the rest of the year the pale yellow horn would be wrapped in white silk and hidden at the back of the Ark behind the Torahs. Nobody would dream of breaching its sanctity by taking it out to demonstrate or even to practise. In earlier times it had been used much more often, to announce the start of sabbath on Friday nights village by village, for example, but not now. Its infrequent appearance added to its potency, for this was not magic nor witchcraft but the heart of a people, before words and beyond understanding. To handle the horn was itself a *mitzvah*, to blow it a terrifying responsibility, to hear its cry an awesome challenge which year by year made him shiver.

An air of self-congratulation hovered about Daniel's neighbours instead of the anxiety of a few minutes before. Two rows ahead he could see the shawled shape of Simon Rotblatt visibly relax. In middle age Simon had become quite *frum*; a true adherent, who paid well for his better view. It was a sentiment Daniel did not share as he watched Reverend Siegel mount the podium and adjust his robes, ready to deliver his sermon.

Through the high windows the September sun slanted in. One side of the synagogue soon became warm and stuffy. The wood of the pews where the sun lingered turned hot to the touch. Upstairs women in their best hats and the latest fashions fanned themselves discreetly and passed around a bottle of lavender water. A fly buzzed lazily at a window. Daniel could see Maurice Feinstein squint against the light and try to shift away from its merciless passage but without success. Above them Morrie's new girlfriend in a ridiculous bit of millinery dabbed her throat with a lace handkerchief.

'My dear friends. Our New Year has begun. For two days we do as our forefathers commanded, as it is written: *And in the seventh month, on the first day of the month, ye shall have a holy convocation; ye shall do no servile work; it shall be a day of blowing the horn unto you.* And again, *Blow ye the trumpet on the new moon, in the time appointed, on our solemn feast-day. For it is a statute for Israel, an ordinance of the God of Jacob.*'

Daniel half smiled as he saw Siegel raise his head from his notes to reclaim the attention of his flock. *No servile work*: so all Jewish-owned shops and businesses were closed, as was his own, their proprietors united in worship. About him a muted hum of conversation had risen and fallen then rose again, never sufficient to be intrusive. They had heard every syllable so many times before. The text was lifted straight from Leviticus, Numbers and Judges. Identical hallowed phrases had been uttered in every Jewish gathering including the Temple in Jerusalem since time immemorial. '*When the trumpet is blown, hear ye!*' Isaiah had thundered. They heard, though avoiding their Minister's direct gaze, but on the whole they heeded not.

'*Happy is the people that knoweth the sound of the trumpet.*' Daniel smiled to himself. Siegel with his rounded voice, those guttural vowels, was finding his stride. '*In the light of thy countenance, o Lord, shall they walk. In thy Name shall they rejoice and in their righteousness shall they be exalted. For thou art the glory of their strength, and in their favour shall our horn be exalted.*'

Daniel did not feel exalted. Not yet, anyway. And he dreaded Yom Kippur itself in ten days' time. From dusk to dusk nothing whatever could then pass his lips, not even a drink. Throughout waking hours he would feel absolutely and devastatingly *hungry*. The entire day would be spent in the synagogue, in this seat, supposedly in prayer. *In the seventh month on the tenth day of the month, ye shall afflict yourselves.* By late afternoon he would be faint and tired. Only the sick could be excused, their reasons discussed in ghoulish whispers as they shuffled out.

By the end of the drawn-out festival, despite his refusal to believe a single word of the whole mumbo-jumbo, both body and spirit (if that was what it was) would be wearied and knocked about as if pummelled in a boxing match. And yet: he had to admit that some years, if the fast were easy, he came to its end curiously calm and refreshed. The pious believed that during the Ten Days of Atonement God was near, as if He hovered invisible in the synagogue's dusty air. For Daniel that was altogether too close to the transubstantiation of the Catholics. If he felt light-headed, that was hardly surprising. If virtuous, perhaps it was merely the self-discipline, the knowledge that he could still do it, wasn't too decrepit just yet. In this year of grace, decreed by the rabbis as 5,724 since the creation of the world, Daniel Majinsky asked for no great uplift. He would be thankful for a cigarette and his dinner on the table when it was over.

And perhaps the prayers did some good. If God existed, then He might be taking notes. If not, no harm was done. So Daniel, like most of his acquaintance, attended without fail and insisted on the whole family's appearance together in their finery. The observance had serious purpose: partly to show off to friends and customers, but mainly to demonstrate solidarity. Even had he hated every second he would not have put the community at a disadvantage by not turning up. The more swollen the numbers the better. Should the synagogues ever empty the community would die.

But he did not hate it. Daniel stretched out his painful leg and tried to ease the cramped muscle. Best to concentrate on something outside his own body: then its aches were endurable. The service was too extended, of course, but that was because of repetitions of the good bits as well as a heap of tedious material and poor poetry that could have been discarded. No one in centuries had had the authority to delete any-thing, so it kept getting longer.

Much of it was superb: beautiful psalms and phrases, reminders of the sages who had toiled over them in aeons gone by. *O remember us on this Day of Memorial to vouchsafe unto us a life of happiness and of peace.* The choir was lovely to listen to, and of a far higher standard since women had been admitted. His daughter Helen had been one of the first; more recently she had pleaded pressure of school work and he had not made a fuss. The mixed choir meant that the most Orthodox rabbis refused to attend this synagogue. That suited Daniel, as he guessed it did most of his fellow members. The pliant Reverend Siegel, with his cheery manner, affection for humankind and lack of diplomas was far more endurable as a sermoniser than some narrow-minded bigot with a chewed-up beard and an impenetrable accent.

'The reason we sound the shofar,' Reverend Siegel was explaining, 'apart from the injunctions from our forefathers was best set out by the Rambam, Maimonides. *"Awake, ye slumberers from your sleep, and rouse you from your lethargy. Make search into your deed and turn in repentance. Remember your Creator, ye who forget truth in the trifles of the hour, who go astray all your years after vain illusions which can neither profit nor deliver. Look to your souls and mend your ways and your actions: let every one of you leave his evil path and his unworthy purpose."'*

Somewhere at the back where the sun had left an overheated corner a slumped figure emitted a slow, complacent snore. Simon Rotblatt twisted around to chide but the soft rumble continued. Daniel suppressed a

chuckle. A man with a clear conscience, no doubt: an object more of
envy than disapproval.

But what of himself – had he 'gone astray after vain illusions' or anything else? Daniel pondered. In the Rambam's terms the answer must be
yes. He did not attend services regularly – indeed hardly ever other than
for High Holydays and official rituals such as Barry's barmitzvah. To do
so more frequently would have bored him, since his lack of belief
offered no hope of salvation.

Bizarre, this. An atheist slouched in a synagogue pew on a sunny
weekday morning under the interminable flow of a learned sermon,
contemplating with a twinge of unease his own lack of grace. Daniel
had no guilt about his atheism nor had he tried to reconvince himself,
not since his youth. It stood to reason. The existence of the world was
a random event, controlled by no great intelligence but by sheer chance.
Darwin's description of a universe in which the winners wrote history
was unanswerable, bleak but accurate. That fly and its somnolent buzz
were an accident. There was no eternal or spiritual life, only this one.

Hedging one's bets a little, Daniel reflected. If he were mistaken and
God really existed, he'd find out soon enough; any God worth believing in would forgive an honest disbeliever. He found it impossible to
accept the more lurid warnings of hellfire or punishment after death.
What would be the point? How could such punishment be an effective
deterrent unless one knew for certain it was on the agenda? In the
absence of such knowledge, the God that punished a man who had
behaved honourably but agnostically was vindictive, and not worthy of
worship.

A vengeful Old Testament God who wreaked havoc for any misdemeanour or slight was to be derided. An indifferent God was to be
despised and best ignored. The Catholics' convolutions over original sin
and the temptations of Satan seemed to him laughable nonsense, based
on panic about women and sex. They had allowed their theology to be
captured in its earliest days by a bunch of mystics and misogynists. The
Church of England, so pragmatic, so earnest, was the more admirable,
yet it lacked fervour as if it doubted its own compromises. Not that
Daniel would have been remotely interested in conversion. Religious rituals served mainly to identify the tribe. He knew which tribe he
belonged to.

Let the ignorant round the globe placate their jealous deities. Let
them create their Gods in their own image, their frailties and inconsis-
tencies writ large. Let them pray for their desires and needs, and sing
hallelujah! when some small trifle came their way: if nothing happened
they'd go on praying. That kept priests in hot dinners, an outcome to
which he had only the mildest objection.

Daniel shifted. The pain would not go. His atheism drew strength
from more than science. No merciful God would have permitted the

Shoa, but no other kind of God was credible. No mighty super-spirit was needed to create the Hitler regime, nor the Cossacks and their pogroms, nor the myriad persecutions and cruelties of one man against another. Human beings were quite capable of dreaming up such atrocities all by themselves.

Yet his conscience did chafe, try as he might to ignore it. He *had* gone astray – or at least, he had a nagging awareness that he had lost his way. Let himself down, somehow. Long ago. Not so long that, if he tried, he might remember, and in so doing either take steps to put things right, or failing that at least to comprehend, and to calm that inward ache.

What was it? Once he had been a fiery young man. He had campaigned to change the world; his dreams had been of politics, of a public career, of offering leadership albeit in a small way to comrades and workmates. All that had faded, but he could not remember how or why. Somewhere along the line he had given up. That had been his overweening sin. These days the question for himself was whether he could be bothered even to think the matter through again; or whether, like the slumberer in the corner, it mightn't be easier and safer to drift oblivious through the rest of his life to its close.

Maybe the children would do better. Helen especially. She was so smart and had such chances. Daniel wriggled his shoulders stiffly under the prayer shawl. Barry was not a problem; a lazy personality, he would readily fit into whatever grooves his fate pre-determined for him. But Helen: Helen was more like himself, the way he used to be when he was young. She questioned everything and was not satisfied with terse answers. With touching innocence she read widely and strove to create a philosophy of life for herself – much as he had done, though she, armed with a better education and teachers from both the religious and secular worlds, had already travelled far further intellectually than he had been able to. And she operated in an environment far more conducive to originality and personal quest. The sixties were turning into a decade when nothing was sacred. That'd suit Helen, though instinctively his daughter would be wary of excess. God, how he envied her.

Let her go, then. Let her go, and bless her, whatever path she chose to follow. Let her go, and wish secretly that you could go too.

No, that could not be. Fatherhood demanded a different approach. Annie was right, when she expressed fears about the child's recklessness. Whatever one believed about the faith, the synagogue and its trappings, the fact remained that they offered a coherent way of life which brought stability and joy – yes, joy – into the lives of its adherents. And it was undeniable that if girls like Helen departed – whether by conviction or, God forbid, intermarriage – what remained could be fatally weakened. Not at once of course, but in a couple of generations. Survival of the fittest, it would be, and Judaism could be amongst the fallen. If everybody of quality left, the Jews could vanish from Europe.

Hitler's work would have been completed. That couldn't be allowed to happen. Helen had to see that. She had to be made to see.

That ache again. What was it – remorse? Disillusion? No – something stronger. Anger with himself, for wishing to deny his daughter the opportunities he had lacked, and for trying to rationalise that refusal. Anger with the uncompromising faith, its absolutes and arbitrariness: though piety without rules and rituals was a void that could give no absolution. Impotent fury, that he could accept the strictures and duties of parenthood without putting foremost the one that mattered most: to love your children as yourself, and to want what they wanted.

But just as he had chosen to stay – or had been persuaded to, all those years ago – so he would oblige Helen to do the same. Her responsibilities were identical to his own. She could attend a local university if she insisted but otherwise must remain in the fold. There could be no more argument.

Siegel was wagging a finger. Ten days stretched ahead in which to rewrite their fate before the Day of Atonement, *Yom Kippur*. The metaphor was severely, intensely precise: on high surrounded by angelic advisers the divine Judge held three scrolls of paper on which he was busily writing names – on the first, those who would survive another year, on the second, those who would definitely perish, and on the third those for whom no decision had yet been taken, depending on whether they truly repented their sins against God and man:

> *On the first day of the year it is inscribed, and on the Day of Atonement the decree is sealed,*
> *– how many shall pass away and how many shall be born;*
> *– who shall live and who shall die, who at the measure of man's days and who before it;*
> *– who shall perish by fire and who by water, who by the sword, who by wild beasts, who by hunger and who by plague, who by strangling and who by stoning;*
> *– who shall have rest and who shall go wandering, who shall be tranquil and who shall be harassed, who shall be at ease and who shall be afflicted;*
> *– who shall become poor and who shall wax rich;*
> *– who shall be brought low and who shall be praised.*

The worshippers rose to their feet, tugged prayer shawls closer, avoided the eyes of those nearby who might not make it till next year and crooned the response:

'Ooseshoovah, oosephilah, ootzedokah,

– *By penitence, prayer and good deeds shall you avert the dread decree.*'

*

Michael heard the shofar as he entered the mail room. It emerged as a strangulated squeak from the wall loudspeaker which was tuned to the American Forces network. As a mark of respect the transistor radio had been switched off.

He stood quietly until its ululations ceased. Shorty the mailman jerked a thumb at the wall as the horn's wail was replaced by sonorous chants and the hushed tones of a commentator.

'Creepy, ain't it? Not my kinda trumpet call. Gives me goose flesh up my spine. Gimme a tuneful Christian hymn any day.'

'That's because of the way we were brought up. I find it scary, I must say – like I'd recognise it when I get to the pearly gates, quaking in my shoes and wishing I'd been a better boy my whole life.' Michael smiled but spoke awkwardly. It was not in him to mock another religion. 'Any mail for me?'

Shorty turned his back as he reached for the contents of Michael's pigeonhole. 'Me, I think religion should be about praise and brotherly love. You should come outta church on Sunday morning happy and thanking God for being alive on this earth. That's why that Harlem gospel music is so fine: despite their hardships the Negroes still love the Lord.'

Michael flicked through his post. A letter from Helen, with her distinctive hand – the safest way for them to communicate when they could not see each other. He grinned at Shorty. 'You a regular churchgoer, then? I've not seen you at service on base.'

The man laughed without rancour. 'Hell, no. Maybe when I get older like my Paw and a bit closer to meeting St Peter. But for the moment, if it's Sunday, it's either on duty or off; and if it's off, then I stay in bed. Free will, man, can't beat it.'

Michael strolled away but as soon as he was out of sight he sat down on a box and tore open Helen's letter.

He could not phone her at home. That had taken some getting used to; in the States it would have been the natural mode of communication. The wealthier girls there had their own phone in their bedrooms and could drive a guy wild with dirty talk in low whispers when their mothers assumed they were writing essays for school. Occasionally she could phone him or leave a message if an arrangement had to be altered, but he knew she had to put on her coat and find a call-box, with the worry she might be spotted and questions asked. Nor could he write to her direct at her address: her mother would promptly interrogate her and demand to read the letter. Instead when necessary he could leave notes for her at the Post Office near the school. It was all so scrappy, and not what he'd been accustomed to.

After a few moments' reading his eyes widened in delight. She would slip away from the synagogue that afternoon, if he could possibly meet her. At the far end of Calderstones Park, under the trees. It was walking distance from both her home and the synagogue: she dared not risk a bus ride on such a day. It would be peaceful and quiet and they could talk, though not much else.

Michael smiled to himself, stuffed the letter back in its envelope and headed with renewed purpose towards the gatehouse.

Back in the vestry Reverend Siegel and the young ordinand disrobed and chatted as they hung up their white silk garments and velvet hats and placed black *yarmulkahs* on their heads.

'White,' commented the Minister. 'I can never make up my mind about it. White for a wedding, maybe. We bring in the New Year like a bride. But I'm more comfortable in my usual purple – that's a colour for princes and priests.'

'White for the sepulchre, for the shroud,' the young man intoned. 'To remind the faithful that the Day of Atonement approaches, that some will be condemned if they do not repent.'

What a comfort you are, Siegel reflected, but he kept it to himself.

The visitor combed his hair and beard with his fingers. On holy days it was unlawful to carry a comb. 'You were the most senior man present today?' he asked. 'No rabbi?' Siegel nodded and explained about the mixed choir. He wondered what was coming.

'I heard it was more than that,' the young man muttered. 'The *Jewish Chronicle* says there's been quite a row in this part of Liverpool. The Rabbi and the ecclesiastical court have banned kosher caterers from the new Liberal synagogue hall just up the road from here, isn't that so?'

Siegel nodded again, miserably.

'And some members of this congregation have opposed him?'

'That is correct. They take exception to the Beth Din dictating to them where they can and can't operate. Some of them are my subscribers, yes.'

'Dictating? Is that how you see it? But don't you agree that we must fight the Reform and Liberal movements? They represent the greatest danger Judaism faces. They undermine family life, and that's a fact. We must do whatever we can to eliminate them and to ensure that the Orthodox have nothing to do with them.'

'It seems so hard, that's all,' Siegel mumbled. 'My members hate it. And so do I. My fear is the ban is motivated at best by malice and at worst by a spirit of – well, I can only call it intolerance. Jew against Jew. It's terrible. And to be frank I find it impossible to set about preaching to my flock this line that the Liberal *schul* is a destroyer of Jewish family life. Not when the caterers are booked for *simchas* like weddings.'

The young man bridled. His scrawny chin jutted forward. The beard bobbed up and down in time with his strictures.

'Family life is Judaism's most sacred institution. The Liberal sect contributes daily to the destruction of the faith by permitting the admission of non-Jews after the most trifling of instruction. *Goyim* who want to marry our girls. And they allow it, instead of setting their face against intermarriage as we do in Orthodoxy.' He stuck his face into Siegel's. 'They encourage it. Intermarriage! Miscegenation, that's what it is. Disgusting. Bah!' And he went to spit on the floor, caught the Minister's look of alarm and desisted.

'But it's counter-productive. The Rabbi announces he doesn't want the Liberal synagogue hall to become a place where Jewish youth might meet. Then he blames the press if comments of that sort drive the younger generation away.'

'Your Liverpool Rabbi is absolutely right.' The visitor's voice rose. 'If we let our young girls and men slide away, there won't *be* a younger generation. Then where will Orthodoxy be?'

'But they're Jews,' Siegel persisted half-heartedly. 'I mean, have you met any? We're talking about them like they're minor functionaries of the Nazi party.'

'Of course I've met them,' the young priest retorted bluntly. His eyes had taken on a hard light. 'I have many friends among Liberals. But I would not like to say that some of my best friends are Liberals. Indeed not. Now what about lunch?'

'So: cast your sins away yet?'

Maurice Feinstein jumped. He should have turned smoothly, smiled and made some quip about not having committed any sins, or at least not yet. He should have gazed regally down from his greater height at Vera, then taken her hand in a gentlemanly fashion and walked her to a more secluded spot. They were officially engaged, or at least Sylvia told everyone so, though he could not recall having popped the question – not exactly.

They were in Calderstones Park on the afternoon of the first day of the New Year for the performance of *Tashlich*. Heaven knew where these myriad rituals came from but this one was less onerous than most. '*Thou wilt cast their sins into the depths of the sea*' instructed the prophet Micah, but the stricter rabbis warned that the ritual smelled of Kabbalah and magic. Didn't the ancient Greeks hold that rivers and pools were inhabited by pagan deities? Never mind; the shop was shut for the holy days so a stroll in the park with a little embarrassed shaking of the garments at the side of the lake accompanied by a frantic chorus from displaced ducks and a few psalms would pass an hour quite pleasantly. If only Vera hadn't decided to come too.

Every eye was on them. Feinstein groaned inwardly. Not that Vera disgraced him; on the contrary, she was smartly dressed in a cool fawn dress and jacket and had discarded the cartwheel hat which had so distracted him that morning in the synagogue. Moreover she had taken the hint and toned down the make-up: she was clearly doing her utmost to satisfy him. There was a womanly, ripe air about her which he found distinctly attractive, yet still terrifying.

He ought to be impressed and flattered but instead could not shake off a sense of oppression. As a couple they were supposed to be warm and romantic together, but he felt neither emotion and hadn't the foggiest idea how to fake. Yet a bubble of excitement rose in his throat when he saw her like this, and a twinge of pride that she was at his side. Might this be the start of love? The sight of her certainly made his body twitch inwardly. He found his hands moved independently as if wanting to touch her. It was an effort to keep them at his sides.

The couple strolled down the path to put distance between them and the Minister who had commenced a short service. A light breeze rippled the lake surface; the first fallen leaves skittered across their path. With delicacy she avoided the splodges of green slime deposited by the Canada geese. Unlike most females she seemed to have no fear of the big birds, or indeed of anything much. That both impressed and oppressed him further.

She squeezed his arm. 'You in *schul* tonight?'

'I ought to go, yes, though I've done my share of praying today.'

'You don't have to go.'

'What else would I do?'

'Oh, come on. Do I have to spell it out for you?'

He stopped dead. She snuggled up to him, in full view of the nearby throng. His mouth opened but no sound came out. He could feel his pulse beat suddenly faster.

'Maurice,' she wheedled, 'I know you're a bit uncertain. A woman like me can tell. You've been on your own ages, and you've got used to solitude. You've got used to something which isn't good for you. By that I mean, sleeping alone.'

He swallowed hard. Was this what it meant, a modern woman? Did they all talk like this? Wasn't he supposed to take the lead – with her demure and shrinking? Wasn't she at the least going to *pretend* it was new and mysterious to her? She'd never been married, after all. He felt shocked to the core, but the excitement rose once more.

He had his back to the crowd and could sense gimlet eyes directed at his shoulder blades. In his shadow, much smaller than he, Vera could not as easily be observed.

'Come on, Maurice,' she murmured. With a sly movement she brushed her hand across his thigh, then back again, slowly. He froze and stared down at her in horror. Her voice seemed to come from the top of her curled head.

'You've got what it takes, Maurice, I know you have. How about a trial run? No time like the present. Today. Tonight.'

Oh, God. He wanted to flee but everyone would see. If she carried on like that he'd have an erection in full view. Then even to walk would be a torture. 'Stoppit,' he hissed, and reluctantly she slid her hand away.

But he did not want to refuse. The skin where she had touched him glowed and tingled. Every hair on his arms and legs was aroused and he could feel with an astonishing intensity the weave of his suit move over his limbs. Darn it. She was so – what was the word? Sexy. Yes. Not the way his wife had been, so tiny, so pretty. Not the way of starlets in films, who sometimes made him lick his lips in the darkness. Not the way he'd imagined: in fact, come to think of it, he had never really put sex as one of his priorities when he had acquiesced in Sylvia's schemes. Yet that was now on offer from Vera, and it was clear from the flush on her cheek that she expected a speedy response.

'All right.' He sighed heavily.

'Great! When? Where? Your place or mine? My mother's away for the holiday with my Auntie Minnie. Your choice, *chéri*.'

'Not tonight.' He held up a hand at her pout.

She twirled away from him. 'I'm very good at it, Maurice. Your worries will vanish. You'll be ringing Reverend Siegel to book the *chuppah* –'

'Not tonight,' Maurice Feinstein repeated firmly. It took some adjustment; he would have to think more carefully about the entire project and its next steps. He took her elbow and steered her back towards the safety of the throng. The *Tashlich* ceremony appeared to be over. 'Maybe next weekend.'

From her expression Vera was about to object, so Feinstein bent and kissed her quickly on the lipsticked lips. She tried to entwine her arms round his neck but he stepped smartly back.

Then he forced himself. 'And I shall look forward to it, Vera. Yes. I really shall.'

I heard it as I hurried down the street. I paused in front of a shop selling televisions. Pye and Marconi, the dearest twenty guineas. In the window several sets were switched on to demonstrate. The biggest was twenty-four inches across – it looked as vast as a cinema screen up close. You could see the red and green dots if you pressed your face to the window pane. They flickered at you, and left your retinas dazzled.

One TV had a piece about the Jewish New Year. Through the glass if I listened hard I could hear snatches of somebody prattling on about sin and atonement. An old man with wispy grey hair, his head covered in a funny white shawl with navy edges, raised the horn and blew. The commentator said it did not have to be a sheep's horn, but it definitely couldn't be a cow's because of the Golden Calf which the Israelites worshipped as Moses descended the mountain, the Tablets of stone in his hands. Like it had only happened yesterday.

The old man was frail and everything about him seemed silvery and insubstantial. He had a dreamy air about him, but solemn, as if he believed he'd once glimpsed God. He looked as I imagine God must look. Pity nobody ever suggests that God could be female – that'd be blasphemous. Yet it'd be nicer when you prayed, sometimes. When you had to explain, or ask for guidance: there are lots of subjects you wouldn't broach with a man. And you'd always worry that a male God would take the man's point of view. That old bloke with the horn wouldn't understand: he'd probably be a bit deaf, or condemn me, like Father O'Connor. His eyes'd flash fire and he'd command me to behave and sin no more. Too late for that. Too late.

Miss Plumb said go to the doctor. She wasn't as on the ball as I'd hoped but she had a point. I couldn't go to my own doctor. Wouldn't have trusted him to deal with me straight, or to keep it to himself. The address was in the phone book. 'Family Planning Association', it said. I should have come earlier. 'Pregnancy testing'. Somebody at school told me they were all women doctors, and kind. Wouldn't yell at you or call you stupid or a whore.

I phoned. They told me to bring a sample taken early morning the moment I woke up, before breakfast. I had to wash out a jamjar with a lid. It was in my satchel. The whole day I was in a panic that somebody nosy would find it and make a fuss. Or that I'd drop it and smash it – the smell alone'd find me out. And why else would a girl be carting around a sample like that?

It was a lady doctor. She had gold hoop earrings and faint down on her upper lip, a dab of powder on her nose. She wore a white coat but loosely over a dress as if obliged to prove she's properly qualified. She had me on the examination couch and felt around a bit, though I winced when she went inside, and she apologised for her cold hands. I told her I'm eighteen. She didn't pester me about who it was. None of her business anyway. And given the result it doesn't make much difference.

'Your baby is well and healthy, as far as I can tell, Colette,' she said. I'd told her my correct name; no reason why not, now. She has motherly eyes with crows' feet as if when she's not at work in the clinic she laughs a lot. She probably has a pleasant life. Maybe she has a daughter my age. 'You're about four months gone. That means you should register soon at the maternity hospital – I can give you a note.'

I didn't say anything. She leaned forward but did not start to write. 'You ought to attend ante-natal classes, you know. It's not only the breathing exercises. They'll check your blood pressure and weight each time you go, and tell you about proper diet so that both you and baby will be strong. And how to feed and care for him afterwards. It doesn't come easily to any of us; motherhood has to be learned.'

Still I kept quiet. I couldn't think what to say. She and I might have been on different planets for all the sense she was making. My fault, not hers: I wasn't listening. I knew getting caught for a baby was a possibility, of course. But I could not wrap my head round what she had so calmly told me.

They're not daft, though. She waited a moment to see if I'm going to open my mouth, then very softly she spoke.

'Colette, you're not thinking of trying to get rid of it, are you? Because if you are, let me just make one or two points. Firstly it's strictly illegal. We do not permit abortion in this country – not yet, anyway. There are people in the back streets of Liverpool who would do the operation for money – struck-off doctors mostly, or old crones who claim to be midwives. They use dirty instruments and have no idea how to prevent infection. It is highly dangerous – I cannot over-exaggerate: one wrong poke and they'll perforate your bladder, or you'll haemorrhage till you have to be admitted to hospital as an emergency. We still lose women like that every year. Butchers. They never remove everything either. The number of women I've seen ripped to shreds internally – well, my dear, that's why I give two days a week to work here. I'd rather a thousand times you girls didn't get pregnant to begin with if you're not ready to have a baby and give it a good home.'

She talks about them as if they were puppies, I thought. I was numb.

'So: shall I give you a note for the hospital?' Her voice had become matter-of-fact once more.

I had to get out of there, so I nodded. She uncapped her pen and scribbled, glanced my way, found an envelope and put the note inside. The envelope had no mark on it, nothing to identify it. I took it and mumbled a word of thanks. She had done her best. It wasn't her fault. It wasn't her problem.

Outside in the street I walked down a block then stood there like an idiot for ages. The lady doctor, this time without her white coat, came out, got into a small car parked at the kerb and drove off. She didn't notice me with her envelope in my hand. She didn't toot her horn or wave. I might have been invisible.

I don't know what to do. I want to tear the letter up, and scream and shout, and yell to everybody: for God's sake, help me. Maybe I should go to this ante-natal clinic, but I know I won't – that's the last thing I'd do.

Yet I can't do nothing: the baby is there, and soon I'll begin to feel him. Once he kicks he'll be a person, not a condition. He'll talk to me in the night and keep me awake. Already he's a presence who insists on taking priority. I can't concentrate. That's why I fainted at the Philharmonic and made a fool of myself, but I told them it was 'flu, silly, and they accepted it.

Her and Miss Plumb. You'd think women would be easier to confide in, but not a bit of it. Nobody has any time. Nobody has any inkling. And for me, time is running out.

They met under the trees, in the shade of a gnarled oak which must have been two hundred years old, its craggy bark covered in ivy. She had chosen well: the spot was high up and airy. Figures could be seen in the distance on the far side of the lake, but here it was isolated, with the path a bit steep for casual strollers.

'Hi – thanks for coming.' As ever, Helen was slightly shy at their first contact. Michael bent and kissed her gently on the cheek, then guided her to a small hillock. He took off his leather jacket and they sat down on it, she with her legs curled under her.

'My,' he said, 'you do look smart.'

Helen was wearing a green woollen suit, its boxy jacket with a round Chanel neck and velvet trim, and a pretty blouse with a frill for the collar. New shoes, stockings, a pair of leather gloves completed the ensemble. No handbag: to carry anything was forbidden.

She smiled sheepishly. 'Best bib and tucker. I'm supposed to be a miniature version of my mother. Wouldn't it be wonderful if we kids could wear our own styles, and still be regarded as properly dressed? But no. My Dad offered to make me an outfit, but his always end up like a schoolmarm's. I persuaded them to let me buy this one in Blackler's.'

'I like you best in that gingham dress. Makes you look so cute – mouth-watering.' He ran his finger over her calf, up and down the fine stocking. She did not stop him.

'Not posh enough for today. It is the holiest day in the entire calendar, bar only the Day of Atonement next week.'

'Yeah, I heard the ram's horn. What a weird sound! Doesn't it make you tingle?'

She looked down. 'Oh, yes. It's a summons, and a reminder. To me it sounds like tears – all the murdered souls.' He raised her head in a now typical gesture, his finger under her chin, to make her gaze directly at him. He saw her eyes were moist.

'What is it, sweetheart?' His voice was gentle.

'Oh, Michael, what is to become of us? Here we are, skulking in a public place, nowhere to go. When I fell in love with you I thought you were – all right. Well, I thought you were Jewish. It was only afterwards

I discovered you weren't, but it doesn't stop me loving you, not a bit. In fact, it probably makes me want you all the more.' She stopped, confused, then continued in a lower voice so Michael had to strain to hear. 'I feel wicked at times, for defying my parents, and for lying to them. Mr Mannheim – my father's tailor – said I'd feel guilty and he is so right. Yet what else is there? I love you so much, and I'm certain you are worthy of that love. The more I know about you, the more sure I am of that.'

Michael took her hand and stroked it gently, then put her palm to his lips and kissed it. 'It is a struggle for me to understand too, Helen, and to come to terms with,' he responded. 'You are still so young, and your parents have their duty. I'm close to my own parents – especially my Pa. I can grasp very easily the value of responsible parenthood, and appreciate it. If your parents didn't care about you, they would lay down no rules, take no interest in your welfare. But they do.'

She was silent and he could see that her eyes were misty. 'Look at the dangers I pose, dear Miss Majinsky,' he spoke wryly. 'I'm a foreigner, scion of a foreign power, virtually – despite the friendly rhetoric – in occupation in your country. No doting father would welcome such a stranger. And I'm not from the faith, so I pose a double threat, though I can't say I admire such attitudes.'

'You're a man, that's the biggest problem,' Helen whispered. 'When I'm with you, I don't feel as if there's a five-year gap between us, but it's obvious from your – your size and appearance, that you're no kid, no pushover, and that my relationship with you must be an adult one.' A rueful laugh broke from her. 'I've often wondered what kind of man my Dad might prefer for me, but I've never been able to form a clear picture. If my chosen spouse were an accountant only interested in profit and loss, or a shy teacher, Dad would despise him at heart – he'd want me to marry a bigger, stronger personality. More like himself, I suppose – or as he was years ago. But if I picked a forceful character he'd fight, almost instinctively. He'd fight me being taken over by somebody else – by another man, by an equal.'

Michael frowned slightly. 'He'd not be the first father to love his daughter so much that nobody would be good enough for her. Those rivalries are well documented. And knowing you, sweet Helen, I can see perfectly why he should want the best for you. Here, come nearer.'

She curled herself at his side, with his arm about her. In the distance a small crowd had gathered at the lakeside and appeared to be throwing something in, together. She had forgotten about *Tashlich* when she sent the note, but she and Michael were too far away to be recognised. The dumpy figure in the black robe must be Reverend Siegel. To distract herself, she explained the ancient ceremony, which made Michael laugh out loud.

'Terrific, if it was that simple to cast our sins aside,' he chuckled.

'What a medieval religion you come from, Helen. Perform a little dance, and all is forgiven.'

'It's medieval in more ways than one. We skirt round it, Michael, but there is no way my parents would accept you. Not in a million years. Even if you converted, we wouldn't have a ghost of a chance. There are other Jewish groups like the Liberals and Reform who'd say fine, welcome in, brother. But not the Orthodox.'

'What'd happen, if . . .?' He left the question unfinished.

'We'd be ostracised. Not invited to anything. No contact of any kind, probably, if my parents' resolve held out. If we invited them, they wouldn't come. If we turned up, say, for someone's funeral, we'd get the cold shoulder from most people. They would not speak to us. Oh, one or two might, but they'd be a bit shame-faced about it, and would prefer it if we didn't show up. It'd be much the same if I appeared alone, to be honest. And heaven forbid if I had a child of a mixed marriage with me. They'd say how pretty she was, with regret in their voices.'

'My God.'

'They'd only be pleased if the marriage broke up and I returned to the fold. Then they could say, I told you so.'

'No, no.' He took her in his arms and rocked her, backwards and forwards. She wept on his shoulder and he felt the tears damp through his shirt.

'It is wrong, Helen,' he hissed, and held her away from him at arm's length. 'You do believe it's wrong, don't you?'

She nodded blindly. 'Of course I do. It's prejudice, pure and simple. In any rational discussion, you, Michael, or somebody like you, would be exactly what my parents would seek for me. But they're not on the same wavelength – you're anathema to them, and if I made a – a permanent liaison with you, I would be too.'

He breathed hard as he brought her into his embrace once more. Shorty's parting shot came back to him. 'Free will: we have free will in all of this. That is the Almighty's gift to us. We don't have to be cruel to other people. They don't have to be cruel to you, Helen. They could say – fine, that wouldn't be our first choice, but it's OK by us. Couldn't they?'

'They won't. Wouldn't.' He sensed that she did not want to trap him into any assumptions.

He grinned ruefully. 'Never in my life have I been rejected by anyone, for any reason. I guess I've always assumed a cool superiority to every person I've met. It sure feels odd to be on the receiving end of prejudice.' He peered down at her. 'So now I know how it feels to be discriminated against. And I do *not* like it.'

For answer she pressed her hand to his body, over his heart, and let him feel the warmth of her fingers.

He kissed her gently, on the lips. 'Oh my, Helen. All I want to do is make love to you, and hear your laughter in the same room. Never mind anyone or anything else.'

'Yes, I know.' They talked a while longer, then Helen rose to her feet and brushed down her skirt. 'I have to get back.'

'I'll walk a while with you: it's gone a bit breezy.' Michael put on his jacket. Side by side but not touching they headed for the far gates, the long way round to her house.

The tobacconist was on the corner. A gust of wind blew sweet wrappers out of a litter bin in their path. As they passed in front of the shop the door opened suddenly and a tall moustached man emerged and bumped into them. With a flustered apology he turned to face them.

'Dad!'

'Helen?'

'What are you doing here?' The girl stopped dead. Beside her Michael took a step back and stood, confused.

'Me? Oh, Lord. I was desperate for a smoke. If I went home for one your mother'd make a fuss. Don't say anything, will you?'

He had transgressed twice – not only in wanting to smoke, but in carrying money. That would have slightly shocked the younger Helen and should have amused her today, but her reactions were to start and cover her mouth. She struggled to recover control.

Her father had pulled out his lighter but was having trouble in the wind. Michael automatically stepped forward and offered the front flap of his jacket as shelter. The flame caught and Daniel puffed grate-fully for a minute. 'Thanks.' He offered the packet. 'Want one?'

'I don't smoke, no, thanks,' Michael said gravely.

Daniel looked from one to another. 'American? Don't I know you? I've seen you somewhere, haven't I?'

Helen intervened. 'Yes, I think so. This is Michael Levison, Dad, of the United States Air Force. He's one of the GIs who comes to Harold House. I think he was in the crowd in the Rembrandt the night we were there. With Aunt Gertie.' She emphasised the *Levison*, the first two Jewish-sounding syllables.

Her father was gazing in puzzlement at Michael's casual clothes. On this holy day his dress gave him away – as a non-observer, at the very least, or possibly worse. Helen heard alarm notes screaming in her ears. Michael was trying to take his cue from her, but as at the Rembrandt she shook her head imperceptibly at him.

Ostentatiously Michael checked his watch. 'Gotta get back to the base – I'm on call later tonight. It was good to bump into you again, Miss Majinsky. And to meet you, sir.' Formally and as coolly as he could, as if this were a chance acquaintance which did not matter to him, Michael shook hands with them both, then strode hastily away.

Helen quickly linked her arm with her father's and began to steer him in the direction of home. The still-glowing cigarette put Daniel at a disadvantage both moral and physical and he coughed once or twice.

'Slow down. I can't keep up with your young legs.' She obeyed and they strolled more casually. Fifty yards from their gate Daniel sucked greedily on the dying stub and threw it away. Then the puzzled expression returned and he looked back over his shoulder. Michael was nowhere to be seen.

'Who was that exactly, Helen? What did you say his name was?'

Chapter Eighteen

Fall

'God! My poor feet.'

'Mine too. D'you think anybody'll notice if I slip my shoes off?'

The plump solidities of Sylvia Bloom and her sister Rita Nixon collapsed gratefully into the chairs of Reece's elegant café. Carrier bags with the names of the city's most exclusive dress shops, crammed full, were deposited on a spare chair. The crystal vinegar bottle and condiments were pushed back, an ashtray found and Sylvia lit a cigarette.

'What'll it be, ladies?' The waitress trudged towards them and came to a halt, notepad ready. She would be about their age, Rita noted, though far more careworn. A wisp of frizzy hair escaped from under the lace cap and was pushed back.

'Tea, lots of it, and none of your teabags. And we'll see the cakes, please.'

Rita unfolded a new blouse from its tissue paper and held it up. 'Not bad for twenty-seven and eleven,' she remarked. She leaned forward. 'So come on, tell me. How was the conference in Blackpool? It looked a proper bellyful of laughs on the TV. Lord Hailsham ringing the bell and making a fool of himself . . .'

'Everybody made a fool of himself,' her sister answered crisply. 'Absolute shambles. I don't know what the party's coming to. Poor Mr Macmillan in hospital with his prostate. They couldn't wait till he'd resigned. Like ruddy performing seals. Now what have we got in his place? Lord Alec Douglas-Home, that's what. A blinking aristocrat. That'll go down well in the Dingle, and I don't think.'

'Mr Wilson's having a field day with him.' Rita mimicked the Labour leader's Yorkshire vowels. '"After 'alf a century of democratic advance the 'ole process has ground to a halt with a fourteenth Earl of Home."' She pronounced it correctly, Hume, with a drawn-out vowel, lips pushed forward.

'I liked the answer, though. "And I suppose Mr Wilson, when you come to think of it, is the fourteenth Mr Wilson."' Sylvia shook her head. 'But you're right. We Tories have taken leave of our senses. Anyone'd think it was still the nineteenth century when people tugged their forelocks as the nobility swept by. Those times have gone. But not in the upper echelons of the Conservative party.'

'It won't help in the elections.'

'It won't. I think Wilson'll win, God help us. End of an era.' Sylvia took a quick pull of her cigarette and left a ring of scarlet lipstick around its end. 'And you can see why: the working class used to vote Tory not out of deference so much, as because they believed a man should strive for himself and his kin, then keep the fruit of his labours. But look what goes on down the docks these days. Those as work hard are idiots. Power lies with the unions. The shop steward decides who's in a job, who's blacklisted, who's out on strike. So the ordinary bloke might as well vote Labour. No Tory government's going to face down the unions, is it? And if they won't nobody will.' She prodded her sister. 'You and me, we were brought up to graft. Gone out of fashion, it has. Specially in a dump like this.'

The two women poured their tea, chose two cakes each and concentrated on eating them without unduly scattering pastry crumbs and squirts of jam and cream over their clothes.

'Not everybody's doing badly,' Rita perked up. 'The Mersey Beat has put Liverpool back on the map. Roseanne keeps me informed. The Beatles are gear, she says. We have to "get with it".'

'Saw them on TV on *Sunday Night at the Palladium*,' Sylvia sniffed. 'Not impressed. They're held up as a collection of lovable mop-tops but they're only four scruffy yobs – or were, till Brian Epstein got his hands on them. Did you see the photos of his wedding to Barbara Matteson in the *Echo*? There's a man with style. Next they're going to be on the Royal Variety Performance, God save us. I hope they behave in front of the Queen and Queen Mother. If they act cheeky it'll shame us all.'

'Roseanne wants to leave school and follow them round. Apparently some girls queue the whole night for tickets for their concerts. Then when they're inside all they do is scream their heads off. You can't hear a thing. So why go, I asked her – why not stay home and listen to their records? Because they're fab, Mum, she says, and acts like she's about to swoon. Teenagers! I'm sure we were never like that.'

'Not even over Mario Lanza?'

'No,' Rita answered firmly.

The roomy café, on a corner in the centre of town, was quiet after the lunchtime rush. The waitress sidled back, her raised eyebrows questing for additional orders. She rested her weight on one foot and nodded in vigorous agreement. 'The time and money that goes into their antics. I wish somebody'd devote a fraction of it to looking after us poor housewives. Did you see that chap from MANWEB warned there'll be electricity cuts on Christmas Day if everyone cooks their turkeys at the same time? Country's short of power stations. Do 'em the night before, he suggested. Disgusting, I call it.'

Sylvia was about to demur that since she and her sister were Jewish they were not affected, then thought better of it. 'I have a gas cooker,' she smiled instead.

'That'll make it worse,' the waitress added darkly as she began to clear plates. 'It said in the *Echo* that it'll take seven years to replace the gas lamps still in use in Liverpool with electric light. You'd think they'd leave 'em, if we're so short of power? And now they want to build a Channel tunnel. Mad, the lot of them.'

The sisters looked at each other, bewildered but intrigued. Reece's staff were always friendly. It occurred to Rita that had life not been so kind she too might have found herself in a waitress's pinny and pair of battered shoes with a fund of inconsequential remarks.

'Cost a fortune, they say.' Sylvia showed off her knowledge as a man would. 'Nearly a hundred and fifty millions. But cheaper than a bridge. If our government and the French were to decide to go ahead, it could be open by 1970.'

The waitress shuddered. Her arms were full of crockery but her audience sensed that otherwise they would be waved dismissively. 'Ugh! Who wants it? The place'd be full of dirty foreigners in no time. And rabid dogs and what have you. No thanks. We're an island, and we should stay that way.'

The woman had become so heated Rita feared for the dishes. 'I shouldn't worry,' she counselled. 'They'll never do it.' She slipped a sixpence under her saucer.

'I should darned well hope not. Thank you, ladies. Pay at the till.'

'It's not fair. I wish we could vote.' Brenda folded the *Daily Telegraph* with care. As the newly appointed Head Girl of the school she had first claim to read it.

'If Mr Wilson wins, he says he'll give votes to eighteen-year-olds.' This from Meg, who as deputy was next in line for the paper.

'A purely cynical move,' replied Brenda loftily. 'He thinks young people are more likely to vote for him than for the other lot, that's all.'

'He may have a point.' Meg had succeeded in sliding the newspaper from under Brenda's fingers and started to read.

The girls lounged contentedly in the prefects' room, the inner sanctum of Blackburne House. A former parlour, it was comfortably if shabbily furnished with leather armchairs, a rug, bookshelves, a kettle and a gas ring. The gas fire glowed. A toasting fork with blackened crust burnt on to its prongs rested against the fender. On the table a bunch of Michaelmas daisies wilted in water in an old milk bottle. The style, had they but known it, resembled the study of an elderly academic but the atmosphere was more like a gentleman's club. The room was out of bounds to all but the most senior pupils. Even staff would knock and pause before entry.

Brenda put the kettle on the ring, lit the gas and busied herself making two mugs of instant coffee. 'No milk left. It'll have to be Marvel.' She stirred the dried powder into the hot liquid and sipped. 'Ugh, tastes horrible.'

The door opened. Helen Majinsky stood on the threshold, a brown envelope in her hand. Her eyes shone and a grin was spread over her features; her whole body seemed to dance.

'You've got an offer,' Brenda guessed. As Helen nodded happily, Brenda whooped and punched the air in triumph. Generous of spirit, she was instantly delighted.

'It came this morning. Manchester, two Bs, for chemistry.'

'Not bad. You'll get that easily.' It was not their style to hug but Brenda handed over her own coffee and began to make a third.

'The next Marie Curie, then?' Meg meant to tease but as ever the sharp edge of her voice lent sourness to her words.

'I doubt it.' Helen held the mug in both hands and drank. 'Thanks. It's freezing out. I was beginning to worry that I wouldn't hear. It's no great shakes though. I'd have to live with an uncle and aunt. And they are *frum* – I mean, religious. No staying in hall for me, nor out all night either.' She pulled a face. 'Glad I've caught up with you two. You've got your place in Leeds, Bren, and both Liverpool and Manchester want Meg.'

'White heat of the technological revolution, that's us!' Brenda laughed. 'Did you read Mr Wilson's speech? We're in the frame, girls, as scientists. Gonna change the world, us. Watch!'

The three giggled together, but each felt the frisson of pleasure that their endeavours had been so recognised. Chemists might not be as flashy as those who would read English Literature or French nor as dull as the mathematicians. Nevertheless it was resented when their choice of study was derided. Mr Wilson's emphasis on science as the necessary foundation of the nation's future had notably elevated their position in the school and enhanced their confidence in themselves.

'Has Colette had any offers yet?' Helen inquired.

Brenda shrugged. 'If she has, she hasn't said. She'll get in on Miss Plumb's say-so, even if her results aren't brilliant.'

'I'm sorry she wasn't made a prefect.' Helen straightened her prefect's girdle, the blue, green and gold braided belt which was a precious possession. 'I think Miss Plumb made a mistake. It would have given Colette a boost.'

Brenda frowned. 'You can't have a prefect who keeps missing school. We have to set an example. Colette's horrible family stand in the way, too.'

Helen met her eyes briefly for a moment, then dropped them. There had been comment in the corridors as to why Helen herself had not been made Head Girl or deputy but it was generally recognised that, as with Colette, her family background made her not quite suitable.

Some instinct made Helen persist. 'I am terribly worried about Colette. I tried to get her to confide the day of the prizegiving – we went to the Cavern but we couldn't get in. She wouldn't budge: not a word. I take your point about our duties to school, Bren, but as a gang we have obligations to each other.'

Brenda pursed her lips. 'Well, maybe,' she conceded. 'But what the hell action can we take? If a girl makes up her mind that she's going to give up, there's not much we can say to stop her. After all she'd be in the majority. *Most* kids give up, especially girls. It's a few nuts like us that keep going, and to be frank we need every scrap of our energies to succeed.'

'I don't think it's like that. Something's holding her back. Left alone she'd be here with us – in fact she'd be beating us hands down like last year. Something's *wrong* – I can feel it in my bones.'

'It probably *is* that horrible family of hers,' Meg persisted. 'She's inherited her slackness from them.'

'I know what: I'll take the homework round to her place tonight,' Helen resolved. 'It's not much of a detour. At least I'll have satisfied my own conscience. She was my best friend, once.'

Brenda indicated the envelope. 'What about you? You must start putting yourself first, Helen. You'll still do the Oxbridge exams?'

'It'd mean a battle royal with my parents if I got in.'

'Rot. If Oxford or Cambridge makes you an offer they won't prevent you. It's beforehand they apply the pressure. They want you to stay put and be just like them: that's perfectly normal. But if you made it quite plain that you're off, there's nothing whatever they can do. You'll get a full grant, yes? So it won't cost them a penny.'

'That's true. But that's not the issue.'

'You should prance around saying to yourself, *I'll show 'em. I'll show 'em I'm the best. And that they were foolish to try and deter me.* Make your parents proud of you and they can't say no.'

'They are frightened for me – my mother especially. And they can't see that while I'm – apprehensive – I'm not frightened one bit. At any rate, not of what scares them.'

Brenda looked puzzled. 'What do you mean?'

Helen put down the mug. 'Oh, they think I'll face a lot of prejudice out there, away from home. I might, but it doesn't worry me much: I wouldn't value the opinion of anybody who spoke disparagingly of Jews or anybody else. Then they're petrified I'll break with the faith. They don't see that's likely anyway.' She stopped dead, conscious that she had said too much.

Meg pounced. 'You going to stop being Jewish? You planning to convert? What to?'

Helen shook her head. Brenda became gently protective. 'This American boyfriend got something to do with it, Helen?'

Helen glanced at her friends in anguish. 'For heaven's sake, don't say a word. My parents don't know. About him, I mean.'

A glance passed between the other two.

'You should aim seriously for Cambridge,' Brenda suggested quietly. 'Lots of US bases in that part of the country. He could be posted there, then you could kill two – no, three – birds with one stone: leave home, get an education and see him in safety. A million miles from prying eyes.'

The three were silent for a moment then Meg started to laugh. 'God, that reminds me. Last year I was in the Cavern when the Beatles were on stage. John's Aunty Mimi hadn't known what he was up to and she barged in and tried to drag him out. Mrs Harrison – George's mum – was in the audience and she tells Mimi, Aren't they great? And Mimi yells back that she's glad someone thinks so. The two of them nearly came to blows. If Mimi'd had her way there'd be no Beatles. She still doesn't think what John's up to is respectable.'

'There's your justification, Helen.' Brenda assumed a magisterial manner. 'If you follow your parents' wishes you'll never get anywhere. Time to take your leave of them. With or without your Michael.'

Helen rose slowly. Her earlier jubilation had vanished. 'Possibly. Possibly not. I'll go and tell Miss Plumb about the offer.'

Outside in the corridor she found herself breathing fast. Never before had she admitted to anyone other than Michael himself that her intentions were straying so far beyond the everyday and mundane. With Michael the talk of going away had felt like daydreams, the romantic notions that lovers share; aired with her schoolfriends the flight was in danger of becoming a reality. Decisions would be upon her soon.

Helen halted. She wondered if she were quite as brave as she pretended. When the clash came she would have to draw on every ounce of her courage. Untested, she had no idea how strong or weak she might be. It would be much easier to give in and respect her parents' wishes, if only superficially. Most young Jewish kids did precisely that. In time the rebellion dissipated itself. In time they became strictly conventional parents themselves.

Out of the corridor window the sky had silvered; rain threatened. The Mersey's far shore had disappeared in mist from which the tops of the tallest cranes emerged. Ragged trees in the street below bent tiredly against the wind as their leaves skittered into the gutter. Somebody had vandalised one thin birch which whipped forlornly about. As she watched, a small boy tugged at a broken branch in an effort to dislodge it; defeated, he kicked at the trunk then ran off.

'A penny for them, Helen?'

'Miss Plumb. I'm sorry, I didn't hear you.'

'That is self-evident.' The headmistress joined her and gazed out. 'I must admit, I will miss Blackburne House. On the other hand, it may not be here to miss for much longer.'

The girl turned in surprise. 'You are leaving—?'

'Hush. Not announced yet. I was approached in a manner that would enable me to return to my roots in Kent. An independent grammar school. It seemed appropriate for me, as I should wish to retire to that area eventually.' Miss Plumb's veiled expression suggested she was not telling the whole story. Helen wondered whether the offer had come quite out of the blue or had been engineered by Miss Plumb herself. Perhaps the teacher had simply applied for a job she had seen advertised? But that would be too prosaic for Miss Plumb. Words must have been exchanged, hints dropped. That was how it was done.

'About time,' Miss Plumb elaborated. 'In the nick of time, I suspect. This school, its brother institution and St Paul's secondary modern school are to merge as a single comprehensive, if the Council proceeds as proposed. Selective entry will be abolished in this city. You're the last of a species, my dear. I'm afraid it also leaves little room for the likes of me.'

'I wish I could understand why they're doing it.' Helen traced a finger sadly on the window. 'This school has meant so much for over a century. I mean, it's helped people like me most, from ordinary backgrounds, hasn't it? My parents could never afford fees for private tuition. But selective schools give clever working-class children a serious chance.'

'Yes: the chance to better themselves, and leave their class behind,' Miss Plumb translated coolly. 'That's why the Philistines mean to destroy us.'

'But . . .' Helen struggled. The teacher waited patiently and did not interrupt. 'I mean, if I better myself, and can train for work which requires qualifications, everyone's better off. The most ignorant and ill-educated societies are also the poorest. Aren't they?'

'It doesn't follow, of course, that the wealthiest societies are the most liberal: America proves that,' Miss Plumb said dryly. 'But you are correct, Helen. Poverty and democracy make uneasy bedfellows. The richer a nation the more effectively it can both satisfy its people and play its part on the world stage.' She patted the girl on the shoulder. 'And you can play your part too.'

'I hope so.' The girl showed the envelope. 'I was on my way to tell you. An offer from Manchester. Honours, chemistry.'

'Splendid. No more than I would expect. But hang on till Oxbridge. You will be called for examination and interview. Your name has been aired, Helen. Don't let me down.'

The girl turned away. 'I'm going to pop into Colette's tonight on the way from school. To see if – anything's up. She's been so peculiar lately.'

The headmistress said nothing for a moment. Then, 'I feel it ought to be my job: but if I knocked on their door they'd regard that as blatant interference. Better one of her friends. Thank you, Helen: I'm not surprised it's you.'

I didn't go to school today. I couldn't face them.

The letter came two days ago to say I could go to Birmingham if I get two As and a B. Set my grades higher than everybody else's. Doubts about whether I'll stick at it, probably. No mother, broken home, council flat. It's not right: they should make allowances, not raise the barriers. Pull up the drawbridge, the hoi polloi are in sight. What is the world coming to when scruffs like Colette O'Brien can go to university?

Except that it won't happen. Not unless I get my grades. The way I am now it'll take a miracle to finish the term.

He was at it again last night. I cried and told him he was hurting me, to get off. But he just pulled back a little and said he'd forgotten to open me up properly. After he finished there was blood and I hoped I might lose it. God forgive me, I wanted to lose my baby. That'd have been quick, and he wouldn't have guessed. He was legless as usual.

I can't tell him. If he knew he'd make damn sure I'd lose it. It's not difficult. He'd rub my belly till he found the spot: you can feel quite a lump now, low down. That means it's a boy, they say.

Then he'd pull his good arm back and give me a real thump. He doesn't go to work much but he's got plenty of muscle. One blow'd be enough. Hard as he could, just the once. He'd say it was for my own benefit. He wouldn't think about it. He'd probably swear a bit if I screamed then say he was sorry.

I am ashamed that I didn't answer Helen's questions. She was simply trying to be a pal. What could I say – that I'm expecting, and what's inside me is my half-brother? That his dad is my dad? That my father's grandchild is my son? What kind of information is that to land on your best friend, a girl from a nice family?

That's the heart of it: he's my Dad. They'd put him in prison. First they'd make me go into the court and tell the whole world. And who would be believed? They'd call me a temptress and get it twisted. I'm his flesh and blood – I couldn't do that. He can't help it. He declares he loves me, and maybe he does in his own strange way. He says I remind him of my Mum when he first

met her, when she was beautiful, before she cleared off. Anyway
it's probably my fault, somewhere, though I don't know how.
I am so scared. God in Heaven. What is going to happen?
What is to become of me? And my baby?

The doorbell rang. Colette started, then scrabbled about to hide the exercise book. The bell rang again. Outside it was getting dark. Beyond the balcony starlings and gulls wheeled noisily, seeking roosts for the night. Soon it would be time to cook her father's supper.

The two girls stared at each other across the threshold.

'Helen! What on earth are you doing here?'

'Colette – I wasn't sure you'd be home –'

'Well, you'd better come in.'

The flat was dire. There was no other word for it, Helen thought grimly. The fact that it was ten floors up was disorientating and felt unnatural. But the heaps of dirty clothes on the floor over which she had to step, the frowsty odour of unwashed sheets from the bedrooms, the chill, the stink from the toilet, all announced an ill-kempt home which turned her stomach.

Helen held out the folder. 'I brought some work you missed.'

'Thanks.' Colette led the way into the kitchen which had the advantage of warmth. She took the folder and glanced through it, then pushed away half a loaf and the bread-knife and put it down on the kitchen table amongst the crumbs.

Helen waited. Her stance, solid and dependable, suggested she was not willing to go yet. Wearily Colette motioned her to a chair but did not offer refreshment.

Helen gestured. 'Who looks after you here?'

'I do, when I can. I haven't been too bright lately so it's a bit neglected. As you can see I'll never make the world's best housewife.'

'What about your brothers?'

'Them? Not here much now they've both got girlfriends. But if they were they wouldn't do a stroke. Women's work, they'd snort. It's me and my Dad on our own.' The pinched face turned towards the fluttering above the balcony. 'You get used to it, you know. When I get totally fed up I talk to the birds.' Her voice trailed away.

'You ready to talk to me yet, Colette?' Helen's tone was full of concern.

'I can't. I'm sorry. I know you think I'm brushing you off. It's not that way.'

'Do you need help?'

'Oh, Christ.' Colette pushed a lock of hair out of her eyes. Helen could see swollen lids as if she had been crying.

'There's help available. Nobody wants you to quit school. You're clever, Colette. You'll do that homework in half the time it takes the rest of us. You'll get into college. You can leave this behind and start afresh.'

'Not any more. My brain has got completely addled. I'm no good for anything.'

'Don't talk bilge!' Helen bit her lip. 'I may be out of my depth here, Colette, but I sense that something's going on. I know what it's like to be leaned on. I know what it's like to have to keep secrets – my parents don't know anything about Michael and I'm not going to tell them. Not yet, anyway. I've got to approach our Minister to get some ideas sorted out in my own mind first. Is that the kind of problem you've got?'

'Wish it were.' For the second time, as she had in Lewis's, Colette refused to meet her friend's eye. Yet an explanation was owed and both girls knew it.

'What is happening is too – too bad to tell, and it's mostly my own fault,' Colette whispered. 'I can't explain – you'll have to take my word for it. It's far worse than you and Michael. I don't think any decent people would believe me. I'm quite sure they wouldn't accept my version of events, and it's a ghastly muddle anyhow. So I can't say anything.'

Helen's expression showed she was completely mystified. Colette tried again. 'If I speak it'll mean my family breaks up and my Dad'll go to prison. I don't want that.'

'Your Dad's a bit of a bastard, from what you've said of him before,' Helen countered bluntly. 'You might be better off without him. You wouldn't be put into a home, you're past the age. What have you got to lose?'

'Everything. You don't understand.'

Helen frowned. 'You're right. I don't. But I'm worried about you, Colette. So are Meg and Brenda at school – well, Brenda is. And Miss Plumb. She wants the best for us.'

'Miss Plumb?' Colette snorted, then slumped in her chair. 'Oh, sure, she wants what's best for us. But her own little world is so limited, she can't see an inch beyond it.' Helen began to demur but Colette waved her away. Her next comments, seemingly disjointed, were spoken in so low a tone that Helen had to strain to hear. 'He loves me, see, my Dad. Whatever he's – doing, it's because he loves me. So I can't point the finger at him, can I?'

Helen sighed and rose to leave. 'I bet that means your Dad's up to no good. Stealing, maybe – or stolen property, though from the state of this flat, if you don't mind me saying so, precious little money's found its way back here. I smell criminal action and I don't like it. But we can't solve your worries, Colette, if you keep refusing help. Got enough of my own on my plate right now, and that's the truth.'

'But – thanks for trying.'

Helen waited, but there was no more. She stepped over a pile of grubby laundry, hesitated, took one more lingering glance about her, and left.

For a while Colette occupied Helen's thoughts on the bus home. It certainly looked as if the flat were being used for some kind of nefarious activity, which Colette knew about but did not participate in. Given the casual attitude of her relatives to legality it could be almost anything; the fact that Christmas was soon suggested that a lorry hijack might be in the offing, with cartons of drink and cigarettes to be stored in the bedrooms until they could be off-loaded in local pubs. Colette could have been blackmailed into acquiescence – relatively easily, Helen reckoned grimly, since she would accept the prevailing attitudes towards a sneak. Perhaps the theft had already occurred, in which case inviting Helen inside was a considerable risk. So probably not: whatever was on the O'Brien agenda was still in the future.

It wasn't man trouble. That was the easiest thing in the world to share with your mates. Helen had allowed her friends to grasp that she and Michael were intimate, and that it was wonderful, but had drawn a veil over the details. It meant, however, that she would have been a suitable recipient for confidences about sex – if someone were plaguing Colette, for example, or if the girl had a crush on a bloke. Yet when the straight question was put Colette had declared that she had no boyfriend and Helen saw no reason to doubt her statement.

Nor could it simply be worries about school. Colette knew how smart she was. In any discussion, her originality and discernment drew astonished comments from both friends and teachers. When she was ignorant she would know it, and say so, and absorb the missing information rapidly without need of repetition. She was cleverer than Helen and hit the mark more often and more accurately. She was also modest, and generous with her own understanding.

Yet the pressures on her were to fail. Brenda had commented shrewdly. Most girls didn't bother to stay on, let alone go to college; though at age eleven they were as able as boys, sometimes more so, by school-leaving age of fifteen they had slipped far back and evinced no further interest in education. Girls would claim they couldn't see the point since success for their sex meant the catch of a suitable husband, as if he were a fish on a line. That resulted, as Helen's mother often muttered, in a belief that clever girls – openly clever girls – were at a big disadvantage. The image of an intelligent woman was – was rather like Miss Plumb: condemned to be single, considered to be sexless, repellent to men who in the end ruled the world.

Helen felt she had the inner strength to resist such influences, as had Brenda. Meg would relish challenging them, and would find other models. But Colette had a greater burden, for bred in her, from the poorest sort of home, and a broken home at that, was the desire not merely *not* to succeed, *not* to stand out, but something far more devastating: the desire to fail.

'We all want to conform to those around us,' Helen murmured to herself. 'It's instinctive camouflage – nobody likes to stand out. But in that block of flats and hundreds like it, in the disgusting lifts which don't work and the landings which are never swept, in blocked toilets and stained hallways, the silent voices expect disaster as the norm. Poor Colette. If she doesn't fight it – if she doesn't stand up and scream her head off – then those voices will overwhelm her. And we will see her no more.'

Michael would call it 'dropping out'. But Helen, thinking of that dreadful tenement whose odour clung evilly to her clothes, preferred a different metaphor. 'Falling off the edge' would be a better description entirely.

She grieved for her friend. But as the bus passed her house she squared her shoulders. She had decided to stay on two more stops. Another interview, as tricky as that with Colette, as significant as those for Oxbridge, loomed. It could be put off no longer.

Cautiously Helen opened the main door to the synagogue. With classes in train she had expected to find Reverend Siegel in his office, but his wife said he was pottering about inside.

It felt odd to stand where she was not normally permitted to be. The chamber was bigger than it appeared from the gallery yet more ordinary, as if its magic disappeared without the devotees, the opened Ark, the glitter and lights and prayers.

'Ah! Helen. Come in, come in. You wanted to see me?'

Hesitantly she entered. The door closed on its spring hinge behind her, nearly trapping her fingers.

'Good, good.' The Minister had been counting prayer books, but straightened happily at the interruption. 'Sit, sit.' He motioned to a pew.

'That's my Uncle Simon's seat,' Helen indicated. 'D'you think he'd mind?'

'Of course not. Don't be so foolish. Sit. Have you come to discuss Chanukah? I want a big show this year. Lots of children. D'you think it'd impress if we dress the babies themselves as candles? They are the lights of the future and –'

'I can't help you with Chanukah. In fact I won't be able to help you much more.'

The two sat side by side on the front row, fifty yards from the Holy of Holies, shut and curtained. Something in her tone made the Minister turn and gaze at her.

'You are busy, Helen. Exams coming up. Such burdens they put on you – and a girl, too.'

Helen bridled. She had had no idea how to commence the conversation stored in her mind, but this would serve. 'I think girls should be educated. Don't you?'

'Oh, I do, I do,' the Reverend agreed energetically. 'The sages declare that an educated woman is an educated family. That was how they justified women learning in societies which frowned on the practice.'

'I'd like to learn for myself, not only for my utility to my future offspring.' Helen was startled at how bitter, unintentionally, the remark sounded. 'I want to earn my own living,' she added hastily. 'That's how I'd prefer to be useful.'

'No plans to marry a rich man, then?' Siegel teased, then realised that Helen was upset. 'Come, then, tell me. What's the matter?'

The girl shook her head wearily. 'I don't know. Or rather I do. I feel lost – like a piece of jetsam, cast off from a ship as it passes. Not sinking, not drowning, exactly. Not likely to. But without direction.'

Siegel looked at her shrewdly. 'You surprise me. You always seem to know exactly what you're doing, Helen, plus what you intend to do next. Isn't that the case? Didn't I hear you have a place at university for next year? The community will be very proud of you if you get in, and with reason.' He touched her arm.

'My parents aren't keen. They keep arguing that it's so tough out there.'

'Why, so it is. But you're perfectly capable, like thousands of others. And you know it. That's not what's eating you, Helen.'

She glanced at him sidelong. 'You will be angry with me.'

'For heaven's sake! What are you about to say to me?'

'I don't know.' She could not raise her eyes to him, this sweet-natured wise man, her teacher. Her first teacher: as an infant she had herself been one of the Purim and Chanukah babies. Miss Plumb and those on her side – secular teachers, from a different, newer, dominant culture – had increasingly taken over, especially once Helen had turned eleven. There had come a moment about then, or soon after, when her honest questioning had begun and she had become reluctant to accept what she was told without further inquiry. The struggle in her soul came in part from that conflict, but more so from the contrast in moral values held out to her. Yet if she owed anyone outside her family for her early acquisition of a moral sense, she owed Reverend Siegel.

Best to blurt it out. The two of them could take it from there. Otherwise she ran the risk of sounding as confused and dense as Colette, the worst situation possible.

'Please, why are Jewish people so opposed to intermarriage? I could understand if we were reluctant, if we discouraged it. I could accept the prohibition if we insisted on conversion as the Catholics do, and that children be brought up correctly. But we act as if God has been insulted when a Jew marries a non-Jew. Yet of all the peoples of this earth, we know how dangerous and insane racial discrimination is. Why do we practise it?'

Siegel looked at her, and placed a finger under her chin in an effort to raise her face to his. But she resisted and kept her eyes lowered. She felt rather than saw his weight shift between one tubby thigh and another, hands clasped loosely in his lap.

She continued, 'I could understand if we proselytised – if we went out for converts. There's so much that's superb in our religion – as in most religions, I suppose – but we have the benefit of thousands of years of ethics, poetry, history. Some of mankind's finest philosophers and writers have the same blood in their veins as I do. But we make no attempt to persuade people to join us, and those that might, we deter. I don't get it.'

Siegel sighed heavily. 'You put your finger on it a moment ago,' he said slowly. 'Blood. It's to do with blood – the imperative that like is mated with like. Other people, however worthy, are not of our race. We court danger when we match like with unlike. God told Noah to bring in the animals two by two, each with its mate. It is not for us to play God and mix them up.'

'The science of genetics would say that a little judicious intermixing was very sensible,' Helen answered severely. Miss Plumb had said that once in a discussion on Darwin. 'Too close is incestuous. And too close a community can lead to imbecility and sterility. Of ideas, I mean,' she added hastily.

'Don't start me on science – you know I can't compete with you, my brilliant girl.' Siegel glanced towards the Ark as if for inspiration. 'Look: we have in this synagogue, in these prayer books, a precious inheritance. You know this – in fact you know more about it than most of my flock. Judaism has survived aeons of oppression. Hitler tried to wipe us out. Ferdinand and Isabella tried the same. The year Columbus discovered America the Jews were expelled from Spain: the flower of European civilisation was made to pack its bags and leave. And the Cossacks and Czar Alexander – they don't bear description. What would you do, Helen – complete their hellish task for them?'

'What do you mean?'

'Think about it. If we allow outsiders to be brought in we dilute the blood – and in so doing, inevitably, dilute the culture. That's already going on, in the Liberal and Reform *schuls*. They're so liberated, Helen, they're hardly Jews any more. Their practices make them barely distinguishable from any other of the god-forsaken wishy-washy lost souls outside. And don't forget, that's what *kashruth* and the other taboos and *mitzvahs* are for: to keep us separate. Otherwise why bother? But dilute the blood, or do away with the rituals, and there's nothing much left.'

'Nothing? Not the insights of Maimonides, nor the politics of Marx, nor the music of Mendelssohn? The great men other people mention with reverence? Or the vision of a Theodor Herzl, say?'

Siegel's eyes narrowed. 'Herzl – you thinking of emigration to Israel, is that it? They don't go in for observance much there, that's true. A secular socialist state is what they set up. Well, the Diaspora's main reason for existence is to give support to the new state – to return is what we're charged to do. I'd be a bit surprised if it'd suit you, but if that's in your mind, get your degree first and go later. You'll be more value to them then.'

Helen allowed her gaze to follow the Minister's towards the Ark, then around the synagogue, so familiar, so homely. 'No, not Israel. That's not the answer. I am British, and I feel it. If I left this country, it wouldn't be for Tel Aviv, I'm afraid.'

She turned at last and faced him. A decision had been taken; she would not mention Michael. He had been a catalyst, but she would have come to this stage sooner or later by herself. 'I feel I am being pushed out,' she said. 'I loathe racialism. I abhor discrimination of every kind. It's not only intermarriage, it's the way we treat everybody, in everything we do. Only one sort of person counts with us: ourselves. But I'd like everyone to have the same chances and be treated the same. And I am simply not prepared to practise discrimination in my own life, not in any way. I feel increasingly at odds and out of place in a society which promotes racial separation as a central tenet. In Christianity they don't.'

Siegel's mouth had fallen open. Now he closed it again with a snap. 'If you're arguing that Christian societies don't practise racialism, you're on another planet,' he answered. 'The Russian Orthodox are the worst, but they all do it. What about Alabama and Mississippi this summer? It's ingrained in human nature, Helen, fear of what's different. At least we recognise that fact.'

'But Christianity outlaws it, on principle. Thou shalt love thy neighbour as thyself. This is the first commandment.' Helen took a deep breath. Both knew she was quoting a forbidden part of the scriptures. She must change tack quickly. It would not do to promote a competitor while sitting in a synagogue. That had happened too often in past decades, as rabbis were tortured in back rooms and adherents died in the streets, in the name of God.

'What I can't swallow is that we promulgate it, on principle. If I planned to marry somebody not born a Jew of a Jewish mother, two things would follow. First, everyone'd do their damnedest to dissuade me, and put the guy off by their unpleasantness if he showed his face. Including you, I'm afraid. Then, if that failed, they'd cut me off, wouldn't they? Shove me out the door and slam it behind me. Never darken this threshold again.' She let herself sound angry, but could sense herself trembling.

'That's so,' Siegel answered slowly. 'I would try to dissuade you, yes. But you know why, Helen. If we allow wholesale assimilation the faith will disappear.'

'And if we don't permit any, it'll start disappearing anyhow, because people like me will leave, whether we marry out or not.'

Siegel stood up. '*Gott in Himmel*! What am I hearing? Jews survived where most other small nations perished, because when faced with persecution we knuckled down and refused to convert. Exactly that.'

Helen bit her lip. The last thing she wanted was to hurt him: yet she had embarked on the altercation and desperately needed to conclude it to her own satisfaction, if not to his.

'The outside world would make people like me very welcome. If I were to marry out, I could anticipate that my new husband's family might find it in their hearts to welcome me. There'd certainly be a huge contrast between their attitudes and my family's in reverse, wouldn't there? Even if some of the Christians felt antagonism, they'd believe they had to conquer it. We don't. We regard it as a virtue to reject a non-Jewish partner, however honourable and decent he might be. And I hate it. I hate it!'

Suddenly the strain was too much and she burst into tears. For several moments the Minister let her cry, then fished in his trouser pocket and brought out a large but slightly used handkerchief, which Helen accepted with a wry smile.

'Sorry,' she muttered and wiped her eyes and face. Then she shook her head as if to free herself of pain, and continued. 'I remember what Mr Mannheim once said when he told me about his fiancée in Nazi Germany. He couldn't get her to see that it was unacceptable to live under a regime which divided people up into Aryans and the rest. It made racialism the law, see? To him it didn't matter whether they were likely to be victims or not – it was simply *wrong*, and a dreadful place to be. If she'd taken any notice, she'd have escaped. She'd have walked away from it.'

'You are being very hard, you know.' Siegel kept his voice mild. 'Jews have fought racialism throughout the world. In the front line.'

'Then why do we practise it? Oh, I can't go over it again. I keep going back to this same question, over and over. I do *not* accept it, and I will not live by it.'

Siegel put his hand on her head, as if he would bless her. His dispute with the young ordinand came back to him forcibly, and silenced him. His hand fell to his side. Helen rose, tears still in her eyes.

'And I suspect I'm not the only one, though most young people won't agonise quite so much about it. Why should they? They'll drift away, find somebody nice to marry, and be lost.'

'If you're right, the religion will shrink. I hope to God that won't occur. Samuel Butler once said you can do very little with faith, but you can do nothing without it. All the creeds are facing the same problem,

Helen. People have stopped believing – in God, in the power of prayer, in the strength of a community if it acts together. They don't see the weakness of the individual. They don't see the emptiness within, if there is no faith, no moral code. Where the religious life is suppressed – as in the Soviet Union or Poland – it flourishes underground as a symbol of resistance. Like ours did, I suppose. But take away the pressure and what is left? Only kindness, and we can suffocate in that in no time without even realising.'

'But I have faith,' answered Helen simply, as she moved to go. 'More than my father, I suspect. It simply doesn't involve choosing my friends on the basis of *their* parentage. And if that means that eventually I have to part company with the people I love, who raised me –'

Her mentor, his face grey and drained, leaned on the door as if physically to prevent her exit.

'You will do Hitler's work for him,' he repeated sombrely. 'After what we have gone through, you can simply turn your back on us? You can deny your heritage? What is it – you are ashamed of being a Jew? I hoped never to hear it, Helen. Not from you.'

'I am not ashamed. But you must not try to – to blackmail me, sir. What Germany did was terrible. But it cannot be undone. Nothing I do with my future can bring six million murdered people back. But they mustn't be – be resurrected from the grave, to prevent the next generation living a normal life. Otherwise we are all victims and it'll never end. Mr Mannheim wouldn't want that, nor would his dead wife, I am certain.'

She had no idea where the words came from; words of an unfamiliar maturity which drew on some unknown inner source. Her absorption of Michael's attitudes which so chimed with her own, and of the vocabulary that helped her articulate them, accounted for some part. Or perhaps, she pondered later, they originated from the faintest of spirits, which floated in the synagogue's dusty air and whispered through her.

'You must not allow the dead to imprison us,' she said softly but stubbornly. 'You must not permit our enemies and those who would exterminate us to make us hate in the same way. We forget how many other men and women sacrificed their lives to make this world free. And in my freedom, sir, I prefer to live in friendship with others – all of them, as far as they will allow: Jews and non-Jews alike.'

With a quietly determined move she reached past Reverend Siegel for the door handle, turned it, and went out.

He sat for a long time in the unlit chamber, a tubby man in a black silk robe, his head bowed and eye-sockets dark. Helen was not the first, nor would she be the last, to express such sentiments. If the rumours he had heard were true, her father Daniel Majinsky must once have felt the same. The difference was that persuasion had brought the one back into the flock, but the other, he feared, was rapidly moving away, beyond redemption or return.

Chapter Nineteen

Autumn Leaves

'See, the geese are flying.'

Annie dried her hands on her pinny and pointed out of the kitchen window. It was Friday morning, early, a crisp bright day, with the pink flush of dawn still in the sky. She turned to her daughter. 'Canada geese. You see them in Calderstones Park. Savage creatures – they'll bite your arm if you get too close. They're off home.'

Helen stood with her mother for a moment, munched a piece of toast and watched the arrowhead formation winging its way west. 'Thank goodness we don't have to do that.'

'It's in their natures. Every autumn I watch them and each year I'm reminded of when I was carrying you. You were such a big baby, and so reluctant to come into the world. Now look at you.'

Helen stopped in mid-bite and blinked at her mother. So seldom were expressions of affection uttered in the Majinsky household that Annie's remark was startling, yet it created a moment of danger. Helen sensed that if she stayed the conversation would revert quickly to the unwisdom of her leaving. She would rather not put up with it any more; the tension and pain of the bitter argument with Reverend Siegel was sufficient.

She swallowed and quickly washed her buttery fingers under the kitchen tap. 'Must run, or I'll be late. If there's any post for me, don't open it, will you?'

'Would I do that?' Annie called after her, as Helen pulled on her duffel coat.

'Wouldn't you just, Mum,' Helen murmured but kept the reflection to herself. 'You'd apologise afterwards and say it was a mistake, that you thought it was for you. You still don't see your children as separate people, entitled to a life of their own. And to their own secrets.'

It was to prove a strange morning. Though outwardly composed she was restless and unhappy. After the confrontation with Siegel she felt drained; so many questions remained unasked, yet the Minister, good man that he was, had answered her all too effectively.

Nor could she get Colette out of her mind. Her heart yearned to find a way to cheer and support her, but first her friend had to want that too. Colette appeared briefly at school but did not speak to Helen. The visit to the O'Brien flat had not worked; instead of rapprochement Helen felt estranged and a little cross. Out of her depth, she had said, and it was apparent from Colette's stony expression that whatever murky world the Irish girl moved in now, Helen's presence was not desired. To be rejected when she was trying to be kind was hurtful. She would not be so bold again.

For months Helen had envisaged a parting of the ways as still to come – a crossroads to be approached with the greatest care, but not as yet reached. It had to be faced, however, that her own journey had already taken a unique direction, whatever might happen about the university places.

She, Helen, was not the same person as her three friends. In fact, apart from attending the same school they did not have much in common. She and Colette had been closest; both came from immigrant families, both knew themselves to be outsiders. Both had emerged from an intense, erratic religious environment laced with arbitrary rules – whether 'fish on Friday', or 'no milk and meat together' – outside the English mainstream. Whereas Brenda, Meg and Miss Plumb could assert that *of course* they were British, for Colette and herself that identity was something to ponder. And if they stayed in Britain, it would be a matter of choice, not a matter of course.

She had met very little prejudice in her life. There had been the occasional remark – Brenda's casual pity of her at the beginning of the year, Miss Plumb's description of her religion last month as inconvenient. But the headmistress had obviously regretted the sneer immediately and would guard her tongue in future. Most of the barriers Helen would face would not be over her faith or race but over her gender. It would be far tougher to make progress as an ambitious woman than as a Jew. There hovered in the recesses of her mind the suspicion that coming from Liverpool might also prove a handicap, but for the moment it was hard to judge in what circumstances.

If her parents and the Minister were to be believed, the absence of anti-semitism she had met was sheer luck and could reverse at any time. Her riposte to Siegel had been that it was not luck but the culture of a Christian country which advocated tolerance and compassion. She had offended him sorely by her implication that any philosophy could be finer than his own, but that could not be helped.

The person to whom she felt closest was Michael: how bizarre, for he was a foreigner in every sense. Her community would never accept him: never. As she set up apparatus in the lab for the afternoon's double lesson her scientist's mind turned the issue over, and she smiled quietly to herself.

Scientific method, as followed since Isaac Newton's day, was to fix as many variables as possible then systematically change one and measure what resulted in the others. That enabled the identification of the basic laws of nature – the relationship between heat and volume, between pressure and boiling points, the regular stuff she had absorbed for her exams and could reproduce virtually in her sleep.

So what were the variables for Michael? A father might object to his daughter's choice on the grounds that the man was unsuitable. A layabout, for example. Or unlikely to earn a living. Or unstable, one who might leave her in the lurch holding a baby with no visible means of support. Or a drinker, or gambler. Even she might hesitate if a boyfriend revealed such weaknesses.

As far as she knew, however, those variables were not in play in the case of Michael R. Levison. Indeed his prospects financially and socially were, as far as she knew, far better than her own family's.

That made him more, not less, of a challenge. Her father could not object to him on any grounds that might be persuasive. Had any such been present, she would not have met Michael again, nor fallen in love with him. Perhaps she had inherited some of her mother's cautious nature. There were similarities between the two men – their independent pattern of thought, their directness, their strong characters and dignified sense of justice. Were Daniel to permit himself to meet Michael properly and get to know him, he'd recognise those fine qualities which Helen had originally learned to respect in her father. The comparison made the rejection much more painful. For only one characteristic remained on which her father could or would try to deny her her choice: Michael was a Christian, and therefore taboo.

'A full-blooded Christian, no less,' she reminded herself. 'And strong enough not to be deterred by opposition. Not one jot.'

It was wise to stay well in with her parents. Not merely out of self-interest, for the time being, but because it was the right thing to do. Michael would approve; had she had a row with her family without good cause he would have rebuked her, even if sympathetic. The self-discipline of holding her tongue applied as much to herself as it did to Miss Plumb. Reverend Siegel was different, because he was a serious thinker and equipped to respond to the heart-searching of his flock. But her family she should treat as she wished to be treated by them, at any rate for as long as it was possible.

She resolved to spend her brief lunchtime with Daniel in his workshop. A little courtesy never went amiss and she still loved her father even though she increasingly felt distanced from him. As she climbed the stairs to the showroom she heard voices; Daniel was in the throes of measuring a customer.

It was Maurice Feinstein. Helen stared from one to another. Maurice turned away shyly, clearly embarrassed.

'Arm up, Morrie,' her father urged. 'Bend it at right-angles. That's it, then I can get the outside arm measurement. Now relax – don't hold yourself in. Your trousers need to be comfortable. That's better. Belt or braces? I recommend both –'

'The only spare time I could get,' Maurice justified, too loudly. He must have left Nellie McCauley in charge.

Helen grinned at him. 'New suit?'

'Correct,' Daniel answered for his client. 'At last one of my bridge partners has realised that Burton the Tailors' off-the-peg outfits do not satisfy every need. He's chosen a splendid piece of worsted. Suitable for a wedding, hey, Morrie?'

Daniel bent to measure the inside leg and took rather long about it while Maurice wriggled and blushed. Helen's grin widened. 'Mazeltov. Is it the lady we saw on Rosh Hashanah in *schul*? I loved her hat. She was certainly making eyes at you.'

'Nothing's settled yet,' Maurice grunted defensively. 'I simply needed a decent suit. Vera nags me about what I wear.'

The two Majinskys exchanged amused glances. Helen strolled about pretending to admire while the hapless grocer was held and twirled by her father.

'It wouldn't have bothered Nellie,' Helen commented mischievously.

'Nellie?'

'Nellie. At the delicatessen. Don't you see her mooning over you sometimes? She adores you for what you are, Mr Feinstein sir, not for what you wear.'

Feinstein gulped and opened his mouth to reply, but Daniel swished at his daughter with the tape measure. 'Don't be cheeky. If you want a sandwich they're in the box on my desk. And if you're free at four-thirty I can give you a lift.'

Helen complied, pleased that the teasing had lifted her own spirits somewhat. As she walked back to school she saw she had gone a trifle too far: but she had worked in the shop on Sundays now for several years, and concluded that it would do no harm if Mr Feinstein realised someone else held a candle for him. It might make him less hasty about this Vera, who seemed a great deal more artificial than the dependable and friendly Nellie.

Though perhaps Mr Feinstein already knew, more than he might be willing to admit.

Later that day and back at the shop Nellie McCauley could be found grumbling angrily to herself. She had so chewed the end of her pencil that bits of sodden wood had disintegrated from it into her mouth. With a sigh she spat them out and wiped her lips on the back of her hand.

The accounts were a nuclear disaster zone. It had not been her intention to spend Friday afternoon after Mr Feinstein had vanished and the shop closed in a titanic struggle to disentangle them, but her conscience would not permit the disarray to continue.

An element of self-protection drove her. She it was who took the brunt of rows over money. It was all very well Mr Feinstein being so distracted. Bills had not been paid for ages; creditors had begun to show up furiously waving bits of paper. Some were genuine, some not. When he couldn't hide he'd pay the most persistent, who might not be the most needy or urgent. Nellie feared the message'd get round. Soon the demands would come from the Inland Revenue: then where would they be?

She had provided herself with a half-bottle of Polish vodka and a tin of Jaffa juice out of the shop to keep her going, but the first taste of the strong liquor had brought Pete vividly to mind and she had put it to one side. What she had meant to do was pack. The air tickets lay in their glossy blue folder before her on the table, a reminder of the wonderful fresh start which awaited her. Which she had chosen, and which soon would be hers.

It was getting dark; Nellie rose and switched on the lights, then cut herself a hunk of cheese. This job could take all night.

The Spanish sunshine alone would make the move worthwhile. She loved the sun, on her shoulders, on her bare back. The sun didn't shine much in Britain so resorts were full of things to do and places indoors to eat. In Spain people ate outside, even in the evening. During daytime in summer it was so hot everyone stopped what they were doing and curled up for a snooze. Siesta, the Spanish word. Would she have to learn the language? But it sounded like heaven.

Nellie grunted. That was probably precisely what Mr Feinstein was up to right now: curled up in bed. Not upstairs in his own bed, where he had a right to be. He was with his snooty lady friend in Queen's Drive, the house he'd probably move to when the pair of them were wed. The mother was away. He'd been dropping boyish hints this morning about how he was to spend the weekend. 'Sorting things out', he called it, with a roguish wink to the male customers present. The atmosphere at times had been like one of those French farces. Nudge, nudge. God, what schoolboys they were. Ridiculous, grown men fooling around like that. Then he'd gone off to town, and not reappeared since.

Nellie began to add up a long column of numbers, her lips moving. Halfway down the pencil lead broke and with an oath she resharpened it and tried again. Three times she computed and three times a fresh answer emerged. For a long few seconds Nellie stared at the paper without seeing a single digit.

Then she pushed away the unfinished orange juice, folded her arms on the untidy piles of paper and pencil shavings, laid down her peroxide head, and wept.

In the car on the way home Helen and her father were quiet but companionable. Daniel switched on the heater and their feet soon gently toasted. The low roar allowed them to sit silent but content when conversation languished.

'D'you think Maurice Feinstein will marry this lady, Dad?'

'God knows. If she has her way, yes, from what I hear of her. It was set up by the matchmaker, you know, so he must be intending to get hitched again.'

'Crikey. But she doesn't strike me as right for him.'

Daniel shrugged. 'Not for us to say. Who knows what attracts a man to a woman or vice versa? But you shouldn't have mentioned his shop assistant. That wasn't fair.'

The car had stopped at traffic lights. Helen snuggled down into her duffel coat. 'Not suitable because she's a *shikse*, I suppose.' But her tone was wistful rather than strident.

'People have to be compatible. They should share the same values. All you've seen of – what'sername – Nellie – is the few hours you've spent helping out there. You've no idea what she gets up to, say, tonight. And neither has he.'

Above their heads the traffic lights winked. It occurred dimly to Helen that she might not get another chance of a private conversation with her father in this old amicable mode they used to take for granted. There was something she wanted to know.

'What about you, Dad? Would you ever have contemplated a *shikse* as a girlfriend?'

Daniel shot a side glance at her as they moved away from the junction. 'Good Lord. What prompted that?'

'I dunno. Came out of the blue.' That was true. 'I don't mean to pry. But might you have – before you were married, I mean?'

Her father seemed to be having trouble changing gears. 'Has my sister Gertie been spinning you tales, then? I was never a great romantic, Helen. My health wouldn't allow it.'

'Mm, I know. Mum says you courted her right through the war but you still needed a nudge to propose to her.'

Daniel chuckled. 'That's about it.'

'Is that why you didn't emigrate? Because you decided to get married and settle down here?'

'More or less. It might have been different, I suppose, if I'd met some dishy American Red Cross girl from a kosher family. But I didn't. So here I am, and here you are too.'

It was a subject better left. She sensed also that before long her father might quiz her on Michael: his curiosity had not been allayed and he seldom forgot. But before Helen could dream up a more anodyne topic her attention was caught by sudden rapid movements to her left, under a street lamp down a narrow side road. It was a mean, gloomy cul-de-sac with terraced houses crowded straight on to the pavement. Otherwise it was deserted. She stared hard, brow furrowed then quickly put her hand on her father's arm.

'Dad – stop a minute,' she commanded.

'What's up?' he asked, but complied and drew the car into the kerb. Behind them a lorry honked.

'Some kids and an old man – I think they're trying to rob him,' was all she could say as she opened the door and jumped out.

The man was small and dressed in a shabby black overcoat of an old-fashioned style, a muffler at his neck and a battered trilby hat insecure and crooked on his grey head. He had his back to Helen as she raced up, and was clutching the lamp-post to keep himself upright. Around him four or five scruffy boys aged around ten or twelve circled and yelled at him. One, the biggest, held a stick in his hand with which he prodded the bowed figure; another with a piebald mongrel on a lead urged it to snap at their victim.

'Go on, push off,' Helen shouted in her most authoritative manner. It worked with the roughest girls at school and these underfed mini-yobs were a lot smaller. Her heart pounded but she did not have time to think. She reached for one of the boys and hauled him fiercely to her by the neck of his pullover so that his feet dangled an inch above the ground. 'Does your mother know what you're up to? Clear off, or I'll take the stick to you myself. Get out of here.'

Reluctantly the boys pulled away, shouting obscenities, then ran off and disappeared around the corner chased by their own dog. A light went on in a window opposite and a woman could be seen banging on the window and shaking her fist at the fleeing children. Nobody emerged. The front doors remained shut tight.

Helen found herself sweating hard. She turned to the old man. 'You OK?' she asked. 'Do you live near here? Can I take you home?'

The hat slipped off and the figure raised its head.

'Yes, not far,' he began to reply, then stopped. 'Why, it's my *schöne mädchen*. Helen, is it not?'

'Mr Mannheim?'

It was. As she picked up the tailor's hat and gently took his arm he explained that he'd recently rented inexpensive rooms nearby, and that the boys had often taunted him but generally did no harm and eventually allowed him to go. But there was terror in the watery eyes, and he kept looking over his shoulder in an agitated way.

'Once I made the mistake of giving them some money, so now they expect it every time. Sometimes they ring my door bell and vanish before I can open it. They think it is funny,' he elaborated sadly.

'My Dad's here with the car. We're on our way home. Perhaps we can give you a lift. Or would you like to come to our house for some tea?' Helen felt sure her mother would repeat the invitation when the incident was described to her.

Mannheim hesitated then raised a finger and stroked her cheek. 'Knight in shining armour, eh? It would be churlish to refuse. If your father says so. Come, let us speak to him.'

Daniel had been forced to stay with the badly parked car but had speedily seen that the situation was not as dangerous as had first appeared, and that Helen was in control. In a moment Mr Mannheim was installed in the back seat and the Vauxhall had resumed its journey.

Daniel checked in the mirror and waited until his new passenger had closed his eyes. He nudged his daughter and whispered. 'You see, Helen? You think it's such a pleasant world out there, that Jews will find a welcome wherever they go. Well, it's not so. What happened in Nazi Germany could happen in Britain quite easily. You've just seen an example.'

A deep sigh came from the back seat. Helen twisted around anxiously. Mr Mannheim opened his eyes.

'No, no, Daniel. Don't get it wrong,' came the remonstration. 'Those boys did not chase me because I am a Jew. They don't care about that.' *Zey don't care about zat.* 'They chase me, they ring my doorbell, they try to make my life a misery, because I am a helpless old man. Because I am old. And that is far more terrible, do you not see?'

The envelope was there, ostentatiously placed by the telephone in the hall. A rectangular brown envelope with a prominent Oxford postmark. Helen touched it gingerly.

In the fuss over Mr Mannheim and the necessity to set an extra place, it was put aside. But as her mother asked for the incidents to be described for the fourth time and expressed once more her alarm that both of them might have been injured, Helen found the excuse she needed to leave the table.

'Mum, I didn't think. Like I said, there wasn't time. But if I had thought about it, I'd have done the same. I hope.'

And, she added under her breath, it wouldn't have mattered if it hadn't been Mr Mannheim. As far as she was aware when she went pelting down that street, it wasn't him, anyway – she didn't know that till afterwards. Her mother could not get her head round that: it would be family legend for ever more that Helen had spotted somebody she knew from *schul*, and that this was the entire explanation for her behaviour.

'It's over, Mum. Please leave it alone,' she protested as she pushed away her plate. 'I'm not a hero, but I'm not a fool either. If they'd been bigger than me I'd have yelled for the police. Now where's that letter?'

She took it upstairs, switched on the bedside light and sat down on the bed with it. Her fingers shook slightly and it took an effort to calm herself. Would it be an interview? Might she expect to travel to one of the oldest universities in the world, to sit at the table with their most eminent tutors, to meet their gaze levelly and show what she was made of?

It was a standard printed letter, that was immediately obvious. A cursory examination showed no inked-in words with dates and times. It was not personally addressed and had not been personally signed. She guessed its contents almost before she read the first line.

'Dear Candidate
Thank you for your recent application to this college. I regret to have to tell you ...'

A rejection. They did not want her at Oxford. They did not bother to ask to see her. They would not give her the ghost of a chance.

Maybe because she was too young: her seventeenth birthday was in a few days. Both Oxford and Cambridge expected applicants to be eighteen already and nearly nineteen on arrival for their first term. She knew nobody there, and nobody knew her. And there were so few places for girls, and a plethora of applicants, not only more mature but vastly abler than herself.

A cold sensation gripped her; an element of delayed shock, probably, from the confrontation with the street urchins. It would be sensible to go downstairs and drink some more tea. But not yet. She did not want to wallow in self-pity, but it would take a while to absorb the empty news.

Helen lay down on the bed and switched off the light. A sick feeling of dreadful disappointment and rejection seeped from the pit of her stomach. How she wished Michael were near to talk to. He would cheer her and hold her tight; he would remind her she was on the lists at other universities and could reasonably expect to take an honours course and complete a degree. 'Miss Helen Majinsky BSc' was still on the cards.

But her hopes of escape by this route were fading, it seemed. If she accepted her lowest offer, from Liverpool, then she'd still be sleeping in this same bed the day she took her finals; still jousting with her parents, still failing to make herself understood, especially by her mother. Still a child. She would have to apologise to Reverend Siegel and withdraw her criticisms. She would have to bite her lip whenever her father was around. Or else life would have become a permanent battleground of pain and anger, and that would have been intolerable.

The higher offer from Manchester carried much the same implications. Uncle Sammy and Uncle Abbie, her mother's younger brothers,

both lived there and would jostle for the right to house her for the duration. Both had married correctly; both as prominent businessmen kept
strictly kosher homes. Neither was as widely read even as her father.
Conversations over dinner in their establishments would be exceedingly limited. She would not merely be frustrated there, she would be
bored out of her mind.

What about staying in Hall? Out of the question in Liverpool, of
course; the grant for a local university would barely cover the bare
expenses of staying in her own home. And the row which would ensue
with the family if she suggested it in Manchester! She shut her eyes tight
and shuddered. She would have to take on not only her mother but two
uncles and their wives, all deeply hostile to the whole idea, who would
allege that she wished to ignore their hospitality and live in a tower
block of students so that she could stop eating kosher and misbehave in
other unnameable ways. Which would be precisely true, though she
would deny it vigorously. Everyone would be terribly upset, cut to the
quick, and they would go on about it. For ever.

And in those scenes there'd be no room for Michael: none at all.

There was still Cambridge. No news was good news. Next week
Miss Plumb might telephone her friend Dr Swanson and check privately if the rejections had gone out, and the dates set aside for
interviews. But Cambridge had fewer places for women than Oxford,
and was held to be less progressive. The odds were stacked against
her.

Cambridge, then, it had to be. That was her only hope. But it had
become alarmingly, terrifyingly, a slim one.

It was a mistake. Right from the start, Morrie Feinstein knew it.

Not that he was averse to trying. A little experimentation was fine; he
was prepared to be a modern man, or at least to do his best. And he was
a man, with few doubts about his virility. The existence of his son
proved that.

Nor did he jib at sex outside marriage – not if, as he argued to himself, it was truly sex *before* marriage – a trial marriage, you might say.
It was sensible to check whether he and Vera could get along, especially
in that particular field. Neither would be well served had they tied the
knot and it proved a disaster, too late. Divorce was still frowned on.

There was nothing unattractive about Vera: on the contrary, a great
deal about her appealed to him. She wouldn't be the perfect stepmother
to Jerry but that was probably no longer necessary. She was about the
right age, too. Not so advanced that she would embarrass him – indeed
his pals would call him a lucky cuss to capture a pretty younger woman.
Nor was she such a child that he could be accused of cradle-snatching
or make himself look ridiculous. No, in many respects she was ideal.
Far more so than Nellie, say, in the shop.

Vera had gone to a lot of trouble with the dinner. A beautiful embroidered cloth, a single silver candlestick with a tall pink candle, a pot of late rosebuds rescued from the garden, a bottle of Italian wine chilled and opened: his heart had leapt as she had shown him in, and fluttered more than somewhat as she dimmed the lights. That was a new scent she wore – exotic, musky. The house was stylish with a few good pieces of furniture, though Vera's mother's taste ran mainly to G-Plan. The chandelier in the dining room was grander than any he had seen in Liverpool. Its facets twinkled enticingly and were reflected in the sparkle of the wine as she poured.

Consummation. Funny word. He tried to explore it as the lamb, pale and moist, appeared on first his plate then his fork. It meant food, by which he earned his livelihood: people always had to eat so he would never starve. But it meant – something else, as he eyed Vera across the rim of the glass. It meant the completion of an act, of a process started by both in hope, driven along by loneliness: or at least, by a dragging awareness of being incomplete alone. *Consummation*. He rolled the word around his mouth with a second, then a third glass of wine, and ate the last green pea and mashed potato with relish. Then Vera stood up and held out her hand to him.

'We'd be more comfortable upstairs, Morrie.'

His mouth went dry and he rose a little unsteadily. 'What about pudding?' he asked uncertainly.

'Later,' she answered. 'This way. I've put the hot water on. We can have a bath together afterwards if you like.'

At the top of the stairs he tripped and she lifted his arm. 'I hope you don't think I'm always like this,' he muttered thickly. 'Don't drink much as a rule.'

'Don't worry. You won't be the first I've put to bed in a state,' Vera replied, matter-of-factly. Fuzzily he wondered how to respond, then decided to focus on the next few minutes. It was years since last time. Would he remember what to do? Would it be in working order? Lord almighty, was he supposed to impress her?

At the top he drew himself up to his full height but Vera had stepped smartly ahead and with a swish of skirt and perfume disappeared into a bedroom. He stumbled after.

His tongue felt strange, with a winey taste. His knees and legs wanted to operate independently of each other and of his intentions. The bedroom, with its startling rose-pink plush, was lop-sided. The pink light bulb in the bedside lamp was on, but no other illumination. Liked pink, did Vera. The wallpaper covered in scarlet peonies moved as he moved. It seemed wise to grab the bedpost.

'That's right,' came Vera's voice. It was muffled by the layers of taffeta of her skirt which oddly had found their way up over her head. She was undressing alarmingly quickly. He did not feel one bit prepared.

'You relax on the bed. I'll do everything. You'll have a ball, believe me.'

With relief he sat on the bed with its slippery magenta eiderdown which matched the peonies, found a couple of pillows and lay back. Flat out, would have been nice. He liked a snooze after a big meal. He could feel his eyes closing.

Then she was on him, surprisingly strong, in her bra and knickers. The black lace bra was unlike anything he'd seen before; it was low cut and pushed her breasts up like two melons. It looked tight and uncomfortable. The skimpy knickers matched and revealed her belly button. It stuck out a bit. He found it extraordinary and pointed at it. The words slurred.

'My panties? You like them? Bought the set in Paris. We'll take them off in a minute. First, you have too many clothes on, Morrie. Lift up.'

She knelt astride him, one firm thigh planted on each side of his pelvis, an arch of tanned flesh which towered over him. Above him the vee of the panties stretched and a few pubic hairs escaped. They were curly and exuberant and intensified a panicky sense of helplessness. Her fingers had unbuckled his trouser belt and were unzipping his fly.

Obediently he lifted his hips and she slid his trousers away from him on to the floor. His one and only good pair, he wanted to say, they should be hung up, but she was unbuttoning his shirt. At his neck his tie was unbearable and he tore it undone himself. She laughed delightedly.

'No rush, no rush, Morrie,' she soothed. Her fingers slid inside the elastic of his underpants and pulled them part-way down his legs. What was she up to? Wasn't he supposed to lead? Or was this the same as her dancing in which she seemed to know every move, and with those firm arms pushed him in the direction she wanted him to go? A sob came into his throat: 'Vera –!'

Her head bobbed and disappeared. Then he felt her tongue and he yelped. 'What are you doing?'

She was squatting over him, both hands now enclosing his limp organ. She squeezed her thighs together at his sides. 'Making sure you're in hand,' she murmured roguishly and bent her head again. Then to his horror she put his penis in her mouth and began to slide it in and out.

He could feel the edge of one of her back teeth. His own skin was suddenly horribly sensitive and he tried to pull away. She held on more firmly with one hand and placed the other flat on his stomach so he could not wriggle away. Her strong knees dug into his ribs like a vice.

The sucking intensified. It sent shock waves through his whole body. He could feel himself swell and rise to her. With it came a mounting horror. He put both his hands on her head and tried to push her off. 'Don't, Vera. Don't do that. It's not nice. Please don't.'

The ceiling above him swayed drunkenly. Vera's face reappeared above his own, her expression incredulous.

'Don't you like it? Most men love it. Come on, you mean you've never had one? Blimey! Well, lie back and think of England, Morrie, this is your big night tonight.'

And she lowered her head and set to once again.

'Oh, please, don't,' Morrie wailed miserably, then realised dully that he must sound like the traditional reluctant virgin. 'I mean, what happens if it works and I – I – you know, I come in your mouth?'

'Oh!' She sat up again, but this time her hands kept moving up and down, her thumbs on him expert and independent. He felt as if he was on fire and yet dreadfully sick. 'If that happens, Morrie, I'll swallow it.' She grinned wickedly.

At once he found his anger, and knew what had most disturbed him about her. 'You've done this before, haven't you?' he accused, and with a shove half sat up and pushed her away. 'You've done this lots of times, and with lots of men. You've done it for money.'

'Not for money. No. Don't be so po-faced, Morrie,' she wheedled. 'I've always done it for fun. Nothing else. That's what it's supposed to be – fun. Sex is terrific, if you know how. And I do.' She bent as if to continue.

'It's love I'm after, Vera. If I wanted that kind of sex I could've gone every week to a prostitute. Plenty of them down the docks.' He sat upright and began to swing his legs over the edge of the bed. His erection, he noted, was exactly the same shade as the puce counterpane. He had never noticed it before: with Rosetta his wife he had not looked at it, only at her, at her sweet face, and like her been glad to finish and enfold her in his arms and sleep.

'Thanks, Vera, but no thanks. A big mistake.' He was on his feet and falling over, unable to locate his underpants till he found them around his ankles. His shoes, socks and best trousers were in a heap on the floor: with as much dignity as he could muster he dragged them on. The zip came up with a satisfying finality. His belt he could not find in the alcoholic haze and decided to abandon it.

Any remaining ardour deflated halfway down the stairs. Vera, once convinced he was serious, screamed vicious epithets from the rumpled bed: 'You shit! You prize bummer! You led me up the garden path! Wait till I tell my mother about you – you'll be the laughing stock –' His head rang with the noise but he did not turn back to argue. In the kitchen he vomited up his dinner into the sink and washed out his mouth with two glasses of cold water from the tap. He wished he could do the same with Vera's mouth. It should never have been used in that way. And he hoped never to hear again such foulness from a woman. Not his kind of woman. Not ever.

Still unsteady, with drops of water staining his shirt, Maurice Feinstein shambled out into the leaf-strewn front garden of the house in Queen's Drive. The fifteen minutes it took to walk carefully back to the shop helped clear his head a bit. He must have drunk a lot, and too speedily, through nerves. He was not used to it – the booze, the feminine aggression, the hunger, the steamy knowingness of the woman. The stink of perfume, her sexual smell. He did not want to get used to it. At the corner he was obliged to pause, and looked back briefly. No sign of Vera – it seemed her recriminations were confined to the boudoir. He was well out of it; there was no going back.

A light was on at the back of the shop. Feinstein slowed. No lights upstairs so it could not be Jerry – and anyway, the boy was away at camp this weekend. Feinstein shuddered; had the attempted seduction taken place on his own premises, he'd never have got the vixen out, and would have had to go through with it. At the memory of that tough lip-sticked mouth his manhood shrank and his hand went protectively to it. Thus he most resembled a small chilled boy at the door when he realised who was inside.

Nellie lifted her head and rubbed her eyes. 'Oh, it's you. I was sorting out the books. Well, trying to. Had a good evening? Didn't think you'd be back tonight.'

Feinstein sat down heavily. 'Awful,' he said. His eyes met Nellie's. 'She was terrible, Nellie. A man-eater. Literally.'

Had Nellie not herself been in a deeply unhappy frame of mind, she might have laughed out loud; had she succumbed to earlier temptation and swallowed the vodka, she might have said something cutting and cruel. But she was stone cold sober, and sad, and she valued Maurice Feinstein and his fine qualities more than anything else in her entire world.

His misery cut her to the quick. She rose and came to him, lifted him up, and held him, at first clumsily, then close. Her head rested on his breast, her hand on his arm, the other lightly around his body. He could do no more than stroke her tangled hair, and note that her cheek felt soft, and that she wanted to do nothing but be with him and love him.

'Nellie,' he said. 'Nellie.'

Chapter Twenty

War's End

Not autumn but the depths of winter. Not 1963 and the dawn of a new generation, but 1945, with a new day still to come.

'Jack – Jack! Oh, there he is. Jack!'

Not for the first time Annie Feldman cursed her diminutive height. Around her jostled a frantic crowd that would do credit to the football terraces. Lime Street Station was crammed to bursting with noise, smoke and shouting figures, grey-faced but excited in the early light, with more arriving every minute. Burly policemen fought to restrain the surging throng, but the atmosphere was determinedly good-humoured. Annie's throat stung from the acrid air. Even on tiptoe she could see hardly anything.

With clouds of billowing steam, as if aware of its own inflated importance, the train chuntered slowly into the station. Suddenly doors opened and they were pouring from the carriages. Young men and not so young tumbled out, in uniform, khaki mainly but with a sprinkle of Air Force blue and a few navy overcoats, faces drawn and stubbled, some with bandages or arms in slings, one or two on crutches or helped by a comrade, kitbags slung over shoulders, caps askew. The engine uttered a great hoot in triumphal salute; blackened jets of smoke soared to the grimy roof. Then with cries and tears, like a spring tide soldiers and families flung themselves into each other's arms.

Her brother hesitated then spotted her and swept her into his embrace. 'Golly, Annie, it's good to see you. Where's the wife?'

'At home. Waiting for you. She didn't want to leave the babies and it's a bit cold for them being winter, and still dark. Your cooked breakfast will be on the table. And your job's waiting too, as soon as you can get demobbed.'

The two linked arms and walked jauntily towards the exit. In Lime Street Jack gazed about. 'The street lamps are back on! Terrific. No more groping our way around.' He headed for the taxi queue. 'As for the job: not yet, I'm afraid. May have to go back.'

Annie stopped, concerned. 'But you've done your bit. You've been in four years. This is the first time we've seen you since we waved good-bye before D-Day. Isn't that enough? You marched right through France, and Belgium and Holland. About bloody time you got some leave. And as a married man and father you should be let out now.'

She squeezed his arm. Through the khaki his butcher's strong muscles seemed to have wasted and his bouncy manner had vanished. A streak of white hair above his ear was new, though he was not yet thirty. It occurred to Annie that her big brother had witnessed many brutal sights, including (as he had briefly written in a heavily censored letter) the death of friends at his side in battle. However ghastly their collective miseries under bombardment in Liverpool, nothing would match the experiences of a citizen army made to carry guns a long way from home.

Corporal Jack Feldman sighed. 'My unit is on the German border, Annie. Monty will be pushing on. It's a race between the Americans and the Russians to get to Berlin first. If it's Patton's Third Army then the future of Germany will be decided by us. If it's General Koniev the place'll go Bolshevik. Then there could be another war.'

'No!' Annie halted, her hand to her mouth.

'Enough of that,' Jack muttered. 'I'm famished.' He glanced down at his sister's small feet clad in their wartime fur-lined boots. 'You game? Either we can stand here and freeze for half an hour, since nobody seems to have considered how we get home before the buses are running – or we can slog it. I've tramped across half Europe with no hearth to welcome me. C'mon, sis, let's go.'

Lady Mary Wortley, twenty-nine years old and former Debutante of the Year, rolled over and sleepily opened one eye.

'Oh, Christ. What time is it?'

'Six. I have to get cracking. We clock in at seven-thirty at Berman's, you know.'

'Frightful. I don't know how you cope, sweetheart. You slave for ten hours a day over a hot pair of shears, then fire-watch duty three nights a week, then me. No wonder you're so thin.'

'Then you. Best part of all. It's worse today – I have to go to court this afternoon as a witness. Time off work and no pay.'

'Mmm. Entertaining though. Mind you aren't taken for a black mar-keteer and sentenced to three months. Today I'm idle, but tomorrow I do the teas at the American Red Cross Club. Mrs Quincy Wright from Chicago will speak to GI brides on everyday life and customs in the USA and answer questions. Oh, *my*.' She purred the last word in imi-tation of an American drawl.

'That's in Mount Pleasant, isn't it? I expect my two cousins will be there. Landed a Yankee Doodle, both. Say hello to them.'

'Sure thing, sweetie. D'you realise that in a couple of months they'll be talking like *this*?' She drew the word out, southern-style, until it had three syllables. 'Bye bye, England.'

He reached for his clothes. 'Is the blackout shut tight? I'll switch on the light.'

She reached out a languid arm. 'No, don't. Open the curtains. I'd like to watch you get dressed.'

He laughed quietly. 'God, Mary, you have such strange ideas. Most women don't like to look at a man. They put up with what we need to do with their faces averted. But you're forever wanting to see, and to touch. I can't get over it. Your idea of sex is – I dunno – great, incredible. I've never known anything like it. Not that I was such a Romeo before you came along.'

'It is supposed to be fun. Not simply the act of procreation. Come here.'

He paused naked beside the bed, clothes in hand, shivering slightly. The bed was low, not more than a camp-bed, standard issue for those bombed out. Lazily she stroked his calf, then ran her hand round and up his thigh. He was wiry and narrow chested; the apparently endless stamina that came from such a scrawny frame was a source of surprise to those who knew him. She made to caress him but he moved gently away and patted her hand.

'Well,' she murmured. 'You're something very special for me. In more ways than one. I've never slept with a circumcised man before.'

'Does it make a difference?' He pulled on his underpants and trousers, a trifle hastily.

Lady Mary pondered. 'I don't think so – depends on the overall size, I suppose. And the skill of the operator.' She giggled infectiously. 'It certainly looks tidier, I'll give you that. Your priests do a neat job, though I think the whole practice is barbaric.'

'It's recommended for health reasons, Mary. Some poor fellows have to have it done when they're adults. I'd much rather be cut at a few days old – scream a bit then it's finished.'

'Ugh.' She shuddered. Then she pushed the bedclothes down to her hips and examined her own smooth body. 'I am glad we women don't have to be mutilated, for health reasons or any other. I like my tiddly bits the way they are.' She rubbed her palm over her breasts and tweaked each nipple so that it stood up, hard and rosy purple in the early morning air. Then she grinned up at him as he fastened his shirt, inviting his admiration.

'Lay off, Mary. That's not fair – you're trying to get me going again. I have to be on time. We run enough risks as it is.'

He bent and tucked the covers up around her chin. On the pillow her dark hair spread out, natural ringlets, curls and tendrils. Usually she wore it scraped back in a severe bun under her velour hat as befitted a charity volunteer. Its riotous freedom in bed symbolised for both the few hours of untrammelled pleasure snatched week by week, the memory of which was milked to give sweetness to every waking minute.

'War'll be over soon. What will you do then?' Mary crossed her arms behind her head. The action lifted her breasts again so one became uncovered, but it was merely the careless action of a sated female.

'Haven't considered.' That was a lie and both knew it.

'Will you stay in that factory? You can't, you're made for much better things. You could stand for Parliament, you know. There's bound to be a General Election as soon as Germany surrenders. The Labour Party would have you, with your Pier Head talents. I know Sir Stafford Cripps and the Webbs: I can put in a good word for you.'

'Me an MP? Don't be daft.'

'Why ever not?' Mary sat upright. On her bare shoulders the light turned her skin a delicate gold. 'Look, I agree it wouldn't have been likely before the war. But after this war's over, a lot will change. I shouldn't say this with my father in the House as a National Government supporter, but the coalition will collapse and Churchill will lose. He is trusted as a wartime leader but not for afterwards. They're afraid he'll fight on and there'll be no end to it.'

'And they'll vote for a welfare state and a national health service. The New Jerusalem. Churchill would never agree to that: Attlee would.'

'Exactly. There are eleven parliamentary divisions in Liverpool. The Tories currently hold eight. It'll switch over, you'll see – Labour are bound to win a couple or more. Of course you should put yourself forward. You've always called for the new generation to take their place in government, haven't you? Well, that's you. Step forward.'

He was fully dressed, his muffler wound about his neck, his cap in his hand, but still he dallied. Mary had unerringly focused on issues which had begun to churn in his own brain. He sat on the edge of the cot and picked up a lock of her hair which he curled absent-mindedly around his finger.

'The end of the war. It seemed impossible, once, didn't it? Especially when our house had a direct hit last year. I never thought I'd get out of that alive.'

'Your father didn't. Or any rate, he was alive when we got him out, but dreadfully injured. You didn't see him then because you were in such a state yourself, but I did. Shan't forget that night in a hurry.'

'An old man, God rest his soul. Never hurt anybody.' Daniel took her hand in wordless thanks. His voice had an edge of bitterness. 'I'm so glad my poor mother was not still alive to see it. Nobody can tell us that war is only for soldiers – it's civilians who bear the brunt, and without complaint. But that wasn't what I had in mind. You know what the end of the war will mean for us.'

She nodded, her eyes luminous. He had found it impossible to decide what colour they were, whether green, or hazel, or a soft light brown but for two years now he had wanted no more than to gaze into them with wonder. His Mary, his own love: aristocratic lady, Red Cross volunteer and district organiser who had braved danger repeatedly without a thought for herself, and had been in his neighbourhood so frequently during the bomb raids, her actions selfless and heroic, that it had been natural to invite her out for a drink, and then for another.

In wartime barriers fell, taboos were broken: people grabbed at whatever affection could be found. In the devastated cities a man, a woman might be blown up at any time. Circumstances had made both solitary and lonely, but each had been drawn by the other's intelligent interest in the outside world. Much of their conversation, to their joint amusement, was the exploration of ideas to improve the society from which in each other's company they sought temporary respite. Each found the other fascinating. That they came from competing extremes of the social spectrum made their relationship a source of intrigue and achievement for both, and added a roughened urgency to their mutual attraction.

He had not been the first man she had taken up with. On that she was totally open, but for the last eighteen months he had been the sole incumbent. Words of love had passed between them which both, cautiously and awkwardly, tested for honesty. They had grown to care greatly for each other: that was beyond doubt now, though of necessity the affair had been kept discreet. Appearances elsewhere had been maintained and other friendships continued, if more remotely. Neither had deceived the other. Yet the moment of truth would soon be upon them.

'It means Rupert will come home.'

He turned away. She had never before put it so bluntly.

'Will you be glad?'

'Oh, Christ. I don't know. Pass me my cigarettes.' He did, and struck a match for her, cupping the flame in his hands. It made her cheeks alive with colour for a single flickering second. She cleaned a flake of tobacco from her lips with a fingernail and stared upwards.

She continued, 'Naturally I'll be glad. He's had two ghastly years in a prisoner-of-war camp. That's if the bastards don't kill our fellows before the Allies reach them. But those already liberated have been all right – the guards gave themselves up to the prisoners. So it's not unreasonable to expect him to appear. Sometime in the next couple of months.'

'And then?'

'Oh, don't. It doesn't bear thinking about. I shall feel a lot happier if

I know you're OK. I could then go back to my dearly beloved husband with an easy conscience.'

'If he were dead it'd be a different matter.'

She took a drag on the cigarette. 'He won't be – he's a survivor. Anyway, he's a decent cove and I was frightfully fond of him. I expect we can carry on where we left off. This time I won't refuse his desire to have children. Give me something to occupy myself with when we're bored stiff with the peace.'

'You wouldn't think of –?' He left it unsaid.

'Leaving him?' she finished, and paused. 'I have thought about it. A lot. What if it doesn't work out, too – chaps are coming back terribly altered. But divorce is a horrible business. And what kind of life would it be for you, with a divorcée as girlfriend or even wife? The Labour Party'd turn up its nose at you as a candidate, what with the Catholic voters in Liverpool. You'd be denounced from the pulpit. You wouldn't stand a chance.'

'I'd take my chance with you, Mary.' He stroked her face, touched her lips, dreamed wildly of staying with her.

'Don't. That sounds too much like a proposal. Your family would have a blue fit. To them I'm a – what do you call it? – a *shikse*. The title and a lineage back to the fourteenth century might impress some people, but not them. And frankly, darling, my father would go spare if we were to get hitched. Register office – a Lovat Fraser? You must be mad, certifiable, he'd say. Cast me off without a penny. We'd be a miserable pair, you and I, poor as church mice. No, darling, it wouldn't wash.'

He rose. 'It could if we both wanted it to.' Yet the hope was slipping away. Outside the light grew stronger. No church clocks or bells yet: they would come with the ceasefire.

'You should marry, though.' Her face was hidden from him and her voice sounded muffled. 'Marry and have lots of kids. And a little house and be perfectly respectable. That girl, Annie – she's sweet on you. She'd have you – a nice Jewish girl, that's what you need. Not a god-awful second-hand hag like me.'

'Oh, Mary, don't talk like that. It hurts me so.'

She took pity on him, reached for the ashtray, stubbed out the ciga-rette and held out her arms to him. 'So, Mr Daniel Majinsky, you with the lop-sided smile and the moustache and the burning eyes and fever-ish brow, let's make the most of the weeks we've got, shall we? What time do you finish tonight?'

Simon Rotblatt and Daniel Majinsky were hard at work when Annie slipped into her place between them, face flushed and hair awry. Simon wagged his shears at her.

'Heavens, Annie, what time is this? I told the gaffer you weren't well. You'll get shot. Don't you know there's a war on?'

In a trice Annie had tied on the leather apron and pulled up the box to stand on. 'My brother Jack came back from Holland, five this morning. I took him home and came straight here. Mother's like a dog with two tails – that means all her children are safe.'

For a while they concentrated on the tasks in hand. Simon helped Annie lay out her cloth but thereafter she could manage herself. Daniel seemed preoccupied.

The bell rang for teabreak and the three strolled to the canteen. Simon walked with Annie, Daniel pensively followed, alone.

Simon had the previous night's *Echo* with him. 'It's fearsome out there. Your brother's well out of it. It says that the Allies are flying over four thousand sorties a day to German cities. Imagine! But only twenty-five of our planes went missing last weekend compared with nearly two hundred of Jerries'.'

Annie cast a sidelong glance at Daniel. She wanted to provoke him to join in. 'They're taking a hell of a pounding. Did you see Nuremberg on the newsreels? Our bombers got the chemical works and oil refinery. Went up like fireworks. The American airmen said you could see it from a hundred and forty miles away. And then the German High Command squawked about "the enemy's senseless mania of destruction". What a nerve, after what they did to us.'

The trio peered at the flimsy four-page newspaper. 'It's not senseless,' Danny muttered. 'But it's brutal. Bomber Harris wants to show off what his murderous machines can do. We know all about that in Liverpool. It won't break the people's spirit – it didn't here. But it could leave them sullen and resentful, much harder to rehabilitate. Anyway, if the war's going to be won it'll be on the backs of the poor bloody infantry – like your brother, Annie.'

The three drank their tea. Annie found her courage and prodded Daniel. 'You need cheering up. How about a film? *Love Story* is on at the Trocadero. Margaret Lockwood, Stewart Grainger. I missed it last week. Fancy a night out?' If she noticed the flash of misery in Simon's face she did not acknowledge it.

Daniel shook his head. 'I may go to the Tatler. They're showing that discussion documentary, *What to do with Germany*. More in my line.'

'We haven't beaten them yet. Bit previous, isn't it?' This from Simon. He addressed himself to Annie. 'I'd like to see *Love Story*. Let me take you.'

Daniel rose abruptly and moved away. The bell for the end of break rang. Annie gazed sadly after Daniel's back. She had not answered Simon.

'He's in a pickle, that one,' she said quietly. 'You heard the stories, Simon? Got himself a fine lady, a *goy*, but her husband'll be home soon. If he finds out he'll kill him. And she's giving him ideas way above his station about standing for Parliament. He told me a bit about it. Claims she's Labour: God! What does she know about poverty? Her sort never had to scrimp to buy medicine for a grizzly child. Makes me sick. He could go badly wrong, adrift like that, when the war is over.'

'Maybe he'll emigrate,' Simon replied diplomatically. He hung back. 'Like those cousins of his. And he has a sister in the States, hasn't he? She'd help.'

'His cousins? Big joke that is.' Annie laughed shortly. 'Miriam's got pregnant to catch herself a fat New York sergeant who's been once married before, and Eva's knocked four years off her age. I hope they'll be very happy.'

'That's a bit unkind. Why shouldn't they seize their opportunities? Not much for them here.' Simon looked uncomfortable as he chided.

'But they're heading out into the wide unknown. Wouldn't suit me. I'm too conventional, I suppose. I'd like a three-bedroom semi-detached house in West Derby with leaded windows and space for a garage. See – there's one in the For Sale column at £1,200 – that'd do. And a bit of garden, and English seasons with showers and cool summers. What'll the Majinsky girls get? A flat in Brooklyn if they're lucky, a mother-in-law they've never met and *schwarzes* as neighbours. Maybe I shouldn't say that but you know what I mean.'

'Oh, forget them, Annie. Will you come to the flicks with me tonight or no? Please?'

The first Quarter Sessions of 1945 at St George's Hall was formidably busy. Wartime and the black-out had stimulated illegal activity on an unprecedented scale; a record number of cases were set for trial. Despite the lofty ceilings and marbled corridors the atmosphere was stuffy, though on the staircase the faces of those newly come in were pinched and cold. Barristers in black gowns and wigs, policemen with helmets under their arms and polished boots, solicitors with armfuls of papers and battered briefcases, worried relatives, bleary accused and mackintoshed reporters mingled and mouthed at each other. Nobody seemed to listen much to anyone else.

Daniel paused bewildered at the top of the stairs, unsure which way to go. He stopped a young woman to inquire.

'Haven't a clue,' she said brusquely in an Irish lilt. 'I'm here looking for my husband, Joseph O'Brien. You seen him? Drunk and disorderly last night and pinched two hundred cigarettes from a sailor. An' that's not all.' She pushed past and disappeared.

A stout woman in a black robe with a badge of office and a clipboard in her hands bustled up. 'Which court are you?'

Daniel consulted a paper. 'Court three. I'm a witness. The Chinese case.'

'Ho, ho. Lots of excitement.' The official's eyes glittered. She gave Daniel a quick approving look; apparently his neat if shabby suit passed muster. Her voice took on a confiding note. 'Miss Rose Heilbron's defending. What will she say in mitigation for a bunch of Chinks caught in an opium den in Berry Street who set to and beat up the police? I've carried in the evidence – knives, sticks, a shovel, a chair and a motor tyre pump. One of the bobbies is still in hospital. How did you get involved?'

'I was on firewatch. Saw one of the Chinese climb out of the window down a rope. There was a hell of a row going on. I ran down and grabbed him.'

'You'll get a commendation for that. It'll be heard about three. They'll get sent down – six months' hard labour and a bit more for possession. Over there.'

The usher seemed in no mood to rush off. Daniel indulged his curiosity. He nodded at the long line nearby. 'What are they here for – same case?'

'Goodness, no. They're mostly Miss Heilbron's, though, she does get some dodgy ones. Lovely lady, so clever.' She pointed at a young woman. 'That one's been absent from work without reasonable excuse. Her boyfriend was home on leave from the merchant navy, she says. She'll be fined: two guineas each count and four guineas costs, most like. Hard-faced bitch if you ask me: been here before, different bloke each time. And him –' Her finger indicated a wiry man who sat, shoulders slumped, staring at the floor. 'Theft. Big increase in burglaries this winter. And he's in a separate case too: an appeal against a sentence of two months' hard labour for unlawfully wounding his wife. *He* claims he was drunk and didn't mean to hit her with the plate. Cracked the poor woman's skull, but he'll get off with a fiver fine because it's a quarrel between husband and wife.'

The official started to walk down the line and lowered her voice. Daniel kept pace. 'Then in court five we have the black marketeers. Everyone else pulls their weight, but not them. That one in the striped suit – he's a Mr Frank John Morgan – a market fruit trader. Found in unlawful possession of four pounds of mutton, three pounds of pork, two pounds each butter and marge, two-and-a-half pounds of sausages, a pound of cheese and a pound of lard. Plus four hundred coupons. He says he sold his customers extra fruit and they looked after him in return. He'll be fined – a tenner, probably – and if he can't pay, a month in clink.'

'They all think they can get away with it,' Daniel murmured encouragingly.

The woman snorted. 'Don't they just – and the rest of us keep to the rules. Lord knows I hate rationing, but you have to live with it. Best is tomorrow, if you have the time. The jam factory managers. William Hurst and Sons of Wigan. Should have had a lot more sense.' She flicked over a couple of pages and read out in a loud whisper. 'Ministry auditors found that *most* of the firm's five hundred customers had had excessive deliveries of jam. Nearly fifty tons of sugar had disappeared into thin air. It's reckoned that over three hundred tons of jam have gone on to the black market – that's a profit of £3,500. Nice work if you can get it.'

'What'll happen to them?' Daniel asked.

'Prison,' the woman answered with satisfaction. 'Now I must get on. His Honour'll be back from dinner soon. You sit here and keep your ears open. But don't talk to the other witnesses in case you get nobbled. Nasty lot, these Chinks.'

To Daniel and his workmates it had felt as if the war would never end. As the hours of daylight began to lengthen, however, he followed with more hope, and a mounting sense of unease, the progress of the conflict. Night after night the press detailed Allied sorties, up to 6,000 planes at a time. The streets of Liverpool were peppered with the uniforms of forty Allied nations, but especially Americans, Canadians and Poles in transit eastward. The *Liverpool Echo* told him that USAF Burtonwood held 18,000 men, and he became accustomed to the bashful New Yorkers who had been captured by his cousins.

He went as often as he could to the cinema, usually alone, but frequently left before the main feature. His objective was the newsreels, increasingly vivid and uncensored. By mid-March it was clear that the Nazis were abandoning their bases on the western border of Germany; Patton, fourteen miles from Mainz, told reporters that Allied planes had destroyed over 1,400 motor vehicles and as many railway cars. As the Wehrmacht tried to save what it could, Allied fliers spoke in clipped if proud terms to the cameras of the 'utter turmoil and chaos' in front of General Alexander Patch's US 7th Army. The 4th Armoured Division captured Bad Kreutznach where the civilians were reported 'very hostile': Daniel reflected ruefully how he might have reacted had the invasion been the other way round. In Cologne the Chief of Police who had been imprisoned for anti-Nazi views in 1933 was restored to office (to the applause of the cinema audience), while his local factories were repaired sufficiently to start churning out boots, soap and blankets for the advancing troops.

When he heard that rations were enforced at 1,500 calories a day for German civilians, about one third of the American level, Daniel wondered whether to write in protest to General Eisenhower: but his attention was then held by the pinched faces on the screen of the refugees who streamed in the opposite direction. Especially Poles. Damn the Germans. The Americans were at times not much better. Under February's Yalta agreement Poland was to be handed over to Russian control, as if a dying Roosevelt had forgotten why war had broken out in Europe in the first place.

Column after column in the *Liverpool Echo* kept Daniel, Annie and Simon informed, with official maps. By 19 April the Germans had evacuated Frankfurt and blown up the bridge. Russian and American armies were about equidistant from Berlin. *'Another two days' advance will bring Patton so close to Koniev's troops that it will become dangerous for either side to use long-range artillery'*, warned Reuter's. Montgomery was on the Elbe, the Russians on the Oder and Neisse. The three tailoring friends quivered as they heard that nearly three million troops were embroiled in the concentric attacks on the Reich capital. Annie's brother had been recalled as they had feared, and was somewhere in that mêlée near Berlin. Moscow radio spoke: *'The entire world is holding its breath as it watches the curtain falling on the European war.'*

During tea-breaks at the factory the prime topic of conversation began to shift. The cessation of the conflict could not come soon enough. Then it would be time to catch up with unfinished business at home, those reforms of housing, health and welfare which had been avidly and thoroughly discussed by voters including the three friends and their workmates. Apart from Daniel, their support for the conflict, always faintly conditional, was waning; its continuation further afield no longer seemed a matter for them. Of course they knew that the fire-bombing of Japanese industrial cities such as Nagoya and Osaka had only just started. Should the Japs fight as tenaciously on their own soil as the Germans had done, it could take a further eighteen months to defeat them. But despite Mr Churchill's desire to make a show in Burma, the truth, as voiced increasingly often in Berman's canteen and elsewhere, was that many of his countrymen and women were not interested. Once Victory in Europe (VE) day was behind them, they intended to get on with more pressing matters.

Daniel loitered at the bus-stop by the bombed-out St Luke's at the bottom of Leece Street. He and Mary were to attend the Saturday afternoon concert at the Philharmonic Hall which had miraculously escaped major damage. In his hands was the new Labour Party manifesto: 'Let us Face the Future: A Declaration of Labour Policy for the Consideration of the Nation.' The thin white pages with the confident red 'V' on the cover and the dense print seemed too fragile to bear the weight of such portent. The back page invited readers to join the party for 6d per month.

After a minute Daniel realised that a tubby middle-aged man waiting for the bus was examining him and his pamphlet with undisguised curiosity. The man was small and unshaven and had no coat, but his eyes were sharp.

'Whatcha got there?' The accent was ripely Liverpool.

'Oh, nothing much,' Daniel replied politely. You never knew who

you might be speaking to in wartime. Mary was nowhere to be seen. He
showed the man the pamphlet, then took it back and flicked over the
pages to pencil-marked passages. He read aloud:

'*The Labour Party is a Socialist Party and proud of it. Its ultimate
purpose is the establishment of the Socialist Commonwealth of Great
Britain – free, democratic, efficient, progressive, public spirited.*'

'You a socialist?' the man asked. His tone was friendly.

'I'm not sure,' Daniel mused. 'I suppose in one sense everybody is,
these days. Our gallant Russian allies have shown that ordinary folk,
what Marx called the proletariat, could take power and govern themselves.'

'Nah,' the man sniffed. 'Dictatorship of the proletariat? Load o' rubbish. Dictatorship of the bosses, more like. Only they're different bosses,
that's all. Gimme our system any day. We Brits can give socialism a
human face, given half a chance.'

'Yes, but –' As ever, Daniel found himself enjoying the argument for
its own sake. 'It's difficult, isn't it? A chap who says he's *not* a socialist
these days is tantamount to saying he wants government as of old by the
upper classes. And I don't. Those were the leaders who appeased Hitler,
and who brought ruin and hunger during the Depression to this city and
my family. *They* didn't suffer, much – the nobs disported themselves at
the Adelphi and on the Cunard and White Star liners, while we queued
up at soup kitchens.'

'Swilled champagne poured by stewards on ten bob a week, slept in
beds made up by chambermaids paid even less,' the man agreed. 'Oh,
aye. I know all about that. I was one of those waiters before the war.'
He squared his shoulders. 'But you still say you're not a socialist?'

'I just wonder,' Daniel murmured, and indicated the pamphlet, 'if
they go too far. Throwing the baby out with the bathwater. We must
have private property and enterprise. The state can't do everything,
and I don't want it to try. And fail.'

The man began to remonstrate. Daniel listened, then interjected.
'You seem to know a lot about it. You involved in politics?'

The stolid figure filled out with pride. 'You could say. I was having
you on a bit: I know that manifesto. I live over by Ormskirk. I'm a
Labour Party member – humble as you like, but I get to do my bit.'

'Ormskirk? Who's your candidate?'

'A Mr James Harold Wilson. Brainy bloke, spent the war in the
Ministry of Supply. Yorkshireman. And we'll get him elected, you'll see.'

The bus drew up and the man, still declaiming, climbed on board. As
the vehicle drove off he waved and called back at Daniel:

'It don't matter what you think! Just make sure you vote the right
way –'

Daniel watched the bus churn smokily up the hill and stroked his
moustache. His face had a wistful expression.

'Hi! Sorry I'm late.' Suddenly Mary was there, a perfumed flurry, pert hat on head, dressed to go out. 'Goodness, isn't it warm? I didn't need my furs.'

'I'll carry them for you,' he offered, awkwardly, and went to shove the pamphlet in his pocket.

'What're you reading?' She pounced, alert and inquisitive.

He showed her. 'Hot off the presses. I thought I'd better find out what we're going to vote for.'

They began to walk up the street. 'Some of it I can swallow quite easily,' he continued. 'It says Socialism is to be applied gradually, with public ownership of fuel, power, inland transport and iron and steel as the priorities. But you won't like the last bit, Mary.'

'I will,' she countered firmly. 'I shall do my utmost to get them into office. No virtue in being a stick-in-the-mud.'

He halted, took out the pamphlet and pointed. *Labour believes in the nationalisation of the land, and will work for it.* Precisely how much land does your family own, Mary?'

'Lord, couldn't tell you offhand. Twenty thousand acres in Scotland for a start, and the farm in Suffolk's about two thousand and there's more in the Staffordshire moorlands. And did you say iron and steel? We have a steel mill in Warley and a couple of pits in Derbyshire. Done well out of the war, to be honest – munitions means coining money.' She shrugged. 'They'll pay compensation. Daddy'll take the cash and go rough it in the Bahamas. He's often said he'd retire after the war.'

'What if there's no compensation – or not much?'

'They couldn't do that.'

'They could. If they've a big enough majority in Parliament. They'd say funds were too short, or promise deferred payments or whatever. This is politics, Mary, not barter at face value.'

She looked uncomfortable then tossed her head. 'If we're going to be poor we'll have to get used to it. I've learned such a lot in the last few years, Danny: how to lay a fire and keep it lit, how to make omelettes with dried egg and eat peas out of a tin. How to drive a lorry, though I wasn't awfully good at it! I mend stockings I'd have thrown away and am proud of my darning skills, and I get on famously with lots of amazing types I would never have met. I'll cope.'

Daniel was dubious. 'People like you will find a means to preserve your position. Of that I'm certain. Maybe you should stand for Parliament yourself.'

Her laughter rang out, a merry peal which cut him to the quick. 'What, me? Gracious, no. That's no job for a lady. Look what a fool Nancy Astor has made of herself. Anyway, I shall be off soon.' She put her hand to her mouth.

'He's coming home.'

'Yes. As soon as he's fit to travel.'

'It had to happen sooner or later, I suppose.'

They climbed the hill in step, but Danny knew he would not be listening to a note of Kathleen Ferrier.

'I have made up my mind, Danny, to be content with my lot. I took my marriage vows freely and though I've been hopeless at keeping them while he was away, I must make the effort now. Rupert should be back for Victory Day, whenever that is – it can't be long. We shall spend it in London.'

'Not here?'

'Not here. No.'

The news from the front became more strident and steadily dottier, as if the Allies could at last ridicule the enemy they had so grimly feared. When Admiral Engel, second in command of the North Sea fleet was captured at Buxtenhude, reported Reuter's, he was well prepared by his wife. In his five suitcases she had meticulously packed wines, food, newly pressed clothes and 500 cigarettes. On 23 April, St George's Day, the British Second Army's mixed bag of captures included a circus with two bears and two elephants; Marlene Dietrich's sister; two genuine werewolves; 500 German WRENs in bell-bottomed trousers, and another admiral. The bears had been wounded, but no further explanation emerged about the 'werewolves' which remained a mystery. In Italy the enemy fled. And the Red Army was within two miles of the centre of Berlin, fighting street by street, whole districts ablaze.

Then, quite suddenly, it was over. On Saturday 5 May newspapers throughout the country showed German girls in tears as 100,000 prisoners of war were taken in one day by the British. Hitler was dead, the brutalised bodies of Mussolini and his mistress hung upside down from a Roman lamppost. As Admiral Dönitz and Field-Marshal Keitel led the surrender party, the scale of their defeat and their ignorance of it were made manifest. Dutifully Montgomery set forth his terms based on a detailed plan of the front line. 'When they looked at the map they were shocked,' he commented dryly to *The Times*. 'They did not know. Von Freidberg burst into tears.'

But at home confusion reigned, not least because of the weekend. On the Monday night a few tentative bonfires were lit in Everton and Anfield but were extinguished by the National Fire Service as still forbidden. On the drizzly Tuesday morning, 8 May, Daniel, Annie and Simon with many others arrived for work to find the gates shut and padlocked and a notice pinned to them with a border of red, white and blue bunting.

The workforce milled excitedly around and questioned each other. In the distance a band could be heard playing 'Tipperary'. A man rounded the corner, his arms clutching a large stuffed effigy of Hitler. After him marched a child with a battered petrol tin suspended like a drum from thin shoulders, beating time vigorously with two sticks. From behind a cloud the sun emerged and a cheer went up, ragged at first, then with whoops and screams; the younger men and women clasped hands and began to run towards the city centre.

Simon Rotblatt read the few words then let out a yell. 'It's today! Victory in Europe! Today and tomorrow. Mr Churchill will broadcast to the nation this afternoon. We'll be able to hear it from the Town Hall. It's over! Oh, dear God, it's over!'

And he jumped around, and kissed every woman in reach including the older hands who dimpled and blushed. Annie watched him in amazement: kind as he was, Simon was not normally demonstrative. As he lurched towards her she sidestepped closer to Daniel who appeared dazed.

Annie decided to take charge. She held out her hands and took to her right Simon's, to her left, Daniel's. 'I have the two finest-looking Jewish boys in Liverpool,' she announced to nobody in particular. 'And we are going to celebrate. Together.'

Their path took them past the Cathedral where a throng had gathered, unplanned, from the dawn hours: thousands of ordinary citizens who spontaneously wished to give thanks to God. In the absence of the Bishop who had inexplicably gone to Plymouth, Canon Soulby flapped about for a while then admitted them for improvised services every hour, the packed congregations calling out the names of hymns they wanted to sing. Somehow the Canon, a lump in his throat, managed a short sermon: 'Our cause prevailed by our doing the plain and obvious thing – playing a straight bat.' After a struggle the flags of every Allied nation, the Dominions and Colonies were unfurled in the centre of the nave. In the War Memorial Transept people quietly placed slips with the names of loved ones lost until the little chapel seemed covered in small white butterflies.

As the sun rose high the city broke out in a riot of colour. Annie squealed with delight as shopkeepers hammered up beribboned V signs across windows and doors, some from the rafters to the ground. Bunting and streamers appeared as from nowhere; if they turned back to look, a street monochrome grey as they had passed through it had become a blaze of patriotic hues as they reached the end. Rain threatened yet few walkers carried umbrellas, and shelter was willingly given during showers. Whisky and gin, bourbon and rum were repeatedly offered, so that by the time the three friends reached the Pier Head they were distinctly tipsy.

And there they gaped: from the Landing Stage as far as the eye could see, flags had broken out on tugs, ships, ferry boats, on cranes and dockside warehouses, a fantastic and merry sight. A favourite banner was a composite of the Stars and Stripes and the Union Jack. Every ship's hooter was in play, each to outdo the other. 'Marvellous,' breathed Annie, and felt ready to cry.

In front of the Royal Liver Building a drum-head service was in progress. Annie slowed, and tied her scarf around her head. The preacher, Reverend Cocup of the Royal Navy, was reminding the respectful worshippers that the conflict had not ended, especially at sea. The band struck up the sailors' hymn:

> *'Eternal Father, strong to save,*
> *Whose arm doth bind the restless wave,*
> *Who bidd'st the mighty ocean deep*
> *Its own appointed limits keep:*
> *O hear us when we cry to thee*
> *For those in peril on the sea.'*

To Annie's consternation she heard Daniel's voice raised in unison though he did not know the words well. Irritated, she nudged him. The hymn may mention only God, not Christ, but it was Christian and Jews were not supposed to join in. He ignored her and sang on. Fortunately it finished quickly. Before she had time to remonstrate the National Anthem struck up. Here there could be no debate. Backs straightened, hats were off, arms snapped to sides, salutes were held firmly at brows. The lusty sound lifted over the quay and floated across the waters:

> *'God save our gracious King*
> *Long live our noble King*
> *God save the King!'*

The impromptu event finished with three noisy 'Hurrahs!' though it was not clear whether they were intended for the King and Queen, the sailors, soldiers and airmen or everyone in general; a passing cargo vessel let out a great hoot which made everybody jump, then laugh, then disperse, chattering gaily.

'To the Town Hall. We can grab a good spot.' Annie had rediscovered the bossier elements of her nature. The boys seemed content to tag along in streets awash with happy people. They came into the square then settled on the steps of the Bank of England building nearby.

Annie hugged herself and gazed about, thrilled at the banners and flags, but could not avoid noticing also the boarded-up windows, the blackened façades pitted by shrapnel, the burned-out roofs open to the sky. This part of the city had been ravaged, though not quite as badly as the devastated docks and railheads. Only Herculean efforts had kept everything moving. Nowhere in central Liverpool had emerged unscathed. How much the war had destroyed: the burden of reconstruction would be horrendous. And it was not only buildings and the bodies of those caught in them which had been mangled beyond recognition, but their own hopes and prospects.

The loss was permanent. These vanished years could not be replaced, years when they should have been rearing families and arranging photographs on the mantelpiece. She sighed inwardly. Some of the old conventions and assumptions would be re-established very quickly, including the curbs on female ambition and independence. Once the men were demobbed they would take precedence for employment, naturally. It would be back to the kids and the kitchen for women.

She herself had been twenty-one when the war broke out. Another year or two and she would be thirty. The boys – men, really, Daniel and Simon, as dear to her as brothers – were a couple of years older. They should both have had wives in pinnies, and little sons with dirty knees and cheeky faces, and modest insurance policies and mortgages. Instead their progress had stopped dead. Daniel lodged in two draughty rooms where, reliable gossip had it, he was soothed by another man's wife, while Simon was still with his mother and sister. The fracture of their lives would scar them for ever. Under her lashes she examined first one man then the other, but when Simon tried to catch her eye she smiled vacantly and glanced away. She did not want to share her musings, at any rate not with him.

The space before the Town Hall had filled quickly. Over hastily erected loudspeakers martial music blared scratchily and unidentifiably. Dignitaries emerged on the balcony in robes and chains of office, their visages red and sweltering in the bright sunshine. The Labour leader of the Council, Alderman Luke Hogan, appeared with his son, also Luke, a recently returned POW. The tall young man leaned over the parapet and waved, his pale gaunt face so like his father's. The Lord Mayor, the Earl of Sefton, seemed to fill the balcony by himself, his beaming Countess at his side.

The crowd began to sing and drowned out the victory marches: ditties to pay tribute to those who had stood by Britain in her darkest moments – 'Oh Susannah', 'Waltzing Matilda' and the like. A clock struck three, to three energetic cheers. Then, unmistakably, the tones of Winston Churchill boomed through the air. Silence fell.

'*Yesterday morning, at two forty-one am, at General Eisenhower's headquarters . . .*' To the crowd's slight disappointment there followed an interminable list of defeated dignitaries and Allied heroes who had signed the surrender documents. As usual Churchill rolled every syllable and lingered between phrases, prolonging the moment they so desired. The listeners became faintly restless. It had been announced that the text had been agreed and the identical statements were being made simultaneously in Washington and Moscow but nevertheless – when would he say it – when?

'*Hostilities will end officially at one minute after midnight tonight, Tuesday the eighth of May . . .*' A premature shout went up and was hushed instantly. '*. . . celebrating today and tomorrow, Wednesday, as Victory in Europe days.*'

There was a pause. Churchill raised his voice.

'*The German war is therefore at an end.*'

'Yes!' Simon threw his cap in the air, grabbed Annie, and gave her a bear hug. 'Marry me! I'll buy that house in West Derby – we'll live happily ever after!'

She pushed him away, face scarlet. 'Shush. He's not finished yet.'

Churchill could not stop himself adding a few words of laudatory self-congratulation. '*After gallant France had been struck down, we from this island and from our united Empire maintained the struggle single-handed for a whole year, until we were joined by the military might of Soviet Russia, and later by the overwhelming power and resources of the United States of America. Finally almost the whole world was combined against the evil-doers who are prostrate before us . . . We may allow ourselves a brief period of rejoicing. But let us not forget for a moment the toils and efforts that lie ahead – Japan with all her treachery and greed remains unsubdued . . .. We must now devote all our strength and resources to the completion of our task –*'

The gravelly voice had risen a whole octave; a clear tenor floated out from the loudspeakers to the hushed multitudes.

'*Advance Britannia! Long live the cause of freedom! God save the King!*'

A broadcast blast of trumpets from the buglers of the Scots Guards ceremoniously sounded the victory. The music started; bells pealed out from the seamen's church, St Nicholas, then other belfries took up the signal, and soon the whole city was ringing for joy; the crowd burst into raucous song, the Lord Mayor waved his feathered tricorne hat, kissed the Lady Mayoress, shook hands with a tired Sergeant Logan and his father; waved again, and uttered into the microphone words lost in the cheers and celebration below; and the crowds began to dance with each other, in and out of the bollards, around the Town Hall, down to the Municipal Annexe, in and out of shops and arcades and halls, by trestle tables being set up in streets for the following day's parties, around the market place and along the Pier Head, jumping, clinging, screeching, free. Free: and at peace.

Annie was not sure what time they stopped and slumped in a doorway, only that it was nearly dark, and their clothes were damp from rain, and she was not entirely in control of herself. That the three had managed to stay together was a minor miracle, but somehow it symbolised the comradeship of the conflict itself, those qualities of gritty endurance which had seen them through. It had been a remarkable time, for all the pain. All over.

Time to start again.

Simon had acquired a half-bottle of cheap sherry in a brown paper bag. He took a swig and handed it to Annie, who shook her head. 'Had enough,' she slurred. 'Not going 'ome in this state. Bit *shicke*, I am. Stay out a bit. My mother won't worry. Not tonight.'

'Annie: Annie. Listen to me. I may never be able to say this when I'm sober.' Simon had her arm. She wriggled but he held tight. Daniel rose shakily and strolled away. About fifty yards from them he leaned on a doorpost, hands in pockets, head down.

'Whatissit?' At last Annie gave Simon her full attention. He spoke rapidly, as if he had rehearsed the words but could not get the flow quite right.

'I'm going to leave Berman's at once. Get out while the going is good. My uncle has some cash and we'll start our own firm. Trousers for the mass market – no more bespoke tailoring for me. I shall make money, Annie, I'm set on it. Here in Liverpool. Will you join me? I meant what I said about the house. I love you dearly, Annie, you must know that. I've loved you for ever. I know you can love me. Marry me. Please, say yes. Please.'

With a hurried movement he was on one knee, still talking urgently. 'I haven't got a ring yet – I didn't know it was going to be today, nobody did. But I'll make a wonderful husband for you, Annie, and I'll devote my life to making you happy. On my knees I swear it. You deserve the very best. Say yes.'

Annie stood and tried to lift Simon, but he resisted and stayed down, his face upturned in the bluish lamplight. Their hands entwined for a minute, then she slid hers away, and walked slowly and deliberately to Daniel's side.

The drizzle had restarted; fine silvery drops on his hair and shoulders gave him a ghostly sheen. His face glistened with what she suspected might have been tears. He took his hand out of his pocket and word-lessly wiped his face with his open palm. She slipped her hand into his before he could hide it again.

'Did you hear that, Daniel?' she asked softly. He nodded.

'He's decent and worthy and I'm very fond of him, as you are, but he's not the man for me. It's you, Daniel, it always has been. You, all mixed up and passionate, trying to deny your heritage, dreaming of being something you're not: but good and honourable, and so in need of a decent home it breaks my heart to watch you. Alone in the world – your father dead, your cousins about to emigrate. Your girlfriend back in her stately pile – she'll have forgotten you already. But I'm here. I can help you. I can make that home. I am the right partner for you, Daniel. And you for me.'

He looked down at her. The tears flowed down both their faces and neither attempted to hide them. 'Take Simon,' he said brokenly, and made to move away. 'I am no use to you. He will make something of himself – I never will.'

She stood in front of him, small and fierce. 'I'm not as clever or as bookish as you, Daniel Majinsky. I'm not some smart society lady, but so what? I know what you need. You know what you need, dammit. I love you. I worship you! For God's sake, stop arguing. You're not on your soap box now. This is a real future I offer you. The head of a family – a name for yourself, which you've never had. Love for decades, for the years ahead – not just for this month or next. Oh, Danny, it has to be. Otherwise I swear I'll not get wed at all, and neither will you. If you say no, what else is there for you? Come on, be sensible.'

He laughed quietly at that, gazed down at her small hand held in his for a long moment and massaged the fingers, as if erasing a memory. Then gently he took the tiny girl in his arms, and kissed her, and held her close.

When they turned to look behind them, Simon had gone.

In the library of a Georgian house two hundred miles away, Spanish sherry sparkled in a decanter on a silver tray as Waterford crystal glasses were clinked together. The ancient butler, bowed but with his lined face creased in pleasure, glided out. A rangy setter dog loped into the room and sat at their feet, its head across the shoes of its newly returned master.

'Darling. Here's to the peace.'

'To peace. And to Mr Churchill. And to our brave boys – all of you.'

The two drank. His hand trembled and he glanced away.

He leaned back on the sofa. 'You must have had such adventures, old girl. We'll have to catch up. Was Liverpool too frightful? You are such a brick. What a place to have to go.'

'Better than Stalag IIB at Fallinghestel, I'll bet.'

'Rather – but I don't want to talk about that. Isn't Liverpool supposed to be crammed with characters? Here, sit beside me. Your spouse may be a heap of battered old bones but there's nothing amiss with my sense of humour. Did you meet any interesting coves? Tell me.'

'I met a few.' Her voice was calm. 'Some wonderful people. Such stoicism, even as their little terraced houses crashed about their heads. I came to love them, in a way.'

'Anybody special?' He was teasing, but his eyes were cloudy. It occurred to her that he might prove a far more jealous and orthodox husband in future. There would be no more adventures, no pre-war open marriage from here on.

She pondered, head on one side, and brushed a stray curl off her brow.

'No, darling, of course not. Nobody remarkable at all.'

PART FIVE

'He quickened the heart and mind of the nation, inspired the young, met great crises, led our society to new possibilities of justice and our world to new possibilities of peace and left behind so glowing and imperishable a memory.'

Arthur M. Schlesinger Jr.,
A Thousand Days – John F. Kennedy in the White House
(André Deutsch, 1965)

Chapter Twenty-One

Saturday 17 November

Birthday. Seventeen. Cards from her parents and, unexpectedly, from Auntie Gertie with a $20 bill folded small. The scribbled note told her to take it into a bank. It would be worth over £4, more than she could earn in a week. To Gertie that was probably small change. And to Michael, and his family.

Before breakfast, still snuggled into the bedclothes, she started a letter to her Aunt with the usual stilted phrases of gratitude. Then it felt as if the old lady herself had entered the room, her skirts a-swish, her eyes inviting confidences. Helen began to write more freely.

> *Neither one thing nor the other, seventeen, is it, Auntie? Old enough to sleep with a man; old enough to wed. Old enough to hang, come to that, though nobody that young has been sent to the gallows in years. At seventeen you'd already gone off with your sailor and been brought back. But I'm still not old enough to do anything truly independent, like sign a cheque or vote. That'll have to wait till my twenty-first. It seems a lifetime away.*
>
> *Strange how it works in this country. When are we old enough to make up our own minds, and what about? In law I can consent to sex, if I want to. If I were a boy, though, and queer, sex is banned at any age. But a girl who fancies another girl can get cracking at age sixteen. Is it the same in America? I suppose it differs from state to state. Apparently Queen Victoria was so taken with masculine men, that to her it was unthinkable for a woman to love another woman. So, I read somewhere, the Act of 1885 ignored lesbianism and it wasn't ever banned. Not that it's to my taste, but don't you think that's odd?*

Helen giggled at herself. It was a bit early in the morning to be thinking so much about sex. But Gertie would not be startled and would answer her somehow. Maybe in person, if she, Helen, could manage to get across the Atlantic, even if only for a short trip. From downstairs came the sounds of clattering plates and cutlery. Hastily Helen laid the letter aside and threw off the blankets.

On the early bus into town Helen felt cramped and out of sorts. She was not ill, or she would have telephoned Boots the Chemist to cry off. The summer job had metamorphosed into regular Saturday employment at the flagship store in town, which suited her fine. It was less likely that members of the community on their way from sabbath service would pop in and embarrass both of them with their furtive handling of forbidden money. And the big shop was busy, with better pay and more to keep her occupied.

The Boots people were friendly. Mr Clay the pharmacist from Allerton Road must have had a word with his city centre counterparts for she had been spoken to twice and had the sense of being nurtured, cautiously but deliberately. Pharmacists might be defensive about the invisibility of their profession, but (they murmured) they were readily employable. A chemist – druggist, Michael would say – was always valued, especially when doctors were revered but not entirely heeded. Should her exam results be inadequate, if Cambridge and other seats of learning should decide against her eventually, she could do worse.

Yet every instinct rebelled. To spend a lifetime doling out cough sweets and painkillers to whinging customers was not quite basking in the white heat of the technological revolution. There was no point in striving so hard just to be ordinary, to disappear in a white coat into the pharmacist's den, that neon-lit cupboard behind the counter. By contrast the *creation* of those new pills, the research into the new frontier of medicine and antibiotics: that would be a worthier objective. Her heroine Marie Curie with radium, or Dorothy Hodgkin who had unravelled the mysteries of penicillin and Vitamin B12: those women benefited humanity, as much as any man. Compared, say, with the men who invented the H-bomb, rather more so. Mr Mannheim would agree.

The pressures were on. Childhood was slipping away. A sunlit pasture was passing and the future seemed alternately fantastic and murky. Soon she would have to earn her keep, accept her responsibilities and adapt herself to citizenship. Before many more weeks had elapsed choices would emerge, concrete and urgent.

Birthday.

Her mother had inquired tentatively over the porridge whether she wanted a few friends round for a little party, but without Michael it would have been no fun and with him impossible. The suggestion had made Helen smile inwardly, but she was tactful with Annie. To her mother she was still a small girl, and maybe always would be.

Children never grew up in their parents' eyes. It made teen life excruciatingly difficult.

It meant there was nobody older around to talk to, with whom to share her fears and unease. At times as she rode on the top deck of the bus to a few hours of simple, undemanding certainty, she felt panicky. Most people would dozily stay on the bus for ever and go to easy jobs, day by day, with no more anxieties than the size of the pay packet on Fridays. That would be true of the bulk of the girls at school, whatever ambition Miss Plumb had tried to instil. Most people were content to be ordinary. She was not, and it hurt and frightened her.

Only Michael. He would grasp what troubled her, and guide her gently to greater trust in herself. Michael, here and now, not Aunt Gertie, remote across the ocean. Michael would advise her not to be put off by her own isolation. Michael. But he, indeed, was both a part of the solution, and part of the problem.

Saturday. School hop on tonight. Six schools are invited, so the kids'll have to come, plus the staff. Our teachers are trying to get with it, I suppose. Makes you sick. If they'd any sense they'd know there's so much real music on in Liverpool. Their clumsiness shows they haven't a clue.

The governors wouldn't fork out for a proper group – that'd cost a hundred pounds – so we have the Institute's skiffle boys. Awful. Awful! Plus records. Peter Paul and Mary, if the teachers have their way. Except they don't notice the words.

Part of the ancien régime, *they are. Like in France before the revolution. The teachers, for all they try their best. And politicians. They don't know what's brewing. They have no grip. It's as if they expect to apply the standards and mores of an old world, pre-war virtually, without realising the forces gathered to sweep them away. The wind of change is blowing through Africa, said Mr Macmillan, but he looks and sounds more like that old buffoon of the First World War – Kitchener, I think. The winds of change are blowing right here.*

Nothing much has altered in this city since I was born. It never recovered from the bombing. Gaping holes still, waste sites, burned-out houses. Feels sorry for itself. Thinks it's owed a living by everyone else. Yet it's dying on its feet wherever you look. It's so obvious. Death and decay in all around I see.

I can't go to the dance. They'd notice. Anyway I have to visit the nuns. They wanted me to come Monday morning but I'd miss even more school, so this evening it is. After confession. But will they listen?

My belly's bigger. I'm so scrawny everywhere else that it's becoming noticeable. Lucky it's winter: my school mac billows around and hides most of it. I've avoided games since the start of term. Can't go on much longer. Have to make some decisions, and soon. That's why I have to plead with the nuns.

The world is falling apart for me. I've felt it for months – not just because of the baby. Like when we went on the ferry last summer. The other girls joked, and teased each other about their plans for next year, and later. They spoke the same language. I didn't. I wasn't part of it. It was as if I was on a different boat, at the mercy of some capricious zephyr, swirling out to the edge of the unknown universe, never to return.

They're heading for the next stage of their lives, full of grand hopes and dreams. My ship is driven towards an abyss. I can't see when or where. I can't see. It is all darkness.

'I am sorry, Michael. I have to go to that darned school dance whether I like it or not. As a prefect I am a hostess.'

Helen shifted the phone to her other ear. Her tea break was ten minutes. The call box on the corner near Boots was draughty and her feet were frozen.

'Gee! What's a prefect, Helen? I wanted you to come to the base. We got some guys leaving and there'll be quite a shindig.'

She laughed, a trifle nervously. 'Maybe it's fortunate I can't come, then. But the dance packs up about half past nine. The younger children can't have a late night. Why don't I meet you later? In town? Gerry and the Pacemakers are on at the Cavern. Their record's gone to number one – we're lucky to get them.'

'*When you walk through a storm*
Hold your head up high
And don't be afraid of the dark –

'Heavens, sweetheart, that's ancient. My mother sang it to me when I was a kid. *Carousel*, isn't it – Rodgers and Hammerstein? Nowhere but a crazy country like England could that be a hit.'

'It's sold a quarter of a million copies in ten days. And Cilla's got a Top Twenty hit now too – "Love of the Loved".' Helen spoke with lofty dignity. 'See you there later, or not?'

Michael mused. 'I can't hear myself think in that smelly dive,' he admitted. 'Better at the pub – The Grapes, is it? – opposite. As near ten as you can make it. And happy birthday, sweetheart. I haven't forgotten. OK?'

Maurice Feinstein ran his finger down the entertainments listing in the *Echo*.

'I fancy *Brides of Dracula*. Peter Cushing and Andrée Melly. Liverpool girl, she is.'

Nellie clicked her tongue. 'You sure? Bit gory, isn't it?'

'No, it's a laugh. My son Jerry saw it with his girlfriend. He said the whole cinema fell about. You're not supposed to take it seriously, Nellie.'

She peered at him. '*Mutiny on the Bounty*'s more in my line. Or *The VIPs* with Burton and Taylor. I can't believe how gorgeous that woman is. Provided you don't spend the rest of the night sighing over her finer points.'

'There are bare breasts in *Bounty*, I'm told,' he murmured roguishly, and reached across the table for her hand. 'Or we could stay in, if you prefer.'

'Later, Maurice. I want to go out. As long as you don't mind if we're seen in public.'

'I don't mind, if you don't. I've put those sort of worries behind me. If we bump into Sylvia Bloom I'd simply tell her I'm no longer in the market. She'd get the message.'

'Won't you lose customers?' Her face was grave.

He considered. 'I don't think so. Maybe one or two'd close their accounts but they'd have to clear them first. And there isn't another decent kosher delicatessen between here and Manchester, so I reckon we're safe.' He held her gaze. 'I don't care, anyway, Nellie. I've found you, and I'm happy. I only wish I'd realised years ago.'

'Me too,' she said simply, and let him stroke the inside of her arm, and tickle her palm till she wriggled.

A moment's silence ensued, as if both were still unsure how to express their emotions. Then Maurice spoke slowly.

'I can't marry you, Nellie. You must see that.'

'Course you can't.' She did not want him to say why not. She did not want to hear him put into words and thus make permanent her status as an outsider. Quickly she added, before he could interrupt, 'Because I'm already married.'

His jaw dropped. Astonishment gave his face a boyish look. 'Did I know that?'

'You must have known I was married. I don't call myself "Miss". P'raps you assumed I was divorced. Well, I'm not.' Briefly she explained about Pete, and the robbery, and Spain. There would be plenty of time to tell him more, if he wanted details. He would sympathise, of that she was certain.

'I nearly lost you,' was all Maurice could answer. 'Another couple of weeks and you'd have been away. It was that close.'

'And you'd have been hitched up with that cow.' The two began to giggle again, but Nellie watched him carefully. He might still be easily hurt. She did not yet know him well enough to be sure of the boundaries. Young lovers they were not, exactly.

'If we don't shift we'll miss the features,' she announced at last, and folded the paper. '*Brides of Dracula*, if you insist. On the way back we'll collect a couple of brown ales and I'll make you fried egg and chips when we get home. How does that sound?'

The gym hall was decorated, but scrappily. A few balloons, a streamer or two of crêpe bunting, all somewhat forlorn. Orange squash and biscuits were ready on a side table for 6d. Coloured spotlights had been erected and focused on the platform. The main lights were full on: prefects had been warned not to switch any off in order to discourage illicit petting in corners. The toilets were to be checked regularly, and the bushes behind the hall. It might be chilly outdoors but nobody wanted any goings-on. Not at the Blackburne House school dance.

To the pupils' relief the skiffle group were not bad. This was how the Beatles had started, and Rory Storm and the Hurricanes and the Merseybeats and the Swinging Blue Jeans and countless other groups now household names. The tacky instruments, some amateurishly cobbled together, didn't matter. It was the beat, the noise they could make, the riffs they could lay down and the amps their home-made loudspeakers could drive into the ether. The boys put on a brave show, sufficient to furrow the brows of teachers who stalked the hall like sentinels, but which pleased the hundred or so youngsters obliged to turn up.

As for the players, Helen knew that the payment of a fiver for the night would be gratefully pocketed. Better than an early morning paper round in the dark and wet with a bagful of dailies, *Beano* and the *Radio Times* for ten bob a week.

She did not have a partner, so busied herself as a hostess, trying to ensure that as far as was possible in the artificial atmosphere the kids could enjoy themselves. She wore the gingham dress nipped in at the waist that Auntie Gertie had liked. It was Michael's favourite, too – he said it made her look like a regular American girl.

Next week at the prefects' meeting she anticipated that the entire body would put its foot down and petition Miss Plumb, and through her her successor, not to order a repeat the following year. At least the Head had had the grace not to appear which would have killed proceedings stone dead, but had left it to Mrs Egerton, fresher-faced and more motherly, who had children of her own and was marginally more human. School dances were passé and stupid. The authorities had not the faintest notion how the young conducted themselves. It was time to bury the tradition.

The whole point of places like the Cavern and the dozens of other clubs which had mushroomed was that only under twenty-fives could grasp their magic. If adults were shocked, that was the idea. For the first time in history, young people would set their own standards, do their own thing. The old guard were not to be in charge, not any more. Instead strenuous efforts would be made to obtain then ensure their exclusion.

It was a question not merely of style: something more fundamental was at stake. It showed in the dancing. As the band assembled its ramshackle equipment Mrs Egerton, spectacles on her nose, checked her written instructions and put the 'Tennessee Waltz' on the turntable. A youth from Merchant Taylor's, the head boy in his school uniform, dutifully approached Brenda as host head girl, bowed formally and asked her to waltz. Brenda was too polite to refuse, but for the entire number the couple were pointedly left to circle the dance floor alone.

As the record finished Brenda marched swiftly to Mrs Egerton and whispered to her. She beckoned Helen to join them.

The teacher removed her spectacles and gazed from one to another helplessly. 'Then you take over,' she said. 'If you must have rock and roll, I wash my hands of it. But if there's trouble, a riot or fight, you will be held responsible.'

And that was how the sounds of Freddie and the Dreamers, the Dave Clark Five and Presley and Chubby Checker filled the hall, though the new disc jockeys decided against the Crystals' 'Then He Kissed Me' or Mike Sarne and Wendy Richards' 'Come Outside' as a fraction too suggestive. This was not the juncture for a full-scale revolution.

Hesitant and self-conscious at first then with evident pleasure, pairs swung out on to the floor and began to jive. Mrs Egerton stood with hands on her hips, then chuckled.

'We used to call it the jitterbug,' she remarked. But nobody heard her.

By nine the band were at full pitch. The music was deafening, the gym hall crowded and hot. Half-bottles of cheap rum and vodka were passed secretively around among the bolder lads. The teachers had retired to the staff room where they sipped tea and bemoaned the disappearance of their status and influence with every crashing chord.

'Wanna dance?'

Behind the hatch Helen cursed. She had preferred to busy herself in the kitchen to avoid undesired attention. And if the facilities were kept tidy she could slip away quickly at the close. She raised her head. The gangly youth looked familiar.

'Met you before, haven't I?' He twitched awkwardly. From out of the sleeves protruded his wrists and hands, large and knobbly, with bitten nails. 'That day at the Cavern. I've not forgotten. Name's Mack.'

She gave a suitably withering glance but he was not put off.

'Come on. Just one. I like that frock. I promise I won't be a pest.'

His tone was wistful. Merchant Taylor's had meanly insisted that their pupils attend in uniform but his tie was askew and his blazer hung off his shoulders. Had Miss Plumb tried any such injunction her pupils would have refused to appear. There was a world of contrast between the offspring of conventional wealthy suburbanites and the street-wise inner city.

'Oh, well.'

It wasn't him she wanted. Not a tall, skinny schoolboy. Not an Englishman. His father was probably a bank employee and he'd be one in his turn. He'd adjudicate solemnly on the lives and proposals of those twirling around him in years to come as they negotiated the shallows of mortgages and bank loans. Despite the beads of sweat on his forehead and his efforts to keep to the rhythm he was ultra-respectable, committed to doing what was correct however meagre its appeal to him. He'd make a great pharmacist. He'd ride the bus till he could afford a car, then sit in the morning rush hour till he retired or keeled over with a coronary. Boys like that did not feel the rhythm. They did not know what it could mean.

'Drat,' Helen grumbled. She had failed to move away adroitly enough. The band, perspiring freely, had started to play a slow tune. Her partner made a lunge and dragged her into his arms.

'Your cheatin' heart – will tell on you –'

'But I'm not cheating,' Helen muttered savagely to herself. Her nose wrinkled against Old Spice aftershave mixed with body odour. She was stuck, enfolded by thin arms and sticky palms. She wanted to yell, and shove him away.

It was not merely that she was with the wrong boy, whose presence made her body revolt in fury and anguish. Such a lot was in the balance. It was as if a timebomb set seventeen years ago the day she was born but held in abeyance during her minority had begun to tick, loudly. Things were about to happen, mostly beyond her control. It was a strange and uncomfortable sensation: exhilarating, necessary, unavoidable. And quite terrifying.

To distract herself Helen examined the boy. His acne had worsened since their first encounter. An inch from her eyes a large pustule was about to burst. She gazed concentratedly at the scarlet hillock, then felt ashamed. She ought to have pity. He must hate being adolescent, was probably as disgusted by his skin condition, by his general state, as she was.

What would he know about sex? In all probability he had well-thumbed magazines, *Playboy* and similar, hidden in secret places away from prying parental eyes. Some such, and others brought in from Germany and France, circulated in most Liverpool schools. But the nearest he'd have got to a live female form would have been a quick grab in the dark after a dance such as this, a squeeze of a brassiered breast, a tug at knicker elastic. He'd never have dared buy a contraceptive; his cheeks would have flamed, he'd have fled in panic. If he wasn't careful, that kind of boy got married young to somebody he didn't love, and was trapped in his turn.

Two decades before boys like him on National Service would have learned their business in Aden or Cyprus. Michael hinted as much, since Uncle Sam depended on conscription. Their service in the military educated men in more ways than one. But not this boy, who might never perform sex with skill and joy, as Michael did. How different they were: how far she had come.

So Helen gyrated with a fretful air, and saved her energy for Michael, and itched to get away.

'Reverend Mother, the next girl is here.'

'In a minute. How have you been today, sister? Better, I hope?'

'I cope, Reverend Mother. This is the cross women must carry.'

'The punishment for the faithlessness of our mother Eve. God's curse, indeed.'

'But worse at a certain age – at the change of life.'

'For some. It means we understand suffering, sister. Far better than men. It brings us closer to Our Lord. However, your trials will terminate eventually, be sure of that. Pray for fortitude. Send her in.'

'Yes, Reverend Mother. Thank you, Reverend Mother.'

'Good evening. My name is Mother Ignatius but you can call me Reverend Mother. What are you known as?'

'Colette, Reverend Mother. Colette – Thomas.'

'Indeed. It says O'Brien here. Father O'Connor knows you?'

The girl bowed her head but did not reply. In her hands was a small handkerchief twisted tight. The knuckles showed white. Reverend Mother pursed her lips.

'Never mind that. Do I need to ask why you're here? Speak up, child, I can't hear your mumble.'

'I'm having a baby.'

'Are you now. And not married? Who is the father?'

'I – I can't say.'

'So *he* is married, is he not. Otherwise it's a wedding you'd be seeking, not a bed for your confinement.'

The girl shifted uncomfortably and glanced around as if seeking a means of escape. Her voice was a low monotone, but took on a pleading note. 'I have a while to go but I can't stay at school till the end. Or at home. I thought –'

'Yes? Do speak up. Goodness, they get worse each time. What is it you thought? Pity you didn't think a bit sooner, young lady, and avoided this pickle from the start.'

'I – I wondered if I could come and work here, skivvying, anything, for my keep, while I wait.'

'Hmm, you wouldn't be the first. Mostly they're straight off the boat. You don't look like you're used to scrubbing floors.'

The girl bridled. 'I can work. I'd do whatever I was asked.'

'You'd do whatever you were told, if we admitted you early. This home is for confined pregnant women. It's not a rest cure. And we'd expect you to confess your sin, and give us the name.'

'I know I've sinned, Reverend Mother. I'm a good Catholic – I go to confession. I've just been, but there was a long queue.'

'The name, then?'

Mother Ignatius waited, pen in hand, but Colette slowly shook her head. The nun's wimple rustled crisply.

'Ah, what's the use? You might not even have it, if you've had carnal relations with several men. Mortal sin – do I need to tell you? Evidently yes. If it weren't my God-given duty to save your soul, young woman, I would not stoop to try. But this order will strive mightily to bring you to redemption through the blood of our Saviour. Then there is the matter of the adoption.'

It took a long time before the girl would reply, but her hands were busy, twisting and straining at the handkerchief.

'Yes, Reverend Mother. That will be for the best, anyway.'

'Well, you're not capable of bringing a child up yourself, are you? You'll be able to see the baby, of course. We're not ogres here, we don't steal the infant wet from the birth-bed. But a fortnight after delivery, barring hitches, it'll be handed over to a God-fearing couple. A Catholic family. You can rest assured that your child'll be brought up properly.'

'He will go to kind people, won't he? Where they'll love him?'

'Huh. *You* are in no position to make that proviso since you can't provide any kind of home yourself. Make up your mind: once it's gone you will never see it again. Never. Is that clear?'

'Why won't you?'

'Because. That's why. Not until we're married.'

'Oh, come *on*, Roseanne. That's a completely out-dated attitude. Nobody believes that nowadays. I'll be careful, I promise.'

Roseanne Nixon eyed Jerry Feinstein grimly and wondered how long her refusal could be maintained. He had called at her house in Menlove Gardens to collect her; newly decorated, it smelled of paint. The aim had been to go to the cinema, probably the Odeon at Allerton for *The Day of the Triffids*. Jerry liked what he called sci-fi, though Roseanne had other preferences.

Her parents however were due at the JNF dinner and had no intention of being late. The Braddocks were the main guests, the new Leader of the city council and his wife the MP, one of the handful of women elected to the House of Commons. Their presence had led Mrs Nixon to consider not going at all. Then her sister had suggested that these scions of the Liverpool Labour party could best be humiliated if government supporters flaunted their finery as demonstrative of a world of which the Braddocks and their ilk were both ignorant and critical.

'That'd show 'em,' Sylvia had urged, and discussed which of their cherished fur coats – the silver fox or her beaver lamb – would fill the bill most effectively.

So Rita Nixon, dressed to impress in brocaded silk, a diamond pendant and the fox, her husband fidgety and irritable at her side, had departed the moment Jerry had arrived, with admonitions to the children to lock up properly and mind the paint before they went out and not leave any windows open.

Jerry had made appropriate soothing noises. As soon as the car had vanished down the road he took off his own coat and scarf, hung them casually on the knob at the end of the banisters and pinned Roseanne's warm, plump body against the fresh wallpaper on the hall wall.

'No,' she repeated primly. 'Apart from anything else, they could come back any minute. You know my father's ulcer plays up.'

'He uses it as a convenience. I mean, I'm sure he has one, but it only plays up when he's had enough.'

'Probably. All men are the same, my mother says.'

His right forearm was firmly placed on the wall above her head, his left about her waist. Around them the smell of paint and wallpaper paste was mingled with Coty's L'Aimant. She could not easily evade his advances. Nor, to be truthful, did she mean to. The trick was to get him where she wanted, and it wasn't here. She was not scared of him; if the worst came, he could be kneed in the groin and put out of action for a day or so. Roseanne, like most Liverpool girls, could take excellent care of herself.

Jerry's eyes flickered. He bent and began to nibble her earlobe. 'Please,' he whispered. 'Please let me. I love you, Roseanne. You're gorgeous. It's driving me nuts.' Suddenly he put his tongue in her ear and she squealed.

Coolly she planted her hand on his chest and pushed him off. 'Are we engaged?' she demanded. 'Like you said?'

He shrugged. 'Sure. I just can't afford a ring, yet.'

'Well then.' Roseanne pondered. Jerry leaned towards her and pressed his erection into her. She yelped and struggled a little, but did not remove herself. 'Well: you can't go the whole way. But you can have a bit of a feel, if you like. Will that keep you happy for the time being?'

Jerry groaned. 'God, then I'll be like this for hours. Or else I'll come and make a mess on my trousers. When your parents get home they'll guess. At least, your Dad will.'

'Can't help that. Halfway or nothing at all. And don't ask me to play with your – thingy, or touch it. I don't even want to see it.'

Jerry bent again, pulled her to him, and covered her lips with his own. From the way he thrust his tongue into her mouth Roseanne gathered he was genuinely hungry for sex. Not that Jerry especially wanted it from her – she was under no illusions about that. But the tensions of his writhing body told her firmly that should she continue to deny him he'd find what he craved elsewhere. Prudence nevertheless ordained that if she succumbed too readily she would never be Mrs Jerry Feinstein, with no guarantee that anything better might ever walk in.

'You have to accept, Jerry,' she introduced a note of solemnity as she drew the lounge curtains, 'that this is a decent house and I am a nice girl. A virgin, and I intend to be a virgin on my wedding night. I am not an easy lay, or a tart. Not like some I could name.'

Jerry lounged back on the pale blue sofa. 'Like who? Come and sit here and relax.' On a sudden thought he undid his laces and slipped off his shoes. The session could get gymnastic and sweaty. It would not do to leave scuff marks on the furniture.

'Like – oh, like that Helen Majinsky. You used to fancy her, didn't you? Too hoity toity today. But I'm certain she's sleeping with that GI of hers. Same as her Dad's cousins. My mother said, one twang of an American accent and the Majinsky knickers were off. My mother is a bit vulgar but I bet she has a point.'

Roseanne had stopped fussing about the room and seated herself beside him. Jerry ran his fingers up the fleshy thigh until he found the skin above the stocking top. At his touch it reacted satisfyingly into goosebumps. She was not entirely immune. 'Umm, sounds like a great suggestion to me.'

'The question is,' Roseanne ruminated as she allowed him to fiddle unproductively with the buttons of her blouse, 'what are we going to do about it? It demeans all our friends to have that – that *looseness* going on. She doesn't think any of our boys are enough for her. Don't you think we should tell somebody? Older, I mean?'

'Yeah, if you say so,' Jerry concurred as he nibbled at her neck. Its smoothness was surprisingly attractive, with a clear view of breasts with the same yielding curve. With a quick nip he sucked in the hollow of her shoulder-blade and left a purple mark. 'You've got some explaining of your own to do now. I've given you a love bite. Now let me get this straight – how far will you let me go this time?'

The city centre pub was dark, cramped and very dirty. On the planked floor scattered sawdust absorbed spills and expectorations. Customers leaned heavily on the bar, their elbows in patches of wet, cigarettes on lower lips, boots resting on brass rails. Disputes flowed freely over the day's football, insults were traded. The air was a fug.

Helen and Michael squeezed behind a corner table, he with a pint and she with a Coca Cola. He kept his flyer's jacket on despite the warmth; one or two customers had been eyeing it.

'I shouldn't be in here. Eighteen is the age.'

'I'm not about to complain. In some states, Helen, it's twenty-one, and you'd have to show an ID. On liquor the US is more puritan than Europe. That's why we boys try to be posted over here. Though one day pubs like this'll sell cold Budweiser, and then you Brits'll know what beer is.'

'I don't mind a lager and lime. That's a woman's drink.'

'You want one?' He half rose.

She shook her head. 'No. Let's talk. It's so great just to see you.'

'Especially today. Happy birthday! I've a present somewhere.'

He rummaged in his jacket as she watched him, amused and content to be in his company. The gift was wrapped in coloured paper. She unwrapped it and broke into a broad smile.

'Oh, heavens. Black Magic. Lovely. You shouldn't have.'

'Box of chocolates. Not much, I'm afraid. But if I bought you perfume or a slip or something, your mother'd notice. If you'd been free tonight we could have had some fun at the base.'

She knew she seemed withdrawn without her usual vivacity. He would spot it at once.

'What's the matter, Helen?'

'Nothing. Everything.'

'Go on. Tell me. If I can help –'

'You can't but thank you. The next few weeks – I shall go bananas. Certifiable.' This was the opportunity she had needed. She lifted her drink and swallowed. 'I chide myself I mustn't worry, just do my best. I have offers from Manchester and Liverpool universities – both would mean an education, but no escape. I'd be stuck. The rest have come through as refusals – perhaps they think I'm a bit young, or they don't believe the exam grade predictions. The Oxford rejection really hurt, I must say. On Monday I'll know whether I'm called for interview at Cambridge. The test papers last month weren't too bad – I felt I'd done fairly well. Almost confident, in fact. Now I'm not so sure.'

'Do you want me to tell you yet again that you're one smart cookie, and that you'll do brilliantly? Have courage, have faith in yourself. My God, Helen, what kinda society is it that so squashes you down? It's as if every other sentence I hear in Britain has "can't" in it. Americans are joshed for our "can-do" mentality. I didn't know what that meant till I got here.'

'I am supposed to conform.' Helen intended the remark to emerge laconic, dry, but instead it sounded desperate and bitter. She followed the train of reflection out loud. 'I love my family but I can't live with their limitations and restrictions on me. I respect religious people like Reverend Siegel but if I stay we'll start to fight; my disapproval and dislike will grow. I'm scared my belief in God – or in anything – will be wiped out. Like with my father, I suppose.'

Michael said nothing but his expression willed her to continue. A customer carrying two full pint glasses pushed past. Beer spilled in a sloppy puddle on the floor. Helen gazed after the man with a sigh.

'I love Liverpool and its scousers. Honestly. Our humour and kind-ness are legendary, yet they make me miserable with their endless moans and their inability to see the virtues of sheer hard work. I do genuinely like most of the people I live with, but they want me to be the same as them, to stay here, ossify. I can't. And I can't bear it.'

Michael sipped quietly but did not interrupt.

'And when I sit there in that interview – if it happens – I'll have to conform to a whole new set of norms, those set by upper-class Cambridge dons, and I haven't the foggiest what they are. Will they be snooty and stare down their noses at me? Will they take umbrage at my accent? Will I be anywhere near what they're looking for?'

Michael was chuckling at her, as if she were talking nonsense. She ploughed on, 'Oh, Miss Plumb tries to prepare us, but it's as if we're studying another planet with misted-over telescopes. Yet if I'm spot on in that one half-hour, this time next year I won't be sitting in a scruffy pub near the river Mersey but in a panelled dining hall in one of civili-sation's oldest universities. On my way, but Lord knows where.'

'Will it help if I urge you simply to be yourself? It seems to me you fulfil Aristotle's maxim to the utmost.'

She sat up, puzzled. 'What's that?'

Michael grinned. 'I'm not claiming to be a classics scholar. But my Pa quoted it to me: President Kennedy often says it to young people when he makes awards at the White House. Let me think. It's Aristotle's def-inition of happiness – *the full use of your powers along lines of excellence*. The whole quote is longer and mentions virtue too, but that's the gist of it.'

She lifted her glass in a mock toast. 'I like that. It sets out what a person like me should do: firstly use whatever talents I have, not neglect or suppress them, nor pretend I don't have any, 'cause I have, period. Then aim to use them not merely to the full, which begs the question of what that means, but use them according to the highest external stan-dards. There are absolute measures of excellence – or at least, there's wide agreement. But those standards keep moving on, don't they?'

'Sure. What is excellence? Each age has its own convictions. The next batch reject their elders' notions, as we are doing over pop music. But in each society there's a revolutionary genius whose work was con-demned as rubbish by the establishment of his day.'

'Picasso. Mozart, I suppose. Solzhenitsyn today.' She adored this sort of conversation and strove to match Michael's parries. It reminded her warmly of the discussions she used to have with her father. Not that she and Daniel had talked much recently. There didn't seem to be much to say.

'Michelangelo – used to get into terrible trouble with the Pope. Leonardo da Vinci – died in exile.'

'Galileo. Darwin, for heaven's sake – I am supposed to be a scientist. D'you know he finished *Origin of Species* in 1844 but hid the manuscript for fifteen years because he could foresee the consequences? Scientists have always shaken the tree and been bashed on the head by the falling apple. Yet we never give up.'

Michael smiled. 'Chatter away like that in your interview and you'll have them eating out of your hand. But keep Aristotle in mind. He taught Alexander the Great, remember, so he knew about getting results.'

'Thanks. I'll look the original up at school. Could be very handy. Something's missing about that maxim, though.' Head on one side she contemplated her Coke. 'Let me think: ah, got it. Nothing about *purpose*. It implies that the purpose to which you put your brain is irrelevant. I don't agree. It's not enough to be smart. I want to be useful too. We should try to justify our existence. Service to others is a worthwhile objective. That much I've absorbed from school.' The discovery, though pompously expressed, intrigued her; she felt oddly pleased with herself.

'This time next year I could be in Washington,' Michael mused. 'I'll save up some furlough, tug a few strings and get myself on to the campaign. I'd like to do my bit to get Kennedy re-elected.'

Helen laughed. 'I can see you taking it up as a career.'

Michael did not laugh in reply. 'Maybe. Kennedy's next term could be terrific. He'll wipe the floor with Goldwater. He'll gain a much stronger mandate than in 1960 – maybe even a landslide. That'd mean progress with reform, on poverty, on race.'

A door opened, admitting a blast of chill air. A customer at the bar swore crudely, somebody responded similarly and the door banged shut. The streamers of tobacco fumes swirled and settled.

'As long as foreign policy doesn't overwhelm you,' Helen commented quietly, 'as it did over the Bay of Pigs.'

'Cuba's quiet, thank heaven. The administration's learned some painful lessons. The military will be reined in much more, my Pa reckons. Give them their heads and they'll bomb everything that moves. Give 'em a new toy like napalm and they're determined to try it. That's not a policy, that's the negation of a policy. Kennedy knows that.'

'You don't think those assassinations in Viet Nam will make any difference? Madame Nhu was a horrible person but the situation is hardly stable, is it? The furthest I've ever been is a school trip to Bruges so I shouldn't comment, but I loathed the sight of those Buddhist monks burning themselves. Sooner or later that regime was bound to fall apart.'

'That's probably true, Helen, but the Kennedys know Viet Nam. Remember they went there in 1951. That dope General de Lattre de Tassigny told 'em the French army could not be beaten and that Ho Chi

Minh and the Viet Minh'd be wiped out. Jack and Bobby knew better –
in Saigon they couldn't get out of town because of the insurgents. On
his return Jack did a radio interview in which he allied himself with the
'have nots' and declared that Communism cannot be defeated by force
of arms alone. In his opinion the USA should not buttress the status
quo, when that implied the French hanging on to the remains of their
empire.' Michael waved his finger in the air for emphasis. 'This
President knows more about Indo-China than most commentators. He
won't get us embroiled. As long as he's around, we'll ensure the
Mekong delta stays non-communist without thousands of our troops
being entangled. You'll see.'

'The Kennedys. You speak of them in the plural, Michael. As if
there's a whole tribe.'

'But there is. The father has an unsavoury reputation around
Washington: when he was ambassador at your Court of St James he
advocated peace with Hitler. But he's out of it now. Bobby I have a lot
of time for – he's eight years younger than the President and a harder-
edged, more emotional personality. He's got loads to learn if he wants
to be President, including how to get on with those he has to deal with.
My Pa says he and the Vice-President are barely on speaking terms and
Bobby makes sneering remarks behind LBJ's back – that'd have to stop.
And a third brother is in the wings. We could have Kennedys in the
White House till the end of the century! Americans are not averse to
dynasties. The Roosevelts, for example.'

Helen drained her glass. 'Long way from boxes of birthday chocolates,' she teased gently. 'But I do admire him. Kennedy is the most
imaginative and intelligent figure of our day; while he's in charge, you
feel the forces of good are in the saddle, don't you? His heart's
absolutely in the right place. You sense that he himself'd like to move
faster and it's the reactionaries who are preventing him, but given
enough support he'll win through. Best of all, he's *young*. In Europe all
we hear are old men like Mr Macmillan, or de Gaulle, or Douglas-
Home or Konrad Adenauer! Old, and grotty, and out of it. Kennedy fills
me with – oh – hope, I suppose. Yes, that's it – hope.'

Michael rubbed his eyes in the thick air, then glanced at his empty
glass. 'If Kennedy succeeds in what he's trying to do, Helen, he'll go
down in history as one of the great Presidents – he has the potential.
You remember the inaugural?'

'Oh, yes. Who could forget?' Helen smiled, and touched her lover's
hand. 'Kennedy reached out and spoke for us – the young, the next
generation.'

'*Ask not – what your country can do for you –*'

She joined in. '*Ask what you – can do for your country.*'

A fight had broken out a couple of tables away. Two men, both
hopelessly drunk, staggered to their feet and ineffectively swung their

fists at each other. A stool crashed to the floor followed by a beer mug. Their companions joined in the shouting, but made no attempt to separate them.

Michael raised his glass in rueful salute. 'Amen to that. Time for another drink?'

Helen winced as one of the drunks managed to land a blow on the unshaven jaw of the other. It would take some manoeuvring to avoid the altercation and reach the exit. 'No, I don't think so,' she murmured, and swiftly gathered up her coat and chocolates. 'It's about to get a mite unpleasant in here. Sorry, Michael, but this is Liverpool. Time to leave.'

Chapter Twenty-Two

Monday 19 November

Outside the study window the clouds scudded through an untidy sky. The sash frames rattled with gusts of wind; drops of rain worked their way through the thin putty and trickled down the inside of the pane. The squall was the tail end of a hurricane which had nearly but not quite blown itself out as it crossed the Atlantic. Helen shivered and pulled her cardigan cuffs down over her wrists. It would be rough at sea.

'Well, Helen. Are you ready?'

The call from Cambridge had come. Miss Plumb smoothed the tweed skirt over her thighs and tightened the narrow belt a notch. Her shoulders became square, her gaze bold, direct, almost stern. To Helen the gestures were unmistakably masculine as if the headmistress were the captain of a warship steadying his men before a great naval battle.

'Part of me is paralysed with terror, to tell you the truth, Miss Plumb. But I'm as ready as I'll ever be. You've prepared us thoroughly.'

The teacher acknowledged the compliment. 'You've certainly been reading widely. What was that I saw you deeply engrossed in yesterday – Aristotle?'

'Yes – the Nichomachean Ethics. I found it at the back of the library here.' Helen felt herself blush and lowered her eyes. She did not intend to boast but rather hoped the teacher's response would guide her to the correct pronunciation of the book's title and more information about it.

Miss Plumb's mouth twitched. 'Did you follow it?'

'Up to a point.' Helen bit her lip. The teacher had failed her test; the girl lacked the courage to inquire directly on such a triviality. 'Fortunately I found what I needed in Book One. And there was a detailed commentary.'

'Aristotle: the greatest teacher of all. If my profession had a patron saint it should be he. Politicians too – have you got as far as what he says about them?'

Helen shook her head.

'I can't recall it exactly, but it's on the lines of: "Politicians have no leisure, because they are always aiming at something beyond political life itself: power and glory, or happiness."'

The girl made a note. 'That's true for most of us, isn't it? We aim not merely to live day by day, but towards ultimate objectives.'

'No, I don't think so,' the teacher responded briskly. 'Not if you mean that *most* people operate that way. Rather the opposite. *Most* people – the working classes, or what the Greeks called the *hoi polloi* – George Orwell's proles – live from day to day, buffeted by a fate they regard as quite beyond their control. Oh, they have objectives. Survival is their main objective. Staying obscure and keeping their heads below the parapet are the means they adopt. Exposure is danger: the tall poppy is cut down first. Happiness, if obtained, is a bonus that comes by accident. Other motivations are frequently instinctive, not rational: both love and hatred of their fellow men, and such obvious drives as – as greed, and necessity.' The headmistress fixed her fiercest stare on the girl. 'But you're far ahead of such people, Helen. At least, if anything you've learned at Blackburne House has sunk in, and I'm sure it has.'

Helen waited. Miss Plumb had not mentioned duty. Or love of one's family, or the love of a man and a woman. Above the schoolyard two grey seagulls fought to combat the wind, their cries muted and inter-mittent. Miss Plumb tapped a forefinger on the desk.

'Your life *is* under your control. You can do with it what you wish. The sole limitations are your inherent abilities, your determination, your stamina. This school should have equipped you to leave the pro-letariat behind. You will not be ordinary, unless perversely you choose to be. You'll do more than merely survive. The stairway upwards beckons.'

'Up to where – to what?' Helen itched to return to the forthcoming interview but sensed that the discursive remarks were important. Michael singing 'Three Steps to Heaven' as the two lounged on a grave-stone came vividly back to her. Miss Plumb had unerringly struck recognisable chords. A conflict appeared inevitable between ambition and service. The struggle made her feel disloyal and horribly selfish. Yet Michael often said much the same as he urged her to cut loose from the world she knew.

But to what? How would she know if her talents were equal to her ambitions? How could you tell whether you could do something until you'd tried it? What should she try? And what happened if she failed? Miss Plumb who came from afar like Michael would have broader ideas than her parents but the teacher's world was limited in its turn. The experience of everybody she knew was so restricted.

Miss Plumb was sitting upright, her gimlet eyes fixed on her pupil. 'It's up to you. What is it you want from life? Upwards to academic excellence if you wish, as a don. Or elsewhere in education – you could become a headmistress, Helen, though I fear the authority of the role is about to diminish. Or an administrator, like our distinguished Mr Magnay who gave you your prizes at the Philharmonic Hall.'

The girl pulled a face. Miss Plumb laughed. 'Now, now. Without men of his vision – and adaptability – Liverpool would never have had the fine schools for which it is renowned. Though he is due to retire shortly and I believe may leave the city. However – where was I? Ah yes, your choices. Well! If your aim is a high salary I would advise accountancy or the law. Girls are now accepted as articled clerks. The wealthiest parents I know are solicitors and barristers. Women like Recorder Rose Heilbron are celebrated. In all of these, Helen dear, a Cambridge education is invaluable. It will open many doors.'

'But that's not why I want to go there,' the girl answered slowly. 'At least . . .' She stopped. 'I mean, it seems a bit shallow to want so little afterwards – a well-paid job or money in the bank. I want to be a useful member of society, but first I want to learn for its own sake. If I was only interested in a degree for vocational reasons I'd read chemistry at Manchester. But at Cambridge I can go into *any* lectures and sit in *any* classes. So I could be a scientist and a – a rounded human being too. I want to read, and think, and listen at the feet of the great. I want to sample *everything*. Otherwise how will I know what suits me?'

'Admirable. A hungry mind is the most precious possession. But you do have to earn a living at some stage also. Very few families round here can afford to support a perpetual student.'

The teacher was gazing at her oddly. In that book-lined study with the river in the distance, the Atlantic beyond, the gulls wheeling and crying so near the glass that their individual feathers were visible, to dream did not seem absurd. Helen's voice dropped. 'I live in a community of closed minds, Miss Plumb. While I can, I want to explore. Then I shall feel less like an idiot. And it's a practical matter too. If I'm to reject the philosophy I was brought up with, I have to replace it with – well, something. If I'm to have a purpose in life, I want it to be my own, not someone else's and particularly not one foisted upon me by my ancestors.'

With a sense of urgency, of having grasped an essential principle which could gain strength through articulation, Helen rushed on:

'Look: if I get to Cambridge I could attend lectures by a Nobel Laureate in the Cavendish Laboratory where the structure of the atom was discovered. But next day I could sit at the feet of F.R. Leavis and ask him about – the influence of Aristotle, I suppose.' She halted. 'D'you think they would regard me as a complete moron if I did that?'

'I'm sure Dr Leavis would be impressed,' the teacher responded smoothly. In the face of Helen's burst of enthusiasm her expression had been thoughtful. The girl had not mentioned her religion directly but it was plain that dissatisfaction with its tenets formed part of her frustrations. That was not a matter on which Miss Plumb felt able to advise. 'However, I would recommend that you first read just a *little* more. Here –' Miss Plumb walked to the tall bookcase and rummaged on a shelf. 'Try this. Bertrand Russell. You'd probably find his *Wisdom of the West* an entertaining and lighter version with its pictures and diagrams, but *The History of Western Philosophy* should keep you engrossed on the train down. He has the most remarkable encyclopaedic knowledge: you would find him an excellent guide.'

Helen accepted the book shyly. She sensed she was being mildly teased. 'I don't want to sound a fool.'

'You won't. You aren't. The sole thing that'll put them off, my dear, is if you don't sound at all. They're not interested in solid dependable types with nothing to say for themselves. They are seeking precisely that spirit of inquiry which you have enunciated so effectively, and the power to express it. The gift of the gab, my friend Dr Swanson called it – frightful phrase, but that'll captivate them. You have it. So keep your brain working as busily as it usually does; jot down in advance some points you might wish to make; have a couple of questions handy in case, and don't be frightened.'

'Easier said than done,' Helen whispered, but her hour was up. In her hand the small closely printed book felt formidably weighty. She collected her papers and went slowly out.

For a long moment after Helen had gone the headmistress sat on. Thirty years before Elizabeth Plumb had thirsted in the same way. Her options had been so much more narrow. To be a career woman then had been a path of sacrifice and unconventionality: for many people the spinster headmistress was an object of both awe and pity. Neither sentiment would affect Helen. Miss Plumb fidgeted and tidied the items on her desk, and deeply envied the good fortune of the new generation.

That evening after supper Helen showed her parents the printed instructions from St Margaret's College at Cambridge. The journey entailed the slow train towards London and a change at Bletchley, then another train to Cambridge; then back home via Bletchley once more. Miss Plumb had given her a travel voucher. An overnight stay was necessary.

'You'll get to know this Bletchley place pretty well,' commented Daniel from behind his newspaper. 'Sorry I can't drive you, but I can't close the shop. You'll ring your mother when you arrive, or she'll worry.'

'I'll give you some threepenny bits for the phone.' Annie's hands were restless. She started to stack dishes but her husband had not finished and motioned her to stop. He continued to read the paper and eat left-handedly at the same time.

'Don't worry. I'm not going to the moon. It's still England.'

'But it's so far.' Her mother began to twist her apron in her fingers. 'What I don't understand is why you can't take your degree in Liverpool and live at home? It'd be much cheaper.'

In the pit of her stomach Helen felt the ache which gnawed whenever her parents began to talk about her staying put. In bed at night it would surface and invariably made her weep. How could she reveal to them the extent of her rejection of their life, their beliefs, of them? It was kinder not to. Provided she could indeed escape.

She tried another tack, though her smile was tight. 'Did you never want to spread your wings, Mum? Never want to do something different from what everybody expected of you? Or you, Dad?'

Annie tossed her head. 'No, never. I was completely satisfied. I wanted a house, and a husband, and a family. I didn't trouble myself with silly fancies.'

Daniel raised his eyes and looked at his wife quizzically for a moment. To his daughter he shrugged. 'It was harder then, Helen. The war. And circumstances – we'd call it poverty these days, I suppose, though everybody was in the same boat then. The opportunities didn't exist.'

'Well – didn't you ever stand up for yourself, then, Mum? Never try to *be* somebody a little different? Never defy –?' She paused and her voice faltered.

'Never defy your parents, was what you were going to say.' Annie flapped her apron at her wayward daughter. 'Stubborn, you are. Won't learn sense. No of course I didn't. I accepted what was arranged for me by my family. We had no choice in those days. Your Dad's right.'

Daniel chuckled softly. 'Your mother's forgotten. She had her moments. You get some of your spirit from her.'

It occurred to Helen that these were old issues alluded to, long buried. Perhaps it was cruel to resurrect them but her curiosity was strong. Whatever she might learn could be armour in conflicts to come.

'Don't talk rubbish,' Annie replied crossly. 'You get your stubbornness from your father, not from me. Never would be told. And your bits of wildness. D'you know he had plans once to go to Parliament? Him, an ordinary working boy and with half a lung after the TB. If that isn't plain daft, I don't know what is.'

Helen switched her gaze from one to the other in astonishment. Daniel had taken refuge once more behind the *Echo*. She touched his shoulder. 'Did you, Dad? I never heard that before. I knew you were interested in politics, but I never thought you –'

'I didn't,' he answered shortly. 'Other people suggested it, but a bloke with no money had no chance. Even Labour MPs in those days came from the moneyed classes.'

Helen's reading told her that was far from true but she did not correct him. It sounded like a well-rehearsed but slight excuse for inaction. A faint cloud of injustice seemed nevertheless to cling to her father and left her saddened. She wished she had known about it earlier; when they were closer, she could have questioned him. But it was ages since they had talked discursively. When she needed to unburden herself Michael was altogether more *au fait* with her feelings.

Annie prodded her daughter. 'I can't understand why you need more than you see around you. Women were made to be wives and mothers. They're at their best and happiest when they have someone to take care of. Even those women who never married – look at them, the devoted way they look after elderly parents. Women biologically have a caring nature. We're not suited to jobs and careers, except temporarily. Have your fling but then be ready to settle down. You should be doing like your friend Roseanne Nixon – getting engaged as soon as she's eighteen. She'll be married before she's twenty when they've saved a bit, then she'll make her mother a grandma. Now what more could any girl want?'

That sort of wedlock sounded more like a trap, Helen reflected, something to flee, not to seek. A flicker of memory brought back Gertie's remark about her mother as a martyr. Annie's normal expression was hardly one of unalloyed satisfaction nor had it ever been. A touch of panic was more characteristic, tinged with discontent. Gertie had hinted that her mother did not like sex and did not believe it could be a source of joy. On that Helen already had her own views. Perhaps sex was the problem: but it was hardly a matter one could raise, now or in the future. Talking intimately with your own mother was virtually impossible.

'I am not Roseanne Nixon, and I don't want to be her,' the girl responded firmly. 'And you don't want me like that, surely. She's lazy, and sly, and a tease. She plans to live off her husband's earnings – and if it's Jerry Feinstein she might find that tougher than she expects because he's as idle as she is. Not a fine example to hold up, Mum, sorry.'

The noise behind Daniel's paper might have been a chortle but he said nothing. Annie gave him a despairing tap with her tea towel. With or without her husband's assistance her duty as a mother was still uppermost. She tried one more time.

'This stuff about education can be risky, Helen,' she urged. 'Fills you with ambitions above your station that could leave you restless and miserable. You've got to realise, as your Dad had to, that people like us don't do things like that – Parliament and such. We're ordinary folk, working class and proud of it. There's nothing wrong with being working class, you know. Salt of the earth, we are. And you want to turn your back – but it won't bring you happiness, you mark my words.'

Daniel folded the newspaper. 'You should listen carefully to your mother,' he concurred. 'She's seldom wrong. People like us have no capital, nothing to back us up. If you get into trouble – in debt or whatever – I can't help you, I don't have it. Oh, I know those who have it, but at a price. And part of our family pride is not to have to ask. So stay small, don't stick your neck out and you won't fall over.'

'That is a very restrictive philosophy, Dad,' Helen countered, then wished she hadn't as she saw the spark of annoyance in Daniel's eyes. She hurried on, 'But it won't work for me, or my future. I have to take risks, but if I've got the backing of a good education – the finest I can get – the risks diminish, don't you see?'

Her parents glanced at each other rather than at Helen who rushed on regardless. She tried desperately to keep her tone calm but her voice trembled. 'An education is the one thing that was denied to both of you, wasn't it? So you don't see its benefits. What you've never had, you've never missed – you can't appreciate. It's intellectual capital, see. It's – it's like training a racehorse for the Grand National. Whatever its natural inheritance if it's well trained it can jump higher and more cleanly, can't it? Then it's more likely to be a winner.'

'It won't make you happy,' her mother repeated slowly. Helen wanted to scream at her that Annie's way of life seemed to have brought in its wake only dismal acquiescence. There had to be something better than this, this living room with its cheap furniture, the remains of an ill-cooked dinner, her father slumped tired in his chair, the newspaper propped up on the salt cellar, her mother in her apron. There had to be.

Helen rose and came to Annie's side and put her arm round her mother's thin shoulders. 'But you'll wish me well, won't you, Mum? I know Dad does, though he doesn't say much. I'd far rather go to the interview with your blessing than without it.'

'You will be lost to us,' her mother muttered. 'It will be goodbye.' But she set her mouth square. 'Of course I wish you well. You're my only daughter. Even if I don't agree with what you're up to.'

The college board room had been built in the 1930s in a minimalist style long regretted. The starkness of its plain cream walls was barely alleviated by portraits of former Principals, stern females with hair in buns and voluminous academic gowns. Outside its tall small-paned windows a grey rain was falling. At the far end mackintoshes dripped and umbrellas stood open like cartwheels.

The main furniture was a massive mahogany table donated by a brother college. Around three sides were eight women. Dr Edith Swanson, her grey hair cut severely short for the occasion, the man's watch on its black strap prominent on her wrist, sat to the Principal's right. Then the delicate Mrs Rossotti, so pretty, clever and shy. Opposite her the philosophy tutor, a wraith-like figure, twisted her thin limbs around the back of her chair in an agony of self-expression. Further down came the maths tutor, on loan from another female college since St Margaret's did not have one of its own; then the Honourable Maud

Sheppard, President of the Senior Common Room, a bag of boiled sweets before her, whose father the Earl of Westmorland had been a substantial donor when his third and plainest daughter had to his relief immersed herself in the College; and finally two younger research fellows so overawed at the honour of representing the junior teaching body that they said very little.

The Principal opened her folder. Lady Donington was a large woman with a soft body which had spread relentlessly since her thirties. Wispy hair framed a broad forehead, pink cheeks and a generous mouth. Marriage had produced four children on or about the same dates as her First, her doctorate and publication of the standard tome which had led to her appointment at St Margaret's. However unconfined she might be physically there was nothing ill disciplined about the Principal's brain, while her heart brimmed with affection for her students, her staff and humankind in general.

'Good morning. Natural sciences next. Edith, you'll lead.'

'Thank you, Principal, but I don't quite see why. My discipline is English. Mrs Rossotti, surely?'

The chemistry don shook her head and twittered dissent. Barely thirty with fluffy hair, her combination of brilliance and femininity perpetually confused her colleagues. Dr Swanson did not encourage the discussion to continue; it suited the Dean perfectly to dominate the event. At least this way one might ensure that one's own preferences, honed by careful consideration of test papers and personal contacts up and down the country, would be selected for admittance.

The Principal referred to jottings on a notepad. 'I should remind you that we have about one hundred places to offer and a thousand candidates from throughout the world. We also have certain – ah, obligations, which so far, I regret, we have failed to meet.'

Every face around the table turned respectfully. 'Obligations? What do you have in mind, Principal?' Dr Swanson inquired. She was familiar with the answer.

The notepad was tapped. 'Governing Body wished us to increase the uptake of state-educated girls. Our applications are running at eighty per cent private and public school. If you count the girls from private academies overseas it's higher. And to date, ladies, the offer rate is about the same. If we want to satisfy the governors we need more state school pupils.'

'But that implies discrimination, Principal,' the Hon Maud observed frostily. Her long nose twitched in distaste. 'Surely that could not be justified – to turn down better candidates in favour of some from – shall we say – a more dubious background – merely to meet the latest fashion?'

'Oh, I wouldn't put it that way,' the Principal replied. She leaned back in her chair which creaked alarmingly and put her fingertips together. The other dons watched the contest with open pleasure. 'The

view is taken that discrimination has already occurred – that it has
been endemic for years. So the grammar school girls are deterred from
applying. It is up to us to put the balance right.'

'So what do we do if we have two applicants of equal merit, but one
is from Christ's Hospital or Benenden and the other from –' the Hon
Maud consulted her notes '– an obscure city-centre grammar school in
Liverpool?'

The Fellows shuffled their papers. The maths don, being from
another college, smiled in private amusement. The Principal leaned forward and her chair creaked once more. This time she planted podgy
elbows on the polished table and gazed magisterially at each in turn. But
it was the Dean of Admissions who spoke.

'We will make no special allowances. That would be quite unfair and
the President of the SCR's reservations would be correct. But we must
bear in mind that our offer to that young northern girl might be her
chance of a lifetime. The scion of a wealthy family could do quite as
well at – ah – Nottingham.'

The Hon Maud sniffed loudly but was silenced by the Principal's
lifted eyebrow. The philosophy don murmured something indistinct
which might have been a Sanskrit proverb then clutched her chair for
reassurance. The Hon Maud subsided, took a boiled sweet from the
packet, unwrapped it noisily and popped it into her mouth while glar-
ing over the Principal's head.

'It might nevertheless', the philosophy tutor continued in English,
'help the women's movement hugely if vigorous strident northern girls
were admitted. Amazons indeed! Did you see the Cambridge Union has
at last admitted women as full members? I went to the debate last
week. Only twenty-eight have joined so far, but just think! The *Daily
Telegraph* wrote that we might even see "over the blown-up hairdo of
an earnest young female debater the misty aura of a future woman
Prime Minister". I confess I didn't see one. But the very next girl to
come into this room could be that person.'

She paused for breath, eyes shining. Dr Swanson pursed her lips.
Their job was to educate the girls, not to elevate them.

'None of us like it,' the Principal sighed. 'But we must give these
young women their chance. It will change the nature of College, I grant
you that. Fresh blood and what-have-you. But we should be prepared
for the unexpected, and welcome it when it surfaces.' She nudged the
Dean for reassurance and was gratified to receive several vigorous
grunts. 'Fine. Then we have fifteen this morning, and another eighteen
this afternoon. Onward!'

Helen leaned against the wash basin in the ladies' toilet on the main corridor of St Margaret's. It was only Thursday but it felt like a year since
she had left home.

She was the washroom's sole occupant. Slowly she washed her hands and wiped them on the towel hanging on a hook. The striped fabric was not particularly clean. Her hair was wet but there was no way to dry it, nor was there time to change her blouse. The maroon lino on the floor was in need of a scrub and the mirrors were marked with splashes. One cubicle was locked with an old dog-eared notice pinned to the door proclaiming it out of order. Her mother would have disdained using such facilities. Helen bit her lip. Cambridge life so far was not nearly as glamorous as she had hoped.

That was not the only illusion discarded. The journey had been an endurance test of alternately chilly and overheated carriages laden with smoke from tobacco and diesel engines, infused with damp clothing and buffeted by repeated contact with too many bodies. Once she had glimpsed Brenda and Meg on a windswept distant platform and had called but to no avail. To the bewildered girl who asked for assistance – which platform, what time, how much – blank faces were turned, heads shaken. The result for Helen was exhaustion and disorientation. Added to the growing sense of not knowing where she was going – or rather, her awareness that this was her mother's criticism – the girl had arrived at St Margaret's as dishevelled as her fellow travellers and with a bleak and disordered air.

Her own distinctly grubby hands had left a mark on the towel. Cross with herself, she rewashed them thoroughly till the soapy water ran clear, then combed her hair tidily and picked lint off her navy-blue skirt. It was good not to be in school uniform. One tap was marked 'Drinking Water'; she found a glass nearby, rinsed it and drank.

Slowly her good humour returned. Washing of the hands: the effort to keep clean soothed her. She was not about to succumb to the debilitating pressures of the weather or the journey, nor to the nagging desire to run away, straight back home. The flow of tepid water and the drink was refreshing. Wherever she planned to go the voyage would be arduous. A little accumulated dirt would not deter her. It could be washed off. She would arrive her own person. She would go into the interview as respectable as usual. She would be a credit to her mother, to her upbringing.

The face in the mirror half smiled back at her through the streaks. She straightened her shoulders. Daft, really, that her mother's prejudices on personal appearance should fortify her daughter in a place where such priorities would be derided as keeping people down, especially women. Annie relished her home comforts precisely because their acquisition had been so hard won, their lack so acutely remembered. The central heating installed two years before meant no more frozen mornings clearing the grate. Hot tap-water in kitchen and bathroom was a reminder of black-leaded ranges and boiled kettles. A washing machine was still cooed over, while the house had no fewer than two toilets, one upstairs, the other outside, both spotless and smelling of daily Harpic.

Was it possible to hold both sets of values at once? To be both working class and an intellectual, to be both a Liverpool girl and an aspiring Cambridge undergraduate? At home most people believed these were contradictions in terms, mutually exclusive. *Most* people, most of those she knew, especially the older ones, in all honesty would not have started out on her journey even if given a push. They'd happily win the pools: that was an acceptable route to success, as was luck in business. Academia was despised where it was understood, but mainly it was dismissed with a wave of the hand as impossibly airy-fairy and pointless.

Was she going too far – being altogether too ambitious? An Icarus flying too near the sun? Maybe Annie was right. Yet surely one did not have to exchange one philosophy for another – it must be possible to meld the best of both, of the past and of what St Margaret's could offer.

The solemn brown eyes in the mirror pondered. Why not? Those old work ethics and traditions of cleanliness, graft, a whiff of materialism were leavened with a powerful sense of community. A place like Liverpool had a grand history not least because, however ragged a family, there were neighbours willing to help. At least, that had been true in her parents' childhood. It had to be admitted that such traditions were under threat. Colette in her dirty flat came to mind forcefully and Helen sighed. The fight in the pub which had cut short her evening with Michael was more typical than the prizegiving at the Philharmonic. *Brighton Rock* had displaced the *Ragged-Trousered Philanthropists*. And she herself, sprung from one of the most ancient cultures, could upbraid its Minister with fundamental challenges, as she had done with Reverend Siegel. When she had left the synagogue that afternoon, her questions confirmed by his inability to answer them to her satisfaction, it had felt as if she had closed a door on more than just a consecrated house. She had shut it on a part of herself for ever.

Her father's attitude had been more ambiguous than her mother's. Annie had set ideas of a woman's role, which on the whole was not to swan about and study but to prepare for wedlock and motherhood. Helen feared that it would indeed prove tricky to combine a home and a career – but if it were remotely possible, she would try. That would be her aim.

But Daniel? Helen rubbed her fingers on the mirror as if hoping his image might appear to help her, but the steamy glass was blank. Her father would have been clever enough to go to college, she had no doubt; that he was prevented by lack of means was so obvious it didn't need explanation. Poor boys from Liverpool's slums didn't get near. Poor boys got TB and were judged unfit even for war service, as her father had once commented with some bitterness. Yet he was an enigma. All the family stories – Gertie's among them – hinted that he had once been energetic and optimistic. Somewhere along the line he had had the stuffing knocked out of him. He had become the passive character she knew, unwilling to do more than argue superficially over the headlines after supper. He'd chosen to let the world pass him by. It was not his fault but it was his fate: and he had long since abandoned the struggle.

So he would warn her about the pitfalls and wistfully if half-heartedly pressurise her into giving in. Maybe he wanted to legitimise his own choices. If his clever daughter, generally reckoned to take after her father, turned her back too on the temptations of the outside world it would make his failures less acute. Yet somewhere deep down he must ache for her to fly. If only he could have brought himself to enthuse and support her. If only he could dredge up some of that positive approach to life he must once have had. But it was lost, or he was unable any more to put it into words. The tiniest scrap of encouragement would have sufficed, and would have made Helen love him dearly.

Instead her father sat at the gate like a blind man who could not see beyond his nose. His role as guide had been filled by substitutes like Miss Plumb and Michael. Except that Michael was not a substitute for anybody.

'I am my father's daughter, and I am not,' Helen murmured to the blurred face in the glass. 'I am Michael's girlfriend and I am much more than that. I come from my mother but I will never be my mother, nor much like her. *Never*. I am of Jewish blood but I wasn't born in Lvov or Frankfurt but England; I am English, but I am not a Christian. I am from a class which is disappearing anyway, so I am not alone. I am a child of the past but I am not a prisoner of it. I'm – I'm – Oh, Lord.'

She stopped and pointed at the mirror. 'What am I? Who am I? I'm Helen Majinsky, that's who, sufficient unto myself, and I'm about to walk into the most important fifteen minutes of my life with my head held high. Right! Here we go.'

And with a big grin, but her heart beating fast, she marched out of the washroom and headed down the corridor.

The Fellows of St Margaret's College raised their heads from their folders and examined the young woman who had quietly presented herself. The brow of the Hon Maud Sheppard furrowed as the Dean Dr Swanson acknowledged the newcomer and motioned her to a chair.

Majinsky, H. Aged seventeen, just. A bit young. Hair damp at the edges. Not yet taken her A levels. Not a single higher qualification to her name, yet. The Liverpool Institute for Girls: Blackburne House. The Hon Maud flinched inwardly. So this was one of the northern grammar-school girl scientists pushed forward by an overly enthusiastic Dean (one could not criticise the Principal). One had to be modern, but there were limits. Barriers should not be reduced unnecessarily. Protective walls once breached might lay the entire edifice open to destruction.

Majinsky was of medium height and build, open-faced and brown-haired with large dark eyes. Semitic blood. The Hon Maud privately acknowledged that that augured well, strangely enough, better than were the child a simple Liverpudlian with an accent redolent of pop music and bad comedians. The university was littered with erudite men and a few women who had escaped the Holocaust and found sanctuary. Their guttural accents added spice and their academic quality was generally superb – they were quite a gain, in fact, as were their emerging offspring. More of the same was not absolutely undesirable.

Beyond the windows rain pattered fitfully. The light had taken on a searing quality as if the sun were trying to break through. The young applicant was seated, her head up, her hands clasped steadily before her, at the far end of the table facing the Principal. Number twenty in a heavy day.

The Dean commenced. 'Good afternoon, Helen. Welcome to St Margaret's. Your entrance papers reached a high standard. Now we want to ask you some questions.'

The girl's eyes were bright. 'Yes, I'm ready.'

'But first – did you have a good journey? What were you reading?'

The inquiry was delivered with a deceptive smile. Helen blinked. 'Bertrand Russell. *The History of Western Philosophy.*'

'Really? But I thought you were a scientist.'

'I am. I'm also interested in the universe beyond science. Anyway, there's a lot about the philosophy of science in it.'

'Are you finding him enjoyable?'

Helen grimaced then shrugged. There was no mileage in pretence. 'Enjoyable is not exactly the adjective I'd use. But he makes me think, it makes me better informed, and I like that.'

Nods of approbation all round. A neat start. Notes were made in margins. The Principal turned to the mathematics tutor.

'Well,' the don drawled, 'now for the obvious question. Why do you want to come to St Margaret's?'

'Because it is there, is the obvious answer.' The crisp reply drew a laugh. Everyone began to relax. 'I mean, because this college is among the top-rated in the finest university I could aspire to. And like asking a mountaineer why he climbs mountains, I'd say that I want to obtain the very best education I can. So – I was advised to come here. If you will allow me.'

'Then why science?'

'That's harder to answer, because I suppose I might have chosen something else. Partly because I find it relatively straightforward – my maths are OK and my grades have been fair straight through. I enjoy studying what is not common knowledge: most people know so little about science that it's like a secret garden which I feel privileged to be able to explore. And it's useful. Plus I shall be able to get a job.'

The prosaic conclusion brought a further ripple of laughter. Helen frowned. The Principal signalled her to continue.

'My family don't have any money so to be employable afterwards does matter. But that's not my prime intention, as I don't know what I'll do when I finish – that's too far ahead to tell. What I especially like about science, though, is the quality of certainty it conveys. The world is changing so fast, but an aldehyde is an aldehyde, an atom is an atom. That's set, once it's discovered and described. The laws of nature can't be bent or twisted. And I like that too.'

'You find it comforting, do you?' This from the chemistry don. In the strange light her hair shimmered about her head, but her expression was intense. 'Yet the process of discovery is uncertain, is it not? And much of that process unpicks what we believed to be certainty before.'

'That's true,' Helen countered, and thanked her lucky stars that a similar discussion, much of which she had but dimly grasped at the time, had been part of Miss Plumb's tutorials for the scientific quartet. The don's observation about the effects of the process of discovery also reflected something of which she was suddenly quite sure in her own mind: *it did unpick certainty, but could not be prevented for all that.*

'But were I to read politics or history, for example, the situation would be far more fragile. There, nothing's fixed. Human behaviour alters under different pressures – research into what were believed to be historical facts turns them upside down. The very process of observation changes things – the existence of a free press, for example, makes a huge difference. Whereas in science there's no argument about, say, Newton's Law of Gravity. You can't have competing viewpoints on it. It's fixed and other laws revolve round it. So science gives us something absolute to hold on to, which history doesn't.'

Eyebrows were raised. Mrs Rossotti murmured, 'I think you may revise your views once you commence particle physics,' but indicated that she had finished.

The Dean, one of the scientific illiterates at the table, opened her mouth. 'But surely there are absolutes of human behaviour. Don't you believe in anything absolute?'

Helen pondered. Her pulses were racing, but she was conscious that every eye was on her. 'No-o. I don't think so. Except absolute zero. You can't get temperatures below that.'

'Capital!' The chemistry don slapped her palm on the table as if she had won the point herself.

The discussion ranged more widely for several moments over those who had challenged the accepted order. Helen promptly brought in both Darwin and Galileo; it was as if Michael's spirit sat on her shoulder whispering. Her acquisition of myriad facts and surmises, seldom

understood first time but retained and pondered over, settled into
steady patterns of thought and response. Her brain felt cool and deliberate, her speech a well-honed implement. Back in the washroom the
child had entered and vanished for ever; the new Helen had emerged,
outwardly calm, assured, self-confident, womanly.

The Principal lowered her head and gazed at her. 'But you must
believe in something. What do you think underpins human behaviour?'

Helen spoke slowly. 'Survival. Greed. Fear. Hate, if you consider the
Nazis. The love of one's family. Loyalty – blind loyalty, sometimes.
Emotions like that. But I can't answer for others, nor would I wish to
judge them. For myself, I try to guide my own behaviour according to
Aristotle.'

'You do, do you? Which bit?' The philosophy don sat up.

'I think the exact quote is "The good of man is the active exercise of
his soul's faculties in conformity with excellence or virtue." From the
Ethics. But I like President Kennedy's version – "the full use of your
powers along lines of excellence". It's a bit selfish, I suppose, but that's
what I try to do.'

As usual when she engaged in a conversation which stimulated and
excited her Helen's face had become faintly flushed, her eyes wider. Her
hands would not keep still but flitted with the rhythm of her words as
if in independent agreement. One Fellow was scribbling rapidly but she
had the total attention of the others.

The Principal intervened. Behind her the sky lightened; the rain had
petered out. 'What I would like you to explain to us, Helen, is how a
pupil from –' she placed her spectacles on her nose to check, then
removed them '– the Liverpool Institute High School for Girls learned
all that?'

The girl let her Scouse accent creep into play. If they were to accept
her, it had to be for what she was. 'I attend a remarkable institution.
Blackburne House, its colloquial name, was the first girls' day school in
the country when it was founded in 1844. Our brother school started
while King George IV was on the throne. It was philanthropic education
of that kind that helped make Liverpool great. The successes of that
great sea-port in turn made this country rich. And able to afford . . .'
She let her eyes roam around the room as a shaft of weak sunlight
touched the gilded picture frames. 'All this.'

She did not add, 'So there.' She did not need to, but gently softened
the riposte with a smile.

'Bravo,' Dr Swanson murmured.

The mathematician decided to have one more try. 'Then why not go
to Liverpool University?'

Helen took a deep breath. 'Because Cambridge is the best, as I said
before. And because, if I am to be truthful to you, I would prefer to get
away from what I have just described. I need to leave it behind. This is

my way to – to escape, and to accomplish it with such dash that nobody could be cross with me.'

'Really? So if we offered you a place you would accept it?'

Helen wanted to shout out – yes, yes, of course I would. But some devil was at work. It would not do to sound too eager. She put her head on one side, then smiled. 'I could suggest something better.'

'You could? What do you mean?'

The girl glanced about, slowly, from one adult face to another. An inner voice urged her on: the room seemed filled with rosy light and air, as if they were no longer in a cavernous room built on bare earth, but suspended above it, unbound and free. Her voice was low but clear.

'Please: you need to understand. You are absolutely right – my parents would love me to stay close to home. A simple place here would not impress them much. But if you offered me – oh, heavens. If you offered a scholarship, they could not refuse.'

'They couldn't?' The Principal's mouth had dropped open. Nobody had ever bargained before.

'No. 'Cause I'd have my photo in the *Liverpool Echo*, you see, and that'd convince them that I'd made it.'

And her smile widened, self-deprecatingly, but in complete accord with every person around the table. A slight hiss of breath, a glance here and there was exchanged, then silence reigned for a few seconds. The Principal beamed and closed her folder.

'Well, Helen. Miss Majinsky. We will have to bear that in mind. Thank you for your attendance. You will be hearing from us in a couple of days.'

Later that evening she lay on the narrow bed in the student lodging. The ceiling overhead was covered in a maze of cracks, but the pattern was unfamiliar and lacked comfort. A brown patch betrayed a forgotten leak from the room above. A great lassitude overcame her. For the first time she knew loneliness, and the ache of despair.

Her performance, she could now tell, had been over the top: undignified, crass and stupid. She had overdone it. They must have found her ludicrous, with her silly answers, her parade of discordant scraps of knowledge. The shallowness of her comprehension, the superficiality of her ill-acquired veneer of education must have been painstakingly obvious. And all delivered in that unmistakable accent. The dons were probably laughing about her even as she dozed. Her antics would be the talk of High Table for weeks to come.

She needed to think it through more, but both mind and body were drained. Those queries she had fluffed came hazily into her head and were batted half-heartedly away. There would be no re-run. So it would be Liverpool and her parents' house, or Manchester and an uncle's, depending on her grades. The door to freedom had slammed firmly shut.

If she stayed put alone she would have a restless and miserable night. Wearily she rose, tidied herself and made her way along the hall to the lounge used as a junior common room. Inside, a kettle was boiling merrily and coffee was being spooned into mugs. A group of young women sat on the rug in front of the electric fire, or lounged on armchairs. The television in the corner was switched on, though nobody was paying much attention.

'Hi! You're one of the candidates, aren't you? How do you like your coffee?'

NEWSFLASH. What was this? The newscaster appeared, his face solemn. He began to speak. A hush fell.

Everyone froze. A little cry came from one girl, a sob from another. An empty mug fell to the floor with a crash and broke but was ignored.

'We have the latest news from Dallas, Texas. President Kennedy has been shot. He has been rushed to hospital but doctors fear for his life. We will bring you more news as it comes in. I repeat, President Kennedy has been shot in Dallas . . .'

Chapter Twenty-Three

Sunday 25 November

'Oh, God, Pa. What's happening? What's happening to us?'

Michael fought back the tears. Had he been with his father instead of in a chilly corner of the postroom with the telephone receiver pressed tightly to his ear, he would have wept openly.

The crackly voice at the other end was sombre. 'I don't know, kid. None of us knows. One minute you're planning the re-election campaign and tossing around next year's legislative programme. Next you're on a windswept airfield as a coffin is brought out with a dead President inside. Forty-six years old. Everything yet to come.'

'Ma said you were over the Pacific when you heard?'

'Yeah, that's right. A big crowd of us – on a delegation to Japan, trade, security, that sort of thing. Six members of the Cabinet including Dean Rusk, Dillon and Stewart Udall. Turned that aircraft straight round and came back. The atmosphere was real jittery. Nobody knew whether there wasn't a bomb on the plane too. Boy, were we glad when we touched down.'

'I was in my bunk, waiting for supper. The base went berserk – everybody running around, completely crazy. Except for one Louisiana guy who hates him. Had to be put in the cooler for his own safety.'

'He was dead on arrival, I reckon. The surgeon claimed they found a pulse but Senator Yarborough told me half his head was blown away. The bits of bone flew up into the sunlight. What you saw splattered on Jackie's couture jacket were his brains. He never had a chance.'

'They're talking about conspiracy, Dad.'

Colonel Levison sighed. 'Yeah, they're talking about nothing else. I dunno. Oswald was crazy but his schoolmates on TV say he was a loner. That stuff about him going to Russia and his Russian wife. If he'd really been an assassin under orders he'd have kept his head down, stayed inconspicuous – yet he popped up in official files all over the place. Got court-martialled twice in the Marines and discharged.

Cleared off to the Soviet Union and couldn't make a go of things there either. D'you know State Department had to lend him $435 to get home? Then he finishes off his big day by killing a patrolman – so he was gonna land on Death Row one way or another. Doesn't sound like a professional conspirator to me. A mediocrity his entire life I reckon, until its spectacular conclusion.'

'Christ! Why couldn't he have gone and shot somebody else? Why Kennedy? Why?'

'Because JFK was President, that's why. Because the President was a success and handsome and rich, and a war hero – everything Lee Harvey Oswald was not. Because this was a man to look up to. If you mean, why was Kennedy taken from us: well, son, I have no answer. That's a matter for priests and pundits, not for mere foot-soldiers like us.'

There was silence for a moment. Michael sagged against the wall and passed a hand over his brow. He desperately wanted Helen and wondered if he dared phone her. Behind him a small queue had formed: only one overseas call per man was allowed and the other phone was equally busy. The airmen waited patiently, faces tinged with grief. One boy blew his nose and snuffled softly.

'It scares me, though, Dad. Oswald was arrested barely two hours after the shots and now he's dead too. So he can't talk.'

'He never admitted he did it. Not a word. But think, Michael. Who benefits from Kennedy's death? Nobody. The Soviets know our system isn't undermined: Khrushchev's not stupid. Kennedy's not the first – we've had four Presidents assassinated. Johnson was sworn in before the corpse was cold. We have a new President. Continuity is assured. Life goes on.'

'But what about the Cuba connection? The papers are full of it here. Oswald called himself a Marxist and was secretary of the Fair Play for Cuba committee. Don't you think Castro might have been involved?'

His father grunted. 'Huh. They're wild enough, I grant you. But the only people who'd have slit Kennedy's throat were some of the guys abandoned in the Bay of Pigs – anti-Castro, not the other way round. Anyway there was no chapter of the Fair Play committee in that area, so Oswald was fantasising. And that, in my view, is what he was doing all along.'

'Till it became reality. And Ruby got him.'

'Yes. And I tell you what worries me. Let's hope this sort of thing ain't catching. We don't want any more lunatics on the sidewalks of America gaining fame for five minutes by shootin' up whoever momentarily excites their jealousy.'

Michael turned his back on the line which had begun to murmur and shuffle its feet. 'Tell Mom I love her, and you too, Pa. Be careful. D'you think Johnson'll make a good President?'

'Can't tell. Heart in the right place. But he knows bugger all about foreign policy – never took any interest. His passion is the poverty pro-gramme: he wants to be the new Roosevelt. Sharecropping white southerners, Appalachians, urban poor. So South East Asia'll be left to the generals. Could get nasty.'

'No more Bay of Pigs, though.'

His father snorted, with a hint of bitterness. Michael could hear the tiredness in his voice. 'No, and Castro'll be around for ages yet. Let's hope we do a better job in Viet Nam. So long, son. Keep in touch.'

Daniel had declined to go but Annie was keen, and Helen at the last minute volunteered to accompany her mother. Hastily concocted prayers had already been offered during the sabbath service on the Saturday morning for the President and his family, but the congregation was invited to the synagogue hall on the Sunday afternoon. The men, assuming at least ten turned up, would *daven* a *kiddush* for the dead. A short eulogy would be preached. Then the Ladies' Guild, of which Annie was a member, would serve tea and cakes.

Attendance, despite wet weather, was far greater than anyone antici-pated. The mourning was genuine, the desire to pay their respects deeply instinctive. A Book of Remembrance was opened and dedicated. It would be illuminated in gold script and delivered later to the US Vice-Consul in Water Street. Yet it was not for the repose of the mur-dered President's soul that they prayed, but for their own.

Though Kennedy had not shown himself particularly close to the Jewish people he had many Jews in his administration and had given unstinting financial and political support to the state of Israel. The position of Jewish people in America was secure. Why, a Jew would even be the next Republican candidate – Barry Goldwater whose family came from Konin in Poland, the same strain as many British Jews. America had welcomed the world's persecuted: it was right and proper to honour the memory of its dead chief. And in so doing, to ease the ache in every breast at his dreadful demise.

'So young, so young.' Sylvia dabbed her eyes with an embroidered handkerchief. 'What a tragedy. May God rest his soul.'

Annie bent her head and busied herself with the Madeira cake. 'They take such risks when they go into politics,' she murmured. 'Do take a piece, Sylvia. I baked it myself. I couldn't think of anything else to do. Made me feel a little better.'

Sylvia chose the largest slice and crumbled it on to her plate. 'A strange, dangerous world they live in, the famous. I mean, we could get run over by a bus but it's not the same, is it? We wouldn't be on the front pages. Nobody's likely to come searching for us with a gun. It's as if the gods are wilful – on a whim they cut down the finest in their prime. If I remember my schooldays it's because they don't care for the competition. So pride goes before a fall, et cetera.'

'Hush – that's pagan. We're in *schul*,' Annie reminded her.

Sylvia shrugged. 'Still, I suppose we can be proud that the murderer Oswald was done away with by a Jewish man – Jack Rubinstein, wasn't that his proper name? Even if he was a night club owner. Murky. I'm not sure I believe an ounce of what I've heard. Terrible business.'

They were joined by her sister, cup of tea in hand, a home-made biscuit balanced in her saucer. Helen had made herself useful on the far side in the cloakroom among the damp coats. In the background the hubbub was subdued. Everyone spoke in hushed tones.

'I hear the American bases are on full alert,' Rita remarked. 'World war three, it could be. Just like the Cuba missile crisis.'

'No. Honestly?' Annie put down the plate anxiously. 'How do you know?'

'Well, there'll be no youth club at Harold House tonight. It's closed partly as a mark of respect, but Roseanne told me that when Jerry phoned around the boys at Burtonwood told him they couldn't come anyway.'

Sylvia and Rita exchanged glances. Both waited for Annie to react but she did not. Rita raised her voice. 'Pity. Those lads from the US Air Force have made a wonderful difference to our young people. Don't you agree, Annie?'

Their companion looked bewildered. 'I suppose so. We met a couple of them in a restaurant when Gertie was over. I didn't know they were still going to the club. You'd think they'd have plenty of other places to go – more sophisticated, perhaps.'

'They fancy our girls, I believe.' Sylvia tilted her head inquiringly.

It was obvious that Annie was unable to rise to their bait. Her brow furrowed as she struggled to keep up with the conversation. Then she laughed. 'History repeats itself, doesn't it? That camp used to be a hotbed for young girls desperate for a way out of Liverpool. Why, my husband's two cousins met their future husbands there, though I must say they seem to have been happy stateside. Years ago, of course.'

'Hotbed is the right word.' Rita placed her cup and saucer carefully on the table and folded gloved hands across her ample middle. Annie flushed. 'It's still going on. I'm surprised you've not heard.'

'Oh? Are we expecting a *simcha*? Somebody getting engaged?' Annie was flustered but polite. She had never had the same taste for gossip as the two matrons before her, who were notorious.

Rita satisfied herself that Helen was out of earshot then laid a hand on Annie's arm. 'We thought *you* might be telling *us*. Your daughter, Helen. So pretty, so brilliant. Still waters run deep, my dear. She's been seen around a few times with an American.'

'What, our Helen? You sure?'

Both women nodded, smirks playing around their mouths.

'My Roseanne told me,' Rita continued. 'Quite a nice boy he is.

Man, rather. Quite a bit older, I shouldn't be surprised. You mean to say she's not mentioned it?'

Annie pursed her lips but laughed again as lightly as she could. 'Dark horse, my daughter. She doesn't say much.'

'Roseanne thinks they're quite smitten with each other. But Helen was hoping to go to university, wasn't she?'

'Yes. She's had an offer from Liverpool but we are waiting to hear from last week's interview. I'm sure she'll be sensible. Her education comes first.' Annie began to clatter plates together. She had a sudden urge to bring the conversation to a close. The priorities she had just expressed were not her own but her daughter's. Or were they? Doubts assailed her, but it was not wise to display them before Sylvia and Rita. Otherwise the chatter would be around town in no time.

Rita turned away with a shrug. 'My Roseanne can't wait till the end of school,' she commented over her shoulder. 'We'll have the engagement party at the Adelphi. You should have a heart-to-heart with your Helen and find out what's up. Maybe hers'll be on board a ship, out in the Atlantic on its way to New York.'

To Rita's satisfaction Annie's mouth dropped open, then was quickly snapped shut. A parting shot could not be resisted.

'She's always had big ideas, your daughter. You brought her up a bit hoity toity, if you don't mind my saying so, Annie. Liverpool never satisfied her. Nor Liverpool boys neither.'

The head of the household was asleep. Daniel had pottered about till the women were gone from the house then put on his slippers and settled in an armchair with the previous night's *Echo*. It had not been long before the pages slipped from his grasp and he had slumbered. The shrill ring of the phone, when it came, startled him.

'I'm coming, I'm coming,' he grumbled as he lurched out of his seat. His calf had cramp and he pinched it to bring back the blood flow. In the hallway he could hear pop music from Barry's bedroom. '*Roll over Beethoven –*' That boy could live through a revolution and neither hear it nor care. Answering the phone was not in his repertoire.

'Childwall three six one nine.'

'Hallo?' The voice was male, masculine, American.

'Yes? Who is it?' It must be a wrong number.

'Ah – good afternoon. I'm sorry to trouble you. Is that the Majinsky household?'

Daniel took the earpiece away from his ear and gazed unfocused at it, as if it would identify the caller by itself. Some faint memory stirred then slipped away. He spoke again, testily. 'This is Daniel Majinsky. Who's that?'

The caller did not enlighten him. 'I'm trying to contact Miss Helen Majinsky. Is she available, please?'

'No, she's not. She's out. At the synagogue. A do for President Kennedy. Who wants her?'

'What time might she be home, sir?'

Sir?

'Look – who the hell is this? Who wants Helen? Is this some kind of joke?' The memory jangled again. Didn't he know that voice? His mind was still fuzzy from sleep. Not a customer. But where from? When?

'No. No – I'm sorry to have bothered you. Good-day to you.'

'What? D'you want me to tell Helen you telephoned? What name –?' The line had gone dead.

With a grunt Daniel replaced the handset and padded back to his armchair. People these days acted so oddly. Not leaving a name, even. His arches teased him with pins and needles. He bent and massaged his toes, then stretched and pointed his foot, but the effort brought no improvement. Circulation was so poor, the doctor said. Best to rest it. But his sleep from that point onwards, though resumed for a further forty minutes, was fitful and disturbed, and plagued by snatches of voices with accents from far away.

My Dad found the exercise book.

I'd heard him scrabbling about for another bottle of whisky. Money's been short the last few weeks, with no overtime as the nights draw in. He kept muttering he was sure he'd had a spare bottle hidden, in the back of the cupboard. That's where he went with an old torch. The miracle was that the torch worked. So he found his liquor, and my diary nearby.

Nobody's around. Not any more. My brothers have cleared off, probably permanently. They've got themselves a couple of girlfriends. Floozies, more like. They meet up on the ferry, on those riverboat shuffles. Late night cruises, in a wide circle round the estuary. The decks are awash with beer and vomit. The men piss over the sides and don't care who they splash. Hardly a romantic moonlit night like in films. The O'Brien boys love it, but it's horrible.

'What've we got 'ere?' Dad asked, and sat down on the floor. He unscrewed the cap on the bottle and took a swig, didn't bother with a glass. It'll all be gone by this evening. He takes his time drinking, not too fast. That way he seldom gets sick. Only drunk. Then he'll hit out at anything that crosses him.

My Mum used to hide. In the house we had then, there was a cupboard under the stairs. She'd shove me in and tell me to stay put till it had gone quiet. Sometimes she'd hide there herself. Once she whispered in the dark, 'It's not that he drinks a lot. He's not a bad man. But he can't hold it when he does.' Her voice was very sad.

But my Dad knows what drink does to him. He knows it makes him aggressive and belligerent. That's what he wants. Underneath he's timid – he's frightened of the loose cranes on the dockside, terrified of an accident. When his mate Jimmy – the one who was kind to me – fell into the ship's hold, or if a ganger gets smashed up at work, the bloke who comes home white as a sheet with his hands shaking is Joseph O'Brien. He drinks to give himself courage. He's a coward underneath. But really he drinks to make himself a man. That's what the booze does for him. And it always works.

So my Dad said, 'What 'ave we 'ere? You been writin', our Colette? Whatcha gonna be, then – a lady novelist or sum'pn?'

And he cackled, and took another swallow, and began to read bits out loud.

I felt myself go panicky inside. My breath came in short bursts. He was sprawled in the hallway so I could not get out without stepping over him. His eyesight isn't too perfect so he misread some words – luckily. He thought at first it was merely random scribbles and chuckled boozily to himself.

I went into the kitchen. I was scared and in a muddle. On the table sat the remains of stew for Sunday dinner; he'd been quite complimentary about my cooking. I was wearing what are now my everyday clothes, a loose skirt with the top button left unfastened hitched over my bump and a big sloppy sweater on top. That hides my condition pretty well. I kept nudging against corners of furniture with my belly and it hurt.

I tried to wash the pots and ignore him but I couldn't concentrate. I was so tired, and his chunter and grunts were a distraction. I needed a clear mind, but instead a faintness came over me. I stepped on to the balcony to get some air. It was cold and drizzly out, the atmosphere acrid and full of soot from the power station. In this damp weather it'll be going full blast.

A bird was singing sweetly somewhere. That was unusual. I leaned over the balcony and tried to see it. One bird with not much to sing about, I dare say. The notes came from a ledge above my head – there's an old lady on the twelfth floor feeds the birds with a few spare crumbs. They're mostly scavengers: crows, a couple of magpies, or pigeons, dirty things with twisted red legs, and gannets which scream and peck at her. The old woman doesn't seem to mind. Lonely, probably. Sometimes I hear her talking to the birds and telling them her woes. Bit like me.

Then I saw it – it flew quickly down and past, and on to the roof opposite. A tiny brown scrap with a perky stance, its short tail held smartly, and a high trilled song. I stared at it fascinated.

*Then I recognised it. It was the bird on the old farthing. A wren,
that is. The smallest British bird for the smallest coin. They're
permanent residents in Britain, they don't fly off for the winter.
They stay. They could leave, but they don't. They stay.*

*The birdsong lifted my spirits a bit. I could breathe more
easily, though my heart pounded at the least noise from inside.
Baby kicked me, hard. I put my hand to the bump to soothe
him. Darling baby: is it a sin to bring him into such a dread,
unhappy world? I don't believe so, even if it was a sin that
created him to begin with. But he can grow up as good and pure
as anyone. I'm certain of that.*

*I realised I was hungry. Must keep up my strength. I tiptoed
back into the kitchen, cut off a hunk of bread and nibbled a
piece. Another slice I broke into bits and scattered on the lip of
the balcony. The wren must have a nest nearby. Maybe it'll come
and whistle for me, as it does for lady upstairs.*

*Beyond the door it was quiet. I peeked into the hall. He'd
dozed off, the half-full open bottle clutched tightly in one hand.
The blue exercise book was on his knee. He hadn't got very far.
But I guessed if I tried to retrieve it or squeeze past he'd be
awake in an instant. No chance. No escape there.*

*So now I'm in the living room. The panicky sensation has
subsided and all I feel now is a weary listlessness. The sofa
stinks of chips and vinegar from last night's supper. Empty beer
bottles are stacked up in a corner. Both the curtains are torn. No
wonder my brothers have done a bunk. No wonder, come to
that, my friend Helen wrinkled her nose. What a pigsty we live
in. After baby is born I won't come back. I'll consider my
options, as they say: but afterwards.*

*The TV is on and the sound turned down. That's safe, and
comforting. A weekly news review, extended. From the hallway
I can hear the rumble of intermittent snores. An unwelcome
commentary.*

*They are showing pictures of the funeral. The President's been
lying in state two days since the coffin arrived in Washington,
but this morning he was buried in the military cemetery at
Arlington. A horse draped in black walks alone, stirrups crossed
over the empty saddle. A single drum, so mournful: no music.
Young cadets line the route. And thousands of people. I couldn't
see Jackie's face beneath her heavy veil, but the small boy, John,
stood to attention. Three years old and lost his daddy.*

*Ah, the children. Once the President was making a speech out
on the terrace of the White House and his daughter Caroline
emerged behind him, clumping around in her mother's high
heels. The child stole the show as the international leaders fell*

*about in stitches. Kennedy was a loving father. He wanted more
children but their babies died. It made the two of them more
human: Jack and Jackie, such important people yet they couldn't
have things exactly as they wished. But they had the daughter
and the little boy, and as his daddy's coffin passed he saluted
and tried to be brave.*

*I cried then, I did. I expect everybody cried who saw him.
That brought it home. A life has been snuffed out, prematurely:
hope, too, possibly. Millions of people, grief-stricken throughout
the world. The future will never be as bright, not after this, not
with the young leader gone. We weep together tonight.*

*Our Prime Minister was present, and Prince Philip. I think
the Queen should have gone: kings and queens from Europe,
Greece, Belgium were there, on parade with grim faces. And
President de Gaulle, upright, proud and rigid. Algerian refugees
have tried to assassinate him too. The Americans had warned his
safety couldn't be guaranteed but he insisted on attending.
That's courage.*

*Then the news showed the other man, the assassin. I itched to
turn it up but didn't dare. Yet you could see what was going on.
The killer had been killed in his turn, but the TV could not let it
go, and showed the clips of both murders, of Kennedy and
Oswald, over and over. The crush came out of the narrow
doorway – it was an underground passage, a car park maybe.
The police were trying to get him out quickly, I suppose. They
wore white Stetson hats, but the man Oswald was bare-headed.
He had on a black sweater and a shirt, no tie. He had a weird
expression on his face – almost pleased with himself. He stared
straight at the camera. As if he were saying,* Remember me.
There was a lot of pushing and shoving.

*Then somebody elbowed a space so that a hefty shoulder
obscured the camera. A thick-set man in a dark suit, with an
everyday hat with a dark-coloured band. But you could see his
hands. He prodded Oswald as if to make sure he'd got the right
guy, and then shot him. Just like that, quickly, so no one could
intervene. You could see the flash and the gun, the gleam of light
on the metal barrel. Oswald opened his mouth to scream but
with the volume off nothing came out, only this dreadful silent
shriek from a gaping mouth. The entrance to hell. Like that
picture by Edvard Munch. Exactly like that. And he fell down.*

*I pressed my fingers to my eyes. To see a man shot like that –
it was awful, ghastly. I felt exhausted. I put my head back on the
smelly cushions and tried to rest a while.*

*In a minute I'll slip out and check if Dad's properly asleep. If
he is, I'll take my chance. Baby's been kicking again while I've*

been sat here. The doctor says I'm small for dates. She means
the baby is, but he's lively enough. My bag is packed, under my
bed. If I can reach it, and creep past Dad without waking him
up, I could get out. I could go to the nuns tonight.

It won't be wise to stay in the flat a moment longer, not when
my Dad's got the hang of what I've written.

He's no idiot. He will know it could put him behind bars for
ever.

The four friends had assembled as usual for bridge. None had suggested otherwise – the game had been cancelled in the past when one or
other had suffered a personal bereavement, but Kennedy was hardly a
relative. Annie, tired after the afternoon, had laid out supper and retired
early to bed. The children were in their rooms reading.

Yet within twenty minutes it was plain that the card-players' regular
pleasure could not be summoned up. Simon missed two tricks and
Maurice had to be reminded to bid. At last Mannheim folded his cards
and laid them face down.

'I cannot,' he said. 'I am too touched by sorrow. I feel I should be in
schul offering prayers for the dead.'

'It's like sacrilege,' Maurice Feinstein agreed. 'My Nellie is in floods
of tears. She's used up a whole box of Kleenex. She wanted to shut the
shop this morning but I told her life goes on, we gotta earn a living. But
the customers stood around saying how terrible it was and not spending money, so we didn't gain much.'

Daniel rose and fetched the Scotch and two more glasses. He topped
up Maurice and Simon's drinks and without asking poured for himself
and Mannheim. He raised his glass.

'We should drink to – to what? To his soul, and to the good he has
done, *olvershalom*. God bless and keep him.'

The quartet solemnly drank. Daniel pushed the bottle into the centre
of the card table. Mannheim refilled their glasses.

For a moment they were alone with their thoughts. Simon swirled the
liquid in his glass. 'Surprising coming from you, Danny. I thought you
didn't believe in the eternal soul and such? You didn't come to the
commemoration this afternoon.'

'Not an eternal soul, correct. No life after death, heaven and hell and
that rubbish. But there is something about a man – call it spirit if you
like – which drives him to do good, I suppose, or evil if it goes wrong.
I do believe in free will. We aren't predetermined. We can choose
whether to spend our lives well or not. I reckon, for all his faults, John
Kennedy made that choice. So I admire him.'

'People like us don't have the same choices, do we?' Maurice was
content to pursue a subject away from the assassinations. The atmosphere in the kitchen behind the shop was leaden and tragic. He leaned

back in his chair. 'I mean, nobody we know is going to be President of
the United States.'

'Mr Wilson is likely to be Prime Minister soon and he's one of our
local MPs. Yorkshireman, yes?' Mannheim reminded them. His watery
eyes crinkled briefly in a half-smile. 'Nothing special about his background.'

'Maybe it could've been you, Danny,' Simon teased. 'D'you remember? You had dreams once.'

Daniel dismissed them with a wave of his hand. 'Load of nonsense.
My Annie says people like us don't do things like that. She's right.'

'But the young people today – they have chances we never had.'
Simon jabbed a finger. In the absence of bridge a lively discussion would
be some consolation. He would be stolidly argumentative. 'An education, grants, scholarships. How's your Helen getting on? Any decisions
yet?'

'She'll go to university here in town and stay home. That's best.'

Maurice frowned. 'I thought you had bigger expectations for her,
Danny. Cambridge, wasn't it?'

'Not me. She had plans for herself. Went for interview. But she didn't
get anywhere with it. Or at least, we've heard nothing since.'

'She will leave, your daughter,' said Mannheim quietly. *She fill leaf.*
'You will not keep her. Your son Barry, yes. He will never go far from
home. Nor will Jerry – he likes Liverpool, isn't that right, Morrie? But
beautiful Helen will fly the nest.'

All eyes turned to the old man. 'What do you mean?' Danny tried to
keep the irritation out of his voice. He feared that sides were being
taken, against him.

Mannheim spread his hands. 'Maybe we are not the settling kind, we
Jews. We are restless. We wander. We seek challenges, we are too intelligent to accept the status quo without question.' *Vizzout qvestion.* 'We
are kept down by terror of being hurt, but when no such danger
exists –'

'There is danger out there,' Danny said shortly. 'Look what happened
to you when you were beaten up. If she seriously believes she'll be
made welcome in the *goyische* world, she's got another think coming.'

'And she would not leave her heritage behind, surely,' Simon joined
in the protest. 'She came top of the *cheder* class in Jewish studies a
couple of years ago – I presented her with the prize myself – and she has
an O level in Classical Hebrew, which is more than any of us. She's been
well prepared for her future. She won't abandon the faith, you'll see.
Maybe for a short while, but she'll return to it. They all do.'

'She will leave,' Mannheim repeated ominously. 'It might hurt you,
my dear Daniel, to say so, but deception in the end will hurt you more.
There is nothing to stop her, nothing to keep her. The wide world
beckons.'

The friends fidgeted with their glasses and cards and avoided each other's eyes. Daniel fetched the plates of cake and cheese sandwiches and busied himself clumsily with side plates and paper napkins.

'The best ones leave,' Mannheim continued slowly. 'The brave ones. Like emigration – it is the most far-sighted, the most determined and ambitious who are keenest to pack their bags. The foolhardy stay behind. Sometimes they are murdered.'

'Sometimes it is the brave who are murdered, like Kennedy,' Morrie pointed out, gently. Mannheim's lined face told the company that unhappy memories had been stirred. 'But if you are correct then Judaism is under threat as never before. Death from kindness, from comfort, from ease.'

'From lack of terror.' Simon had his mouth full. 'And that's wonderful. God forbid we return to the old days. Give me Liverpool any time. Our community will survive provided the children keep the faith. That means not intermarrying, of course.' He stopped dead and his eyes swivelled to the grocer.

'We will not be getting married, so you needn't worry about that,' Morrie answered with dignity. 'I love my Nellie, I don't mind admitting it. If I'd met her when I'd been younger then yes, marriage would have been a possibility. But not now. And I must say I'm glad my Jerry is engaged to Roseanne Nixon. She's a nice Jewish girl, a *balaboster*, though there's not much else to commend her. But her family'll make a big *simcha* and we'll both be pleased to get the youngsters safely off our hands.'

Simon nodded in agreement. 'Don't worry, Danny,' he soothed. 'Your daughter will do the same. It's merely a question of her finding a suitable chap. From Leeds or Glasgow. The lure of the unknown.'

'My Jerry's future aunt Sylvia Bloom will be delighted to assist, I'm sure.' Maurice chuckled good-naturedly. He had entertained the group with Sylvia's antics and some of Vera's, though the intimate detail had been omitted. The final showdown still made him blush with hot shame. 'But Jerry said she already has a boyfriend. An American, isn't it? From the USAF base. You'd be well in there, Danny, with a rich son-in-law.'

'No-o, I don't think so. Or at any rate, she's said nowt.' Danny looked thoughtful. He pushed away his plate. He had almost forgotten the phone call, or when he woke up believed he had half imagined it. Suddenly he had it. A broad-shouldered young man in a leather jacket on a holy day. An illicit cigarette on a windy street corner. Helen's white face. Was that –?

'I admire your Helen. A great deal goes on in that pretty head of hers.' Mannheim raised his glass. 'I give you a toast. To the young ones. May they have happier and easier days than we had.'

Glasses were clinked. Mannheim glanced sideways at Morrie. 'The next generation won't have your scruples. They will marry out. They won't see why not, and they won't care.'

Maurice shifted uncomfortably. He was not about to tell his friends that the woman he lived with was not free to marry. 'I can understand,' he said at last. 'If my boy brought home a *shikse* – a nice girl, mind – and said they were engaged I don't suppose I'd throw either of them out.'

'Thank God I'm never going to be faced with that choice,' Simon muttered.

'Why, what would you do?' Maurice challenged them all. 'You can't cold shoulder your own kith and kin. What other people think doesn't matter – at least, not as much.'

Simon shook his head. Mannheim leaned forward. His skin was unusually flushed after two glasses of whisky. 'In the old days in the *shtetl* when a son or daughter married out the father would hold a funeral service. For a girl especially because she takes with her her ability to bear Jewish children. They would offer the prayers for the dead as she walked away.'

A chill fell on the group. Simon turned in curiosity to Daniel. 'You wouldn't do that, would you? I mean: supposing what Morrie says is so and some of the gossip is true. Supposing she does have an American airman for a boyfriend. Like your cousins at the end of the war, it's not so strange. But unlike theirs he's not Jewish. A respectable boy. How would you react?'

Daniel stood up suddenly and his chair fell over with a crash. He reached for the card table to steady himself. 'No,' he whispered. 'It couldn't be like that.'

Morrie shrugged. ''Course it could. If you'd told me ten years ago I'd be shacked up with a *shikse* I'd have hit you in the mouth. But here I am, and I'm happy.' The alcohol had made him garrulous. 'They're made the same way, you know. Same bits in the same places. Not an alien species. Same hearts. Same – souls. Nicer than our own people, often.'

'You can't stop her,' Mannheim warned, but his voice seemed to come from a great distance. 'She will go her own way. You're her father, Danny, but she has left you far behind. So what will you do if it is true? Will you declare her *persona non grata*? Will she be dead for you?'

Their host, standing, looked from one to another, his cheeks drained of colour. His hand groped for his empty glass as if it were a link to reality. 'No, no,' he said again, almost to himself. 'She would not do that to me. Not after all we've done for her.' His eyes swivelled wildly. 'Walk out on us? Pack her bags and leave? With some *goy* in tow? Reject us in favour of *that*? No, no. We keep the rules in this house. We always have.' He shook his head, a bewildered expression on his face. 'But dead? God. Dead?'

Simon banged his hand on the table. 'You hold prayers for the dead for your Helen, Danny, and you can count me out. I won't come. Lovely girl, just like her mother. She will do you proud some day, you'll see.'

'Nor me,' Morrie agreed brusquely. 'Nellie'd kill me. But you'd get some to do it. Religious fanatics. The rabbi'd lead the prayers. In this very room. You'd be honoured.'

'There have been enough dead.' Mannheim rose slowly to his feet and balanced carefully, fingertips spread out on the green baize. 'Enough. If she leaves, if any of them leave, we wish them a long life. A prosperous life. With our blessing.' For a moment he held Danny's eye, then peered around. 'Where is my coat? I have no more taste for cards tonight.'

Daniel stepped forward and remonstrated but the old tailor pulled his scarf around his face, insisted on going for the bus and made it clear he could not be prevented. It was early yet, he would be home by ten. With a leaden manner Daniel showed his guest out into the gloom then returned to the main room. Simon and Morrie had their heads together over the remnants of cake and another Scotch and were whispering, but abruptly fell silent when he entered. Then Simon spoke.

'So, Danny. The world turns, things are not the same as yesterday. If it is true, what will you do?'

It was dark, must've been about nine. I'd meant to stay alert but I'd dozed off on the sofa. When I heard the noise behind me I opened my eyes. The television was still on, its black and white images flickering but no sound. A variety show with dancers. I switched it off and watched as the tiny dot shrank and disappeared. I wished I could go with it, and vanish into the ether.

I felt drugged and groggy from sleep. And hungry again. I'm forever hungry now – the baby I suppose. Eating for two.

For a minute I lay back in the dark. I didn't want to put the light on yet, but I wanted not to be dizzy when I stood up. Then I heard again the noise which had disturbed me. I remembered my Dad was in the hall with my diary and the liquor. It must have been him.

'Colette?' His voice was grating but soft. 'Colette? You there?'

I stood up then and peered around the door. 'Here, Dad. What is it?' I could see my bag packed under the bed on the far side of the hall. My coat was on the hook on the front door. My gloves were in the pocket and I had my shoes on.

'Colette.' His tone was wheedling but there was menace in it. He had been slumped across the hall but now was upright, though he had to lean on the door jamb for support. He switched on the light. The bottle was in one hand. Empty. The

exercise book was in the other, his dirty thumb keeping his
mark. He'd read a lot of it. He'd read it. I could tell from his
face.

My heart was thumping so loud you could've heard it. That
disturbed baby who began to kick. My mind was distracted and
I struggled to think. It seemed safest, though, to act casual. I
turned my back on him and went into the kitchen. I felt wobbly
with hunger; if I was to make a run for it now or later, I was too
weak without something to eat. I didn't want to fall over as I
ran down the staircase – it'd be quicker than waiting for the lift
to get up this far. And I could run faster than him, with a pint of
whisky inside him. Of that I was sure.

The loaf was on the table and the breadknife where I'd left
them. I picked up a crust and chewed it slowly. It reminded me
of earlier. The wren would have nested though starlings were
scrapping around outside, fighting over perches. There's so
much light in these flats they get confused and think it isn't night
yet, when it is. I hoped my Dad could not see that my hands
were trembling. I couldn't help it.

He staggered a bit and lurched into the doorway of the
kitchen. Then he made an effort and squared his shoulders. He
plonked the bottle hard on the table but it did not break. His
eyeballs were reamed with red veins and his mouth was wet and
smelled of sour drink.

Then he seemed distracted. He never could concentrate on
much for long. 'God, I need a fag,' he said. There was a packet
of Woodbines and matches on the table and I pushed them over
to him.

While he lit up and appeared for a moment to forget what
he'd meant to say I opened the fridge. Margarine and a bit of
ham. That'd have to do. I started to cut the bread, keeping my
head down. I didn't want to look at him.

Then he grabbed my arm. 'Colette. Our kid. What've you got
hidden in there?' He poked my bulge. He'd ignored it till now –
though he should have noticed. But then we never talked much.
'Gotta little bastard, have you? A baby, no less. That's what it
says.' He indicated the exercise book. 'An' you think it's mine,
do ya?'

I didn't answer. I held on to the loaf to stop myself from
falling. My hair came forward and hid my face.

'Answer me!' He gave me a shove. He was scared: he knew
he was in trouble too. 'It can't be mine. I'm your father. It can't
be. You shouldn't say such things. It's probably some other
bugger. Somebody you can't even remember, most like.'

I stayed silent but he began to shout. Then I spun round and confronted him. The breadknife was still in my hand. 'Of course it's yours, Dad,' I told him, as calmly as I could. It was like in a dream, like slow motion. 'I haven't been with anyone else.'

'You have. You must have. It's not natural, a girl like you.' He tried to keep his voice down. The walls are paper thin. He didn't want the neighbours to hear.

'It's yours, Dad. And I'm going to have it. I'm going to the convent. It's all arranged. Don't worry, it won't cost anything.'

His eyes opened wide. 'You're goin' where? You been telling them nuns about me? You given them my name? Why, you bitch. We'll see about that –'

And he gave me another vicious shove, but this time it was aimed at my belly. I stepped back.

'Don't, Dad,' I pleaded. 'I want to have this baby. I'll have him adopted, he'll have a decent home. Then I can take my exams and – well, that's for the future. And I haven't told anybody about – that it was you. Not a soul on earth, I swear. But it's my baby as well as yours, and he has a right to be born.'

'No he hasn't –' he spat at me, and drew back his arm. He was going to punch me hard, I know he was. I tried to slip out of the line of fire. He yelled at me and threw the book on the floor and stamped on it. His eyes were down, his body hunched. He was going to destroy the evidence. He was going to kill the baby. He was, and he wouldn't have cared much if he'd killed me in the process. He had that crazed look about him, of a man about to do a terrible act.

I put my arms before me and backed off, trying to put the table between us. He was in my path if I wanted to run out now, between me and the door. I had the big breadknife in both hands, held tight, pointing at him. In front of my baby, to protect us both. It wasn't very sharp, but it was all I had.

'I'll sort you out, Miss, once and for all,' he ranted, and launched himself at me. A kind of charge, it was. I suppose he expected me to drop the knife but I didn't. I don't know why, I just held on to it for dear life.

The table was light, it didn't stop him. He knocked it aside and came at me headlong, fists up. But I stood still and closed my eyes and held on tight.

Then it happened.

There was a noise of tearing cloth and a jerk as the blade hit bone, then a slight hiss, as if the knife had slid into a yielding joint of fresh meat. I could feel the fabric of his shirt jammed hard and wet against my knuckles. I opened my eyes and he was stopped a few inches from me, his mouth opened wide, his tongue lolling, a gape of complete astonishment on him. His eyes *bulged and turned purple. He struggled but he was stuck, impaled on the knife. He must have hit the point dead on. As he twisted he screamed. Then blood came out of the cut, dark red, not a spurt but a glutinous flow. It fell down his front and stained his shirt. It covered my hands. He coughed, and a trickle of brighter blood came from his mouth.*

I yanked the knife away and he half fell on me. 'Colette – what have you done?' he croaked, and held his hand to the wound. When he lifted it the palm was covered in his own blood. I tried to hold him up and away from me. His face went pallid and he began to gasp. Then suddenly he heaved himself upright and shook his bloody fist in my face.

'You fucking bitch! You piece of dirt! What have you done? My God, I'll sort you out. And your fuckin' bastard. Come here –'

And he began to stagger towards me. The veins in his throat swelled like ropes. The knife clattered to the floor. He yelped and picked it up. 'Right, miss. Now it's your turn.'

He had strength from somewhere. He put one foot in front of another, clutching his stomach, the foam on his lips flecked with scarlet. He meant to destroy me. I had nowhere to go. I could not get past him. I took a couple of steps backwards and found myself on the balcony.

Around my head the starlings flapped in angry protest. They scrabbled furiously about, sweeping low as if they would carry me off. Away from here. Away from the cold-faced nuns. Away from my father, father to my child, grandfather to his own son.

To a better place. There has to be a finer place than this. There has to be.

He was in the lighted doorway, his face livid. Then he lunged.

And I was in the air, not falling, but flying, over the ledge ten floors up, not falling at all, but flying, me and my baby, free as the birds who swooped and cried about my head and body. Free at last of pain and fear. Free to be together.

Free, free, for ever.

Chapter Twenty-Four

Monday 26 November

'I don't want any breakfast.'

Annie hovered, frying pan in hand. 'What's the matter? You were tossing and turning last night. Aren't you feeling well?'

'I'm fine. Don't nag.'

Daniel shook the newspaper like a shield and buried himself in the sports pages. His surly demeanour told its tale. With the smallest movements possible Annie toasted bread and put the plate before him. Then she sat down opposite.

'Danny. Something's eating you. Can't you tell me?'

A hand reached out from behind the newsprint and picked up a piece of toast.

'Daniel Majinsky!' Crossly Annie swept the paper aside. 'What is it? If you're not well you should go to the doctor. And if you are, then speak to me. Stop acting like a child.'

Her husband allowed the paper to drop. With a glower he answered her between mouthfuls.

'Acting like a child? It's your child that's the matter. Your daughter. Her behaviour. We're about to be disgraced, Annie, if you but knew it.'

Annie began to stack dishes nervously. 'My daughter? Why – what have you heard?'

Daniel stared at her until Annie could bear it no longer. 'Stop goading me, Danny. What have you heard about Helen?'

'She's going out with an American boy. An airman from Burtonwood.'

Annie glanced away. 'You've heard that too?'

Daniel grunted. 'I saw him. I should've known. We both met him, Annie, that night at the Rembrandt with Gertie. Only our daughter didn't introduce us. Then Morrie Feinstein tells me all about it. He got it from his son Jerry. Everybody knows but us.'

Annie, realising at once that her source was the same, kept her own counsel. Whereas her husband would regard his informant as reliable, hers would be seen as tellers of tales.

'Well!' Annie continued, primly positive, 'I'm sure if there's anything serious in it, Helen will bring the boy home to introduce him. Are we saying we can't trust our own daughter?'

'But, Annie. Why might she keep it a secret – have you considered that?'

Miserably his wife concurred. 'I wondered, ever since I heard the rumours too. She hasn't said a word.'

'Has it occurred to you that the reason could be that we would disapprove?'

'Not if he was a nice boy from a good family,' said Annie, stoutly. Then she gaped. 'He's not – black, is he?'

'Christ. No. I tell you, I've seen him. Bumped into the two of them some weeks ago. He pretended he didn't know her well, and when I questioned Helen she poo-poohed the idea. God help us.' Daniel recollected himself and decided not to tell Annie any more about the encounter outside the tobacconist's. 'But there's one obvious explanation which is staring us in the face.'

'Don't say it.'

'Come on, Annie. You know what I mean.'

'I don't believe it. She's a good girl.'

'Oh, not *that*. She's got too much sense to get pregnant. Something else. Suppose he isn't Jewish.'

'No. Surely not. Not our Helen.' Annie's voice betrayed her doubt. She placed a hand on her husband's arm. 'You'll have to put it to her – get to the bottom of it.'

Daniel stood, his expression despondent. 'I don't want to in case I find out the truth. We'd have to put our foot down. Can't have the kids marrying out. We have a position to keep up in this community. Rules are rules. It won't do.'

'When will you see her? Best as soon as possible. Tonight? I think she's going out later.'

'So I'll come home early and catch her.' With that, Daniel made ready to leave for work and in a few more moments was gone.

Alone in the kitchen Annie debated whether to eat the cold fried eggs with their congealed butter then decided against. Waste not want not, but she was neither hungry nor greedy. She made another slice of toast, buttered it and spread marmalade, and made a fresh pot of tea.

What would her husband say? He'd lay down the law, certainly. Come the heavy-handed father: he would feel he had no option. Yet there surfaced the vexatious notion that it might not succeed, and that it was dangerous to have no alternative stance. If Danny threw his weight about to no avail – if Helen was determined to ignore them – then their authority would have been permanently shattered. And that would leave the girl rudderless, directionless, just as she entered the adult world and needed their guidance most.

Annie, perplexed, drank the tea slowly. What if she were Helen – how would she feel? What would she expect? The love and regard of her parents, of that the mother was sure. The child was not rebellious by nature. Spirited and independent, yes. As she herself had been. So many similarities between herself at that age and her pretty, troubled daughter came to mind that Annie smiled ruefully, and poured another cup.

When she had been young she had tried to please her parents, for example by leaving school and working for Auntie Ida Bernstein in that awful shop. It had been up to her to better herself and she had triumphed: after, warm plaudits had come from her family – apart, of course, from Auntie Ida.

But once her needs were met, resistance had been abandoned. She knew where the barriers lay and kept her distance from them. While she had sought advancement, defiance for its own sake had not attracted her, nor had she developed the slightest inclination to test those barriers for height or strength. And not at all to peep over the top. It was never apparent to Annie that the grass was greener on the other side. The grass was much the same everywhere you looked. What was smart was to improve your lot as much as possible within the confines of the life into which you were born. To seek anything else was foolhardy, and mostly led to misery and despair.

So her husband would be doing no more than his duty to dissuade Helen or somehow prevent her from leaving – from intermarriage, or from contemplating such a cataclysmic step. It was not clear however what sanctions they possessed any more. Helen was a young woman in reality, perfectly capable of tossing her head and storming out. Old enough to earn her own living: why, at seventeen Annie had been into her third job with better money, and so were many other girls today. As for university, with public support and scholarships a student could manage without parental approval if necessary, though it was seldom satisfactory.

But would she? A well-brought-up youngster, taught to honour her father and her mother – the fifth commandment? A scion of the *schul*, who could quote scripture at will, who'd been a star of the choir? Who could acquit herself splendidly in discourse with Reverend Siegel, and was lauded and admired by him, and held up to others as an example of a fine modern Jewish girl? Surely she would not walk away from such richness. Helen could not slough off her heritage and the hopes pinned on her by so many like a discarded outgrown skin. The child was too genuine for that. She would surely not do it.

With increasing anxiety Annie washed up. Memories had been stirred. The arguments she had put to her husband the day the war ended came to mind but had not been exactly the same. There'd been no need to describe to Daniel what he would lose if he eloped with his Lady Mary. He had known better than anyone – and that liaison had had no substance, had been a romantic dream, an adventure. He had hurled himself against the barriers and found them insurmountable. But Annie had wanted him the more because he was tempted to run off; the romance in her own soul had responded to the urge to save him from himself. That had inflated Daniel into a much more desirable figure than earnest, predictable Simon, however much rosier the latter's prospects were. Dear kind Simon, who still carried a candle for her, and of whom she was so fond.

She'd guessed Daniel would never be a commercial success. In pleading with him to marry her she had given up expectations of wealth and ease. Instead she'd plumped for doing what was proper. The element of sacrifice had heightened her satisfaction rather than diminished it. To be respected and worthy were the best options. Preferably in the eyes of your neighbours also, naturally. That worried her occasionally for these days, it appeared, it was money that counted; the worthy poor man who kept his obligations had slipped badly in the hierarchy.

Danny would have married out, given half a chance. If his Mary had been single or widowed – if, say, her husband had died in captivity as many did – it could well have happened. In those days he would have scoffed at the criticism that it was wrong on principle to assimilate. He would have been disgusted at racial prejudice, would have rebuked his friends and spoken angrily. Yet here he was, about to act the paterfamilias and enforce precisely that view. And would convince himself that he agreed with it.

Annie shivered. If her husband had forgotten (or had resolutely put those events from his thoughts) then he would take a hard line with his daughter without recalling the magic of what was different. Or maybe the girl was in love: though Annie had merely a passing acquaintance with passion and largely distrusted it, she could grasp how it could drive people to their own destruction.

Were Helen indeed in love nothing would stop her, but the end result could be dreadful. At the worst, she could throw up her education, abandon home and religion to go chasing off after this American boy, only to find she'd pursued a will-o'-the-wisp and that love had evaporated in the night as love often did. Or she'd discover she didn't like America and was homesick for a family that had closed its doors and wanted no more to do with her.

For Danny was capable of that, Annie was certain. The strains and contradictions in his personality, ossified by middle age and exacerbated by whatever disease it was that disrupted his sleep and caused him more pain than he would admit, made him irritable and erratic. He could be caring and wonderful one day: erudite, charming, liberal-minded. The next he'd make a fuss about some petty matter and insist on things being just so, though similar lapses had not been a problem the previous week. It made him hard to live with; in the Majinsky household, it seemed, love had been replaced by blind loyalty. Plus adherence to a set of religious diktats which, Annie admitted to herself, Daniel the atheist did not regard as gospel.

There was another way. They could as loving parents support their daughter in whatever choices she wanted to make. If the child acted foolishly they might point it out, but still tell her that they loved her, and that she would for ever be welcome in their house, that it would be her home for as long as she needed it.

It was possible. She could tell her husband not to be so silly. She could tell her daughter to respect her father, and to reflect on the future with care and common sense. She could push Danny not to be so absolute in his judgements. She had persuaded him before, forced him to use his better judgement: once, long ago. As a last resort she could defy him herself and announce that whatever Danny might do she, Annie, would support her lovely girl and make welcome whichever partner she picked.

But that would mean taking Helen's part against her father. Wives should not do that. Wives should back up their husbands especially when the pressure had become almost unbearable. Children should obey their parents, as wives promised in their wedding vows to obey their husbands – as she had promised, and meant it. The alternative would be ghastly, chaotic disorder. Society would fall apart as they knew it, and neither marriage nor religion nor authority would hold sway any more.

So there would be no defiance, not by her. No opening of another flank of battle. It would not be fair, nor correct. She would stand by the man she married. She had made her bed decades before when she had taken him, warts and all. She would not cross him: not now, not ever.

Instead Danny would shout, and Helen would cry or be sullen, and the battle of wills between father and daughter which had simmered for ages would come to its climax and its conclusion. If one of them weakened, reconciliation was possible. But if neither did, then Annie knew the household would be riven from top to bottom, and her heart would ache till the day she died.

The atmosphere at school was listless and downhearted. For the younger girls the assassination of the President of another country meant little but they felt the sadness of their elders and the fear of calamity. So for once the lower forms behaved themselves though by the end of the day boredom would set in. They would be as boisterous as usual on the morrow.

The prefects' den at mid-morning break was also quiet, with most of the usual occupants supervising playtime. Only the head girl and Meg were present.

The gas fire blazed, creating a pool of warmth in the dank chill. The table was covered in that morning's newspapers and the weekend's. With a determinedly purposeful air Brenda busied herself for want of something better to do by clipping articles about the American tragedies and pinning them on the noticeboard. She had brought with her a black ribbon and stapled it around the President's picture. The theatricality of the gesture gave a sense of condolence.

Brenda assembled cups and dried milk. 'How did you get on at your interviews?' she inquired over her shoulder.

Meg stretched out her legs towards the fire. 'OK, I think,' she said, with a show of brashness. 'But they do expect us to be geniuses, don't they? They asked me about the relationship between high pressure and temperature in the manufacture of ammoniacal compounds and I hadn't a clue what they were on about. That's degree-level stuff. But I tried to reason from first principles so I hope they were satisfied.'

'Makes you wonder why they bother,' Brenda sympathised. 'They probed some of my answers to the written paper but I'd swotted it up, fortunately. You'd think the A level results would be sufficient for them as they are for the other universities. But no, both Oxford and Cambridge have to set their own exams then follow them up with inter-views. Give themselves masses of slog, and for what?'

'The true tests are outside the classroom,' Meg observed dryly. She accepted a mug of coffee. 'At dinner in hall, for example. I was warned they watch how you eat. Do you know the correct etiquette? Do you tuck your napkin into your neck instead of over your skirt? And d'you call it a napkin or a serviette? D'you know what the various knives and forks are for – do you eat your peas off your knife? Stuff like that.'

'Surely not.' Brenda giggled. 'From the state of one or two dons I met they eat their food with their ties. And that was the ladies. The men were worse. Barking mad, some of them, I'd say.'

'So it makes you wonder why *we* bother, doesn't it,' Meg continued. 'Why do we go to that extra effort, entering more exams, hours writing essays, studying stuff which won't be a scrap of use to us when we're project managers at ICI? Kant, Wittgenstein – I ask you! I answered their questions, but it'll be out of my head in three weeks' flat, I'm sure.'

'Culture, that's what it is. They desire us to be more than mere scientists. I suspect they'd rather we weren't scientists at all. Educationists in this country have never got their noses round the fact that civilisation depends not only on poetry and Shakespeare but on sturdy bridges and new fabrics and pesticides and ships and the like.'

'And railways. We had the first passenger railway in this city, don't forget. In 1830. If I were a boy I'd have gone in for engineering, but there's no point. Girls in that subject are as rare as swallows in winter.'

'You? You'd have adored being the single woman on a course. A pioneer.' Brenda was curious.

'P'raps. But it can be grotty, being on your own. Constantly being teased and treated like a separate species. Who needs it? I'll read chemistry, then later if my employer agrees I could take a second degree in something – more masculine.' Meg grinned, and yawned. 'God! The quicker we hear "yes" or "no" from those dreaming spires and what-not, the better I'll like it. How did Helen get on, does anybody know? And where's Colette? I haven't seen her this morning. She's spectacularly late.'

'Helen's on playground rota. She's not said much. She's desperate to get away, you know. If she has to stay at home I think she might throw it all up and emigrate. They don't fight openly but her people are totally at loggerheads with her.'

Meg picked her fingers then began to chew a nail. 'She's lucky to have people. They might not encourage her to do what she wants but at least they notice her. There are times when I'm glad my parents split up but when you want to talk to somebody there's no one around. My Mum only ever wants to talk about herself.'

Brenda frowned. 'Haven't you anybody else – grandparents?'

'Them? Christenings and funerals, that's when I see them. Cards at Christmas and a two-pound postal order. I haven't seen the Wirral grandparents since Easter – they don't get out much. I'm not sure they'd recognise me in the street.'

The head girl paused indecisively, hands on hips. On the table her half-empty coffee mug sat cooling. To her irritation the air of gloom had pervaded the prefects' sanctuary. Meg in a self-pitying mood could be unendurable; the girl would think up negative ripostes to everything. If the dialogue lasted long enough Brenda herself, ever optimistic, would start to suffer also from self-doubt. That would not do.

'Damn!' Brenda muttered. 'I think I'll go to the Library. See you later.'

But as she opened the door Helen met her, her duffel coat still on, the gold and green scarf wrapped loosely round her neck, gloves in one hand. Helen's cheeks were ruddy from cold and her mouth was set.

'We're wanted. Miss Plumb's study. Now.'

'Oh? Is it our results? Who is wanted?'

'You, me and Meg. Nobody else. Miss Plumb called to me from her window. She was being ultra mysterious but when I asked she said it wasn't anything to do with Oxbridge. Bit early yet. She seemed – I don't know – strange, agitated. I'll hang up my coat and see you there right away.'

It needed all Miss Plumb's self-control, every last ounce of it, but still she felt herself perilously close to breaking down. She motioned to her visitors. Her voice quavered, then she swallowed and tried again. 'Let me handle this to begin with. Will you want to speak to them separately?'

The taller of the two men spoke gravely. 'Only if they have something to tell us. We'll see.'

Miss Plumb had offered to take their mackintoshes but both men had demurred and sat with the beige folds covering their trousered knees, their belts trailing on the rug. Their hats were placed politely on the table in front of them, revealing short-trimmed hair and lined faces. The taller man was about her own age, Miss Plumb judged, his thinner colleague with the narrow moustache about thirty. The older one took the lead while the other painstakingly made notes in a flipover notebook. After some shuffles they had placed their chairs slightly to one side. Together, Miss Plumb reflected, the three of them must resemble an impromptu Inquisition. But who was in the dock? Was it herself? The school? The girls?

The headmistress felt totally bewildered and inadequate. And, obscurely, guilty. An iciness had begun to seep through her, as if she had always known some terrible disaster would occur in this God-forsaken hole and she had failed to take steps to prevent it. But what exactly had occurred? The men had been reticent. The barest details had been imparted and she could make no sense of them.

A tap came at the door. Maybe the prefects would know more. They'd been pals and confidantes. With alacrity and to lessen the tension Miss Plumb leaped forward and turned the handle. 'Come in, come in,' she urged the puzzled schoolgirls.

'This is Detective Inspector Cummings, and this Detective Sergeant Clarke,' she indicated. 'Liverpool CID.'

The two men grunted, half rose in their chairs, settled down again. The inspector cleared his throat and gazed gravely from Brenda the leader to Meg to Helen and back.

'Good morning,' he said briefly. 'I won't trouble you for long. Could each of you tell me when you last saw or spoke to Colette O'Brien?'

Brenda counted. 'Wednesday. She was in school then. I was away Thursday and Friday – we three all were. She hasn't been in today.' The other two murmured their agreement.

'Why – where's Colette? Has she disappeared?' Helen asked anxiously.

'Now why should you ask that, Miss?' The inspector's eyes glittered under heavy brows.

'She's not been well recently. Is she OK?'

The inspector pondered then looked at each in turn once more. 'Did any of you know she was pregnant?'

A cry broke from Helen. 'Oh, God, that was it. We should have realised. When she collapsed at prizegiving.' The three girls, open-mouthed, reached for each other.

Brenda steadied. 'We knew she was off-colour as Helen says, but we had no idea that she was – expecting. She never said anything to any of us. Did she?' The girls shook their heads.

Miss Plumb clutched her chair and sat down heavily. From her handbag she took a handkerchief and pressed it to her cheek. Eau de Cologne scented the air, faintly, like incense.

Helen stepped forward. She looked directly at the inspector.

'You said she was pregnant. Past tense. Does that mean she isn't pregnant any more? Has she lost it – is she in hospital? Please tell us. Has she been beaten up or something? We know she had a miserable time at home and was unhappy but she never told us much. But if we can help her I'm sure we'd do our utmost.'

'It's too late.' The sergeant's voice was reedy with suppressed excitement. He spoke with a pronounced Scouse accent.

'What do you mean?' Helen demanded fiercely. Brenda's hand touched her arm to restrain her but she shook it off. 'How can it be too late? Has she had an abortion, is that it? Because if she has, I'm glad for her, but I don't have any information on the abortionist for you. None of us has, I'm sure.'

'Helen.' Miss Plumb came to her side. 'Listen to the police officer.' The teacher's mouth opened and closed without a sound, then she covered it with her handkerchief. She turned to the men. 'Don't keep them in suspense, please. This isn't a game. You'd better tell them.'

'Well, Miss.' The inspector rose to his feet. The announcement was too portentous to be made seated. He coughed once, then his voice took on a gentler tone. 'Your friend Colette is dead. She was found late last night at the foot of her block of flats. It appears she fell off the balcony. She'd have been dead the moment she hit the ground. And she was about five or six months pregnant, the police surgeon reckons.'

'And that's not all,' whined the sergeant quickly. 'In the flat upstairs was another body. Her father, Mr Joseph O'Brien. He was dead of a stab wound to the upper abdomen. One wound. Died of shock and loss of blood. Kitchen knife, we think. Her fingerprints were on it. The flat was awash with blood everywhere.'

'Clarke, that'll do.' Sharply.

But it was out, and the younger officer smiled secretly at the reaction he had produced. With a yell Meg ran from the room and banged the door after her. Brenda pursued her; their voices could be heard arguing furiously in the hall beyond. Helen sagged in Miss Plumb's arms, then bent her head on to the teacher's shoulder.

'Colette – pregnant? Dead? And her father too? But she never had a boyfriend, Miss Plumb. She was a virgin. I'm sure of that.'

The two women's eyes met.

Helen started to scream. 'Oh, no, no. Oh no. It can't be. Oh, God.'

*

It would be hushed up. Inspector Cummings had given that assurance. Since no one else was sought in connection with the two deaths, a hue and cry was not appropriate. The girl's pregnancy would come out at the inquest. Her demise would be put down to accident or misadventure. There was nothing to suggest she had been pushed. The man, her father, had a record of petty thieving and drunkenness but not of violence. The level of alcohol in his blood was high but not unusual. Half the district were drunks; every street corner sported a pub. Nothing remotely inexplicable there. An open verdict, most likely.

There'd been a domestic quarrel: that much was self-evident. Police would have been reluctant to interfere even had a concerned citizen heard the row and called them out, but no one had. The force had enough to occupy them without intervening in the endless altercations of tenement dwellers. That would have made them piggy-in-the-middle every night.

An exercise book had been found on the kitchen floor which appeared to be a sort of diary, but it had been caked in blood and nearly unreadable. Inspector Cummings, a kindly man at heart, had tried to prise open its pages, his features twisted in distaste. He had decided eventually that it contained no more than the wild jottings of a youngster who probably didn't know who'd made her pregnant and under cross-examination would not have told – had she still been alive to question.

The inquest would be in a month; whatever the police regarded as sufficient would then be reported in the *Echo*, and no more. No editor would upset his local Chief Constable by publishing unduly salacious material. What went on in families was private and best left so. Who would gain by incest being broadcast, if that was indeed the cause?

There were other members of that family and neighbours to consider. Plus her teachers and her friends, who must have realised what was going on but stayed mum. Nobody would be helped by a public laundering of dirty linen. Some things were better unsaid.

He had closed the pages with a deep sigh and washed his hands in the kitchen sink. His search for a clean towel proved fruitless so for a moment he stood shaking the drops from his wet fingers. Another life, gone. Two, rather. Or three, if you thought about it.

Meanwhile a multiple affray down on the docks required his attention; six men were in the infirmary and one in the morgue. Real criminals, not domestic fights. Then it would be all hands on deck for Christmas and the New Year. He would get no leave before February. He must remember to book a table at Reece's for St Valentine's night. If he forgot again this year like last, his wife would scream blue murder.

'Mum, can I have an aspirin?'

Annie peered up. 'You got a headache? Or is it your period?'

'No.' Helen fetched a glass and filled it with water from the tap as her mother rummaged in a drawer for the aspirin bottle. 'We had some terrible news today at school. D'you remember my friend Colette O'Brien? The Irish girl, green eyes, black hair. She was in my chemistry class and we used to go to the Cavern together.'

'Y-yes,' her mother answered uncertainly. The only girls she knew well were those Helen felt confident to bring home, which did not include non-Jewish people. This O'Brien sounded like a Roman Catholic.

'She was found dead last night. The police came to school. Said it looks like an accident. She fell off the balcony ten floors up. Oh, Mum, it's so horrible. She was so clever, and could have gone to college. Now she's gone – snuffed out. I can't believe it.'

Helen swallowed two tablets, her head averted. It was wiser to spare her mother some of the more gruesome details, or the dreadful conclusions at which the three friends and their headmistress had arrived.

Annie made sympathetic sounds while preparing supper. 'Your father will be home soon,' she remarked non-committally. 'He wants a little chat. Why don't you go upstairs and get out of your school uniform? Then you'll be more comfortable.'

The headache dulled Helen's reactions. 'Yeah, good idea. Has there been any post?'

'From Cambridge, you mean? No, nothing. Don't fret, I'm sure you'll hear soon.'

Helen trudged up the stairs and donned a pair of jeans and a thick sweater. Gradually the medication soothed the throb behind her brows but left her giddy and light-headed. She had intended to go out that evening and had told her mother so the previous week. An assignation with Michael had been planned but until the bases were released from their alert that would be impractical. Instead she would find a telephone box and phone or leave a message. Or find somewhere quiet to write to him in peace.

But there could be no peace. Michael would want to discuss the Kennedy murders and agonise about Johnson and the future. Helen desperately needed to talk about Colette: it came to her with a shock that under normal circumstances she would have been able to talk *to* Colette, as they used to. In recent months the two girls' friendship seemed to have cooled. Helen had wondered whether the reason was the divergent directions in which their lives appeared to be travelling. Now, she saw, it was the pregnancy, its cause, its probable aftermath. Colette had been dragged where her companions had never ventured. Colette had found hell.

And if her guess were right about the father of Colette's baby – the horror of it was beyond imagination. What were the correct terms? Incest, yes, and rape, for certain. Repeated rape, over and over again – Helen felt sure it had not been a single isolated incident. No wonder

Colette could unburden herself to nobody. That was not a criticism of Helen as a friend; that was a simple matter of fact. Ah, poor girl: what she must have gone through. Maybe after such cruel torture the leap from the balcony was a blessed relief.

Helen shook herself. Colette was not the type to fling herself to her death. Suicide? No, never. She would have considered the baby. She would not have wanted to kill him too. Nor was there a note, nor any evidence that the balance of her mind was disturbed. But what if she were under attack and her escape route barred – what if no other way out existed? That made more sense. But it also meant that Colette had stopped fighting. The girl had given up. Maybe for a brief instant, but that was enough.

The car nudged into the narrow driveway. The garage doors were opened, their edges trailing and grating on the path. It was not yet dark: this was an unusual time for her father to come home. What had her mother said – that he wanted a chat? How peculiar. Not like him at all.

Perhaps this would be his last attempt to persuade her to give up too. To stay put, not to abandon them and their ways. It was with considerable unease that Helen picked up the hairbrush and brushed her hair.

The garden outside her window seemed unduly noisy. A struggle was under way for the best spots under the eaves; the trees, nearly leafless, offered the birds little shelter. A big seagull flapped angrily a few feet from the glass as if demanding entry, then circled away with discordant cries. Nasty beasts, seagulls. They devoured the eggs of smaller birds, snatched rubbish from dustbins and dumps, lived off other creatures' weakness. Survival of the fittest, Darwin dubbed it. No wonder he tried to suppress the knowledge once he had it.

Ignorance would not hold her. Once a person had eaten of the tree of knowledge, he could not be divested of what he knew. That was the essence of the Genesis story. Armed with knowledge Adam and Eve had had to leave the garden where innocence had been their sole raiment. A parable for adolescence itself: out into the world, aware and ashamed. But *not alone*. Armed with some knowledge and, far more importantly, with the fruit of that other tree in Eden – the understanding of the distinction between good and evil, which enabled the race of men to rival the gods.

'Helen! You up there? Come down a minute.'

He was in the parlour, the front room. The television was off. 'Sit down. I want to talk to you.'

Her father had a preoccupied air. The aspirin still made her feel fuzzy as if she were covered by gauze. She slid into an armchair and cudgelled her brain to concentrate.

'Your mother said you had some bad news at school today. One of your pals died?'

'Yes. We don't know what happened. An accident.' The phrases were automatic already. A year ago had such a thing occurred she could have shared her turmoil with him, but not now. Their assumptions would have been contradictory, their attitudes at cross-purposes.

He waited, then said simply, 'Well, I'm sorry about her. You all right, apart from that?'

'Yes, Dad. Thank you. What is it you wanted to talk about?'

'No news from Cambridge yet?' His voice was unnaturally bright.

'No. Nothing. Miss Plumb says it could be later this week.'

'Ah.' Daniel did not know where to begin: that much was obvious to his daughter. The headache was threatening to return and she yearned for some fresh air.

'Is that all, Dad? Or is there something else you wanted to discuss?'

'Well – yes. You, actually. I hear you've been seeing a boy from the USAF base. Is that true?'

She did not answer, but opened her mouth and breathed through it, made her lungs work, her eyes fixed on the blank television screen. If she did not breathe deeply she would faint.

'Who told you that?' A whisper.

'Never mind.' He drew himself up to his full height, his back to the fireplace. 'It's common knowledge. Several people have mentioned it to us. If you wanted to keep it a secret you've been a bit careless.'

Helen said nothing but kept her head turned away. Daniel repositioned himself into her line of sight.

'It was that young man in the leather jacket I saw on Rosh Hashanah, wasn't it? I should have known. And what I'd like to know now is why you should want to keep secrets from us, your parents? What's going on, please?'

'Nothing's going on.' This was delivered in a low voice but was so patently untrue that Daniel began to remonstrate.

Woodenly Helen rose and moved away. A distant part of her brain noted that it was fortunate that there was no instrument in the room which could cause injury, like Colette's knife. Whatever took place in the next few moments, whatever mortal damage was inflicted on this home, it would most likely be verbal in nature not physical. That was a blessing, given the mixture of bitterness and animosity that darkened her father's face.

'You're going out with some bloke we've never met, some foreigner, an American with his pockets stuffed with dollars I expect, and you tell me nothing's going on? You've made your mother and me the laughing stock of the entire community. Nobody was talking about anything else this weekend. I wasn't born yesterday, my girl. Now will you tell me or do I have to drag it out of you?'

'You aren't a laughing stock, Dad,' she protested wearily. 'Or at least, not for anything I've done.'

His eyes narrowed. 'He phoned here. Yesterday. When you and your mother were out. Did you know? Wouldn't leave a name. Wouldn't speak to me – oh no, your father wasn't good enough for him. So who is he, this – this Chuck, or Bud, or whatever his name is?'

Her father's face had gone crimson and he had begun to pant.

'Michael.'

'What?'

'His name's Michael. Not Bud or Chuck. He comes from a New England family and his father's a colonel in Washington. You'd like him.'

'I might. I might indeed. So why haven't you brought him home? Come on, why? Why?'

They both knew the answer. For a split second a look passed between father and daughter, a look of love and of the highest regard, which cut through the hatred and malice of accumulated centuries, through the fog of furious rivalry between generations. In a sudden flash Daniel saw how like Mary his daughter was, and how she resembled her mother at her best twenty years before; and he knew that he worshipped his daughter exactly as she was, wilful, honest and pure. Her free spirit above all endeared her to him and rendered her irreplaceable.

In that same instant Helen saw how Daniel alone would be the model for any man she would ever care for, how in his younger days he must have been much as Michael was now, and how her future husband, whatever his name or country, the father of her children, would have to measure up to this man her father, or be forever found wanting.

'Because he's not Jewish, Dad,' she replied quietly.

Then Daniel came up to her and she thought he would cry out: but she stood her ground and faced him, cool, sad and determined.

'So. You going to get engaged, or what?'

'I don't know. Not yet, certainly. I must finish my education first.'

'And then? Will you marry out – after everything we've taught you? Is that it?'

'I told you, Dad, I don't know. It's too far ahead. University first.'

'Pah! I thought to hear better from my own flesh and blood. You're ashamed of us, that's what you are. We brought you up properly and you reject us.'

'No, it's not like that. He's OK, Dad. You'd like him. You've taught me wonderful values. I wouldn't get involved with somebody you and Mum wouldn't like, except –'

'Except. That we would never receive him as a son-in-law, never. Till eternity. And you knew that all along. You've always known it. You defied us deliberately. You knew what you were doing.'

'I didn't, as it happens. Not at first. I thought he was Jewish because of his name and only found out later. But it makes no difference to me. You're well aware, Dad, that I can't accept that. We're all equal. He's as fine a man as anybody. I won't make that distinction between one person and another. I won't.'

'My God! As long as you live in this household, you will. As long as you carry my name. This is an Orthodox Jewish home. That is how you were brought up, and our ancestors before us for thousands of years. It is a gift and a burden. It means a huge amount, Helen. It is an obligation I accepted when I married your mother. If I could accept it, so can you. You have to carry it on. You especially.'

'I won't be made captive like that. It's racialist, and I won't do it.'

'Racialist? How dare you!' Daniel swung round, face distorted and purple. 'What are you accusing me of – your own father? The Nazis were racialist. They tried to wipe us out and nearly succeeded. How can you say such things?'

Helen was conscious of the solemnity of the moment. She spoke slowly and coolly. 'Because it's true, Dad. If I select my future partner on the basis of his race – if I pledged only to marry another Jew – then I'd be working on much the same lines as the Nazis did. Or any other anti-Semites. Don't you see – you can't condemn racial separation and selection when it functions against us, only to apply it to *other people*.' She raised her eyes to him. 'I know you can see that. And I won't do it. I refuse. I don't know whether I'll marry Michael or not or anybody else, but I will *not* make my choice the way you insist. I won't do it. I won't.'

He came to her then, up very close, raised his left hand and slapped her hard across the mouth.

'Don't be disgusting. That's for calling me a Nazi. I am appalled. I don't know what to say. Get out of my sight.'

Her mouth stinging, Helen fled from the room into the hallway. She could taste her own blood, licked it, swallowed. She would not give in. She would not.

Annie jumped back from the door where she had been hovering. 'What did he say?' she hissed, but her daughter started to push past her towards the empty kitchen.

Her lips throbbed. In a moment they would swell; her father had hit her with the full force of his arm. She sucked at the wound inside her cheek, where the flesh had caught a tooth. The slight salt taste, the warmth of the blood was almost soothing. It was as if she had deserved the blow. Catharsis, not nemesis. She had not merely provoked her father but had confronted him with his own intolerance. She had cut him to the quick, of that she was fully aware. He had no defence. That was why he had hit her.

The glass of water used for the aspirins was still on the sink unit, half-full. She reached for it, her hand shaky and began to sip. Noises jangled loudly in her head. She felt dazed and battered, but her mind was at last as clear as ever in her entire life.

Her mother's voice came to her from the hall. 'Helen! Come back. Don't be stupid. There's a phone call for you.'

Phone call? Might it be Michael again? The girl turned and virtually ran to where the handset rested by the receiver. In the parlour she could see her father seated on the sofa in the gloom, head bowed, his cigarettes unopened before him, hands clasped together as if in prayer.

'Yes?' She was breathless, disordered.

The voice at the other end was disappointingly Scouse, a woman's voice, elaborate and affected.

'Hello? Is this Miss Helen Majinsky?'

'Yes. I'm Helen. Who is this?'

'Operator speaking, Liverpool Central exchange. I have a telegram for you. Shall I read it out?'

'What? Oh, yes.' Maybe Michael had despaired of finding any other means of communication. She would call him tonight, somehow.

'Are you ready? It's from Lady Donington, St Margaret's College, Cambridge. That mean anything to you?'

'What? Oh. Yes. Please go on.'

The operator cleared her throat as if about to read the lesson in church.

'*Delighted offer you place St Margaret's stop subject to two As and a B in A levels stop plus scholarship worth two hundred fifty pounds a year stop letter follows please confirm.* How nice. Do I say congratulations?'

'Read it again.' Helen rubbed a hand over her eyes and pleaded with her mind to steady. The operator re-read the telegram, emphasising the scholarship and the money with a distinct smacking of the lips.

'Thanks,' Helen muttered and replaced the receiver.

It was over.

Whatever else she might do in her life, the battle at home was finished. And she had won.

To Annie's queries she murmured 'I got in, Mum. I'm off to Cambridge in October.' No sound came from the lounge. Annie would inform him and he would know he had been defeated. No joy would come of that. There would be no celebrations.

Helen walked quietly into the kitchen and through the back door. Out in the garden she turned her hot face to the violet sky. It was dusk, almost dark, though the outlines of nearby roofs and telegraph poles were visible. In one house the television was on for children's programmes: the blue flicker lit up the garden fence. Lights came on in lounges. The odours of a cooked meal at Mrs Williams' house floated tantalisingly through an open grille. Meat they would eat, as every night, followed by prunes and custard then tea, gallons of it. No nonsense about not mixing meat and milk. They had other shibboleths but not those which had so chafed Helen. Which she could discard in totality at Cambridge and which would never hamper her again.

How she wished she could tell Colette about her good fortune. Michael would be thrilled, though he might also guess that her success meant she would stay in Britain, at least for the next three years. They would keep in touch, they would see each other, they would write marvellous letters. She might save part of the scholarship money to visit him in America, or in Germany were he to be posted there. Further afield, though, would be beyond her reach. She hoped he would not be sent to Viet Nam as his father predicted.

Helen remembered Meg and Brenda. In the morning at school she would discover whether they had been lucky too, or whether the parting of the ways had come as they headed instead for provincial universities or London.

Whatever the outcome the quartet had broken up. Colette would never share in all this bewildering change. The Irish girl had been trapped in her misery and had been unable to find a way out, let alone a path as worthwhile, as enticing as a Cambridge scholarship. Where Helen had been faced with too many alternatives and had been forced to make choices she would have preferred to avoid, Colette had had no choices at all.

Twelve months before the two of them had ridden on the bus back to school from the Cavern session, best mates despite the contrast in their backgrounds. They'd argued about pop groups, indulged in sheer triviality. The options before them had been similar. Now Colette was gone, and the memory of her full of anguish.

Tears obscured Helen's vision and she shut her eyes. Her lip stung. The damp breeze was comforting on her flaming cheeks.

The big seagull was still causing a rumpus. With a squawk it dived towards her as if to investigate. The swoop disturbed the smaller birds already nesting who flew up with little cries. One fluttered blindly into her face and instinctively Helen clutched at it. Her fingers closed over it, and she held the bird in her hand.

It lay trembling in the cup of her palms, its wings spread out to balance, its heart beating rapidly. She could barely see the tiny creature in the light from a window, only that it was very small and drab brown, but vibrantly alive. Helen lifted her hand nearer her nose to examine it and wondered idly what it might be. It looked familiar, as if she ought to know its identity.

She opened her hands to the sky. The tiny brown bird paused then rose above her head, fluttered, whistled a sweet song for a few seconds then flew off into the night.

It was time to go indoors and start the rest of her life. Helen watched the bird go then turned and entered the house.

Glossary

'To transliterate Yiddish into English is to risk upsetting someone, either the Jewish layman who clings to the traditional Germanized spellings, or the academic Yiddishist who favours the codified rules of orthography laid down by the scholarly YIVO Institute for Jewish Research. Many authors have acknowledged the problems, grappled with them, and apologized for whatever sins they may have committed. I must now join them.'

Theo Richmond, *Konin: A Quest* (Jonathan Cape, 1995)

Most of the following are Yiddish, German or Hebrew with a Liverpool accent, as I remember them from my childhood.

aliyah – (lit, to go up) – emigration to Israel
bagel – hard white bread roll with hole in middle
balaboster – a fine woman who keeps a kosher home
barmitzvah – religious ceremony performed for boy at thirteen
bat-mitzvah – similar, for girl (not Orthodox)
bimah – raised platform in middle of synagogue; pulpit
bris – circumcision of boy at eight days old
chalah – best quality plaited loaf
Chanukah – December festival of lights
Chassid, chassidic – ultra-religious Jews
cheder – religious part-time school or classes (lit, room)
chometz – containing leaven, not allowed at Passover
chuppah – the wedding canopy; a wedding
cuchon – soft white bread bun
daven – to pray silently while rocking backwards and forwards
Eretz Yisroel – the land of Israel
erev – eve of (as *erev shabbos* = Friday night)
fleischich – meat foods (containing meat products)

frum – religious, pious

frummer mensche – a religious man

gonif – thief

goy – non-Jew (usually male)

goyim – Gentiles

goyische – gentile

Kaddish – prayers for the dead; holiest part of service

kashrut – dietary rules

kiddush – (lit, blessing) – drinks offered to congregation as part of festivities

kinnenhorror – God bless him/her; may he/she have good health

kosher – prepared according to dietary rules; permitted

matzoh, matzos – unleavened bread like water biscuits

mazeltov – (lit, good luck) – congratulations

Megillah – order of service for *Purim*

mem – the Hebrew letter M

mensch – a man, a fine man

mezzuzah – metal or wooden seal screwed to doorpost of Jewish home, containing extracts from the Scriptures

mikvah – ritual baths

milchich – milk foods (containing dairy produce)

minyan – ten men to form a quorum for prayers

mitzvah – (lit, the Law) – a good deed

nun – the Hebrew letter N

olvershalom – may he/she rest in peace (said of the dead)

payers – uncut hairlocks retained by ultra-religious male Jews

pesadich – cutlery and plates for exclusive use at Passover

Purim – spring festival commemorating success of Queen Esther

Rebbe – rabbi

Rebbetzin – rabbi's wife (or wife of Minister)

Rosh Hashanah – (lit, head of the year) – Jewish New Year

sabra – native-born Israeli

schlemiel – scoundrel, good-for-nothing

schmaltz – (lit, fat) – *schmaltz* herring is pickled in a mix of oil and brine

schöne mädchen – beautiful girl

schul – synagogue

schwarzes – blacks, Negroes

seder – main meal of Passover festival

Sefer Torah – (lit, book of the Law) – holy scroll

shabbos – sabbath (Saturday)

shadchan – marriage broker

shicke – drunk

shikse – non-Jew (female)

Shoa – (lit, catastrophe – Hebrew) – the Holocaust

shochet – kosher butcher

shofar – ram's horn, blown on *Rosh Hashanah* and *Yom Kippur*

shtetl – Eastern European market town with a Jewish community

Shulchan Aruch – (lit, arranged table) – sixteenth-century codification
 ˙ of Jewish law

simchah – a celebration, a family party

Tashlich – ceremony of casting away of sins

Talmud – collection of religious writings from second and third
 centuries AD

treife – not *kosher*, forbidden

tzimmes – spicy beef stew with carrots

wursht – German-style sausage

yarmulkah – skull cap

yeshivah – centre for religious and rabbinical studies

yiddishe – Jewish

yiddishkeit – everything to do with being (Orthodox) Jewish

Yom Kippur – Day of Atonement

Author's Note

Fact and fiction are so interwoven in this book that it might help the reader to know what is historical and what is not.

Census details show that the population of the city of Liverpool fell from 791,000 in 1951 to 450,000 in 1991, a fall of 43 per cent. A further drop is expected at the next census in 2001. The main part of this decline came in the 1960s when 136,000 people left the city followed by a further 100,000 in the next decade. The only other location in the United Kingdom to show a similar fall is Belfast.

Amongst those who left were Dr Heenan, prelate of Liverpool, who was elevated to the See of Westminster and a cardinal's hat in September 1963. As his train left Lime Street Station 10,000 people lined the platform and sang 'For He's a Jolly Good Fellow'. Harold Swindale Magnay left in 1964 for Paris where he became adviser to OECD on education. He died in 1971. Professor Dr Semple remained and lives in retirement in Gateacre.

In the early years of this century tuberculosis accounted for more than one death in three among men aged 15–44. Liverpool at 135 deaths per 100,000 population and Bootle at 161 (1931) were amongst the worst in the country. Lady Ida Titchfield (Duchess of Portland) was active in the National Association for the Prevention of Tuberculosis and its chairman from 1938. She lived to be 94 and was honoured with the DBE for her charitable work. The fears of dependency (Chapter Five) were expressed by NAPT after-care committees quoted in *Below the Magic Mountain* by Linda Bryder (Clarendon Press 1988). Dr Leadenthall is remembered by my mother. Special thanks are due to Professor John R. Ashton, Regional Director of Public Health, North West Regional Health Authority and Dr Sally Sheard of the Department of Public Health of Liverpool University.

Burtonwood USAF station was closed in 1965 but was reprieved in February 1967 after President de Gaulle took France out of NATO and ordered the removal of US troops from French soil. It was handed over to the RAF in 1992 and declared surplus to UK requirements the following year. Marks and Spencer's M62 store is now situated over the main runway; a commemorative plaque and flags decorate the stairs in the staff area. Warmest thanks to Aldon P. Ferguson of the Burtonwood Association, to Sheldon A. Goldberg of the Air Force History Support Office, Washington DC and to Mr A. Leigh, Curator of Warrington Museum and Art Gallery, and staff including Polly Arthurs for their tireless assistance.

The remarks of the 'young ordinand' in Chapter Seventeen are based on quoted comments of Rabbi Z. Plitnick in the *Liverpool Jewish Gazette* of summer 1968.

The British Museum newspaper library at Colindale, Liverpool Public Libraries and the House of Commons Library staff also deserve my appreciation for their prompt and efficient efforts. Any errors are my own.

EC September 1997

The author gratefully acknowledges permission to quote lyrics from the following songs:

All Alone Am I Words and music by Hadjidakis and Altman. Copyright © 1962, Hadjidakis and Altman. Reproduced by permission of MCA Music Ltd (co-publisher)

Be-Bop-a-Lula Words and music by Gene Vincent and Sheriff Tex Davis. Copyright © 1956, Lowery Music Inc., administered by Unichappell Inc., USA. All rights reserved. Reproduced by permission of Lark Music Ltd, Iron Bridge House, 3 Bridge Approach, Chalk Farm, London NW1 8BD

Can't Help Falling in Love Words and music by George Weiss, Luigi Creatore and Hugo Peretti. Copyright © 1961, Gladys Music Inc., administered by Williamson Music, New York, USA. All rights reserved. Reproduced by permission of Lark Music Ltd (address as above)

Fever Words and music by John Davenport and Eddie Cooley. Copyright © 1956, Jay and Cee Music Corp., all rights assigned to Fort Knox Music Co. Inc., New York and Trio Music Co. Inc., California, USA. All rights reserved. Reproduced by permission of Lark Music Ltd (address as above)

Hey Baby Words and music by Bruce Channel and Margaret Cobb. Copyright © 1962, Le Bill Music Inc., USA. Reproduced by permission of Peter Maurice Music Co. Ltd, London WC2H 0EA

I Walk the Line Words and music by Johnny Cash. Copyright © 1956, Hi-Lo Music. Public performance rights for USA and Canada controlled by Hi-Lo Music Inc., a BMI affiliate. All other rights for the world controlled by Unichappell Music Inc. (Rightsong Music, publisher). All rights reserved. Reproduced by permission of Carlin Music Corp., Iron Bridge House, 3 Bridge Approach, Chalk Farm, London NW1 8BD

Let's Jump the Broomstick Words and music by Charles Robbins. Copyright © 1958, Kenny Marlow Music, all rights assigned to Kentucky Music Inc., administered by Unichappell, Inc. All rights reserved. Reproduced by permission of Carlin Music Corp. (address as above)

Lollipop Words and music by Berverly Ross and Julius Dixon. Copyright © 1958, Edward B. Marks Music Corporation. All rights reserved. International copyright secured. Reproduced by permission of Anglo Pic. Music Co. Ltd

Love Letters in the Sand Music by J. Fred Coots and words by Nick Kenny and Charles Kenny. Copyright © 1931, Bourne Co., USA. Reproduced by permission of Francis Day and Hunter Ltd, London WC2H 0EA

Memphis Tennessee Words and music by Chuck Berry. Copyright © 1959, Arc Music Corp. All rights reserved. International copyright secured. Reproduced by permission of Jewel Music Co. Ltd

Please Help Me I'm Falling (in Love With You) Words and music by Hal Blair and Don Robertson. Copyright © 1960 Ross Jungnickel Inc., all rights assigned to Anne Rachel Music Corp., administered by Unichappell Inc., California, USA. All rights reserved. Copyright renewed. One-half word rights assigned to Don Robertson Music Corporation. Reproduced by permission of Carlin Music Corp. (address as above) and Don Robertson Music Corp., PO Box 150976, Nashville, TN 37215-0976